Larry McMurtry

THE EVENING STAR

A NOVEL

Simon & Schuster
New York   London   Toronto   Sydney   Singapore

Simon & Schuster
Rockefeller Center
1230 Avenue of the Americas
New York, NY 10020

First Simon & Schuster trade paperback edition 2003
SIMON & SCHUSTER and colophon are
registered trademarks of Simon & Schuster, Inc.

For information about special discounts for bulk purchases,
please contact Simon & Schuster Special Sales at
1-800-456-6798 or business@simonandschuster.com

Manufactured in the United States of America

2   3   4   5   6   7   8   9   10

The Library of Congress has cataloged
the hardcover edition as follows:
McMurtry, Larry.
The evening star / by Larry McMurtry.
p.   cm.
Sequel to: Terms of endearment.
I. Title.
PS3563.A319E94   1992
813'.54—dc20   92-2596

ISBN 0-671-68519-8
0-684-85751-0 (Pbk)

FOR
GRACE DAVID,
MYRTLE BOONE,
AND CURTIS

I

The Children
and the Men

1

On their monthly visits to the prison, Aurora drove going and Rosie drove home. That was the tradition, and there was good reason for it: seeing her grandson behind bars, being reminded yet again that he had killed a woman, realizing that in all likelihood she would be seeing him only in such circumstances for the rest of her life, left Aurora far too shaken to be trusted at the wheel of a car—particularly the sputtery old Cadillac she refused to trade in. Aurora managed the Cadillac erratically under the best of circumstances, and visiting Tommy in prison could not be called the best of circumstances.

Rosie and everyone else who knew Aurora felt sure the Cadillac would be the death of her someday, but it would not have been wise to reiterate this fear on the return trip from Huntsville, when Aurora would have been only too happy to die on the spot.

Aurora, in the midst of a bitter fit of sobbing, nonetheless reached up and twisted the rearview mirror her way, in order to regard her own despair. It was an old habit: when sorrow beset her, as it now did regularly, she often grabbed the nearest mirror, hoping, through vanity alone, to arrest it in its course before it did her too much damage.

This time it didn't work, not merely because she was crying so hard she couldn't see herself at all, but because Rosie—a woman so short she could barely see the traffic in front of her, much less that which she knew to be in pursuit, immediately grabbed the mirror and twisted it back.

"Don't do that, hon, I got to have my mirror!" Rosie said, panicked because she heard the sound of a huge truck bearing down on them, but lacked a clue as to exactly how close it might be.

"There's an eighteen-wheeler after us—if that sucker ran over us we'd be squished like soup in a can," she added, wishing they were in Conroe, so perhaps Aurora would quit crying, shaking, and scattering wet Kleenex around.

The prison where Tommy was doing fifteen years to life was in Huntsville, Texas. Conroe, Texas, thirty-two miles to the south, down an Interstate rife with eighteen-wheelers, was the nearest point at which Aurora could reasonably be expected to regain control of her emotions. Until then, all Rosie could do was stay out of the fast lane and drive for dear life.

"I just wish you'd do something I ask you for once in your life and buy us a Datsun pickup," Rosie said. "We'd stand a lot better chance on this racetrack if we had a vehicle I could see out of."

To her relief she noticed the eighteen-wheeler sliding smoothly past them on her left.

Aurora didn't respond. Her mind was back with Tommy, the pale, calm boy in the prison. He had always been the brightest of her dead daughter's three children. His grades had never been less than excellent, unlike those of her other grandchildren, Teddy and Melanie, both such erratic scholars that it was hardly even fair to use the word "scholar" when referring to their academic careers.

"We're almost to Conroe," Rosie said unwisely, hoping it might cause Aurora to stop crying a little sooner than usual.

"Who gives a fuck where we are!" Aurora yelled, flaring up for a moment before crying a fresh flood.

Rosie was so shocked she almost rear-ended a white Toyota suburban. Only three or four times in their long acquaintance had she heard her employer use that particular word.

Shortly after they sped past the first Conroe exit, Aurora calmed a little.

"Rosie, I'm not a robot," she said. "I do not have to stop crying just because we happen to be passing Conroe."

"I wish I hadn't brought it up," Rosie said. "I wish I hadn't never been born. But most of all I wish we had a Datsun pickup—the seat of this car is so old it's sinking in, and if it sinks in much farther I won't be able to see anything but the speedometer. Then an eighteen-wheeler will probably run over us and squish us like soup in a can."

"This car is not a can and we will not be squished like soup," Aurora declared, sniffing. "You've chosen a bad figure."

"Yeah, I was always flat-chested, but I didn't choose it, God did it to me," Rosie said, thinking it odd that Aurora would mention her lifelong flat-chestedness at such a time.

"Oh, figure of speech, I meant," Aurora said. "Of course you didn't choose your bosom. What I meant to point out is that there's nothing souplike about either one of us. If you get squished, it'll be like a French fry, which is what you resemble."

Aurora felt no better, but she did feel cried out, and she began to mop her cheeks with a wad of Kleenex. She had already scattered several wet wads on the seat. She gathered these up, compressed them into one sopping mess, and threw the mess out the window.

"Hon, you oughtn't to litter," Rosie admonished. "There's signs all up and down this highway saying don't mess with Texas."

"I'll mess with it all I want to," Aurora said. "It's certainly messed enough with me."

When her vision cleared a bit more, she noticed that a stream of cars and trucks was flowing past them. Looking back, she saw with alarm that a very large truck seemed to be practically pushing them.

"Rosie, are you going the correct speed?" she asked. "We're not exactly leading the pack."

"I'm going fifty-five," Rosie said.

"Then no wonder that truck just behind us has such an impatient aspect," Aurora said. "I tell you every time we come here that the legal speed is now sixty-five, not fifty-five. You had better put the pedal to the metal, if that is the correct expression."

"The pedal's to the metal, otherwise we wouldn't be moving at all," Rosie said. "Why do you think I been bugging you about a Datsun pickup? I could push the pedal through the radiator and this old whale wouldn't go more than fifty-five. Besides, the speed limit's only fifty-five when you're going through a town, and we're going through Conroe."

"Don't be pedantic when I'm sad," Aurora said. "Just try to go a little faster."

Rosie, in a daring maneuver, attempted to pass the sluggish white Toyota just as a truck behind them pulled out to pass them. The driver honked, and Rosie instantly whipped her arm out the window and gave him the finger. Then, not appeased, she actually stuck her head out the window, turned it, and glared at the truck driver.

Unimpressed, the truck driver honked again, while Rosie, pedal to the metal, inched grimly past the white suburban.

"Well, you don't lack spunk—you never have or I'd have squished you myself," Aurora said.

The trucker, perhaps annoyed, perhaps amused, began to tap his horn every few seconds, and Rosie—definitely not amused—stuck her arm out the window and left it there, with her middle finger extended for his benefit.

The sight of her maid sustaining a rude gesture while virtually beneath the wheels of a giant truck made Aurora laugh. A vagrant bubble of mirth rose unexpectedly from inside her, but she had no more than started a little peal when sorrow came back in a flood and overran amusement, just as her Cadillac seemed about to be overrun by the eighteen-wheeler.

"I hope it kills us, then this will be over!" she cried, as she was crying.

"I'm from Bossier City, and I ain't about to be bullied by no truck," Rosie said. She calculated that she now had at least a three-or-four-inch lead on the Toyota and was nerving up to make her cut to the right.

When Aurora calmed for the second time they were well down the road past the airport exit—she could see the skyscrapers of downtown Houston through the summer haze.

"I can no longer laugh without beginning to cry," she reported, rolling down her window. She proceeded to mess with Texas to the extent of another fifteen or twenty Kleenex.

"You wasn't really laughing, you was just mainly crying," Rosie said.

2

"The unbearable part is that he likes being in prison," Aurora said, finishing her second pig sandwich.

In the bleak hours after a visit to Tommy, the two of them had formed the habit of stopping at the old Pig Stand on Washington Avenue, in the hope that a little something to eat would help them lift their spirits off the floor.

Rosie, true to her recently acquired vegetarianism, which she hoped would enable her to live to at least one hundred, had a salad. Aurora ate an order of onion rings and two Pig Stand sandwiches.

"You won't be the first person to commit suicide by eating fatty foods," Rosie informed her.

"I'm serious," Aurora said. "I think Tommy likes being in prison."

"He don't really like it," Rosie said. "I doubt anybody really likes being in Huntsville."

"No, but he prefers it to being outside," Aurora said. "That's the tragic fact. He prefers it to being out, which means that you and I totally failed him."

"Maybe so, but you need to stop gnawing on it," Rosie

said. "Gnawing on it's worse than eating pig sandwiches. We done the best we could, and that's all anybody can do."

Aurora, realizing that it would be a biological outrage to consume three pig sandwiches at a sitting, nonetheless called the waitress and ordered a third.

"Well, I feel weak and empty," she told Rosie. "You're a wisp, compared to me. I can't survive on desiccated lettuce."

As she waited for her sandwich, Aurora reviewed—in memory—Tommy's life, and realized sadly that she could not really remember having seen a truly happy look on his young face.

She had seen smart looks, though, and had hoped he might go on to win intellectual distinction, a hope that was probably ended by a single gunshot in a house in the Austin suburbs. Tommy shot at a rival dope dealer and hit the man's girlfriend in the head. The girl, whose name was Julie, was from a military family in San Antonio, and had been Tommy's first real girlfriend, whatever being a real girlfriend meant in contemporary terms.

"If only he hadn't met that girl," Aurora said, angered that such a mouse of a girl had brought such a harsh and bitter destiny upon them all. That Julie had been in some ways more than a mouse was borne out by the fact that $134,000 in cash and half a kilo of cocaine had been found in her closet, hidden beneath her large collection of stuffed animals.

Though Rosie's heart ached for Tommy, too, she felt she had to take a stoic line on his tragedy, otherwise Aurora would mope for hours, behavior she couldn't afford. Tommy was not the only problem they had to deal with.

"I didn't much cotton to Julie either, but she's dead, let her rest in peace," Rosie said. "Tommy was a dope dealer. Them kinds of things just happen to dope dealers.

"If you ask me we're lucky he didn't shoot two or three people," she added. "Tommy's been mad at the world ever since his momma died."

She thought for a moment, and amended her conclusion. "Actually, Tommy's been mad ever since he was born," she said. "He's one of those people who are just born mad, and it don't do no good to look for a why because there ain't no why you can find."

"Thank you for your advice, O fount of wisdom," Aurora said, casting her eyes toward the pies—there was a long line of them, in gleaming pie racks. Somehow, through the magic of lighting, the gleaming racks seemed to magnify the pies' appeal. She knew the pies couldn't possibly be as good as they looked, but that didn't mean they weren't fully good enough to eat. She waved at Marge, the waitress, and decided on mince, with pistachio ice cream.

Rosie watched Aurora eat the pie and the ice cream with silent, austere disdain, secure in the knowledge that she herself weighed only ninety-six pounds—whereas the other customers of the Pig Stand, a typical assortment of human flotsam and jetsam, most of them possessed of a fatigue not yet quite emptied of curiosity, merely wondered why Aurora, a woman who looked like she had enough money to eat elsewhere, kept showing up at the Pig Stand in the company of a frizzy-haired little old lady who, in their acute estimation, was some kind of Louisiana cracker.

Like many residents of the north side of Houston, most of the Pig Standers tended to take life steady and take it slow. A few chubby Don Juans in Hawaiian shirts mustered snap enough to flirt with Marge or one of the other waitresses, and a few truckers or delivery men, all too well aware that time is money, strode in, ate a cheeseburger or a few eggs, and strode out. But the majority of the customers were in no hurry; from long experience they had learned that the best way to handle the Houston humidity was to ease through it slowly, one step or one thought at a time.

Aurora was not quite ready to let go of her anger at the treacherous Julie. To her annoyance, Tommy himself had no interest in her anger, and would not react at all when Julie was mentioned.

"Julie was a little squirrely," he had said, and that was all he said.

"There are often problems in military families," Aurora remarked. She finished her pie and took out her mirror, but she could not muster enough interest in her appearance to do anything about it. What was there would have to do—perhaps forever, but at least until they got home.

"The General's from a military family," Rosie reminded her. "He's as much trouble as five or six military families, but I doubt he's lost a wink of sleep in his life."

"You're quite wrong," Aurora said. "I've caused him to lose thousands of winks of sleep. One of the few powers I can still claim is the ability to upset Hector sufficiently to keep him awake until I'm ready for him to start snoring."

General Hector Scott, Aurora's resident lover—a category not to be confused with that of the several nonresident aspirants—was eighty-six, and not happy about it; he was even less happy about the fact that only three weeks before, he had managed, in defiance of all the known laws of physics, to turn a golf cart over on himself, breaking both legs and one hip. He was recuperating, at a pace much too slow to suit him, on the glassed-in patio next to Aurora's bedroom, on the second floor of her house.

The fact that he was in de facto confinement on the second floor was another thing General Scott was not happy about. Aurora had had him carried upstairs over his stern, almost violent, protests. The boys who brought him home in the ambulance, perhaps unaware that he had been a four-star general, took their orders from Aurora and ignored the thumps he attempted to give them.

General Scott at once concluded that Aurora could have had only one motive for consigning him to the second floor: she intended to make free with her other suitors on the first floor, where he could neither see, hear, nor interfere with anything she might decide to do.

The most threatening of the other suitors was a little Frenchman named Pascal, an attaché at the French consulate. The General couldn't stand Pascal, and didn't conceal the fact—indeed, General Scott concealed few facts, and in the past few months had even ceased to conceal certain parts of his own anatomy that both Aurora and Rosie would have preferred that he conceal.

This new propensity of the General's was on both women's

minds as they left the Pig Stand and prodded the old Cadillac along its homeward path, toward the well-tamed forests of River Oaks.

"Has he flashed lately?" Aurora asked. "Sinner that I am, I hardly thought that I could have committed enough sins to earn me a grandson in jail and a flasher on my patio."

"Yep, he flashed this morning," Rosie said. "Then he had the gall to complain about his eggs."

"How, exactly, did he flash?" Aurora asked. "For an ancient person on crutches he's developed quite an extensive repertoire."

"He left his pajamas unbuttoned," Rosie said. "I think the next time he goes that route I might spill a glass of ice water in his lap, or a little hot tea or something."

"Yes, do that," Aurora said. "At least he didn't pull the crutches trick, which he's very prone to pulling when I'm his target."

"What's the crutches trick?" Rosie asked.

"He hoists himself on his crutches and then contrives to let his bathrobe fall open," Aurora said. "Then he just stands there grinning. He looks like a mummy on crutches."

"Well, he's eighty-six," Rosie said, softening her stance a bit.

"Why is that relevant?" Aurora asked. "You yourself are not exactly a maiden, but you don't stand around lolling out of your bathrobe."

"I'm too flat-chested, there's nothing to loll," Rosie said. "We may not be no spring chickens but we ain't really old like the General, either."

Aurora gave her maid a quizzical look. "I'm afraid I don't quite take your point, if you have one," she said. "Is there any reason why the old shouldn't be expected to behave as well as the middle-aged?"

"Middle-aged?" Rosie said. "Do you think we're still middle-aged?"

"Well, why aren't we?" Aurora asked. She opened the glove compartment and poked around in it hopefully—she had the vague suspicion that she might have hidden some money in it at some point.

"You're kidding yourself," Rosie informed her. "We ain't been middle-aged for twenty years."

To her delight, Aurora discovered just what she had been hoping to find: twenty-four dollars, tucked into a city map.

"Why, there's my twenty-four dollars, let's stop at the flower shop," she said. "As for middle-aged, you're quite wrong. There's a category called late middle age which has rather indefinite boundaries. I think we're both still well inside them—or at least I am."

"The backyard's nothing but flowers, why do you want to buy more?" Rosie asked. She was not keen on stopping at the flower shop.

"You're right, go home—flowers are a job for Pascal," Aurora said. "I'll call him and tell him to bring over twenty-four dollars' worth next time he shows up."

"What if he don't want to? Pascal ain't rich, you know." Rosie said.

"No, but I don't see anything extravagant about asking him to bring me twenty-four dollars' worth of flowers, since that's the precise amount I found in my glove compartment," Aurora said, grinning. "How could anyone argue with the logic of that?"

Rosie didn't care about the logic—it was the first time Aurora had smiled since leaving the prison. If it cost Pascal twenty-four dollars, it was worth it.

Still, she had not quite finished making her point about the General and his new fondness for flashing. That was one subject, but it was connected to a second subject, and the second subject—of profound interest to Rosie—was whether Aurora and the General still had sex.

Obviously the General was plenty randy in his head, but that didn't necessarily mean he was randy elsewhere, nor did it offer the slightest clue as to Aurora's position on the matter. And Aurora, no prude, and no enemy of plain speech, either, had ceased to be either forthcoming or plain about that aspect of her life with the General.

Rosie ached to know, partly out of simple curiosity and partly because a little more information might help her with a dilemma of her own—her boyfriend, C. C. Granby, once as feisty as a rooster, seemed to be losing his roosterlike propensities at an alarming rate. Rosie couldn't figure out if it was her fault or his, and could not quite get up her nerve to apply to Aurora for an opinion.

"What I meant about the General not buttoning his pajamas or letting his bathrobe flop open is that we're all getting old, and I guess old people have a right to get their kicks some way," she said nervously.

They had just pulled into the driveway of Aurora's home. Rosie covered her nervousness by beginning the lengthy business of aligning the Cadillac with the narrow doors of the garage. The car was nearly as wide as the opening—there was only a little more than an inch to spare on either side: another reason Rosie's automotive fantasies were so focused on a Datsun pickup. Aurora, who otherwise could scarcely drive, always whipped the Cadillac right into the garage, whereas Rosie, who stubbornly refused to have her cataracts attended to, could scarcely see the width of the front seat and was always in terror of crumpling one of the fenders or scraping one of the doors, in which event she expected to be dismissed instantly despite more than forty years of faithful service.

"Stop!" Aurora commanded, looking at her maid sharply.

Rosie was just on the lip of the driveway; she liked to align the Cadillac as a golfer might a long putt, before committing herself to an approach that wouldn't work.

"I'm getting it centered, I ain't gonna scrape nothing," Rosie assured Aurora, edging ever so slightly to the left in her approach to the garage.

"You stop!" Aurora said. "I want to talk to you and I want to do it right now. You can destroy my car a little later."

Rosie stopped and sat looking at Aurora's nice Spanish Colonial house. She had helped maintain it for so long that she considered that it was, in a sense, hers, too. At the moment she longed to be inside it—from the look in Aurora's eye it seemed likely that her remarks about the aged and their kicks had not been well received.

"I ought to know when to keep my mouth shut, I guess," she said, hoping to blunt the force of whatever attack might be coming.

"Oh, stop cringing," Aurora said. "You ought to consider changing your hairdo. At the moment it's far too frizzy."

"I wish I was bald and had a wig," Rosie said. "I've tried my hair every way there is to try hair, and look at it! Lots of wigs are nicer than my hair, but I don't know . . . I guess I just ain't the wig type. Every time I try one on I get the giggles."

"I agree you probably aren't the wig type, but there are always new hairdos one can try," Aurora said. "I've tried quite a variety myself. Now, what was that you were asking about my sex life?"

Rosie sighed deeply but said nothing. She didn't want to admit that she had asked Aurora about her sex life.

"They say curiosity killed the cat," she finally ventured.

"Good lord, Rosie," Aurora said. "We've known one another for more than forty years. I'm not going to maul you just because you asked me about my sex life. The truth is, I thought you never would ask me about it."

"I'm asking, what about it?" Rosie said.

"It's a short story—Hector can't do it," Aurora said.

"Oh," Rosie said.

They sat in silence for a minute as the shadows of the great trees began to extend themselves across the house and the yard.

"I knew that stuff you read in magazines was probably lies," Rosie said.

Aurora looked at her calmly. "What stuff?" she asked.

"That stuff about men being able to do it until they're ninety-five or a hundred," Rosie said.

"Yes, we've been reading the same magazines," Aurora said. "In other words, the ones I subscribe to. Those stories do give a rather misleading impression of male capacities, at least as I've experienced them."

"You think you've got problems? C.C.'s just sixty-eight and he won't even try," Rosie said. "Trying to get him to do something is like trying to corner a bobcat. Sometimes I feel like giving up."

"I've considered it myself," Aurora admitted.

"Yeah, but you got beaus," Rosie reminded her. "You got Pascal, and then there's Louis and Junior and Cowboy Bill."

It was Aurora's turn to sigh. "Just hearing their names depresses me," she confessed. "There was a time when I could command a more impressive assortment. I rather like Pascal, but it must be admitted that he's mostly talk."

"I think he's scared of the General," Rosie said.

"I'm afraid the truth is he's scared of me," Aurora said. "Of course the fact that Hector lives here probably does discourage my beaus. Unfortunately, the fact that they seem a little too willing to be discouraged is beginning to arouse my contempt. I may clear the deck of the whole lot of them pretty soon, Hector included."

"Maybe the General's just in a slump," Rosie speculated. "They've got all these new medicines for your glands now. Stuff a few of them down him and see what happens."

The shadows touched the car and Aurora's mood turned. She remembered Tommy's face, so young and so closed; she remembered the stolid guards who led him away.

"Put the car in, it's getting dark—you'll knock down my garage," she said.

Rosie, who had been thinking the same thought, edged forward, correcting her course by minute degrees as she neared the garage.

"I shouldn't be thinking of these things," Aurora said. Her mood was sinking fast. "I'm an old withered thing now, what does it matter?" she asked. "You're younger, of course you should be concerned about C.C. But I've got a grandson in prison, another grandson who's in and out of mental hospitals, and a granddaughter who's pregnant and is not even sure she can identify the father. Why should I care about male capabilities, or male anything? I should just forget it."

They edged safely into the dark garage.

Rosie, exactly one year younger than her boss, reached over and squeezed Aurora's hand.

"Hon, you got to think of yourself sometime," she said. "You're human, like the rest of us. You got to think of yourself sometime."

"What I think is that I wish you'd hit that pillar so this garage would fall and make an end of me," Aurora said. She gathered up her purse and her box of Kleenex and quickly got out of the car.

3

"Another bad thing about Hector's state is that I now dread going up my own stairs," Aurora said. She had more or less finished another long cry, and was in her kitchen, drinking tea.

Rosie, who had become a news junkie in her late maturity —a phrase gleaned from the very magazines that had contained the misleading information about male capabilities— was peering through her contacts at her idol, Tom Brokaw. "Lithuania's not looking so good—I hope Gorby knows what he's doing," she said.

Aurora had little patience with Rosie's late-blooming interest in world affairs. In her view, Rosie was not so much a news junkie as an anchorman groupie, and, to make matters worse, had fixed her affections on the wrong anchorman to boot. She herself much preferred the urbane Peter Jennings.

"Lithuania will have to look out for itself—anyway it's Truman's fault," she said. "If General MacArthur had had his way all those communists would have been dealt with long ago."

"You better not let General Scott hear you talking about

MacArthur," Rosie cautioned. General Scott had once been a subordinate of General MacArthur's, and it had not been a happy experience, to hear him tell it—and Rosie had heard him tell it many times.

"I have no doubt that whatever happened between Hector and General MacArthur was entirely Hector's fault," Aurora said. "Besides that, he was jealous."

At least the gumbo they were making for dinner smelled good. She sipped her tea and enjoyed the good smell. She had always loved her kitchen—but then, she had once loved her whole house. Now it seemed the kitchen was the only place she was likely to feel happy. It was to the kitchen that she repaired when she needed to recover some sense of esprit.

Once she had made the window nook in her bedroom her haven, when seeking to recover a bit of esprit, but the window nook was no longer reliable in the way that it had been. Hector Scott was far too likely to hobble in and scatter whatever little blossoms of spirit she had managed to gather.

"Come to think of it, everything bad that happens in this house is Hector's fault," Aurora said with a flash of bitterness. "I once loved going up my stairs, but now I dread it because I never know what I'll find at the top of them. Even if Hector doesn't decide to flash, he'll be angry because I went off and left him."

She sipped a little more tea. "Old men are so dreadfully selfish, and there's little one can do about it," she said. "They can't simply be put down, like old dogs."

"You better go up and speak to him, selfish or not," Rosie said. She was waiting patiently for NBC to cut back to Tom Brokaw. She herself had never been to Lithuania, or anywhere farther from home than Las Vegas, where C.C. had taken her for a giddy weekend when their relationship was just firing up—but from what she could tell, life in Lithuania consisted mostly of standing in crowds in front of parliament or somewhere else official, protesting for more freedom and better government.

Actually, from what she could tell, life in most of the rest of the world consisted of standing in just such crowds, protesting for more freedom and better government. An exception was Israel—or perhaps it was Palestine; she was not entirely clear about the distinction—where youths with handkerchiefs over their faces threw stones at soldiers, who then shot tear gas at them.

Rosie had long since decided that if the U.S. government ever threatened her freedom, or raised taxes one more time, or did much of anything she didn't like, she would join a crowd of protesters herself and see if it did any good—or, at least, see if it was any fun.

From what she could tell, though, protests always seemed to be rather similar. She was always glad when Tom Brokaw came back on and told them how things were going with the protesters.

Aurora contemplated going upstairs and informing Hector that he would have to leave. Several times in the last year or two she had composed a little speech on that subject, and once had even made a tentative approach to it by asking him what he would do if she abruptly died.

In her thinking about her own demise, Aurora always supposed it would be abrupt. She did not propose to linger in a hospital as her beloved daughter Emma had. Poor Emma had taken months to die, but Aurora had no intention of following her example. Something would happen that she didn't feel, and she would just be gone.

She outlined just such a scenario to Hector one afternoon. He had looked startled, and his Adam's apple wobbled for a bit. He looked at her as if he considered that she had almost lost her mind. He seemed momentarily to be about to cry; but he didn't cry—nor did he speak. He had been watching a golf tournament, and he resumed his watching.

"Hector, we really should think about it," Aurora insisted. "I certainly shall die someday, I imagine. Hadn't you better be thinking of arrangements? I know they have some very nice military homes for distinguished old soldiers such as yourself. You could sit around with your peers and talk over the Battle of the Somme or something."

"Aurora, I was eight years old when the Battle of the

Somme was fought," the General said. "You need to get your world wars straight. There were two. The Battle of the Somme was in the first. I fought in the second."

"You would be pedantic just when I'm attempting to discuss something serious," Aurora said. "We weren't talking about which war you fought in, we were talking about my untimely demise."

"I wasn't talking about your goddamn demise," the General said. "I was watching my golf tournament. Who says your demise will be untimely anyway? You're no longer a young woman, you know."

"I recognize that I am now in late middle age," Aurora said. "Nevertheless, my demise will be untimely, whenever it occurs."

She reflected for a moment on poor little pregnant Melanie, on Teddy and his lithium, on Tommy in his cell.

"I know I shouldn't complain," she said. "It was Emma's demise that was untimely, and look what woe it bred."

"The ruin of those children, that's what it bred," the General said. "I tried, you tried, Rosie tried, and nothing worked. One's crazy, one's a criminal, and one's pregnant. Thank God there weren't more, I say."

"I refuse to regard Teddy as crazy," Aurora said. "He's just having a rather hard time finding himself."

The General, too, grew sad at the thought of Teddy, a boy he had always had a deep soft spot for, even though he didn't entirely approve of his own soft spot.

"No, and he'll never find himself as long as he can find a pharmacy and get more pills," the General said. "He's a perfectly healthy boy—I'm opposed to all those pills. I wish he had taken my advice and joined the army. The army would have straightened him out in no time."

"No, the army would have crushed him—he's already more or less crushed," Aurora said bitterly.

Her tone alarmed the General. He thought for a moment that she was accusing him of crushing Teddy.

"*I* didn't crush him," he insisted. "I love Teddy. I took him fishing, remember?"

"Yes," Aurora said. "I remember.

"I don't know why talking to you is so difficult now, Hector," she said, after she had recovered herself for a bit.

"Well, I'm old and cranky," the General said. "I can't help it. I wish I was young again but I'm never going to be. Knowing that makes me cranky."

"All right, suppose I drop dead," Aurora said. "That was what I was attempting to talk to you about. Then there'll be no one to care for you but Rosie, and Rosie has her hands full with my grandchildren and her own. Difficult as you are, I would still like to think you'll be well looked after when I catch the tide. Don't you think you ought to look into the possibility of a nice military home?"

The General clicked off the TV and looked at her out of eyes that still occasionally had the piercing quality that generals' eyes were supposed to have.

"I see what you're up to now," he said. "You want to be rid of me. You want to pack me off to the old soldiers' home."

"As usual, you're quite unjust," Aurora said, flaring up. "I was merely thinking of your own welfare. I'm sure some of those homes have golf courses. You could be playing golf with your cronies, rather than sitting here glued to a stupid television set."

"Oh, yes, my cronies from the Battle of the Somme," the General said. "It's plain you know nothing about old soldiers' homes. That idiot MacArthur should have been court-martialed for saying what he said about old soldiers."

"Hector, I'm aghast," Aurora said. "Whatever your differences with General MacArthur, I'm sure he did not deserve to be court-martialed."

"Yes, for saying old soldiers never die, they just fade away," the General insisted. "Of course old soldiers die. Most of them die the minute they retire, or at least within a few days. I have no cronies, Aurora. They all died."

"Hector, please don't exaggerate," Aurora said. "You know perfectly well you have some cronies left in California. We visited them ourselves."

"That's right, two cronies," the General said. "Joe's still hanging on in Pebble Beach, but they won't let him on the golf course because he chews tobacco and spots up the greens when he spits. As for Sammy, I guess he's still alive. He's down in Rancho Mirage. All Sammy was ever interested in was bimbos. I told him he ought to move to Las Vegas, but he claims he finds plenty of bimbos in Rancho Mirage."

"I'm sure you'd find a better class of old soldier in some of the nicer military homes," Aurora said, wondering why she was bothering to keep such an unedifying conversation going. Hector clearly wasn't eager to commence negotiations with a military home.

"You aren't listening," the General said. "The point I'm making is that there are *no* old soldiers in military homes. The old soldiers have all died. There are only old soldiers' *widows*—talk about living forever. Some of those old biddies look like they're three hundred years old. I've seen them with my own eyes. Battle of the Somme, nothing—some of those widows probably knew Napoleon."

"Hector, I'm sure that's not possible," Aurora said. However, her vision of Hector playing golf with a number of trim ex-officers blurred suddenly, to be replaced with the less appealing vision of Hector playing bridge with a number of vivacious widows.

"Besides that, they're the horniest women in the world," the General said. "Their husbands were never around much to begin with, and then they died—those women are looking to make up for lost time. They'd be on me like sharks—I wouldn't last a month."

Then the General remembered a particular widow he had once encountered in Washington, and his own vision of aged biddies dissolved. This widow, a lively Southern blonde, had seduced him immediately, without even suggesting that he leave his wife and marry her. "What the heck, Hec," she said, the minute they entered her apartment. "Let's have a little fun."

The General had not thought of the woman in years—her name had been Lily something. A lot of time had passed, but it seemed to him that they had had quite a bit of fun. It had been the only easy seduction of his entire life; he hadn't had to do a thing except undress. Seducing Aurora, on the other hand, had taken the better part of five years, and what had it got him, other than constant harassment?

The General's vision of life in a military home came back into focus, only this time it was a much more pleasant vision, with Lily in it. She hadn't been especially old, then. Perhaps she was still around; perhaps she was even still interested in fun. And if she wasn't, so what? There must be other attractive widows in some of those homes.

The thought made him smile, and Aurora saw the smile. She realized she had been a little dense in allowing her own imagination to people the military homes of America entirely with trim colonels—the only kind of colonels she herself would have been likely to take an interest in. There would also be widows, a few of whom might also have remained trim themselves. Some might even have remained quite attractive. Hector obviously thought so, or he wouldn't be grinning like an idiot. Her spirits began to slide, and the General noticed.

"Ha," he said. "Hoist on your own petard, am I right? You were ready to pack me off, but you overlooked one big fact: women live longer than men."

"Normally, I suppose you're right, although any number have failed to live longer than you," Aurora said. "Your dear wife, for example. She didn't live longer than you, and it's unlikely I shall myself, considering how much you enjoy breaking my heart."

"The sledgehammer has yet to be forged that could break your goddamn heart," the General said crisply. "I had an affair in a military home once, if you must know. I tell you that so you'll realize I won't just be drooling on golf courses if you pack me off. I intend to find a girlfriend within a week if you carry out that threat."

It had been, Aurora reflected, a highly unsuccessful conversation. The bitterest cut had been Hector's smile. Every day she flashed him her best lights, offered him her gaiety, her optimism, her mischief, her fun. It seemed to her no small thing that she could continue to summon any mischief or any fun at her age, considering all the grief she'd had with the grandchildren.

Yet she did summon them, but it brought her no smiles from Hector, when a few smiles from Hector was all she really hoped for.

"Why won't men smile when you want them to?" she asked Rosie. "Almost inevitably, they fail to smile just when one wants them to most."

Rosie was still hanging on Tom Brokaw's every word, although now he was talking about something called the European community, a topic that didn't interest her much.

"Speak for yourself," she said. "Mine's got the opposite problem. All C.C. can think of to do is grin. If C.C.'s grinned at me once he's grinned at me a million times."

"I have noticed that C.C. seems to have difficulty getting his mouth over his teeth," Aurora said. "I suppose it would get old, being confronted with nothing but teeth, day after day."

"I keep pointing out to him that there's ways to have fun in this life that don't involve grinning," Rosie said, getting up to inspect the gumbo. "You want some more tea?"

Aurora's mind was on the General. He was up there, as he always was, waiting for her to appear and entertain him. The likelihood of his being in a decent mood was very slim. In the hour before dinner he seemed to feel his age the most.

"At least I don't feed him off a tray," Aurora said.

A table had been moved to the patio with a tablecloth, place settings, candles. There were some things she wouldn't give up. She herself did not intend to eat off trays, nor would Hector, even though it meant a lot of carrying for herself and Rosie.

The phone rang, and Rosie took it. She listened a moment, looked at Aurora, shrugged.

"Honey, stop that boo-hooing and get on over here," she said. "I'll take care of Bruce, if he shows up before you do. I'll make him wish he was someplace nice, like in jail, before I'm through with him."

She listened a bit more.

"We're having gumbo," she said. "Don't run no red lights on your way over, either. That little one don't need to be in any car wrecks."

"That was Melly," she said when she hung up. "Bruce has been hassling her agin."

"I couldn't have guessed," Aurora said.

4

When the evening news ended, Aurora rinsed her teacup and forced herself to go upstairs and change. She was urged on by Rosie, who flogged her with platitudes whenever her spirits sunk to threatening depths.

Rosie considered that her floggings were mostly delivered out of self-interest: when Aurora's spirits sank they often carried her own to the bottom with them. Aurora's invariably floated back to the surface sooner or later, whereas her own were apt to dwell on the bottom for days.

"Life has to go on," she commented, as Aurora was rinsing her cup.

"It seems to go on, but that doesn't mean my mood has to accompany it," Aurora said. "I wish I hadn't invited Pascal to come by for dessert—now I'm not in the mood for him."

"It don't take a Frenchman long to eat dessert," Rosie said.

"No, but it takes this Frenchman a long time to pay court," Aurora said. "I wish Trevor hadn't died. Trevor always favored the shortest distance between two points, and there were only two points that interested him, where human beings were concerned."

"Which two?" Rosie asked. Besides being interested in whether Aurora and the General still had a sex life, she was also curious about the sexual behavior of Aurora's former boyfriends.

"Which two would you suppose?" Aurora asked. "You should have been named Nosie, not Rosie."

"You didn't answer my question," Rosie pointed out.

"The male point and the female point," Aurora said, heading upstairs. Trevor had been a yachtsman—he was very old school. After forty years of yachting he had choked on a bite of lobster while dining with his eighteen-year-old girlfriend at a restaurant in New York. Aurora had almost married him once; sometimes she found herself wondering whether marriage to Trevor, considered as a whole, would have increased or decreased her life's load of misfortune.

She would have been the first to admit that her life's load of misfortune had been far lighter than the load many, perhaps most, humans sustained; nonetheless, hers weighed quite enough. Trevor had been both charming and devoted, but, as his six marriages and innumerable romances suggested, he had not been noted for his willingness to shoulder anyone's load for very long. He far preferred to bob about on the seven seas, putting into port now and then in order to indulge in heavy meals and light seductions.

Still, Aurora missed Trevor, and the fact that he would never be showing up again to buy her any of the heavy meals, or attempt any of the light seductions, did nothing to lighten her tread as she pulled herself upstairs.

General Hector Scott, on his crutches, met her at the head of the stairs. To her surprise she saw that he was actually dressed. He wore a clean shirt and his bright red bow tie. For a second, Aurora was hit by an intense feeling of déjà vu; was this not a moment that had occurred long ago at the head of her stairs?

"My goodness, Hector, you're up," she said. "You're dressed. I believe you've even shaved. "I'm witnessing a miracle."

"It's no miracle," the General said. "I'm sick of feeling old and ugly. I'm trying to reform. I decided to start my reform by getting dressed. How was Tommy?"

"Oh, Hector," Aurora said, and before she knew it she was crying again. Every thought of Tommy brought it on. The General spread his crutches and took her into his arms for what proved to be a short cry.

"I mustn't mess your shirt, now that you're wearing one," Aurora said, resting her wet cheek against it anyway.

"My shirt's expendable," the General said. "I know how you get when you go see Tommy. I thought I'd make a special effort. Did he seem all right?"

"No, he just seemed the same," Aurora said. "He's always the same. It makes me want to shake him. I'm afraid though, that even if I shook him, Tommy would be the same. Nothing anyone can do affects him at all."

She drew back and looked at the General. Despite his improved appearance, he seemed subdued.

"Hector, you look quite wonderful," she said. "Still, you don't seem to be quite yourself."

"No, I'm usually cranky," the General said. "Tonight I'm not cranky. I'm making a special effort."

"Ordinarily I would consider that a good sign," Aurora said, wondering why she didn't consider it an especially good sign.

"Of course it's a good sign," the General said.

"I can't quite convince myself that it is," Aurora said. "I'm not sure that it's good that you've decided to restrain your strong preference for being cranky. What if it brought on a stroke?"

"It won't bring on a stroke," the General said. He wanted rewards, not questions, but he was getting questions, and it was all he could do not to slip back into his normal cranky state.

"I don't want to be packed off, it's as simple as that," he said. "I decided to clean up so maybe you'll let me stay. I also decided to stop being cranky. I don't want to go to the old soldiers' home. I wouldn't last a year in one of those places. I'd miss you so much I'd just die."

Aurora was struck to the quick.

"Now you've spoiled the one nice moment of the day," she said, abruptly drawing back. "Do I appear to be the sort of woman who would simply pack off my companion after putting up with him for twenty years?"

"Well, I can tell you're thinking about it," the General said. "You as much as suggested it, just the other day. I've got my pride, you know. I don't want to stay where I'm not wanted."

"Pride such as yours goeth before a punch in the nose—or it should," Aurora said, getting angrier. "I only once mentioned a military home to you, Hector, and if you'll recall I mentioned it strictly in the context of my own unfortunate demise."

The General, who had shaved and dressed in the specific hope that if he did he and Aurora might get through one evening without a fight, was annoyed to realize that they were heading straight into a fight.

"Your death, you mean," he said. "Don't keep calling it your demise."

"Yes, my death, Hector," Aurora said. "I don't see why I can't choose my own name for it. Demise, departure, death —I don't care. If you're trying to reform, you're not succeeding. I scarcely got up my own stairs before you started picking on me."

The General felt, as usual, that his tongue had betrayed him. Despite his best effort to say only the right things, invariably whatever he said turned out to be the wrong things.

"I'm just going to die, when I go," he said lamely. "I'm not going to demise."

"Yes, but that's you," Aurora said, cooling slightly. "Hector Scott, plain soldier. Of course you're just going to die, although I imagine you'll expect America to give you a twenty-one-gun salute, or whatever number of guns is appropriate to your age and attainments."

"Oh, they hardly ever do that anymore," the General said. "I doubt it would occur to them to do it for me. They'll just drop me in a hole and that will be that."

The thought that his own burial would lack ceremony made the General feel sorry for himself; he *had* always supposed he would have a military funeral and a twenty-one-gun salute. The fact was, he had lived too long: even towering figures, even an Eisenhower, would be lucky to get that kind of attention nowadays. He himself had not quite been a towering figure and could not expect much.

"Hector, we must stop this quarreling," Aurora said. "We'll be too upset to eat. Now we're even quarreling about dying, when the obvious fact is that neither of us *is* dying, demising, departing, or going anywhere at all. We're living on forever, quarreling every step of the way. I'm sure if there turned out to be an afterlife you'd get there first and lie in wait for me. You'd ambush me, just as you did tonight, and we'd resume our quarrels."

She walked into her bedroom and stood by her window nook, trying to gain control of her emotions. Hector had the irritating habit of being at his best and his worst at the same time; on countless occasions in their twenty years together his best and his worst had manifested themselves within a few seconds of one another. Just as she had softened toward him for taking her into his arms and allowing her to cry about Tommy, he had made an insulting remark about her packing him off.

The General hobbled into the bedroom behind her, feeling very low in his thoughts. He was saddened by his own propensity for angering Aurora, even on occasions when he was making a special effort to keep her in a good mood. Special efforts didn't seem to count for much in this life—not really, the General concluded. Whatever ground one gained by a special effort was rarely ground one could hold for more than a few seconds, after which it was back to trench warfare. Aurora's chance reference to the Battle of the Somme didn't describe his life as it might be in a military home. It described his life as it was with her. Mud, barbed wire, and sudden death were likely to be one's portion.

He crutched himself over to the window and stood beside her silently. He didn't know what to say.

On the sidewalk below them, under the streetlight, two squirrels sat facing one another as if in conversation.

"Do you think those squirrels are happier than we are?" the General asked. Aurora loved animals and could sometimes be distracted by references to them.

Aurora knew he was trying to atone for his wounding remark, but she still felt wounded and did not intend to be led into a discussion about the happiness of squirrels.

"It's not my fault that I'm younger than you, Hector," she said. "That's why you're mad at me, isn't it? That's what people nowadays refer to as the bottom line, isn't it? I'm younger than you, and I always will be. I have quite a good chance of outliving you. Is that what you're mad about?"

It was, although at the moment the General didn't really feel angry.

"I know I'm lucky," he said. "You've been wonderful to me for twenty years. If you want to know the truth, you've been the best part of my life. You've been better than soldiering and a lot better than being married to Evelyn. It makes me mad that it has to end.

"Of course, that's not your fault," he added hastily. "It's just what happens. It's just life and death."

Aurora blew out her breath in a kind of resigned sigh. It made the General nervous. More and more, the course of their life together was being punctuated by Aurora's long sighs of resignation. The General didn't like it. In his twenty years with Aurora she had passed through a great many moods, some of them hundreds of times, but the one mood she normally skipped was resignation. She might be buoyant, she might be sad, she might be furious, but she had never been resigned.

But now she had begun to sigh her new sigh, and to the General it bespoke resignation. More than once he had wanted to ask her to stop sighing, but he was afraid to. She might take it wrong. Over the years he had said a great many things that she had taken wrong—so many, in fact, that he could not understand why she had not just kicked him out.

While they were standing together at the window, a small

car pulled into the driveway and Melanie, Aurora's grand-daughter, got out. She was chubby, and her short hair, to the General's annoyance, seemed to be green.

"Is her hair green?" he asked Aurora. "I thought it was pink."

"It was pink, now it's green," Aurora said. "Are we going to have to quarrel about that, too?"

"It's just that I was finally getting used to it being pink," the General said. "Now I have to get used to it being green. Before that it was orange. It makes my head spin.

"Melanie's hair was beautiful once, when it was blond," he added.

Aurora was thinking the same thought. When she was a small child, Melanie's shining blond hair had delighted everyone who saw her. Indeed, Melanie herself delighted everyone who saw her. She had only been three when her mother died, and for the next several years her liveliness, charm, and self-confidence had kept them all going; in those years it had been hard to stay gloomy with Melanie around. She had defied all opposition, particularly Aurora's opposition, and Aurora's opposition was the only serious resistance Melanie encountered as she skipped and darted through her early youth, getting her way nine times out of ten.

But then the teenage years came, and almost at the moment of their arrival Melanie lost her liveliness, charm, and self-confidence, retaining only her defiance. From being skinny and quick, she became chubby and slow; she dawdled end-lessly, missing her school bus morning after morning. At thir-teen she began to disappear from school for hours at a stretch; at fourteen she became addicted to amphetamines and had to spend most of a summer at a substance-abuse camp. Only Rosie could exercise any influence over her at all. By then Aurora had lost so many battles with Melanie that she had more or less ceased battling, from sheer exhaus-tion. Melanie's boyfriends had been a succession of rich louts, uniformly intolerable, at least from Aurora's point of view. Melanie became pregnant by one of them; Rosie per-suaded her to have an abortion. Shortly afterward, she ran away for the first time, though only to the home of a friend who had moved to Dallas. When she was seventeen, the stress in the house rose to such a level that Aurora consented to her getting an apartment. She graduated from high school early and enrolled in a media program at the University of Houston, but dropped out and began to work at various fast-food jobs. Then she punked out and quit working. She was now pregnant again, a fact she had only informed them of the week before. Aurora argued for another abortion, but Rosie —mother of seven and grandmother of six so far—wanted her to have the baby: one abortion was okay, two were not. Besides Rosie was frankly gaga about babies and was still vaguely bitter about the fact that she herself had not had a few more.

"Shouldn't we ask Melanie up?" the General inquired. "She may be in trouble."

Aurora sighed again. "Leave her to Rosie for a bit," she said. "She only comes to see Rosie anyway."

"I'm getting pretty hungry," the General admitted. "I've been nervous all afternoon. I get nervous when you go to the prison. Then I get hungry when you finally come back."

Aurora, still digesting three pig sandwiches and a large piece of mincemeat pie, sat down on her bed. She felt like a nap, but knew she couldn't have a nap just then.

"We're having some excellent gumbo," she informed him. "And I'm having Pascal for dessert."

At the mention of Pascal, the General saw red.

"You're what?" he said. He not only saw red, he turned red. Even in the dimly lit bedroom, Aurora saw him flush.

"Excuse me, I'm having him *over* for dessert," she amended. "I myself just had some wonderful mince pie at the Pig Stand. You just control yourself. On top of everything else I've had to deal with today I don't think I can bear one of your jealous fits about Pascal."

The General didn't speak for some time—he was doing his utmost to rein in his fit. Aurora looked exhausted and depressed, and a fit just at the moment would be sure to make things worse.

42

"You might come to like him, if you'd try," Aurora said. "You eventually came to like my other boyfriends—only now they're all dead."

"Well, they weren't exactly boys," the General reminded her. "Some of them were nearly as old as I am."

Aurora began to remove her rings. She needed a shower—nothing else was likely to revive her.

"They may not have been young, but they had boyish qualities I'm afraid you've always lacked, Hector," she said. "There's very little of the boy left in you."

"How could there be, I'm eighty-six," the General pointed out, in what he thought was a reasonable tone. "Besides, I've sent men into battle. Those things age you."

In fact, he could only occasionally remember the battles he had sent men into, but he liked to remind Aurora that he had been a soldier. None of her other boyfriends had sent men off to die.

"Yes, they aged you, and now you've insisted on aging me," Aurora said. "I wish I had Charlie back, and Trevor and Vernon and Alberto. You're so rude to Pascal he won't even stay around to play cards. I'm sure if we had a couple of my boyfriends to play cards with we wouldn't quarrel so much."

"I might like Pascal if he weren't French," the General said. "I fought in France, you know. The women are pretty but the men are much too prissy. They're always saying 'Vive la France!' I've heard all I want to hear of 'Vive la France!' if you don't mind."

"What does it matter what I mind? I'm going to shower," Aurora said, hoisting herself up with the aid of one of the General's crutches.

"I hope you aren't mad," the General said. "I guess I could make a special effort with Pascal. If only he won't say 'Vive la France!' I might come to like him."

"Well, we'll see, Hector," Aurora said, switching on the light in her bathroom. She paused at the door for a moment, looking at the General, who felt that on the whole he was trying hard and not succeeding where Aurora was concerned. He began again to feel a little sorry for himself.

"I said I'd make a special effort," he repeated.

"Yes, dear, I heard you," Aurora said. "I believe I've heard you utter the phrase 'special effort' a half dozen times since I came up. I don't want to seem unappreciative, but there are times when your special efforts are more trouble than they're worth. There are times when I'd trade them all for a good card game."

"You *are* unappreciative, though," the General said. "I'm doing my best. It's not your fault that you're younger, and by the same token it's not my fault that your boyfriends died before I did. I know you wish I'd died first so you could get a younger man to live with, but I'm stubborn, and I didn't. That's the way the goddamn cookie crumbled."

To his annoyance Aurora looked at him and sighed her sigh again—it was the last sound she uttered before she shut the bathroom door. In a second the General heard the sound of the shower. There was nothing for it but to hobble back to his patio and wait for dinner.

As he hobbled he reflected that he had hit the nail squarely on the head when he said what he had about Aurora wishing he had died first. After all, he was a worn-out old man—any younger woman would prefer someone with more vigor, particularly more vigor of what one might call the bedroom type.

That was undoubtedly the nail, and he had undoubtedly hit it on the head. The problem was that, with Aurora, hitting nails on the head was not necessarily the right thing to do. But what *was* the right thing to do? Did she expect him to spread a red carpet for his own successor? Making things easy for rivals had never been his way, either in love or in war.

Aurora, in the shower, experienced a sharp touch of remorse. Hector *had* made a special effort, but for some reason it had activated her cruel streak. Ordinarily, even when a little tired, it was her habit to sing arias in the shower, but the persistence of her cruel streak, where Hector was concerned, left her aria-less this time. Try as she might to be appreciative, the fact was that Hector irked her intolerably at such times, and he always had. It seemed to her that her cruel streak had emerged even oftener, and with more force, when they had both been younger and Hector better able to defend himself.

The horrible thought struck her that, due to some perversity in her own character, she loved Hector Scott only when he was cranky. At his worst he had certainly been as cranky as she was cruel, and yet she had accepted him as her lover when she might instead have accepted several men who were, by comparison, meek as mice: her boyfriends, the ones who were all dead.

Thanks to her prison visit she was too cried out to wax very sentimental about her lost boys, or to deceive herself that, as suitors went, hers had been a particularly spectacular group. Charlie Norris, her most recent loss, had been a Cadillac salesman; their courtship had consisted of many test rides in gleaming, new-smelling vehicles that Charlie had hoped to sell her. He had won her affection mainly by incessant flattery, but she was not so won as to spend tens of thousands of dollars on one of his cars. The General rather liked Charlie because he played golf, and in fact had been standing beside Charlie Norris when he hit his last tee shot and fell dead of a heart attack before the ball even hit the fairway.

Prior to Charlie there had been Trevor, Alberto, and Vernon. Trevor choked on the lobster, Alberto—once a brilliant tenor—died of a brain tumor, and Vernon, her helpful if hopelessly inhibited oilman, had met his death in the crash of a bush plane in Alaska—or at least it was so assumed. No trace of the plane, its pilot, or Vernon had ever been found.

Of her four fallen friends, only Vernon's death struck her as truly sad; or, rather, not his death but his life, or lack of a life. Trevor had had his yachts and his women, Alberto had had his great voice and his early fame; even Charlie had had his gleaming cars, and a certain hearty, attractive bonhomie.

But Vernon had had only his aloneness, and all her wiles —back when she had wiles in abundance—could not induce him to leave it. He had been the most helpful man she had ever known, arriving time after time to get her out of trouble or help her survive crises; but once the trouble ended or the crisis passed, Vernon left. The next time he called he might be in a hotel in Riyadh, or a hut on the North Slope: curious, friendly, even wise at times—but distant.

"Here is my conclusion, Hector," she said when she emerged, refreshed, repaired, and dressed for dinner.

The General had been sitting on the patio but had not turned on the light. He felt too gloomy even to turn on a light. Try as he might, he could not manage to ignore Aurora's moods. She had hundreds of moods. He knew it was foolish to allow himself to react to every one. After all, at his age, what did one more female mood matter? If it got too bad, he could always die.

But he didn't die, and he continued to react to Aurora's moods. If she was in a bad mood when she shut herself in the bathroom, he would be in a worried state until she came out.

From the sound of her voice, announcing that she had reached a conclusion, he knew she was in a better mood, and his own spirits rose, though he had no inkling as to what her conclusion might be and could not even remember what subject they had been discussing when she shut herself in the bathroom.

"My goodness, can't you even turn on the lights for yourself anymore?" she asked, turning on several.

"I'd rather be in the dark when I'm depressed," the General said. He had just remembered what they had been talking about before Aurora took her shower.

"I was depressed because you don't seem to like my special efforts," he said. "You're always badgering me to make them, and then I do and you don't like them."

"Hector, are you comparing me to a badger?" Aurora asked briskly. "We're dining shortly. I hope you won't spoil my digestion by comparing me to a rodent."

It was the General's turn to sigh. After his sigh he grabbed the dictionary and began to look up badger. Lately he and Aurora quarreled so often about what words meant, or what

46

things were, that he had taken to keeping the dictionary handy.

"A badger isn't a rodent," he informed her. "It's related to the bear."

His eyesight was untrustworthy at times and he had not actually yet found the word "badger" in the dictionary, but he was pretty sure a badger was a member of the bear family, so he decided to bluff.

"Are you doing this to avoid hearing my conclusion?" Aurora asked, highly annoyed. Nothing irked her more than to see Hector Scott take refuge in a dictionary.

"No, I forgot you had a conclusion," he said simply. "I'm glad you're in a better mood."

"Too bad for you, now I'm not in it anymore," Aurora said, although the thought of gumbo and the pleasing ceremony of dinner and the fact that she was dressed and looked nice perked her up more than she was ready to admit.

"You don't deserve my conclusion but I'll give it to you anyway," she added. "My conclusion is that from now on, when we're angry, we should just slug it out till one of us drops."

Now that he was convinced she was in a good mood, the General was not particularly interested in her conclusion.

"You mean have fist fights?" he asked mildly. "How'd you come up with that one?"

"You see, you don't take me seriously," Aurora said. "As it happens, I don't take you seriously, either. I'm apt to be quite cavalier about your special efforts—in fact, I just was. But you're equally cavalier about my tender feelings."

"Your what?" the General asked, startled.

"My tender feelings," Aurora repeated. "Don't sit there pretending you didn't hear me. I have tender feelings quite often, thank you very much."

"Well, I make special efforts quite often too," the General said. "Thank *you* very much."

"You see, this very discussion proves my point," Aurora said. "Your special efforts make no impression on me, and my tender feelings make no impression on you. So why are we bothering? From now on you have permission to be as cranky as you want, and I'll be as difficult as I can. That way we'll know where we stand."

"Where *you* stand, you mean," the General said. "I can't stand, unless I have my crutches."

"Don't interrupt me," Aurora said. "There is one last part to my conclusion and it's the surprising part. Are you ready to be surprised, Hector?"

"Sure, every day's a new day," the General said.

"I'm afraid I've concluded the opposite," Aurora said. "If one happens to be living with you, as I appear to be, every day is pretty much the same day. We quarrel and then you sulk. In fact, it's the sameness of the days that has led me to my surprising conclusion. I think we should go into therapy."

The General considered that he knew Aurora thoroughly, and did not expect to be surprised by anything she might conclude. He was so convinced of this that when she said they should go into therapy he assumed he had misunderstood her. Though admittedly a little hard of hearing, he distinctly heard the word "go" and assumed she must be planning to drag him off on a trip to some ridiculous island in a part of the world he wouldn't like.

"Where is it?" he asked.

"Where is what, Hector?" Aurora asked, exasperated by his lack of reaction.

"The place you mentioned," the General said. "I think you mispronounced it. Isn't it in the Maldives, or somewhere?"

"I pronounced it quite correctly—it's scarcely a hard word," Aurora said. "T–h–e–r–a–p–y. Therapy. And it isn't in the Maldives, it's in the Medical Center."

"Oh, therapy," the General said.

Then the concept sank in, and his jaw dropped. "Therapy?" he said. "You mean you want us to see a psychiatrist?"

"Correct," Aurora said. "In fact I was thinking we might want to try psychoanalysis. I wouldn't be surprised if a little psychoanalysis had a good effect on our quarrels."

"You've lost your mind," the General said. "I'm eighty-six

years old. What goddamn good would it do for me to be psychoanalyzed now?"

"For one thing it's said to be quite good for one's memory," Aurora said. "I've concluded recently that we have a memory problem. Half of our quarrels start because we disagree in the area of memory. I remember things correctly and you remember things incorrectly, and the next thing you know we're quarreling. Psychoanalysis might prompt you to remember much more accurately than you do now and I don't see why we shouldn't try it."

"*I* remember things incorrectly?" the General said. "Who is it that's always forgetting where she put her car keys or her earrings? You must have lost a thousand earrings just in the years I've known you."

"Hector, I won't stand here and listen to your exaggerations," Aurora said. "You've heard my conclusions and I mean to implement them. I intend to have us in analysis so quick it will make your head swim."

"It won't be a new feeling," the General said. "You make my head swim every day."

"Excuse me, Hector, you know how I hate to bicker on an empty stomach," Aurora said. In the course of her shower she had somehow gone from full to empty, and could hardly wait to taste the gumbo. Without giving Hector Scott a chance to issue further complaints, she sailed downstairs to start carrying up the dinner.

5

While the General and Aurora were having their discussion, Rosie, in the kitchen, had been trying to help Melanie get a grip on herself. For starters, she made her a chocolate milkshake and slipped a couple of raw eggs in it. When left to herself, Melanie's diet seemed to consist mostly of potato chips and Diet Pepsi, not exactly ideal fare for a mother-to-be. Rosie seized any chance to improve it.

"Weren't Bruce's parents both drunks?" she asked. Melanie sat, or rather slumped, at the table, smoking and looking desperately unhappy.

"They go to AA," Melanie said. "Bruce doesn't even live with them now. He lives with his new girlfriend."

"I wouldn't worry too much about the new girlfriend," Rosie said. "The fact that he's got one might be a blessing in disguise."

"Easy for you to say, you've got a boyfriend," Melanie said, annoyed. People were always telling her she ought to be glad she had lost Bruce.

"I *have* got C.C., but that don't mean you can't do a lot better than Bruce," Rosie said. "Anybody that would beat up a pregnant woman is a good person to stay clear of, if you ask me."

"He didn't really beat me up, he just shoved me, and I fell over a chair," Melanie said. "I was upset when I told you he beat me up."

Although she hated Bruce at the moment, she didn't like to hear Rosie criticize him. Neither Rosie nor her grandmother understood anything about her life, and it irked her when they made criticisms.

"Getting shoved down could be the first step in getting beat up," Rosie said. She was in no mood to relent where Bruce was concerned. "Once men start shoving you around they don't know when to stop."

"Did your husband beat you?" Melanie asked. She could only dimly remember Rosie's husband, who had died about the same time as her mother. Her main memory was of the man's stomach, which was huge.

"Not on your life, he didn't," Rosie said. "I told him while we were engaged that if he ever raised his hand to me I'd kill him. He only hit me once, and that was self-defense."

"Self-defense?" Melanie asked, interested. In her memory the man had been almost a giant—at least his stomach had been as big as a giant's. Why would he have needed to hit a tiny woman in self defense?

"Yeah, I discovered he was screwing a slut," Rosie said. "I tried to stab him with a butcher knife. He beat me off and then one of his own friends stabbed him with a butcher knife anyway—Royce nearly died that time."

"Why did his friend stab him?" Melanie asked. A few minutes before she had wanted to die; she was convinced she would never be attractive or happy, and that no one would ever love her as much as Bruce had, when they first met. But now she felt a little better. She was thinking of asking Rosie for another milkshake.

"The friend that stabbed him had been screwing the same slut," Rosie said.

"I guess I shouldn't call her a slut," she added more gently, after a moment's reflection. "She visited Royce in the hospital—it could be she was just crazy about him. When he died she called and asked if she could come to the funeral."

"Did you let her?" Melanie asked.

"Yeah, I let her," Rosie said. "I thought it was nice manners on her part to call and ask, even if she did wreck mine and Royce's marriage."

"I don't think you would really have stabbed your husband," Melanie said. "May I have another milkshake?"

"Just because I'm small don't mean I'm harmless," Rosie assured her. "I would have killed Royce right there in the bathroom if he hadn't punched me in the snoot."

Melanie tried to imagine Rosie stabbing her fat husband with a butcher knife, but she couldn't. Then she tried to imagine herself stabbing Bruce with a butcher knife because he had decided to live with Beverly, a girl who had once been her best friend.

Neither of her imaginings worked. Rosie and her grandmother couldn't get it through their heads that she still loved Bruce. She had cried for a week when he started living with Beverly, but that hadn't made her want to stab him. She didn't even stop loving him, mainly because she suspected that he didn't really like Beverly that much. The real trouble was that Beverly's folks were too rich. They were so rich they had given Beverly a Ferrari for her birthday.

Bruce's big weakness was sports cars. He had hardly said two words to Beverly before she got the Ferrari, but a week later they were living together. Bruce just wasn't the sort to pass up a chance to drive a Ferrari. Unfortunately he wasn't as good at driving sports cars as he thought he was, and had had an accident almost at once. The accident was basically just a fender bender, but Beverly's parents promptly freaked out—they didn't like Bruce anyway, and had given Beverly strict orders not to let him drive the Ferrari. They started yelling at Bruce. They told him he had ruined an eighty-thousand-dollar car, and that he had to pay for every cent of the damage or else go to jail. Bruce didn't even have a job at the time—how could he pay for an eighty-thousand-dollar car, or even one fender of one? Plus, Beverly was real spoiled and expected Bruce to take her dancing or to nice restaurants at least five or six times a week. Bruce was happy just eating pizza and didn't have the kind of money it took to take Beverly out every night. The only way he could get that kind of money was to be a dope hauler, running loads of pot up to Fort Worth or Dallas; but Bruce really didn't like being a dope hauler because of the possibility of being caught, sent to prison, getting raped, and dying of AIDS.

He had just come by her apartment to borrow twenty dollars from her, but Melanie knew he meant to spend the money on Beverly, which was why she got so mad. She freaked out and started yelling at him, which scared him so badly he shoved her over the chair. Bruce wasn't nearly as tough as he pretended to be.

"Don't, I'm going to have a baby," Melanie said. That had been enough to calm Bruce down. The shove really wasn't that big a deal, and she had begun to regret even mentioning it to Rosie.

Besides, she didn't feel all that bitter toward Bruce; she felt bitter toward Beverly's parents. Didn't they know a Ferrari would attract a lot of attention? Beverly herself didn't even much like cars, but she had tiny tits and knew perfectly well that having a Ferrari would make it easier for her to get boyfriends.

Had it not been for the Ferrari, Melanie reasoned, Bruce would never have left her, and she wouldn't have lost her self-esteem. If she hadn't lost her self-esteem, she would never have slept with either Koko or Steve. Koko had been her best friend for years; he was a sweet Thai boy, just your basic pal, someone who was always there in emergencies and a great person to listen to music with or just hang out with when there was no emergency. It had not been entirely right to sleep with him, she wasn't that attracted, but Koko was, and now he was madly in love with her. Also, it had increased the confusion about whose baby it was she was pregnant with. The fact that Steve had happened to come home from college just when she was at her very lowest ebb increased this confusion still more. Steve was just your basic spoiled-rotten yuppie brat. Melanie had dated him for a month or two in high school. He popped into town pretty much at the exact moment she hit bottom; she felt so desperate for someone to be with, even if it was just for five minutes, that she slept with Steven too.

Just thinking about the fix she was in made Melanie feel tired—so tired she would have liked to sleep for a week. Often she *would* sleep through most of the week—heavy sleeps that lasted ten or twelve hours at a stretch. In her view there was no reason not to sleep: she didn't have a job, and had dropped out of her media studies program because she was too fat and not pretty enough to be an anchorwoman—for years being an anchorwoman had been her secret dream—and Bruce only came to see her when he had had a fight with Beverly, or needed money, or maybe just wanted to smoke a joint with his old girlfriend.

"Do you ever hear from your father?" Rosie asked. If ever there was a child who could use a father's attention, it was Melanie, but Rosie was under no illusions that Flap Horton, Melanie's father, would come through with very much attention, very much money, or very much anything. Flap taught English literature in Riverside, California; Melanie adored him and had hoped at various points to be allowed to go to school in Riverside, and perhaps even live with her father, but it was one of those things which was just not coming to pass. Lately, as far as Rosie could tell, Flap had stopped giving Melanie any encouragement at all—very few rays of light came from his direction.

In the first few years after Emma's death, Flap had tried hard to be a decent father to Melanie and the boys, but then he remarried and acquired three stepchildren; he and his new wife had a child of their own, and Flap's attention had drifted away—farther and farther away from the children he had had with Emma.

To an extent, Rosie was not disposed to blame him too much. No one could pay attention to everything they were supposed to pay attention to; her own record as a mother had not been spotless. Two or three of her own children had not really received the level of attention a child should get, and she knew it. But at least she had managed to focus on them in emergencies or in periods of profound need. Melanie was in just such a period at that moment, and Flap, it seemed to Rosie, was doing a very poor job of focusing.

"He never calls," Melanie said bitterly. "He said he'd help me pay for my car, but he never sent the money. Teddy was sort of interested in going back to school this semester, but Daddy never sent him the tuition money either."

"I'm sure your granny would pay for Teddy's tuition," Rosie said. "Teddy's and yours too. She'd love to see both of you kids in school."

"I know, but Daddy says he'll do things, and then he doesn't do them," Melanie said. "He always sounds like he means to, but then nothing ever comes in the mail. He doesn't really love us now—he just thinks we're a lot of trouble. He's never even been to see Tommy since Tommy got sent to jail."

"Out of sight, out of mind," Rosie said, imagining how nice it would be if Tommy were sitting at the kitchen table with them just then. More than any of Emma's children, Tommy haunted her—haunted her so profoundly that she rarely allowed even a wistful daydream about him to slip into her consciousness. She couldn't afford such daydreams—they soon would be followed by many sad, guilty thoughts. Though she faithfully accompanied Aurora to the prison in order to drive her home, she could rarely psych herself up enough to actually go into the bleak visitors' room and see Tommy. Most of the time she sat in the car, feeling like a sick, cowardly rat. She felt as if she were letting both Tommy and Aurora down. After all, Aurora hated going there, too, and came out destroyed; yet, time after time, month after month, Aurora went in, whereas Rosie only managed to psych herself up that high two or three times a year, though she loved Tommy every bit as much as Aurora did.

"Daddy liked me when I was little," Melanie said. "He gave me books to read. Now he never sends me books. He never sends me anything. I wish my mom hadn't died."

Melanie could only dimly remember her mother, but she did have a memory or two of her mother combing her hair, and she thought she remembered her mother singing songs to her. Mainly, though, she remembered that when her mother was alive she and her brothers had never felt alone—and now they did.

Rosie had to gulp and blow her nose. She turned to the sink and began to wash a dish that was already perfectly clean in order to have a moment in which to master her emotions. Emma Horton, the children's mother, Aurora's daughter, had been Rosie's favorite person, more beloved to her in some ways than her own exceedingly difficult children. Melanie looked almost exactly as Emma had looked when she was a teenager; sometimes the mere sight of Melanie caused sorrow to well up in Rosie, forcing her to gulp and blow her nose and wash perfectly clean dishes, until it subsided.

She knew quite well that she and Aurora had done their best by Emma's children; she suspected that their best was a good deal better than many other people's best—and yet she also knew that it hadn't been enough. Tommy and Teddy were cripples, in their different ways, and Melanie was sad.

Still, sad was different from broken, she reflected. Melanie wasn't broken. She would soon be having a baby, and a nice little fat baby might make a huge difference in Melanie's life.

"We better take dinner upstairs," she said, remembering her duty. "Your granny and the General need to eat on time. It's when they get too hungry that they have their biggest fights."

Just as she said it, Aurora walked into the kitchen. Her eyes immediately lit on Melanie's cigarette.

"Melly, I do wish you'd not smoke," she said. "It can't be good for little Andy."

Melanie gave Rosie a guilty look and stubbed out the cigarette.

"I was nervous," she said. "Do I really have to name him Andy if he's a boy?"

"No, dear, of course not, you can name him Plato or Aristotle, if you prefer," Aurora said, hugging her sad-looking granddaughter. "It's just that I've always wanted an Andy in my life, and none has ever come my way."

Actually, Melanie loved the name—she just wished she had thought of it instead of her grandmother. Her grandmother was always taking over—it left very little for the rest of them to do.

"I've been dreaming of twins lately," Rosie commented. "It might be twins. Wouldn't that be fun, having twins running around the house?"

"Or it might just be a girl," Melanie said. "If it's a girl I want to name her after Mom."

"Oh," Aurora said. She had been lifting the gumbo off the stove—the thought of Emma coming round again threw her off so much that she almost dropped the pot. Rosie took it just in time.

"Don't you like that, Granny?" Melanie asked. "Wouldn't that be nice?"

"Yes, dear," Aurora said, but in a very different voice from that she would have hoped to project. The thought that she might soon have a great-granddaughter bearing the name of her daughter jerked at her heart; she was afraid to say more for fear that what would come out would be the voice of an old woman.

"Oh, well, I like to be surprised, myself," Rosie said. Aurora's moment of shock had not been lost on her. "I'd take an Andy or an Emma, either one."

"Of course, so would I," Aurora said, recovering. "But that's a very nice thought, Melly—appropriate, too. I think we should adopt it. If a girl emerges, we'll name her Emma."

"How's the General?" Melanie asked, getting up to help carry the dinner.

"Very quarrelsome, as usual," Aurora said. "Could you carry the gumbo? You're the youngest and strongest. Rosie and I will hobble along with the rest."

"Sure, do you have a Pepsi?" Melanie asked, as Rosie began to cut the bread.

6

After dinner, Rosie and Melanie hung around for a while, playing dominoes with the General over the din of CNN. Encouraged by Rosie, the General had become a news junkie too. Following the news with Rosie allowed him to demonstrate his superior knowledge of world affairs—superior not merely to Rosie's but also to that of a long parade of reporters and analysts who pontificated night after night about things the General felt he understood far better than they did.

"Yes, the war clouds are gathering," he said, after consuming a nice chunk of walnut cake. "Russia's going to go for sure, and I think China might go."

"Go where, Hector?" Aurora said. He was always saying that the war clouds were gathering, a phrase which for some reason irked her.

"China's a rather populous country," she added. "Where could it possibly go?"

"Well, civil war could break out," the General said. He had spoken rather automatically, and now regretted it. He did not in fact think China would go, but then again it might, and what did Aurora know about it, anyway? They had visited China together, and, except for a few art-historical high spots, Aurora had scarcely noticed the country. In Beijing she had complained because there were too many bicycles and no way to make them stop so she could cross the street; her mood had only improved once they got back to Hong Kong, where she could shop all day.

Aurora had been polishing her rings on a napkin as Rosie and the General exchanged tidbits of speculation about what might happen in the trouble spots of the world. This happened every evening now, so regularly, indeed, monotonously, that she had almost come to regret her decision to install Rosie as the permanent occupant of the guest house in the backyard.

True, her decision had rescued Rosie from the violent Denver Harbor neighborhood where she had survived by dint of tooth and claw for most of her adult life; but the downside meant having her dinner table turned into a political-science seminar run by her maid and her boyfriend.

She was about to deliver herself of a blunt comment notifying them as to what they could do with China, not to mention Lithuania, when the doorbell rang.

"Thank God, it's my date, just when I need him most," she said, brightening. "Last chance for walnut cake."

The General, considering how best to employ his double six, ignored her remark about the date, but hastily whacked himself off another piece of cake. The second he did, Aurora took the plate and headed downstairs.

"I don't know why I put up with this," he said, once he felt sure Aurora was out of hearing distance. "It's your move, Rosie."

"Granny's just a big flirt," Melanie said. "She really loves you best."

The General chuckled. He was well aware that both Melanie and Rosie gave him a lot of credit for tolerating Aurora's willful ways.

"If she loves me best, God help the rest of them," he said. "Play, Rosie. You're the only person I know who has to use a calculator to play dominoes."

"Its batteries are about to go, that's why it's flickering," Rosie said. "I skipped third grade, that's probably why I'm no good at addition."

Melanie yawned. She thought she might go by Teddy's for a while. The apartment where he and Jane lived was only a few blocks from her own apartment. Teddy and Jane were always up, studying Sanskrit or some other language.

Aurora had prepared a little snack for Pascal—a pear, a mango, some of the walnut cake, a little Camembert, and a half-bottle of Burgundy. She set it out on a small table in her downstairs study before bothering to go to the door to let Pascal in. Over the years she had found it best to let Pascal settle his nerves for a few minutes before letting him in— otherwise he might jump at her in his eagerness to show affection. He was a mere five four, and when agitated displayed something of the jumpy character of a small French dog.

Pascal Ferney, waiting with increasing discouragement just outside the door, wondered if this would be the night when Aurora wouldn't let him in at all. With any other woman he would have been ringing the doorbell furiously every few seconds, but he had done that once, in his early days, and Aurora had responded with a fury so violent that ever since he had had to screw up his courage to a high pitch before even ringing the doorbell once. What if he pushed too hard and the doorbell became stuck? What would she do then?

"Goodness, Pascal, just in time," Aurora said, opening the door and giving him a hug in one smooth motion. Hugging him immediately was also likely to reduce the likelihood of his jumping at her. Looking over his head, she noticed that, as usual, he had left the lights of his small crumpled Peugeot blazing brightly.

"Am I late or early?" Pascal asked. "I lose all sense of time when I visit you."

"You're more or less on schedule, but once again you've left your lights on," Aurora said. "I do hope they aren't stuck. I wish you would remember to turn them off, Pascal. The rest of humanity remembers to turn their lights off, and I'm sure you could, too, if you concentrate. My reputation will suffer, if it hasn't already, if my lovers insist on coming over here and leaving every light blazing."

"Oh, *merde!*" Pascal said—it irked him that once again he had forgotten to turn off his lights. He raced across the lawn, whacked them off, and slammed the car door violently. Then he raced back across the lawn and arrived again at Aurora's side. Encouraged by the fact that she had moved him, at least conversationally, into the category of lover, he tried to resume their hug, but with no success. Aurora merely caught his arm and ushered him inside.

"I lose all sense of time when I visit you," Pascal repeated. He was a little breathless from his double dash across the lawn.

"I lose all sense of everything when I visit you," he added. "Everything becomes—topsy-turkey, is that correct?"

"Topsy-turvy," Aurora corrected, amused. For all his faults, Pascal had a twinkle, and some resilience; slapped down a million times, he would still come twinkling back, and she had never been able to entirely resist men who managed to twinkle, General Scott, on the other hand, had yet to twinkle his first twinkle—or, at least, his first in her company. She had upbraided him for this inability many times, but to no avail.

Aurora kept a firm grip on Pascal's arm until she had him firmly installed in the study—if left to roam unchecked, Pascal was apt to dart upstairs for a minute in a misguided attempt to be sociable. Once there he was apt to burst out with niceties which were more or less the moral equivalent of "Vive la France!" His sudden appearances startled both Hector and Rosie, neither of whom ever knew what to say. Once, in a moment of embarrassment, Rosie asked him to join them in a domino game, an invitation that ruined everyone's evening. Pascal had chattered so that neither the General nor Rosie nor her calculator could add accurately, causing the General to lose his temper and stomp off to bed. That, of course, had been back in the days when he could stomp.

"What do they do up there?" Pascal asked, glancing hastily upstairs as Aurora marched him along.

"Oh, don't mind them, you know how serious they are," Aurora said. "They're sorting out the fate of Lithuania, or perhaps Lebanon."

"They should talk to me then," Pascal said. "I was once in Vilnius for three years."

"I don't want to hear the word Lithuania out of you tonight, Pascal," Aurora informed him. "If I hear it again you're out on your ear. Sit yourself down and eat this food. I'd like to hear some gossip about Madame Mitterrand, if you have any, and if you don't, then how about some gossip about Catherine Deneuve?"

"Madame Mitterrand is very serious," Pascal said cautiously. He had a sense that this was one of those times when he had better be careful. He had better try to say what Aurora wanted to hear, and yet he had no idea what that might be.

"I don't know if Catherine Deneuve is so serious," he added.

"You *are* from France, after all, Pascal," Aurora said. "What makes you think I care whether they're serious or not? Who are they sleeping with? Who is anybody sleeping with? Here I sit, dying for a little gossip, and you won't give me any. I guess it's not as easy to be a lewd old woman as I'd always hoped it would be."

Pascal was so startled that he almost dropped his pear. Aurora had a reckless look in her eye. She wanted to talk about movie stars or presidents' wives sleeping with people. She had even suggested that she wouldn't mind being a lewd old woman. Could she be doing what Americans called "coming on"?

Watching her closely, Pascal decided that that was exactly what was happening—why had he been surprised? His life-long assumption, borne out many times, was that all women wanted him: Aurora had just taken longer than most to let him know it. He took a sip of wine and grasped her hand. He expected that this first sally might be rebuffed, but it wasn't. Aurora let him keep holding her hand.

"If you want to be lewd we should be upstairs," Pascal said, smiling. "*They* should be downstairs—people can talk about Lithuania anywhere. Upstairs we could be lewd all night."

"All night, at your age?" Aurora said, aware that two of her suitor's appetites had just come in conflict with each other. Pascal was trying to finish his Camembert while keeping a firm grip on her hand—rather too firm a grip, in fact, if seduction was his purpose. She felt an old restlessness take her— it was no doubt quite immoral for her to lead this little man on, but she was doing it anyway, as she had many times in her life, with men small or large, just to see what would happen. Would Pascal Ferney at last fight his way through her taunts, or would he retreat to cheese and wine?

"If we were upstairs you'd be surprised," Pascal said. "Not all of me is old."

"Not all of me is dumb, either," Aurora said. "As you correctly point out, people can talk of Lithuania anywhere, but I don't believe that's the *only* thing that can be done anywhere. In my youth I knew people who were capable of committing lewd behavior in a quite surprising variety of places. In fact, I rather frequently found myself doing that sort of thing too—all over the house, or even out-of-doors, if the mood took me. If you don't mind my saying so, Pascal, the notion that carnal actions of a lengthy duration can only occur in a bedroom on the second floor of my house is rather un-Gallic, is it not? Somehow I had imbibed the myth that the French can do it anywhere, anytime. What a pity it's only a myth."

Pascal was thunderstruck. Convinced as he was that all women *did* want him, and want him a lot, he could scarcely believe his ears. This woman, who had never given him more than a kiss and a squeeze now and then, was accusing him of being too conventional in his approach to sex.

"Besides that, we're not arm wrestling," she said, before he could collect his thoughts. "Stop squeezing my hand so hard. Having my fingers crushed is not my idea of foreplay."

Pascal turned red in the face, dropped her hand, then immediately tried to take it again. Aurora jerked it away. Pascal had been about to take a swallow of wine, but the jerk caused it to slosh out of his glass and splash his tie. All the while, Aurora was looking at him in a reckless way, a way that he had not seen her look before. He felt a coward—she was making him feel a coward with her reckless look.

"Pascal, you seem to be falling apart before my very eyes," Aurora said. Her demon was out, and she was in a mood to destroy him utterly, since nothing else was happening. "Now you've managed to waste my wine and ruin your tie in the same motion. Isn't that the tie I bought you in Paris?"

Pascal jumped up in a fury. "I'll throw you on the couch!" he said. "You'll see what happens then."

"Pooh, sticks and stones, " Aurora said. "I don't believe you'll throw me anywhere, or do anything else very interesting, either."

Pascal felt a blind rage coming over him. He rushed around the table, meaning to grab Aurora by the throat and still her merciless tongue forever. He *did* grab her by the throat, but before he could get on with the business of strangling her a young voice at his elbow said, "Hey, what do you think you're doing? You behave, Pascal."

To his horror he saw Melanie standing at his elbow, holding a silver soup tureen.

He immediately took his hands off Aurora's throat.

"Oh, mademoiselle, thank God you came," he said. "I didn't know what I was doing."

"You certainly did know what you were doing—you meant to strangle me," Aurora said, rubbing her neck. On the whole she felt rather pleased with how things had gone. She lifted her eyebrows and grinned at Melanie.

"Oh, no, no, it was just a fit," Pascal said meekly. "It was *amour fou.*"

"You needn't explain to my granddaughter," Aurora said. "She knows what brutes men are—she was just cruelly beaten by one herself, scarcely an hour ago."

"Oh, Granny," Melanie said, "I wasn't cruelly beaten, I was just shoved over a chair. What did you do to make Pascal so mad?"

"The same thing she always does!" Pascal exclaimed. "Taunts—she only taunts me. She doesn't mean a word. I love her, but so what, as you kids say."

"It's just that my demon got loose and decided to make a snack of this unwary Frenchman," Aurora said. "Pascal, that's excellent cake—I think we might just table the passion question for a bit. I suggest you go to the bathroom and run a little cold water over that tie you just soaked in wine. If you want to soak your head at the same time, that's no business of mine, but in my view it wouldn't hurt you. Then come back and eat your cake."

Too embarrassed to argue, Pascal trundled off.

"My God, Granny, what was that all about?" Melanie asked. She knew life was full of surprises, but she had never expected to come downstairs and find her grandmother being strangled in the study.

"Just a contretemps, a very small one," Aurora said. She reached across the table and took what was left of Pascal's wine. "I was just trying to get him to make love to me on the couch. In my heyday I was made love to a great many times on couches, and I suppose I had in mind to try it once more. Unfortunately, Pascal chose to strangle me instead."

She took a sip of wine. Now that her anger had passed she was feeling a little discouraged.

"It's a lesson you should take to heart," she said, looking at her chubby granddaughter.

"What lesson?" Melanie asked. She was stunned by the thought that her grandmother had apparently been willing to fuck Pascal on the couch in her study. She knew her granny was eccentric, but she had never supposed she would do anything *that* eccentric.

"Given the option, men will frequently try to murder you rather than make love," Aurora said. "There are exceptions, but not too many."

"Granny!" Melanie said, again. "You were going to do it on *that* couch, with Pascal? What if the General had come downstairs and caught you?"

"I would have been very angry," Aurora said. "Hector knows me well enough to realize that there are times when

65

he should leave me well enough alone. It points to another lesson, which is that it's unwise to incarcerate yourself with a man nearly fifteen years your senior. I've done it and now I'll have to make the best of it—for all I know Pascal may be the best of it, too.

"Chew on that for a while," she said in a lighter tone. She noticed that her granddaughter was struggling to assimilate some rather shocking information.

"I'll chew on it for years," Melanie said, as Pascal came back into the room. He looked disconsolate, and his tie was dripping wet.

"I can't believe it," Aurora said. "When I directed you to run cold water on your tie I naturally assumed you'd take it off first. I thought you French were supposed to have savoir faire. What happened to yours, dear?"

"It has been a strange evening," Pascal said. "At this moment I am not myself."

He sat down and began to apply himself to his walnut cake.

Melanie took the soup tureen to the kitchen. She came back to the study for a moment, gave her granny a kiss, and left. She could hardly wait to tell Teddy and Jane what she had just witnessed—talk about blowing their minds!

"Good night, dear," Aurora said. "Remember little Andy and try not to smoke."

Pascal ate his cake in silence while his tie dripped on his pants. Aurora was watching him quietly—she did not seem to be angry, but then she had not seemed to be angry when he arrived, either, and yet within ten minutes she had goaded him into a violent act.

"What's the matter with you now?" Aurora asked. "I hope you aren't preparing to sulk or weep or produce any other manifestations I'm not in the mood for."

"Why can't you come to my apartment?" Pascal asked. "In my apartment there would be nobody but us."

"That's quite true," Aurora said, smiling at him. "On the other hand, if I were in your apartment, I might faint from the stench and the squalor. You must admit that you seem to lack housekeeping skills along with savoir faire and various other things.

"Though perhaps that's what you want," she added, kicking him lightly under the table. "You want me to faint. Then you'd have a passive body to work your will on. But that's not the way it's going to happen, if it happens."

"I want it to happen!" Pascal exclaimed. "I want it to happen."

"Well, if it should, keep in mind that this is not a passive body that you're looking at," Aurora said. "Nobody's getting any fun unless I get some too."

"I will get a housekeeper," Pascal declared. He lived in a tiny studio apartment near the zoo. The fact was that he had allowed it to become rather grubby over the years. The one time Aurora had visited it she had held her nose the whole time. It was hard to seduce a woman who was resolutely holding her nose.

"I will make it spotless! Spotless!" he declared—his soon-to-be-hired housekeeper would make the house spotless, and Aurora would come. He felt better just thinking about it and reached for the wine bottle.

"You'll see," he said. "I'll even buy new sheets. You'll see."

"New sheets, Pascal?" Aurora said. "I hardly know if I deserve quite that much savoir faire."

He was still talking about his housekeeper and his soon-to-be-spotless apartment when she tucked him into his Peugeot and sent him home.

7

Teddy and Jane met when they were both patients at a psychiatric hospital in Galveston. Soon after they fell in love, both were released from the psychiatric hospital—on the same day, in fact. They felt it was a happy omen and for some months they weighed the question of marriage before deciding against it. Then they weighed the even weightier question of children and decided they wanted one—or possibly two. Roughly a year after they took the second decision, Jonathan arrived. Jonathan was now nearly two and had yet to speak—or, to be more accurate, had yet to speak in English. One of the things that convinced Teddy and Jane that they were perfect for one another was that both had been majoring in classical languages when they began to go wrong in their heads. Jane had been at Bryn Mawr, Teddy at the University of Texas. Jane's parents and Teddy's grandparents both lived in Houston, and that was where they had retreated when they dropped out. After a few months of getting crazier and crazier, they had both agreed to be admitted to the hospital in Galveston.

The fact that Jonathan, whose nickname was Bump, had

yet to speak in a recognizable language worried Aurora considerably, but didn't worry Teddy or Jane at all. For one thing, he could draw some of the Greek alphabet in his coloring book, and had recently shown an interest in the Cyrillic alphabet as well.

"I don't care how many alphabets he can draw," Aurora said. "I want him to say something I can understand."

"Maybe he's just waiting until he has something interesting to say," Teddy suggested. "Wittgenstein didn't speak until he was four."

"Wittgenstein wasn't my great-grandchild either," Aurora said. Jonathan was a beautiful child—he had curly blond hair, unlike his mother, whose hair was blond but straight—and was apparently quite happy. He had alphabet blocks in a variety of alphabets, procured from a special store in Cambridge, Massachusetts, and when he wasn't amusing himself with them he played what appeared to be quite complicated video games on a TV set that was used for no other purpose—Teddy and Jane objected to American TV on the grounds that the sets weren't high resolution and thus produced images that were visually degraded. They felt that they were being ripped off by American TV manufacturers, who could have easily made high-resolution TV sets if they had wanted to.

Aurora also objected to Jonathan's nickname, Bump. She felt it was a very inadequate nickname for such a beautiful child.

"Bump suggests a bump on a log," Aurora pointed out. Sometimes she would show up in the middle of the afternoon and sit on the couch in the little apartment for a while, watching Jonathan amuse himself with his many alphabet blocks. He was by no means a withdrawn child—he loved to crawl all over his great-grandmother and to sit in her comfortable lap and have stories read to him. He made approving or disapproving sounds, he giggled, laughed, yelled, and cried, much as other children did. He just declined to converse. One of Aurora's theories about this worrisome fact was that Jonathan was silently protesting his own nickname.

"Why should he speak to people who call him Bump?" she asked one day. "The fact that he can draw all those alphabets suggests a strong sensitivity to language. He probably hates his nickname. If you two would start calling him by his right name he might be talking a blue streak in a matter of days. Nicknames can be dangerous, you know. Perfectly nice people get stuck with dreadful nicknames, often for their whole lives. What if he wants to be president and people are still calling him Bump?"

Teddy and Jane thought that possibility too slim to take seriously. Jane was rather more prone than Teddy to taking things seriously—at times even too seriously—but she wasn't worried about Jonathan's political career being sabotaged by his nickname.

"He just looked like a Bump, even when he was still in me," Jane said. "He didn't even weigh six pounds when he was born."

Jane was a very quiet woman—very quiet but very smart. Aurora approved of Jane and had a great deal of confidence in her. Jane was modest, spent nothing on clothes, said little, fed Teddy and Jonathan admirably, kept the apartment tidy, and seemed to be to both a competent and responsible young woman.

Indeed, Aurora felt slightly intimidated by Jane. All her life she had been slightly intimidated by people who were both competent and responsible. She could not have imagined that such a person would end up in her family, though to her chagrin Patsy Carpenter, her daughter's best friend, had predicted something of the sort.

"Teddy may go crazy now and then, but when it comes to a mate he'll pick well," Patsy said once, when she and Aurora were discussing the fact that neither of them had done a particularly brilliant job of picking.

"Why would you think so?" Aurora asked.

"Because all of his girlfriends have been nice," Patsy said. "All of his girlfriends have been a lot nicer than *any* of the people my own kids have been attracted to."

Patsy had three children, a son and two daughters, by different marriages. They were roughly the ages of Emma's children, and none of them had the knack of choosing well. Her son Davey had already married and divorced two shallow rich girls, while her daughters, both of whom had temporarily believed themselves to be Maoists, showed a strong preference for working-class louts.

Patsy was acutely aware that she herself lacked the knack of picking well. Jim, her first husband, had been an inoffensive but not exactly brilliant yuppie nerd—a yuppie nerd long before either term had been coined—who managed to lose his entire and considerable inheritance in a computer business just when other, brighter yuppie nerds had begun to make billions in computer businesses.

Tomas, her second husband, had seemed a great deal more promising, and for a time had actually *been* more promising. He was a very elegant and blazingly arrogant half-Spanish architect whose weird, severe houses had enjoyed about a ten-year vogue in L.A. and some of the tonier beach towns. The two of them had produced two bright, lively daughters before Patsy surprised Tomas in the pool house one day being sucked off by a sixteen-year-old gardener's assistant. Patsy had just turned forty and was no country girl—she and Tomas had run with the Hollywood elite for more than a decade, during which time she had thought some thoughts and seen some sights. Interrupting the sex startled her, but it startled her far less than the deadly beating Tomas proceeded to give her for having presumed to interrupt his pleasure.

It was a dark day for their marriage, because Tomas discovered that he enjoyed beating Patsy far more than he enjoyed making love to her. After that he beat her frequently and inventively, until she took her girls and left.

Two years later, before the lawyers had even finished working out their complex property settlements, Tomas tottered feebly up to her door, a dying man. A few months later he became the first prominent L.A. architect to die of AIDS. Patsy took care of him in his last months, though she could see in his eyes that if he had had the strength he would have liked nothing better than to beat her again.

It was at that juncture that Patsy moved back to Houston and picked up the threads of her old, old relationship with Aurora Greenway, and with Emma's children. Her sexual confidence, such as it had been, was lost; she was so convinced that she would never pick well that for over three years she simply ceased picking. Though her heart went out to fat little Melanie, the child of Emma's that touched her most was Teddy. He treated Patsy like a beloved aunt, and, even when he himself was shaky or more or less out of his head, had the knack of soothing her when she was upset.

Bereft of confidence that she or any of the children would ever manage to mate successfully, she fixed her hopes on Teddy, and he did not disappoint her; besides which, it was no small pleasure to point out that she had seen something in Teddy which Aurora missed.

Teddy and Jane supported themselves by working different shifts at a 7-Eleven on Westheimer. Aurora, Rosie, and Patsy were all horrified that they had chosen such a dangerous profession; in Houston, as elsewhere, convenience store employees were natural targets, and targets which were frequently hit—but Teddy and Jane simply walked around these protests.

"That's the reason we work different shifts," Jane told Aurora. "If one of us gets killed the other will still be there to raise Bump."

"Yes, but it would be a great deal nicer for Jonathan if you were *both* there to raise him," Aurora pointed out.

The 7-Eleven was only two blocks from their apartment, and was owned by a nice Vietnamese who sold spring rolls and good soups as snacks, something Teddy and Jane approved of. Jane often made the soups herself. Mr. Wey, the Vietnamese, was teaching her Vietnamese cooking. Teddy usually worked the night shift, midnight to eight; he had been held up twice and had had a few other nervous moments, but on the whole he and Jane liked the convenience of working at their neighborhood convenience store. They knew almost everyone who came in and felt that they were serving a useful role in their community—the lower Westheimer community, to be specific. It was a little dangerous, but no more so than being crazy, they felt. In her worst year Jane had tried suicide three times; in his worst, Teddy had tried it twice. The arrival of Bump had removed that possibility—both were very devoted to their child.

But neither had forgotten how they felt on the days when they had tried to die, and they went about their work at the 7-Eleven with a serenity matched only by that of Mr. Wey, who had left Vietnam on a boat that had sunk in a storm, drowning his wife and two of his three children. He lived with his surviving daughter, a girl named Nani, who had started high school in Houston knowing almost no English and a mere four years later won a full scholarship to Princeton.

Teddy and Jane considered that in Mr. Wey they had lucked into the perfect boss. He appreciated their efficiency and politeness; besides teaching Jane Vietnamese cooking, he was helping Teddy learn the language. Over the years, Teddy's linguistic interests had drifted eastward—from Greek to Farsi, then Hindi, then Sanskrit. He thought they might drift ever farther eastward, and was delighted to be working for a man who could give him a toehold on Vietnamese.

It was not quite time for Teddy to go to work when Melanie came tromping up the stairs and burst in with the news that Pascal Ferney had just tried to strangle their grandmother. Bump was sound asleep in the middle of the floor, hugging a stuffed raccoon. Teddy was reading a page or two of Horace—he didn't want to let his Latin slip too far—and Jane was combing her long blond hair and wondering if a cup of tea would keep her awake.

"He did what?" she asked, when Melanie burst out with the news of the attempted strangling. On first blush it seemed a little too weird to be believed.

"I saw him!" Melanie insisted. "He had his hands around her throat and he was strangling her."

"What happened next?" Teddy asked. *Something* out of the ordinary must have happened, because Melanie was looking more animated than she had looked in months. She was really excited, which in Teddy's view was good. One of Melanie's big problems was that she had lost the capacity for excitement when she was around fourteen—her loss of interest in her own math skills was an example. In junior high Melanie had been one of the three top students in the city of Houston in math skills—she could have gone free to virtually any college in the land. But then she just stopped doing anything at all with her math. Teddy was a big believer in keeping one's skills honed, which was one reason he was reading Horace. Also, of course, he *liked* Horace, in the way that Melanie had once *liked* calculus, but now Melanie didn't seem to like anything very much, not even her stupid lover, or former lover, Bruce.

"What happened next was that I told him to cut it out," Melanie said.

"Did he cut it out?" Jane inquired, getting up to make tea. It looked as if she was going to be up for a while anyway.

"Yeah, he quit strangling her," Melanie said. "He got all embarrassed and went to the bathroom and ran water on his tie. I guess he just flipped out or something."

"Aurora likes to goad people," Jane observed. "Maybe she just goaded Pascal once too often."

"That isn't even the interesting part," Melanie said. "When Pascal left the room I asked her what had been going on and she said she had been trying to get him to make love to her on the couch."

Teddy and Jane received this information calmly—a little too calmly for Melanie's taste. Teddy and Jane made a big point of being unshockable—it could become a little irritating. All Teddy did, when he heard the news, was pick Bump off the floor and deposit him in his bed, which was about three steps away. It wasn't a large apartment. Bump didn't wake up, nor did he lose his grip on his raccoon.

"Don't you think that's weird, Teddy?" Melanie asked. "Our own grandmother trying to get a guy to fuck her on the couch? He isn't even her main boyfriend, either."

"Maybe her main boyfriend's getting too old to cut the

mustard anymore," Jane suggested. "I hope not—I like Hector—but I guess he is getting up in years."

"She went to see Tommy today, too," Teddy reminded them. "She gets a little crazed when she goes to see Tommy, and you can't blame her. I get a little crazed when I go see Tommy—we all do."

"That's because Tommy's too sad," Melanie said, remembering how after her last visit to the prison she had felt so weird and frenzied that she had wanted just to turn her car north and keep driving for days until she got to Wisconsin or somewhere. The part that made her feel frenzied was that Tommy wouldn't even try not to be sad. He wouldn't even try to look forward to anything—like getting paroled or something. Of course he wouldn't be eligible for parole for five or six more years, but still, five or six years wasn't forever; he could permit himself some little ray of hope, only he wouldn't.

"You're both making it too complicated," Jane said. "Maybe she just plain wanted to get it on with Pascal."

" 'Get it on' is one of those phrases that makes me shudder," Teddy said. "Just say she wanted to fuck him. Why torture the language?"

"Sorry," Jane said mildly. "I keep forgetting you hate that phrase."

"What I really hate is that you don't hate it," Teddy said.

"I don't see why I'm supposed to hate it," Jane said, "It's just a phrase."

"I can't get the thought of Granny doing it on the couch out of my mind," Melanie admitted. "Do you think old people kiss?"

Neither Jane nor Teddy seemed to have any opinion on the likelihood of old people kissing.

"What if they kissed and one of them had false teeth and the false teeth started to come out?" Melanie asked. "Yuk."

Jane laughed. She didn't often laugh, but she had a deep, delightful laugh that sort of filled the room, once she released it. People who got to hear Jane laugh realized immediately that this was a hearty woman laughing, and after that, when they were with Jane, they waited for her to laugh again. Sometimes they had a long wait. Jane was not a person who could be called giggly or tittery. She either laughed or she didn't.

"You should be a writer, Melly," Jane said. "That's the kind of thing a writer would think of. I doubt Aurora would let false teeth stop her if she really wanted to kiss somebody."

"No, and neither would you," Teddy said, looking at Jane. "You'd just kiss him—or her—wouldn't you?"

Jane handed Melanie a cup of tea.

"You bet I would," Jane said, giving Teddy a kind of stern look—a look that, in Melanie's view, sort of said Watch it, buster. Teddy had a way of saying things that went a little too far. He had made a number of remarks about Bruce that went a little too far, also. Jane lived with Teddy—it was probably good that she could hit him with a stern look when his remarks got out of hand.

"Maybe I ought to go home," Melanie said.

"No, have some tea," Jane said. "Teddy has to go to work in five minutes."

A few minutes later, Teddy did go to work. He had an old green scarf that he wrapped around his throat when he went to work. Teddy was very prone to sore throats—he had many allergies and really needed a drier climate than Houston's, but he wouldn't leave the city.

"If I got you a new scarf for Christmas, would you wear it?" Melanie asked. "You've been wearing that scarf ever since you were in grade school—you got it when we still lived in Nebraska. Wouldn't you like a new scarf?"

"Well, I might," Teddy allowed. He seemed to be a little moody—a little low. Teddy rarely did anything dramatic when he was low—he didn't have fits anymore, or disappear for days at a stretch—but it was not hard to tell when he was depressed. Melanie's notion was that Jane's stern look had done it, but then, why shouldn't Jane have given him the look? He had sort of hinted that Jane was bisexual. Of course, Teddy and Jane were a pretty advanced couple, but Melanie had never given any thought to Jane being bisexual until Teddy made his remark, which sort of implied that Jane would be just as likely to kiss a girl as she would to kiss a boy. Melanie looked at Jane, wondering if it could be true.

"Don't give him a new scarf," Jane said. "Give me a new scarf. I'll wear it. Teddy plans to wear his green scarf for the rest of his life. He doesn't like change."

"You have to admit it can be upsetting," Teddy said. "I think I'll go see Granny tomorrow. Maybe I can find out what's going on between her and Pascal."

It was true that their granny told Teddy stuff that she never told anyone else, not even Rosie. Teddy had taken a course in memory while he was still at the University of Texas, and he had talked to their granny about some of the memory concepts he had learned—storage and retrieval and other stuff that Melanie, who had not had a memory course, didn't fully grasp.

Somehow the stuff Teddy told their granny about memory had given Aurora the weird idea of trying to remember every day of her life. She called it her memory project and announced that she fully intended to remember every day of her life before she was done. She had had a room over the garage fixed up to do her memory project in, and had even hired people to go up in the attic and bring down boxes full of old engagement calendars and baby books, and her husband's desk diaries and stuff. She even had engagement calendars and diaries and journals that had belonged to her mother and grandmother—maybe even her great-grandmother. Aurora really seemed to think that when she settled down and sorted out all the calendars and diaries she could do a complete chronology of her entire life and remember every single day; and all this started because Teddy happened to have a free elective and had decided to take a course on the structure of the memory.

Just before Teddy went out the door to go to work Jane went over and gave him a kiss and bit his ear. "Sell a lot of spring rolls," she said.

"Bye, Melly," Teddy said. He seemed a little glazed. Getting a bite on the ear from his wife didn't seem to perk him up much.

"Teddy's weird," Melanie said, the minute he went out the door. The thought occurred to her that Teddy and Jane might break up someday; other couples broke up, and so might Teddy and Jane. If that happened, Jane might take Bump away. Between sips of tea Melanie began to bite at her hangnail. Teddy and Jane breaking up would just make a bad situation worse.

"Teddy's fine, stop biting yourself," Jane said.

"Do you think you'll ever break up with him?" Melanie asked—she couldn't hold back the question. Teddy and Jane were really important to her. Except for Rosie, they were the only people she could go to when she got really strung out. Of course, that left out Koko, who had helped her through strung-out periods a million times, but her relationship with Koko had become confused the minute she slept with him.

"Get a grip on yourself," Jane said calmly. "Just because he got in a little dig about my kissing habits doesn't mean we're going to break up. I might even be pregnant right now. We want at least one more kid."

"You'll have to get a bigger apartment," Melanie said, brightening immediately. That was great news—Teddy and Jane wanted more kids.

Still, when Jane got yawny and Melanie left and was driving through the late-night mist to her dump of an apartment off Fairview Street, she didn't feel any too calm. She had seen Teddy go to pieces before—he might go to pieces again. Rosie seemed to think that Jane had been crazier than Teddy at the time the two of them met. Underneath the surface there *was* something kind of wild about Jane. It would be pretty horrible for Bump if his mother and father went to pieces again.

Melanie parked in front of her apartment and started to get out and go in—but then she didn't. She stalled. What she usually did when she went into her apartment was call somebody to take her mind off what a mess the apartment was; but the only person she could call at such an hour was Koko, and if she called Koko he would want to come right over. Then, if she let him, she might not be able to get him back to being just her basic pal.

Also, if she was in the apartment, she was definitely home, but if she was still in her car the situation was was sort of less definite—she could con herself into thinking that she might be about to go somewhere else, even if it was only to the Westheimer 7-Eleven to buy a pack of cigarettes from her brother.

Technically she knew that it was really not that safe to spend the night in your car—some rapist or girl killer could always come by and spot her. But in fact, with the deep mist wrapped around the car like a cocoon, she felt safer in the car than she did in the apartment. That was a great thing about Houston: those deep mists. You could put on a tape and sort of listen from within your cocoon of misty fog. Melanie put on a tape of one of her favorite groups, *Pump Up the Volume*. She didn't turn it up very loud—she didn't want a passing rapist to find her in her cocoon. She had her old poncho in the backseat and she wrapped up in it and let the music and the mist and the little red light on the tape player sort of coax her into being drowsy. It wasn't really sleep, but to Melanie it was more restful than being upstairs amid her mess. If she went upstairs she might start missing Bruce; she might start crying and cry too long, or she might start having hate thoughts about Beverly and her stupid Ferrari. At the very least she might lie there feeling zingy all night, worrying about people going to pieces. On the whole it was just better in her car—being drowsy under her poncho, hearing the music, and feeling sort of safe and cozy because of the mist.

8

After she dispatched Pascal, Aurora wandered into the kitchen, there to discover Rosie, who was watching CNN. To Aurora's annoyance she seemed to have finished off the walnut cake.

"Yeah, I got nervous and ate it," Rosie admitted. "We still got that extra piece of mince pie you brought from the Pig Stand in case of emergencies. Remember that piece of pie?"

"Of course I remember it—who do you think bought it?" Aurora said. "I just happened to be more in the mood for walnut cake, but that mood has now obviously been frustrated, along with all the other moods I've had this evening."

"I'm sorry," Rosie said. "C.C. ain't called for two days, that's why I got so nervous I finished off the cake. Maybe he's quit me."

"Nonsense, why would any man quit you?" Aurora asked. "Most of them would far rather quit *me*."

"Well, we both got the same kind of tongues," Rosie pointed out. "The mean kind."

"Do I have to hear the news every time I come into my own kitchen?" Aurora asked, taking the mince pie out of the refrigerator. Now that she was holding it in her hand it looked every bit as appealing as the walnut cake.

"A whole mountain fell on top of a little town down in South America," Rosie informed her. "It was just a little village full of real poor people, and now it's gone and they're all buried in mud, except for one baby they managed to get out. It's awful."

"It certainly is, but I'm not looking at it," Aurora said. "This is suffering I can't possibly redeem, and I object to having to confront it in my own kitchen. There's quite enough suffering I feel I must at least try to redeem—falling mountains and smothered villages are far more than I can cope with."

Rosie immediately clicked off the TV. It was obvious that Aurora was in no mood for any news, really.

"I turned it off," she said apologetically. Aurora's mouth was already full of pie.

"That's what I hate about television," Aurora said, pausing at the halfway point of the pie and wishing she had brought two pieces home instead of one.

"What's what you hate?" Rosie asked, when no comment followed. Aurora sat with her fork in her hand, looking annoyed and unhappy.

"What I hate about it is that it brings every suffering face in the world into my kitchen," Aurora said. "I don't want to see Chinese suffering, Romanian suffering, Palestinian suffering, South American suffering, or any other suffering. I'm up to my gullet in suffering right here at home—you saw how sad Melly looked. I'll try to take care of my own but I'm not going to sit here and feel responsible for China or Romania or anywhere else."

"That's the most pie I ever saw you eat in one day," Rosie commented. "Three pieces of mince, and then there was that piece of chocolate cream that you ate this morning before we went to the prison."

"So what, it's the only appetite I can satisfy by myself," Aurora snapped. "No males or their organs need be involved. Just me and my pie."

"Oh," Rosie said, "Did the General flash you or what?"

"No," Aurora said. "Pascal ran cold water on his necktie without bothering to take if off first, and then he attempted to strangle me. I'm so disappointed in him I could cry, and I would if I weren't already cried out."

"I know what you mean," Rosie said, "I'm about ready to give up on C.C. I *would* give up on him, only the next bozo to come down the pike might be even more of a washout than he is."

Aurora didn't answer, so Rosie got up and left. She liked to leave a perfectly clean kitchen, but in this case holding out for perfect cleanliness meant waiting for Aurora to finish her mince pie and then washing the pie plate and returning it to the cabinet. Rosie decided she better not risk it. Aurora did not look to be in the mood to appreciate having her pie plate snatched from her hands and washed.

"Good night, hon," Rosie said, going out the back door. As soon as she got to her cottage in the backyard she meant to switch CNN back on and see if any more babies had been rescued from the fallen mountain in South America.

Aurora knew Rosie would have liked to snatch the pie plate; she had been prepared to tear her limb from limb, verbally, at least, if she tried it. But when Rosie left, the fighting spirit went out of her at once, and her appetite suffered such a sharp falling off that she could scarcely finish her pie. In fact, she even left a curl of crust on her plate, something she rarely did. She almost regretted chasing Rosie off. When the two of them were together they at least generated enough human energy to bicker, and there were moments when bickering with Rosie seemed a good deal better than doing nothing with no one.

But Rosie was gone, the pie was eaten, her irredeemably sad grandson had been duly visited, Hector had been rude, Melanie had been depressed, and Pascal had disgraced his nation, more or less. There were moments when she felt she might someday achieve a living, more or less complete relationship with Pascal Ferney, but those moments were few and far between. And yet, if not with him, who could she achieve a living, more or less complete relationship with?

Discouraged, she put the pie plate in the sink and surveyed the contents of her refrigerator for a moment, hoping to spot some especially enticing leftover that might revive her appetite. People were constantly pointing out to her that all she did was eat, and it was more or less true; but eating was at least a real pleasure and it seemed hardly to matter any more whether she put on weight. She had never been exactly tiny, and now that she was older, she felt that weight was one worry she could safely dismiss.

"I'd rather be strong than thin," she said, when Rosie and Melanie chided her about her eating. Fortunately, Hector Scott knew better than to chide her about it, and in any case he had long been attracted to women of a certain heft, herself included.

She trudged up to her bedroom and opened the curtains. Invariably Hector closed them, and just as invariably she opened them again, because she liked the way the streetlight at the end of the block made circles in the mist—circles that were like little moons of luminosity. Hector, whose circulation was now so impaired that he had taken to sleeping in socks, gloves, and a nightcap, was snoring away. She preferred to ignore the socks and the gloves, but it was hard to ignore the nightcap, which made him look far too much like a character out of Dickens—Ebenezer Scrooge or Silas Marner or someone.

Aurora washed her face, got into her gown, and crawled into bed. She didn't feel sleepy; she felt empty, absent, idling—as if she had strayed into an area of life that she had not really been able to make her own. Often she read most of the night, mysteries and one thing or another. She had been making a late assault on Proust, but when she felt so absent she could rarely quite focus on Proust. Occasionally she might amuse herself with an old staple—movie magazines—but lately movie magazines hadn't been working quite as well as they once had. The stars now seemed ridiculously young, their antics and the romantic complications they got themselves into seemed adolescent in a way that had ceased to be appealing. Even their beauty had ceased to be appealing; she didn't know why, exactly. Perhaps it was because physical beauty was never likely to make an appearance in her life again—it was vaguely annoying that there seemed to be an endless supply of it running around Hollywood and behaving badly.

When she slipped into bed, Hector's body immediately edged over toward hers, as if in tropic response to her size and her warmth. His body did that every night. Aurora sat up in bed, looking out at the streetlight and the little moon it had created around itself. She felt Hector's hand fumbling for her hand. Every night he fumbled for her hand. Aurora removed his glove and flung it on the floor before allowing him to take her hand, at which point, to her annoyance, he woke up.

"What happened to my glove?" he asked.

"I took it off, Hector," Aurora said. "I don't feel like holding hands with a glove, if you don't mind."

"Yes, but you don't like it when my hands get cold, either," the General said. "I'm caught either way I go."

"You're no more caught than I am, you know," Aurora said. "Either I'm holding hands with a glove or I'm being fondled by an icy claw. It's very disappointing that this is how life ends."

"Ends?" the General said. "That's nonsense. Your life isn't ending. *My* life is a lot closer to ending than your life is. I'll be lucky if I last five years, and I imagine you'll last at least twenty."

"Those are just numbers," Aurora said. "In other respects this is how life ends, and I have every right to be disappointed, if not indignant."

"Did anything happen with the Frenchman?" the General inquired. He noted sadly that Aurora seemed subdued. Difficult as she was when she wasn't subdued, he still hated to see her subdued, and it seemed to be happening more often. It was not uncommon for them both to find themselves awake in the middle of the night feeling subdued. In the General's thinking, it was all because of sex, too. If he hadn't petered out, no pun intended, they would have something to do in the middle of the night if they both happened to be awake.

It might not be all that it had been, but would probably have been enough to keep them from feeling so subdued.

"Well, he came and ate and made a fool of himself," Aurora said. "Anything is a rather vast category, Hector. If you mean did I manage to stumble through the amenities, yes. On the other hand, if you mean something more sinister, no, nothing happened."

"Well, that's too bad, I guess," the General said.

"Too bad, you guess?" Aurora said, stung. She snatched his nightcap off and threw it in the general direction of his glove.

The General realized from her hostile tone that in all likelihood he had misspoken, but he was just waking up and didn't quite have his mental bearings; he knew it was foolish to speak when he didn't have his mental bearings, particularly if Aurora had hers—and she usually did have hers—but he often failed to stop himself in time. This was particularly likely to lead to trouble if Aurora was feeling subdued when he popped off.

Besides speaking in a hostile tone, she jerked her hand away, a sure sign that she was miffed, or worse. The General decided to pretend that he had just made a very general remark with no very specific intent. This might not work, but it was about the only option he had open to him.

"I just meant it was too bad you didn't have a more agreeable evening," he said, and then he began to hum a patriotic tune, something he had taken to doing with increasing frequency in moments of stress. Since almost all moments were now moments of stress, he found himself doing a good deal of humming.

In this case the patriotic tune he started to hum was "There's a Star-Spangled Banner Waving Somewhere," a tune he associated with the Second World War, though it seemed to him he had also heard it a good many times during the Korean engagement.

"Stop that stupid humming, Hector," Aurora said. "Every time you fumble the ball nowadays you start humming unrecognizable melodies from your distant youth. I much prefer that you just admit that you fumbled the ball, as you did. Humming, as you prefer to engage in it, won't help you recover many fumbles, if I'm using the right terminology."

"That wasn't an unrecognizable melody," the General protested. "That was 'There's a Star-Spangled Banner Waving Somewhere.'"

"Shut up about the stupid song," Aurora said. "Didn't you just imply that you wished I'd slept with Pascal?"

"Of course I didn't imply it," the General said. "I didn't imply any such a goddamn thing."

It occurred to him that perhaps he had implied it, but if so, what was to be gained by admitting it?

"Then what did you mean when you said it was too bad that nothing more sinister happened between Pascal and myself this evening?" Aurora asked. "Were you hoping he'd murder me? Was that what you meant was too bad, that he didn't murder me?"

"Aurora, I just woke up," the General said. "I don't know what I meant. I probably said something stupid. We quarrel all day as it is—do we have to quarrel all night, too?"

"Get out from under me, Hector," Aurora said. He seemed to be trying to wedge himself underneath her—it was another of his new habits.

"And stop lying, too," she added. "My hearing has not deserted me, thank you, and I very distinctly heard a remark suggesting that I am now free to seduce my admirers willy-nilly, and furthermore that I can count on your sympathy, if one lets me down, shall we say?"

"I thought I was supposed to be sympathetic to whatever happened to you," the General said. "You're always complaining about my lack of sympathy, but the second I show some I get attacked. I'd like to know what the rule is. Am I supposed to chortle with glee every time some fool disappoints you?"

"Yes, that's exactly what I expect you to do," Aurora said. "You've hounded me with your jealousies for more years than I can remember, and I won't have you wimping out now."

"Doing what, now?" the General asked.

"Wimpery, wimping out," Aurora said. "It's something Melanie often complains about. Now that it's happened to me I've decided that it's a very useful term."

"What's it supposed to mean?" the General asked.

"It suggests a failure in the area of manly behavior," Aurora said.

"Oh, impotence," the General replied. "Here we go again. If that's what you're complaining about, why not call a spade a spade?"

"Because in fact that wasn't what I was complaining about, Hector," Aurora said. "I was speaking of a certain desertion of principles, where I am concerned. Annoying as your principles have always been, I still expect you to hew to them. You're not French, you know, and you are not required to adopt a French attitude toward my infidelities. When I behave badly I expect wrath, not sympathy."

"Your what?" the General asked, suddenly sitting up in bed. "I didn't know you committed any goddamn infidelities. I thought you said nothing happened."

"Nothing did, but that's because Pascal is a fool," Aurora said, glancing at him to see what, if any, effect she might be having.

"I know he's a fool, I've been telling you that for five years," General Scott said. "What does that have to do with what we're talking about?"

"Merely that I had every intention of seducing him on the sofa," Aurora said lightly.

"You what!" the General said. Despite the heated argument he found himself in, his head felt cold, and he leaned out of bed and tried to reach his nightcap with one of his crutches, hoping to drag the nightcap within reach. Unfortunately Aurora had heaved it nearly into the bathroom, and he couldn't retrieve it.

"Well, you've always had a lot of goddamn cheek," the General said. "Now my head's cold. I might get pneumonia and die, in which case I have no doubt that you'll immediately start screwing some little fop from Europe right here where I'm lying. You won't have to bother about sofas if I get pneumonia and die."

Aurora retreated into an aloof silence, her favorite form of silence.

"Too goddamn much cheek," the General repeated. He wanted his nightcap, but he didn't quite want it badly enough to get out of bed, which was now nicely warmed by Aurora's body, and he didn't want to ask her to get it for him, either. Asking her to get his nightcap for him was one of those things he just didn't want to do.

"How long have you been planning this little seduction?" he asked. "I thought you were acting odd, but I never thought you'd go that far, with Melly and me right upstairs."

"I didn't plan it at all, my demon just happened to escape," Aurora said. "I assure you I long ago learned the folly of planning, where men are concerned. One can plan till one faints and still be very likely to draw a blank."

At the thought of all the blanks she had drawn in her life, Aurora suddenly felt overwhelmed. She sighed her sigh and put her face in her hands.

"What's the point?" she said. "Everything I've ever done has failed."

The General gave up on his nightcap. He hated to see Aurora sad at any time, but he particularly hated it when she slipped into one of her everything-I've-ever-done-has-failed moods, which seemed to him to come over her much more frequently now. Probably that was his fault. Probably everything was his fault. He should have gone to Masters and Johnson's clinic in St. Louis the minute he began to have trouble getting it up; he had suggested that very thing to Aurora, but at the time she wouldn't hear of it. She said it would be far better for them to enjoy a peaceful old age than for him to involve himself with sex doctors. But a year and a half had slipped by, and they weren't enjoying a peaceful old age at all—they quarreled day and night, and Aurora spent half her time sighing or deciding that her whole life had been a failure, or crying or sulking or being anything but the jolly woman he had known for so long. Very likely it was all his fault; he should have overruled her and headed straight for Masters and Johnson at the first sign of trouble. Sammy, his friend in Rancho Mirage, had gone to a sex doctor of some sort when he began to flag, and the doctor had turned Sammy right around and made it possible for him to continue his pursuit of bimbos.

"I knew I should have gone to Masters and Johnson," the General said. "Here you are, a comparatively young, lively woman, stuck with an old geezer who has to wear a nightcap. In my youth they had these goat-gland operations—they advertised them as gorilla glands, but I think they were really just goat glands. They wouldn't have been able to catch that many gorillas, for one thing. My Uncle Mike had one of those goat-gland operations—he had to go to Mexico to get it—but it must have worked. Uncle Mike got married several times after that. If he weren't dead I'd call him up and ask him about it. With all these transfers and transplants they do now I wouldn't be surprised if they've improved the goat-gland operation."

"Hector, go to sleep before I strangle you, like Pascal tried to do me," Aurora said, taking her face out of her hands. "Why would you think I'd be interested in receiving the products of alien glands?"

"It might be better than receiving no products at all," the General said. He was thinking how nice it would be to go to Mexico for a few days—he had always liked Mexico, anyway—and come back potent. That prospect intrigued him so much that it took a moment for him to react to the fact that Aurora had said Pascal tried to strangle her.

"Did you say he tried to strangle you?" he asked. "Tried to strangle you how?"

"With his hands, Hector, a common method," Aurora said, glad that the gland issue had been disposed of. It had come up frequently during the months of Hector's decline. Evidently his Uncle Mike had made a big impression on him, although in her view several marriages might point more readily to the failure of such a method than to its success.

"Let's see your neck," the General said, turning on the bed

89

light. He had to put on his glasses to see her neck clearly; and when he did put on his glasses he could see nothing out of the ordinary about her neck, or about the bosom just below it. Now that he had his glasses on, he rather preferred to look at the bosom.

"He doesn't seem to have done you much damage," he said.

"No, he has small French hands—he's virtually hopeless as a strangler," Aurora said. "I wish you'd stop leering."

"Well, why'd he do it?" the General asked, reluctantly turning off the light.

"When I saw he was going to thwart me I became merciless," Aurora said. "As you know yourself, I can ill abide being thwarted."

"It probably fired him up, though," the General said. "He's a lot younger than I am. I doubt he would have got as far as strangling you if he wasn't pretty fired up.

"I wish you liked the Midwest more," he said; his mind reverted to Masters and Johnson. It was a pity Aurora didn't approve of the Midwest. If there was only some way to get her interested in St. Louis, or even Chicago, he might be able to slip in a few visits to Masters and Johnson. A few visits might well be enough—with science advancing practically every day, fixing him up might be a simple matter. Obviously Aurora was never going to sit still for the goat glands, but perhaps now they had pills or injections or something.

While he was thinking of sights Aurora might possibly want to see in the Midwest—he had given up on the Gateway Arch; whenever he mentioned it, she yawned—he grew tired and went back to sleep sitting up, with his mouth open.

Aurora felt relieved—quarreling about sex or the lack of it with Hector in the middle of the night was not her favorite way to spend the middle of the night. Far better to read Proust, or merely sit with the light off looking out the window at the moon above the streetlight, fantasizing about a time when Tommy might be out of prison, when Teddy and Jane might be back in school, when Melanie might be happily married. If even one of those fantasies would come true, she could sleep at night rather than spending so much of it staring and fretting.

Meanwhile they weren't coming true, and there was Hector. When he was asleep she found she still occasionally had nice feelings for him, even if he happened to be sleeping with his mouth open. Cranky and irritating as he was, at least he was there beside her and was sort of staying the course—not an easy course, she knew, and not one too many men would have wanted to stay. It was something, and, when she thought about it, it still touched her.

She got up, went around the bed, and found his nightcap, which she managed to get back on his head. Then she turned back the covers and began to try and scoot him into a reclining position; it was difficult but it was also necessary. He had gone to sleep sitting straight up: the military posture that had once thrilled her so was now something of a burden—depending on which way he tipped, he could easily fall out of bed, and if there was one thing Aurora was sure of at that hour, it was that the two of them didn't need any more broken bones.

9

In Huntsville, in his cell, seeing that Joey, his cellmate, had
finally gone to sleep, Tommy got his notebook from under
his bunk and began to work on his code. Teddy, his brother,
was the only one who knew that he was devising a code in
which to write a book about prison life that would freak out
the world.

"Why a code?" Teddy had asked, when Tommy first mentioned his plan. In fact, Teddy was thrilled that Tommy was
interested enough in life even to contemplate the creation of
something as ambitious as a code.

Since Tommy had been about fifteen, his only ambition
had been to have no ambition. His main way of being himself
was to refuse to try to do anything that society might consider
worthwhile. Teddy considered Tommy to be the brightest
person he knew—he was even brighter than Jane, and Jane
would have graduated summa cum laude from Bryn Mawr if
she hadn't gone crazy one semester before graduation. But
for all his brightness, Tommy had barely graduated from high
school and had refused to stay in college more than a few
weeks. He just wouldn't try: he felt that all ambition was

cooperation, and that cooperation was corrupt. At one point Teddy had engaged Tommy in many conversations about ambition and corruption and the capitalistic system, as well as all sorts of matters related to trying, and he was convinced that his brother was absolutely pure in his beliefs, which meant that he would never try anything. Teddy had been the one person in the family who wasn't shocked when Tommy killed Julie. Though he had never told anyone his deepest suspicion—not even Jane—Teddy didn't really believe the official account of the killing, which was that Tommy got rattled in an argument over drugs and accidentally shot Julie instead of the dope dealer she was then going with. Teddy had never seen Tommy get rattled enough to shoot the wrong person in a quarrel. In Teddy's view, Tommy probably shot Julie because she had sold out and betrayed the no-ambition ideals they shared, or seemed to share, when they were first going together. Julie wasn't pure; she was conniving. She wanted money, and lots of it. Teddy had never liked her and didn't mourn her—she just wasn't smart enough to deal with a person as dedicated to silence and nothingness as his brother Tommy. She should have known Tommy would kill her if she didn't stay out of his way. Tommy didn't try to make disciples, but of course he wasn't absolutely smart in *all* areas of life: he had been hustled by girls more than once.

Tommy had gone almost a decade, all through the latter part of his adolescence, hardly doing a single thing to further himself in the world. Twice he had starved himself to the point where he had to be institutionalized and force-fed. He only permitted himself actions that he perceived to be essentially terroristic—such as selling cocaine to white upper-middle-class kids. Tommy believed that white upper-middle-class kids were the trash of the planet; helping them destroy themselves seemed to him a worthwhile goal. He was no rabid ecologist, no particular friend of the planet, but he did consider that turning rich white kids into mindless freaks was the sort of service that he shouldn't disdain.

Tommy did like working on his code late at night, when

the prison was asleep. Teddy, who owned more than a hundred dictionaries and grammars, had provided Tommy with Xeroxes of a good many alphabets and twenty or thirty grammars from which to form a basis for his code.

Actually, Tommy had no real interest in devising a super-sophisticated code that would require hundreds of years to decipher. Once, when he was about twelve, their father, who was an English professor, dragged all his kids to England and made them go to all the boring literary shrines that he himself had always wanted to see. The one thing that interested Tommy was at the Bodleian library. It was the diary of Samuel Pepys, written in a weird shorthand. Part of the diary just happened to be on exhibit the day they were there. Tommy had never heard of Samuel Pepys, but when he got home and tried to read the actual diary he couldn't get too interested. The only really interesting thing about Mr. Pepys was that he had chosen to make up his shorthand. From the very moment that he had seen the fragment of the diary in a glass case at the Bodleian, Tommy had had the urge to develop some form of secret writing. In high school, when he still liked to read, he had ripped through quite a few books on codes and cryptology. He read about the Brontës and their secret script, and about the great codemasters and code-breakers of World War II, some of whom, he had to admit, were supersmart. Obviously you had to have a brain to do that kind of stuff.

But then, about the time he starved himself the first time, and had to go through the ridiculous force-feeding routine, he turned off reading. It was too much his dad's kind of thing; for years his dad had always pressured him to read this book or that: *Nostromo*, for example. His dad seemed to think life would shape up and be all hunky-dory if he would just read *Nostromo*, so one weekend Tommy did read it. Then he took a paper cutter, cut the book into a million shreds, and sent it to his dad in a shoebox. No note, just shredded Conrad. After that, his dad never mentioned reading again; in fact, his dad never mentioned much of anything again—not to Tommy. He was too pissed by having this great classic turned into confetti. This was about the time Tommy had his second bout of force-feeding, after which he gave up on starvation. If society wasn't even going to let him have control of his own digestive tract, then the time had come to pursue more aggressive ways to hit back at it.

After he shot Julie and got sent to prison he refused to read any books except those written by people who were actually in jail. Even with that limitation he was still left with a lot of books. Jane and Teddy drew up a list and got the books for him. It was their dream, he knew, that he would use his brain to write stuff as good as Dostoevsky or Cervantes or Defoe or Genet or whoever, but Tommy didn't plan to. He just wanted to use the code to sketch out his beliefs about murder and rebellion, and he didn't even plan to explain the code to Teddy and Jane. He felt that true rebellion had to be undertaken absolutely alone; the minute you started sharing your plans or recruiting allies you just started society all over again. He meant to keep his plans for rebellion entirely in his own head, because his own head was all he could trust. After all, even his guts had complied with the system; they had processed the mush shoved down him when he was hospitalized.

Working a little bit every night on his code excited him. It was *his* work, and not a soul except himself knew what it meant. The prison shrinks, who kept grinding the gears of their little brains trying to think of activities that might get him motivated, hadn't the faintest idea that he had his own work and did it with exact discipline every night.

Of course his cellmate Joey, a Mexican kid who had killed his brother and his best friend, both in one wild fit, occasionally woke up and noticed him scribbling in his notebook, but Joey had no curiosity about anything except sex and automobiles and had asked him about the notebooks only once. Joey was just twenty; he usually woke up long enough to masturbate before drifting back off to sleep to the music of Mexican rock, which he listened to night and day through his earphones.

Why Joey needed to masturbate so much, Tommy didn't

know, unless he was just a maniacally oversexed twenty-year-old. Joey's nickname on the cell block was Cunta—he had acquired it because he was so easy. He was the little whore of the block, available for very little—a joint, a cassette, a can of hair spray—to anybody who wanted him, even scummy old murderers or child rapists who had been in for twenty or thirty years, men who had done every act, taken every drug, had every disease, and probably still had a few diseases, old and new.

Tommy rather liked Joey—in many ways he was an ideal cellmate—and attempted once or twice to warn him about AIDS and other dangers, but Joey paid no attention. He continued to fuck everybody. He was young, cute, and careless; he liked his music and he liked fucking. Some nights he cried like a baby because he missed his mother. Joey had gotten only fifteen years and probably wouldn't serve more than four or five. Crowded as the prisons were, they weren't going to keep a young Mexican too long just for eliminating other Mexicans who might just soon have become part of the prison population themselves. In fact, the prison personnel treated Joey very well; they took the attitude that he had sort of saved them money and freed up beds by killing his brother and his best friend.

Also, Tommy knew, Joey whored with the prison personnel just as happily as he whored with the inmates. Joey basically fucked his way through his prison term. Tommy, on the other hand, had been celibate since the day he threw Julie out. Joey though he must be sick or something—sometimes it bothered him a little that Tommy had never shown the slightest interest in coming on to him—but Joey had sense enough to leave well enough alone. Tommy was a guy you didn't press, whether you were his cellmate or not. He was a little like an alien or something—a little spooky in the eyes. It was okay with Joey if Tommy wasn't interested; plenty of other people were.

Their cell was on the fourth tier. When Tommy worked he could look out across the large open space in the center of the building. Some of the personnel referred to the prison as the Huntsville Hyatt; being on the fourth tier and having the space to look across was a little like being in one of those Hyatt hotels that had a high lobby.

At night, looking into the space gave Tommy a certain sense of peace. He could always jump into the space someday, and that would be that. Of course, he'd have to be sure to do a proper dive and land on his head. An Indian had done that once—a chief called Satanta. An old chain-smoking guard named Mack Mead, who had worked at the prison all his life, told Tommy about it.

Mack Mead collected prison lore and was eager to tell it to Tommy. Not too many prisoners were interested in prison lore. When Mack detected that Tommy had more curiosity than the ordinary murderer, he became loquacious and told Tommy more than he really wanted to hear. He even got special permission and took Tommy one day to the place in the old prison where Satanta had made his fatal jump.

"It don't look too high," Mack admitted, squinting upward. "But old Satanta was smart. He dove perfect. He hit right on his head and died instantly."

Tommy filed that piece of information away. The solution to the system was a perfect dive. Sometimes he played cards with Mack in order to pry out of him whatever he could remember about other prison suicides. It didn't take much prying. Mack loved to talk about notorious convicts who had done horrible things to themselves or to other convicts. One man had become befuddled by prison evangelists to such an extent that he cut off his own penis because he believed it had caused him to sin too much. But most of the prison suicides Mack told Tommy about were just ordinary suicides: hangings, throat cuttings, shootings—the same kinds of suicides that people resorted to whether inside or out. None of them were precise or political in the way Satanta's had been.

Tommy looked at the space in the center of the prison often, at intervals between working on his code. He wanted to acquaint himself with the space—to let it become familiar and comfortable. He behaved very well in prison, mainly because he didn't want to get moved. He wanted to stay on the fourth tier with the space two steps from his cell. The space was a resource he didn't want to risk losing. He needed the space more than he needed anything or anyone else, and that was because he was working around to the conclusion that there was only one pure form of rebellion. Once, bored to tears in his father's house in Riverside, California, he had picked up a book by Camus and ended up reading most of it. It was called *Resistance, Rebellion, and Death,* and it interested him enough that he bought and read two or three other books by Camus. It seemed to him that they were all suicide books. At the time he had just come out of the hospital after his second attempt at starvation; the Camus books disturbed him because they made him realize that he probably hadn't wanted to die. If he had been ready to die, why had he chosen such a sloppy method, when so many definite methods were available? His conclusion was that he *hadn't* wanted to die—he just wanted to make sure that the system had had to go to some trouble to keep him alive. To make matters worse, all this took place at an expensive white-bread hospital in Austin, a perfect embodiment of everything he wanted to attack.

Now that some time had passed, Tommy saw his starvation attempts as things to be ashamed of. Of course he had known, from the very fact that he was in a hospital, that he wouldn't be allowed to die. If he had really respected himself then, he would never have let them get him in a hospital in the first place.

He worked on his code a while, fiddling with some Turkish words. Perhaps his code would never be finished, but the discipline of working on it was important, anyway. Now and then, in little respites, he stared at the space in front of his cell—the space that had become his freedom.

He heard a rustling above him—Joey was awake and was fumbling for some of the cookies Aurora and Rosie had brought that morning. Tommy had immediately given the cookies to Joey—he always immediately gave away the things his grandmother brought him. He was honest about it, too. He told her he didn't want anything from her and that he would immediately give away whatever she brought; still, month after month, she brought him cookies or books or cassettes of classical music or something. Maybe she went home and imagined him eating the cookies or reading the books or listening to the music. She was a stubborn old woman. No matter how many times he rejected her offerings, she kept trying.

"Man, your granny makes good brownies," Joey said, from above him. "Tell her to make chocolate chip next time."

"You tell her," Tommy said.

"Man, I can't tell her, she's not my granny," Joe said, munching. "They ain't gonna let her visit *me*."

Tommy said nothing.

"Want a cookie?" Joey asked. "They're real good brownies."

"You eat them," Tommy said.

10

On his good nights the General dreamed of golf. On his bad nights he usually dreamed of abandonment—in those dreams Aurora was usually the person who abandoned him, and she usually did it in airports, in countries where he didn't speak the language. Of course, there were a great many countries where he didn't speak the language—almost all the countries fell into that category. Often Aurora seemed to abandon him in Lisbon; she *had* once abandoned him in Lisbon, after a terrible fight, and the memory of his depression in the hot little Lisbon airport infected his dreams like a virus.

This time he had a good night, though—he had just hit a perfect tee shot down the fairway when he woke up. He had seemed to be golfing with Bing Crosby, whom he actually had golfed with once, during the war—he would have liked to ask Bing a few questions, but before he was able to get any questions out he woke up, only to discover that Aurora was sitting up in bed, staring at the Yellow Pages.

"I was golfing with Bing Crosby," the General remarked. "Did you ever meet him?"

"Certainly not—why would you suppose I'd want to?" Aurora replied, in a tone that suggested that she might not have had an especially good night herself—she rarely did after visits to the prison.

"Well, Bing was a celebrity once," the General said. "I believe he liked to hunt quail. I was once invited to hunt quail with him in Georgia, but the hunt didn't come off."

"Hector, I haven't been forced to think about Bing Crosby in years," Aurora said. "Why are you inflicting this on me when I'm trying to concentrate?"

"You still look cute in the mornings," the General said, noting that her bosom, at least, had not suffered as the result of the bad night.

"I know you think that's a compliment, but as it happens cute is not a word I care to have applied to me just at this moment—or ever," Aurora replied. "Once we're psychoanalyzed I hope all this will change."

The General had forgotten that Aurora wanted them to be psychoanalyzed. He was not quite clear as to what was involved, but he knew it was expensive and that you lay on a couch and talked about your parents' sex lives, or your own sex life or something. It didn't sound too bad—it might be a good idea to try it just to show Aurora that he was trying.

"I guess it will be easier than shock treatment," he said. "I don't think I'm ready for shock treatment."

"I've found the name of a therapist named Bruckner," Aurora said. "That sounds Viennese to me."

"Vienna is in Austria," the General reminded her unnecessarily. He took off the one glove she had allowed him to retain.

"I hope this Doctor Bruckner can do psychoanalysis," Aurora said. "There aren't many therapists in the phone book who sound Viennese to me."

"Personally, I don't see what's the hurry," the General said. "I never knew much about my parents' sex life anyway."

"Who said anything about your parents' sex life?" Aurora asked, looking up from the phone book. In the morning light the General looked a good deal like a mummy, but he spoke in his customary grating tones.

"Well, I think that's what you do when you're being psychoanalyzed," the General said. "So I've been given to understand. How much do you remember about *your* parents' sex life?"

"Nothing, blessedly," Aurora said. "I don't even remember my own, why should I be expected to remember my parents'? Do you think Bruckner is a Viennese name?"

"I guess, why?" the General asked.

"Because our analyst should be Viennese, of course," Aurora said. "That's where the whole business was invented, if I'm not mistaken."

"Right, in Austria, as I said," the General replied.

"Perhaps this man will do, I think we ought to try him," Aurora said.

"If he's a strict Austrian—and most of them are strict—he's not going to like it if we don't know beans about our parents' sex lives," the General said. "I believe your mother had a lot of affairs, didn't she? You probably got quite a few of her genes."

Aurora carefully wrote Dr. Bruckner's name and phone number on her little pad before turning to deal with the General's last remark.

"I didn't mean that quite the way it came out," the General hastened to say—he thought he had probably let his tongue get the best of him again. "I just meant that you're both lively women who liked your jollies."

"I liked them when I could get them," Aurora said, meaning to give him a few sharp verbal raps. After all, he had just implied that both she and her mother had been loose—to use the word her mother would have used. But, before she could deliver the raps, she was seized with such a sharp longing to be with her mother again that she couldn't speak. She wanted to be in her mother's arms again—she hadn't been in almost fifty years. What peace it would be to be a girl again, if only for a few minutes, if only in a dream—to be small, to be protected by her unshakable mother, to be just awakening to life again rather than awakening to Hector Scott.

The urge, she knew, was crazy—a lifetime, or much of one, had passed since she had last touched her mother's living hand. Yet the urge to go back, to escape the years, to be her mother's young child rather than the crabby grandmother of her dead daughter's children, was so sharp that tears came to her eyes. She flung the phone book off the bed and buried her face in her pillow. Hector Scott must not see what she was feeling—it was too crazy, and he'd think it was his fault.

The General *did* think it was his fault, and he was horrified. What had he done now? Things were getting impossible. He and Aurora were both so sensitized on the subject of sex that the most casual reference to it was likely to send them over the edge. He didn't really know a thing about Aurora's mother's affairs, and even if she had had a lot, so what? That was in New Haven, and a long time ago. Besides, Yale was in New Haven, and people who lived around colleges were always apt to be having affairs. Being at Yale was not like being at the Point. Now he had hurt Aurora's feelings, and they hadn't even had breakfast. If the slightest reference to sex was going to cause her to burst into tears, he might as well move out—but where would he go? He had no children—he and Evelyn had kept putting it off, and then Evelyn got too old. Teddy was the only one of Aurora's grandchildren who really liked him, but Teddy was at least half crazy and could barely manage his own life. It was a grim picture he faced, filled with nothing but old soldiers' homes, endless bridge games, and widows who probably wouldn't turn out to be half as interesting as Aurora. And even if they were half as interesting, he loved Aurora, not them. She'd get another boyfriend, she'd never come to visit, and he'd be alone. Perhaps he'd do better just to join the homeless, once he got off his crutches. The papers maintained that most of the homeless were Vietnam veterans, and he had to admit that a good many of the homeless he'd spotted in his drives around Houston looked as if they might be veterans. Well, he was a veteran himself—he could go back to his own and live in a tent in a park when Aurora threw him out.

The grimness of it all reduced the General to a state not far from tears. He had never supposed he would end up in a tent in a park—he had never been very good at erecting tents, for one thing. Most enlisted men could erect tents far more efficiently than he could. It might be that he'd have to pay one of the homeless enlisted men to set up his tent for him. That would be rather a sorry pass for a general to come to, but if that was the best he could do, then so be it.

Aurora felt the General fumbling for her hand and let him hold it, but she didn't immediately remove her face from the pillow. She enjoyed, for a few moments, the ridiculous fantasy that her mother was once more holding her in her arms, as her mother had often done during her childhood. It was a *ridiculous* fantasy, but at the same time it was deeply comforting, and Aurora clung to it as long as she could before reluctantly raising her face and resuming the taxing life of someone who had miserable grandchildren and a played-out lover.

Looking over at the played-out lover, she noticed that his Adam's apple was quivering, a sign that he was in distress. Hector's Adam's apple quivered only on those occasions when she had vexed him almost to tears. Now it seemed to have happened again, although, as she recalled, he was the one who had accused her and her mother of being loose, an accusation to which she had made only the mildest reply. What could have happened to hurt the man's feelings now?

"Hector, are you getting ready to cry, and if not, why is your Adam's apple behaving that way?" Aurora asked.

"Sorry," the General said. "I guess I just never thought I'd end up in a tent. Old age is full of surprises."

"*Life* is full of surprises," Aurora said. "They are apt to come at all ages, in my observation. I must say I was quite surprised to look over just now and see your Adam's apple bobbing like an apple in a barrel. What's the matter? All I was doing was looking up psychoanalysts in the phone book. Are you going to begrudge me even that mild pleasure?"

"No, no, you can have all the analysts you want," the General said. It was perfectly obvious that she had had her little fit and was now in a good humor, and yet the fact that she had surprised him in a low mood was as likely as not going to cast *her* back into a low mood, and this time she would blame him. Sometimes it was so hard to get through a morning, not to mention a day, with Aurora that on the whole he thought it might be easier to be homeless and live in a tent.

"I was just worrying about my tent," the General said, not quite able to detach himself from the grim vision he had just conjured up.

"What tent?" Aurora asked, surveying her nice sunny bedroom. "Have you been dreaming of the Battle of the Somme again? Does this look like a tent we're quarreling in?"

"No, it's a bed, but I've decided to go live in a tent in Herman Park when you finally throw me out," the General said. "For one thing, I won't last long in a tent, and a short end is about the best prospect I have to look forward to now."

Aurora saw to her amazement that the man was genuinely upset, and for no reason—when had she ever said anything about throwing him out?

"A tent in Herman Park would be a damn sight better than one of those stupid old soldiers' homes with no old soldiers in them," the General said, his Adam's apple still aquiver.

"Hector, I'm baffled," Aurora admitted. "You brought up my mother, and the thought of her undid me for a moment. I loved my mother very much and she died much too young. I think I have every right to be undone by her memory, but that's all that happened. I don't have the least desire to dispatch you to a tent in the park and I don't know how you can have conceived such a notion. This convinces me that we had better make an appointment with Dr. Bruckner quickly. You might be beginning to drift off your moorings or something."

The General was both relieved and annoyed: relieved that Aurora was no longer angry, annoyed that she kept slipping into nautical metaphors.

"Aurora, I'm a general, not an admiral," he reminded her, for at least the hundredth time. "Generals do not drift off their moorings. Generals aren't moored. Even admirals aren't moored. Boats are moored."

"Well, touchy, touchy," Aurora said. "Perhaps the word I was seeking was 'mired.' You can hardly deny that we're mired in a rather quarrelsome embrace."

"The hell we are," the General said. "This isn't an embrace. I remember our embraces. I wish I was dead. Then you could embrace anyone you could catch."

"I can anyway," Aurora informed him. "It's obviously not doing me much good, but I've always claimed the right to embrace people at will. That's where this conversation started, remember? You said I was loose, and my mother before me."

The General recalled that he *had* said something like that. He said it not long before he decided to go live in a tent. Now he couldn't remember why the subject had come up in the first place. They had been talking about Vienna or something and then the quarrel started.

"Well, I suppose I popped off," he admitted. "Did she have affairs or didn't she? Let's get this settled."

"She loved the gardener," Aurora said. "Before he arrived I certainly hope she had a few affairs. What's a girl to do?"

"What do you mean, what's a girl to do?" the General asked. "She was married. Why can't a girl who's married sleep with her husband?"

Aurora was remembering a conversation she had had with her mother once—it was after a concert in Boston. They were walking across the Commons and it was snowing. She could not remember the program, but it seemed to her Brahms had been on it. Her mother confessed to a considerable weakness for Brahms. The evening snow was beautiful, falling on the Commons; the air was wintry and clean. Her mother, Amelia, had evidently been somewhat more stirred by the music than Aurora—just about to marry her beau Rudyard—had realized. Out of the blue her mother made a startling statement.

"I ought to tell you that your father has abandoned my bed," her mother said. "The truth is he abandoned it eleven years ago."

Aurora did not immediately comprehend.

"Why?" she asked. "Isn't it a comfortable bed?"

Her mother, who rarely looked happy but even more rarely looked sad—who made it a point of principle never to look sad, in fact—pursed her lips for a moment and gave her daughter a look that was unmistakably sad.

"It's not the bed he finds uncomfortable," she said. "It's the woman in it. It's me he doesn't like."

Aurora did not remember how the conversation ended, though now she wished she could. As soon as she got her memory project really cranked up she meant to go through her vast collection of old engagement books and concert programs and pin down the concert. If she could recover the program, she might be able to recall the end of the conversation. The two things she was sure of were that her mother had used the word "abandoned," and that she had mentioned eleven years.

"My father didn't sleep with her for eleven years, or possibly longer," Aurora said. "My mother lived for six years after she told me that—so it was probably more like seventeen years that he didn't sleep with her. What do you think of that, General?"

"If you're thinking it's some kind of record, forget it," the General said. "I went more than twenty years without sleeping with Evelyn."

"But did you dislike her?" Aurora asked.

"No, not particularly," the General said. "She was a little chirpy, but I didn't exactly dislike her."

"Then what happened?" Aurora asked.

"I really have no idea," the General said. "We just lost the habit, somehow. There came a time when I don't think it would have occurred to either one of us to go near the other sexually. Otherwise we got along pretty well."

"Goodness," Aurora said. "I believe I'll have to think this over, Hector. If nothing else it explains why you were so enthusiastic when we were first getting to know one another. At the time I was quite swept away by your enthusiasm."

"Swept away, my ass," the General said. "It took me a good five years to seduce you. Or to convince you to seduce me, whichever it was that finally happened."

"I remember it as me being swept away," Aurora said. "If you didn't sleep with your wife for more than twenty years, then it's no wonder. I hope we can discuss this matter with Dr. Bruckner at our first session, if that's what you call them. I find it intensely interesting, particularly in light of what I've just been remembering about my mother. I want to hear more about it."

"We just stopped sleeping together, there isn't any more to hear," the General said. "I'm sure it happens to a lot of married couples."

"Did you have girlfriends, at least?" Aurora asked, watching him closely.

"One or two," the General said. "Not enough to make much difference."

They heard the slam of a car door from the street below, and Aurora raised herself up to look. Patsy Carpenter, dressed in exercise garb, was walking up the sidewalk.

"Here comes Patsy to steal my maid and make her jump around," Aurora said. "I think I better go down to see if Rosie's made us anything to eat before she goes off to jump around."

"I'd like two boiled eggs and corned beef hash, if it's not too much trouble," the General remarked as he felt around for his crutch.

"Well, it'll be a lot of trouble if Rosie hasn't already made it, but we'll see," Aurora said, grabbing her robe and heading for the stairs.

11

"Good morning, Patsy—do you know anything about psychoanalysis?" Aurora asked, sweeping into the kitchen. Rosie sat on a stool by the television, chewing her nails.

"Things are no better in Bulgaria," she said.

Patsy Carpenter was dribbling honey into a cup of tea Rosie had waiting for her. Their aerobics class began in half an hour. She had formed the habit of having tea at Aurora's while Rosie got her news fix. If Aurora was up, she would frequently contribute some of the local news—that is, what was currently happening vis-a-vis the General or Pascal or some of her other suitors.

"I was in analysis for six years after I left Jim," Patsy said. "I lived in Mill Valley then. Every human in Mill Valley was either in analysis or had been. What do you want to know about it?"

"Everything," Aurora said. "The General and I are taking it up. We plan to start today."

Patsy, at fifty, was still a beautiful woman, or would have been if she could have managed not to look disappointed, Aurora thought. Disappointment, particularly self-disappointment—the variety Patsy suffered from—did not do good things for the female face. Tragedy might have added a kind of *gravitas* that would have made Patsy commandingly beautiful, but self-disappointment was merely making her look irrelevantly sad.

"The General's going to be analyzed?" Patsy asked, letting the steam from the tea warm her face.

"Yes," Aurora said, glancing at the stove to see if any corned beef hash happened to be there. None was, just at the moment.

"Rosie, do you think you could avert your eyes from Bulgaria long enough to boil the General a couple of eggs?" she asked. "He's in an egg mood and he doesn't like the way I do them. I will take the responsibility for the corned beef hash if you will just do the eggs before you desert me to undertake your jumpings."

Rosie promptly got the two eggs out of the refrigerator, but she didn't avert her eyes from the TV for more than a second or two at a time. The newscaster, the divine Peter Jennings, had just turned his attention to El Salvador, where things were also dicey.

"What if we invade?" Rosie asked. "It's all jungle down there. It'll just be another Vietnam, and we can't afford no more Vietnams."

"What could you do to a boiled egg that the General could possibly object to?" Patsy asked Aurora. "I don't eat boiled eggs, but aren't they usually pretty much the same?"

"Not to a man of Hector's sensibility, they aren't," Aurora said. "I don't know how many fights we've had about the way I boil, or mis-boil his eggs."

"He is strict about 'em," Rosie commented.

"Okay, but can't you just set the timer?" Patsy asked. "What else is involved in boiling an egg?"

"I'm far from certain, but that's not the point," Aurora said. "If you were psychoanalyzed for six years, what's it like?"

"Good lord," Patsy said. "Do you have an analyst picked out?"

"Yes, a Viennese," Aurora assured her. She discovered to

her relief that she had a can of excellent corned beef hash in her pantry; or, if not already excellent, it undoubtedly would be, once adorned with Rosie's eggs.

"Just the fact that he's from Vienna doesn't mean much," Patsy said. "Is he Freudian or Jungian or Adlerian or what?"

"I haven't asked him," Aurora said. "Besides, I don't much care. I just want him to straighten Hector out. We've already had a fight this morning, and it's scarcely the breakfast hour."

"Aurora, analysis isn't going to make you and Hector stop having fights," Patsy said. "You should get that notion out of your head."

"No, thank you, that's precisely the notion I want in my head," Aurora said. "I can't face many more years of these fights."

"I can't either," Rosie said. "Them fights poison the atmosphere."

She began to bounce around the kitchen, limbering up for her aerobics. Then she did a few stretching exercises, meanwhile keeping a watchful eye on Peter Jennings, who was, at the moment, describing the capture of a serial killer from Illinois.

Aurora popped the corned beef hash into a pan, got herself some tea, and sat down at her table to confront Patsy, a woman of whom she had never entirely approved—not that Patsy had ever entirely approved of her, either. Yet here they were, once again at the same table in the same kitchen, as they had been periodically since Patsy had arrived in Houston as a freshman in college, many years before. Then, of course, Emma had been with them—Emma, as well as Rosie. Now Emma was gone, and Patsy was still turning up in her kitchen. Life was odd. Quite argumentative, even testy, in earlier years, Patsy was now on the whole rather subdued. Her life had not turned out quite as she had hoped; and yet, Aurora reflected, what life did? Patsy's daughters, Aurora had to admit, were nice young women; nice, and more or less stable, despite their outré dress and violent political opinions. On the whole Patsy seemed to have done better with her children than she and Rosie had managed to do with

Emma's. None of them had been institutionalized, none of them had killed anyone; none of them, as far as she knew, had even been pregnant out of wedlock.

"How is Jorge?" Aurora asked. Patsy's beau for the past two years was a rather dashing Chilean architect. Patsy always managed to have someone who was both elegant and creative, an ability Aurora envied.

Patsy made a face. "We broke up," she said. "I can't believe I got involved with another architect, knowing what I know about them—and another Latin architect, to boot, knowing what I know about *them*. But I did, and now it's over. So much for Latin architects."

"Drat," Aurora said. "Now I suppose he won't come to my dinner parties, and he's the handsomest man in Houston. Couldn't you have hung on another year or two until I'm ready to give up dinner parties?"

"No, thanks," Patsy said, looking at her watch. If there was one thing she didn't mean to discuss, it was the failure of her most recent romance. She got up, went to the sink, rinsed her teacup, and turned to Rosie, who was peeking at Peter Jennings from between her own legs, as she stretched.

"Let's hit it, Rosie," Patsy said.

"Let's hit it," Rosie echoed. The egg timer chimed just as she spoke.

"Just remember to cut the tops off," she said to Aurora. "What pisses him off is that you never remember to cut the tops off."

"Yes, and I'm quite likely to forget to cut them off again," Aurora said. "Only it won't be because I forget, it'll be because I refuse."

"Well, you better, or you know what will happen," Rosie said. "It'll set him off for sure."

"You mean he really won't break his own eggshells?" Patsy asked, amused. Life at Aurora's house had its nineteenth century aspects, and it always had. Some scholar of past times should come and study it, before it vanished forever.

"Yes, that is the revolting truth," Aurora confirmed, popping up to stir the hash. "A four-star general is too squeamish to break his own eggshells. It's enough to make one a feminist."

Patsy laughed. "Aurora, when you become a feminist I think I'll run for president," she said. "But if you do go to an analyst be sure to tell him about the eggshells. He'll get a year or so out of that."

"I'll be back in an hour and a half," Rosie assured Aurora. She felt guilty about going away when a fight was brewing and was tempted to dash upstairs with the eggs and break the eggshells herself; on the other hand, the woman who ran the exercise class was really strict about starting on time.

"That's fine, but I still say you look ridiculous in that leotard," Aurora said, stirring the hash. "You make a very unlikely ballerina."

"Bye, Patsy," she added. "You didn't help me much with my psychoanalysis, I must say."

"Well, give me the analyst's name, and I'll check him out," Patsy offered.

"Bruckner," Aurora said. "Please check him out without delay, if you don't mind. Hector and I are panting to get started."

"Good lord," Patsy said again.

12

Patsy Carpenter's sensible Honda station wagon was equipped with racecar-driver seat belts, and an air bag that Patsy had had specially installed. Getting buckled in made Rosie feel a little bit like an astronaut, and the way Patsy drove made her feel even more like an astronaut. Even her son Tillman, who had been a stock-car racer from the age of about twelve, and who now owned a small stock-car track outside of Shreveport, didn't drive as fast as Patsy drove. When he wasn't racing a stock car, Tillman sort of meandered, but Patsy never meandered. Soon they were smoking out the Southwest freeway, toward Bellaire, where the exercise class was held.

"Did you always drive this fast?" Rosie asked, as Patsy blazed by five or six semis and lots of ordinary cars. The thought of the air bag was a comfort at such times—or sort of a comfort. Rosie still had a few reservations about air bags. What if one started to smother you, for example? Could you bite through it, and if you couldn't bite through it, how did you keep from being smothered?

"I'm not driving that fast," Patsy said, grinning at Rosie.

"This car is a lot smaller than that boat you ride in with Aurora. In this car it seems like you're going a hundred when you're really just doing about eighty-five. Thanks to my air bags we could probably survive a head-on collision at that speed," she added.

"I just asked," Rosie reminded her. "I've been known to speed myself."

"I'll tell you a secret, if you won't tell Aurora," Patsy said. "It's a minor secret, but I still don't want Aurora to know it—she'd manage to use it against me, somehow."

"What is it?" Rosie asked. She loved secrets, although they could be burdensome. She had been the recipient of hundreds of Patsy's secrets, none of which she was supposed to tell Aurora, and of thousands of Aurora's secrets, none of which she was supposed to tell Patsy. All those secrets were a big responsibility. Rose knew the day would come when she would forget whose secret she was guarding and tell it to the very person she was supposed to be guarding it from. After that happened, no one would ever speak to her again, except her children, who only spoke to her when they were in trouble as it was. Still, she couldn't wait to hear Patsy's secret.

"When I drive fast I don't grind my teeth," Patsy said. "I grind my teeth when I sleep, I grind my teeth when I read, I grind my teeth when I have to deal with my mother or my children, but I don't grind my teeth at speeds exceeding seventy miles an hour. What do you think of that?"

Rosie shrugged, although when strapped into the racecar seat belts it was hard to manage much of a shrug.

"Well, when you're going this fast, you need to keep your eyes on the road," she said. "I guess your teeth figure it's time to give it a rest."

Patsy curled off the freeway, curled again into the parking lot of the health spa, parked, killed the motor, and released her seat belt. She looked at her watch.

"We've got five minutes," she said. "What about Tommy?"

Rosie slowly undid her seat belt. Everyone asked her the same questions about Tommy: the General asked her, Patsy

115

asked her, and several of Emma's old Houston friends asked her, whenever she ran into them. She had come to dread the questions because she had no answers. Tommy was in jail. Tommy had always exerted a remarkable hold on people, and his tragedy had apparently done nothing to weaken this hold. Everybody wanted to know about Tommy—only there was nothing to know—or nothing, at least, that *she* knew.

"Aurora went in, I just sat in the car," Rosie said. "Jails give me the heebie-jeebies. My kids was never in many— just one or two for fights on New Year's Eve or something. I can't handle Huntsville. I just can't. Aurora goes in and I sit in the car and feel like a coward and a rat. I love Tommy too, I ought to go in, but I feel like I might throw up the minute I get inside them bars."

"Sometimes I'd like to shake him," Patsy said, thinking of Tommy. "I have the irrational feeling that if I could just shake him I could turn him back into the nice boy he used to be. I'm sure that's folly, but it's how I feel. It's like he sits in that cell and controls us all. None of us will ever be happy while he's there, and he knows it. I think he likes knowing it. I don't think he wants any of us to be happy, ever. It makes me just want to smack him."

Patsy had once been on Tommy's visitor's list. He had cut her off because she kept bringing him books; yet Aurora brought him books and he didn't cut *her* off. Of course, Aurora was blood kin, but the fact that Tommy wouldn't let Patsy visit him in the prison anymore left her feeling wretched. She lived, always guiltily, with the knowledge that she loved Tommy more than she loved her own son, David. Tommy had the right kind of brain—or, at least he had the kind she had always been a sucker for—and Davey didn't. When Emma Horton was dying, she had almost given Patsy her children to raise, but Aurora fought for them and won. Of course, it would have been wrong to separate the three siblings, and Patsy couldn't really fault Aurora, who had probably done about as good a job as any grandmother could do. But it still rankled that she hadn't gotten to raise Tommy. After all, he had said his first word to her, one night when she was baby-sitting for Emma and Flap. It was just a mess, what had happened—a mess that was probably never going to get rectified.

"We better get in there," Rosie said. "Gwen don't like no laggards."

"Sorry—I guess I fell into a reverie," Patsy said, opening her door. "The thought of that boy just throws me off."

"We can't break him out of jail," Rosie told her. "It's just one of those things we're going to have to live with."

She popped out of the car and did a handstand in the parking lot. One of the self-discoveries she had made since she started accompanying Patsy to various exercise classes was that she had a talent for gymnastics. She was small, limber, uninhibited, and equipped with near-perfect balance.

Rosie had gone through most of her life being a mother, wife, and maid. She had never supposed she had a talent, but in fact she did: a talent for doing handstands and other gymnastic feats. She immediately became the star of every exercise class she joined—invariably, if the instructor had to choose one pupil to demonstrate some tricky new exercise, the instructor chose Rosie. Indeed, two health clubs and several instructors had tried to *hire* Rosie to teach exercises full time. Apart from the fact that Rosie was really good, they needed an uninhibited seventy-year-old to persuade other, less uninhibited seventy-year-olds that it was okay to do bends and stretches and twists that they might otherwise have considered too unladylike to attempt.

On the way to the gym, Rosie did several more parking-lot handstands, to the astonishment of a number of deliverymen and early-morning shoppers. The sight made Patsy giggle. A couple of cops, gossiping and drinking coffee beside their patrol cars, began to eye Rosie suspiciously.

"Oh, stop it," Patsy said. "Those cops are looking at you. They don't see many ladies your age doing handstands in parking lots. They may think you've just been let out of a bin of some sort."

Rosie righted herself and glared across thirty yards of asphalt at the policemen, who repaid her with hostile looks of their own. They wanted to enjoy their coffee and not have to deal with anything out of the ordinary for a while, and an old lady in a leotard doing handstands in a parking lot was out of the ordinary, and, in their view, suspicious. They thought it best to keep an eye on her.

"I can remember when this country wasn't no police state like Romania," Rosie remarked loudly, as she brushed the dust off her palms.

"Well, I don't know that it *is* very much like Romania," Patsy said. "They haven't arrested you or beat you or anything."

Rosie was not mollified. The thought that policemen would look at her suspiciously just for doing a few handstands made her want to join a demonstration as soon as she could find one. Maybe Peter Jennings would be around to report on the demonstration for ABC. Maybe he would even get to ask her a question or two as she was being handcuffed and booked. She had seen women not much younger than herself being handcuffed and booked, and she was sure it would happen to her as soon a she began her life as a demonstrator. She hurried on to the exercise class, eager to get some exercise. She wanted to be in tip-top shape when she started her career as a demonstrator for the rights of men or women or Americans or blacks or pregnant women or whatever. After all, she was tiny, and many cops were large. Unless she was in good shape and had mastered a few resistance techniques, some big ugly cop would probably just pick her up like a sack of flour and carry her off.

"I ain't gonna go like no sack of flour," she said, turning to Patsy, who was tying up her hair. Patsy had had long hair all her life—Patsy with short hair was a sight no one had ever seen. But long hair was a drag when she exercised, so she usually arranged it in a bun as she was walking into class.

"Go where? This is just an exercise class," Patsy said. "What are you talking about?"

Rosie realized that she had let her imagination carry her away a bit, down the stream of fantasy and into the police state America that she felt she was living in—or, if she wasn't yet, that she would be living in any day.

"Oh, nothing, I just hate cops," she said, before doing a back flip onto the gym floor.

13

Melanie had just washed her hair and was indulging in the first Diet Pepsi of the day when she heard a car outside. She looked out the window and saw Bruce pull up to the curb in the Ferrari. He eased up right behind her car until the bumper of the Ferrari was just touching the bumper of her Toyota.

The sight made Melanie sort of hopeful. That was a special thing she and Bruce had done when they were first dating—they always left the bumpers of their cars touching as a symbol of their love. Kissing cars, Bruce called it. The fact that he had just kissed the bumper of her Toyota with the bumper of Beverly's Ferrari gave her a jolt of hope. She wished she hadn't washed her hair just then—it seemed to her that she looked fatter with her hair wet—so she hastily got a big towel and wound it around her head. It was only eleven o'clock, and Bruce wasn't usually even out of bed by eleven o'clock. Something weird must be happening. Also, why was he in the Ferrari, when Beverly's parents had made it quite clear that he wasn't even welcome to *ride* in the Ferrari?

Bruce didn't get out of the car immediately and start racing up the stairs or anything. Bruce was prone to being a little slow and a little indecisive. He didn't just hop out of his car and let you know what was on his mind. Half the time he didn't know himself what was on his mind. He was kind of like a person that had a stutter, only Bruce didn't stutter when he talked, he stuttered when he acted. Moving in with Beverly right after she got the Ferrari was one of the most decisive things Bruce had ever done. He knew he wanted access to that Ferrari.

But usually, when it came to action, he stuttered. Teddy's take on Bruce's indecision was that it was the result of the fact that Bruce's father thought Bruce was a worthless person. Bruce's father was a self-made oilman, and he saw no reason why Bruce couldn't be more ambitious. He wanted Bruce to pop right out of high school and either go to college or get to work becoming self-made. Plus, when Bruce's parents divorced, his mother promptly married a Cuban billionaire who didn't treat her any too nice, or his stepson Bruce any too nice, either. Bruce's parent situation was just not a great situation; Bruce mainly handled it by taking drugs and staying out of sight as much as possible.

Probably the reason he wasn't out of his car yet was that he had a tape on and was waiting for the song he was listening to to be finished. Or he might be waiting for the whole tape to be finished—in fact, he might sit there half the morning listening to tapes, and then start the car and drive off, if he thought of some scene he wanted to check out. He might be so stoned that he didn't realize it was her car he had kissed with the bumper of the Ferrari—there was just no knowing, with Bruce. After several minutes had passed, Melanie began to have a hard time hanging onto her hopeful feeling. Bruce was so unpredictable—sometimes being in love with him was real unrewarding. She knew he liked the fact that she was loyal to him, but there were times when that didn't make the situation a whole lot more rewarding.

To her relief he did get out of the car and start up her stairs —he didn't look any too happy, though. Melanie felt herself starting to get nervous. It was horrible to have to get nervous every time the one person she really wanted to see came to see her, but it was happening.

She liked it that he was tall, though—tall and with a lot of hair. One thing that made it hard to take Koko seriously was that he was short and had a crew cut—great pal though Koko was, he did look sort of Boy Scout age, which kept her from getting into it too much sexually. That was not a problem she could imagine herself having with Bruce.

Melanie thought maybe she ought to pretend she didn't see Bruce kiss bumpers—he might have just done it out of habit or something, and it might piss him off if she made a big deal out of it. She was going to try to be cool and wait for him to knock, but then she got so excited at the thought of this early visit that she yanked the door open before he even got to the top of the stairs.

"Hi," she said.

Bruce smiled. He saw that Melly was trying to be cool but couldn't handle her own excitement. That was one thing he really liked about Melly—she could never handle her own excitement. It just sort of overflowed and made her do all sorts of impulsive things that weren't necessarily in her own best interest. This trait might not be so smart, but it was part of what he really liked about Melanie. Nobody could ever accuse her of not being vulnerable to her own feelings—they just kept getting loose from her and overflowing. An example was her telling him right off that she had slept with two other guys the week she got pregnant. If she had had more cool, she would have tried to hook him back to her by pretending that he was her one and only lover so that he would feel he had to marry her or at least help her pay her bills. But Melly just came out point-blank and admitted that she didn't know whose child it was, letting him off the hook immediately.

Of course, Melanie's taking the hook out wasn't quite the end of it, though—not really. At first he had felt a huge relief, but, to his surprise, within an hour or two the relief started dribbling away. For one thing, he didn't really believe Melanie had gotten pregnant by anyone but him. He was the one Melanie had had the hot act with—Koko and Steve were just accidents. Despite himself he started to believe it was his baby, which sort of removed the area of relief. What was Beverly going to say when Melanie had a baby that looked like him? She was already madly jealous because one night he had let slip that Melanie had no trouble having orgasms —a skill that Beverly had not yet entirely mastered. Actually, Beverly was pretty constrained in that department—she wouldn't do or let him do a number of things that Melly had no problem with—in fact, that she liked a lot. Bruce had the feeling that if he added many more causes for jealousy, such as a baby, to what Beverly was already dealing with, something was probably going to crack.

Add to that the fact that her parents really thought he was the scum of the earth, and you had quite a few problems to stack on top of the ones he already had with his own parents. Bruce felt that the stack of problems was getting too high, and the only person who understood that and really cared to help out and see that he had a few moments of enjoyment now and then was Melanie.

" 'lo," he said, when she yanked open her door.

"I just washed my hair," Melanie said.

"How's the kid?" Bruce asked. In the night he had had a terrible dream in which Melanie's baby came out too soon and they both died. He was even dreaming about the funeral when he finally woke up; then he didn't want to go back to sleep, for fear he'd dream the dream again. He remembered that he and Melly had had a fight, during which he'd sort of shoved her, causing her to fall over a chair. He had heard that little accidents such as that could cause women to lose their babies, so he spent quite a bit of the night worrying that Melanie might have had a miscarriage. It was an unnerving dream, but it made him realize that maybe he had more going with Melly than he thought.

Then Beverly woke up and he was so blanked out from his dream that he actually told Beverly that he had dreamed Melanie had had an accident. Even blanked out, he had had sense enough not to mention baby or miscarriage or anything, but Beverly freaked out anyway, and kept on freaking out until he wanted to pop her. He thought a little sex might make it possible for her to stop freaking out, but Beverly couldn't come, which made matters even worse.

"I hate her, I hate her, I hate her," she said, referring to Melanie.

Bruce didn't say anything. Fortunately Beverly wasn't able to freak out too much longer because her mother was taking her to New York that day on a shopping trip. Beverly's mother was from New York and went back at least once a month to get in a little shopping. Beverly's dad had a private plane and pilot and everything, so it was no big deal for them to hop up to New York for a little shopping.

Then while Beverly was dressing she got worried that Bruce would go back to Melanie while she was gone; she left him the keys to the Ferrari, despite the fact that she had been strictly warned never to let him behind the wheel of the Ferrari again. Beverly did it anyway—she was thinking how horrible it would be if she got back from New York only to discover that Bruce had gone back to Melanie. Maybe a whole day with the Ferrari would make him love Beverly more, or something.

When Bruce asked how the kid was, Melanie had to think a minute to realize he meant the kid inside her. Even though she knew very well that she was pregnant, and spent many hours a day wondering what the baby would look like and how she'd do as a mother—what if she got distracted and let it fall off the bed and it broke its neck or something?—there were other times when it went out of her mind so completely that she was apt to be surprised when someone reminded her of it.

But once Bruce reminded her of the baby she remembered their fight and the fact that she had fallen over a chair—probably that was why Bruce had come so early, looking so guilty. He was worried about her, a thought that touched Melanie so much that she just wished Beverly didn't exist, so they could be together again.

"I was worried because you fell down—I thought it might have hurt the baby," Bruce said, looking out the window as he said it.

"I shouldn't have shoved you," he added. "I know it's bad to shove someone who's pregnant."

Melanie couldn't believe her ears. Now he was actually apologizing to her, or at least coming close. Bruce had never apologized to her before—when they had a fight he usually just stalked off, and when he finally showed up again he would pretend that nothing had happened. This was the first time since they began dating that he actually acknowledged that something bad had happened, and that it was his fault.

"Hey," Melanie said. "You don't have to worry. The baby's just fine. It's not like you knocked me down or anything. I just sort of fell."

Bruce kept looking out the window. He was feeling that he couldn't take it anymore—his father always putting him down because he didn't have a job; his mother always complaining that he wasn't in college; Carlos, his mother's billionaire, always griping about the fact that his mother gave him money; Beverly always crying and freaking out if she didn't happen to come, calling Melanie a fat whore and stuff. Plus his friends were always bugging him to haul dope around—even the ones in college were more into drug dealing than they were into getting educated. It just seemed like a lot, and Bruce could see no end to it unless he did something radical. One reason he had come to Melanie was that she was the only person he knew who might have the guts to do something radical, if she happened to feel like it.

Bruce kept feeling tight inside—he really didn't feel like he could take it anymore. He'd just as soon be dead as take it anymore; on the other hand, he didn't really want to kill himself or anything and he didn't want to desert Melanie and their baby, either. The one good thought he had was that Melanie might want to go away with him. America was this free country—why couldn't they go away? His own parents, when they had first married, ran away from Corsicana and went to Midland and got rich; but they hadn't been rich or anything when they were doing the running away part.

The one thought that seemed to be positive was that maybe Melanie would want to run away with him. Of course, it was a big thing to ask of someone pregnant. He had to psych himself up for the question, but then he began to feel silly—how long could he stand there and look out the window?—so he turned around and made an attempt to get the words out. "Let's get out of here," he said. "Let's just get out of here right now."

"Okay, can I just dry my hair?" Melanie asked, thinking he meant to go to breakfast, or maybe it would be lunch by the time they actually left.

"Bruce, did you kiss bumpers on purpose?" she asked then. He was sort of pacing around, he really seemed wired; she thought she'd just go on and ask. She wanted to know, and if it *had* been an accident, they could still go out and eat.

Bruce turned his grin on—he had a great grin. It made you realize how sweet he really was.

"I didn't know if you'd noticed," he said.

"So did you?" Melanie asked again—she felt nervous all of a sudden.

"Yeah," Bruce said, coming toward her.

Next thing they were hugging, then kissing; a little later it was like he had never been gone. Melanie couldn't believe that her dream of bliss, her nicest hope, was coming true; but her body believed it—just for a moment she wondered what the baby inside her was thinking about it all. After the lovemaking Bruce fell asleep and she had a nice time, just lying beside him, feeling lucky. Maybe they were back in love; maybe they'd even get married and raise the baby like normal people. Melanie felt that she *was* a normal person, mainly—at least she felt herself to be more normal than Teddy and Jane, although she loved Teddy and Jane and had to admit that they did a good job being parents. Also, she was more normal than Koko, who spent far too much time playing computer games on his computer. Of course some of that could be because she wouldn't let him move in and be her lover.

Bruce took a while waking up. Melanie didn't care, although she was actually getting a little hungry. She could have absorbed some Mexican food, but she didn't wake him. He had been really wired, and she had unwired him, which was good. The thought of the Ferrari was a little troubling, though. The fact that he was driving it sort of implied that he still had some connection to Beverly, but Melanie decided not to worry about that too much—yesterday she had had no hope but today there definitely was hope.

When Bruce woke up it took him about twenty more minutes to get the yawns out of his system. He lay on her bed and yawned, watching Melanie brush her hair.

"So are we going to get out of here?" he asked, realizing she hadn't the faintest idea what he meant when he'd asked the question the first time. It was going to be interesting to see how she reacted when she got the point.

"Sure, are you up for Mexican food?" Melanie asked. "I could go for a bean burrito."

"I knew you didn't get it," Bruce said. "What I meant was do you want to get *out* of here. I don't just mean eat—I mean *leave*. Go live in another town—L.A. or somewhere."

"L.A.?" Melanie asked. "You want to go live in L.A.?"

"Well, we could," Bruce said, waiting to see if the idea was really going to hook her, or what.

"In the Ferrari?" Melanie asked—she still felt a little uncertain on that point. If they headed out to L.A. in Beverly's Ferrari she was pretty sure they'd wouldn't make it. Beverly's folks would have the cops on them in a minute.

"Naw, I just borrowed the Ferrari," Bruce said. "Beverly's out of town. I guess we'd have to go in my Mustang and maybe tow your car. Once we're out there we're going to need two cars, in case we both get jobs. It's a big town."

"It's a big town," Melanie echoed. Actually she was sort of stunned by the prospect of moving to it. More than that, she would be moving with Bruce—it sounded as if he intended for them to live together, once they got there. The thing that was amazing was how quickly life could change. Only last night she had sat in her car and cried, convinced that she would never even get to kiss Bruce again, never even get to touch him, maybe. It had been a bleak prospect—also, she was pregnant, which made that prospect even more bleak. Now, just a few hours later, they had not only kissed again and made love again but he had asked her to run away with him to Los Angeles.

"My dad lives near L.A.," she said, remembering that fact and wondering if it would make their living together awkward or something. Her dad was not exactly prudish, but her stepmother, Magda, definitely wasn't any too fond of her, and there was no telling what either her dad or Magda would think of Bruce—he sometimes didn't make too good an impression on adults.

She saw Bruce watching her a little anxiously; she hadn't really answered his question, maybe he was thinking she didn't really want to go. But that wasn't what she was thinking at all. It was just such a shock to realize that Bruce wanted her to go with him and wanted her to *live* with him that her thoughts sort of spun around for a few seconds; it was such a shock that she actually felt a little dizzy, but it was a happy, amazed dizzy, and when she came out of it a little she didn't waste any time on doubts or questions.

"I'll go, Bruce," she said. "I love you."

"I just sort of knew you'd be up for it," Bruce said, yawning in relief.

14

When Melanie called, breathless, and told Teddy that she and Bruce were moving to Los Angeles, Teddy was in the midst of refereeing a dispute between Jane and Bump and couldn't give this dramatic news the sort of awed attention he knew Melanie would like to have it receive.

"That's a surprise I can't deal with right now," he admitted to his sister.

"Why not, what's happening?" Melanie asked. Teddy was trying to sound calm, but in his voice she heard reminders of a time when he had not been calm.

"Jane wants to spank Bump and I'm arguing for clemency," Teddy said. "I have to hang up or there won't be clemency—she'll spank him. I'll call you back later."

Jane had just come in from work at the 7-Eleven and was not in a serene mood. An asshole had hassled her about change just before her shift ended, and then had had the gall to follow her for almost a whole block, trying to get her to go out with him. The man had looked like a Cajun, though he claimed he was from Florida.

"You have the most beautiful long legs I've ever seen," he

said, as he was following her. "I know how to do the dirty dancing." He was combing his hair as he walked.

"I know how to squirt you in the eye with my Mace, too," Jane said, taking her Mace out of her purse. He made so bold as to touch her elbow, so she pointed it at him, a threat that immediately cooled his ardor.

"Don't Mace me, goodbye," he said, departing. "I just fell in love with your beautiful long legs."

Jane did have beautiful long legs and was a little bit vain about them, but her legs pretty much got taken for granted by Teddy; it annoyed her that a Cajun who couldn't even count his change paid more attention to them than her husband. Then she got home and started to make tea, only to find a sopping-wet Sanskrit grammar in the sink. For the past few months she and Teddy had been working on Sanskrit together. Bump's main flaw was that he craved attention—indeed, he craved it so much that he would attempt to destroy anything that distracted either of his parents' attention from him for long. Although he liked his own books, and usually kept five or six of them in his bunk bed with him so he could look through the stories whenever he wanted to, he didn't like his parents' books, any one of which was likely to distract his parents' attention for long periods of time.

Lately, though, his main rival had been the Sanskrit grammar. His parents spent long hours poring over it or talking about it; when they were devoting themselves to the book he would have to have a fit or scream to get their attention at all. First, he tried merely hiding the book—he hid it under a shoebox in his mother's closet, but she soon found it. Then he managed to tuck it under the washing machine, but again the book was found. Bump was ingenious at wiggling into places a parent couldn't go, pushing the book ahead of him to hide it as far away as possible, but there weren't that many good hiding places in the apartment, and his parents always found the book. They seemed to find it amusing that he was jealous of the book and wanted to hide it—also they seemed to enjoy letting him know that they were Bigs and he was a Little, which meant that they could always find anything he tried to hide.

Bump didn't find this amusing at all, but he thought he had solved the problem of the book one day when his father was napping. It was raining hard and the window was open, so he pushed the book over the windowsill and watched it fall into the rain. When his parents discovered the mushy book lying in a puddle below their window they shook their heads at Bump and looked sort of pleased. The fact that he had so cleverly disposed of his rival, the book, seemed to convince them all over again that he was a child with a quite high intelligence.

Bump was glad he had pushed the book out the window. He assumed that he had disposed of it forever and became very annoyed when his father came home, a few days later, with a book that seemed to be exactly like the one he had pushed out the window. He immediately tried to stab the book with a pencil, but his mother just took the pencil away from him and put the book on a high shelf where he couldn't reach it.

Then the old, annoying pattern started repeating itself. Every day his father or mother or both spent too much time looking into the book, ignoring him completely at such times unless he threw a tantrum or hurt himself in some way. He tried to stab the book with pencils and knives and once even made a small cut in it with a kitchen knife he had snatched, but none of these attempts really worked. Once, trying to climb up the bookshelves in order to get the book, he fell and split his lip; this got him some sympathy but didn't mean that the book was gone. Bump watched it on its high shelf and intended to attack it again if he got the opportunity, but no opportunity had come until that afternoon, when his father, who was making a phone call, momentarily relaxed his attention and left the book on a chair. Bump grabbed it and took it to the bathroom, and threw it in the big people's toilet. His father discovered it there only a few minutes later, but a good deal of damage had been done. The book was almost as mushy as the one Bump had pushed out the window. His father merely looked at him in a funny way, twisted his mouth a bit, and shook his head. His father didn't grab him or shake him or anything; his father never did such things, even when Bump ignored his potty and peed wherever he happened to be.

"This isn't going to keep us from learning Sanskrit, you know," his father said, carrying the dripping book to the sink.

Bump didn't know why they liked the book so much—it didn't have pictures in it, as his own books did—but he knew that they wouldn't like it *as* much, now that it was wet through and through. He ignored his father's remark and sat at the foot of his bunk bed, studying his book with a tiger in it—the tiger book was one of his own favorites. He felt happy, now that his parents' bad book had been disposed of again, and when his mother came home he ran to meet her and got picked up and kissed. Bump loved the way his mother smelled and was happy for a while, cuddling and smelling her.

But when his mother saw the wet book in the sink, the atmosphere immediately changed.

Bump saw her face grow angry—he immediately ran and burrowed into the closet amid his mother's shoes. It was the safest place in the apartment, but this time it wasn't safe enough. His mother just kicked away the shoes and pulled him out. Bump began a silent resistance; he kicked at her as hard as he could, but kept a smile on his face. His mother was not very gentle, though. She held him and shook him; she was very angry and didn't smell nice anymore.

"Don't you dare ever hurt one of my books again, Jonathan!" she said. "It wasn't your book and you mustn't get it wet."

His father came and tried to take him away from his mother. Bump stretched out his hands to his father but his mother refused to let his father have him. Then the phone rang and his father turned to answer it. Bump really wanted to get away from his angry mother. He wiggled as hard as he could in an effort to demand that his mother release him so he could run to his safe father, but his mother imprisoned him in her lap and ignored his kicks and wiggles. Bump could hear her breathing like a beast—when she became angry enough to use his other name, Jonathan, she often breathed hot breath on him like a beast—like some of the big dogs they met on the sidewalk during his walks. Sometimes when she held him as she was holding him now, and breathing hot breath, he wondered if his mother was really a tiger. She didn't have stripes and a tail, but Bump thought she might be some sort of tiger anyway because of the way her teeth looked and her eyes looked and her breath came when she was angry. Perhaps the tiger in his book was only one kind of tiger and his mother another kind. He felt himself to be a match for his father but he knew he wasn't a match for his mother, and he thought it was probably because she was really a tiger. "You little fucker, that's two Sanskrit grammars you've ruined!" she said—she often spoke in such tones to him when she became angry enough to use his other name.

"Yes, but it's just a book, after all," Teddy said, hanging up the receiver so quickly that he dropped it and had to fumble a bit before he got it back on the hook.

"Please don't spank him," he added.

Jane had been holding Bump on her lap, watching him struggle and wiggle, while he eyed her with a kind of maddening calm that replicated Teddy's own maddening calm in every way. When Teddy asked her please not to give Bump the spanking he deserved, she immediately flipped the child over like a pancake and whopped him twice on his behind with her open hand. Then she sat him on the floor and watched him flee. In seconds he was back in the closet amid her shoes, hiding.

"I wish you hadn't done that, but you did it," Teddy said.

"Yeah, I did it, and it's over," Jane said, still very angry. In a detached part of her brain she was wondering what sort of place the Cajun would have taken her to if she had gone with him. Would he have paused at a dance hall for a little dirty dancing? Or would he have just made straight for some crummy apartment?

"Maybe it's over and maybe it isn't," Teddy said, a little angry himself. "Maybe twenty years from now he'll murder us both because of what you just did."

"Oh, fuck you," Jane said. "Do you think I'm going to sit

here and practice the Socratic method with a two-year-old? Anyway, I'm sick of the Socratic method, and the reason I'm sick of it is because it's the only method you know."

"I don't think I practice the Socratic method, particularly," Teddy said. "I just don't believe in spanking kids. Do you really think swatting him on the behind is going to make him respect our Sanskrit grammar?"

Jane didn't say anything. She was wishing, just for a moment, that she had a different mate. She always thought of Teddy as a mate, not a husband. A mate was easier to get rid of, but harder to replace. She thought again of the Cajun, who, for all his obtuseness, had an attractive smile. There would have been no problem about the Socratic method with him—he had clearly been a disciple of the Warren Beatty method.

"What's wrong with you?" Teddy asked. "You came in looking annoyed, and now you've spanked our child."

"I'm tired of your concern, Teddy," Jane said. "Mind your own business."

"Well, but Bump *is* part of my business," Teddy pointed out.

"Look, I was spanked, and I didn't turn into a murderer," Jane said. "How many Sanskrit grammars do you propose to let him ruin before you put a stop to it? You know perfectly well he just does it because he doesn't want us to study. He wants all our attention, and he can't have it.

"When I want to study Sanskrit, my child is not going to stop me," she added. "I don't want him to be one of those children who has total control of his parents."

"I still don't think it's a good idea for parents to hit children," Teddy said, feeling a little sad. He wasn't going to win the argument, and for an old reason: Jane might not have more conviction than he did, but she had more emotional energy to put behind whatever conviction she was pressing at a given moment. He could hear Bump in the closet, beating a shoe against the floor. He hadn't really been hurt, or even particularly scared, and the two splats Jane had given him on his bottom probably hadn't even registered with him

134

—they bore no comparison to the stinging spankings Teddy's father had given him when he had been five or six. His father had spanked him as if he had been responsible for everything bad: his mother's death, the Vietnam war, you name it; and, if anything, the spankings Tommy got were even worse. Teddy remembered the spankings as a vague but ominous turning point, though, in talking to many shrinks, he had never been able to define the nature of the turning to his own satisfaction. Mainly, it was at that point that life became frightening, and it had continued to be frightening ever since.

"I just don't want him to be scared of us," Teddy said, seeing that Jane was still looking at him angrily. "Besides, I'm the one who caught him red-handed."

"Right, and you should have spanked him on the spot, only you didn't," Jane said. "You left the dirty work to me."

"Do you think he knows you spanked him because of the book?" Teddy asked.

"Look, I don't want to talk about this anymore," Jane said. "Are you ever going to learn just to let things happen and be over?"

"Not when it involves justice," Teddy said. "I'd like for Bump to know he's been treated justly, that's all."

At that moment the doorbell rang. Bump crawled out of the closet and ran to the door—he loved to answer the doorbell. He peered through the bamboo screen that hung on the door and saw his Big Granny and Rosie standing on the steps.

"Oh, gosh," Teddy said. "I forgot that Granny said she and Rosie might drop by."

Jane went to the door and let the two women in. Aurora swooped Bump up and gave him many kisses before passing him to Rosie, who did the same. Aurora noticed tear tracks on the little boy's face.

"Has he been laughing so hard he cried, or is it the other way around?" Aurora asked.

"I spanked him," Jane said. "Teddy doesn't approve. You two look experienced—what do you think?"

"What was the crime?" Aurora inquired, fanning herself—

the air conditioner on her old car had chosen a bad moment to stop cooling. She noticed that Teddy looked somewhat on the defensive. It was her instinct to side with her own whenever possible, and Teddy was her own, but common sense had not exactly been his strong point; frequently, in matters of domestic judgment, she found that she was more likely to agree with Jane.

"He drowned our Sanskrit grammar for the second time in a month," Jane reported. "He hates for us to study."

Bump, noticing that his mother was no longer breathing like a beast, reached out his arms to her and was taken back.

Teddy felt relieved and a little silly.

"Well, I was a jealous child myself," Aurora said. "I didn't like for my mother to play the piano, although she played it beautifully. Still, I suppose I felt I was even more beautiful. I used to stick pencils between the keys. So I'm afraid Jonathan comes by his jealousies honestly. It's this business of genes."

"Shoot, if I hadn't spanked mine, they'd have been in jail before they started kindergarten," Rosie said. "I spanked and I spanked. I doubt I'd ever spank this little boy here, though. He's too full of sugar."

"Maybe I overreacted," Teddy admitted. He was glad his grandmother and Rosie had arrived when they did. Jane had stopped being angry.

Aurora watched Jonathan making up with his tall, beautiful mother in the middle of the small apartment that always seemed to be a trifle too orderly. She wondered if the bedroom was too orderly too—perhaps one reason the door to it was always shut when she came was that it was a total mess. She rather hoped it was a total mess, as her own bedroom often was. She never felt quite comfortable in Jane's and Teddy's apartment because some element of orderliness put her slightly off balance.

The decor was simple—just an old couch she had given them, a plain table they had bought at a garage sale, a good if well-worn rug they had brought back from a trip to Afghanistan, and bookshelves filled with books—and she could never quite figure out why the place put her off balance. Perhaps it was because in the simplicity there was too much of a suggestion of restraint—and restraint was a quality she had never been drawn to, although she was brought up around Yale, where there was plenty of it.

"How about some iced tea?" Jane asked. "You two look a little overheated."

"We accept, or at least I do," Aurora said. "My car has betrayed me again, just as Rosie predicted it would."

"I'm still trying to talk her into a Datsun pickup, but I ain't making no headway," Rosie said.

It disturbed Aurora to note that Teddy had a slight case of tremors. He appeared to be calm, but if one looked closely one could see that his hands were shaking just the slightest bit. She noticed it when Jane brought the iced tea and Teddy reached for his glass.

Bump, more curious about his Big Granny than he was about Rosie, walked over and showed her a block he had with four Greek letters on it. Rosie he felt no hesitation with —he was sure of Rosie's approval—but Big Granny was not someone he felt he could be quite sure of. He offered her the block with some diffidence—if she wasn't interested, she didn't have to take it.

"You should be talking, young man," Aurora said, accepting the block and pretending to study it closely. "Carrying around a block with Greek letters on it is all very well for a one-year-old, but you are no longer a one-year old. I do think it's time you faced up to your conversational responsibilities."

Bump looked to his mother for guidance. His Big Granny was a lot of fun and could blow amazing bubbles out of a magic jar she kept in her bathroom, but there were times when he didn't know quite what to make of her. She always talked to him as if he were a Big himself, when it was obvious that he wasn't. He was just a Little. Sometimes his father also talked to him as if he were a Big, but his father never kept it up for long. His father would soon drop back into tones the Bigs customarily used when they talked to little people—

tones Bump preferred. His mother spoke to him in those tones too, except when she was angry and became a beast.

But Big Granny had old eyes, and old eyes were different from the eyes of his parents. Big Granny's eyes seemed to look all inside him, even when she was being playful. Often when she looked at him, Bump felt like hiding in the closet, and sometimes he did hide in the closet, although he liked Big Granny, mostly. He particularly enjoyed visits to her bedroom, when she would bring out the magic bubble jar, and also let him bounce on her bed. The old Big that lived in Big Granny's bedroom didn't approve of Bump's bouncing, but Big Granny ignored him and went on blowing bubbles or talking on the phone. Bump was allowed to bounce until he wore himself out.

"It will serve you right if this child starts speaking Greek," Aurora said, handing Bump back his block.

"You never gave us your views on spanking," Jane pointed out. "Do you think it will ruin Jonathan if I whop him on the butt once in a while?"

"Of course not," Aurora said. "Hasty spankings have little effect on the child, but they often make parents feel better. There's nothing wrong with it—parents often need *some* way to feel better."

Aurora watched the beautiful little boy wandering around the room and wondered at her own lack of real interest in him. Somehow she felt she had failed to connect where Jonathan was concerned. Obviously he was a bright child; Aurora liked best the cunning looks he fixed on adults when he thought adults weren't looking. He was trying to figure out what life involved—the task all children had set for them—and he seemed already to have concluded that his mother was stronger than his father. It was also clear that he had developed an act designed to soften his mother when he felt she needed softening.

What disturbed Aurora slightly, watching Jonathan wander around, was that she felt no urge to grab the child and bind him to her. She felt no need to tilt or choose in the little quarrels that arose between Teddy and Jane, over spanking versus not spanking, toilet training, or any of the other issues young parents had to grapple with. For the first time in her life as a parent or a grandparent, she felt destined to be a spectator. Jonathan was the third generation—perhaps the third generation was simply beyond her. Maybe she had simply run out of gas, emotionally, in the way that her car had, two days previously, right on a freeway. Maybe she had no gas for Jonathan—but what did that *mean?* He was certainly a beautiful child, and she had never been immune to good looks, but in Jonathan's case, she felt a little bit So what? So what? was not the attitude she was accustomed to feeling about members of her family.

"I doubt I shall be a distinguished great-grandmother," she reflected a little later, as Rosie was driving her home.

"Who asked you to be?" Rosie asked. The sun was bright, the traffic fierce. With no air conditioner to cool her, she felt in no mood to listen to Aurora feel sorry for herself.

"No one asked me to be—are you going to be impolite?" Aurora said, pricked by the note of impatience in Rosie's voice.

"Great-grandkids are a little too far down the ladder," Rosie observed. She had three herself but rarely saw them.

"That is exactly as I would have put it, had you given me the opportunity," Aurora said. "They're a little too far down the ladder. Still, I never thought I'd be so indifferent to a direct descendant. Who do you suppose bosses in that household, Teddy or Jane?"

"Jane," Rosie said. "Teddy wasn't designed to be no boss."

"Did you know I lost a son?" Aurora asked, holding her straw hat out the window and trying to direct some of the air flow onto her sweaty face and even sweatier bosom.

Rosie was inching up to the light at Buffalo Speedway and missed the question. She was considering a criticism her beau C.C. had leveled at her that morning, which was that she made too many suggestions. What she was wondering was whether he meant it generally or if he meant something more specific. Did he resent her telling him which muffler shop to use, or did he resent her making suggestions designed to slow him down a bit when they made love, on the ever more rare occasions when they *did* make love?

Aurora saw that Rosie had not heard her. She sighed and decided not to repeat herself. She had been foolish to say it, anyway; if they discussed it, she'd cry, and what could be more pointless than a sweaty old woman sobbing at a stoplight, over a miscarriage that had occurred so many years before.

Rosie finally turned the corner, and soon they were shaded by the great trees of River Oaks. Five seconds later, as if in response to the shade, Rosie's brain coughed up Aurora's remark. Looking over, she saw that Aurora was straining in the way she strained when she was trying to hold back tears. Rosie immediately reached for her hand.

"I'm sorry, hon, I was thinking of my own problems," she said. "Was it that miscarriage you had when you and Rud had the car wreck coming back from Galveston? Wasn't you about five months?"

"Five months . . . a little boy," Aurora gasped. "He would have been Emma's brother. He might have looked rather like Jonathan. I suppose that's what made me think of it. I dreamed about him for years. I even dreamed he graduated from Yale."

With a great effort, she got control of herself; she didn't cry. Soon they turned into her driveway and stopped. Rosie began the slow business of aligning the car with the garage.

"Perhaps I wouldn't have lost him if they had had seat belts then," Aurora said, quite illogically, since her seat belt, as usual, was unbuckled. Nonetheless, the thought held some slight comfort. She blew her nose.

"Hon, that was quite a while before seat belts got thought up," Rosie said, as they slid into the deep shade of the garage.

"I know, but Rud would have made me wear one if they had been thought up," Aurora said. "Rud was always careful that way."

15

"Uh–oh, do you see what I see?" Rosie asked. They had just emerged from the garage. Aurora was putting on her dark glasses for the brief walk to the house, but Rosie didn't need dark glasses to see what she saw.

The General, naked except for his casts, was standing just inside the front door, waving one of his crutches at them frantically.

The ridiculous often had a calming effect on Aurora, and the sight of Hector Scott with no clothes on waving his crutch at them certainly struck her as ridiculous.

"The monster's broken out of his crypt," she observed coolly. "Why do you suppose he's waving his crutch like that? Could it be an air raid?"

"No such luck, we ain't at war," Rosie said. "Aurora, he's naked. How did he get downstairs?"

"Perhaps he fell out a window," Aurora speculated. "Why don't you duck in and get a sheet or one of the extra table-cloths so we'll have something to wrap him in."

"What if he won't let me?" Rosie asked. "He might have flipped out. Flashing's one thing, but that old boy is all-out naked."

141

"Yes, yes, Hector, we see you, sight that you are," Aurora said, moseying up the driveway. Rosie took off on a flanking movement toward the back door.

"Aurora, hurry, I have bad news," the General yelled. He had never seen anything as exasperating as the slow way Aurora was moseying. He had gone to the extraordinary trouble of hobbling all the way down the stairs so as to bring her the news at once, but the woman was hardly moving at all. She was still ten yards away, standing coolly on the grass watching birds or something when Rosie suddenly darted out of the kitchen and started trying to wrap him in a tablecloth. It was the last straw: they might ignore his news, but they weren't wrapping him in a tablecloth. He began to poke Rosie back with his crutch.

"Now, Hector, stop that," Aurora said, closing the distance between them in a dramatic burst of speed. "It's just a tablecloth. It's not a straitjacket, and no one's coming to take you anywhere, even if you are insane."

She and Rosie managed to get the tablecloth more or less around the General, but because he was still on his crutches the effect was rather like installing him in a small tent, with his angry face sticking out above it.

"Will you stop it, goddamnit!" the General said. "You're the ones who ought to be in straitjackets. All I've been trying to tell you is that Melanie's run away."

"Oh, shit," Aurora said, dropping her end of the tablecloth. "What else is going to happen?"

"Even if Melanie left, it don't mean we need nudists running around the house," Rosie insisted, sticking to what she felt to be the first task. She ducked the General's crutch and soon had him swaddled, or at least entangled, in the tablecloth.

"Can't you two get it through your heads that I *am* a nudist now?" the General remarked, a little more calmly. "I decided to become one just after the two of you went shopping. It's a perfectly respectable thing to be. I think Calvin Coolidge was a nudist."

He felt the claim might be a little inaccurate, but he *had* once seen an old nudist magazine that contained a picture of someone who had looked a lot like President Coolidge.

"Well, we can argue that one till the cows come in," Rosie said, wishing she had a safety pin. As it was, she had to stand where she was, holding the tablecloth, and well within whacking distance of the General's crutch.

"I believe you're a disciple of aerobics," the General remarked. "Why can't I be a disciple of nudism?"

"Because I don't want to be having to look at no do-whangs when I'm waxing the floor," Rosie said. "It's hard enough doing these floors without distractions like that."

"Please, both of you," Aurora said. "You're driving me mad. First you say Melanie's run away, and then you start arguing about nudism. *When* did Melanie run away, and is it just to Dallas, or is it worse?"

"Well, she said they were leaving this afternoon," the General said. He had momentarily forgotten Melanie and was more interested in dealing with Rosie's stated objection to his nudism. It had been both milder and more specific than he had anticipated; perhaps if he showed a willingness to compromise when she was waxing the floors his main goal might be achieved.

"Oh, if that's the only problem, then I suppose I could wear my pajama bottoms on the days when you're doing the floors," he said, looking at Rosie hopefully.

In fact it was just that morning, annoyed by the inordinate amount of time it took him to get his pants on over his casts, that he had decided to become a full-time nudist, though he had been gradually inching toward that decision for several weeks.

"Hector, you will not just wear your pajama bottoms on the day Rosie does the floors," Aurora informed him. "You're going to wear normal dress, as you always have, as long as you stay in this house. Stop pestering us about nudism and tell me where Melly thinks she's running off to."

"To Los Angeles, to live with her boyfriend," the General said, annoyed. Just as he had decided to strike a compromise with Rosie, Aurora had to butt in. "I could have told you that long ago if you hadn't started wrapping me in the tablecloth. I'd rather be naked than look like a goddamn mummy, which is what I look like now."

At first he had been so alarmed by Melanie's call that he had wanted to go call the police and have them either arrest the young couple or go find Aurora and Rosie; he had struggled all the way down stairs in order to get word to Aurora at the earliest possible moment. But once downstairs, with no one there to give the news to, his alarm gradually subsided, while his pleasure at having decided to live a healthy life in the nude had swiftly risen, causing him to more or less forget Melanie for longer and longer stretches of time. Fortunately he had remembered her when he saw Aurora and Rosie drive up; his responsibility fulfilled, he was eager to continue savoring the joys of nudism, only to have Aurora and Rosie overreact and wrap him in a tablecloth.

"I don't know why I work here, this is a crazy household," Rosie said. She took the belt off her own slacks and tried to loop it around the General to keep the tablecloth from falling down.

"This *is* a crazy household, who could deny it, Hector," Aurora said accusingly, just as the phone rang.

"Maybe that's Melly," she said. "Let's all cross our fingers."

"Aurora, that's just a superstition," the General said. "Facts don't cease to be facts just because people cross their fingers."

"Melanie and Bruce might have broken up before they could get packed," Aurora said. "I broke up with Rudyard several times and almost divorced him once because of difficulties he made about my packing. I'm sure the same thing could have happened to Melanie."

She left Rosie to make what she could of the General and the tablecloth, and went to the kitchen to answer the phone. She felt she might feel more peaceful in her kitchen, since frequently that was the only place where she felt peaceful at all.

"Hello, you're not going to go, I won't hear of it in my

present state," she said into the receiver, assuming she had her granddaughter on the other end of the line.

"I wasn't going," Pascal informed her. "I'm just having a drink. I got the new sheets today, you should come and see."

"Pascal, bad timing," Aurora said. "In fact it's quite the worst timing you've ever managed to achieve, which is saying a lot. I haven't a moment for you just now, and anyway why would I care about the fact that you've changed your linen? Hector's just become a nudist and my granddaughter is running away from home. Only a person with a very odd world view, such as yourself, would distract me with talk of bed linen at such a time."

"But we talked—I'm making plans," Pascal said, deflated. No matter when he called Aurora, and no matter what he said, it always seemed to be bad timing.

"Well, I'm sorry if I've punctured your little balloons again," Aurora said, wondering for a moment what his new sheets might look like.

"My balloons?" Pascal asked, confused.

"Yes—I see your fantasies about me as being rather like little balloons," Aurora said. "I'm always puncturing them."

"Yes, puncture," Pascal said. "Everything I try, you puncture right away. Don't you want me?"

"Well, I don't know the answer to that," Aurora admitted. "At the moment I can't say definitively that I don't, but I can say definitively that I don't want to talk about it right now. Goodbye for the moment."

She hung up, only to have the phone ring again before she could even scan the contents of her refrigerator to see if she had anything edible ready to hand. In all the emergencies of her life, her first instinct had been to eat, and it was, in her opinion, a perfectly healthy instinct. After all, no fuel, no fight.

"Granny?" Melanie said, when Aurora picked up the phone. Even in that one word, Aurora heard a new note of hope.

"Hello, Melly," Aurora said, feeling nervous. Puncturing

Pascal's balloons was one thing—she didn't want to puncture Melanie's if she could help it.

"I guess I'm rather hoping you haven't left yet," she added, cautiously.

"We left but we've just gone a little ways," Melanie said, very surprised that her grandmother's response was so low key.

"We're just in Flatonia, getting gas," she added.

"Flatonia sounds more like a place where one would get flats," Aurora said. "Are you quite sure about this decision to go live in L.A.?"

"Yeah, we're going," Melanie said, with such a note of happiness in her voice that Aurora immediately gave up all thought of talking her out of it. All that she had been meaning to say—all the proper cautions, all the fruits of her own experience, all the wisdom of the ages couldn't counter Melanie's hopefulness; nor, in her view, should those things be allowed to interfere with it. Since she'd become an overweight teenager, Melanie had almost never sounded either happy or hopeful—her life had been a matter of small losses and small defeats. Now, suddenly, a boy had wanted her enough to ask her to run away with him. Though usually much wanted herself, Aurora had no trouble imagining how wonderful Melanie must feel. Someone had actually wanted to embark on a grand adventure with her.

Melanie was nervous, and when she was nervous she chewed on her lower lip. The phone booth she was standing in was hot, sweat was pouring off her face, and she was partly really wanting to get the call over with, and also partly really wanting to talk to her granny. Part of the nervousness was just her fear that somehow her granny would manage to overrule her and make them come back; it was sort of a surprise that she wasn't trying. Melanie had expected that she would immediately blast off at Bruce a few times—her granny had not been all that impressed with Bruce, though Rosie liked him and had pointed out to Melanie long ago that if she intended to keep looking for a beau her granny *was* impressed with she'd probably be looking all her life.

"I imagine it must be wonderful—you do sound wonderful, Melly," Aurora said in a very quiet voice. Just in time she had mastered herself and refrained from saying all the things Melanie expected her to say.

"Oh, Granny!" Melanie said, so startled she almost dropped the phone. There was a silence, as both women, the young and the old, struggled with their emotions, trying to make them conform to what might safely be said over the phone.

"I wanted to come by for a hug, but I was afraid, and anyway you weren't home," Melanie said. Bruce had finished gassing up and was leaning on the car, waiting for her. Bruce was in great spirits, though—he wasn't rushing her or anything.

"No, dear, you were quite right just to leave," Aurora said. "You're a very large part of my life, you know. Selfish as I am, if you'd come by for your hug, I might not have been able to bring myself to let you go."

"I guess that's what I was afraid of," Melanie said. Something in her grandmother's sad tone made her almost want to give it up, to turn and go back to take care of her granny. But she didn't want that, either, and even her granny seemed to be saying that *she* didn't want that.

"Have a good time in California and let me know when you've brought your living quarters up to my standards, so Rosie and I can visit," Aurora said. "Drive safely and give me a call by and by."

"Oh, Granny!" Melanie said, bursting into tears as she hung up.

Aurora sighed and sniffed. Then she got up and rummaged in her refrigerator until she had put together a respectable snack—a little chicken salad, a hunk of cold lamb, a good tomato, and a little custard that she had hidden behind the milk. She had the conviction that she had left a piece of mince pie for just such an emergency, but exhaustive research failed to turn it up. Few things were more welcome in emotional emergencies than a solid chunk of mince pie.

"Which of you ate my mince pie?" she asked, when the

General and Rosie, unable to stand the suspense any more, made their way cautiously into the kitchen. Rosie had procured a few safety pins and now had the General wrapped so securely in the tablecloth that he did look rather like a mummy.

"Oh, I ate that, right after I took up nudism," the General admitted. "It was there, and I didn't see your name on it. Besides, I was nervous because Melly was running away and I couldn't reach you."

"Is she running away?" Rosie asked.

"Yes, and she sounds really happy," Aurora said. "I have decided, for once, to let be."

"Why?" Rosie and the General asked, almost in chorus.

"Because I want her to have that happiness," Aurora said sharply. "It may not last, of course—but then, what lasts?"

"Well, we've lasted, sort of," the General said.

" 'Sort of' is right," Aurora said.

16

The next morning Aurora woke in a state of low spirits, of the sort most apt to afflict her when she managed a more or less noble act—in this case, letting Melanie leave them to pursue her own life. It was the right thing to do, and she considered that she had done it with at least a bit of grace; yet the fact was, Melanie was now gone and she missed her already. Also, Melanie was pregnant, and who would be there now to see that she stayed on a proper, healthy prenatal course? Young people were apt to place too much confidence in their bodies; they assumed things would turn out all right, and yet, often, when babies were born, things didn't.

She crawled out of bed, being careful not to wake the elderly nudist sleeping beside her, went downstairs, made tea, and brought a pot of it back to bed with her. It was just light. A rosy tint showed over the treetops to the east. Aurora repaired to her window seat to drink her tea and watch the dawn develop; she felt no less low. Very little was right in her life, she knew. Her granddaughter, by now, was far to the west, perhaps sleeping in a cheap motel with her young man. To Aurora, Bruce hadn't seemed much, but at least he had been capable of an impulse. One of her grandsons would be just finishing his shift at the 7-Eleven—at least he would be, if he hadn't been murdered on the job. Another grandson, seventy miles to the north, had the job of being a prisoner, because he had murdered. All of her dreams for those children had been cruelly shattered—what would any of them ever amount to?

While she was sipping and reflecting, Hector uttered a strangled groan and woke up briefly. "Turn me over, I ache," he said. "I need to change sides."

Aurora put down her tea and helped him change sides; before she had quite finished he uttered another groan and went back to sleep.

"Hector, I do wish you wouldn't groan, it makes you seem so old," Aurora said, but he didn't hear her. Sometimes she thought he just looked normal, but other times she thought he looked very old, and this morning he definitely looked very old. She had many years of life before her—at least she hoped she had—but it was obvious that Hector didn't have very many—not a reflection that helped her low spirits much.

C.C. Granby's station wagon was parked at her curb, as it always was on the rare nights when Rosie could persuade her jittery beau to spend the night with her. Aurora had peeked into the car a time or two and had pronounced it a mess. C.C. sold oil-field products of a mysterious nature and the station wagon was always littered with them. A neat man in person, he seemed to let chaos reign in his car.

Aurora had no more than glanced down at the car, taking note of the fact that Rosie's boyfriend had at least showed up. But something didn't seem quite right about the car, so she glanced again. The light was not strong; she wasn't sure, but the car seemed to be trembling slightly. It struck Aurora as very odd: parked cars rarely trembled. She looked again, and sure enough the car was trembling—in fact, it was almost shuddering. She recalled that oil-field work sometimes involved explosives; perhaps C.C. had left some form of explosive in his car and the explosive was about to go off. It seemed rather alarming. She was about to grab the telephone and call Rosie to tell her to wake her boyfriend and get him out there before his station wagon exploded all over her lawn, waking the neighbors and very likely bringing the police; but then, peering more closely, she thought she saw a human form, or forms, in the car. A passing cloud had just obscured the sun, making it difficult to see; also, she was high up and the car well below her. Perhaps it wasn't about to blow up; perhaps someone was inside, trying to steal whatever C.C. sold. She had heard that there were even methods by which cars could be started and stolen by people who didn't have keys to them.

Peering more closely, Aurora managed to convince herself that human movement of some sort was taking place in C.C.'s car; she was on the point of reaching for the phone to call the police, when to her astonishment one of the rear doors of the car opened and her own maid, Rosie, got out, tucking her bathrobe around her tightly. She was barefooted, and she was also nervous. Aurora immediately drew back from the window, and in the nick of time, too, for Rosie glanced nervously up at the very spot from which she had been peeking.

Aurora moved to a more secure vantage point from which to watch the enthralling drama taking place on her lawn. This time she peeked from behind a drape and was rewarded with the sight of C.C. himself, his shirttail not tucked in, buckling his belt. He seemed to be in an affectionate mood—he kept reaching for Rosie's hand and trying to put his arm around her. He had rather a large belly, Aurora observed, but then so had Rosie's husband, Royce Dunlup.

Rosie, for her part did not seem to be in a particularly affectionate mood—she kept glancing up at Aurora's window, nervously. After a bit of shuffling around on the dewy grass, Rosie finally gave C.C. a perfunctory kiss. Then she virtually raced across the lawn to the back gate and disappeared. C.C. also glanced up at Aurora's window a couple of times, tucking away at his shirttail all the while. Finally he got in his car, started it, and turned it slowly around in the street, as he always did when he got ready to drive away;

only this time, instead of driving away, he sat in the car for a moment, eased it back to the curb, killed the motor, got out, checked nervously to see that his fly was buttoned, and trudged slowly back toward Rosie's little cottage.

Aurora, still peeking, realized with a flush that she had almost witnessed a sex act. She felt quite sure one had taken place right in front of her house, in C.C.'s messy station wagon; he had been one of the participants, and her own beloved Rosie had been the other. If she had been able to see a little more clearly in the dim morning light, she would have *seen* them doing it, in a car parked at her curb. The thought was startling, perhaps even shocking—on the other hand, she couldn't deny the thought, or the fact, that somehow it had produced a certain immediate excitement.

Meanwhile, unaware of the storm gathering nearby, the General had quietly awakened. Turning him over had relieved his ache, and once his ache was gone he began to feel wakeful. To his surprise he noticed that Aurora wasn't in her window nook, drinking tea—that was a departure from habit. Most mornings when he became wakeful she was in her window nook, wrapped so snugly in her bathrobe that nothing significant was showing, but this morning she was peeking out of one corner of her window, her bathrobe hanging open and a good deal that was significant showing, peeking intently at something taking place on the lawn below.

"What's happening, a mugging?" the General inquired. "If it's a mugging, hadn't we better call the police?"

"Shut up, Hector, C.C. might hear you!" Aurora hissed. "He's looking in our direction at this very moment. I feel sure he knows that he's being observed."

"But if it's only C.C., and he isn't being mugged, then he is being observed," the General said. "You're observing him. Besides, what do I care if he hears me?"

"You know what, Hector? C.C. and Rosie just had sex in that car," Aurora said. "I witnessed it myself, or very nearly, and that's why I'm observing C.C. now."

"You mean to see if you want to have sex with him yourself?" the General asked, very startled. "I never supposed

C.C. was exactly your type, although maybe I'm mistaken," the General added.

He decided to scramble out of bed himself and observe this interesting spectacle, but before he could move, Aurora suddenly jumped back in bed and sat on him, an action which startled him so that he knocked his glasses off the night table. He had been reaching for them in order to have a look at C.C.

"What do you mean? They didn't really have sex in the car, did they?" the General asked, a little alarmed by Aurora's aggressive behavior. She very rarely sat on him any more, and there *was* the matter of his injury.

"How do you know they did?" he insisted. "Is C.C. standing there naked?"

"No, but you seem to be naked, thanks to your nudist principles," Aurora said, grinning. "Do you know what *Liebestod* is, Hector? Perhaps if we attempt a few practices right here and now you'll die in the midst of them, at a moment of ecstasy or something. That way I'll save all that money that we were going to spend on psychoanalysis, and besides maybe we'll even have a little fun."

"If you mean the *Liebestod* part, no," the General said. "Of course I don't object to the fun, if I can manage."

"At least you're not against ecstasy," Aurora said, rummaging around a bit beneath herself. "You know how I hate to be the one to miss out. Perhaps it's only a lack of imagination that's been causing us to miss out. It would never occur to either one of us to turn my car into a boudoir, would it? Does the thought excite you? As you can tell, it excites me a good deal."

The General could tell. His heart was racing so rapidly that suddenly *Liebestod* seemed a real possibility—why was Aurora hurrying so? But thanks to the racing, it seemed that at least a little blood was pumping elsewhere—but would it last long enough for Aurora in her wild mood?

"I'd never manage in that car, not with these crutches," the General said, hoping everything would keep racing and pumping for a few more minutes. He felt more smothered than ecstatic, but the chances were he'd be even more smothered if Aurora came away frustrated from this endeavor. "Anyway, you don't need to think of your car as a boudoir, you have a boudoir," he reminded her.

"Yes, and we're in it, but for the present purposes I'd prefer to imagine that we're in my car—no, not that, either—for the present purposes I'd prefer to imagine that we're in C.C.'s car," Aurora whispered in his ear.

The whisper *was* exciting. Aurora, usually so ladylike, had long had the habit of whispering rather raunchy suggestions in his ear—she had at one time done it often, but in recent years she had seemed to run out of suggestions. The General had forgotten how exciting it was to have her whispering in his ear.

"Oh, C.C.'s car," he said. "It's a station wagon. I suppose I could manage in that. I didn't expect this to happen."

"It's happening, if you'll shut up and move a little," Aurora said.

17

Rosie felt so miserable that, for once, even the news failed her. Peter Jennings didn't look interesting. Tom Brokaw didn't look interesting. Dan Rather didn't look interesting. In desperation Rosie tried CNN, but no one on CNN looked interesting, either. Demonstrations of unrest continued, pretty much throughout the world, from Beijing to Washington, D.C., but Rosie found that she didn't care. She watched Kermit the Frog for a few minutes—Kermit was one of the few performers on TV who seemed to get as depressed as she did, but she couldn't really concentrate on his troubles because C.C.—the last person in the world who would have been likely to be able to cheer her up at that moment—kept trying to cheer her up. Or, if he wasn't exactly trying to cheer her up, he was at least trying to get her to assure him that *he* wasn't the sole cause of her depression.

"I didn't know it would turn out this way, I didn't mean to do nothing wrong, please don't cry," C.C. said twenty or thirty times, as Rosie cried.

"C.C., it wasn't your fault, you didn't do a thing wrong, I'm just depressed," Rosie said twenty or thirty times. "Why don't you just go on to work?"

"Because if I go off to work with you crying I'll just worry all day—I'd rather kill myself and get it over with," C.C. said. Indeed, he himself looked so miserable that Rosie almost wished he would kill himself, or kill her, or somehow put one or both of them out of their misery. It wasn't going to happen, though. C.C. kept turning up his cuffs and then turning them back down, a habit that drove her crazy.

"C.C., just leave 'em alone!" she pleaded.

C.C., in the process of turning down his cuffs, had no idea what she was talking about.

"If I apologize will it make it better?" he asked. He was a short, stocky man, with a head so nearly square that Rosie sometimes wanted to ask him if his mother had put a box over his skull when he was a baby to make his head become square.

"You done apologized till I'm sick of hearing it," Rosie said discouragingly. "After a while I'll cry myself out and then maybe I'll get better, but you sitting there apologizing and rolling your stupid shirtsleeves up and down ain't gonna have any effect, except the effect of making me wish I could find a boyfriend who had sense enough just to leave me alone when I get like this."

At that, C.C. began to act a little huffy. "Well, I was brought up to believe there ain't nothing wrong with saying you're sorry," he said, rolling his cuffs back up.

"There ain't nothing wrong with saying you're sorry, but after you've said it ten or fifteen times, that's *enough!*" Rosie shouted. Out her window she could see Aurora pacing up and down on the downstairs patio, pretending she wasn't eavesdropping or paying any attention to what might be going on in Rosie's cottage, although she was obviously nearly dead with curiosity.

"Particularly since you didn't do nothing to apologize for even once!" Rosie added, also loudly.

C.C., red-faced, close to tears, and at his wit's end, finally gave up. He made an awkward attempt to pat Rosie on the shoulder, and an even more awkward attempt to give her a kiss before rolling his shirtsleeves down one more time and standing up to go.

"Have it your way—I just hope you feel better—call you later," he stammered, as he left. Crossing the yard he kept his head down, so as not to have to speak to Mrs. Greenway, a person who terrified him.

Aurora busied herself with some geraniums, but watched C.C. go out of the corner of her eye. Moments later, Rosie stumbled out of her cottage, wiping her eyes and trying to get her apron tied, but before she got three steps she dropped her apron and fled back to her house in tears, shutting her door firmly behind her.

Aurora retrieved the apron and went and made a substantial breakfast. Rosie had looked shaky; she would require sustenance at some point, and she herself required it immediately. Hector, still upstairs, had sunk into such a state of post-coital gloom that feeding him seemed almost beside the point. Nonetheless, she boiled him a couple of eggs, whacked the tops off them and carried him up a tray equipped with his egg spoon and also coffee, orange juice, and bacon.

The General was on his chaise, and his gloom had not abated. Before Aurora and the tray even cleared the top of the stairs he began to find fault.

"I don't want those eggs, they haven't been done properly," he said. "What's the matter with Rosie that she can't even do my eggs properly?"

At that a dangerous light came into Aurora's eyes, and the General noticed.

"Well, maybe I can get one of them down anyway," he said hastily. Aurora set the tray down and carefully lifted one of the eggs out of the egg cup. He had a feeling she might be going to throw it at him, but instead she held it over his head and squeezed it until the yellow ran into his hair. Then she picked up the tray and went back downstairs, taking the other improperly broken egg, as well as a lot of other food he would have been perfectly happy to have eaten. The General tried to throw his crutch at her but by this time egg yolk was dripping down his face, and he missed.

Aurora didn't say a word, though she heard the crutch hit the railing. She went back to her kitchen and ate every bite of the breakfast she had prepared for the General, minus only the egg she had squeezed over his head. Then she ate the breakfast she had prepared for herself, and was rather guiltily beginning to annex portions of the breakfast she had made for Rosie when Rosie made a shaky entrance.

"Good, I was about to eat your English muffins and now I won't have to—you can eat them yourself," Aurora said.

"I'm sick, I can't eat a bite. Besides, I lost my apron," Rosie said, dropping into a chair. Actually, the English muffins did look delicious. She particularly liked them with marmalade, and a nice pot of marmalade was handy on the table.

"No, I rescued your apron," Aurora said. "I was afraid a bird might carry it away. Why are you sick?"

"Because nothing I do ever works out," Rosie said, digging a knife into the marmalade. "Seventy years of not having a thing work out is a lot of years of nothing working out."

"Rosie, I'd like to point out something to you," Aurora said. "You have seven children, am I correct?"

"Yeah, seven," Rosie admitted.

"I'd like to point out to you that all seven of your children have turned out splendidly," Aurora said. "They grew up, they pursued educations, all but two of them married—and I'm sure those two will get around to it eventually. They're responsible citizens, several of them own their own businesses, and for all we know they may all get rich."

"Oh, yeah, true," Rosie said.

"Well, here I sit, listening to you complain," Aurora said. "My daughter is dead, and not a single one of my grandchildren has done even as well as the least successful of your children. How dare you sit at my breakfast table and tell me that nothing you've ever done has turned out right! It looks to me like everything you've ever done has turned out rosy, no pun intended."

"Well, it's true, I've got my kids to be proud of, I guess I overlooked that part," Rosie said.

"Overlooking seven successful, healthy children is like overlooking Mount Everest," Aurora said. "You have no idea how happy I'd be if even one of my grandchildren exhibited the kind of competence your children have. I'd think I was in heaven.

"But I'm not in heaven," she said, looking down. She had long been shamed and puzzled by the achievements of Rosie's children in contrast to the failures of her own.

Rosie knew that Aurora envied her her healthy, reliable children—anyone who had raised children and knew what the odds were *would* be likely to envy her, she knew. They *were* her children, she had raised them, in anxiety and strife, and yet nowadays she could rarely sense her own hand in their lives or their successes. Somehow it had just happened; one by one they had left her behind and gone on to inhabit worlds where she herself would never live. The kids had once been a part of her, but, for the life of her, she could no longer feel a part of them, and when she thought of them now it was mainly to be glad that they weren't miserable, as she was.

"Do you see what I'm getting at?" Aurora asked, shaking off the bitter mood that had been about to sweep over her.

"I see," Rosie said. "You're right. I'm luckier than you. I'm luckier than anybody. I ought to be the happiest old woman on earth. That's one of the reasons I'm so damn miserable. I ought to be happy but I ain't—I ain't at all."

"Well, I'm not either, don't look at me," Aurora said. "I squeezed an egg over Hector's head. He's upstairs, snarling and flailing about even as we speak. He'll probably shoot me with his army pistol in my own bedroom if I'm not careful."

Between the marmalade, the muffin, Aurora's lecture, and the surprising news about the General and the egg, Rosie began to feel a little better.

"You squuz an egg over his head?" she asked in wonderment. Aurora's capacity for inspired retaliation had always amazed her. Why hadn't she thought to cook an egg and squeeze it on C.C.'s head? It would have surprised him so much he would probably have croaked on the spot. The thought made her smile.

"That's better," Aurora said. "However, I must inform you

that there's no such word as 'squuz.' There ought to be, but there isn't."

"I guess there is, if I said it," Rosie commented—Aurora's pickiness about words often annoyed her. Still, she was feeling a great deal better suddenly and she slavered a great hunk of marmalade on the next English muffin.

"That's not a correct attitude, but never mind," Aurora said. "May I ask what happened to make you so unhappy?"

"Oh, well," Rosie said. "I'd like to forget it, if you don't mind."

"Of course I mind," Aurora said. "Did you and C.C. have sex in the car, or am I mistaken?"

"Oh, no, you did see—I knew you'd see!" Rosie said. She dropped the muffin—it hit on its edge and rolled several feet across the kitchen floor—and buried her face in her hands. She'd been discovered, and now she'd never, never live it down.

"Now, now, I didn't see," Aurora said, wishing she had. "It's merely that I inferred that such practices might be taking place. You surely don't think I'd peek on your intimacies, do you?"

"I sure do think you'd peek," Rosie said. "I *know* you'd peek. Who wouldn't? I told him you'd peek. Now I want to kill myself."

"Rosie, please don't overdramatize," Aurora said. "I'm the one who gets to overdramatize. We can't both get away with it, and I've had a lot more practice."

Rosie kept her face in her hands. She *knew* Aurora would see! She had told C.C. Aurora would see! But he begged, she gave in, Aurora *did* see, and now she would never live it down.

"The one thing I'm not is prudish," Aurora assured her, when Rosie had hidden her face and held her silence for a considerable while.

"People fortunate enough to have active lovers can have sex wherever they want to without a word of complaint from me," she added. "When I was younger and luckier I had it in a wide variety of places myself, as I informed Pascal the other evening, in no uncertain terms. Surely you're not thinking I'd begrudge you your good luck?"

Rosie put little stock in Aurora's tolerant stance. Besides that, she had no intention of sitting still for the suggestion that what had happened to her amounted to good luck—what had transpired between herself and C.C. that morning was anything but lucky, in her view.

"What good luck?" she asked, raising her face briefly. "The fact that C.C.'s got this weird thing about doing it in cars is the curse of my life. It ain't good luck at all, and if you think it is, try it sometime!"

"It's odd that I never suspected that you were suffering under this curse until today, when I happened to look out my window just at the right moment," Aurora said. "I didn't even know C.C. was weird—I just thought he was lazy, like Hector and Pascal."

Rosie looked disgusted, but didn't answer.

"Why does he like doing it in cars especially?" Aurora asked, after a decent interval.

"Because that's where he done it with his first girlfriend," Rosie said. "When they got married, C.C. was a boomer and they traveled around a lot and kept on doing it in cars. C.C. got in the habit and now he can't break it. What you got to remember is that C.C. still thinks like a teenager, even if he is sixty-eight years old."

"He's by no means the oldest teenager in the world," Aurora pointed out. "The one that threw the crutch at me this morning is even older."

"I don't know," Rosie said. She felt that she would never enjoy even one day free of confusion in her whole life.

"Don't know what?" Aurora asked.

Rosie sighed. "Maybe it's just that C.C. was raised in cars," she said. "He's just about worthless once you get him in the house."

"Hector is nearly worthless too, and he wasn't raised in cars," Aurora said—she thought it was about time to switch the conversation back to *her* problems.

"I get nervous in cars," Rosie admitted, ignoring Aurora's

ploy. "I mean, I oughtn't—it's the same thing you're doing, whether you're doing it in a car or a bed. But I get nervous and then I try to hurry and you know what happens when you try to hurry."

"The men hurry faster, that's what happens," Aurora said, remembering that Rosie had not looked exactly replete when she stepped out of the station wagon. "Believe it or not I was confronted with the same phenomenon this very day," she added.

Rosie peeked through her fingers at the floor she had mopped so often. Fortunately, at the end of its roll across the floor, her English muffin had landed marmalade side up. She retrieved it and took another bite.

"Since all you seem to want to talk about is sex, let me ask you a question," Aurora said. "On a scale of one to ten, how would you score your little frolic in C.C.'s station wagon?"

"What?" Rosie asked. "Score it?"

"Sure, score it," Aurora said. "Why not?"

Rosie suspected a trap of some sort. If she were to give her morning's lovemaking a grade such as one got in school, she would undoubtedly give it an F, but F happened to be the letter a certain four-letter word started with. Was Aurora trying to trick her into saying the word, and if so, why?

Then, remembering her nervousness and her frustration, she ceased to care about Aurora's motive.

"On a scale of one to ten I'd give it a zero," she said bitterly. "All I got out of it was a raw back from C.C.'s old scratchy seat covers, and besides that I gouged myself on a screwdriver he left on the seat. Even a zero might be putting it too high. It was more like a minus two."

"No wonder you cried," Aurora said. "I suppose I fared somewhat better, although not much."

Rosie had thought Aurora looked sort of cheerful. "Does that mean the General finally perked up?" she asked.

"Slightly, but only slightly," Aurora said.

Rosie considered that it was just one more unfair instance of Aurora getting more than she herself did of life's pleasures. In the forty years she had been with Aurora there had been thousands of such instances, but that didn't mean she had stopped resenting them. That Aurora had done better with the General, who was *really* old, than she had done with C.C., who wasn't, was no cause for joy; and, besides that, if Aurora had seen the station wagon shaking, the whole neighborhood had probably seen the station wagon shaking.

"Seventy years of keeping up a decent reputation, and now it's gone," she said. "I wish I could just quit and go live in a neighborhood where people don't start looking out their windows before it even gets light."

"Oh, hush," Aurora said. "I didn't see a thing, and no one else did, either. I'm just a good guesser. Hector wanted to look but he couldn't find his crutches in time, so you're quite safe. Anyway, if you would devote yourself to the study of history even for a few minutes you'll find that even the most respectable people do ridiculous things now and then. I've done several ridiculous things myself, and no one's more respectable than I am."

Rose finished her muffin—life had to go on, or at least it hadn't yet stopped going on. Someday, she knew, it *would* stop, for her if not for others, and that would be that. Her main hope was that she'd be fully clothed when she died. Now and then, in low moods, she found herself worrying that she might die naked, in the bathtub or somewhere. That would be too much—she cringed at the thought. But it hadn't happened yet, and perhaps it wouldn't happen; meanwhile, all she and Aurora could find to talk about anymore was sex. For most of the years that she had worked for Aurora they had rarely mentioned sex; now they rarely mentioned anything else.

"I've heard old women get nasty-minded," she said, wishing she had another English muffin. "I sure never thought it would happen to us."

"Me neither," Aurora admitted. She picked up her hairbrush and proceeded to give her hair a thoughtful stroke or two.

"On the other hand, I'm sure neither of us supposed we'd be making do with what we're making do with, either," she said.

"Right, a nudist and a maniac who can't keep it up unless

163

he's in a backseat," Rosie said. "We deserve better. If there's anything I hate, it's starting the day with a minus two."

She noticed that, in fact, Aurora didn't look all *that* cheerful.

"How about you, on a scale of one to ten?" she inquired. She had never asked her employer such a question, but since they couldn't seem to stop talking about sex, she thought she might as well.

"Oh, I don't know—perhaps a one and a half," Aurora said, brushing more listlessly. "Certainly no higher than a two."

The phone rang. Aurora ignored it.

"Want me to get it?" Rosie asked. "It could be Melly. They could have had a car wreck."

"No, it's Hector, I'm sure," Aurora said. "I don't wish to speak to him, but you may if you like."

Some months before, after weeks of quarreling, she had consented to the installation of a second phone line. The General complained that she spent so much of her time on the phone that he could barely squeeze in his business calls. Also, as he often reminded her, the day might come when he could no longer manage the stairs—he wanted to be able to call down to the first floor, in case there was an emergency of some sort. Now he was in the habit of calling down eight or nine times a day, mainly to inform them that he was lonely.

"Hi, General," Rosie said, picking up the phone.

"Am I to be left here to starve just because I complained about my eggs?" the General asked, in moderate tones.

"He wants to know if he's being left to starve because he complained about his eggs," Rosie said to Aurora.

"No, but coming on top of a meager one and a half, it was certainly unwise of him to complain," Aurora pointed out. "After all, I didn't complain about the one and a half. Besides, he threw his crutch at me. Let me have the phone."

"Hello, Hector," she said coolly, once she got it.

"Aurora, I'm sorry I complained," the General said. "I miss you. I wish you'd come back upstairs."

"Why, so you can conk me with your crutch?" Aurora asked. "What if I'm not in the mood to be conked?"

"I won't conk you—I love you," the General said. In times

past he had seldom declared his love so directly, but now he often had to declare it directly several times a day, just to keep things on an even keel. Even then, they didn't stay on a particularly even keel. It was rather a disappointment that life was just as uneven at the end as it had been at the beginning and in the middle. He had always supposed that passion would eventually subside, and that when it did life would be calm. He had once rowed a little boat across the Bay of Naples at sunset, and when he thought back on the experience he realized that he had hoped that was more or less how old age would be: serene, beautiful, calm, with sky and water in harmony.

But here he was, his hands shaking, calling from the second floor of Aurora's house to the first floor, pleading with her to come back up and see him and, if possible, bring him a scrap of bacon, or *something* to eat. It wasn't much like the Bay of Naples at sunset with the evening star bright in the sky.

"Well, perhaps you do—perhaps I'll come in a moment," Aurora said. "You should be getting dressed now. We're going off to see our analyst in about an hour."

"Oh, drat," the General said. "I forgot about that. I haven't had a bite to eat, you know. You threw that egg on my head and took my breakfast away."

"Rosie says I squuz it," Aurora said, with a giggle.

"There's no such word as 'squuz,' " the General informed her.

"Yes, I made that point," Aurora said. "Did you wash your hair?"

"Of course I washed my hair," the General said. "What choice did I have? Did you think I want to go through life with egg all over me?"

"Hector, I was merely thinking of our poor analyst," Aurora said. "If I brought you in with egg in your hair, the poor young man might give up on us before we even get started. We wouldn't want that to happen, would we?"

"No, but the point is, I'm starving," the General said. "Do you think Rosie could at least make me some oatmeal?"

"Well, I don't know, her day has had a tragic beginning, or

very nearly," Aurora said. "I refuse to put your case—you'll have to put it yourself."

She handed the phone back to Rosie, who listened patiently to the General's request.

"Okay, but there's no brown sugar, I forgot to get any," Rosie said. "You'll just have to eat it with plain old white sugar, much as you hate it—or else you can have honey."

"A little honey will be fine," the General said.

18

Bump hated it when his Bigs shut the bedroom door. First they locked the screen door so he couldn't escape down the stairs and into the yard. Then they plopped him in his bed with some books and toys, told him to be nice, gave him a kiss or two, and then abandoned him. No matter how he tried to get them to play, or how hard he cried, or how loud he yelled, his Bigs ignored him and disappeared behind their door.

Often this happened in the morning, not long after his father got home. Everyone would be sitting on the couch and for a while Bump would be the center of attention—his mother and father would kiss him a lot and laugh at the things he did. It was usually when they started to kiss one another that he got abandoned. He knew this and would try to stick a book between their faces if he thought they were going to kiss, but his Bigs just laughed and ducked under the book. They kissed anyway.

Then they locked him in the house, but out of their bedroom. Sometimes it made him feel lonely, but mainly it made him feel angry. Once or twice he lay on the floor and tried to peek under the door, but all he saw was his father's shoes and a heap of clothes on the floor.

Sometimes he yelled, but nobody answered. Sometimes he listened, but all he could hear was jiggle sounds from the bed. They were the kind of sounds he made when he bounced on his Big Granny's bed. If his own Bigs just wanted to bounce on their bed, why wasn't he welcome to bounce with them? Once his mother was in a hurry and didn't manage to get the door completely shut, and he slipped in for a second; the bed was making jiggle noises, but his Bigs weren't bouncing nearly as high as he imagined. Before he got two steps into the bedroom his mother came rushing at him naked, even more like a beast, and flung him into his bunk bed so hard he cried for a long time. She slammed the door to the bedroom so hard it made Bump want to run away. He got a pencil and tried to poke a hole in the screen door—he wanted to squeeze through like Peter Rabbit and run away, but he could only make a tiny hole, and then he broke the pencil.

Bump liked it in the early mornings, before his father came home. He and his mother would lie on the couch together and play games. His mother would yawn big yawns and sometimes even go back to sleep. She wore a loose gown and sometimes one of her breasts would come out of the gown. Bump would always be naked—he hated his pajamas and would always take them off as soon as he woke up. Sometimes he would try to pull his mother's gown off so they could be naked together; but his mother would never take her gown off. She didn't particularly care if one of her breasts fell out, though. She wasn't so beastlike when she was playing with him in the mornings. She smelled good then— Bump would often lie on top of her and smell her.

But soon his father would come home and the two Bigs would start talking. Sometimes they would just go right into their bedroom and leave him alone and make him feel helpless. They didn't seem to realize how bad it was to feel helpless, if you were a Little. The one thing Bump found to do that would let them know how angry he was at being shut out was to drag his toy box across the room and throw all his toys at the bedroom door one by one. He expected his mother to come raging out like a beast when he threw his toys, but she never did. Sometimes they would yell at him to stop throwing the toys, but Bump didn't stop. He threw every toy in his toy box—sometimes he even tried to butt the door open with a little wagon he had, but it didn't work. Nothing worked, not even crying and screaming and kicking the door with his feet. The Bigs just stayed in the bedroom, not caring a bit that he felt helpless.

"I wish you'd told me Melanie was leaving," Jane said. "I'm going to miss Melanie. We should have gone and seen her off, or something."

They were lying in bed, lovemaking over, listening to Bump use his little wagon like a battering ram against their bedroom door.

"That little boy of ours is determined," Teddy said. "Listen to him try to break down the door."

"For one thing, Melanie was our ambassador to Aurora," Jane said. She had learned to blank out Bump's attempts to get into the bedroom while she and Teddy made love. At first they had irritated her and thrown her off, but she adapted. Where sex was involved, Jane liked to think she could always adapt. She wasn't going to be cheated out of the big pleasure, not by Bump or anyone. Sometimes she wished Teddy weren't so placid, though. Sex with Teddy was fine, but sometimes she felt it could be even better than fine if he would occasionally be more antagonistic, or get a little angry or something. It was just a thought—maybe she was wrong—but it was a thought she kept having.

"I don't think Melanie wanted to be seen off," Teddy said, wishing his son would stop banging the wagon against the door. Jane was very appealing to him at that moment—despite a thumping orgasm, she seemed a little restless. He felt there might be more sex in the offing, but it wasn't going to happen if Bump kept banging the wagon against the door.

"Maybe she felt if she went through too much seeing off she might lose her nerve and not go," he suggested. He reached down beside the bed, found one of his shoes, and threw it at the door as hard as he could. The tactic worked. Bump stopped butting the door with his wagon. There was total silence from the other room.

"I think I trumped him," Teddy said.

"It shouldn't be hard, he's only two," Jane said. "At least he gets mad and lets us know it."

Teddy raised up on an elbow and looked at his wife. "Is that comment directed at me?" he asked.

"Yeah," Jane said. "Sometimes I wonder if you'll ever get mad again. You wanted to yesterday, when I spanked Bump, but I guess you didn't have the nerve."

Teddy decided it was unlikely there was any more sex in the offing—not that there needed to be, necessarily. But, having quelled Bump, he didn't know if he still had the energy to quell Jane. Something had left him when he threw the shoe at the door.

"I just threw a shoe at the door," he pointed out.

"Big deal," Jane said. "That was tactical. There's a difference between tactics and emotion."

"Right," Teddy said. "But the last time I crossed the line I got put in a straitjacket. You weren't around to see that. That was before we met, and also before I discovered lithium."

"I wish I had been around to see it," Jane said. "I'd like to see you get so mad you had to be put in a straitjacket."

"Why?" Teddy asked.

Jane shrugged. "Maybe I just would," she said.

"It's stupid to romanticize anger," Teddy said. "I don't think you'd like it so much if you saw it."

"We'll probably never know," Jane said.

19

Despite his conviction that going to an analyst was ridiculous —at his age, Aurora's age, or any age—General Scott had cleaned himself up admirably for the occasion. He wore his best suit and the red bow tie with tiny spots that Aurora had picked out for him in London.

The sight of Hector in his best suit and his red bow tie lifted Aurora's spirits to the level that was apt to cause arias from her favorite operas to float out of her mouth. Several floated out of her mouth between her house and the distant Bellaire street where Dr. Bruckner had his office.

Hector's response to her singing, unfortunately, was not quite on a level with his appearance.

"Don't sing those goddamn arias when you're driving," he said. "You can barely drive adequately when you're quiet. If you want us both to live to get this analysis started I'd advise you to shut up."

"Hector, it's very unfortunate that you have so little appreciation of my singing," Aurora said. "Singing is a very healthy thing. I'm sure Dr. Bruckner will back me up on that."

The General's spiffy appearance belied his mood, which was black. Despite a hearty, if belated, breakfast, his post-coital gloom had not passed—if anything, it had deepened. He could not rid himself of the conviction that the morning's brief intimacy had been his last hurrah—and not much of a hurrah at that. The minute it ended he had started having the feeling that he and Aurora would never make love again, and the feeling wouldn't leave him. He felt completely drained of juice—he was just an old bone.

"The first thing I'm going to tell that psychoanalyst is that I can no longer ejaculate," he remarked. They were at a stoplight on the edge of Bellaire, and Aurora had stopped singing. For some reason she considered it inappropriate to sing at stoplights.

"You're not going to tell him any such thing," Aurora said. "I forbid it. There's a great deal we can talk about with this nice young man other than your ejaculations."

"I don't have any ejaculations," the General said. "That's what I just said, and that's the point I intend to stress. Nothing comes out, and you know what that means."

"No, I'm not sure I do," Aurora said. "I'm not sure I want to, but I am sure I don't want you mentioning our problems along that line to the nice doctor."

"How do you know he's nice?" the General asked. "We haven't even met him."

"No, but I spoke with him, and he has a soothing voice," Aurora said. "His voice is the exact opposite of yours, Hector. Your voice rarely soothes me, and the fact is I often need soothing."

"Well, yours doesn't soothe me, either," the General said. "Particularly not when you sing arias in the car. Go, why don't you—the light is green."

"Hector, it just turned!" Aurora pointed out.

"Well, but when it turns, it means it's time to go, immediately," the General reminded her.

"I just like to give it a second or two, to be sure it means it," Aurora said, going.

"Right after we made love this morning I got the terrible

feeling that we'll never make love again," Hector said. "The feeling won't go away, which is why I'm so depressed. Can I tell that to the psychoanalyst?"

Aurora didn't answer. She did not like the suburb of Bellaire—indeed, she was opposed to the whole concept of suburbs, though it appeared that suburbs were where most people now lived. In her youth it had been different. There were cities, towns, villages, and the country, with none of this muddle of stoplights, convenience stores, and small ugly houses in between.

"If I can't tell him about my feeling that we'll never make love again, then I don't know what I'm supposed to tell him," the General said. "My parents have been dead for over fifty years—I don't think I can say much about them.

"It's going to be a sad life if we never make love again," he added.

"Hector, why can't you be an optimist instead of a pessimist?" Aurora said. Actually, she had also had the feeling, after their early morning intimacy, that something was over —namely her long, twenty-year romance with Hector Scott. Passion *had* quite probably made its last appearance in their lives—the passion, that is, that had been theirs.

It was not a happy thought. She wished that she could simply be still and content, at rest in her heart, as the elderly, or at least the late middle-aged, were supposed to be, but in fact she never felt still, content, or at rest. Not only had the fever of life not abated—in her it seemed to be glowing ever more hotly. Instead of feeling calm she felt agitated and needy, too alive to sleep, and often troubled by thoughts that were unladylike and, in fact, distinctly lustful, about unlikely men or even more unlikely boys. One such boy came to cut her grass. He was Hispanic, wore shorts, and had wonderfully sturdy legs. His name was Jaime and every time she happened to glance down from her window and notice his sturdy legs she was apt to have lustful stirrings. Very often these stirrings followed her into the depths of sleep, causing her to have to get up and pace the house in her restlessness. Of all afflictions, lust was the one she had least expected to be beset by, at her age, but there was no doubt that lust was the affliction that beset her.

"I'm a pessimist because I'm old and useless," the General said. "We'll see how optimistic you are when you're my age."

Despite his spiffy appearance, he did look shockingly old to her at times. For years her eyes had lit up at the sight of General Scott in a uniform, or General Scott in one of his crisp summer suits; not every man wore clothes as well as Hector. But now he didn't so much wear them as huddle in them, issuing gloomy statements.

The General happened to glance out his window and he saw a little green sign on the lawn of a house they were passing. It said, "Dr. J. Bruckner, Therapist." Aurora sailed right on past the house.

"Whoa," the General said. "You just passed our doctor's office."

Aurora looked out her window and saw nothing on either side of the street except ugly little suburban houses. It was certainly not the sort of block where she supposed their psychoanalyst would have his practice. She had envisioned a tasteful glass office building, with good carpeting and discreet receptionists. There were hundreds of such tasteful glass buildings in Houston, many of them housing doctors. Certainly it would be a lot easier to sort through the tangle of Hector's psyche if the sorting were taking place in a tasteful building with possibly a bank or two in it.

"Stop, I said," the General said. "You passed the house."

"We're not looking for a house, Hector—we're looking for a doctor's office," Aurora said.

"I know, we just passed it, I've now told you that three times," the General said. "You'll have to turn around."

"Not until I spot a building that looks as if it ought to have a doctor's office in it, I'm not," Aurora said. "This is the kind of street salaried people live on—I don't think we'll find a respected psychoanalyst installed among a lot of salaried people."

"What a ridiculous snob you are," the General said. "I'm

telling you again, we just passed Dr. Bruckner's house. He had a sign on his lawn. I read it plain as day. It said 'Therapist,' and therapy is what we're after. We're getting farther and farther from it every second. Couldn't you try being reasonable, for once?"

"Hector, I've been to doctors before, I know what a doctor's office is supposed to look like," Aurora said. "An analyst is only a sort of doctor."

In explaining her position, Aurora ran a red light, and unfortunately a patrol car happened to be lurking right at the intersection.

"Now you've done it," Hector said, as the patrol car swung into action and began to make a loud sound and to blink a bright light. Aurora gave up and started to ease toward the curb, but she didn't ease quite close enough to suit the patrolman, who instructed her several times, through his loudspeaker, to pull over.

"He wants you to pull over," Hector said, to her intense irritation. Whenever she got into difficulties with the traffic police Hector invariably took the patrolman's side—she had almost broken up with him over this issue several times, and she now began to wish she *had* broken up with him. If she had, not only would she not have to watch her own lover cravenly ally himself with the authorities, but she wouldn't have to see him huddling in his suit, looking infinitely old.

"Hector, for your information, I *am* over," Aurora said. "It's not gallant of you to pick on me when I'm in trouble, either."

"If you'd done what I told you and turned around five blocks back you wouldn't *be* in trouble," Hector informed her. "If you won't listen to me, what can I do?"

Aurora, who had had a lifelong phobia about scraping her tires against the curb, eased gradually nearer the sidewalk, expecting to hear a hideous scraping sound at any moment.

"Please get out of the car!" the officer behind her said several times through his bullhorn.

"Why do you think he wants me to get out of my car?"

Aurora wondered. "They rarely insist that I leave my car. Do you think he's going to shoot me just for running a red light?"

"He probably thinks you're some kind of maniac, but he's not going to shoot you," the General said.

"Hector, why would he think I'm a maniac?" Aurora asked, extracting herself from her seat belt and opening her door. Unfortunately she had not yet put her car in Park, and was continuing to drift slowly curbward. When she noticed her error she slammed the gear shift over to Park, causing the car to stop abruptly. Hector, who had his seat belt on, jerked forward but didn't quite bump his head.

"I don't know about him, but *I* think you're some kind of maniac," the General said. "We *are* on our way to a psychiatrist and it's a goddamn good thing. We probably should have gone years ago."

Aurora got out of her car with as much dignity as possible, only to be confronted with a small redheaded policeman who looked at her skeptically, as they all did; though, actually, once she focused on him, she noticed that his skepticism seemed to be mainly directed at her car, which, much to her surprise, was still quite some distance from the curb.

"That's not exactly what I call pulling over," the patrolman said. "If this was a time of day when there was much traffic you'd be obstructing it. Have your eyes been checked recently?"

For a moment Aurora couldn't quite grasp what he meant: people checked their coats, but why would anyone check their eyes? Then she realized that the redheaded officer had merely spoken imprecisely: he was attempting to inquire about her vision.

"My vision is fine, thank you, Officer," she said. "It's just that I have a little phobia about scraping my tires against the curb. In fact, that's why I was hurrying to my doctor, to see if he could do something about my phobia."

"Is that why you ran the red light?" the officer asked. "Is this some kind of medical emergency?"

"Why, yes, it could be considered in that light," Aurora

said. "As you can see yourself, I have quite a serious phobia. I'm nowhere near that curb, but I assure you that in my head I heard a kind of continual screech, such as tires make when you scrape them. An imaginary screech of that intensity can be quite distracting, I assure you."

The small policeman looked at her wryly and shook his head.

"Nice try," he said, and began to write her a ticket for running the red light.

"Not nice enough, evidently," Aurora said. "If you're going to give me a ticket the least you can do is help me find my doctor's office. His name is Bruckner and he's a psychoanalyst. I'm very hopeful that he can help me with my phobia."

"I hope so too," the officer said. "Otherwise the next time you run a red light and don't bother to pull over you'll probably get a double ticket, one for the light and one for blocking traffic."

"Do you know where Dr. Bruckner's office is, at least?" Aurora asked, feeling rather incensed.

"Yes, you just passed it," the officer said, handing her the ticket. "Once you turn around it'll be on the left, about three blocks back. It's a little green house with a sign in the yard. Please try to stop at the stoplights, ma'am."

Aurora got in her car and immediately executed a sweeping U-turn, right in front of the patrolman, who watched her skeptically, it seemed to her.

The General, too, watched her skeptically, although the light in front of her was red, and she politely stopped at it.

"I'm not sure U-turns are legal in Bellaire," he said, but the look in Aurora's eye—a look with which he was long familiar—advised him that it would not be wise to raise too many questions about legalities in Bellaire—not just at that moment, at least.

"Hector, we must look for a little green house with a sign in the yard," Aurora said. "I expect it will appear on our left at some point."

"That's right," the General said.

"No, not right—left!" Aurora insisted.

"I meant right in the sense of correct," the General informed her. "The word has more than one meaning, you know."

"Hector, I'm merely trying to follow the officer's directions," Aurora said. "I don't want to get into the question of multiple meanings. I'm sure our analyst may want to, but I don't."

"Aurora, there it is, right there—see!" the General said, pointing excitedly as they approached the house. "It's the one I tried to get you to stop at in the first place."

Aurora looked and saw a more or less normal ugly green ranch-style suburban house. Reluctantly she executed yet another sweeping U-turn and pulled into the driveway.

"What a disappointment!" she said. "Why would a respected psychoanalyst from Vienna live in a dump like this?"

"It's a perfectly normal house," the General observed. "People have to live somewhere, you know. Anyway, we're hiring him for his brain—who cares what kind of house he lives in?"

"I care," Aurora confessed. "I suppose it's silly of me, but I can't help it. I just had rather a different image of what Dr. Bruckner's office might look like." She sighed.

"Now don't start sighing," the General said. "We've decided to do this and let's try to go into it with a positive attitude."

Aurora sighed again.

"I wish you wouldn't keep sighing," the General said. "I hate it when you sigh. Why do you have to sigh so much?"

"Because you're the last person who should criticize me for the lack of a positive attitude," Aurora said. "I've met virtually every day of the last twenty years with a positive attitude—even a cheerful attitude, in most cases. And a lot of good it's done me."

The General, feeling trapped, said nothing.

"I feel like crying," Aurora announced, to his horror.

"Aurora, we're at the doctor's office," the General said.

"We're parked in his driveway. He's probably looking out the window at us right now, wondering why we don't come in. Don't cry now."

"Well, I feel like it," Aurora said again. "The thought of all my wasted cheerfulness makes me want to cry."

"It wasn't wasted," the General said. He was feeling a little desperate.

"It was—you never stopped being depressed," Aurora said, beginning to cry. "All my cheerful attitudes just got smashed on your depressions. You're the most negative man I've ever known. I wish I hadn't even thought of psychoanalysis, because I know it won't work. None of the thousands of things I've suggested we do together have ever worked, and it's because you don't like anything and you don't want to do anything, and if I persist and work up some gallant little initiative, you smash it."

She cried briefly; the General felt too crushed and guilty to say a word. He racked his brain, trying to think of some gallant initiative of Aurora's that he had actually responded to—something that had worked out well. But just at the moment his mind was blank, and he couldn't come up with anything.

After one or two bursts, Aurora's crying subsided.

"The last thing you should ever do is accuse me of lacking a positive attitude," she said, wiping her eyes. "*You* lack a positive attitude—you, you, you!"

"Well, you lack a few things too," the General countered. "Are we ever going to go in and be psychoanalyzed, are or we just going to sit in this man's driveway all morning and have our usual quarrels?"

"I guess we must go in," Aurora said, screwing the rearview mirror around so she could hastily repair her eyes. "I doubt I would have cried when I was looking so nice if I hadn't been cruelly disappointed in this man's house. I'm so disappointed in it I hardly feel like letting him psychoanalyze me now."

"Aurora, we're here, let's try it, at least," the General said. "The man's expecting us."

"People often expect things that don't happen," Aurora said. "Look at me. I've been expecting happiness on a daily basis all my life. But the days keep passing, and where is it?"

Somehow they pulled themselves together, walked up the driveway, and rang the bell. The door opened immediately, before Aurora had quite finished composing herself. I'm not quite ready for this, she thought, when she saw the door opening. So many things in life happened before one was quite ready: Emma, for example, had been born two weeks early, before she was quite ready, and she had always supposed that this slight prematureness was what had caused her to be such a nervous mother, at least for the first few years. She preferred to be quite ready before things happened, but all too often they began to happen anyway while she was getting inwardly prepared for them; and that was just what was occurring with her psychoanalyst's door. It was opening, though she was not quite ready.

In the door stood a rumpled man, perhaps in his early forties, with a shock of graying hair and the largest, saddest brown eyes Aurora had ever looked into. He was wearing a corduroy coat with patched elbows, and Levi's, but the shock of seeing a doctor in Levi's was offset by the look in his eyes —a look that was far more welcoming than the look in most doctors' eyes.

Looking back on her time with Jerry Bruckner, after his death, Aurora felt it had all happened because from the first moment he had made her feel welcome—immediately and completely welcome—to a degree that no man, before him or after him, had ever done.

"Howdy, I'm Jerry Bruckner, come on in," the doctor said. He had a rather husky voice.

"Howdy?" Aurora asked, stepping inside. "Do psychiatrists from Vienna really say howdy?"

"Probably not, but who said I was from Vienna?" Jerry Bruckner asked, shaking the General's hand.

"That's fine with me, I hate Austria," the General said.

"But I thought you must be," Aurora insisted, though her

vision of a classical psychoanalysis was rapidly slipping away. "The name sounds so Viennese."

The doctor looked slightly amused.

"I'm from Las Vegas, Nevada," he said. "I doubt there are too many psychiatrists in Houston who are actually from Vienna."

"No, but there can't be vast numbers from Las Vegas, either," Aurora commented, looking around the waiting room, which was nothing more than a rather shabby living room with an orange couch that needed recovering along one wall.

"I should get that couch recovered," Dr. Bruckner said, echoing her very thought.

"Goodness, you just read my mind," Aurora said, smiling at him. "I hope you'll do that some more." She immediately forgave his living room, as she had forgiven the Levi's. He had a nice smile—and a nice smile meant a lot.

"She expects a great deal," the General put in, nervously. He thought the doctor ought to know that right away—at any moment Aurora might start criticizing the man's clothes, or his furniture, or the wallpaper, or something else.

"I don't know about reading your mind, but I can offer you coffee or tea," the doctor said.

"But where's that charming receptionist I spoke to when I made the appointment?" Aurora inquired—she had never been in a doctor's office that seemed less like a doctor's office. Where was the usual staff, the ones who stuck your finger or inquired about your insurance policy?

"I think her name was Simone," she added, to the General's annoyance. Did she think a psychoanalyst wouldn't remember his own receptionist's name?

"I believe I did do Simone with you," Jerry Bruckner said. "You sounded like you might prefer someone French. Sometimes I do Simone, sometimes I do a Magda, and sometimes I just do Marjorie, for people who prefer to deal with a plain American receptionist."

"I don't follow you at all. What does this mean?" Aurora asked.

Jerry Bruckner smiled his welcoming smile again. "I can't afford a receptionist and I'm not sure I'd want one around even if I could afford one," he said. "I was an actor for a while. I'm pretty good at voices. For you I did Simone."

"Well, goodness gracious," Aurora said.

20

The letter from Melanie was postmarked Quartzite, Arizona, a place Tommy never heard of. He asked Joey if he had heard of it, but Joey had been sulky for a few days and didn't bother to answer. He then asked a couple of guards, but neither of them had heard of it, either. In terms of travel horizons, the prison personnel were fairly limited. Few of the guards had heard of too many places unless the places happened to be in East Texas.

Tommy let the letter sit for three days before he read it. Often, when he got letters from people on his letter list, he let them sit for anywhere between a week and a month before he read them. The other inmates couldn't understand this—most of them read their mail immediately and obsessively. The fact that Tommy let his sit for a week or more just convinced them of what they already knew: Tommy was spooky, an alien of some sort.

In fact, Tommy had considered telling the prison authorities just to send back whatever came in the way of mail. Communications from the outside world were not events that he welcomed—they were more likely to be events that he dreaded. He allowed members of his family to visit, but at the same time he made it clear that he was not *encouraging* them to visit; and he didn't encourage them to write, either. The things that they wrote were too apt to be like pleas for him to change himself, to become a person he had never been and didn't want to be. He really didn't want to think about such changes or such ways of life anymore. When he thought about them he experienced conflicting vibes, or even got migraine headaches. Far better just to concentrate on his own plans, his own forms of rebellion, his own way of being. It was a weakness that he hadn't yet hardened himself to the point of rejecting all visits, as well as all mail. The fact was, he just got tired of seeing no one except criminals or the prison personnel—and most of the prison personnel were fantasy criminals, or criminal groupies. The more horrible the criminals, the more the guards and the shrinks were apt to kowtow to them.

The letters that Tommy had the hardest time dealing with were those from his brother Teddy, who couldn't seem to admit that Tommy wasn't interested in giving him advice anymore. As the older brother and the stronger personality, Tommy had casually dished out a lot of advice over the years, and now Teddy didn't want to admit that Tommy had basically tuned out. Teddy's letters were all about his fears that Jane was going to leave him and go live with a woman she was having an affair with. If she did, Teddy was convinced he would crack up and have to go back to the mental hospital.

Tommy never made any reply to Teddy's letters or his pleas for advice. He maintained a strict silence, assuming that Teddy would eventually realize that he no longer had the slightest interest in domestic shit like that. Who Jane was sleeping with, or not sleeping with, or whether Teddy was in or out of his head, were just not concerns he felt like making space for in his consciousness. Even before he killed Julie and went to prison he had stopped wanting his consciousness to be filled up with family trivia of that sort. He preferred simply to be left out, but no one seemed willing to leave him out—which was why he let their letters sit, often for weeks.

Still, the thought of fat little Melanie being in a place like Quartzite, Arizona, was sort of intriguing; before he opened the letter he went to the prison library and looked the place up in an atlas. It was just a tiny dot in the middle of the desert, not far from California, which probably meant that Melanie was making an ill-advised effort to go see their father. Maybe she thought the mere fact that she was pregnant would soften the man up enough that he would help her go to school or something.

Knowing his father, Tommy knew Melly was making a big mistake if she thought anything of that nature would happen. Professor Horton—as he and Teddy preferred to call him; Melanie was the only one of them who still called the man Daddy—would just be horrified that Melanie had turned up, since when any of them turned up his present wife got pissed and had a fit, to make him pay for having dared to have children by anyone but her. Also, the thought that another child of his descent was on its way into the world could only be a downer, from Professor Horton's point of view. It just meant that he might ultimately be asked to contribute money toward the child's welfare, which would piss his wife off even more and cause her to throw worse fits.

Joey hated it that Tommy didn't read his mail right away. Seeing letters lying there for four or five days unopened made him want to beat Tommy up for being such a selfish prick. He himself almost never got letters, only a few scrawls from his mother or one of his crazy aunts once in a while. Every one of his letters made him cry and want to go home, but Tommy didn't even think enough of his family to open his letters. Joey didn't like being in a cell with such a person, but he didn't beat him up, either: he was too afraid that if he did, Tommy would figure out a way to kill him some night in his sleep.

Tommy knew that Joey disapproved of his discipline about the letters, but then Joey would never block any impulse—the fact that he couldn't was why he was in prison—and could not even grasp the concept of discipline, much less exercise any. Even if Tommy had wanted to read the letters immediately, he would have let them sit for a bit, just to make his point with Joey; but, after three days, curiosity about what had caused his kid sister to write him a letter from a remote town in the Arizona desert got the better of him and he opened the envelope and read the letter:

DEAR TOMMY:

I'm in this town in Arizona—boy is it an ugly dump, but there are all these big saguaro cactuses around, they're kind of interesting to look at.

Bruce drove all the way from Houston to here without stopping, and now he's so tired he can't wake up. I think maybe we should have stopped a little sooner, I've never seen Bruce this tired. But he was really interested in putting some distance between himself and his parents, so he just kept driving.

Anyway, we're nearly to California, our ultimate destination. We just sort of fell in love and ran away. I'm not really too sure what we're going to do in California—I guess we'll just get jobs and try to be grownups and make a living and stuff. Maybe that sounds silly to you, but Bruce and I are eager to try it.

The biggest surprise was that Granny didn't try to stop me. I expected her to freak out, but she didn't. Granny will surprise you sometimes.

We'll have to get a real cheap apartment to begin with—we don't have much money to start out our new life with.

Tommy, I guess this means I won't be coming for visits for a while. I was getting pretty discouraged about the visits anyway—it just seemed like visits were a kind of form of pressure, from your point of view. Part of the reason I'm writing is to let you know the pressure's off, at least where I'm concerned. It's kind of scary, being this in love with somebody—I'm so obsessed with Bruce right now that I feel like waking him up—it's crazy, but I even miss him when he's asleep. It's wild, being that obsessed, but I can't help it, I'm out-of-control in love. I'll just be glad when we get to L.A. and find a place and sort of get settled in.

I'm gonna stop now—I know you don't like long letters.
Anyway, Bruce just rolled over, maybe he's about to wake
up. I'm gonna try to get him moving.

I guess that's my big news, Tommy. Please be careful. I
love you.

MELLY

"What's your sister look like?" Joey asked, when he noticed that Tommy was finally reading his letter. Another
weird thing about Tommy was that he kept no pictures of his
family. He himself had snaps of every one of his sisters and
brothers—even one of the brother he had murdered—and
his mom and his aunts and his three best girlfriends. But
Tommy had none.

"She's a little chubby," Tommy said, putting Melanie's
letter back in its envelope.

"I wish I could meet her," Joey said wistfully. "She sounds
like just my type. I don't go for no toothpicks.

"You know, skinny girls," he added, not sure that Tommy
had taken his point.

"That's what I thought you meant," Tommy said.

II

The Decorative
Woman

II

The Decorative Woman

1

Knowing that Rosie Dunlup's loyalty to her boss was absolute, Patsy thought it best to take a cautious approach to inquiring about Aurora's new lover—if he *was* her lover— Jerry Bruckner, whom she had met the night before at a dinner party Aurora had given for him. Aurora had been radiant —she looked fifty-five again—and the minute she met Jerry, Patsy felt sure she knew why. He was a seriously attractive man—"seriously attractive" being a term she had brought home with her from L.A. Implicit in the definition was the suggestion that seriously attractive men were seldom serious about women. They were not where one applied if one were looking for long-term loyalty, but Patsy had ceased to suppose that she could afford to spend too much more of her life looking for long-term loyalty; she could easily be dead before she found it, and even if she did find it there would probably be a price to be paid in the area of serious attractiveness.

The dinner party had been lively, the food excellent. Poor old General Scott had gone sound asleep in the middle of it, but that hadn't slowed anyone down—least of all Aurora. For much of her adult life Patsy had an inkling that sooner or later, unless they were lucky, she and Aurora might clash over a man. Aurora was obviously just better at finding men than she was; the odds were that sooner or later she might find a man they both would want. Aurora, after all, was a great forager; she grazed her way through herds of men, all the while keeping a firm grip on someone like General Scott, or Emma's father, Rudyard, if only for the sake, as she had once admitted, of having some sort of continuing presence of the male sort in her house.

"It's one of the few things that can be said for marriage," Aurora had once remarked. "It provides a continuing presence of the male sort—if one likes such a presence, of such a sort, as I happen to."

She had admitted this to Emma and Patsy on a rainy Houston day many years before. Emma had just married Flap, and Patsy herself was just about to marry Jim. They were discussing bridesmaids' dresses, but she and Emma—both passionately curious about Aurora and her boyfriends—did she sleep with all of them? did she sleep with none of them?—had managed to turn the conversation toward the great haunting questions that they themselves discussed virtually nonstop whenever they got together to contemplate adult life: marriage, boyfriends, adultery—and was the last really fatal, in the moral sense, at least?

"What we really want to know is, do we have to throw ourselves under trains if I ever sleep with someone other than Flap, or if Patsy ever sleeps with someone other than Jim?" Emma asked, timidly.

Aurora had given them a long, wicked look, in which, for a moment, a kind of challenge had flickered. But the challenge, if that's what it had been, faded quickly, to be replaced by Aurora's standard infuriating patronizing gaze.

"You two should be out selling Girl Scout cookies," she said. "Instead, you're sitting in my kitchen trying to find out how wicked I am."

"Right, why can't we know?" Emma asked.

"Only those I'm wicked with know how wicked I am," Aurora said.

"I bet you're plenty wicked," Patsy said, annoyed by the woman's patronizing tone.

Now, nearly three decades later, driving Rosie home from aerobics class, she still found Aurora's tone annoying, only this time she had the notion that she might do something about it—something on the order of taking her new boyfriend away. She knew herself to be a much less forthright seducer than Aurora; more than once she had let other, more aggressive women lead her to the men she wanted. Sometimes she waited patiently for the romance to stall before interposing herself; other times she had not felt like waiting that long. If she sensed that the man was getting interested and might be ripe to switch, she would sometimes lay a timid, modest kind of ambush—often her very reserve would convince the man that he was the one doing the ambushing.

Jerry Bruckner had hardly flirted with her at all during the dinner party, but that was okay. Aurora had given him few chances. But a couple of times Patsy had caught him looking, a good sign. She didn't know if she believed he was a real analyst, whatever being a real analyst meant in this day and time, but he did seem to be some kind of therapist, which left a ready-made opening. Over the years she had tried every kind of therapy, from primal scream to mud baths; a little therapy with Aurora's new boyfriend surely wouldn't hurt, whatever brand of it he practiced. She could make an appointment some day and tell Jerry Bruckner the sad truth about her most recent Latin architect, though really, in that case, the truth was more silly than sad. The man owned two perfect, gorgeous Dalmatians, and was more interested in spending time with them than he was in spending time with her. Nothing as dramatic as discovering him being sucked off by a gardener had occurred; she just got tired of competing with a couple of spotted dogs.

Rosie seemed despondent. As usual, she had performed brilliantly in aerobics class, but now she was staring blankly out the window of the car, indifferent to the fact that Patsy was doing her usual eighty-five. They had decided to go to a Vietnamese market over near the Ship Channel and reward themselves with a Vietnamese breakfast before going back to Aurora's house.

"Had you met the guest of honor before?" Patsy asked.

"Which?" Rosie asked. C.C. Granby was hopeless, she had about decided to break up with him, but the question was, if she did, would she ever be able to get another boyfriend?

"The guest of honor at the dinner party?" Patsy repeated. "Aurora's shrink."

"Oh, Jerry," Rosie said. "Yeah, I met him before."

Patsy waited, but Rosie didn't elaborate. She stared blankly out the window some more.

"What's the matter?" Patsy asked. "Why are you clamming up on me? Are you forbidden to talk about him?"

"Talk about who?" Rosie asked. Her mind had been tugged back to C.C. Granby—it was as if her mind was a paper clip that kept getting flattened against the magnet of C.C.'s intractability. He was already talking about making love in the car again and had even shyly proposed what he thought might be an ideal solution to the problem of the car's rocking noticeably: oral sex.

It did not strike Rosie as an ideal solution, but the mere thought of it, and the certainty that C.C. would return to the proposition again and again, as regularly as he rolled his shirtsleeves up and down, made it difficult for her to keep her mind on Patsy's questions.

"I ain't supposed to talk about anything, specially to you, but when has that ever stopped me?" Rosie asked.

"It's stopping you this morning," Patsy said.

"Naw, I'm just distracted," Rosie said. "I'm getting where I'm distracted more and more. Aurora thinks I need therapy myself."

"That's interesting," Patsy said. "With Jerry Bruckner or with somebody else?"

"With Jerry," Rosie said. "One thing I'll say for him, he can cook. He's come over and cooked dinner a couple of times. If I ever had a boyfriend who could cook I'd think I was in heaven."

"Me too," Patsy admitted.

"What does General Scott think about all this?" she asked, a little later. They were on Canal Street—the mist off the Ship Channel was cut by strips of sunlight.

"The General ain't been himself lately," Rosie said. "Half the time he calls me Aurora, or Aurora me. He's gettin' a little senile, I guess."

"Is he still going to the shrink with Aurora?" Patsy asked. "It's not exactly standard procedure for two people to be analyzed together, if they are being analyzed."

"Naw, he quit after about three weeks," Rosie said. "He says Aurora's driving scares him too much now. She got at least one ticket every time they went to see Jerry, and once she got three in one morning. The General's nerves ain't up to it. He likes Jerry, but he and Aurora fight so much over her driving that the therapy wears off before they even get home."

"I bet she does it on purpose to get the General to stay home," Patsy said. "I bet she really just wants Jerry to herself."

"Aurora don't have to fake bad driving, though," Rosie said. "She drives about as bad as anybody I know. My kids could drive better than she does before they were ten years old."

Listening to Patsy try to probe made Rosie feel sulkier than she had been feeling to begin with. Sometimes she enjoyed gossiping about Aurora's love life, and sometimes she didn't. This was one of the times when she didn't. On her low days it sometimes seemed that she had spent her whole life doing nothing but talking about Aurora and her boyfriends. It seemed to her that there really ought to be a little more to life than trying to figure out whether Aurora Greenway was sleeping with a particular man or not—and anyway, the task was not as simple as it might seem. For all her flaunting of this suitor or that, Aurora could be as secretive as the next person when it suited her to be. Neither she herself nor Patsy nor anyone else had ever been able to determine whether Aurora had actually slept with the man called Cowboy Bill, a tall, craggy rodeo promoter who had drifted incongruously into Aurora's orbit, circled around in it for five years, and was still apt to show up and receive a warm welcome whenever the rodeo was in town.

But how warm was a warm welcome, in Cowboy Bill's case? Rosie didn't know, and neither did anyone else except Aurora and Cowboy Bill.

"What's therapy like?" she asked, hoping to change the subject. She liked Patsy and didn't want to hurt her feelings; she just thought it was a little early to start worrying about what might be going on between Aurora and Jerry Bruckner.

"I ought to be able to answer that question, since I've had every kind known to man," Patsy said. "Sometimes it's pretty helpful and sometimes it isn't. Dr. Bruckner seemed like a pretty relaxed guy. I don't think he's going to solve all your problems, but he might help you with a few of them. It wouldn't hurt you to go see him a few times."

"I only got one big problem, and that's C.C.," Rosie said. "All he thinks about is oral sex, but what's really driving me crazy is that he keeps rolling his shirtsleeves up and down."

"He does what?" Patsy asked.

"He rolls his shirtsleeves up, and then he rolls them back down again," Rosie said. "The oral sex I can take or leave, but watching that man mess with his stupid shirtsleeves is driving me bats.

"It's like he's obsessed with his shirtsleeves," she added, as they pulled up to the little Vietnamese market. In the morning it was a very popular place. Two or three Mercedeses and a dozen or more pickups were already parked at the curb—so many that Patsy had to park a block and a half away.

"It sounds to me like C.C.'s the one who needs therapy," Patsy said. "On the other hand, there might be a simpler solution."

"Like what?" Rosie asked.

"Like buying him some short-sleeve shirts," Patsy said. "When's his birthday?"

2

Before becoming a therapist, Jerry Bruckner had mainly made his living either as a concierge or as a stand-up comic. His specialty as a comic had been analysis routines. In those days he worked mostly in lower Manhattan, where a lot of people appreciated a comic who could mimic Freud or Jung, Adler or Reich or whoever. Jerry even managed to locate an orgone box and did a hilarious Reich routine from inside it.

His crowd-stopper, though, was Anna Freud. When Jerry did Anna Freud the customers knocked over tables and rolled in the aisles, such as they were.

Still, stand-up comedy was hard work, even if one had a well-honed specialty. Jerry was getting a living, but he wasn't getting ahead, and the grime and grayness of New York eventually wore him down. He missed his hometown, Las Vegas, and the sun and the sunsets and the beautiful desert sky. His mother, Lola, had been a showgirl—the star of the Stardust for nearly twenty years. One of the reasons Jerry got interested in psychoanalysis in the first place was that his mother's lover, during most of Jerry's childhood, had been an itinerant psychiatrist named Marty Mortimer. Marty was known in Las Vegas as the Shrink of the Strip; he had not quite managed to get through medical school and was just a lay shrink, but he was a much beloved figure in Las Vegas. He roved from casino to casino, doing his work mostly between the shows. He had eased countless showgirls through anxiety attacks brought on by too much thinking about what would happen to them when their breasts began to sag or their thighs to get fat; he counseled gay costume managers, and high rollers who were no longer rolling so high. Besides all that, he was a pillar of support to Lola and an excellent stepfather to Jerry, whose real father lived in Australia and was seldom heard from.

Marty Mortimer's dream, unrealized, was to be analyzed by some great analyst, preferably a strict Freudian, after which he would become an analyst himself and have a little office in one of the many white stucco buildings on the edge of the desert, where he could do proper analysis. He planned to give very low rates to showgirls, for whom he had a great fondness; but one day, while making his way from the Stardust to the Circus-Circus, Marty pitched over, dead, victim of a heart attack. Lola and Jerry were bereft, and the showgirls Marty had counseled so tenderly and whom he had hoped, with the tool of analysis, to coax into happy lives, were forced to make do with evangelists who offered them Jesus and heaven but were much less sympathetic to worries about breasts and thighs.

Marty's legacy to Lola was the little stucco building in which he had hoped to set up office; his legacy to Jerry was his psychoanalytic library, a good one. Marty's library became Jerry's college—he soon became almost obsessed with the rivalries and feuds of Freud and the early schismatics. By night he made his living dealing blackjack at the MGM Grand, and by day he read his way through the works of a lot of quarrelsome European doctors. A good deal of what he read seemed funny to him. Since childhood he had done minor stage bits with his mother, and he gradually developed the notion of a comedy act based on psychoanalysis and its founders.

Jerry realized, of course, that a comedy act dealing with Freud and Jung and the others was not likely to be welcomed in Las Vegas—a town where even tits and feathers, or lions and tigers, or people being shot out of cannons frequently failed to distract people from the slots or the craps tables for more than a few minutes at a time.

So one day Jerry bought a bus ticket, kissed his weeping mother goodbye, and went to New York, where he survived by doing sidewalk magic and a little short-order cooking until he developed his act, which he worked with fair success until New York ground him down. At least, though, he had risen above buses—when he moved to Los Angeles, to reacquaint himself with sunlight as Westerners knew sunlight, he took a plane.

In L.A. the sunlight was adequate—not as good as you got in the desert but a lot better than you got in New York—but his career as a stand-up comic quickly came to an end. Plenty of Angelenos were in analysis, but for them it was a dead serious business; they didn't want people being funny about it. Sophisticated New Yorkers loved to hear analysis being made fun of, but in Los Angeles making light of analysis was a good way to start a fistfight. When Jerry mimicked Jung or Adler, very few people chuckled; nobody rolled in the aisles when he did Anna Freud. After a few penurious months, which he only survived financially by working at an Orange Julius stand on the Santa Monica pier, Jerry went home to Las Vegas, to deal some more blackjack and help his gentle mother die of cancer.

During most of the time of her dying, Lola lay on a couch in the little house Marty had left her, watching Carol Burnett reruns. Jerry often watched them with her. He sat in a big chair by the couch and held her weak, frail hand. Lola had never ceased to believe in his talent as a comic. Sometimes, for her amusement, he redid Carol Burnett routines, Lucille Ball routines, or Bob Newhart routines. His mimicry was flawless, even though his heart wasn't in it.

"When you were a little boy in school you only liked science, remember?" Lola reminded him, a day or two before she died. "I had it in my mind you'd be a doctor. You're so sweet, Jerry. You'd be a fine doctor. People need someone sweet to be with them when they're sick.

"Look at us," she added. "I've hardly even noticed I'm dying, you've been so sweet to me."

But Lola, star of the Stardust, died despite his sweetness; and in his loneliness following her death, Jerry fell in love with a seventeen-year-old showgirl named Cherry. They had been in love only a week when Cherry got laid off in the late summer lull and decided to use the layoff to go home to Houston, to her little sister's wedding. Cherry had long legs and perfect breasts; she had no worries about getting rehired when things picked up.

After some hesitation, Jerry allowed himself to be taken to Houston. He was still sad about Lola and didn't feel in the mood for wedding-type festivities, but when Cherry wanted something she very rarely took no for an answer, and she didn't take it this time: she had long legs and perfect breasts, and didn't see any reason to.

Jerry Bruckner was a quiet man; Cherry's family, though friendly to a fault, soon proved to be a little too loud for his taste. For that matter, Cherry herself was a little too loud for his taste—she had so much energy that he frequently felt a little overwhelmed. She liked to holler at the top of her lungs when they danced, and she was apt to screech and scream, also at the top of her lungs, when they made love. Her father owned a little welding company specializing in oil-rig repair; her mother was head dispatcher for a local trucking company; and her three tall, perfectly formed sisters also did their share of hollering and screaming. It was all done in the spirit of heartiness, health, and good fun, but Jerry still felt he was apt to be deafened before the wedding even happened, and he became a little depressed at the thought of all the stomping and hollering that would take place at the wedding reception. At Cherry's insistence, they had arrived in Houston a week early so Cherry wouldn't miss a single bit of the partying, which involved dusk-till-dawn honky-tonking and many large meals.

If Jerry was a near genius-level mimic, he was an absolute genius-level hitchhiker. Two days before the wedding he got out of bed, took one last look at the sleeping Cherry's perfect breasts, and took a walk down the ramp of the nearest freeway. Fortunately I-10 was only four blocks from Cherry's family home. Before he had even gone halfway down the on ramp, he was picked up by a black nurse on her way home to Galveston; an hour later he was walking on the gray, almost-deserted Galveston beach, enjoying the quiet. By midafternoon he had a job shucking crabs at a big seafood restaurant on the seawall, and another little chapter in his life had ended: the Cherry chapter.

Jerry spent a happy six months odd-jobbing it around Galveston, ending up as concierge at the only beachfront hotel that even knew what a concierge was. The Texas tips were so good that when he tired of the job he bought a brand-new station wagon and drove back to Las Vegas to sell Lola's little building and pack up Marty Mortimer's extensive psychoanalytic library.

On the long drive across the spacious West, Jerry performed a mini-analysis on himself and concluded that he was not cut out for great loves or high passions. Getting girlfriends had never been a problem; he liked all of them and fell in love with a few of them, but the high passion never seemed to quite kick in, and after a time either he would saunter away from them or they would saunter away from him. Often he would feel a few twinges of loss when he and a girlfriend parted, but no intense regret. His only intense regret was that Lola had died. He spent a good deal of time reflecting on his years with his mother—the things he missed most about her were her gentleness and her good manners. Even in pain and disappointment, neither had ever deserted her.

Jerry moved back to L.A. and got a job as a concierge at a very good Beverly Hills hotel. He was an excellent concierge, well informed, well liked, and well tipped. He immediately went into analysis with a dour, bald Freudian in Westwood, and used tips to pay for his analysis. Nearly four years were spent in discussing Lola and her manners: whether subconsciously he resented them, or merely loved his mother to excess, or blamed her for his absent father, or all of the above. Meanwhile he dated actresses who were still at the waiting-tables stage, almost marrying one named Sheryl, whose breasts were not much less perfect than Cherry's. He liked Dr. Rau, his keen-minded, grumpy old analyst, but the analysis came to an abrupt halt one day when Dr. Rau's wife of some forty-five years greeted him at the door of their home with a loaded shotgun and killed him on the spot. She had just discovered that he had been playing around with a neighbor's teenage daughter.

Mrs. Rau left her husband lying dead in the foyer of their modest West Hollywood home; she went upstairs, ran a bath, got in it fully clothed, and used a pair of nail scissors to strip the electrical cord on her hair dryer. Then she turned the hair dryer on, dropped it in the tub, and neatly electrocuted herself.

The case was big news for two days—longer, of course, in the immediate West Hollywood neighborhood where the Raus had lived. The neighbor's daughter, a well-developed seventeen-year-old, swore that nothing improper had happened, but in the minds of many her protests lacked conviction. One of the many who didn't believe her was a waitress named Norma who worked at a little coffee-and-doughnut shop in the Westwood block where Dr. Rau had had his office. Jerry had consumed quite a few doughnuts there while trying to decide whether to ask Norma for a date. One day, while he was trying to decide, Norma happened to mention that Dr. Rau had made advances, and that she, personally, was of the opinion that he had received more or less what he had coming to him.

"Sexual advances?" Jerry said.

"Yeah, sexual advances," Norma informed him. "What kind of advances did you think I was talking about?"

"I just wondered," Jerry said. Norma, who was named after her hometown, Norman, Oklahoma, had buck teeth and a low flash point. It was the buck teeth that made her look interesting, and the low flash point that kept Jerry from asking her for a date. He knew that quarrels were a part of life, but that didn't mean he had to enjoy them. In fact, he *didn't* enjoy them—perhaps that, too, was attributable to his thirty-five years with Lola. He and his mother had rarely exchanged a cross word, but instinct told him that lots of cross words were going to be exchanged if he took up with Norma—so, in the end, he didn't.

What he did, though, was spend a lot of time thinking about the Raus. How could it be that after all those years of wedded union, Mrs. Rau could get mad enough at the doctor to blow him nearly in two with a shotgun? Was it a last straw? Or the first straw? Had the doctor worn her down with forty-odd years of adulteries, or had he fooled her all that time into thinking he was a faithful husband, only to reveal himself in a fatal moment as a chaser after winsome seventeen-year-olds? Jerry had never met Mrs. Rau and had seen the doctor only in his office; he was not the type to go snooping around the Raus' neighbors, asking them what they knew about the old couple's marriage, which meant that his questions remained pure questions: that is, unanswered. When the doctor and his wife rose in his mind, as they did from time to time, Jerry was of the opinion that it might have been a first straw, or, to put it more precisely, a first-and-last straw, but that, he knew, was just a guess.

Six months later Jerry got a postcard announcing that there would be a house sale of the Raus' effects. Dr. Rau had once shown him his proudest possession, a copy of *Die Traumentung*—Freud's first great book—signed by Freud. The doctor kept the book in his office in a handsome leather slipcase. Jerry decided to go to the sale, hoping to get the book. He wanted it as a talisman, a great text by a great master, something to carry with him through life.

Unfortunately, on the day of the sale he overslept; by the time he got there the book was gone. In fact, by the time he got there, almost everything was gone, though a sizable crowd was still milling around in the house. A few of the cheaper prints still hung on the walls, and some crockery was still piled on card tables in the living room, but by and large the sale had achieved its purpose: the Raus were gone, and so were most of their domestic accouterments. What surprised Jerry was how old and how German the crowd was: apart from a few neighbors and a passerby or two, the whole crowd was old and German. It was a crowd that seemed to belong to the thirties, or at the latest, the forties. Quite a few of the women had cigarette holders, and one fat old gentleman even had a monocle. They weren't tatty, either—most of them were dressed rather well in the Continental manner of decades past; they were a far cry from what one usually saw at house sales in L.A. Jerry would not have been surprised to see Von Stroheim, Von Sternberg, Thomas Mann, or Alma Mahler, or even Dietrich, walk out of one of the empty dusty bedrooms.

He had almost passed up the sale, but soon felt glad that he had gone. He had missed the great book but had gained a glimpse of something even more rare: L.A. as it had once been—smart, tenacious, determined, elegant. The people milling around among the Raus' sparse effects might be a little stooped, a little wrinkled, a little too made-up: but they did not look defeated. They looked as if they intended to be around for a while—such pretty seventeen-year-old Americans as strayed into their paths had better look out. They might be old, but clearly they weren't through.

Wandering out onto the small back porch, Jerry noticed a couch covered by an old bedspread with peacocks stitched on it. He needed a bedspread and picked this one up to look at it more closely—Lola would have loved the peacocks. But it was old and dusty, and he decided against it. Then, in attempting to spread it neatly back on the couch, he realized that he wasn't looking at just another ordinary piece of furniture: he was looking at an analyst's couch.

He bought the couch immediately and stuffed it into his no longer new but still very serviceable station wagon. He was proud of his purchase—in fact, excited by it—but when he put it in his apartment, the one thing he did not do was sit on it. Once a girlfriend named Didi sat on it briefly, and the sight made Jerry so uncomfortable that he suggested they go for a walk. The couch was not an ordinary piece of furniture, to be sat on, slept on, worn out, and eventually plunked into a lawn sale or given to the Goodwill. It was an analyst's couch—a relic, in Jerry's view, of a stricter, more polished, more intellectually rigorous era. It was not for girlfriends to sit on while they watched TV and/or did their nails.

The more or less accidental, last-minute purchase of Dr. Herman Rau's analyst's couch changed Jerry's life—a fact he pointed out to Aurora Greenway one day when she was lying on it but exhibiting signs of restlessness.

She was lying on it facing him, too, which was not the way a patient in therapy was supposed to face. The fact that she was facing him was merely the first of many victories Aurora won in struggles involving proper therapeutic procedure.

"The point is, you'll feel freer to talk if you're just looking into your memory rather than looking at me," Jerry said, when they discussed the matter of which way she should face when she lay on the couch.

"Well, you're the doctor, but it's plain you don't know me very well," Aurora said, smiling at him. He was one of those rare men the mere sight of whom made her smile; she saw no reason why she should lie on an uncomfortable couch and stare at the wall when she could be staring at a man whose slightly gloomy appearance almost invariably cheered her up.

"I know I don't know you very well," Jerry said. "I'd like to know you better, and I hope I will, but if you watch me when you talk to me about your past, then you'll be trying to guess what I'm thinking about what you're telling me. That might just slow things down."

"I certainly will try to guess what you're thinking, if I choose to tell you anything significant," Aurora countered. "If you're my therapist, why can't I know what you're thinking? If you're going to keep secrets from me, what's the point?

"This couch could use some pillows," she added. "I intend

to bring some next time I visit. I may even buy you some new curtains—these you have now are pretty dingy. I don't think I can concentrate on any former traumas if I have to be uncomfortable and look at dingy curtains. I'll be too busy experiencing new traumas to remember my old ones."

Most of Jerry's patients dressed like their moods, and their moods were mainly dull, drab moods, so they arrived wearing dull, drab clothes, and equally dull, drab expressions. Aurora was the complete opposite: she dressed in reds and yellows or bright blues, and her moods were equally vivid. She didn't seem depressed at all—or at least she didn't once the General dropped out of therapy and she began coming alone.

Jerry had pointed out to them on their first visit that it was uncommon for couples to be treated together.

"I told her that," General Scott said. "I didn't think you'd want to do both of us at the same time, but Aurora wouldn't pay me any mind. She never does pay me any mind.

"She made me come," he added. "This wasn't my idea."

"Yes, and I believe I erred, for once," Aurora said.

"There's only one couch," Jerry pointed out, amused. He decided he liked her.

"That's fine, I'll lie on it and Hector can sit in a chair, if he wishes to stay," Aurora said. "It's much easier for him to get back on his crutches if he's in a chair."

"If I wish to stay? What choice do I have?" the General asked. "Do you expect me to walk home in the shape I'm in?"

"No, but there are plenty of taxis in Houston," Aurora pointed out. Now that she had met Dr. Bruckner, she could not imagine why she had insisted on dragging Hector along.

"What's wrong with a taxi?" she added. "You rarely approve of my driving anyway."

Jerry used that opportunity to point out to them that he was a lay therapist. He pointed that out to all his patients on their first visit, informing them frankly that he had never been to medical school and had no degrees of any kind. So far, without exception, his patients had been too depressed to care about his lack of formal credentials. They were there, they hurt, they wanted to talk about it; if Jerry would at least try to help, that was good enough for them.

This response surprised Jerry at first. When the notion first occurred to him to try to be a lay therapist, like Marty Mortimer, he hadn't invested much in the idea. Something told him, though, that L.A. was the wrong town for the experiment; he stuffed the analyst's couch into his old station wagon and headed back to Houston. But he did so with no great expectations about developing a booming practice. From what he had seen of it, he liked Houston—it seemed wide-open and, as cities went, unusually welcoming; it might be the kind of loose, freewheeling place where a lay therapist might have a chance. If it didn't work, he could always go back to the concierge business.

In fact, he *went* back to the concierge business and stayed in it for almost a year while he was trying to decide whether being a lay therapist was ethical, whether he was up to it, whether he should just give up the idea. He bought a house with a study that would make an ideal office. He put the analyst's couch in that office, arranged his psychiatric books —by this time he had over three thousand—had some cards printed, and even had a sign painted. But he didn't take an ad in the phone book; in fact, he didn't even stick his sign in his yard—he left it propped tentatively on his front porch while continuing to work at the concierge trade. He also continued to try to make up his mind. He was forty years old and had been studying psychology and psychoanalysis for nearly half those years. Did he dare try being a therapist, or didn't he?

Evidently he didn't dare; the sign remained propped on the porch, and Jerry continued to be a concierge until one steamy June afternoon, when fate took a hand. He was resting in his dim living room, watching a Mets game on TV, when there came a knock at the door. A small, fat, elderly, drunken woman stood on the porch, smoking and holding the leads of two wheezing Corgis, so ancient they could scarcely shuffle along.

"Hi, I'm Marge," she said, "If you're a doctor, help me. My daughter's had thirty-six strokes on the same side of her brain, and my husband has emphysema so bad he has to be on oxygen twenty-four hours a day. I've been walking past this house for six months, waiting for you to put your sign in the yard, but it's still propped on the porch, and I can't wait any longer. I have terrible problems. If I take the dogs home, can I come in and talk?"

"You don't have to take the dogs home," Jerry said. "I don't mind dogs."

That same afternoon, after Marge left, Jerry put the sign in the yard. In a week he had ten patients; in a month he had nearly forty, all of them, like Marge, people with terrible problems who happened to be wandering around Bellaire, noticed the sign, and grasped it as a last straw. Jerry Bruckner, self-invented therapist, was in business; he knew he wasn't doing analysis or anything resembling it, but he did think he was following in the noble tradition of Marty Mortimer by giving a little informed attention to people whose problems were on the order of Marge's, whose daughter actually had suffered thirty-six strokes on the same side of her brain. It was catch-as-catch-can psychotherapy, but it took away the empty feeling that had been part of his life for so long. He had finally found something that he thought might be his work, and the feeling grew as he struggled to provide at least a little sympathy and a little knowledge to hopeless human case after hopeless human case. Some of his patients only came five or six times, but most of them, like Marge, still came every week—Marge to smoke, chat, reproach her wheezy old dogs, and talk about her terrible problems.

By the middle of his second year as a practicing, if unlicensed, therapist, Jerry had gained confidence enough to put a tiny one-line ad in the Yellow Pages. After the first rush, passerby traffic had slowly trickled off. After all, only so many people with really terrible problems—so terrible that they would just whip over to the curb at the sight of a sign saying "Therapy"—would have any reason to be driving along his little street in Bellaire, Texas. It seemed time to cast a slightly wider net.

Jerry cast it, and the third person who called, once the ad appeared in the Yellow Pages, was Aurora Greenway.

3

"You're falling in love with that young man—don't think I can't tell," the General said, watching Aurora dress. Aurora was singing, as she frequently did, and he didn't know whether she heard him. He had been meaning to bring up the subject of her new love for some time, but somehow his courage always deserted him at the last moment.

So he brought it up while she was singing, half hoping that she wouldn't hear him.

"That's why you didn't want me to keep on being psychoanalyzed," he added.

He liked Dr. Bruckner fine and didn't really mind all that much that Aurora had a crush on him, but he had rather enjoyed chatting with the young man the four times they had gone together, and Aurora's crush meant that now he was denied a pleasant outing. Though Aurora had always been a terrible driver, she, and no one else he had ever ridden with, had driven as badly as she managed to drive on their visits to Dr. Bruckner. It was obvious to him that she was driving so terribly in order to discourage him from going with her. He *had* stopped going with her, but now he regretted his decision. There was nothing to do at home—at least nothing that he had not already done a hundred times. Driving to Bellaire and chatting with Jerry Bruckner had been something new to do—at least it would be, if Aurora could just get him there alive. If not, being dead would be what he had to do, and being dead was pretty soon going to be what he had to do anyway. He didn't want to rush it by getting in a car wreck, but at the same time he felt a growing resentment of Aurora for being so selfish and denying him his little outings.

"I don't get many outings, you know," he said. Aurora had stopped singing, but she was still humming, and she had given no indication that she had heard his thrust about her being in love with Jerry Bruckner.

"Are you going to answer, or are you just going to pretend that you didn't hear the question?" the General asked finally, when his patience had begun to wear thin.

"What you said was a statement, not a question," Aurora said. "I heard it perfectly well, but, as you know, I prefer not to have annoying statements made to me while I'm singing my arias. Now that I look back down the years, I think we would have had a better life together if you hadn't so frequently insisted on making annoying statements while I was singing."

"I have to make statements sometime," the General said. "If you're not singing you're napping, or if you're not napping you're gone, or if you're not gone you're cooking or eating or we're quarreling or something.

"Anyway, I don't know what you think was so annoying about my statement," he added. "I just pointed out that you're falling in love with Jerry."

"Yes, Hector, but the problem of you saying that to me while I'm singing is that it poses a number of questions, and in order to consider any one of them, I have to stop singing, which I wasn't ready to do," Aurora said.

A moment before, when she was singing, Aurora had been looking happy, but the General saw to his concern that she was no longer looking quite so happy. She didn't look angry with him, which was the way she had often looked in the last few years, but neither did she look as happy as she had looked while she was singing.

The change in her demeanor made him regret that he had spoken.

"I'm not mad at you about it," he said. "I guess I was just thinking out loud."

Aurora had slipped into one of her silences, or seemed about to slip into one, and he was willing to apologize or do almost anything else, if only she wouldn't slip into one of her silences. Her silences terrified him—always had. Now she was looking out her bedroom window, a sure sign that a silence might be gathering, but when he said he wasn't mad at her she turned and smiled at him. It was not one of her stunningly happy smiles, but it was a smile, at least, and not a silence.

"What an odd thing for my old boyfriend to be thinking out loud," she said.

"Well, what's so odd about it?" the General asked, relieved that she was at least talking. "If you're falling in love with Jerry, why wouldn't I be thinking about it?"

"You've never been exactly the compliant type," Aurora said. "If I'm falling in love with Jerry and you're not mad, what am I to take that to mean? That you're too far gone to care?"

"Aurora, I'll always care," the General said. "You don't have to put it so brutally. I can't help it if I'm this far gone."

"So you *are* going to be mad if it turns out that I'm in love with Jerry, is that what you mean?" Aurora asked, with a flash of spirit.

"I don't know if I'll be mad—I don't know what I'll be," the General said. "What can I do about it if I do care?"

"The act of caring is doing something—will you never understand that?" Aurora said. Her bosom was heaving and she looked as if she were about to become very angry.

"I don't want you to beat me, if that's how you interpret caring," she said. "But I don't see why I can't know whether you care."

"Why do we always end up talking about whether I care?" the General asked—he felt a strong sense of déjà vu.

"That's simple—because it's so hard to tell if you do!" Aurora said. "You've tolerated a lot of my admirers. More than once I expected you to leave me because of them, but you didn't."

She fell silent for a moment, making an attempt to calm down. The General had no idea what to say.

"That is, I expected you to leave me when you could still walk," she added, in a more kindly tone.

"Well, now I can't walk very well, and I'm not going to leave you," the General said. "You'll have to pack me off if you want to get rid of me."

He waited for a response, but Aurora said nothing. She seemed to be thinking, a fact the General could not help but be alarmed by. Even when Aurora was angriest, he would rather she speak, not think. When she was thinking, all he could do was dread all the awful things she might say or do when she resumed talking.

"Are you going to pack me off so you can live with Jerry?" he asked. The thought was in his mind that that was just what she might do if she was in love with the young doctor, as he was pretty sure she was.

"What makes you think I'm in love with anyone?" Aurora asked, fixing him with a stern look. Her eyes got larger when she was stern. At the moment they were very large and very green.

Looking into her angry eyes, the General wished that he had managed to suppress his last remark—in fact, he wished he could take back all his remarks, all that he had made in the last few minutes, and perhaps most of the remarks he had made over the last few years. He should never have brought up Jerry Bruckner, or anything else, for that matter. In a sense, that was the story of his life with Aurora: he should never have brought anything up. Time after time, when he ventured to open his mouth, the next thing he knew she was looking at him out of large, angry green eyes.

"You're just looking happier lately, or something," he suggested mildly.

Aurora said nothing. She continued to look straight into his eyes in the unnerving way she had.

The General tried to think of something he might say that would at least cause her to break her silence. He hated it when Aurora became silent. Sharp as her responses could be, they were still preferable to her silences.

"You look like you're enjoying life more," he added. "You've got your fun back, or something. There was a time when you didn't seem to have your sense of fun anymore."

"I see," Aurora said. "And you think I could only have got my sense of fun back by falling in love with Dr. Bruckner, is that what you're saying?"

"Oh, go to hell, you're driving me crazy!" the General said, exasperated. "I won't sit here and be badgered like this. You always come back from your therapy looking happy, and I just thought you might be in love with Jerry, that's all. If you're not, you're not—can't we just forget I ever mentioned it?"

"Nope," Aurora said, but in a more friendly, less exasperating tone. "I have to train my memory, you know. Therapy requires one to have a good memory, and besides therapy, there's my memory project."

"Good lord, are you still thinking about that?" the General said. "Do you seriously think you can crank your memory up to the point where you can remember every day of your life?"

"Not unassisted, perhaps," Aurora said. "But then I'm not unassisted. I have quite extensive records, and I absolutely intend to remember every day of my life. My project wouldn't be off to a very good start if I did what you just suggested."

"What do you mean, what I just suggested?" the General said. He knew he had said a number of things in the course of the conversation, but he had no idea which ones he might have said five minutes before.

"That was when you suggested that the only possible source of my renewed sense of fun was that I've fallen in love with Jerry Bruckner."

"Oh," the General said. "I didn't say that five minutes ago. "We've been talking about it for a goddamn hour at least, and you still won't admit it."

"It?" Aurora asked. "Is 'it' supposed to refer to your quaint notion that I've fallen in love with my doctor?"

"Right," the General said. "If you'd just admitted it right off, we wouldn't have had this interminable quarrel, which feels like it's going to go on for the rest of my life.

"Most of our goddamn quarrels have felt like they were going to go on for the rest of my life," he added, recalling all the times when he had that sensation while quarreling with Aurora.

Aurora smiled—a happier smile than any he had seen from her since the quarrel began.

"It's true that I sometimes have to quarrel at length with you, Hector," she said. "Life's just that way. It's unfortunate, but sometimes lengthy quarrels are the only means I have of determining what you feel."

"That's a goddamn lie," the General said, feeling his gorge rise. "I always tell you every goddamn thing I feel, and I always tell you immediately."

"If there was a God I expect he'd strike you dead for a lie of that magnitude," Aurora said. "You've obviously waited days, or perhaps weeks, to bring forth your theory about my being in love with my doctor."

The General had to admit that that was true, though he didn't admit it out loud. He had suspected almost from the first that Aurora might fall in love with Jerry, but he had quietly kept his suspicions to himself.

"I was trying to wait for the right moment to bring it up," the General said.

"In that case, you didn't wait long enough," Aurora said. "You brought it up while I was singing, and now we're having this quarrel."

"We're not going to be having it much longer," the General assured her. "The reason we're not is because I'm sick of it. Just answer yes or no. Are you in love with him or not?"

"Not, as it happens," Aurora said, highly amused.

"You're not?" the General said, very surprised. He had expected her to admit it with her usual brashness—the brashness she always displayed when they were discussing her other men.

"No, not as yet, at least," Aurora said.

The General thought that over for a moment and decided he didn't like the sound of it.

"That's not very reassuring," he said. "When *are* you going to fall in love with him? Tomorrow? Next week? If you're going to fall in love with him you might as well go ahead and do it."

"Yes, but one can't just go and do that sort of thing," Aurora said pleasantly. "I try to be brisk whenever I can, but falling in love is not one of the things one can be brisk about."

"I hate it when we quarrel," the General said. "I wish I'd never asked."

"I know. You'd think you'd learn what to ask and what not to ask, but you never do, dear," Aurora said. Then, seeing that her old boyfriend looked quite exhausted, she took his hand for a bit to show that she meant no harm.

4

The day Aurora decided that the time had come to allow
Pascal to seduce her, she let him make her lunch in his apartment, but restricted him, to his annoyance, to one glass of
wine. She had never allowed him to feed her in his apartment before, and Pascal, convinced that his moment had finally arrived, was beside himself with excitement. He would
have liked a little more wine, both to calm his nerves and to
go with the excellent lamb he had cooked. Aurora devoured
the lamb and his *crème brulée* with relish, but was adamant
about the wine.

"But why not?" Pascal asked, annoyed.

"Because I say not," Aurora said, eating the last bite of her
crème brulée. She looked him in the eye and wiped her
mouth.

"I've often had my fun spoiled by intemperance," she told
him. "It's been a long time since I've had any fun, and I'm
not about to have it spoiled just because you're nervous
about sex and want to glug a lot of wine."

"I'm not nervous about sex—I'll strangle you again!" Pascal said, furious for an instant. He shot up from his chair as if

he'd been sitting on a coil and a wrestling match ensued, during which Aurora, at several points, had great difficulty suppressing her sense of comedy. The new mauve sheets Pascal had so hoped to impress her with were no help in her effort to keep from laughing, but she did end up between them with him, only to discover at the moment of entry that something about the entry was a little different from any entry she had ever experienced.

"Whoa," she said, twisting a little. "What's wrong here? We're not getting a perfect fit."

"I'll explain, it happened when I was a boy," Pascal said. "I'll correct." And he did correct, shifting himself atop her right leg. Aurora felt slightly puzzled, but otherwise, there they were. Pascal was wild in his happiness, the fit improved once he was lying on her leg, and she soon went a bit wild herself.

It was only later, when Pascal's mettle had been proven, more or less, and she allowed him to bring a little cheese and the rest of the wine to bed, that she learned that the slight problem she had experienced at the onset had been caused by the fact that Pascal had a crooked penis.

"It became bent when I was young," he told her, with a rather endearing smile.

"What?" Aurora said. "You mean at my age I've been made love to by a bent dick? This I have to see."

"It's not bent when it's little," Pascal said. "It's only bent when it gets big."

"Then let's have it big," Aurora said. Indeed, there was little to see, as matters stood.

"I don't know about right now," Pascal said, twinkling a little in his happiness. "You should have looked when you had the chance," he added.

"But I don't usually look the first time," Aurora said. "I've never heard of such a thing as a bent penis. Now you've got my scientific curiosity aroused."

"I've got you all aroused," Pascal said, watching her stretch.

"I suppose you have, but I'm not sure I'd have proceeded if I'd known you were deformed," Aurora said.

"No, I was normal," Pascal assured her. "It became bent when I was fourteen. The girls didn't like me then, and I was making love to a hole in the fence. A boy was on the other side of the fence—I didn't know this. He took a piece of board and chopped at my penis. Since then it's been crooked."

"Good lord," Aurora said, setting her wineglass on the table. "If I'd been there at the time I doubt you would have had to be engaged with a hole in the fence."

She gave him a winy, urgent kiss. "Come on," she said. "I remember some of your vast claims. Now I want proof."

"I've taken vitamin E for years," Pascal informed her.

"By golly, it *is* bent—it's a wonder this worked at all," she said, a little later. "It's a good thing you've learned to compensate—I suppose having to compensate is what's given you your resourceful air, Pascal. Your resourceful air is one of the things I like best about you."

"Besides that, I took all the vitamin E," Pascal reminded her.

Later, though, driving home from her tryst, Aurora's exultant mood began to seep away. Little by little it seeped away, until there came a time when the last drop of it had seeped; she felt lonely, disarrayed, dejected, and depressed. She reached such a low state in her feelings that she didn't think it was quite wise to drive, although she was only a few blocks from her house. She pulled to the curb and sat, and before she knew it she was weeping. She had no desire to go back to Pascal, who had already been talking excitedly of taking her to Paris, Morocco, Istanbul, and various other places he felt sure she would enjoy. Lust had been sated, but at what price? She was certainly fond of Pascal, but also, just as certainly, wasn't in love with him, although now she had gotten him ever more madly in love with her. He was jealous, too—he had made as much of a fuss as he dared just because she was going home to Hector. He had already suggested that she shouldn't sleep in the same bed as Hector. Problems of that nature were sure to plague their future relations.

Also, sitting in dejection in her car, she was aware of a certain lurking dishonesty in her behavior. Had she finally slept with Pascal because she wanted to, or because she felt that after years of flirtation she owed him a fling? Or could it be that a darker, more particular fear had driven her into the arms she had spent the afternoon in? She knew perfectly well what the more complex fear was, but alone in her car, she didn't want to think about it—and yet if she went home and tried to talk it out with Rosie, Hector might eavesdrop or get wind of her distress somehow, and what that might lead to in terms of quarrels, sadness, questions, or apprehensions she didn't want to contemplate. Suave and sophisticated as Hector had tried to appear when he suggested that she was in love with Jerry Bruckner, she knew that he was merely putting up a cool front while fishing for information. If she gave him the information, particularly the information that she was having an affair with Pascal, his arch rival, his reaction would be anything but suave and sophisticated. He would be mad as hell, and their life together would be a good deal more tormented than it was already.

Drying her eyes, she noticed that the man of the house whose lawn she had parked in front of had come out to move his sprinklers and was looking at her. To her horror she noticed that the man was Hargreave Goulding, her insurance agent. Hargreave was a very presentable man who sold insurance to half the people in their neighborhood. She hadn't noticed that she was in front of his house when she became too dejected to drive and had stopped to cry. The last thing she wanted was for Hargreave Goulding to come over and ask her what was the matter. For one thing, he was a very attractive man, and the two of them had spent thirty years flirting at parties; if he came over and tried to comfort her while she was in a vulnerable state, she might end up in even hotter water than she was in anyway. He was a widower, too—though well supplied with lady friends, he was also probably the type who felt he could always handle one more.

Aurora started her car with a jerk and turned the nearest corner, causing two children on bicycles to dash up a driveway. Her house was almost in sight, but she didn't go there

—she had a sense that it might be fatal to face Hector, feeling as she did.

Without quite knowing why she was doing it, she drove rather reluctantly in the direction of Bellaire and soon found herself driving just as reluctantly in front of Jerry Bruckner's house. Unable to bring herself to stop, she drove right on past it. Then she circled the block and drove past it three more times, slowing for a moment each time, but never quite working up to stopping.

Finally, on the fourth pass, she did stop, so close to the curb that she felt sure her tires would scrape, although they didn't; she stopped, but refrained from killing her motor—she hoped that at any moment she would get control of her sinking emotions and drive back into her sensible—or, at least, mostly manageable—life. She looked at herself in the mirror several times, but made no repairs. It was getting dark. Soon Hector and Rosie would begin to be worried about her. Her phobia about driving after dark was even more intense than her phobia about scraping her tires. She knew she ought to rush home and reassure them, and yet she felt paralyzed. All she could do was sit in front of Jerry Bruckner's house, twisting her emerald ring round and round her finger while dripping hopeless tears.

While she was twisting her ring, there was a tap on her window. Jerry Bruckner stood there, in jogging clothes. He seemed quite sweaty and had obviously been jogging. He tapped on the window again, looking in with his mild smile. Aurora felt her paralysis deepen. She didn't do anything; she even stopped twisting her ring. She just sat, leaving the matter, and all matters, to Jerry. She didn't even roll down the window; she just sat with her hands in her lap.

After another unanswered tap or two, Jerry came around to the driver's side of the car. Aurora looked at him hopelessly. He made a motion that she couldn't interpret. When she did nothing, he put his face as close to the window as he could.

"Please roll down the window!" he shouted. "Or unlock the door, so I can talk to you!"

Aurora noticed that he was still attractive, though sweaty.

Something about him was a little too doglike, though—she had felt that the first time she saw him and she registered the impression again—but then, there must be something to be said for dogs, or people wouldn't be having them as pets.

She looked at the lock on her door and decided she might as well unlock it. When she tried to roll down her windows they sometimes slipped off their track, which meant a trip to the garage, a place she hated. Rosie had once been capable of putting her windows right, but Rosie was no longer the mechanic she had once been. Now she sometimes took weeks to accomplish the simplest repair.

That being the case, she ruled out rolling down the windows, and unlocked her door.

"Thanks," Jerry said, immediately opening the door. Aurora noticed that he did smell quite sweaty, but then, she had never been one to balk at a little sweat.

"What's the matter?" he asked, squatting by the car and looking up at her. Just then a car swooshed by—Aurora felt quite sure Jerry would be hit and killed if he kept squatting where he was.

"I just slept with a Frenchman with a crooked penis in order to stop myself from sleeping with you," she said.

Jerry Bruckner looked surprised—a little more than mildly so, if she was any judge of surprised men. On the other hand, he was not thunderstruck. In fact, after a pause, he chuckled. Usually his chuckle—deep, like his voice—delighted her, but this time for some reason it irritated her.

"If you want to discuss this distasteful episode, you'll have to get in," Aurora said. "Squatting as you are, I'm sure you'll be killed within the next few minutes."

"That's what I was trying to do to begin with, but you had all the doors locked," Jerry said. He reached in, unlocked the door to the backseat, crawled across it, unlocked the other door to the front seat, and was soon seated in the front seat, where Hector usually sat.

"I was afraid to risk walking around the car," he said. "You might have locked me out again."

"Quite true," Aurora said dejectedly. "An old woman who's capable of sleeping with a Frenchman with a crooked penis might well be capable of other very bad acts."

"I've never seen a crooked penis," Jerry said. "How did it get crooked?"

"A youthful accident caused it to become somewhat bent," Aurora said. "However, if the crook in my lover's penis is all you're interested in, you've unlocked all those doors for nothing. I think I'll go home."

"Be fair," Jerry said. "If someone told you about a man with a crooked penis, wouldn't you ask how it got bent?"

"Not if I had more serious matters to discuss," Aurora said. "I'm not sure you took in the import of my original remark, or if you did then you probably just think it was just one more remark made by another of the many lustful old women you probably have for patients. I think I want to go home."

In fact, she did want to leave. She felt that coming to Jerry's house had been a terrible mistake, one she would never have made had she not been in terrible disarray. She had revealed herself in a way that made her acutely uncomfortable—and so far Jerry had not responded in any fashion that was likely to relieve her discomfort.

"I heard what you said, and I'm glad you said it," Jerry said. "Did you think you had to go to this length to stop yourself from sleeping with me because I'm your doctor?"

"Hardly," Aurora said with a snort. "I don't even think you are a doctor. I think you're just a seducer with a weird couch. In my view it would be a toss-up between that couch and a crooked penis, if one were thinking of amour."

Aurora Greenway had been a surprise Jerry had not quite taken the measure of, but he did know that she was one of the most immediately appealing women he had ever met. Already, despite the age difference, it was often Aurora, not his present girlfriend, Sondra, that he had begun to think of when he was alone and thinking about sex. Sondra, the long, lanky East Texas waitress that he was actually sleeping with, and was also very fond of, scarcely figured in his fantasy life at all.

"I'm not a normal psychiatrist, maybe, but I do make my living trying to make people feel better," Jerry said. He tried to put his hand on Aurora's shoulder in a friendly way, but Aurora flinched and drew away.

"Keep off, and that's a serious warning, Doctor," she said.

"I'm sorry," Jerry said. "I've never seen you this disturbed. In fact, I've never seen you disturbed at all. I'd like to help but I'm not sure I know where to start."

"Start anyway," Aurora said. "If you don't, I'm going away. I was a terrible fool to come here. I've often felt a fool, but I guess this is the first time in my life that I've felt like an *old* fool."

"I don't think about your age when I'm with you," Jerry said. "I doubt that anyone does."

"Oh, someone does," Aurora said. "*I* do. The difference between being a foolish woman and a foolish old woman looms large in my mind. I'm sorry I came here and I'm sorry I disturbed you, but I think you had better get out now. If you wish to help me you're failing, and I had better just go home."

"Would you like to go to dinner?" Jerry asked. He realized that he was going to be very depressed if he let her just drive off—if he could just delay her, maybe her mood would improve. Under the circumstance, asking her to dinner sounded weird, but it was the only thing that came to mind that she might consider.

Aurora was astounded—he was a complete mess, he was in jogging clothes, and he was asking her to dinner. But when she turned to him to tell him how absurd his suggestion was, and why, he looked at her with such a childlike look of longing that, without quite fathoming what the longing might be for, she gave an answer that was less unfriendly than the one she had been prepared to give.

"Do we look in any shape to dine?" she asked. "I'm soaked in tears and you're soaked in sweat. A decent hamburger joint would probably turn us away, looking as we do."

"You've been crying, but you're wearing a very nice dress," Jerry said. "I live in this house you're parked in front of. I could shower and you could fix up a little. We could just go to a Greek place, or a Cajun place or something. We wouldn't have to look too fancy."

"Do you mean this?" Aurora asked. "Are you actually asking me to dinner?"

"Yes, why not?" Jerry said.

Aurora felt a little lifted by the fact that he had noticed she was actually wearing a nice dress. He was right, and his suggestion was sensible, more or less. She *could* wash her face, and they could go somewhere not too fancy. Also, she had experienced a great deal of distress since eating Pascal's lamb. She was hungry.

"I suppose we could go to the Pig Stand," she said. "I always go there after visiting my grandson, the murderer, and I'm certainly not looking my best on those occasions—no one who frequents the Pig Stand seems to be looking their best. They just look how they look, and they eat a lot. In my present mood I believe I could eat a lot."

But then a lurking guilt pounced and made her doubt that she should indulge in this little outing. It was already dark, and she was never out after dark unless she was being driven by someone competent. What would Hector and Rosie be thinking?

"Do you really want to do this?" she asked, almost hoping Jerry had changed his mind. It had grown too dark for her to see his face clearly; she couldn't tell if he still had the look of longing on his face. Oddly, seeing that look had made her less afraid of him; in fact, she no longer felt afraid of him at all.

"Sure, let's go eat," Jerry said. "Ever since you became my patient I've been wanting to have a nonprofessional conversation with you. The dinner at your house didn't count because it was a dinner and you had to be a hostess."

Aurora smiled. "All my talks are nonprofessional, including our so-called therapeutic sessions," she said. "What will we talk about first?"

"About why you think it would be a particularly bad thing if we were lovers," Jerry said.

"It would not merely be a bad thing, it would be a terrible thing," Aurora said. "It would mean I was lost, that's all."

"Come on," Jerry said. "You wouldn't be lost. That's silly."

Aurora was silent for a moment. She was sorry darkness had fallen—she would have liked to look at this man clearly. Of course, she had an appointment with him in two days: she could look at him clearly then. But his last remark was disappointing, and her spirits, which had shown signs of rising at the prospect of several pig sandwiches and a lot of pie, began to sink again. It was not going to happen—at least not with this man, on this night.

"Get out," she said. "Calling me silly was a serious mistake. We won't be going to dinner tonight, I'm afraid."

Jerry was taken aback. "I'm sorry," he said. "I didn't mean that *you* were silly."

"Sure you did," Aurora said. "It's pointless for you to sit there and quibble. What I said about being lost if I slept with you wasn't silly, it was merely true, and if you can't understand that, then I don't think you should be hanging around here playing at doctoring. At the very least, you lack understanding, and understanding is itself the very least one should be able to expect from one's doctor. I now see that I can't expect it from you, and I don't want to go to dinner with you, or to discuss this unseemly attraction of mine ever again."

"Can't I apologize?" Jerry asked, at a loss to know what to do.

"You did apologize, and if there's anything I hate in a man it's the habit of excessive apology," Aurora said. "One apology is quite enough. You made it. Now get out."

Jerry started to try again, but Aurora anticipated him and cut him off.

"Get out, please," she repeated. "That is a verdict from which there's no appeal. If you try to appeal at this moment I'll cancel my next appointment and I'll never speak to you again."

Jerry opened the car door, which made the overhead light come on. He was beginning to feel very depressed—in fact, the depression he felt he might have if Aurora left had arrived while she was still there. He had lived through many quarrels with women, but every time, the depression that always followed struck him with fresh force—and it was now striking him with a lot of force. He thought Aurora might notice, relent, take pity. But Aurora looked him over and did neither. She merely waited silently for him to get out of her car, and finally he did.

He turned and looked in one more time before shutting the door, and this time Aurora's look was not quite so cold.

"Who are you sleeping with now, by the way?" she asked in a flat tone.

"Uh, she's a waitress," Jerry said.

"No surprise," Aurora said. "Please shut the door."

Jerry did, and she drove off.

5

At Aurora's house, Rosie and the General were growing desperate. It was almost an hour after dark and Aurora wasn't home, nor had she called. This was an unheard-of occurrence. They were both in the kitchen—Rosie was pacing and smoking—and, due to her health regimen, she had not smoked in a year. The General couldn't pace very well, thanks to his crutches, and was sitting stoically at the table, an unfinished game of solitaire in front of him. Rosie had the TV on, tuned to a local news channel.

"That way if she's been killed on the freeway, they're bound to show it," Rosie said.

"Bound to show it to you, maybe," the General said. "If Aurora's been killed on a freeway, I don't want to look. Why would she go on a freeway anyway? She hates freeways."

"They say most accidents occur within three blocks of home," Rosie remembered. "Maybe I ought to go up to the corner and look. She could be dead and not three blocks away."

"Rosie, please stop saying she's dead," the General pleaded. "We have no reason to think she's dead, and if she is I don't know what we'll do."

"Well, I don't know what we'll do either, but shit happens," Rosie informed him.

They had already called Teddy and Jane, neither of whom had heard from Aurora that day. In desperation, as dusk was turning to darkness, the General even urged Rosie to call Pascal. He had long suspected that something might be going on between Aurora and Pascal—what had probably happened, in his view, was that Aurora had dumped Pascal in favor of Jerry Bruckner, and Pascal had strangled her.

"The French make a big thing of *amour propre*," he told Rosie. "They murder women constantly. Call Pascal and ask him if he murdered Aurora."

To his astonishment, Rosie did just that.

"Hi, Pascal, did you murder Aurora?" Rosie asked, to the General's horror.

"I didn't mean *really* strangled her," he whispered, as Rosie was on the phone.

Pascal, for his part, was so startled to hear that Aurora wasn't home that he readily admitted they had had lunch—although he didn't admit they had had it in his apartment.

"What if she was kidnapped?" he asked, plunging immediately into wild, irrational worry.

"He thinks she was kidnapped," Rosie told the General.

"But why would anyone want to kidnap Aurora?" the General asked.

But then he too was filled with his share of wild, irrational worries. Perhaps she *had* been kidnapped. What else could keep her out so late?

"Ask him if he has any idea who kidnapped her," the General requested.

"Maybe it had to do with drugs," Pascal said, when asked. It was a wild guess, prompted by the fact that he had recently been in Colombia, where most kidnappings had to do with drugs.

"He thinks she's a drug addict," Rosie reported.

"Aurora?" the General said. "That's the trouble with the French, they always come up with wild theories."

Rosie waited, receiver in hand. "Is that what I'm supposed to tell Pascal?" she said.

"Of course not," the General said. "You weren't supposed to tell him I thought he might have murdered her, either. That was *my* wild theory. Why don't you ask him to come over? Maybe if we put our heads together we can figure this out."

"I will be right there!" Pascal assured them. As he was rushing out the door it occurred to him that Aurora might have driven to Galveston and drowned herself. Though she had seemed to enjoy making love, just as he had, he did remember that she seemed to be becoming a little depressed as she was leaving. Perhaps she had construed their lovemaking as adultery of some sort, become more depressed, and dashed down to Galveston to drown herself in the ocean.

Before he got his Peugeot started, this passing thought had become a conviction—one which made him very nervous. Not only was there the possibility that Aurora was gone forever just as their romance was finally starting, but it would, at some point, entail admitting to General Scott that he had seduced his girlfriend, thereby causing her fatal despair. General Scott didn't like him anyway and might well kill him when he heard this news.

Worries piled up as Pascal dashed away from his apartment building—he wanted to get over to Aurora's as quickly as possible. Nothing he could think of would make him so happy as to rush over there and see that her Cadillac had returned and was parked safely, its rear end sticking out of her garage. If it were only there, he wouldn't have to go in and confess to the General that he had seduced Aurora; he could just turn quietly around and go back to his apartment.

In his hurry to determine if his fate was to be torment or relief, Pascal plunged straight through the stop sign at the end of his block, a stop sign he had run successfully many times when he was in a hurry. This time, though, he realized a second too late that he shouldn't have run the stop sign. A giant thing, a pickup with tires the size of whole cars, appeared out of nowhere in front of him, and the Peugeot plowed straight into it, hitting it just in front of its giant rear tire. Pascal, who in his haste had not bothered with his seat belt, crashed through his own windshield and landed in the back of the pickup, cutting his face badly, cracking his skull in two places, and knocking himself out so soundly that he didn't regain consciousness until more than thirty hours later. When he came to, he was in a hospital, his head hurt, and he had the vague sense that someone had drowned—he just couldn't think who.

Meanwhile, at Aurora's house, no one had any notion that Pascal had been in a car wreck. Aurora still wasn't back, and neither had Pascal arrived to elaborate on his theory of a kidnapping. Rosie had smoked an entire pack of cigarettes and was feeling guilty about it, but not guilty enough to stop her from opening a second pack. The General still sat at the table, his game of solitaire still unfinished, popping with annoyance that Pascal hadn't bothered to show up.

"It's what I've been telling Aurora all along," the General said. "He probably had a date or something. He probably never had any intention of coming. He might have even had a date with Aurora. I thought she might be in love with Jerry Bruckner, but now I think she's probably in love with that lying little Frenchman. They're probably off having a fancy meal right now, while we sit here and suffer."

"No way," Rosie protested. "I know Aurora better than you do. If she was going to go off and have a fancy dinner she'd have come home and changed. She ain't the kind of woman who would wear the same dress to lunch and dinner both."

"She might if she'd just fallen madly in love," the General said darkly. "That's the one thing that might take her mind off her goddamn clothes."

"If that's it, it ain't Pascal, then," Rosie said. "I doubt he could keep her mind off clothes for five minutes."

That sentiment reassured the General somewhat, but not much.

"You know, we have got to go to the prison tomorrow— she's probably upset about that," Rosie said. "She's getting worse and worse upset about Tommy, and you can't blame her."

"No," the General said, reflecting. "Of course you can't blame her for that. You think that's why she's not here?"

"That could be it," Rosie said. "She's really getting where

she hates to go see Tommy—it's just that she hates chickening out about it worse."

"Well, if that's it, where would she go?" the General wondered.

"She'd go to the Pig Stand," Rosie said. "That's where we always go, *after* we see Tommy. Maybe this time she just decided to go there first."

"Oh, that place where she gets the mince pie?" the General inquired. "I went there once. I liked the pork chops. I doubt Aurora would risk it at night, though. You know how paranoid she is about being raped and murdered."

"She'd risk it at night if she was depressed enough," Rosie said. "Once Aurora gets depressed enough she forgets she don't want to be raped and murdered. And if she was hungry, that might push her over the edge."

"I suppose it's possible she's there," the General said. "Do you think we should call and ask?"

"We could," Rosie said. "On the other hand, you know how she hates snoops. If we call and she's there, it might piss her off."

"Undoubtedly, but call anyway," the General commanded. "Do you remember what color dress she was wearing?"

"Yellow," Rosie said. "Why?"

"If she's not at the Pig Stand I guess we should call the police and see if any dead woman in a yellow dress has turned up at the morgue," the General said. His spirits had suddenly taken a downward turn.

"Ain't that a little drastic?" Rosie asked. "She's late but she ain't *that* late."

"Rosie, this is *very* irregular," the General insisted. His spirits had sunk to their lowest point in years, and indeed he was beginning to feel desperate. Even Omaha Beach hadn't made him feel as desperate as he was beginning to feel— though Omaha Beach had been pretty bad. But on D day it had been *his* life that had been in danger; now it was Aurora's. He felt extremely worried.

"The only reason Aurora and I have gotten along as well as we have all these years is because we're both extremely regular in our habits," he said. "There've been lots of fights, but at least both of us turn up when we're expected, in order to have the fights. In all these years Aurora's never failed to turn up, and now she's not turning up."

"You're getting dotty in your old age," Rosie informed him unsentimentally. "That woman's always late, and you know it."

"I know, but not *this* late, and not after dark," the General pointed out. "There's a subtle difference between being late and being *this* late."

At that moment they heard a car turn into the driveway. "That's not Pascal," Rosie said. "He wouldn't dare park in the driveway and risk getting in Aurora's way when she's trying to steer the Cadillac in."

She darted to the front window and saw the familiar Cadillac idling in the driveway. She rushed instantly back to the kitchen, feeling that the General should be the first to know.

"It's her, she's safe," she said, dropping into a chair. Suddenly she felt a little weak in the legs.

"Home is the sailor—no, home is the hunter," the General said, feeling that he might cry. To his surprise, he did cry, a sight that unnerved Rosie so much that she immediately joined in.

"Why is my kitchen full of smoke?" Aurora asked, before she noticed that both Hector and Rosie were sobbing, or very nearly. In fact, she *had* made a hasty trip to the Pig Stand, just managing to consume three pig sandwiches and two pieces of pie before rushing home. She had two extra sandwiches and two extra pieces of pie with her as a bulwark against future emotional emergencies. Now, to her surprise, there seemed to be an immediate emotional emergency right in her kitchen.

"Good lord, what is all this?" she asked, fanning herself vigorously in order to clear a path through the smoke.

"Home is the hunter," the General managed to mutter, accepting a hug. His emotions were still in riot, and he didn't trust himself to say more.

"Poetry, cigarette smoke, and tears," Aurora commented.

"I suppose you two must have concluded that I was murdered—I doubt anything less could cause you to quote Stevenson to me, Hector."

"Pascal said you'd been kidnapped and that he thought you were a drug addict," Rosie blurted out, drying her eyes. Now that Aurora was standing there, a big Pig Stand bag in her hand, it all seemed a little ridiculous, and she was glad to be able to shift some of the blame to Pascal.

"Besides that, he was supposed to show up and help us locate your body, but he ain't here yet," Rosie went on.

"You called the right man, though—locating bodies is more or less Pascal's life work," Aurora said. She noticed that her companions were shell-shocked and saw no reason not to be a little witty at the expense of her new boyfriend.

"He didn't come when he said he would—I despise him," the General said. "He's unreliable, like his nation."

"Hector, I'm right here, alive and well—you don't need to foam and rage at Pascal just now," Aurora said. "Since it's obvious that my tardiness has upset you both, I feel I should be noble and offer you a pig sandwich and a piece of pie as an antidote to your ordeal. Would you like that?"

"I would," Rosie said, sniffing.

"I might if it's a kind of pie I like," the General said. He made a massive effort to regain control of himself, but his hands were still a little shaky.

"That's what I love about you, Hector—picky even *in extremis*, just like me," Aurora said, as she unwrapped the pie.

6

"Would you rather I never came here again, Tommy?" Aurora asked of her grandson. They sat in the visitors' room at the prison. Some small effort had obviously been made to make the visitors' room cheery, but the small effort failed. Aurora could never come into the room without feeling that she herself was a criminal, come finally to be punished for a lifetime of sins, omissions, crimes—all of them irrevocable, irredeemable, and far beyond her power to change or make up for.

She didn't need the unintentionally grim room to remind her that her crimes were irredeemable, either. The evidence was there in Tommy's eyes, and in his indifference—an indifference that was more unyielding than any she had encountered in her long life.

"You can come but you don't have to," Tommy said pleasantly.

Aurora twisted her ring. She was remembering the day they buried Emma—her daughter, Tommy's mother. It had rained that day; she remembered clearly a sinking feeling she had had on the ride home beneath the dripping trees of

Houston. At the heart of her sinking feeling was the fear that, with Emma gone so young, her children might be lost—particularly Tommy. That very night, as she was putting Tommy, Teddy, and Melanie to bed, she had asked Tommy if he would like to go to the zoo in the morning—he had always been particularly fond of the zoo.

"It doesn't matter," Tommy said. "I'll never like to do anything again."

"I will," Teddy said. "I'll still like *Sesame Street*."

"Sessy street," Melanie said.

That moment, as the children were glumly getting into their pajamas, had fixed them all, down the years, Aurora felt: Teddy still liked the zoo and *Sesame Street*. Melanie liked many things—indeed, a few too many things. But Tommy, the oldest and strongest, had been a boy of his word: he had never liked anything again.

Aurora looked up, and Tommy met her eye. He had no trouble meeting her eye—or anyone's eye. On the whole, he liked his grandmother, not for any of the many things she tried to do for him, but because of the way she never stopped living for herself. She kept on trucking at a level that was kind of amazing if you stopped to think about it, and he had thought about it. In the prison, only the worst criminals and the most committed killers kept on trucking inside themselves despite all. Most convicts had stopped trucking altogether; they surrendered to boredom and apathy. In prison the people you really had to watch out for, the ones who could just glance at you and make you feel in danger, reminded him of his grandmother.

"Well, that's noncommittal," Aurora said, looking at him.

"It's neutral," Tommy said. "That's how I prefer to live."

"I know, Tommy," Aurora said. "Probably it isn't your fault. But to those of us who aren't neutral, it's very trying."

Tommy said nothing.

"I think I better give up," Aurora said. "I very rarely have given up in my life, and I've never before given up on someone of my own blood, but I think I better give up on you before you destroy me. There are others who depend on me, among them your brother and sister, and I don't feel I can afford to be destroyed for the sake of someone who prefers to be neutral.

"At least, I won't choose to be destroyed," she said. "I don't think I believe that you *are* neutral—I don't think I believe that humans can be."

"You might be wrong about that," Tommy said mildly.

"I might be, but I'm older than you and I've yet to meet a really neutral person," Aurora said.

"There's me," Tommy reminded her.

Aurora shook her head. "That's just your weapon," she said. "It's what you're using to kill us—or at least to kill me. But I'm a selfish old woman. I'd rather give up than be killed."

She stood up to go. Tommy uncrossed his legs and stood up too.

"Your mother used to stall on me, too," Aurora said, thinking even in her despair of how much he reminded her of her daughter. The brow was the same, and the way he stood. In body and to some extent in manner he was distinctly his mother's son.

"Passive-aggressive, I believe they call it now," she added. "It's a term I picked up from my shrink. Your mother was a master of it—she could remain absolutely resistant for months or even years, and so can you."

"You have a shrink?" Tommy asked.

"Why, yes," Aurora said. "The General and I both went to him for a while, but then the General dropped out. I still go, and I must say I've learned a lot."

"That's probably good," Tommy said. The thought of his grandmother at a shrink's was pretty startling. It was something he was going to have to think about.

"Not necessarily," Aurora said. "He who increaseth knowledge increaseth sorrow, you know? Did you enjoy shooting Julie?"

"I enjoyed shooting well," Tommy said immediately. "I wasn't particularly thinking about Julie one way or the other."

"I'm going," Aurora said. "If you ever wish to see one of us again you'll have to call."

Usually she tried to hug him, to his discomfort, but this

time she merely walked over to the guard and let him know that she was ready to leave. For once she didn't cry.

"You know what I like about your grandmother?" the guard said, walking Tommy back to his cell. The guard was an older man who limped a little from rheumatism.

"What?" Tommy asked.

"She don't wear no cheap perfume," the guard said. "Most of these women that come up here, they douse themselves in cheap perfume. I got a sensitive smeller, and some of that cheap perfume is so strong it makes my eyes water. But your grandmother, she's always real tasteful—and she dresses nice, too," the guard added. "She ain't no old hag like most of the women that visit up here."

A year later, Tommy wrote his grandmother a brief note, telling her about the guard's compliment. The fact that she had made such a nice impression on an old, hardened prison guard was something she would probably like to know about, he thought.

7

On the ride back to Houston, Rosie felt tense, but Aurora seemed resigned. She got in the car and they proceeded almost to Conroe without a word said. Usually, between Huntsville and Conroe, many words were said—most of them by Aurora in criticism of Rosie's driving—and many tears shed.

The fact that no words were said, and no tears shed, did nothing to ease Rosie's tension. She would have been less tense if Aurora had vented some wild emotion. As it was, she had nothing to do but drive along and contemplate her own folly in making an impromptu dinner date with a prison guard with a potbelly, who had simply walked up to the car while she was waiting in the parking lot. His name was Willie, he was about her age, and he had a nice smile. He smiled at her twice, when she was in such a low mood that the smiles immediately robbed her of her normal good judgment.

"If you ain't cute as a chicken," the guard said. "What's your favorite food?"

"Shrimp gumbo," Rosie said. At least it was high on her

list of favorite foods and she was too startled by the question to tell the man that it was none of his business what her favorite food happened to be.

"Mine too. I'm Willie," the guard immediately said. He tried to spiff up by hitching his belt above his potbelly, but within thirty seconds the belt slid back under the overhang.

"So—what would your name be, and why don't we get together and eat some shrimp gumbo late this afternoon?" the man asked. "I get off at three."

"I don't," Rosie informed him. "You'll have to go hungry till around six if you want to eat with me."

"Okey-doke," the guard said. "I'll just munch some M and Ms to tide me over."

"I forgot to say I live in Houston," Rosie said. "It's probably too far to drive just to eat gumbo."

"Hell it is, I live there too," the guard said. "Half the people that work in this jail live in Houston."

Rosie decided the man wasn't likely to take no for an answer, and anyway, she didn't especially see any reason to give no for an answer—C.C. Granby was somewhere on the North Slope and hadn't been heard from in three weeks. Life, boring even when C.C. was around, had seemed especially pointless lately. So far as she knew, she had no reason not to enjoy a bowl of shrimp gumbo with a prison guard named Willie. The prospect, though unexpected, was initially a welcome relief from sitting in the parking lot chewing her hangnail and waiting for a devasted Aurora to show up and cry.

Now, though, in the cold light of forty-five minutes later, her rapid acquiescence had begun to seem rash. It might have been a mistake—even a moral lapse. What if C.C. was back from the North Slope? What if he was waiting at the curb when they got home? He was not going to be too thrilled to hear that she planned to eat shrimp gumbo with a prison guard named Willie on his first night back.

"Besides, I'm sick and tired of potbellies," she said aloud. Her husband, Royce, had had one, C.C. had one, and now Willie had one.

"What?" Aurora asked. She had been sunk in depression, attending to nothing, and suddenly Rosie was talking about potbellies.

"I mean it, Aurora," Rosie said. "At least once I'd like to go out with a skinny man."

"How about Hector, he's skinny as a stick," Aurora said. "I'll deed him to you this afternoon, if you'll take him. He's driving me crazy."

"Me too, he flashed again yesterday," Rosie said.

"Yes, he's reconverted to nudism, I'm afraid," Aurora said.

"Poor old thing, I guess it's horrible being impotent," Rosie said.

"Yes, but he doesn't plan to put up with it much longer," Aurora informed her. "He's got six kinds of potency pills now, not counting vitamins. If they work as well as Hector hopes, I won't be safe in my own bed much longer.

"So far, though, I seem to be quite safe in my own bed," she said. "What prompted that remark you made about pot-bellies?"

"Oh," Rosie said, "I guess I was just thinking out loud."

"About potbellies?" Aurora said. "You don't usually think about potbellies when you're driving me home from the prison, or if you do, you certainly don't think about them out loud. What's going on?"

"A guard caught me with my guard down and asked me for date," Rosie admitted. "His name's Willie and he's got a big fat potbelly."

"Good," Aurora said. "It's time C.C. had some competition, and the stiffer the better, in my view. C.C. has never succeeded in charming me even once, and he's had years."

"Yeah, but what if Willie don't turn out to be as sweet as he looks?" Rosie said. "I ain't up to no date rapes at my age."

"Very few men are as sweet as they look," Aurora informed her.

"Vernon was," Rosie said, remembering her personal favorite among Aurora's suitors.

"Yes, Vernon *was* as sweet as he looked," Aurora admitted.

"On the other hand, he could never get beyond sweet. I'm still annoyed with him for being so unseducable."

"You ain't supposed to be annoyed with the dead," Rosie said. "I'm superstitious about thing like that. When I think of Royce I hardly ever think of all the grief he caused me, carrying on with that slut. I just try to think of the nice times we had when the kids were young."

Aurora looked out the window, watching the pines drop behind them. Many of the pine thickets now had their edges chewed away by mini-malls or clusters of convenience stores and filling stations. Billboards announced the imminent availability of luxury homes, secure within well-guarded enclaves, deep in the pines. They had begun to pass the most outlying Savings and Loan establishments and Cajun restaurants. Once or twice they had stopped at one of the Cajun restaurants only to find that it was run by most un-Cajunlike people.

Indeed, in Aurora's view, the only nice part of the ride to Huntsville was the few seconds it took them to pass the lovely green field where the Goodyear Blimp was often anchored. There it was, anchored in the field, looking quite majestic. Behind the field was a vast hangar, where the blimp usually lived when it wasn't on one of its trips to sports events. Over the years, Aurora had come to love the blimp and to admire its size and beauty. It was an aircraft from another era, and yet it managed to survive and flourish, to retain its dignity and power in their own degraded time. In her happy, confident moments, she felt rather like a peer of the blimp—but today was not one of her happy, confident days, and when they passed the blimp, anchored tranquilly to its guy wires, she looked at it wistfully. In the distance tiny people were admiring it from their pickups.

"Better take a last look at the blimp," Aurora said to Rosie. "We won't be seeing it anymore."

"We won't?" Rosie said, sneaking a look. She, too, liked the blimp and hoped to take a ride in it someday.

Aurora said nothing—she kept her eyes on the blimp,

watching it until they left it well behind and swept on down the road toward the next mini-mall.

"Why won't we, hon?" Rosie asked, worried suddenly. She had a fair notion of what Aurora meant.

"I can't take this anymore, that's why we won't," Aurora said. "Tommy's a cruel child, if he is my own grandson. There's no point in letting him torture us like this that I can see. So we won't have to come this way again. I'm giving up."

Rosie didn't know what to say. She felt scared, and she kept her eyes on the road. It was a good time to take special pains with her driving. Aurora had given up on lots of boy-friends, but Tommy wasn't a boyfriend. He was Emma's old-est child—even if he had killed, he was Emma's oldest child. She tried to imagine how she might feel if one of her grand-children had killed his girlfriend and gone to prison, but she couldn't imagine it, because so few of her grandsons had even managed to *get* girlfriends, and none, so far, had killed one. Besides, she had been the coward of the parking lot for most of the time they had been driving to Huntsville. Aurora had been the one who went in and faced the music. She could only imagine what Tommy might have done or said, but if Aurora Greenway was ready to give up on her daugh-ter's child, then what went on between them in the prison must have been terrible, so terrible that she didn't want to think about it.

"Well," she said, but then could not think of a sentence to go with the word. They drove along in silence for another ten miles.

"Prisoners are allowed to make calls," Aurora said, finally. "I told him he could call us if he wanted or needed us. "I guess we'll see if he does."

"Are you in the mood for the Pig Stand?" Rosie asked.

"Not today," Aurora said. "Let's just go home."

"Well," Rosie said again.

"That's twice you've said that," Aurora observed. "Well, what?"

"Well, I wish I was dead," Rosie said.

"Not only are you not dead, you've got a date," Aurora said. "Look on the bright side."

"I have, and that's another reason I wish I was dead," Rosie said.

8

When they reached the house they were startled to see the General, naked once again, standing in the front door. The moment they stopped the car he began to wave his crutch at them.

"Shit, there's the ancient nudist again," Aurora said.

"I'll sneak around and do my tablecloth number," Rosie said. "We'll have him decent in no time."

"Not likely, he's never been especially decent," Aurora said.

Rosie was worried about Aurora, who clearly was in a worse than usual mood, and thought it best to try to subdue the General as soon as possible. For Aurora to reject the Pig Stand was a bad sign; seeing the General standing naked before his Maker, not to mention the neighborhood, was not something she deserved to have to cope with on such a day.

"He's yelling some gibberish at us," Aurora said. "I suppose it could be good news. Last time he did this Melanie was running away. Maybe this time she's come back."

"I think he's probably just lost his mind," Rosie said, not wanting Aurora to get her hopes up too high where Melanie was concerned. The few times Melanie had called she had sounded almost giddy with happiness, and there seemed little likelihood that she would be arriving back in Houston anytime soon.

They got out of the car, Rosie heading for the back door, Aurora for the front.

"Hector, it's a wonder you haven't been arrested," Aurora told him, when she got within range of the General's increasingly limited hearing. "This is a respectable neighborhood and people really don't expect their neighbors to stand in the front door naked."

"But I know what happened to Pascal," the General said. "There was a good reason why he didn't show up the other night."

"And what might that be?" Aurora asked, just as Rosie arrived with the tablecloth and thrust it between the General and the outside world.

"Oh, no you don't," the General said, trying to poke the tablecloth away with his crutch.

"Oh, yes I do," Rosie said, pulling the tablecloth back like a matador leading a bull. She proved to be the swifter: before he knew it, the General was decently swaddled again.

"Good God, you're both more interested in wrapping me up like a mummy than you are in hearing my news," he said with annoyance. "You'd think neither of you had ever seen a naked man before."

"A more accurate interpretation, Hector, is that we've both seen one too many naked men," Aurora said. "What is this you've found out about Pascal's irresponsible absence the night of my kidnapping?"

"What kidnapping?" the General asked. "You weren't kidnapped and you know it."

"No, but Pascal thought I was, so in a moral sense he was quite irresponsible in not showing up at once to join in the search for my abductors," Aurora said. "I believe the logic of that reasoning is flawless, if I did invent it myself."

"That's what I've been trying to tell you!" the General said. "He tried to come but he had a car wreck. He's been in the hospital knocked out cold for a day and a night. The consulate just called to say he seems to be out of danger, but he did crack his skull in a couple of places, I guess."

Aurora sighed, just the kind of sigh the General hated to hear her sigh. She was not looking her best, in his view, and after her sigh she looked even more discouraged than she had looked coming up the walk. He had meant to confide in her some exciting news, which was that he had had an erection while he was taking his shower, only about an hour ago, but now she was looking so downcast that he thought he better keep quiet about his erection for a while.

"He's not going to die," he assured her, thinking perhaps that his blunt statement about Pascal's cracking his skull had been a little too blunt. "He was just coming to help when he had the wreck."

"That car of his ain't nothing but a soup can," Rosie said. "If he had much of a wreck in that thing he's lucky he ain't up in harpland, playing a harp."

Aurora smiled a wry smile. "I don't know which prospect depresses me more," she said. "Pascal dead or Pascal playing a harp."

"He was just trying to help," the General repeated.

Aurora looked at Rosie. "Why is it men feel compelled to repeat the most obvious statements?" she said.

"Sometimes when they're scared they forget their own words the minute they're out of their mouths," Rosie said. "C.C. will forget his own name when he's scared."

"Are you scared, Hector?" Aurora asked.

"Hell, no," the General said. "I just thought you'd want to hear the news, since you like Pascal so much."

"Maybe I like him and maybe I don't," Aurora said. "If you knew what was good for you, you'd be scared, but I don't believe you know much of anything, so now I'm going upstairs and be depressed. You keep away from me for a while or you'll not only be scared, you'll be struck."

"Good lord, what did I do?" the General asked, when Aurora had indeed gone upstairs. "It's been years since she's threatened to hit me."

"Ssh," Rosie said, trying to lead him into the kitchen. "Her heart's broke, is all. She says she ain't going to see Tommy no more."

"Oh, that's bad," the General said. "I'm afraid that's very bad. Maybe we better call Teddy and see if he can come over and try to cheer her up. Sometimes Teddy's the only person who can cheer her up when she's really low."

"It's worth a try," Rosie said. "We'll have to try it tomorrow, though. This is about the time Teddy goes to work."

They both sat at the kitchen table but could think of nothing to do but sit and fret. Rosie sprinkled a little salt on her wrist and licked it off, a habit she fell into when almost out of her mind with nervousness.

"If I were to eat that much salt I'd have a stroke and die," the General informed her.

"So?" Rosie said, sprinkling more salt. "I ain't you, am I?"

"No, but that doesn't mean you're immortal, either," the General said.

Before Rosie could summon a retort, they heard Aurora coming downstairs. They stopped talking instantly—when she was in certain moods, a single careless word might set her off.

"Don't sit there huddled," Aurora said, annoyed by the mere sight of them. "You know how rabbitlike behavior irritates me."

"All behavior irritates you when you're irritated anyway," the General pointed out. "At least all *my* behavior irritates you. If I could stop breathing right now I would—at least until you get in a better mood, and who knows when that will be?"

"Hector, I'm going," Aurora said. "You could see that for yourself if you could bring yourself to look up from your rabbitlike crouch."

Rosie noticed that Aurora had changed her dress and had a purse over her arm—nonetheless, she herself still felt like licking a few more sprinkles of salt off her wrist and planned to do so the moment Aurora was safely gone.

"I'm not crouched, particularly," the General said. "I'm

bent with age and care. You can go fuck yourself, for all I care. You've been totally rude to me ever since you came home, and I've had enough. Rosie and I are decent human beings who are just trying to do our duty as we see it, and you're behaving like the monster you are at heart. I don't know why I ever entered this house and I'm apt to leave at any time. Besides, I'm not sure you ought to drive in your condition. You'll be the next one with a cracked skull."

"At least my skull has hair on it, unlike some I could mention," Aurora said, as she went out the door.

"She's right about that," Rosie said. "That woman's got a fine head of hair. A crack or two wouldn't even show."

"Shut up," the General said. "This whole conversation has been a travesty."

"Is a travesty one of them wigs female impersonators wear?" Rosie asked—she was vaguely aware of having heard the word travesty but didn't see how it applied to the conversation, which was no different from thousands that had taken place in Aurora's house over the years.

"Turn on the TV before we both go crazy," the General said.

9

Aurora felt almost irresistibly drawn to drive by Jerry Bruckner's house before going to the hospital to see Pascal, and in fact went a mile or two in that direction before correcting her compass and heading for the Medical Center. She knew there was nothing to be gained from her infatuation with Jerry Bruckner, and yet she was also painfully aware that she *was* infatuated with him, even though she suspected that he was a rather empty man. He just happened to be a really appealing empty man, of the sort she had been too frequently drawn to in her life. Trevor, her yachtsman, had been just such an empty man, sailing, marrying, and seducing, to no purpose, his whole life, and yet she had loved Trevor, believing to the end that if circumstances could be budged a little she could fill him out, or up, and make him into a more or less substantial person.

All she really knew about Jerry Bruckner was that he had sad brown eyes and a perfect lower lip; also the hairs on his wrists had an exciting effect on her. He had obviously read a great many books on psychoanalysis, while remaining in most respects a slightly untidy innocent who seemed to know little about life—the sort of person who made a sex life of waitresses and airline stewardesses—not that there was anything wrong with waitresses and airline stewardesses. The flaw was in the man who was attracted to transient women; the attraction so often seemed to be to the transience, not to the women.

Once in the parking lot at the Medical Center, Aurora studied her reflection in the rearview mirror. It was an annoyed face she saw—annoyed that life had left her so vulnerable to sad eyes, lower lips, and sexy wrist hairs. But there was really nothing to be done about it; though she knew herself to be a woman of considerable force of will, her force of will had never been sufficient to relieve her of any of her vulnerabilities, and she didn't imagine that it would be sufficient this time. Meanwhile, there was an aging Frenchman with a bent penis and a cracked skull to think about; she took her time getting out of the car and proceeding with her duty, but she did finally enter the hospital, where, after a few wrong turns, she located Pascal's room.

The door to the room was slightly ajar. She was about to push it open and go on in when she was stopped by the sound of a woman's voice. The woman was speaking French. Peeking through the crack, Aurora saw a young woman with long, casually combed brown hair sitting on the edge of Pascal's bed, clasping one of his hands in both of hers. Where Pascal's other hand was, Aurora couldn't precisely see, but then the young woman wiggled and giggled and bent over to give him a noisy kiss.

Aurora drew back instantly and walked on down the hall in a slight state of shock. Sometimes, in his cups, Pascal had bragged about his conquests of young women, but she had complacently supposed that was just par for the course Gallic bragging, done in the hope of making her so jealous that she would become a conquest herself.

Now she *had* become a conquest—a girlfriend, really, and had just almost walked in on Pascal and *another* girlfriend, a fact that made her feel like a complete fool. Probably Pascal hadn't been bragging all those years; probably any number of young beauties with casually combed hair had succumbed to the same wooing that she had eventually succumbed to. Part of the reason she felt such a fool ,was that she had overlooked an obvious fact: young women were easy prey to older men with some experience of the world. In her youth she herself had once been easy prey for a Philadelphian who had really been after her mother. His name was Morton Needham; she had never regretted the affair, but she did regret that she had forgotten its lesson: young women were pushovers for older men who knew how to push—and quite a few older men did know how to push.

She wandered on down the hall, as far as the hall went, recovering from her shock. Her first impulse had been to leave, but her second impulse was to hang around and get a better look at the girl; the second impulse won. She went back along the hall, tiptoed past Pascal's room, and waited in the little waiting room by the nurse's station. She was leafing through a ragged copy of *McCall's* when she heard the click-click of heels coming with what sounded like Parisian haste from the direction of Pascal's room. The girl passed within ten feet of her. She was skinny and no beauty, but she had a certain chic and a Hermès bag over her shoulder. She looked to be, at most, a year or two older than Melanie, of whom Aurora only had to think momentarily to feel a kind of ache: the ache of missing.

Aurora decided that five minutes would constitute a decent interval between bedside visits, but discontented with the magazine, not to mention life, she cut it to one minute, and went back to the room. Pascal was not in bed when she arrived but she could hear him in the tiny bathroom. She settled herself in a green chair and waited silently for his return. If he emerged looking frail and pitiful she was prepared to forgive all—who could begrudge a frail old Frenchman a skinny mademoiselle or two?

Unfortunately for him, Pascal strode out of the bathroom looking cocky—though all the cockiness left him instantly when he saw Aurora sitting in the chair by his bed. His first feeling was relief—Solange had left. But then, she had only *just* left: what if Aurora had noticed her? Solange would never pay any attention to a woman Aurora's age, even if she had seen her, but what about Aurora? His shock was so great he gasped. He had been feeling vigorous and had even been thinking of asking the doctor if he could go home, but his sense of vigor declined sharply when he caught sight of his visitor. The spring immediately went out of his walk and the blood out of his face. So great was his shock that he ceased to be able to walk straight and had to grasp the railing at the end of the bed to keep from veering off toward the corner where the television hung. Indeed, before Aurora had had time to say a word, he had more or less become the pitiful old Frenchman she had expected to find in the first place.

See that her mere arrival on the heels of his departing guest constituted a kind of overkill, Aurora immediately got up and helped him get around the bed and back under the covers. She felt like saying "Gotcha!" but managed to hold her tongue.

Pascal had no trouble holding his tongue. He had a feeling Aurora knew everything—if she had so much as glimpsed Solange in the hall she would immediately have figured it out. If she knew everything, then he was at her mercy and he had better keep quiet. A false word at such a time would seal his doom. She hadn't kissed him, which probably meant that his doom was already sealed, but while there was a chance, the best strategy was to remain quiet and look sick. Since he suddenly felt quite sick, there was no problem with that part of his strategy, nor, since he was terrified, with the first part of the strategy either.

Aurora sat down again and they both were silent. Pascal considered trying to groan, calling for the nurse, taking a pill, or just keeping his eyes shut, but he did none of these things.

Aurora soon got tired of what felt like a very silly silence. "Well, Pascal, what an old bamboozler you are," she said mildly. "Ten minutes ago you were chattering amorously with your young girlfriend, but so far you haven't said a single word to your old girlfriend. It makes me feel rather unwanted, just when I was hoping to feel wanted."

"I want!" Pascal said, taking hope from her mild tone. "I was coming to save you when I had the wreck. I ranned the stop sign."

"You may have run it but you didn't ranned it, unless you mean rammed it," Aurora said. "You don't have to start talking like Peter Sellers just because I caught you with Mademoiselle. You can speak excellent English, and you'd better, or I'm marching out of here never to be seen again."

"I forgot the stop sign, that was the problem," Pascal said. "I forgot it and I fell into a pickup. It was because I was so afraid you were kidnapped."

"You thought I was kidnapped?" Aurora said.

"Yes, the Mafia," Pascal said vaguely, realizing that in the sober light of day his kidnapping theory must seem a little silly.

"The Mafia indeed," Aurora said. "In fact, on the day in question I merely happened to linger with *my* young sweetie a little longer than usual."

"Oh," Pascal said. It seemed like a simple explanation until he happened to remember what had happened a little earlier on the day in question—at least he was fairly sure it was the day in question. What had happened was that they had made love not once, but twice, in his apartment, on his new mauve sheets.

"What?" he said, thinking he must have misunderstood, or at the very least, have got his days mixed up. If the day in question was the day they had made love twice, then what nonsense was Aurora talking? On such a day all she needed to do was go home, and without giving the matter further thought, he said as much.

"You should have just gone home," he said, feeling a little confused but also a little indignant.

"Now, now," Aurora said. "This is obviously a loose confederation we're in, and you mustn't be telling me what I should have done. If you, at your age, can have a skinny mademoiselle, there's no reason why I shouldn't avail myself of a vigorous young monsieur."

"But," Pascal said, and stopped. He felt himself growing

indignant, the very thing his doctors insisted that he not do. He had been strongly advised to keep calm, but how could one keep calm with Aurora sitting there bragging about the vigor of her young lover? In view of his health, which he had sacrificed in an effort to save her from the Mafia, she should not be talking such talk.

"But there is no need!" he said, making what seemed to him a generous—even overgenerous—effort to be reasonable. "You have me."

"Yes, but you have Mademoiselle what might her name be?" Aurora asked.

"Solange," Pascal said automatically.

"Ah, Solange," Aurora said. "My young man is named Sam. They don't quite rhyme but their names do start with the same letter."

"Sam, this is too much!" Pascal said, his voice rising. "How old is this Sam?"

"Why, he's almost eighteen," Aurora said.

"Eighteen!" Pascal said, almost yelling. "You sleep with me and then you run around and sleep with someone who is *eighteen?* I am disgusted."

"But why, dear?" Aurora asked. "You know how fond I am of science, and according to the scientists young men hit their natural peak at around eighteen. I don't see why you should find it disgusting that I might want to help Sam enjoy his natural peak."

"You are a monster, you have destroyed me, I thought we were in love," Pascal said in one breath.

"Who says we aren't?" Aurora wondered. "And calm down while you're at it, before you have a stroke. In fact, it wouldn't surprise me if you deserved a stroke, but I don't want to get blamed for it if you have one."

"You should be blamed for everything!" Pascal insisted. He knew he should calm down, but in fact he was getting angrier.

"So I have to compete with an eighteen-year-old!" he said loudly. "At my age this is bad news."

"Really, Pascal, this is America," Aurora said. "We Americans believe that competition is good at any age. It makes one work harder at one's appointed tasks."

"I wish I had strangled you," Pascal said. "You sit there and break my heart when I am sick. I thought you had kindness, but you have no kindness. You just like to break my heart.

"Can't you see that I'm sick?" he added as an afterthought, yelling it nearly at the top of his lungs.

"On the contrary, I can hear that you aren't particularly sick," Aurora said. "Everyone on this floor can hear it, too. Pipe down, or I'm leaving."

Pascal found that he had yelled out the last of his anger trying to explain to Aurora how sick he was. What was left, now that anger was gone, was a profound hopelessness. Aurora would probably never come back to his apartment to have lunch with him and make love on his mauve sheets. Why would she, when she could make love to an eighteen-year-old whose penis probably wasn't even bent?

It seemed to him it was all the fault of the stop sign. If he hadn't run it and hit the pickup he would not be in the hospital and Aurora would not have come to visit, in which event she would not have caught him with Solange. One stop sign, and his life was ruined! One stop sign!

"It was because of the stop sign," he said hopelessly, before beginning to cry.

"Good lord, now you're going to cry," Aurora said. She sat on the bed and put her arms around him, but Pascal went on crying. A nurse peeked in, saw that yet another woman was hugging the patient, and went away.

"Can't you men take a little teasing?" Aurora said, when Pascal was calm enough to listen. "I was just teasing. I wasn't *that* annoyed by Mademoiselle. And there is no young Monsieur Sam, if it will make you feel any better."

"No Monsieur Sam?" Pascal said. "I thought he was seventeen or eighteen—a teenager."

"Pascal, he was just a hasty invention," Aurora said.

"Am I your one and only then?" he asked, wiping his eyes with a fistful of Kleenex she handed him.

"One and only" was an American phrase he had always liked. Just saying it made him feel better. Aurora had allowed him to rest his head on her bosom. She seemed to be feeling sorry for him at last. The only good thing about being in the hospital was that women would come and feel sorry for him.

Following up on that thought, he allowed one hand to begin a feeble probe under her skirt.

"Pascal, you need to change your shampoo," Aurora said. It was a fact she couldn't help noticing, since she was looking at the top of his head. The hand under the skirt she permitted, feeling that perhaps she had indulged in a little too much overkill.

"You are not romantic," Pascal said, still sad. He tossed the Kleenex on the floor in what was meant to seem like a gesture of despair.

"I love you but you are just not romantic," he repeated, hoping she would deny it.

Aurora hugged him, let him fumble a little, said nothing. Her thoughts had drifted to Jerry Bruckner. It was about the time of day when he jogged, and it occurred to her that she might intercept him in his jog. She hadn't talked to him since making him get out of her car, canceling two appointments in order to avoid it. But now it might be time to resume relations. Mainly she wanted a look at his legs, which held promise of being even more exciting than his wrists or his lower lip. It had been a little too dark to correctly appraise legs when he had returned from his jog the other day.

For amusement she gave Pascal a little nip on the earlobe, but what she really had in mind was to catch Jerry Bruckner jogging and have a look at his legs. And if that meant she wasn't romantic, then so be it.

"Very probably you're right, Pascal," Aurora said, slipping off the bed. "Very probably I'm not romantic—very probably I never was. But I am *something*, wouldn't you admit?"

"I admit," Pascal said gloomily, wondering if she'd even give him a kiss before she left.

10

Aurora spent nearly thirty minutes driving around Jerry Bruckner's neighborhood, hoping to spot him jogging, but she didn't spot him jogging. There was a high school not far from his home with a track behind it where a number of people of both sexes were jogging—but Jerry Bruckner was not among them. She parked for a bit, hoping Jerry would miraculously jog past, but he didn't. Teddy, Tommy, and Melanie, while in high school, had competed in sports events on the playing field behind the high school, and Aurora and Rosie had sometimes come to watch them, which was why she knew about the school track. None of them had been very good at sports, but then none of them had cared much that they weren't good, so little harm was done, she supposed.

Another reason why she remembered the track was that one day, years before, while she and Rosie had been looking for the school in order to attend one of Tommy's first sports events, a dismal soccer match in which he managed to get a concussion and a dislocated shoulder at the same time, Aurora had stumbled upon a palm reader named Carmen, who had a sign in her yard featuring a large palm. To Rosie's annoyance, they had missed the start of the soccer match because Aurora insisted on stopping immediately to have her palm read. Rosie, in the course of raising her seven children, had attended several thousand sports events and believed one of the chief duties of a parent was to be on time at such events.

"I never missed a one if one of my kids was playing, and I've never been late either," Rosie had declared at the time. "I don't believe in fortune-telling, and even if I did I wouldn't try it because it might be mostly bad news and if it is I don't want it."

"On the other hand it might be good news, and if it is I *do* want it," Aurora said, marching into the house.

Carmen turned out to be a tiny Spanish woman who chewed gum a bit too loudly for Aurora's taste; she had long, lustrous black hair, which she continued to brush while she gave the reading. Also, she was nearsighted and had to practically stick her nose into Aurora's palm in order to see the future, but these small debits were more than made up for by her frank prediction that Aurora would enjoy a long and richly lascivious future.

"The guys like you" was the way Carmen put it. "You gonna get 'em in all sizes and shapes."

This theme was repeated and elaborated on in Aurora's many subsequent visits. Nearsighted though she may have been, Carmen was quick to perceive that Aurora had no inclination to spinsterishness, nor did she flinch from frank language.

"You're still gonna be doing it when you're eighty, honey," Carmen told her once; it was on the day Melanie dropped the shot-put on her foot, an accident Aurora arrived just in time to witness.

When pressed as to whom she might have found to do it with when she was eighty, Carmen shrugged, smacked her gum, looked wicked, and just said, "Guys"—the ones, presumably, who would come in all sizes and shapes. By the time Melanie finally graduated and there were no more games to go to in Bellaire, the sign with the palm on it badly needed repainting, and Carmen herself wasn't looking so good. The fall after Melanie's graduation, one day while in a low mood, Aurora had driven to Bellaire alone; she and the General were in a slack period and she felt like hearing that she might soon be getting guys in all sizes and shapes. But when she knocked, a portly man with a scar that ran from his eyelid to his lower lip informed her that Carmen was dead.

Now, three years later, sitting in the afternoon drizzle by the sodden playing field, Aurora felt herself losing heart. What was she doing, a woman who was getting on, lurking like a groupie of some sort around a soccer field in a neighborhood she had never really liked, in hopes of catching a glimpse of a man she scarcely knew, for no better reason than that he seemed to have excitingly sturdy legs? As for the guys in all sizes and shapes who were supposed to carry her robustly into her eighties, there were, for the moment, only Hector and Pascal, two sizes and shapes she would gladly forgo if only she had some that were better. Even if Jerry Bruckner did jog by on his excitingly sturdy legs, it wouldn't matter, since she had already resolved to resist him for the sake of her dignity.

Still, important as dignity was, it wasn't everything. Aurora had the suspcion that if her resolve happened to be tested on the right day, or perhaps that should be the wrong day, it might not prove to be such a solid instrument after all. A drizzly afternoon on which she had just caught her new lover with a young girlfriend might be just such a day, too—but Jerry Bruckner, whose timing was not quite in the same class as his lower lip, stubbornly refused to jog past and take advantage of his big chance.

Nonetheless Aurora felt a new reluctance to consider going home, though it was the time of day when she was normally more than happy to go home. For many years she had preferred to spend the end of the afternoon in her window nook, surrounded by light reading on the order of five or six movie magazines. She could sip tea, wonder if movie stars really had that much fun or that much heartbreak, look out the window and observe the neighborhood, talk to Melanie on the phone, or perhaps quarrel with Rosie a little.

All those pleasures, however, were contingent upon Hector Scott being far away on a golf course, hitting his ball around, and now he was never far away on a golf course. Any quarreling that got done would inevitably be done with him, and even if he wasn't annoyed he would be likely just to prattle on about his medications and his correspondent hopes for a late surge of potency, a prospect that seemed more and more unlikely, and that, for her part, she now no longer particularly wanted anyway.

Because of what she and Rosie had begun to call the flasher factor, the thought of spending the late afternoon in her window nook had lost much of its appeal, so, casting one last look across the track field and seeing no Jerry, she started her car and pursued a rather roundabout route to the home of Teddy, Jane, and Bump. Teddy would undoubtedly be at work, but she could see her great-grandchild and perhaps have a talk with Jane about the complexities of life.

Aurora never *had* had a frank talk with Jane about the complexities of life, but she had the sense that Jane at least realized that life was seriously complex, and if she could be induced to talk about it, would probably not be excessively judgmental—in contrast to Rosie, who had a grating tendency to be instantly and unequivocally judgmental about everything Aurora did or hoped to do.

Aurora was uncomfortably aware that in the eyes of many she herself came across as instantly and unequivocally judgmental, though in fact as she got older she felt less and less capable of judging in such a clear-cut way. Such wisdom as had come to her through long experience showed an increasing tendency to blur at the edges; it was getting very difficult to be quite sure about anything. Jane was young and had a sharp eye; a little talk with her might be helpful.

To her surprise, however, it was Teddy, not Jane, who opened the door for her.

"Hi, Granny," he said. Her heart gave a leap at the welcoming tone in which he said it; he was, after all, her very favorite grandchild and had been since he was born. Tommy had been brighter, and Melanie cuter, but Teddy was all love, or all hope, or all despair. He was of a piece emotionally, in a way that Aurora could not resist.

He came out on the porch by the steps and gave her a big hug. They were, unfortunately, positioned just under the drip from the roof, but Aurora didn't care. She felt confusion well up in her; she felt she might cry, but she didn't.

"Bump's got a fever," Teddy said.

"But it's your shift," Aurora said. "Why are you here?"

"Because Jane gets scared when Bump has a fever," Teddy said. "She'd rather risk getting murdered on the night shift than stay with a sick child."

Jonathan was asleep. Aurora marched in and put a hand on his forehead—indeed, he did have a fever, and a fairly high one. When she touched him Bump opened his eyes briefly—the wet eyes of a child with a high fever—but he soon closed them again and slept.

"Laurie came by and played with him," Teddy said. Laurie was Jane's sister. "He gets too excited when Laurie comes. She's his favorite aunt. He almost always gets a fever after she leaves."

"Oh, Laurie," Aurora said. "Does she still have her Senegalese? Jane's sisters do manage to find the most exotic men."

"She's still got him but I don't think he's particularly exotic," Teddy said. "He's basically just a professor."

She noticed that his hands were shaking as he made the tea. Also, there was a look in his eye that wasn't quite right, a look it pained her to see. The look was more sad than wild, but it was not entirely free of wildness, either, and even a trace of wildness frightened her. The years in which the two boys were in and out of mental hospitals had been a hell—one she didn't want to revisit. It was in those years that the edges of everything blurred: the points of the compass whirled, and all she knew was that happiness was now gone; she could not be happy with her grandchildren in madhouses; everything she attempted in those years was spoiled by their despair.

"Ted, if something's wrong, tell me," she said, mustering her courage. "You don't seem quite yourself."

"You don't need to panic," Teddy said, seeing that she was about to. "I'm just coming off a medication and I'm a little shaky."

"What else?" Aurora inquired.

"We're fighting about the night shift," Teddy admitted. "Jane thinks it's bad for me, and I think it's bad for her. I don't need to sleep normal hours, but Jane does. I just let her go tonight because of Bump's fever, but she's not working the night shift regularly, and that's that. But I imagine there'll be a few more fights about it before she gives up."

"What else?" Aurora asked again. She knew there was more. She could tell from the tone of his voice that he was just giving her the skin of the problem—he wasn't giving her the meat.

Teddy grinned and shook his head. His grandmother's intuition amazed him—it always had. There *was* more, but he wasn't sure he wanted to talk about it. His grandmother liked Jane, and if he told her what the trouble was she might stop liking her.

Also, Jane liked his grandmother. Granny might hold her peace, but, then again, she might not, and if she didn't and she and Jane had a big fight there was no telling where it all might end. Jane wasn't going to let him or Aurora Greenway or anyone else interfere much in her life. Jane's first principle was that *nobody* had better try and interfere in her life.

"Come on, tell me," Aurora said. "You can trust me."

"I don't know if I can, this time," Teddy said.

"Have I ever violated a secret of yours?" Aurora asked. She took her tea and settled herself on the couch. She tried to appear calm, but she wasn't calm. Nothing unsettled her so much as the dawn of some new wildness in Teddy's eyes. Confusion she could live with, but she didn't want any more madness—if any more madness came she felt she might lose it and end up mad herself.

"No, but this is a new kind of secret," Teddy said.

"You mean she's having an affair?" Aurora asked.

Teddy was silent, wondering if he looked different in some

way. If he didn't, then how had his granny figured out that there was trouble?

"I raised you, remember?" Aurora said, speaking to his thought. "I do know you rather well. You can't conceal trouble from me unless you stay out of sight and off the phone. And even then I still might figure it out."

Teddy was mainly thinking about what signs might have given her a clue—his shaky hands, or what?

"If she's having an affair that's not really a new kind of secret," Aurora remarked. "I'm afraid it's a very old secret, really, which is not to say it wouldn't be appropriate for you to be very upset—if that is the secret."

"She's having an affair with a woman she went to school with," Teddy admitted—it just took too much energy to hold out against Aurora's inquiries.

"I see," Aurora said with no sign of shock. "It's the same secret, only in skirts."

Teddy felt immediately better, as he always did when he shared some problem with his grandmother. Of course, the problem was still there. But now, at least he had an ally. He knew from his granny's tone that she intended to be his ally. Most of the time he was not disturbed by the fact that Jane was sleeping with Claudia. What disturbed him was that, except for Jane and Claudia, he was the only one who knew it. It was a weight. It overworked his drugs—without something like that added, his drugs kept him pretty stable. He *wanted* to stay pretty stable; maybe with the drugs plus his grandmother, he could.

Bump began to whine, and Aurora went to the bed and got him. She wrapped him in a light quilt and brought him to the couch.

"Could I just have a washrag, please?" she asked. "I believe if I had a wet washrag we could bathe this fever away."

Teddy got her the washrag and she began to bathe the little boy's face and forehead. At first Bump wiggled and resisted, but then he gave up and rested limply in Aurora's lap. His eyes were already less feverish.

"Do you think it's coming down?" Teddy asked. Bump's fevers were big crises in their lives—far bigger, really, than

Jane's affair with Claudia. Jane worried herself sick over the fevers, and he worried himself sick about Jane and Bump.

"Why, yes, a little," Aurora said, feeling Bump's forehead.

"I'm going to phone Jane—she'll be relieved," Teddy said.

Bump looked up at Aurora and she made a fish face at him. Ordinarily when his Big Granny made a fish face at him, Bump dissolved in hilarity, but this time he felt too sleepy to laugh. He smiled a little, though.

"That's better," Aurora said.

Teddy stayed in the bedroom, reporting on Bump's recovery, for some time. Aurora continued to use the washrag to cool down her great-grandchild. When Teddy returned to the room, his eyes, it seemed to her, were less wild. The little boy would soon be over his fever, and perhaps Teddy had slipped past the gates of madness once again. She herself felt rather tired—perhaps now it was time she went home.

"Is the woman nice?" she asked, handing Bump to his father.

"Oh, Claudia?" Teddy said. "Yeah, she is nice. She's a little bit of a slob, but she's nice."

"Far better that it's a woman than a man, Ted," Aurora said. "Just at this moment you may not agree with that opinion, but someday you'll see that I'm right."

"I already think you're right," Teddy said. "If it was a man he'd probably try to take Jane away, and that'd be awful. As it is, about the worst that can happen is that Claudia might move in with us."

"I see," Aurora said. "What does Jonathan think of Claudia?"

"Oh, he likes her fine," Teddy said. "She reads him stories. If she did move in with us, Jane and I could both work days and Claudia could be his nanny. It would actually be kind of good if we could both work days."

"Yes, it probably would," Aurora said. She gave Bump a couple of kisses on his neck—a neck that was still hot. His fever had not abated *that* much, but it would, and she thought it best to anticipate its abatement a bit and relieve his worried parents' minds.

"Jane's family is not without their adventurous bent, I

must say," Aurora reflected. "Laurie's got a Senegalese and now Jane has you and a woman. What about the little one—Betsy?"

"Betsy's gay," Teddy said. "She lives with a girl who's a dental assistant. I like them both a lot, even though Betsy thinks men are brutes."

"Well, except for you and one or two scattered souls, Betsy's right," Aurora said, handing Jonathan to him.

"Did you see Tommy?" Teddy asked cautiously when she stood up to go. Tommy was a sore subject, best approached in a gingerly fashion.

"Yes, but for the last time, unless he changes," Aurora said. "I have other responsibilities, and I can't afford to be hurt that badly. I told him so, too."

"I don't think Tommy will change," Teddy said.

"I don't either, so there's no point," Aurora said. "What do you hear from Melly?"

"We don't," Teddy said. "I guess they aren't able to afford a telephone yet. I told her to call from a pay phone and make it collect, but she won't."

"I'm becoming a trifle worried," Aurora said. "It would be nice to know if either one of them actually has a job yet, and if they don't I'd like to know what they're living on. I wonder if your father's heard from her—I suppose he'd help his own child if it was an emergency."

"I guess he would," Teddy said without conviction.

"At least he would if it were life or death," he added. "If Melly was just broke, I doubt he'd want to hear it. Madga would skin him alive if she caught him giving any of us money. She definitely expects him to spend all his money on her and her children."

"I'm sure—I predicted he'd get that sort of wife," Aurora said. "On the whole it serves him right, but it's no help where Melly's concerned.

"Rosie's quite worried, too," she added. In fact, Rosie was so worried that she wanted both of them to fly to Los Angeles and see for themselves how things stood. They had argued about the wisdom of such a step as recently as that morning.

Teddy felt slightly guilty for not worrying about his sister more than he did, but in fact life at home was about all he had time or energy to think about. Bump was wiggling, meaning he wanted to be put on the floor, which might make his fever to back up.

Teddy put him on the floor and Bump collapsed in a heap, thumb in his mouth, looking not much less feverish than he had when Aurora came in. If his fever actually went up before Jane got home there would be hell to pay, Teddy worried.

"Ted, relax," Aurora said, seeing his anxiety writ plain on his face as he looked down at the child. "We'll just give him a tiny bit of aspirin and I assure you the fever will go down."

"Jane doesn't approve of aspirin," Teddy said quickly.

"I know—shut your eyes and you won't see a thing," Aurora said. She went to the bathroom, broke off a quarter of an aspirin tablet, got some water, and got the aspirin down the child, whom she deposited back in his bed.

"Jane doesn't know everything, nor does she rule the planet," she told Teddy, giving him a big hug before she left.

"I think I'll study a little Sanskrit," he said, looking relieved.

11

Melanie told the young officers that she was pregnant, but they put the handcuffs on her anyway and then seemed to just forget about her while they chewed gum and got the details from the grocery-store employee who had caught her with the two steaks under her sweater. It was all just dumb, completely dumb—she didn't have the right attitude to be a good shoplifter and she had told Bruce so; she just hadn't been able to convince him. He had it in his head that the mere fact that she was pregnant would protect her, although she was only a little more than three months pregnant and really didn't show. But Bruce was in one of his stubborn moods; he wanted her to shoplift some steaks and she finally gave in and did it, or tried to do it, feeling stupid and guilty both.

They weren't even all that totally desperately broke; she still had her little waitressing job at the deli on Ventura. It was just that they had used almost all her tip money, plus Bruce's paycheck from his part-time job at the filling station, to pay the rent on their cruddy apartment, which was an ugly green building on the east edge of Studio City. Even so, they had enough money for Chinese food or some tacos at one of the cheap Mexican places strung along Lankersheim, but Bruce kept insisting that he wanted red meat, and now she was caught; so caught that she was beginning to feel sick to her stomach from worry. The supermarket was on Victory Boulevard, not far from the Burbank airport. Planes kept coming right over her, deafeningly. The cops just left her standing on the sidewalk at the edge of the parking lot while they chatted with the girl from the grocery store—she was skinny but sort of pretty, Melanie thought. Hordes of little Hispanic children milled around, looking at her with her wrists handcuffed—they obviously thought it was a good joke that a fat Anglo girl had got caught with steaks under her sweater. Some of the older women, with kids hanging all over them, wearily pushing shopping carts out to their beat-up cars, didn't seem to think it was so funny—they looked down at the sidewalk when they passed. Nobody was really sympathetic, though; no friendly faces turned her way. The trouble was *her* trouble, and it was clear that none of the shoppers wanted to get near it.

Melanie didn't blame them; it was too stupid, and they were right not to care about it. She wished fervently that she had just stood up to Bruce and insisted that they go get some tacos, or else Chinese; he was going to be pissed, for sure, that she got caught. She had no idea how much it would cost to bail her out of jail, but undoubtedly it was going to cost more than they had—they would have to ask for help from somebody. The anxiety of being arrested, to the extent that she was arrested, was making her feel very tired—she wished they would put her in the police car so at least she would be sitting down, but the officers just went on chatting with the skinny girl from the grocery store and showed no interest in putting her in the police car, or anywhere else.

If only she had stood up to Bruce, Melanie thought again —but Bruce was so disappointed that he had moved all the way to L.A. just to work part time in a gas station that she rarely had the heart to refuse him when he really wanted something. Whether it was sex or steak, she sort of felt he ought to get it if it would put him in a better mood for at least a little while.

Actually, Melanie herself felt pretty disappointed with their life in L.A., but she tried to hide it; somebody had to at least try to be the cheerful one, and it seemed as if it should be her. After all, she had agreed to the move in about ten seconds; at that time she was giddy with love and also eager to get Bruce as far away as possible from Beverly and her Ferrari. But she had never expected just to arrive in L.A. and become an immediate movie star, which is what Bruce seemed to have expected. He was cheerful for about a week, until it dawned on him that he was still a million miles from being a movie star, or anything else different from what he had been in Houston, even though he did enroll in an acting class that met twice a week in North Hollywood.

Melanie had never had the faintest expectations of becoming a movie star, though she still thought she might try someday for a career in television—at least she might if she ever lost weight. But she wasn't going to lose weight until the baby came, so she just started looking for the best job she could get in order to help support them until Bruce got some training and maybe made a little progress toward an acting career.

Still, living in a cruddy apartment on Cahuenga and waitressing and pumping gas just wasn't that different from living in a cruddy apartment on Fairview Street and waitressing and pumping gas. The big difference for her was that she was pregnant, but Bruce wasn't pregnant, and the big difference for him was that he no longer had a Ferrari to drive or a bunch of friends with drug money in their pockets to run around with. Melanie thought maybe she could make some of it up to him with extra good sex, and she did try, but the results weren't too consistent. Once in a while it actually was extra good, but a lot of times it was just normal fucking and it didn't keep Bruce from looking depressed when he went off to the filling station.

Just as Melanie was making a mental checklist of people she might call to get her out of jail—it was a short checklist,

270

she didn't know that many people in L.A.—the cops finished their flirtation with the grocery clerk and turned their attention to her. While they were flirting with the clerk they had both looked jolly, but when they started hustling her toward the police car they got real stern again. Melanie started to feel a little queasy from fear—what if they beat her up or something? Neither one of them was much older than she was, but when they deigned to look at her at all their eyes made it clear that in their eyes she was just total criminal trash. Melanie wished her grandmother were there: it wouldn't take her grandmother long to make *them* feel like total criminal trash.

But of course that was an irrational wish—her grandmother *wasn't* there. She herself was on the way to jail and that was that. The silence in the car was horrible—the cops managed to ignore her in a way that made it clear that they hated her, if only for the inconvenience of being required to drive her to jail. Melanie began to wish they'd read her her rights or something, just to break the silence, although it wasn't actual silence, since the police radio squawked all the time—it was just silence between her and the cops. She looked out the window and happened to notice a familiar green building: they were driving right past her own apartment building! If Bruce would only look out the window he could see her being arrested! But he was undoubtedly just flopped on the bed, watching TV and waiting for her to show up and cook his steak. He probably even had enough money to pay for the stupid steaks; she thought for a moment of telling the cops that, but they both looked so hateful she was a little afraid to speak, and didn't speak. She went back to her mental list of people she could call and immediately ruled out her father. She had called her father only once since moving to the West Coast, and he had not seemed pleased to hear that she was more or less in the neighborhood. She had thought he might at least invite the two of them down for lunch some weekend, but he hadn't, and he sure wasn't going to want to drive all the way from Riverside to get her out of jail.

Melanie decided that the best thing to do was to call Patsy Carpenter's younger daughter, Katie. Patsy's older daughter, Ariadne, was a Berkeley radical-type snob who would hardly speak to anyone who hadn't tried to overthrow the government at least once; she was usually off in some Third World country, finding out more bad things the U.S. government had done. Katie had bopped around the Third World a lot, too, but mainly she preferred to hang out in Westwood, going to UCLA when it suited her and just having boyfriends and hitting the beach the rest of the time. She was a little bit of a snob too, but mainly she was friendly. Katie even came to Texas once in a while to visit her mother, unlike Ariadne, who stayed away from Texas on the grounds that Lyndon Johnson and a lot of people she referred to as pig millionaires came from there. Ariadne was quite contemptuous of her mother for moving back to Texas, a state where Lyndon Johnson had once lived. Ariadne really had a thing about Lyndon Johnson, not to mention a thing about her mother and almost everyone else. The fact that her mother had grown up in Texas in the first place and had quite a few friends there cut no ice with Ariadne—in her eyes, personal things like that shouldn't matter: they could never cancel out the crimes of Lyndon Johnson. Melanie was willing to agree that Lyndon Johnson had probably done a lot of bad things, but she still felt a little sorry for Patsy, who never got to see Ariadne unless she visited her in places like Ethiopia or Sri Lanka.

Katie, though, was a lot nicer—Melanie decided Katie was who she had better call from jail. She couldn't call Bruce because the phone company wanted a two-hundred-dollar deposit before they would connect the phone, and they hadn't been able to afford it yet. Melanie seemed to remember that once you were arrested you were only allowed one phone call—to your family or your lawyer or something. She didn't have a lawyer, of course, but the one phone call business was a really worrisome aspect of the trouble she had gotten herself into. Katie went to the beach a lot, and also she was pretty and popular, and had a lot of boyfriends, and fell in love a lot. What if she was off at the beach with a boyfriend and hadn't left her message machine on? In that event Melanie might waste her one call and never get out of jail.

When the police car passed their apartment building Melanie got the notion that maybe the police station was in Studio City, not too far from their home, but it soon turned out that the cops were just checking a complaint from an Asian guy who had all four tires stolen right off his car while it was parked near the intersection of Vineland and Lankersheim. Sure enough, when they arrived there, a new-looking Honda was sitting there with all its tires off and its belly sort of on the street. The victim was a small Asian man who was extremely upset about the loss of his tires. Melanie couldn't blame him. She could imagine how mad Bruce would be if he got off work some day and discovered that all four of his tires had been stolen.

It took a long time for the cops to calm the man down enough to get the facts from him. Melanie felt tired enough to drop, and also hot and very thirsty—a bottle of Evian would have been a great help just then. The afternoon sun was hitting the car at a real bad angle; the heat and nervousness and everything were making her feel sick, but there was no help for it. All she could do was sit there and sweat.

Then, when the cops did get through getting information from the Asian man whose tires had been stolen, it turned out that the police station they intended to take her to was in Oxnard. Melanie immediately got nervous all over again, wondering what bus she would take if she got released on her own recognizance or something and had to find her way home in the middle of the night. Maybe Katie could be persuaded to come and get her, but Katie lived in Santa Monica and probably had no idea where Oxnard was, and if Katie was off on a date it was going to be tricky getting home, assuming she got to go home.

As they were driving to Oxnard, the cop who wasn't driving finally got tired of being silent and stern and turned in his seat so he could give Melanie the eye. He must have decided she wasn't a serial killer or anything, because he even gave her a little smile. It was just a little smile, but it did give her some hope that they weren't going to beat her up or anything just for shoplifting two steaks.

"I think you're gonna wish you'd stayed home and had macaroni before this is over," he said. He had a little blond mustache, kind of untidy.

"I knew I shouldn't have done it," Melanie said. "I've never committed a crime before and I'm real sorry."

Both cops laughed; they seemed to think it was hilarious that she had apologized.

"Well, I am," Melanie said, feeling a little silly.

"Hey, don't apologize to me," the young cop said. "I wouldn't mind a steak myself. The point is, it's dumb to shoplift on Saturday night, because if you get caught it takes too long to get processed."

"Oh," Melanie said.

"Yeah," the other cop said. "By the time we get you to the jail there'll be a hundred hookers ahead of you."

"A hundred hookers?" Melanie said, startled.

"Yeah, and they'll be pissed because it's Saturday night and they want to go back to work," the cop with the mustache said. "The last place they want to be in is in the slammer in Oxnard."

Melanie had seen several women she thought might be hookers, here and there in the Valley, though no more than she would have expected to see in Houston, in the same sort of neighborhoods. The thought of being in jail with a hundred hookers was startling—if it had been Bruce getting arrested, it might have suited him fine, Bruce was always ogling hookers—he thought they were real exotic.

Still, she thought the cops were probably exaggerating—how could there be a hundred hookers in jail in Oxnard?—and actually they were exaggerating a little. There probably weren't more than forty or fifty women in the room she was put into, but she soon had to admit that forty or fifty annoyed women could easily seem like a hundred if you happened to be in the midst of them, as she was for the next several hours. It was a melting pot of a jail—most of the women in the room where Melanie was put were Hispanic or Asian or black.

There were only about four white girls in the room, but the melting-pot aspect wasn't what bothered Melanie. What bothered her was that the place was crowded and smelly and hot to begin with, and it just kept getting more crowded, more smelly, and hotter. Every few minutes there'd be the click of high heels in the hall and three or four more girls in hooker makeup would be shoved into the room, although it was already standing room only, more or less. Melanie had still not had a drink of water and had moments when she thought she might faint. If it had been cooler and she had been less thirsty and uncomfortable, it might have been kind of interesting to be in jail—certainly it was a good chance to find out how the other half lived—but the discomfort took the edge off her curiosity.

Also, the processing seemed to be going at a snail's pace. Every fifteen minutes or so a couple of bored-looking matrons would take their time strolling down the hall to the big holding cell and would call out two or three names and take two or three girls back with them to be processed, but it was not lost on the crowd of women that newcomers were being added a lot faster than old-timers were being taken out. Most of the women's Saturday-night makeup jobs were melting horribly in the heat, and their impatience was evident.

Melanie didn't blame them. She herself hated to wait— Bruce was always berating her for being so impatient—but in the crowd she was with at the moment she felt she'd better just summon as much patience as she could and not get anybody mad.

A black woman who looked to be in her thirties was positioned right by the cell door, obviously hoping to be next out once the cops came, but the cops came three or four times without taking her, and the black woman began to get too pissed to keep quiet. The next time a cop came and stuck another woman in the cell, she spoke up.

"How many of us do you think you can put in this fuckin' black hole?" she said. "Can't you see it's full?"

The cop didn't change expression or say a word. He just locked the cell and walked away.

"Fuckhead!" the black woman said as he was leaving.

The cop turned briefly and pointed his finger at her. "Watch your language, Denise," he said, and kept on walking.

Melanie began to wish that she could at least make it over to a wall so she'd have the wall to lean on, but every inch of wall space was already taken by women who had been brought in before her, and the very second one of them got taken out, the wall space got filled by women who were a lot closer to the wall than she was. There didn't seem to be any hope of ever getting a spot on the wall, though that soon came to be her dream of comfort.

All she could do was stand there with the other women, hoping that sooner or later her name would be called. An hour passed, or maybe more; she stopped thinking about the time, though now and then she would think about how nice it would be to get a drink of water or to lean against the wall. She didn't really think about anything else—mainly, her mind was a blank. It was a very unusual situation, being in a cell with fifty or so hookers, but she was too tired even to look around. All she really wanted was for it to be over.

Then a time came when she was aware that a pain was cutting through the blankness. It cut through and then diminished and went away, but it soon cut through again, and every time it cut through it got a little worse. It was low down, like a cramp, only worse—it was twice as bad as any cramp she had ever experienced and pretty soon she was squirming and really having to try hard to keep herself from groaning and stuff.

"Wow," she said one time, grimacing when it came real bad.

A small Hispanic woman was standing beside her, chewing gum and waiting stoically, not complaining like some of the other women. But she heard Melanie say "Wow" and saw her distorted face. It seemed to Melanie that she had sympathetic eyes.

"You sick?" the woman said.

"I guess I could be," Melanie said. "I don't know what it is—I'm getting these real bad cramps."

"You don't look so good, honey," the woman said, putting a hand on her arm.

Just then a real bad pain came and Melanie had to yelp a little—it was just real bad. Some of the other women turned to look at her. Up to that point Melanie had been scared of her cellmates—her strategy had been to just keep quiet and not be noticed. But all of a sudden she was hurting too much —it was scary. Her legs began to feel real shaky, she wasn't sure she could stand up any longer; she felt a great urge to lie down. There was a blankness; she felt she might be falling; it seemed like several people grabbed her. Then everybody was yelling so loudly she couldn't think anymore, she just kept falling and let it all go.

12

"Aurora, don't come," Patsy said. "Couldn't you just this once trust me and take my advice? I'm here and Katie's here and Melanie is in no danger. We'll get her back on her feet, and then if you want to come, fine."

"Are you *sure* she's in no danger?" Aurora asked again—the call from Los Angeles had come at 4 A.M. Fortunately, Hector slept through it. The second call came at 6:15; in the intervening two and a quarter hours Patsy and her daughter had managed to get Melanie out of jail and into Cedars of Sinai, a hospital where, Aurora seemed to recall, Elizabeth Taylor had had several of her operations. In her view, a hospital that had managed to keep Elizabeth Taylor alive should be able to deal with Melanie's miscarriage; nonetheless, the hours between the call from the jail and the call from the hospital had been acutely anxious ones. Aurora remembered her own miscarriage—not so much the pain as the sorrow. Rudyard had not been much of a comfort to her—in fact he been *no* comfort to her—in that sorrow. Perhaps it was not really his fault—men were not the ones who had the little one inside them; there was really no way they could feel the loss as a woman felt it—but that very fact only made her sorrow the more lonely and the more acute.

Now Melanie had that loneliness and that sorrow too— Patsy had not even had time to go find Bruce and tell him what happened. Of course it was a very lucky thing—almost a miracle—that Patsy had happened to be visiting Katie when the trouble occurred; she had only arrived in Los Angeles that afternoon. It was lucky, it was a miracle, and yet it only made Aurora feel the more wrong—she and Rosie had been talking for three weeks of going to L.A. to see how things stood; but they had dithered. Rosie had her new, evidently flourishing romance with Willie Cotts, a prison guard, and she herself had her strange, feverish—not to mention pointless and degrading—infatuation with Jerry Bruckner. Almost the worst sin, in Aurora's reckoning, was to let men take precedence over children, and yet she and Rosie, the two people who loved Melanie most, had done just that, more or less—it was Patsy Carpenter who had been there to catch their baby when she fell.

"It don't matter if it was Patsy and not us," Rosie promptly informed her. "She loves Melly too—thank God she was there."

Aurora, unable to bear her anxiety alone, had awakened Rosie and Willie. All three of them, a bleak trio, had sat for two hours in the kitchen, waiting for the phone to ring again. By the time it finally did, Aurora and Rosie were at their wit's end. Willie Cotts had never met Melanie but was at his wit's end, too, from having consumed too much coffee, too early in the day, not to mention from having to be in the company of women who frightened him badly.

"Caffeine makes me jumpy," he said several times.

"Then stop drinking coffee, you're like a jumping bean anyway," Rosie said, annoyed that Willie had not managed to be more of a comfort in this, their first crisis. Just when she needed a steady hand on the tiller, she had yet another man who didn't seem to know how to put *any* hand, steady or otherwise, on the tiller.

"I suppose you're right," Aurora said to Patsy. "I suppose

I should wait a day or two until everyone's calmer. For one thing, if I came now, I might tear the head off that young man for prodding that child into shoplifting. And I might also tear the head off Professor Horton, for not at least seeing that his daughter had money for food."

Patsy chuckled. "Aurora, I'd be happy to snap both those heads off for you," she said. "It'll be like snapping peas."

"May I talk to her at least?" Aurora asked.

"She's sleeping," Patsy said. "I'm sure she'll want to talk to you as soon as she wakes up, though."

Patsy looked over at Melanie, pale in the hospital bed—it was easy to tell that she was quite alive because she was snoring a little. Her own daughter, Katie, had been so tired by the time they got Melanie to the hospital that she had been sent home to bed. The two girls were only eight months apart in age; both of them, when tired or sick, still looked about twelve years old.

"I can't believe they put this child in jail in Oxnard," Patsy said. "How's Rosie bearing up under this news?"

"Ask her yourself, I'm handing her the phone," Aurora said. "Thank you, of course. Thank you."

"Hello," Rosie said. "It's just a miracle you was out there. Are you coming back in time for exercise class, or what?"

Just then General Scott stumped into the room. He was down to one crutch and was feeling much more himself—yet he had awakened with a sense of apprehension. Aurora was not beside him. That was often the case, of course, but this time her absence felt different. He would have been hard put to say how an absence could be different, feel different, yet this one did. He thought he heard voices from downstairs, an unusual thing, since it was still dark. Perhaps a burglar had broken in and was holding Aurora at gunpoint. Or perhaps they were merely chatting. He remembered that a harmless madman had somehow managed to get into the bedroom of the Queen of England—the Queen had chatted amiably with him until help came. Perhaps Aurora was chatting amiably with just such a person, but that theory left several questions unanswered, such as why she had gotten out of bed in the first place, and, more critically, why she had gone downstairs. If she merely needed to go to the bathroom, as she sometimes did in the night, there would have been no need for her to go downstairs.

It was all very puzzling and a little worrisome. He thought he heard Rosie's voice, though he couldn't be sure. If he did, that merely added to the mystery—it certainly wasn't time for Rosie to appear. Besides, now that she had Willie Cotts, her new lover, she frequently didn't appear even when it *was* time for her to appear.

He finally decided he had better get up and see what was going on. In his haste he forgot to take off his nightcap, though he did put on his slippers and his bathrobe. To his surprise, Aurora was sitting at the kitchen table with her head in her arms. Rosie was talking on the telephone, and Willie Cotts, a fellow with whom he was having difficulty establishing much rapport, was there too, nervously drinking coffee.

"Oops, the General's up," Rosie said into the phone. "He's still got on his sleeping cap."

"Why oops?" the General asked, removing his cap. "Why can't I just be up, since I'm up?"

"Hector, don't you be cute!" Aurora said, looking up at him indignantly. "Melanie's been arrested for shoplifting and now she's had a miscarriage. It's no time for witticisms."

"Good lord, I'm sorry," the General said. "It wasn't much of a witticism anyway."

"I agree, and that's all the more reason you shouldn't have made it while we're all in this anxious state," Aurora said, wiping her eyes with a napkin.

"He was looking pretty good, but now Aurora's just chewed him out," Rosie informed Patsy, who had inquired about the General's health.

"Why do you suppose he puts up with her?" Patsy inquired.

"Sex—why does anybody put up with anybody?" Rosie said, giving Willie Cotts a tart look. The look caused him to squirm, and also to slurp his coffee in a way that annoyed everyone.

"Who's she talking to?" the General inquired. "If it's the police, why is she talking about us in this way?"

"It's only Patsy, and Patsy has long since known what a mixed bag we are," Aurora informed him, wondering why Rosie had looked with such annoyance at Willie. From what she had seen of him, Willie was an almost desperately obliging man, rather in the mold of her old admirer Vernon Dalhart, whose plane had gone down in Alaska. Willie was twice Vernon's size, but not twice as obliging. There were not enough hours in a day for anyone to be more obliging than Vernon, a thought that caused her to feel sorrowful, since Vernon was dead. Somehow she had not even managed to seduce him, though surely she could have if only she had summoned a degree or two more boldness. Possibly if she had been able to be just a bit bolder, he would have proved as obliging in bed as he had been out of bed—though, she reflected, there would have had to be a rather lengthy training period before Vernon would have even known what obliging was in the context of bed. The sad fact was that it was often empty men like her therapist, Jerry Bruckner, who turned out to be obliging in bed.

It seemed disgraceful that such thoughts persisted in running through her head, even as her granddaughter lay sick in a hospital far away; lately, to her frequent discomfort, or even shame, her thoughts insisted on running in such embarrassing and unproductive directions, willy-nilly, and at the wrong time. It seemed to her that her will must have been damaged, finally, else such things wouldn't happen. The thought made her look grave.

Her grave look frightened the General, who began rather absently to massage the back of her neck. In times of stress Aurora generally welcomed a bit of massaging, but this time, to his horror, his efforts had the opposite effect.

"Don't touch me!" she yelled, jumping up from the table. Her sudden action scared Willie Cotts so badly that he sloshed coffee all over his pants.

Aurora ran upstairs crying, only to run back down, still crying, but purse in hand, seconds later. Before anyone could say a word she was out the back door and gone.

"Good lord," the General said, feeling lame in every sense.

"The General tried to rub her neck, she ran upstairs, she ran downstairs, and now she's out the back door and I just heard her start the car," Rosie said, giving Patsy play-by-play coverage.

"You should let her go, she's just upset," Patsy advised. "She'll go have a cry and come back feeling a lot better, probably."

"That's your opinion. I think what we've probably got here is a car wreck in the making," Rosie said, wondering why Patsy was always so optimistic.

"That's right. Willie, could you stop her? I can't move fast enough," the General said. "I'm sure she's not in a fit state to drive."

Willie Cotts didn't rise—he got several paper napkins and mopped gravely at the large coffee stain on his pants. Much as he had come to love Rosie Dunlup, his dumpling, as he called her in tender moments, there were times such as the one he was just living through when he wondered if trying to keep loving her was quite worth it. There was certainly nothing wrong with Rosie herself, a little flat-chestedness apart, but the family she worked for was both crazy and scary; just being around them made being a prison guard seem like relaxing work. He didn't know what to say to any of them, Mrs. Greenway least of all.

"You heard the General, stop her!" Rosie ordered, annoyed by the methodical way he kept mopping at his coffee stains while the center of the drama, Aurora, was in the process of putting her life at risk in a car wreck in the making.

"Stop her?" Willie said indecisively. He stood up, but made no move toward the door.

"Stop her!" the General said, louder—Rosie's chance comment about the car wreck caused him to remember what a terrible driver Aurora was, even when she was calm. When she was even a little bit flustered no highway in America was likely to contain her—and it was evident from the way she ran out the door sobbing that she was more than a little bit flustered. The situation was well-nigh catastrophic, yet that man Willie Cotts seemed to be glued to the floor. He wasn't stopping her!

"Stop her or you'll be court-martialed!" the General commanded in a shaky voice, forgetting in his worry that he was no longer in a position to court-martial subordinates.

"What's going on?" Patsy asked.

Rosie could still hear Aurora revving her engine—she always revved it for five or ten minutes to reassure herself that the Cadillac was ready for its task. Time was on their side, since she would need another five minutes to ease the big car out of the garage and get it pointed toward the street, but neither of these considerations made it one bit less irritating that Willie Cotts was just standing there, twitching and still pretending to drink his coffee, most of which he had already spilled on himself.

"Aurora's running off, and Willie ain't lifting one finger to stop her, although I've told him to and the General just threatened to court-martial him if he didn't get a move on quick."

"Court-martial him?" Patsy said.

"Yeah, but if it was me he'd get the firing squad," Rosie said, glaring at Willie, whose immobility had come to irritate her almost beyond endurance.

"You know what? I think you all need to get a grip," Patsy advised. "Melanie is in no danger—she's had a rough night, but we've all had a few of those. She's not going to jail for shoplifting the steaks, and she's not going to die. She's young—she'll get over this. I'd like all of you to settle down and get a grip, starting with you.

"I feel sorry for Willie," she added. "Willie's nice—he must feel like he's fallen in with a bunch of totally crazed people."

Rosie didn't care how nice he was—what was driving her crazy was that he wouldn't move! Aurora had stopped revving, which meant that she must be backing.

"Stop her! Stop her!" Rosie yelled at him furiously, ignoring Patsy's comment—although a little later she remembered it and felt somewhat comforted knowing that Patsy thought Willie was nice.

"Shit, okay!" Willie said, yanking his snub-nosed pistol out of its holster and heading for the door.

"Stop right there!" Rosie said, and Willie stopped.

"I thought you wanted him to go. Why'd you tell him to stop?" Patsy wondered.

"Because he drew his stupid gun," Rosie said. "I don't know if I told you, he's a gun nut. I just want him to stop her, not shoot her!"

"Oh," Willie said. He reholstered his gun, carefully snapping the little strap that went behind the hammer. Then he went out the door to stop Aurora.

"You can sure find yourself some slow ones," the General said, sinking shakily into a chair. "I thought that man would never get a move on."

Willie Cotts had a move on, all right, but the move only carried him a few feet out the door. He saw Mrs. Greenway back the car clear of the garage and swing it in a wide arc, its rear end toward the house. In a moment she completed her backing and paused briefly to put the car in forward gear. He was not more than four feet from her when she paused—he could easily have stepped over and grabbed the keys or the steering wheel or something, but he didn't. He just stood there, watching. Mrs. Greenway noticed him and looked out her car window at him. He thought he saw tears on her cheeks, but she did not seem to be angry with him, particularly—certainly she was not as angry as Rosie had been when he finally ran out of the house.

"Goodbye, Willie, I'm sorry I awakened you," Aurora said, as she put the car in gear.

"That's all right, Mrs. Greenway—drive friendly now," Willie said.

Aurora gave him a bit of a smile. "Your companions in misery don't give me credit for knowing how to drive friendly, I'm afraid," she said. "I'm glad that you have a little more confidence in me."

Then she drove away.

After a bit Willie realized that he would have to go back inside and admit that he had not stopped her. He stood a little longer, gathering his courage, and then went back inside.

"Did you stop her?" Rosie asked.

"No, I didn't, I ain't her boss and you ain't either," Willie said with what firmness he could muster.

"What'd I tell you?" the General said.

13

"It's been my lifelong habit to do this after deaths," Aurora admitted, not happily, as they lay in Jerry's bed. The lower lip, hairy wrists, and sturdy legs, once she finally got to touch them, had been as good as she imagined, though the man himself as a lover was not quite all she had hoped he might be. She had arrived at dawn and had rung Jerry's bell in more ways than one; but now that it was rung, she felt troubled. Her body was at rest, but not her spirit. Her granddaughter had had a terrible experience, and in response she had driven to Bellaire and thrust herself into the bed of a man she scarcely knew, a *faux* doctor of some sort who just happened to have, for her, an intense physical appeal, the very satisfying results of which she could still feel in her body. Not for years, or even decades, had a man tempted her so. Now she had him: why wasn't it bringing her peace?

"I think a good many people do it after deaths," Jerry said.

"Yes," Aurora agreed. "Not a few have done it with me at such times. Some of my least ladylike experiences have occurred right after funerals.

"Sometimes within minutes after funerals," she added, remembering an occasion in Philadelphia. Trevor's beautiful young sister had been drowned in a boating accident for which Trevor was at least partly responsible. At the graveside she had begun to have a terribly mortal feeling—Annabelle was really dead, and dead so young; she herself was only a year older. Her mortal feelings got worse, and Trevor's mortal feelings seemed to get worse too. While the mourners were filing to their handsome black cars, she and Trevor wandered off, glued themselves together, and made love violently on a cot in a little gardener's hut at the back of the cemetery. The body forgets, pleasures and pains alike, and Aurora had forgotten much pleasure and some pain, yet she hadn't forgotten the soaking few minutes with Trevor in the cemetery in Philadelphia. Even now, remembering, she felt a certain stirring, and put a hand on Jerry Bruckner, only to withdraw it a second later. Somehow, in all her doing and forgetting, the expense of spirit was adding up. Jerry was decades younger—what was she doing, touching him? What was she doing?

"Was it different because I'm so old?" Aurora asked, quite unable to repress the question.

"Of course not," Jerry said. He felt restful. It was always reassuring to get to make love to a woman there was a good chance he might never get to make love to. He almost always did eventually get to sleep with those women he thought he might have only a slim chance with, but each time there was an element of surprise that was sort of nice. His answer had been a bit of a lie, because at first he had felt nervous and careful, and it was in his mind that Aurora was the age of his mother. But now he was merely wondering if Sondra would drop by and catch them. Sometimes Sondra did drop by on the way to take her little boy, Timmy, to play school. Sondra was terribly jealous, and if she caught them she would have a violent fit and that would be that—Sondra wouldn't stand for anything less than total possession. If he even let his gaze linger too long on a girl he happened to see in a restaurant, Sondra would notice and have a violent fit.

Her violent fits were tiring, and yet he rather hoped Sondra wouldn't come by and catch him in bed with Aurora Greenway. In his experience the arrival of a new woman rarely meant the departure of the woman who was already there. Aurora hadn't been one bit hesitant about lovemaking, but she *was* hesitant about him. She might be relaxed in her body, but she wasn't relaxed in her mind. She might decide in a day or two to give him a thumbs down—it was what she clearly felt she *should* give him, although she didn't want to. But if she should change her mind, he didn't want to lose Sondra, a possessive shrew who nonetheless had certain perfections, her nipples, for example. Nipples could be all sorts of ways and shouldn't be that big a deal, but Sondra's just happened to be exactly the way his eyes thought nipples ought to be—ditto her shoulders, ditto her legs. One of the ways in which he knew himself to be slightly obsessive was his desire to have the various erotic body parts look *exactly* as he liked them to look. It wasn't that in his actual behavior he was that rigid or exclusive—he had slept with and loved lots of women who didn't have nipples or legs that looked exactly as he thought nipples or legs should look. Still, when someone *did* happen to have exactly the right look, it was a nice extra—nice enough to cause him to put up with such things as violent fits.

"Men should learn not to use the phrase 'of course' when attempting to reassure women about sexual matters," Aurora told him. "I was feeling sad, and what you said didn't help, because it can't be true. It must make some difference to you sexually that I'm thirty years older than you."

"It didn't, though," Jerry said, knowing that he was fudging just a bit.

"Well, if not, it was only because it was our first time," Aurora said, stroking his leg.

"You don't seem to ever say anything true to me," she said, feeling her melancholy deepen. She raised up on an elbow to look him in the eye.

"You open your mouth but all that comes out are statements in the order of 'Of course not,' or 'It didn't, though,'" she said. "If you don't wish to comment when I make a remark, don't comment. I resent being put off with phrases like that. I *am* older, you know—I have my insecurities. If you can't honestly help me with them, then just lie there and look appealing. I'll talk for both of us. Maybe I only want someone who looks appealing, anyway."

"I never know what to say when women ask me about sex," Jerry admitted. It was annoying that women were so unreasonably honest.

Aurora smiled. Perhaps this fellow with the satisfactory legs and great lower lip was empty because no one had ever applied themselves to filling him. The thought made her feel a little better. He seemed very boyish in a gentle, half-shy way. Perhaps with a little application on her part, he wouldn't prove quite hopeless.

"I thought sex was the one thing psychiatrists always knew what to say about," she said.

"Not me," Jerry said, wishing she would just shut up. But he could tell from the look in her eye that she wasn't going to shut up. Even as he wished she would shut up he recognized that the most lovable thing about this woman, and the reason he himself was half in love with her, was because she was determined not to shut up, ever, not till the day of her death. And in the face, she *didn't* seem old—not to him.

"Baloney," Aurora said, scooting closer so that her face was only an inch or so from his. "Sex requires just as much interpretation as any other complicated thing. What's the point of a psychiatrist who won't talk about it?"

"Maybe I should go back to being a stand-up comic," Jerry offered.

"Un—uh," Aurora said, wishing he would kiss her. "You're not sad enough to be a comic, but you are sad enough to be an interesting lover."

Ten minutes after Aurora left, Sondra did show up. Timmy was running a fever so she had left him home with a sitter. She was in jogging clothes and wanted him to jog with her. Actually, she didn't jog, she race-walked, a form of exercise that made Jerry feel profoundly silly—so silly that he had never learned to do it correctly. Sondra was always having to stop and show him how to move his hips and swing his arms.

Having to stop annoyed her; she was capable of race-walking five miles without stopping, and it pissed her that Jerry was hardly capable of walking a whole mile without his form going to pieces.

"If you would just concentrate you could do it right!" she complained the third time she stopped to correct his form.

"Don't pay any attention to me," Jerry said. It was muggy and he felt tired. Although she didn't require race-walking, Aurora took a lot of energy. Aurora required thinking, which was at least as difficult as race-walking.

"Just go off and leave me," he added. Often Sondra did go off and leave him far behind, but then she would do a U-turn and reappear, looking pissed, to correct his form.

"No!" Sondra protested. "We're supposed to be doing this exercise together, right?"

"Well, I guess," Jerry said.

"What's the point of doing something together if the person you're doing it together with is always a mile behind?" Sondra asked.

"I may not know what the point is," Jerry admitted.

"Not only do you have a very bad form as a race-walker, but you don't have very good answers either," Sondra informed him as she was trying to show him how to swing his arms.

Aurora had said almost exactly the same thing to him, not two hours before, when he hadn't been able to come up with anything to say about sex.

"I guess I'm just boring," he had said.

Aurora stared at him with her large green eyes when he said it.

"That's the possum's defense," she said, after a bit.

Jerry decided he liked the line, though. It was sort of pleasant to claim boringness while enduring the scrutiny of women who were not boring.

"I guess I'm just boring," he said to Sondra now, as she was making him swing his arms back and forth in the approved race-walking style.

"That's right, you're boring, you fucker!" Sondra said, as she went race-walking away.

14

After leaving Jerry, Aurora's spirits suddenly lifted. She had done the presumably degrading thing—seduced a man thirty years her junior—and had emerged from it apparently undegraded. Her dignity, as far as she could tell, was intact. It was a little disappointing that Jerry wasn't that expert a lover, since, as far as she could see, he had very little to do *except* become an expert lover; he had the equipment but seemed to lack the temperament, somehow. It was an area of endeavor in which she had always frankly sought finesse; but it seemed that finesse was no easier to find when one was ending up than it had been when one was starting out.

Still, for all that Jerry Bruckner lacked finesse, as well as the lustful temperament, Aurora felt lifted. At least, by golly, she had managed once more to get a man to do what she wanted. She had to make the move herself, but then she had almost always had to make the move herself—it seemed rather a matter for congratulation that she hadn't lost the boldness that it took to make the move.

She decided that a hearty breakfast would be a good way to reward herself, and it occurred to her that it might be nice to take breakfast with Jane, who would be getting off work about then. Against everyone's wishes, she had been doing the night shift lately.

Delighted with her idea, she sped over to Fairview Street, arriving just in time to see Jane sell a spring roll to a man who was delivering beer. The sight of delivery trucks always brought to mind Royce Dunlup, Rosie's long-deceased husband, a man who spent most of his life delivering potato chips in a little blue truck. Aurora herself had crunched quite a few of Royce's potato chips. Royce himself had had a big crush on her, much to Rosie's annoyance. It didn't seem so long ago that Royce had sat in her kitchen, exhibiting his crush as best he could by staring at her worshipfully whenever Rosie happened to leave the room—which wasn't often. And yet it *was* long ago, and Royce was dead, a thought that caused the soaring kite of her good spirits, lifted by the morning and sex, to dip just slightly.

To get her good spirits soaring again, she disembarked from her Cadillac and had a couple of spring rolls herself as preparation for her breakfast.

"Ten years ago you couldn't have sold such a thing as a spring roll in this town," she said to Jane, who looked at her in the cool way that—though a little unnerving—was just Jane's way of looking. At that moment Mr. Wey, the Vietnamese gentleman who owned the 7-Eleven, popped out of a little room at the back where he had been making the spring rolls.

"We sell a hundred a day," he said. Mr. Wey was very proud of the success of his spring rolls.

"My goodness, do you?" Aurora said. "I might take a few home to Rosie and the General."

Rosie had called Teddy about Melanie's difficulty, and Teddy had informed Jane, who was not terribly sympathetic. Much of her time at Mr. Wey's 7-Eleven was spent watching for shoplifters, and the thought that Melanie had been dumb enough to shoplift two steaks annoyed her. Teddy was horrified that Jane was annoyed—he believed in instant forgiveness, no matter what the crime. But Jane didn't. To her, shoplifting meant awkwardness, confrontation, police, and extra bookkeeping; she often scolded Teddy because of his unwillingness to confront shoplifters, even when he caught them red-handed. In her view it was symptomatic of Teddy's unwillingness to confront the messy nature of life itself, which amounted to cowardice. She was feeling quite stony when Aurora breezed in. She was preparing to go home and tell Teddy in no uncertain terms what she thought of his sister's actions, and also what she thought about his wishy-washy attitude in relation to the hard questions life posed. As always, when he was confronted, Teddy's hands would shake and his voice would become high and squeaky. Bump would hide in the closet and talk to Kermit the Frog, his closest companion now, and the day would be off to a stupid start, all because Melanie was a pawn of her boyfriend who was too lazy to pay for the stupid steaks he felt he had a right to eat whenever he wanted.

Thinking about all that made Jane feel fed up. Her mate was a moral wimp and, for that matter, so was her lover. Claudia Seay was just as wimpy as Teddy when it came to such things as shoplifting, or anything else that required difficult action. Jane spent more and more of her time being fed up with both of them. Next time some Cajun cocksman wandered in and asked her to go dancing she might just take him up on it.

Her stony mood wasn't exactly the best mood in which to go to breakfast with Aurora, who waltzed in in what looked like her nightgown and housecoat. Now she had eaten two spring rolls, which she clearly had no intention of paying for, and besides that she was shamelessly flirting with Mr. Wey.

"Oh, come on, Jane, don't deny me," Aurora said, when Jane was acting as if she might decline the breakfast. "We won't talk about Melanie. I'm as annoyed with the girl as you are. She was not brought up to shoplift at the whim of her lover, I can tell you that. When she gets her strength back she's in for a stern talking to from her grandmother, I can assure you."

"What will we talk about, Aurora?" Jane asked, still cool to the notion of breakfast. She gave Aurora a look that was somewhat hostile.

"Lovers," Aurora said. "I just took a new one. I'll tell you about mine if you'll tell me about yours."

Mr. Wey was so startled by the remark that he dropped a spring roll, and the tongs he was holding it with, into a wastebasket. His English was improving, but it wasn't perfect. Perhaps he had misunderstood. Then he concluded that he *had* misunderstood, and hurried to the back of the store to straighten up the paper towels. The spring roll and the tongs remained in the wastebasket.

Jane was always slightly annoyed with herself when she gave in to Aurora. Sometimes she *didn't* give in, but this time she did—it was hard to say no to a woman well up in years who could be that brash about taking a lover. At the Pig Stand no one seemed to notice that Aurora was in her nightgown and housecoat—and no reason why they should, since half the men smoking and eating breakfast were just wearing undershirts and shorts.

"You must come here a lot," Jane said, after the third waitress had said good morning to Aurora, calling her by her first name.

"Yes, I come here to think about my mother," Aurora said. "Also, of course, I eat."

She was, at the moment, eating a plate of scrambled eggs, and pancakes had been ordered.

"Why do you have to drive all the way over here just to think about your mother?" Jane asked. She was having buckwheat cakes and they were, she had to admit, very good. "If I could find a place where I could *stop* thinking about my mother I'd eat there all the time," she added.

"My mother never ate in a place like this in her life, not even in Maine," Aurora said. "There were certain constraints imposed on ladies in her day—she saw little of the lower classes, and yet she took a lover from the lower classes."

"I wish you wouldn't call them the lower classes," Jane said. "That's so snobbish. At least call them the working classes."

"Oh, well," Aurora said, "the terms may change, but the facts are the same. My mother fell in love with a gardener. He was a neighbor's gardener at first, but my mother persuaded my father to hire him, and then he became our gardener. He was a lovely man, one of the finest I've known. His name was Sam. Just the other day I used his name when I needed to invent a lover in a hurry."

"Why did you need to invent a lover in a hurry?" Jane asked, amused. "I thought you *had* a new lover."

"I do now, but I just took him this morning," Aurora said, waving for them to hurry up with the pancakes. "I didn't have him when I needed him for political purposes—that occurred when I discovered Pascal with his hand up a young woman's skirt. I took Sam's name and made him seventeen years old.

"I've often wondered what my mother's life would have been if she'd met *her* Sam when she was seventeen," she said, as the pancakes arrived. "He would have been considered entirely unsuitable. Great pressure would have been put on her to give him up. Still, I think she might have bolted. She was very brave when it came to acting on her emotions. If she'd met Sam a little sooner, she might have bolted."

"I'm glad I wasn't born then," Jane said. "I wouldn't have put up with any of that shit."

"I expect not," Aurora said. "Is your girlfriend nice?"

"Yeah," Jane said, startled, "Did Teddy tell you?"

"Of course. I wormed it out of him," Aurora said. "Do you mind?"

Jane didn't, actually. In a way she was even glad. Crazy as Aurora might appear to be, she was at least tolerant about things most people weren't tolerant about. She clearly didn't think it was a tragedy that she had a girlfriend, whereas her own mother, had she known, would have thought it was the end of the world.

"She's a female Teddy," Jane admitted. "I guess I must be drawn to Teddy types, for some reason. Now I have two of them."

"How fortunate," Aurora said. "The Ted type is actually a very nice type. I wish I had one.

"In fact, I wish I had two," she added.

"So what about the lover?" Jane asked. "Who did you seduce now, Aurora?"

Aurora grinned. "My shrink," she said. "Dr. Bruckner."

"Is that man a Freudian, or what?" Jane asked. She had met Jerry at Aurora's dinner party and thought he was really attractive, almost suspiciously so—he had bassetlike qualities that were pretty appealing, at least. It was sort of a shock that Aurora had actually slept with a man that much younger than herself—although why it should be a shock, Jane didn't quite know. It *was* sort of a shock, though, logical or not.

"Did you really sleep with him or are you two just thinking about it?" she asked.

Aurora looked at her pleasantly, but she didn't answer.

Jane wished she could take back the question. "Sometimes when I'm thinking about it I almost convince myself I've gone ahead and done it, when I haven't," she explained.

"Yep, that's common," Aurora admitted. "I was so attracted to Lord Mountbatten that I almost persuaded myself we'd had a romance on a boat."

"But you didn't?" Jane asked.

"Alas, I didn't," Aurora said. "He was on the boat, though, and I saw him. If he'd ever displayed the slightest interest I would have been putty in his hands, but he didn't."

"Yeah, I met Jack Nicholson at a party once and had the same problem," Jane said. "Is your shrink nice?"

"Nice, but disappointed," Aurora said. "I do think disappointment ruins more people than all the diseases known to man. It ruined my lovely mother. Perhaps that's why I've struggled all my life to keep it from ruining me."

"You don't seem disappointed, Aurora," Jane said. "You look like you've kept your fight."

"I've kept my fight," Aurora said. "I hope you keep yours, Jane. In a few more years you may find that keeping it isn't as easy as it once was."

"It isn't that easy *now*," Jane told her. "Sometimes I get pretty depressed. If it wasn't for Bump I'd probably go crazy again—Bump sort of closes that option."

"Yes, insofar as it's an option," Aurora said.

"Did your mother finally go crazy?" Jane inquired. Aurora occasionally mentioned her mother, but she had never before said anything really interesting about her. Now it seemed a gardener had been the love of her life. It wasn't so hard to understand how that could happen. Most of the gardeners she had met had seemed like pretty healthy guys.

"No, she didn't go crazy," Aurora said. "My father found out about Sam and moved out and never spoke to my mother again. It was rather Lady Chatterley. My father had no interest in sleeping with my mother, but he was highly annoyed that she had slept with a gardener—not once, but often."

"How did your father treat you?" Jane asked.

"He came to my wedding, got drunk, and kissed me," Aurora said. "It was not the sort of kiss a bride is looking for from her father on her wedding day, either. I saw him only twice after that—once at a lunch in New York, which didn't go well, and the other time at his funeral."

"What about your mother and Sam?" Jane asked. "Did it last forever?"

"It did," Aurora said. "Forever was only another five years, though. Sam fell out of a tree he was pruning and broke his back. A doctor did something wrong in the hospital and Sam died. Mother went slightly off, after that. Her last beau was a Portuguese fiddler, who also tried to kiss me."

She felt a momentary sadness from thinking about how sad her mother had looked in her last days. The fiddler had tried to kiss every woman who came to visit, but her mother put up with him.

"Has Pascal ever bothered you?" she asked, realizing suddenly that Pascal looked not unlike her mother's Portuguese fiddler.

"Don't sit there and think bad thoughts," Jane said. "We've eaten, let's go. Pascal is a nice man and he's never tried to kiss me. It's the General who's the flasher."

"I know, just don't look," Aurora said, wondering if the Pig Stand would have mince pie at such an early hour.

"Hector's dotty half the time now," she added. "He seems to think that if he can just manage a return to the golf course his mind might come back, but I think that's a slim hope. On the other hand, when he's not dotty he's the same old annoying Hector. I wonder if hitting a golf ball would really bring his mind back."

"It's a slim hope," Jane said. Most of the time, in her opinion, General Scott was way around the bend.

15

When Melanie didn't come back from the supermarket with the steaks she was supposed to shoplift, Bruce got worried and then more worried, but he didn't know what to do with his worry except smoke dope and wait. Something was way out of order, but he didn't know what. Melly was very anxious to keep him pleased. If she'd got the steaks she would have come right back with them.

By the time three hours had passed, he knew something had to be *way* out of order, and he began to make up disaster scenarios, some of which were pretty paranoid. There were tough gangs in the Valley—some gang members could have been prowling around the supermarket, in which case, by this time, Melanie could have gotten gang-banged, or even murdered. She could also have made the mistake of hitchhiking, though the supermarket wasn't that far away, and she had said she was just going to walk. But if she got lazy on the walk back she might have hitchhiked—she was pretty bold about it—and if the wrong guy picked her up she could also be a corpse. Or, if she wasn't a corpse, she could be in Mexico or Nevada or somewhere.

By the time it was ten o'clock, Bruce was feeling frantic despite all the dope he had smoked. Maybe he had got very mixed up and it was her night to work at the deli—but that couldn't be it, otherwise she wouldn't have marched off to shoplift their supper.

Still, he got so jittery that he had to do something, so he went down to the pay phone at a nearby laundromat and called the deli. Just as he had feared, it wasn't her night to work, and she wasn't there. Since he was already out, he jumped in the car and raced over to the supermarket, but it was closed and the parking lot was empty except for a couple of old people walking their poodles. Bruce felt like running over the stupid poodles, he was so worried, but he managed to restrain himself. He didn't know what to do. There was a hospital not too far from the supermarket—he passed it every day on his way to the filling station—so he cruised over there, thinking maybe she had been the victim of a hit-and-run, but nope—no Melanie Horton had been admitted to the hospital.

Then it occurred to him that maybe Melanie had finally got caught shoplifting. They had been supplementing their diet with a little shoplifting for several weeks, and Melanie kept complaining that she hated doing it and that it wasn't right. Even if it was a big, gross supermarket owned by slimy capitalists who exploited the poor, that didn't, in her view, make it right to steal steaks. Also, just doing it made her feel guilty. The fact that she was shoplifting was bound to be obvious to security people or even just simple grocery clerks: if she kept on doing it, she was bound to get caught, and then what?

Bruce soon concluded that that was probably the simplest explanation for her disappearance, but it didn't help him much with his dilemma. If she had been caught, where was she? Despite performing some minor crimes, such as hauling marijuana, he had never been anywhere near a jail in his whole life and had no idea how to find the one they might have taken Melanie to. Actually, the mere thought of a cop so depraved that he would arrest an obviously sweet person such as Melanie was pretty nerve-racking.

Thinking about *that* made him regret his folly in demanding steaks. There was an excellent cheap Thai place only two blocks from their apartment: they should just have eaten Thai.

But it was obviously too late for that, and his stomach was so upset he had to stop at a convenience store and buy some Maalox just to quiet it down. He went back to the grocery-store parking lot, hoping a miracle would happen and Melanie would be standing there, but the only ones there were more old people walking even worse dogs than poodles—midget Mexican dogs without hair and dachshunds and Pekinese. The parking lot seemed to be a kind of dog-walking sanctuary for old couples with tiny dogs. Melanie was *not* standing there, and he really didn't know what to do. If she was in jail, she couldn't have called him, because of their lack of a phone; she might have called her father, but probably not. She might have called her grandmother, in which case he might as well shoot himself. Her grandmother thought he was scum anyway—what was she going to think now?

Several cop cars passed. Once or twice he thought of flagging one down, but seven or eight passed without his being able to muster the nerve to flag one down. What was he going to say if a cop did consent to stop? Please bring my girlfriend back, all I wanted was a steak?

What he did was drive aimlessly around for about another hour, not getting too far out of the area, in case Melanie crawled out of a ditch or something and appeared on the sidewalk. The mere sight of her would have made him the happiest man alive.

To calm his nerves he stopped at a pay phone and on impulse made a collect call to Beverly in Houston. He didn't really expect her to be home—after all, it was Saturday night —but she was, and not only that, she accepted the call.

"Hi," he said tentatively. He hadn't really expected to get her, and wasn't really prepared with things to say.

"I'm real pissed off at you. Where are you?" Beverly said at once. Like a lot of Houston rich girls, Beverly was pretty up front.

"Uh—L.A.—I'm just out here trying to be an actor," Bruce said.

"What about that fat whore you left with?" Beverly asked. She more or less despised Melanie, although they had once been best friends.

"She's sort of become a missing person," Bruce admitted.

"Good, I hope she stays missing for the next fifty years," Beverly said. She displayed no interest in why Melanie might be missing.

Bruce found making conversation a little difficult. Beverly was totally pissed off, just as she said, and it was sort of hard to get around that fact and have a normal conversation, particularly when he was really worried about Melanie.

"Do you still have the Ferrari?" he asked finally.

"No. Thanks to you my parents sold it, you dickhead," Beverly said coldly.

"So what are you driving?" Bruce asked.

"Just a stupid little BMW, thanks to you," Beverly said.

"BMWs are nice cars, though," Bruce pointed out.

"Not as nice as Ferraris," Beverly said. "Half the kids I know have BMWs. I hate having the same car as half the kids I know."

You'll live, Bruce thought, but he didn't say it. Beverly was ticked enough as it was.

"I heard Melanie is pregnant, is that true?" Beverly asked.

"Uh, yeah, she's pregnant," Bruce said.

"If you marry her, that's it for us," Beverly informed him. "You're not fucking me again if you marry that fat whore."

Bruce didn't know what to say to that. After all, he lived in L.A. and she lived in Houston, and she hadn't much liked having sex with him anyway. Why was she suddenly talking about fucking?

"So do you care whether you ever fuck me again, asshole?" Beverly asked.

"Yeah, sure I do," Bruce said. He didn't feel that he should stop and consider when asked a question like that by a girl. Was he going to tell her he *didn't* care whether he ever fucked her again? No way—better just to lie.

"What if I show up in Beverly Hills?" Beverly asked. "Are you going to be too scared of your wife to get it on?"

"She's not my wife," Bruce reminded her.

"Answer the question," Beverly said.

"Why would you come out here?" Bruce said—he felt he should stall on this one.

"Are you just gonna be dull?" Beverly asked. "My mother comes out there all the time to shop. I could come with my mother if I wanted to."

Bruce was thinking that a pretty big change must have come over Beverly. In Houston she had rarely been too eager to get it on, and when he did manage to persuade her, she mainly seemed interested in getting it over with. Not once had she ever seemed to get *into* it to the extent that Melanie did. Melly was a girl who really got into having sex—whatever was happening, she was *there*; it was not too surprising that she'd got pregnant.

Beverly, though, had quite a few hang-ups in the sexual area. Most of the time she seemed more interested in makeup than she did in sex. So why was she suddenly talking about journeying to L.A. just to fuck him?

"I could probably talk her into coming next week," Beverly said. "Have you got a job, or what?"

"Uh, yeah, part time," Bruce said. "I'm in an acting class.'"

"Big deal," Beverly said. "How do I get in touch with you, if we come?"

"I'm not sure," Bruce said. "We haven't been able to afford a phone. I guess you could leave a message at the filling station."

"You don't even have a phone?" Beverly said.

"Out here it costs a fortune just to get one," Bruce informed her. Sometimes her rich-girlness was pretty hard to take. It was clear she was shocked to discover that she actually knew someone who was too poor to afford a phone.

At that point the conversation stalled. Bruce gave her the number of the gas station, though he wasn't too sure he wanted to get himself involved with Beverly again even if she came to L.A. for the specific purpose of having sex with him. It was a little weird. Of all the people in the world he could have called to calm his nerves, Beverly was probably the number one worst choice. As he now remembered, nothing that happened with Beverly had ever made him calmer. It just made him feel more zingy, usually. At the moment, his big problem was finding Melanie, Beverly's deadly enemy. So what was he doing standing at a pay phone at Burbank and Vineland, talking to a girl in Houston who thought he was an asshole? He had done it himself, but it didn't add up. Now the question was, how to get Beverly off the phone?

"If I come, you better show up, and you better do something pretty special, or that's it," Beverly said, while he was considering the problem of how to get her off the phone.

"You better at least take me to the Ivy to make up for all the trouble you've caused," Beverly said. "I'd still have a Ferrari if it wasn't for you."

"What's the Ivy?" Bruce asked.

"It's a restaurant, dumbbell," Beverly said. "All the movie stars go there. You live in Hollywood—haven't you even heard of the Ivy?"

"We live way over in the Valley," Bruce told her. "We don't get to Hollywood too much."

"We, we, we, and this little piggy went to the market," Beverly said meanly. "I'm looking at my calendar and next Wednesday looks clear. You just better show up at the Beverly Hills Hotel next Wednesday and take me to the Ivy or you're never getting any more from me."

"Beverly, I can't even afford to *park* at the Beverly Hills Hotel," Bruce said. "I just work part time at a gas station. That restaurant probably costs more than I make in a month."

"Are you telling me nothing doing?" Beverly said. The next thing he knew she had slammed the phone down, accomplishing just what he had been trying to think how to accomplish. The phone call was definitely over. Calling her in the first place had been one of his worst ideas in recent times—not as bad as sending Melanie off to shoplift steaks, but not a prize idea, either.

Still, he felt a little jittery. Beverly was perfectly capable of hanging up on him and then expecting him to show up at the hotel anyway even though he had just pointed out that he couldn't afford the restaurant. Beverly had a real blind spot when it came to money—she just assumed he could get it and spend it on her if he really wanted to. If he didn't get it and spend it on her, then all the problems of life were his fault.

Just thinking about Beverly made Melanie seem a thousand times better than he thought she was when she was in the dumps or had had a fight. The phone call shook him up and made him really want to solve the main problem, which was Melanie. It made him want to solve it so badly he even stopped a cop car. He waved his hands and the car wheeled over and stopped. The cop behind the wheel looked at him as if he were a banana peel or something. He did not look even the slightest bit friendly.

"Hi," Bruce said. He felt he had better talk fast before the cop got out of the car and beat the shit out of him. "If someone living in this area got arrested, where would they take her?" he asked nervously.

"What'd she do?" the cop asked. He had a kind of southern voice.

"I don't know, she just hasn't come home," Bruce said.

"*She* who?" the cop asked.

"Her name's Melanie Horton—she's my girlfriend," Bruce said. "I checked with the Valley hospital and she's not there. I thought maybe she got drunk and made a disturbance and got picked up."

"You mean she's a hooker?" the cop asked.

"Oh, no," Bruce said. "She's not a hooker. I just thought she might have got drunk and caused trouble."

The cop who had been sitting in the passenger seat got out and came around the back of the car. He was a hefty white man with a gun on his hip that looked big enough to stop an elephant. Bruce was really beginning to wish he hadn't had the idea of stopping the police car.

"What's this hooker's name?" the hefty cop asked.

"Sir, she isn't a hooker," Bruce said, as politely as possible. "She's my fiancé. She's way late getting home, and I just got worried, that's all. Her name's Melanie Horton.

"She's pregnant," he added, thinking that fact might make the cops a little less hostile to him.

"You think this fucker's a pimp?" the large cop asked his partner.

"Could be," the other cop said. "A pimply pimp."

He smiled at his own wit, but the other cop didn't smile. He took a little sinus sniffer out of his pocket and used it on both nostrils, all the while looking at Bruce as if Bruce were a bug it might be nice to step on.

"Sir, I'm not a pimp," Bruce said. "I work at a gas station on Van Nuys Boulevard."

The cop put the cap back on his sinus sniffer and strolled back around the car.

"Try Oxnard," he said, "If she got picked up around here, that's where they took her."

It took Bruce a few minutes to calm down enough to drive, once the cops left. Talking to cops made him feel some high anxiety even if he was just getting a speeding ticket. Once he had got stopped for speeding when he had marijuana in the trunk; the highway patrolman hadn't looked in the trunk, but Bruce had been so scared he had trouble even driving to Dallas. His legs were so weak they didn't want to work the pedals.

When he finally located the Oxnard police station, five or six women who definitely looked like hookers were standing on the sidewalk, redoing their makeup while they waited for cabs. Inside, he had to wait so long that he almost nodded off; it was hot and boring in the waiting room, and the clerks had a tendency to do absolutely nothing unless you bugged them. He himself had always had a problem with public officials—he didn't enjoy bugging them, or even approaching them. Still, it was obvious he would sit there all night if he didn't bug somebody: every fifteen minutes or so he would head back to the counter and stand there, trying to look polite. Two or three sad Mexican men who looked as if they might be gardeners were also standing there looking polite. Actually, everyone waiting in the police station *was* polite— it was only the clerks on duty who had a don't-give-a-shit attitude.

Finally a fat little white girl clerk took pity on Bruce and looked Melanie up in the computer.

"Oh, she was the one who got sick," the clerk said. "Wasn't she the one they thought had a miscarriage?" she asked, turning to another clerk. The second clerk was counting receipts or something, and took a while to answer.

"Maybe," the other clerk said, not very concerned with the problem.

"'Oh, no!" Bruce said, loudly enough that both women looked at him.

"Didn't they say she went to Cedars of Sinai?" the first clerk said. "I think her mother and her sister came and got her. Two women, anyway. Seems like I remember Cedars of Sinai."

"What's Cedars of Sinai?" Bruce asked.

"Hospital," the fat clerk said. She gave him a friendly look, his first in a while. Bruce could tell she thought he was cute —or else she was just feeling sorry for him.

"Is it in the Valley?" he asked.

"No way," the clerk said. "It's in Beverly Hills or West Hollywood. It's not in the Valley."

It was nearly two in the morning when Bruce found the hospital and persuaded them to let him go up to the room. He had to tell five or six nurses that he and Melanie were engaged—even after that, he got lost and had to retrace his steps. He had figured out that it must be Patsy Carpenter and her daughter Katie who had got Melanie out of jail. He had only met Patsy once, in Houston, and had never met Katie at all, although Melanie was always talking about how they ought to go see her. They had meant to go see her, but kept putting it off—Melanie was insecure about whether Katie really liked her or would just be seeing them to be polite.

By the time he finally found the hall where Melanie's room was, he had built up a little anxiety about having to face Patsy

Carpenter. After all, he had given the order for the shoplifting—she might be pretty mad.

But then he bumped right into her. She was just coming out of the room when he finally found it.

"Oh, Bruce," she said, "good." She looked tired, but she actually gave him a hug—it startled him. She seemed, to his relief, perfectly nice, really nice.

"Melly was pretty sick when we left the jail, we didn't have time to go by and get you—and of course there's no phone," Patsy said. "How in the world did you find us?"

"Just kept trying," Bruce said, very relieved that she wasn't mad.

"Go on in, she's sleeping," Patsy said, "She'll be glad to see you when she wakes up, though. I was just going to look for the Coke machine."

"To the left, I just passed it," Bruce said.

16

Patsy's second husband, Tomas, had made no bones about the fact that he hated creative women—women painters, women writers, women singers. "They should just make dresses," he said. The one creative woman he ever spoke admiringly of was Norma Kamali—even in that case, Patsy never figured out whether he liked Kamali's dresses or her looks. He disliked actresses, ballerinas, ceramicists, sculptresses. His secretary, his receptionist, and all his junior architects were male. The mere suggestion that a woman could ever be an architect sent him into violent spasms of contempt. Patsy had once taken the girls to Washington to see the Vietnam Memorial. When they got home and she began to sing the praises of Maya Lin, Tomas slapped her right in the driveway, in front of the girls—he set one of her suitcases down and slapped her.

Successful as he was at designing houses for producers and rich stockbrokers, Tomas's dream had been to design a museum. He tried for all the local commissions, including the Getty, but was never a finalist. He applied in Dallas, Atlanta, Hartford, Tacoma, and Stuttgart, but when he finally did get a commission to build a museum it was only in Guadalajara. "The last place in the world I want to spend five minutes," he said bitterly. Tomas hated Mexico, hated its poverty and its excesses, hated his own Mexicanness. He went to great lengths to conceal the fact that he had been born in Tijuana. He took the commission, though, and insulted Guadalajara by building them the museum he had wanted to build in Stuttgart. When Patsy tried to remonstrate with him he screamed at her and told her to shut up. "What do you know?" he said. "Mexicans are fascists, like Germans. They deserve a German museum."

It was during the first years of her marriage to Tomas that Patsy let her own small hopes for creativity die. In Mill Valley, once her father died and left her a little money, she had underwritten a small review and published two stories and a poem in it. In Taos she helped a theater group get off the ground and made most of the costumes for it. They did Brecht's *Caucasian Chalk Circle*, to local acclaim. She had started and abandoned three novels, and had written more than five hundred pages of the last one when she quit.

For three or four years she painted; she had a show in Carmel and another in Newport Beach. Tomas refused to go to the openings with her; he refused to so much as look at the paintings and insisted that she keep all of them at her studio, far from the house. He wouldn't even let her hang a small gouache in Katie's room, although Katie liked it and begged him.

At one point he allowed her a kiln; her pot-making was improving, but then, after a quarrel, Tomas broke all her pots. After that, the kiln went unused. Patsy could never summon the spirit to resume.

A wealthy man in Santa Barbara who owned a fairly respectable West Coast publishing company was eager to publish one of her novels, if she would just finish one. He was a nice, sweet man, disappointed in himself in many of the ways she was disappointed in herself; eventually she slept with him, but she never finished a novel.

When she finally gave up on creating, she consoled herself

with the thought that patron-appreciators were important too. She was sleeping with a bright, voluble young poet at the time. His name was Matt, but he called himself Mathias, and he was busy with a new translation of Rilke that the same wealthy man in Santa Barbara was going to publish. Matt told Patsy about all the rich women who had kept Rilke going; for all his brains, Matt was pretty transparent. He obviously thought she should support him in the kind of luxury Rilke had been accustomed to and which the rich Continental ladies had been happy to supply.

Amused, Patsy supplied it to the extent of buying Matt a BMW motorcycle. For a while they rode the motorcycle to the more fashionable dance spots in L.A. That was during the time when Tomas was dying; but somehow, in dying, Tomas managed to cancel her attraction to Matt. It was because, she decided, she was such a snob about art. Horrible and cruel though Tomas had been, he *had* had a gift she couldn't help but respect. Tomas's contempt for almost everything was horribly self-destructive, but he *did* have standards, and he *was* first-rate. Even architects who despised him, and who easily out-politicked him when it came to commissions, respected his work.

Patsy knew that her attraction to the first-rate was snobbish, and that, as far as her own life went, it was as self-destructive as Tomas's far-reaching contempt; but she couldn't get rid of it. Even her girls teased her about it—they themselves had a healthy capacity to deal with all kinds of slop, artwise, and they constantly mocked her high-mindedness. Once they got radicalized, they argued that the sums she doled out to mime troupes or string quartets or poetry reviews could be better spent on shelters for the homeless or Third World relief agencies. Her worst fights with her older daughter, Ariadne, had to do with the relative merits of art charity versus what Patsy called the squalor charities. Ariadne had inherited her father's rich vein of contempt, and also his tendency toward frequent physical violence. She had hit her mother several times in arguments over art versus the wretched of the earth.

Ariadne, though deeply committed to the wretched of the earth, was herself one of the most attractive and animated young women in L.A.; if in town she could be found almost any night with some of the *least* wretched of the earth —at Jack Nicholson's table at Helene's, for example, or at Jack Nicholson's table wherever he happened to be eating. Ariadne had grown up with the stars and saw nothing wrong with partying with them. Then, the next night she'd drag them to Sandinista fund-raisers, or benefits whose purpose might be to save the whales, save the rain forests, save the homeless, save something.

Even when she believed in the cause, Patsy did her best not to show up at the same benefits as Ariadne. She herself chaired benefits for the symphony or the ballet, or the Pasadena Playhouse, or one of the museums. Even after she moved back to Houston, she still came to L.A. for the major benefits, meanwhile doing the same benefits, more or less, in Houston.

Tomas had known how much she hated being thought just a decorative woman, so, as he was dying, he told her over and over again that that was what she was.

"You should have made more babies," he said. "Making babies is the best you can do. Find some little boy poet and make another baby."

Patsy found the little boy poet, Matt, but managed to restrain herself from making a baby with him. In her heart she agreed with Tomas: she was best at making babies, making them and raising them. Her girls were nice girls, even if Ariadne had become a little strident, and her son, Davey, wasn't un-nice—he was just a little uninteresting.

She had persuaded Bruce that Melanie ought to recuperate for a day or two in the little town house that she kept in Malibu, telling him that he was welcome, too. But Bruce declined. He had his job in the Valley, and he had better just stay in the Valley and keep his job: they might make him full time pretty soon.

Melanie was impressed that Bruce had managed to find her in the hospital, but she felt sad about the baby. She had

only felt it kick a few times, but still it was definitely there—
or it had definitely been there. Now it was lost, and she felt
sad; maybe it was just as well that she and Bruce would have
a few days off from one another. Otherwise the sadness might
drag them down. The doctor assured her she could have another baby—she just had to wait three months. Patsy, too,
assured her she could have another baby. Even Bruce assured her they could try again—he didn't have the attitude
that he'd just escaped some onerous responsibility. But Melanie still felt sad about the baby that was gone—it had just
been itself, though she hadn't got to know it. Even if she
started a new one in a month, it wouldn't be the same little
person. *That* little person was lost. She sat in a chair on the
deck of Patsy's little house and cried all day. She asked her
granny not to come out, and her granny, for once, seemed to
understand; she obeyed, at least, and that was even more
rare.

"Do you think Granny's sad about the baby?" she asked
Patsy one morning as they sat on the deck. It was cloudy; the
sea was gray. The surfboarders looked cold, even in their wet
suits. Bruce was going to come visit when he got off work.
He wanted to try surfboarding, and was going to use one of
Ariadne's old surfboards. In her low mood, Melanie was
thinking how terrible it would be if he got knocked off the
board and drowned. But she didn't voice her fear. She had
done nothing but cry for three days; Patsy must be getting
tired of her tears.

"Oh, sure," Patsy said. "Aurora's sad. I can hear it in her
voice. What makes you think she wouldn't be?"

"I don't know," Melanie said. "She doesn't like Bruce too
much. Maybe she thinks that now that we don't have to stay
together for the baby we'll just break up or something."

Patsy was cradling a teacup. She looked a little somber.
But despite the somber look, she still was beautiful, Melanie
thought. She had always wished she could look like Patsy—
sort of skinny and sexy and sure of herself. Patsy looked a
little like Ali McGraw, and Melanie was a big fan of Ali
McGraw's looks—they were the perfect looks, as far as she

was concerned. Now Patsy seemed a little sad, but Melanie still liked her looks.

"Most grandmothers aren't crazy about their granddaughters' boyfriends, you know," Patsy said. "If Bruce stands by you she'll come to like him, and Bruce does seem to be standing by you."

"Yeah, he does," Melanie said. It was amazing to her that Bruce hadn't just freaked out and left. He hated having to deal with police and hospitals and stuff, and yet he had. He had been sitting right in her hospital room with Patsy when she woke up. Actually, he had been nodding—he was obviously pretty tired—but just seeing him sitting there had touched her. It was very reassuring.

Thinking about it made her start crying again—or maybe it was looking at the sea that did it. Melanie wondered if the tides had anything to do with crying—it just seemed that the tears were being sucked out of her.

"Your grandmother and I have never exactly been friends," Patsy reflected. "We've always been slightly in opposition. I suppose it was because of your mother."

"Why? What did Mom do?" Melanie asked.

"Nothing, she was just in between us," Patsy said. "Your grandmother and I both wanted to be the main person in her life, I guess. Then your father came along and neither of us was the main person in her life after that."

She got up, went into her bedroom, looked up Flap Horton's number in her address book, and dialed Riverside, where he taught. She got his message machine, which was perfect: "Professor and Mrs. Horton are not in at the moment; please leave the date, the time of your call, and a phone number, and one of us will contact you. The beep is a little slow in coming, so please wait."

Patsy waited for the slow-coming beep, and when it came she was ready.

"You cocksucker, this is to let you know that Melanie miscarried and could have bled to death in the Oxnard jail Saturday night," she said. "She was in jail because she got caught stealing food. It seems you didn't care to help her.

She's at my place in Malibu, recuperating. I suggest that Professor and Mrs. Horton think this over."

She left her phone number and hung up.

Back on the deck, Melanie was still wiping her eyes—she had put a cereal bowl on top of her pile of used Kleenex so none would blow off and litter the beach.

"Was my daddy nice, when you knew him a long time ago?" Melanie asked, when Patsy returned. She had been worrying about her father lately, mainly wondering if he was going to give her a hard time about the shoplifting. He was never loud or violent or anything—he just had a way of putting people down that was pretty unpleasant. He hadn't done it with her so much, but he was real hard on Tommy and Teddy.

"He was okay," Patsy said. "For a while he had a crush on me, which made it a bit awkward."

Melanie could easily imagine her father having a crush on Patsy—it was easy to imagine any guy getting a crush on Patsy. Even Bruce seemed to be showing the beginnings of one, though up to the night she had got arrested he had always been sort of scared of Patsy.

Still, the issue that gnawed at her was her father—she could remember that he had adored her when she was a kid. He had liked reading to her, or taking her to the park and stuff. But then she became a teenager and got a little chubby, and it stopped. From then on it was pretty clear that what he felt was a kind of distaste, almost as if he thought she was polluted, or something. It was true she was having periods, and after a while she was screwing boys, but after all, that was normal—why did it make her father start disliking her to the point on not even wanting to invite her and Bruce for lunch?

"It's a wonder you even care about me, Aunt Patsy," Melanie said, feeling very lonely for a moment; she wished the little baby inside her hadn't died. If it could have been born she might not have felt the lonely feeling anymore.

"Why's that, honey?" Patsy asked, looking at the sad girl.

"You were in opposition to my granny and in opposition to

my dad," Melanie said. "It's a wonder they even let you see me."

"Yeah, but I wasn't in opposition to your mother," Patsy reminded her. "She made sure there was no nonsense about my not seeing you."

"Oh," Melanie said, reaching in a moment for another Kleenex. Thinking about her mother, with the sea so gray, the sky so cloudy, and the little baby lost, was just too much.

17

"Aurora spends an awful lot of time dressing," the General remarked, trying to choose his words carefully. He and Rosie were playing a little game of dominoes and Rosie, as usual, was busy with her computations.

The General was aware, sadly, that words were more and more often getting away from him, despite his care. There were days when he was fine, when he was his old self—or rather, not his *old* self but his real self. He called Rosie Rosie and Aurora Aurora and could be as precise in his speech as the next man, and a good deal more precise than the women of the household. Aurora of course denied that anyone could be more precise than herself, but he and Rosie both knew that she was hardly ever precise about dates or times or much of anything else.

In particular she had become wildly erratic about her time of arrival—that is, the time at which she would come home. Always before, in good times and bad, Aurora would arrive home before dark; but now, suddenly, there was no telling when she would arrive home. Some nights he tried and tried to stay awake, hoping Aurora would show up and talk with him a bit—maybe even hold hands with him. But usually he couldn't make it. Usually he would go to sleep, and sleep badly. He had gotten used, over twenty years, to a little pillow talk before he slept—somehow he just didn't sleep as well without it.

Often when he got up to hobble to the bathroom in the middle of the night, he would be disturbed to discover that Aurora still wasn't in bed. Sometimes he would creep across the second-floor patio and look out at the garage. The little room where Aurora was working on her ridiculous memory project was over the garage. It was there that she kept all her old diaries, and her husband Rudyard's desk calendars, plus her mother's date books and her grandmother's date books— for all he or anyone else knew, she had diaries and date books going all the way back to the *Mayflower*—though what good she thought her grandmother's date books would do he didn't know: after all, it was *her* life she was trying to remember every day of, not her grandmother's.

But Aurora was finicky about what she called her "memory room." She wouldn't let anyone else in it, not even Rosie. When it needed cleaning, she cleaned it herself, a rare thing. She claimed she wouldn't let Rosie clean because Rosie cleaned too well: in her eagerness to tidy up she might accidentally throw away some invitation or concert program or something that would have allowed Aurora to fill in a vital day from 1936 or 1941 or sometime.

The General had to admit that Rosie *was* likely to throw away things that others might have liked to keep. Several times she had thrown away obituaries he had clipped out of newspapers—obituaries he had meant to save. He had formed the habit of clipping obituaries of old comrades-in-arms—it seemed to him that more of them had died since the war than had died *in* the war. Sometimes the thought struck him that if they kept on dying so regularly he might end up being the oldest living veteran of World War II—that is, if he could avoid dying himself—no sure thing, particularly now that Aurora had become erratic and was leaving him alone too much at night.

Sometimes, peering across the dark yard at the little room over the garage, he thought he saw shadows moving across the windows. Once he thought he heard Aurora singing opera—that was very likely, since she enjoyed pouring forth song whenever the mood struck her. But the shadows moving across the windows were harder to explain. Perhaps they meant nothing. Perhaps Aurora was merely talking to Rosie. They both seemed to have become insomniacs in their old age. Willie, Rosie's beau, had had his shift changed at the prison—he didn't get off until midnight and rarely showed up at Rosie's before 1:30 A.M. Rosie whiled away the time by watching CNN, but of course it was possible that now and then she and Aurora had a chat in Aurora's memory room.

That didn't explain the time she took dressing, though. The General thought he knew what explained the dressing: Pascal had won her away from him at last! It was just a guess, of course, but it seemed to him a shrewd guess. Pascal was nearly fifteen years younger than he was, and Frenchmen had a way of not giving up, where sex was concerned.

Add to that the undoubted fact that he was slipping a little and it seemed to him that you had a recipe for romance.

The General wished there was something to be done about the fact that he was slipping, but he didn't know what it might be. Some days he just couldn't seem to marshal his thoughts—instead of their being marshaled neatly, like a well-drilled platoon, they seemed to wander willy-nilly over golf courses where he had once played, or battlefields where he had once battled. He would begin thinking about something and then lose track of it entirely; his words were apt to behave as badly as his thoughts. Sometimes he called Aurora Evelyn, or Rosie Aurora.

Of course, you couldn't expect a woman to like being called by another woman's name, and yet he couldn't seem to stop doing it except on his clearest days—and even on his clearest days, if he wasn't watching, he might slip up and call Aurora Evelyn once or twice.

Perhaps that was what had driven Aurora into Pascal's

arms. She had probably reasoned that if he couldn't remember her name she might do better to sleep with someone else. It was a position that was hard to argue with—which didn't mean that he wasn't jealous. On the contrary: the less he knew for sure, the more jealous he became. In time he had become so jealous just thinking of Aurora in the arms of the vain little Frenchman that he had taken to keeping his old service revolver in a box by his bed—the same box where he kept his medications. For a time he had apparently nearly driven Rosie and Aurora crazy by strewing his medications all over the house—a habit that meant he was almost never able to find the ones he was supposed to take at the times when he was supposed to take them.

To solve the problem, Aurora had given him an old leather box that had been her mother's—she commanded him to keep his medications in it. After that, he *did* keep his medications in it, which satisfied Aurora and Rosie. They left his box alone, never suspecting that one day when they were shopping he had oiled up his old service revolver and popped it into the box amid the pills. The thought that he had it was soothing when he was lying awake wishing Aurora would come home. At such times he felt bitterly jealous and sometimes got out of bed to see if Pascal might be wandering around on the lawn. If he did turn up on the lawn some night, separated by a safe distance from Aurora, the General meant to shoot him. In fact, there was a particular spot, just to the right of the garage, where he hoped to find Pascal wandering some night. He was pretty sure he could hit Pascal, if he was anywhere near that spot.

But of course shooting Pascal fell under the heading of future pleasures and would have to wait at least until Rosie made her next move at dominoes. She had not responded to his remark about Aurora's spending a lot of time dressing. The fact that she hadn't responded could mean nothing, or anything, depending on whether she had heard him in the first place. The General had such a commanding lead in the domino game that he really didn't care whether Rosie moved or not. He could easily afford to allow Rosie to win the hand,

and was prepared to do just that if he could get her to confirm his suspicion.

"Do you think she's got a boyfriend?" he asked, about the time that Rosie finally figured out that the double six was her best play.

"I don't know, and I wouldn't tell you if I knew," Rosie said, scooting her double six into position.

"Why the hell not, don't I have any rights?" the General asked.

"The hand that signs the paychecks gets its secrets kept," Rosie said. "It's as simple as that."

"You don't know anyway," the General said. "I doubt if she tells you a damn thing. She never tells either one of us a damn thing. She's too goddamn high-handed to bother informing her own household about much of anything."

"Much of anything unless it's something she wants to eat," Rosie said. "If it's something she wants to eat, she ain't shy."

"I think it's Pascal," the General said. "I think he's taken her away from me."

Rosie didn't comment. It was her turn to shuffle, and she was shuffling.

The General saw complicity in her silence, though he did note that Rosie seemed a little strained. She had not been looking too well lately, in his view. Rosie was normally so feisty that he tended to forget that she wasn't a young woman anymore. No one in the household was young anymore. Watching her shuffle the dominoes, it seemed to him that Rosie was definitely slowing down. Usually she shuffled the dominoes a lot more vigorously than she was shuffling them at the moment.

"Are you sick, Rosie?" the General asked, feeling a little frightened, suddenly. He had long held the view that, being eldest in the household, he would die first, but lately, due to his attentive clipping of obituaries, he had become uncomfortably aware of the fact—which he knew anyway, but for long stretches forgot—that people didn't necessarily die in strict chronological sequence. People just died when they died. In the past year he had clipped obituaries for several men who had been junior officers under him. One or two were more than twenty years younger than he was—and yet they were pushing daisies, and he was still aboveground playing dominoes.

The fact was, there were three of them in the household, and there was no predicting the sequence in which they might go. Any day Aurora could perish in a smashup on the freeway. Any day his ticker could stop. And now that he thought about it, Rosie might just keel over. She looked as if she might be about ready to keel over, even as she shuffled the dominoes.

"Are you sick?" he asked. It suddenly occurred to him that if Rosie died he might be left alone with Aurora. All these years Rosie had been their buffer—if she dropped dead there would be no buffer. It was not a cheering thought. On days when the weather was foul between him and Aurora, he could always go down and play rummy with Rosie—or watch television, if she wasn't in the mood to play cards.

"I wish Melly would come home," Rosie said. "I know she needs to go and live her own life and all that, but I miss her, and I still wish she'd come home. I miss her so bad I can taste it."

"Yes, but are you sick?" the General asked.

"Not particularly, unless you mean sick of the same things happening over and over a million times," Rosie said. "We need somebody young around here. We're just a bunch of selfish old people with nothing to do but fuss at one another."

Indeed, she missed Melly terribly—so much that it forced her to realize that she had largely misread the order of things. She had always thought that Melly depended heavily on her —that one part of her human task was to keep Melly on an even keel.

Now she had come to think it was the other way around. It was she who depended on Melly, and it was Melly's task to keep *her* on an even keel.

Besides that, the day before, one of her grandsons had fallen out of a third-floor window and fractured his skull. He survived; the skull fracture wasn't that bad, he wouldn't be brain-damaged or anything, but it was one more thing to worry about, and she had plenty to worry about already.

If that wasn't enough—in Rosie's opinion, it *was* enough —she and Aurora were in one of those periods when they seemed to rub one another the wrong way. Much of the time she liked Aurora—after all, they had been together forty years—and there were other times when they got along fine without giving it much thought. But then there were times when she *didn't* like Aurora very much, when her vanity and selfishness and general high-handedness were almost too irritating to be borne.

At the moment Rosie seemed to be stuck in one of those times when she not only didn't much like Aurora, she could barely tolerate her. Just hearing her sing opera in the shower was enough to make Rosie want to get a butcher knife and murder her, like in *Psycho*. Sometimes she felt like murdering Aurora when she was doing nothing more aggressive than watching soap operas and looking pleased with herself. Rosie was forced to conclude that she must have watched Aurora Greenway look pleased with herself once too often over the course of the forty years.

"The trouble with Aurora, she's a bad winner," she said to the General. "She's a good loser—it's when she's losing that you can't help liking her. But when she's winning it's a different story. When she's winning she ain't interested in nobody but herself."

"I think you're right," the General said. "She certainly isn't interested in me anymore."

Once he thought it over for a minute, Rosie's theory looked better and better. Aurora had always had a tendency toward arrogance, and any sort of success was apt to magnify this tendency.

"When she's winning, it's like dealing with a queen," Rosie commented, as she and the General selected their hands.

"It's like dealing with an empress," the General corrected.

As always, when talking negatively about Aurora, Rosie

began to feel guilty. After all, Aurora had done her many kindnesses. It was Aurora who had sat up with her in the hospital all night when her youngest boy, Little Buster, had almost died of rheumatic fever. In fact, in every serious illness or other crisis with her seven children, it had been Aurora, not the male currently in her life, who had stood by her until the crisis passed.

Only this week Aurora had flown to L.A. to help Melanie and Bruce find a nicer, safer apartment; it wasn't true that she never did anything for others when she was winning. All that was *really* true, Rosie admitted to herself, was that Aurora was now in love with Jerry Bruckner, a man much too young for her; and that, being in love, she had neither time nor interest enough to hear Rosie's complaints about Willie —and Willie was turning out to have quite a serious downside, one element of which was that he was a heroin addict. In his own defense, Willie claimed that all prison guards were heroin addicts, a claim Rosie didn't accept. She didn't see how *all* prison guards could be heroin addicts, but then again, it wasn't her problem. *Her* problem was that the one prison guard she was sleeping with was a heroin addict. Willie had only revealed his problem the week before in the course of a discussion about marriage—Willie was *really* anxious for Rosie to marry him, and Rosie would have admitted that she was considering it if Aurora had demonstrated any interest in hearing the admission. But Aurora hadn't, and—if that weren't enough—Rosie had just discovered that she was about to be a great-grandmother. If Melanie hadn't miscarried, Rosie would have felt okay, knowing that Aurora was going to be a great-grandmother again at more or less the same time; but Melanie *had* miscarried.

Also, the fact that she was staring great-grandmotherhood in the face was a serious element in her thinking about Willie's marriage proposal. Look at it any way she could, it just seemed a little tacky for a great-grandmother to be screwing around. What would she tell her kids and grandkids, not to mention her great-grandkids?

But Aurora, a great-grandmother herself, and certainly

likely to be one again within a year or two, since Melanie and Bruce seemed to have every intention of continuing to try, was definitely screwing around—and with a man who was only going to break her heart, sooner or later. After all, Aurora was thirty years older than Jerry: there was only one way, in Rosie's view, that the story could end.

The General meanwhile was studying his hand while attempting to ruminate about Rosie's new-sprung theory that Aurora was a bad winner. The more he thought about the new theory, the more he decided he believed it. But there *was* one bothersome aspect to it: what was Aurora winning just at present to make her so neglectful of the two of them?

"Why is she treating us this way?" he asked. "I don't see that Pascal is such a prize. I intend to shoot him if I can, but even if I miss and he gets away, there's still no excuse for her acting like a goddamn empress."

"Aw, don't be shooting Pascal," Rosie said. "Pascal ain't so bad. If you shoot him they'll just put you in Huntsville and Willie will have to guard you. You don't need to be in jail and Willie don't need no more murderers to guard."

"Well, I can see that, I guess," the General said.

Rosie sighed.

"Now you're sounding like Aurora," the General said. "Both of you are always sighing. Wait until you're my age. Then you'll really have something to sigh about."

"It's your lead," Rosie mentioned.

The General, perversely, in her view, led with a double blank. It was the equivalent of not leading at all. But then, he was a crazy old man, and Aurora's neglect was making him crazier by the day. Of course, Rosie knew that living with the General and waking up every morning to the sight of him sleeping with his mouth open must be a sore trial. One of her lifelong pet peeves was men who slept with their mouths open. Willie snored like a truck, but at least he snored with his mouth shut.

"That's not much of a lead," she commented, playing a five blank.

"It was my lead, not yours," the General commented.

"Sometimes I think I ought to shoot Aurora and let Pascal live. But I can do without Pascal fine, and I can't do without Aurora."

"You need to get shooting off your dumb brain," Rosie said. "There's never been a gunshot fired in this house, and the first time one's fired I'm leaving."

"Rosie, it's just talk," the General said, hastily retreating. "Don't you ever get the urge to take Aurora down a peg when she's acting like a goddamn empress?"

"Yeah, but not down *that* far," Rosie said. "You're talking about putting her six feet under."

"It was just talk," the General repeated. He realized he had gone too far. Rosie not only didn't look good—now she was looking as if she might cry. He couldn't understand why women were always taking him seriously when he obviously wasn't saying anything serious. Aurora did it too. Aurora had always done it. Let him simply voice some idle fancy, something he would never in his life actually do, and the next thing he knew Aurora would have taken him literally and would either burst into tears or stamp out of the room in a fury.

"It's just talk," he said for the third time. "Can you imagine me actually shooting Aurora?"

"Yeah, I can imagine you shooting her!" Rosie said, feeling herself slipping out of control. "I can imagine *me* shooting her! I can imagine anybody shooting her—that's what's making me crazy! But I ain't the only one crazy. You're crazy and she's crazy and Willie's a dope addict and I don't know what's gonna happen to any of us!"

Before the General could say another word, Rosie burst into tears, swept half the dominoes off the table, jumped from her chair, and tore out of the room. She was having a fit just like one of Aurora's. He heard her sobbing as she ran down the stairs. He felt terrible. All he had been attempting was an innocent game of dominoes, and now, despite all, a woman was having a fit, just because he had muttered some nonsense about shooting Aurora and her latest lover, Pascal. He wasn't really apt to shoot anybody, and Rosie should have known it, but he had touched a nerve, and now the game was over, there was disorder in the household, and he was alone. Rosie was the one person in the world who took the trouble to fix his eggs the way he liked them, too. He wished he could call back his words, but his words were history now, like Omaha Beach. They were not as bad as Omaha Beach, but they were history, just the same. It seemed to him tragic that nothing could ever be changed, once it happened: no word ever taken back, no battle plan revised. Men fell and women had fits and that was that.

The General felt so sad thinking of all the things that could not be changed, or taken back, that for a few seconds his age seemed only to be a source of relief. Soon he would not have to feel such distress in his chest because of a few casual, silly words that caused another woman who was dear to him to have a fit—soon he would be lying with the fallen of Omaha Beach.

It seemed to him it was about time he did just die, but of course he wasn't quite dead yet, and fits, however painful, just had to be lived through. He sat in his chair a few minutes, squeezing his hands together. Often his hands ached; squeezing them seemed to make them better. He hoped that Rosie would shake it off and come back and say hi, or something, so he would know she wasn't too mad.

But Rosie didn't come back and say hi, so the General sat alone, squeezing his hands. He remembered his gun—he could just go shoot himself. It would let the girls off the hook; really, it would probably be the best thing—he had had a pretty good life. He had even made a hole in one once, in Valdosta, Georgia, of all places. Later there'd been some confusion about Evelyn—he'd been so buoyed up by the hole in one that he'd wanted to have sex, though by that time years had passed since he and Evelyn had had sex. Evelyn had been startled—she hadn't really wanted to. After all, *she* hadn't made the hole in one, and wasn't in the mood to change what had been the pattern for years. In the end he went back to the Officers Club and let people buy him drinks. It had been a pretty hole in one.

But that was years ago, before he even met Aurora. It had taken him and Aurora a little more than twenty years to go through it, but now it did seem that they had mostly gone through it. He loved her—wouldn't it just be an act of kindness to shoot himself and let her off the hook? Also, Rosie wouldn't have to deal with his fussiness about boiled eggs anymore.

Of course, the problem was, one never knew how women would react. Even if he left a suicide note explaining that his death was intended to be an act of kindness, the girls might not take it that way. Rosie might blame herself—so might Aurora. They might spend the rest of their lives blaming themselves—he had seen that very thing occur in the families of suicides.

The General sighed a few sighs of the very sort he hated to hear Aurora or Rosie sigh. He had nearly talked himself into suicide, but then, proceeding logically, had talked himself out of it again. He would just have to go on, disorder or no disorder. As a first act in the drama of going on, he carefully got down on his knees and began to gather up the dominoes Rosie had scattered across the floor.

18

"Granny, I'm not criticizing you," Teddy said, wondering if the old Cadillac was going to get so hot it boiled over.

"Perhaps you should be, though," Aurora said, polishing her rings. When in doubt, she polished her rings—lately they had been treated to a lot of polishing.

The two of them were stuck in traffic on I-45, the freeway that led to Huntsville and the prison. She herself intended to remain true to her vow: she did not intend to go into the prison and see Tommy. But Teddy argued that, however perverse Tommy was, he was still one of them. The family could not simply abandon him. He was planning to go in and visit Tommy himself, leaving Aurora in the car. Jane had been against it—she felt Tommy ought to sit and cool his heels until he felt like behaving a little better. Rosie was for it, the General was of two minds, and Aurora herself of at least two minds. Every thought or mention of Tommy upset her.

"Where is the little red needle?" she asked, peering nervously at the Cadillac's temperature gauge. The traffic ahead of them and behind them seemed to be congealed—she was very hot, but of course there was no thought of using the air

conditioner in such a traffic jam. They had been totally im-
mobile for several minutes. Using the air conditioner, even
for a minute, would probably cause the old car to erupt. It
had erupted in similar circumstances several times, but on
those occasions Rosie had been with her, and Rosie seemed
to know what to do about erupting cars. In time they had
always made it home.

Of Teddy's mechanical skills she was far less sure. It
seemed to her Teddy was shaking more; his increasing shakiness was one reason she had agreed to go along to Huntsville. If at all possible, Ted must be kept from shaking
himself back into a mental hospital. His problem was not
Jane and her lover, either. When Teddy showed signs of
becoming destabilized, Jane was as patient and supportive
as anyone could be. Everyone in Ted's life was patient and
supportive at such times. Rosie made him pies, Mr. Wey
helped him on his shift, and Aurora herself made sure that
she spoke with him several times a week.

Still, somewhere inside Ted, the gyroscope was wobbling.
He was seeing Jerry Bruckner regularly now, at her insistence. Despite her doubts about his training, Jerry did seem
to be a helpful therapist. A constant stream of the mute and
the crushed seemed to flow through his office; Rosie's boyfriend Willie, who had stunned them all by revealing that he
had been a heroin addict for twenty-eight years, was now
seeking help from Jerry. Rosie even reported a decline in
Willie's irritability since he had begun seeing Jerry.

"The red needle's okay," Teddy said. "It's not quite touching the H yet. If we can just get some movement, we'll be
fine."

He had no sooner said it than three ambulances screamed
by them, on the shoulder.

"People are dead up there—or else they're dying," Aurora
said gloomily, wiping the sweat off her face. "I don't like
feeling like a hot animal, which is exactly how I do feel."

The traffic surged ahead a few yards, then stopped again.
Teddy decided to get off at the next exit, if they ever made it
to another exit. Driving along the frontage road would at least

be a little bit of an improvement. The car would cool down, and so, perhaps, would his grandmother. She was not an easy person to be with when she was discontented, and at the moment she was pretty clearly discontented. Her new lover, Dr. Bruckner, didn't seem to be working out too well, but she obviously wasn't in the mood to give up on him just yet.

"Nobody's criticizing you," he said again.

"Not to my face, but that's because I'm known to be fierce in rebuttal," Aurora said. "I'm sure you and Jane think it's pathetic, a woman my age throwing herself at a man young enough to be her son."

"You're too hung up on age," Teddy said nervously. The red needle was now touching the H—he thought he might have to take to the shoulder and move on to the next exit. It seemed unfair not to just wait in line like everyone else who was stuck; on the other hand, if the Cadillac exploded, it would only make the traffic jam worse.

Meanwhile, though he denied it, his granny's behavior did sort of bother him—her affair with the young psychiatrist had brought her atavism to the fore, or something. She had always been greedy, but she was usually greedy with flair, making a comedy of her own selfishness; people rolled their eyes and talked about her behind her back, but no one really disliked her for it. Sometimes she shocked people, but most of the time she entertained them and they ended up giving her the benefit of the doubt. Even someone like Patsy, who didn't really approve of his grandmother, usually let her get away with whatever it was she was getting away with.

But then, too, his granny seemed to have pretty good judgment about personal relations. If she wanted something or someone, she would always take things right up to the line, but usually, when she got to the line, she stopped.

This time he had a feeling she might have got carried away and crossed the line. Dr. Bruckner seemed nice enough—he just hadn't impressed Teddy as being too smart. He seemed kind of passive, like most shrinks, but if he was really smart, then he was doing a good job of hiding it. If there was a rub, that could be it. Teddy knew his granny was really smart.

She was the one who had always encouraged him to seek equals as lovers—she had recognized Jane's intelligence immediately and urged him to stick with her, despite knowing that Jane had been in mental hospitals more than once, and had even had to be straitjacketed a time or two because of her suicidal tendencies.

"It's a sad fate, living with someone less smart than oneself," Aurora had told him at the time. "I know, because it has been my fate."

"Was my grandfather dumb?" Teddy asked, rather surprised. His grandfather had died before he or his siblings were born.

"He was not entirely unintelligent," Aurora said. "But he was not as smart as I am, nor was he anywhere near as curious. I like Jane because she's curious about so many things. I hope you'll do your best to keep her."

Teddy had done his best and in fact had kept her. Now he couldn't really imagine what he'd do if for some reason, someday, he failed to keep her. The car inched onward a few feet, giving him enough space to make his cut for the shoulder—the temperature needle was just about to go above the H, which was not good. He himself didn't really mind heat —at least he preferred it to cold—but his granny, who had put on weight lately, looked as if she might melt. The last thing they needed was to have the radiator explode.

Aurora was wondering if she should tell Teddy that Jerry Bruckner was not an accredited, college-educated psychiatrist. She thought probably she shouldn't. Though he had dropped out of college himself, Teddy remained a bit of a snob about schools. In the past he had liked matching wits with psychiatrists who trained at Harvard or Stanford or other such places. Finding out that his new doctor was the son of a Las Vegas showgirl and had simply read his way into the profession might activate this snobbery. Jerry said that Teddy, so passive in life, was a very aggressive patient, very quick in debate, and also very well informed about psychiatric concepts and theories of personality structure.

In fact, though she took care not to ask Jerry anything that would even momentarily tempt him to reveal personal things that Ted might have said—about things that related to his mother, or to herself—she almost regretted getting Ted into therapy with Jerry because she sensed that Jerry was rather intimidated by Ted. At least he was rather intimidated by him intellectually, and the sense that this was the case made her even more dubious about her own situation. Jerry's patients were hardly intellectuals. They were ordinary people, many of them elderly, whose psyches had been mangled by life. They were not well informed about psychiatric concepts, or the structure of their own personalities. They just needed a little sympathy, a little company, and a little common-sense advice. Part of Jerry's appeal was that he was generous with such people; he didn't charge them much, he took them seriously, he did his best to be helpful, and undoubtedly was helpful much of the time.

Still, it was not really comforting to consider that she was sleeping with a man who was intellectually and in some ways socially intimidated by her grandson. She had insisted on the relationship, and was still insisting on it—not that Jerry had really made much of an effort to resist. He was a slow-swimming fish, and it was perfectly obvious that anyone who cared to cast a line could catch him: waitresses, stewardesses, girls who worked in health spas, even an aging woman such as herself. Jerry took almost no initiative, but he also put up almost no fight; when she showed up, he allowed her her way, but it was beginning to bother her that he himself *never* did the showing up. He was never likely to bang on her door in the middle of the night, drunk with love or thick with passion, as Pascal had now done three times since she had taken him to lunch and politely informed him that she was occupied elsewhere.

Yet, the fact was that Jerry Bruckner remained intensely attractive to her physically—so intensely that she tolerated his passivity and lack of initiative, flaws that had caused her to reject or dispose of many, many men when she was younger. She didn't really doubt that Jerry cared for her in his way; for that matter, she knew that he was fascinated by her. She had gone out of her way to *make* him fascinated—it would probably be the last time she was up to that effort with a man, and she had spared no pains. It had worked, and yet it hadn't, because his fascination was too studious, too patient, too relaxed; in some way, it was even too sincere: all in themselves very decent qualities, but not exactly the qualities she would have preferred in a man for whom she harbored such a racking attraction, and with whom she was having what might well be her final fling. She would have preferred him to be a little racked too, or at least a little more unsettlable, or confused, or needy, or something. Yet he wasn't, he wouldn't be. Her grandson, so young and so shaky, was quite mistaken in thinking that she was too concerned with age, when in fact she had chosen to ignore it, and at great risk.

"Fortunately you don't know anything about age yet, Teddy," she said. "It isn't that I'm hung up on it, it's that it's hung itself on *me*. I don't want it. I despise it! I try to give it the back of my hand. But there it is: the skin I wear and the breath I breathe. I just *am* getting old."

Teddy was slipping along the frontage road, passing the miles of stationary cars that were still stuck on the freeway. He had forgotten his remark about age; he had even forgotten, as they sped along and the two of them and the engine cooled, that his grandmother was sleeping with his new shrink. His mind had moved ahead to Tommy, whom he would be facing in another half hour. He didn't mind facing Tommy—he felt that he understood Tommy, and he also felt close to him. His sense of being Tommy's brother was his strongest connection in life, even stronger than his connection to Jane. Tommy just had his own way of being, and Teddy didn't feel there was anything he could or should do about it. He didn't dread going into the prison, as his granny and his sister did. It was just Tommy's place—he had chosen it and adjusted to it, and that was that.

At the prison he managed to find a parking place at the edge of the lot, where there were some trees just outside the fence to provide his granny a little shade. He looked at her to see if she might want to change her mind and come in, but she gave her head a little shake, so he rolled all the windows down and left her in the car.

Watching Teddy cross the parking lot, Aurora felt an old sadness. Teddy seemed so slight—so mere. He was not going to be the writer she had once hoped he would be, nor was he likely even to be the classical scholar he himself had once hoped to become. He was only going to be a nice, lost man, with perhaps enough strength and clarity of purpose to guide and raise his son. It had started, probably, with Emma's death. Teddy had once told her, as a heartbroken little boy, that if he had known how to love his mother better maybe she wouldn't have died.

"Teddy, that's wrong," she said. "Of all of us, you loved her best."

"But she died—I didn't know what to do," Teddy said. The conversation had taken place on one of her visits to Nebraska when the children were still living with their father.

Somehow the orderly, careful way Teddy moved between the rows of parked cars stirred her in her depths. Now and then he paused so that the sad mother or aunt or girlfriend of some other incarcerated boy could squeeze through ahead of him—the prison authorities had not been generous with parking space. It seemed to Aurora that his very kindness and consideration were a measure of his lostness—she was glad when he was out of sight. Selfish as it might seem, keeping her mind on her own dilemma was better, in a way, than thinking about Teddy and his problems.

She had brought the morning paper with her, meaning to study her horoscope and see if anything good could be expected to happen anytime soon. After that, she could devote whatever time was left to doing the crossword puzzle. Fortunately the horoscopes and the crossword puzzle were on the same page.

As she was about to fold the paper, she noticed an item—not a long one—at the top of the page opposite the weather map and the horoscope. The headline said: "Writer's Daughter Killed By Convict Husband."

Aurora glanced at the brief item—just two paragraphs—and discovered to her shock that the murdered girl had been the daughter of Danny Deck, the famous television producer, who had been for a time her own dead daughter's best friend—her lover, even, for one night: the very night, in fact, in which the girl named T.R., who was now dead, had been born.

Painful memories flooded Aurora—she had to put her face in her hands for a moment, to hide her shock. She remembered the very quarrel she and Emma had had—always snoopy about her daughter's life, she had happened to drive by and see Danny Deck's rattly old car parked at the curb in front of Emma's apartment in the early morning. Flap, Emma's husband, the very man who had just ignored Melanie in her distress, had been off on a fishing trip with his father at the time. He had often been off on fishing trips with his father. These absences hadn't suited Emma, but they suited Aurora fine—she even entertained the hope that Danny Deck, who showed at least some promise and might someday be an interesting and successful man, would step on the gas and take Emma away from Flap before it was too late.

But it had already been too late: Emma was pregnant with Tommy, though Aurora had yet to find that out. Emma was stuck with Flap for life, and her failure to escape was one reason Aurora herself was now sitting in a prison parking lot in Huntsville. Danny Deck, after a slow start, had made a great name for himself in television, creating one of her own favorite shows, *Al and Sal*. The show had been off the air for quite some time, but she and Rosie still occasionally watched it on reruns—it was a family comedy, and both she and Rosie identified strongly with Sal, the sex-starved wife, a lovely woman but married to Al, a slug of a man who would rather mow his lawn than make love to Sal.

Now tragedy had struck the comedy master. The girl had been shot down at a filling station, with two other people, by her convict husband, who, through a clerical error, had been released from the very prison whose parking lot she now sat in—and less than a week ago.

It was too much—life was too wretched. Danny Deck had been a rather soft boy. In the quarrel she had had with Emma about Danny and their night of illicit love, Emma had been so defensive that she had missed the point. Aurora had only been trying to encourage her to escape to a better man, but Emma, furious that her mother had spied on her, would talk of nothing but Danny's sorrow and heartbreak. His wife, it seemed, had kicked him out on the very day that their child was born—he had gone to the hospital to try to see the baby, only to be beaten off by his wife's dreadful parents.

So now, for the second time, Danny Deck had lost his daughter—and this time he had lost her forever. Carefully she tore the little story out of the paper and tucked it in her purse. Rosie and the General would be interested. Also, the piece mentioned the name of the town where the killings had taken place. She thought she might just write Danny— in the old days she had called him Daniel, to irritate Emma. She might write him and try to say something comforting. Perhaps he would want to visit sometime. They could all sit around and tell stories about Emma. It might be nice, though of course it would probably have to wait until the first rawness of his grief had passed—if it did pass. T.R. had only been a few months older than Tommy, who might even have known the man who killed her, since until a few days earlier they had both been inmates of the same prison.

Lonely all of a sudden, wondering how she would go about recovering if one of her grandchildren were brutally slain, she looked around the parking lot to see if there were any humans available—a dope-addict guard like Willie, a distraught mother or sister, anyone she might talk to in order to distract herself from the dreadful scene in her head in which one of her grandchildren, rather than Danny Deck's daughter, was lying dead on the greasy concrete at a filling station.

But there was no one—she could only sit and suffer the scene until Teddy came back to the hot car.

"We talked about baseball," he said cheerfully, starting the Cadillac. He saw at once that his grandmother looked even less happy than she had looked when he went in to see

Tommy. It didn't seem to him that Dr. Bruckner could be worth quite so much agony, if he was what her agony was about. But he didn't say it. In fact, he and Tommy had had a pleasant visit. They both kept up with baseball, and it made a good meeting ground. Coming to the prison was really no problem during baseball season. He and Tommy both had total recall of all the recent games; they could forget about the prison and the family and everything else and just analyze ball games. It was very pleasant; he and his brother still talked baseball just as avidly as they had all through their childhood and adolescence. They still had that, and that was sort of enough—at least, when he left the prison, he felt that he still had a brother, and he hoped that when he was back in his cell, Tommy felt the same.

"Did you get really hot, or what?" he asked, looking at his grandmother again. She looked sad—and, for almost the first time ever, she looked *old*, really *old*, which was a shock. Teddy almost backed into a passing pickup, so startled was he by the realization that his grandmother had finally aged. She had always been so attractive and sassy and full of beans that "old" was just not a term he would have applied to her. Jane wouldn't have applied it either, he was pretty sure.

Even when they got rolling and it was cooler in the car his granny didn't look much better. He didn't know what to make of it, except that it was disturbing. It was as if she had lost it suddenly, just in the space of time that it had taken him to go into the prison and talk a little baseball with Tommy. She had always been such a zestful woman that you just weren't inclined to attach an age to her at all—he realized with surprise that he didn't even know how old his grandmother *was*. Earlier in the day she could have passed for fifty-five or sixty; now she could almost pass for eighty. It was very startling.

"Don't look at me that way, Teddy," Aurora said. "I'll be all right in a bit."

She started to reach for her old ally, the rearview mirror, but then decided that in this instance she had better let be. The damage she had suffered was internal—fixing up the exterior wasn't going to help, not this time. She could see that Teddy was shocked by her depression, but there was not much she could do about it. At the moment she lacked the energy to explain about Danny Deck and Emma and all that had happened in those years before he was born, when his mother was just a young bride—only a girl, really.

"Maybe you'll feel better when I get you home," Teddy said.

"Yes," Aurora said. "I'm sure I'll feel better when I get home."

19

"Listen to me, please!" Aurora said that same evening, near midnight. "Stop raving and listen."

"I ain't gonna stop raving," Rosie said, though she was not so much raving as pacing in her distress. Occasionally she paced out of the kitchen into the garage—the latter was reachable through a small laundry room. There she could be heard kicking garbage cans or pounding on the Cadillac or the wall or whatever she could find to pound on, before returning to the kitchen to pace some more.

"May I remind you that I was at that very prison, this very day!" Aurora said, raising her voice. "I was not happy, I can tell you. I opened the paper to read my horoscope and discovered yet another tragedy."

"I don't care. Who cares?" Rosie said. She suddenly grabbed the sugar bowl and threw it through the open door, across the laundry room and into the garage.

"Uh—oh," Willie said, as they heard the sugar bowl smash. "The ants will be into that sugar." He was painfully aware that he was the sole cause of the fit Rosie was having. His addiction had been discovered and he had been fired from

341

the prison, where he had worked for more than twenty years. It seemed, in a way, like the end of the world, and now it had been the end of Mrs. Greenway's sugar bowl as well.

"Rosie, I would have taken *any* drug this afternoon," Aurora insisted. "If a pusher or whatever they're called had walked up to me with a sack of heroin or opium or cocaine or anything I would have taken it."

Now that she had thrown the sugar bowl, Rosie didn't feel quite so violent.

"Baloney!" she said, in response to Aurora's assertion, but she didn't say it with much force.

"Beg your pardon, it is not baloney, it's the truth," Aurora insisted. "Given the opportunity, I would have become an addict, just like poor Willie. In fact, I'd start becoming one right now, if I had the drugs."

"I got some, you're welcome," Willie said quickly, before he thought. After all, Mrs. Greenway had come to his defense at a moment when Rosie was about to kill him, or at least to run him off.

"You shut up, Willie!" Rosie said, her anger flaring anew. "The last thing we need in this house is another dope addict."

"Who are you to criticize us for our weakness?" Aurora said, pointing her finger at Rosie. "You've scarcely set foot in that prison yourself. You've cowered in the car for two years, while I went in. You don't know how sad it is in there. What happened to Danny Deck's daughter yesterday is only one tragedy in thousands. What happened to Tommy is only one tragedy in thousands. We had to deal with our one, but people who have to work there have to deal with them all. No wonder Willie's an addict; I say, more power to him!"

"Now what will we do for a sugar bowl?" the General asked. In a way, he was enjoying the crisis. It was rather like a council of war. He would have enjoyed more crises, actually—it was only when there were fights that he was allowed to be part of the family any more; at least it was only during fights that he *felt* like part of the family. Mostly, when things were calm, he was just left to himself, to putter around until he died. The problem with that was that nothing he was able to putter at was very much fun.

"Hector, it's not the last sugar bowl in the universe, we'll buy another one, so mind your own business!" Aurora said. The man was looking alive, for once, but for some reason, in the mood she was in, that annoyed her. If he still had the capacity to look alive, then he ought to look it more often and make himself really useful, it seemed to her.

Rosie gave up, sat down at the table, and began to cry loudly. She hated to cry, in public or otherwise—her way of crying involved emitting a kind of sucking sound as she attempted to suck the tears back into herself as rapidly as they fell. The sucking sound, rather than the tears themselves or the fact that she was distressed, put a very great strain on the nerves of anyone who had to listen to it—in this case, everyone at the table.

Rosie was crying because Aurora had hit her exactly where it hurt: that is, on the dark bruise of guilt she felt for cowering in the car during all those prison visits. Aurora was right about the sadness of the prison, too. Even on a bright sunny day, the prison was sad, as if an invisible cloud of sadness had settled over it. Even watching people come and go in the parking lot made Rosie miserable—all those ground-down people, suffering for the sins of their loved ones, their husbands or fathers.

Aurora was right—she herself was the coward, and what was the use? Willie had worked in that awful place for more than twenty years; why wouldn't he take dope? The fact that she had worked up her courage and made the big break with C.C. didn't alter the fact that Willie had an awful job. After all, Willie was just a plain man from East Texas, with an eighth-grade education, who had taken the one job he could get at the time, a job he had now lost. So what if she was involved with a dope addict? Her husband Royce had been a beer drunk most of his life, and C.C. Granby had been weird about sex. At least Willie wasn't weird about sex.

"What are you jumping on me for?" the General inquired. Aurora had been annoyed with him for months, and he was getting in the mood to get annoyed back. "Why can't I even make an innocent remark about the sugar bowl without being slapped down?"

"Hector, do I resemble a philosopher?" Aurora asked brusquely. "All you do is question my motives nowadays. I've never enjoyed having my motives questioned, as you ought to know, and I still don't."

"That's right, you've never given two seconds' thought to your goddamn motives," the General said. "You never have, and you still don't."

"So?" Aurora said, lifting her chin. "They are *my* motives, may I remind you? I guess I can ignore them if I want to."

Rosie finished sobbing; the sucking noises subsided. They all fell silent. All four were wondering briefly how it had happened that they had become trapped in a life with the other three. The fact that they had meant that each was stuck in a kitchen at midnight with three insane, unpleasant strangers. Why them, why then, why there, and why the other humans scattered around the table, with whom, for the moment, relations seemed pointless, if not impossible?

"My boss was real nice about it," Willie commented—he had reached a point where he found the silence unbearable. Though usually he was so intimidated by Aurora and the General that he rarely said anything in their presence, the novel experience of being fired made him suddenly eager to talk. In fact, he had scarcely stopped talking since it happened.

"That's good, Willie—I'm glad your boss was nice," Aurora said.

"Well, I doubt you're the first dope addict they ever seen at that prison, and I bet you ain't the last, either," Rosie said, wiping her eyes on the corner of the tablecloth.

"Don't wipe your eyes on my tablecloth—get a napkin," Aurora ordered.

"They gave me a list of these rehab places," Willie said. "I guess I oughta be thinking about rehab now that I got all this time on my hands."

"You better be thinking about getting another job if you expect to keep eating," Rosie said.

"Rosie, what makes you so harsh?" Aurora asked. "Willie is perfectly right. Addiction is a sickness—obviously he needs to get well before he starts looking for a job."

"I just mean I ain't supporting nobody while they sit around sticking needles in themselves," Rosie said. "Rehab's fine if you can afford it, but it ain't no substitute for a paycheck."

"No, rehab isn't fine," the General said loudly. "It's just a goddamn rip-off, if you ask me. Those drug clinics are no better than the nut houses we sent the children to. The nut houses didn't help the children much and the drug clinics won't help Willie much, either."

"What do you think *will* help him, Hector, since you seem to know so much?" Aurora asked. "The reason there are hospitals, if I'm not mistaken, is because the sick are not always able to cure themselves—sometimes not even if they're getting nice paychecks, as Rosie insists that they should."

"A healthy sport like golf that will keep the man out in the fresh air is what I recommend," the General said. "If he doesn't care for golf he could start playing racquetball."

The thought of Willie playing racquetball stunned them all for a moment, and the General mistook their silence for assent.

"Vigorous exercise and lots of it is what I recommend," he said. "It would be a lot better for Willie than sitting around in a clinic with a lot of drug addicts."

"Hector, I hope you don't expect us to treat what you just said as a serious comment," Aurora said.

The General was somewhat startled to find that yet again Aurora didn't appear to agree with him.

"Why can't I expect you to treat it as a serious comment?" he asked, a little defensively.

"Because it's absurd," Aurora said. "Willie has a chemical dependency. He's addicted to heroin. Do you seriously expect us to believe that heroin addicts can cure themselves by playing racquetball?"

"I only meant as a first step," the General said, retreating. "You always twist my words."

"Willie grew up in an orphanage," Rosie revealed. "They

whipped him black and blue, Then, getting that job in the prison was probably the last straw."

She yawned; Willie yawned. Rosie suddenly got up and disappeared into the laundry room. She reappeared in a moment with a broom and a dustpan.

"If you'll come hold the dustpan I'll sweep up that sugar before the ants get started," she said to Willie.

"Oh, come on, leave it," Aurora said. "I think the ant threat is being exaggerated. After all, ants have to eat too, don't they?"

"Yeah, but I'm sorry about the sugar bowl," Rosie said. "I was just freaking out—I never thought I'd be having to deal with stuff like this at my age."

"Yes, I know the feeling," Aurora said. "I'm sure if we all had dollar bills for every time we've had that feeling we'd be in a position to do takeovers and things of that nature."

"You sure about the sugar bowl?" Rosie asked. Suddenly her legs felt so tired she was doubtful that she could even make it to her little house. The moment Willie stood up, she leaned on him.

"I hope we ain't kept you all up," Willie said, putting his arm around Rosie. "I hate to upset other people with my problems."

Aurora gave him a nice smile.

"Don't give it a thought," she said. "There are many times in life when it's rather a relief to be asked to think about other people's problems. One can take a little vacation from thinking about one's own."

Willie just nodded. He had been rendered speechless by Mrs. Greenway's smile—and not for the first time, either. Whenever she chose to smile at him he was rendered speechless, a fact Rosie had not been slow to notice or comment on.

"You got one bad habit now, and that's heroin," she had said to him only that morning. "It ain't the only bad habit in the world, though. There's two or three more you need to watch out for."

"Like what, for instance?" he inquired.

"Like flirting with Aurora," Rosie informed him. "My husband Royce liked to flirt with Aurora, and look what happened to him."

"Well, what did?" Willie asked.

"He died," Rosie said.

"Of flirting?" Willie asked.

"That and a few other things," Rosie said.

Willie decided it was not a matter he needed to pursue any further. If Mrs. Greenway wanted to smile at him, that was surely her business. If Rosie disapproved, she would just have to take it up with her boss. He himself decided to go on enjoying the smiles, but with as little comment as possible.

Hewing to that principle, he managed to steer the shaky Rosie out the door.

"Hector, don't you think it's time you went to bed?" Aurora said, once Willie and Rosie made their departure.

"No, I can sleep when I'm dead," the General remarked.

"Well, no doubt, but a little shut-eye now and then wouldn't hurt you, even if you aren't dead," Aurora commented, getting up to turn on the stove. She felt like having a sip of tea.

"You treat me as if I'm dead," the General said. "At least you do half the time. When you're not treating me like a corpse, you treat me worse. You talk to me as if I were an idiot, or a child."

"Hector, it's after midnight," Aurora said quietly. "Must you reproach me at midnight? I just want a cup of tea. You can have one, too—though I suppose it will just make both of us more wakeful."

"It's because I'm so old," the General said. "You treated me better when I was younger. Now I'm not younger. I'm old. I'm worn out. I'm crabby."

"In your case, crabbiness preceded age, by many years," Aurora said. "You were crabby the day I met you, not to mention thousands of days thereafter."

"Yes, I guess I was, but you loved me anyway," the General remarked. "You thought I was interesting."

Aurora concentrated on her tea, hoping he would just shut up.

"But now I'm an old man," the General said. "You don't think it's worth while to love me anymore."

Aurora had her back to him. He couldn't tell what she was thinking, but he began to wish he hadn't made that last remark. Before he could apologize, Aurora turned abruptly and left the room. She left so quickly that she forgot to turn off the burner under the teapot.

After waiting a minute or two, hoping Aurora would come back, the General got up and turned off the burner himself.

20

"I don't quite know what to do about her," Jerry said—he was referring to Aurora.

"You're not alone," Patsy said. "Nobody's ever known what to do about Aurora."

The two of them had gone to Galveston to eat crabs, and were doing just that at a large, noisy crab house on the sea-wall. The restaurant was full of Future Farmers of America and also Future Farmerettes of America, in Galveston for their annual get-together. All looked as if they had been trucked to the Gulf Coast from very far inland, from small towns in the south or the prairie states. Boys and girls alike were pimply, loud, and in such a state of raw farmland innocence that Patsy had a hard time keeping her eyes off them. They were so innocent-looking that more than once she had an impulse to ask Jerry Bruckner to whisper. The impulse was irrational—no one could hear much of anything in the crab house anyway. Still, Patsy felt it was wrong for Jerry to be spilling the details of his affair with Aurora in the presence of a bunch of kids who were no older and certainly no wiser than Melanie, Aurora's grandchild.

Ambushing Jerry Bruckner had turned out to be quite simple. Several times she had spotted him in Jamail's, the fancy grocery store on Buffalo Speedway—he was usually brooding at the deli, trying to decide between corned beef and pastrami. It seemed to her that it was in his moments of indecision at Jamail's that Jerry seemed most psychiatric. If she hadn't known he was a psychiatrist, she might have guessed it from the way he stood there and brooded.

But she did know, and she also knew that she found him seriously attractive. Still, she wasn't in the habit of just walking up and grabbing every seriously attractive man she spotted. While in the process of deciding whether she should just walk up and grab Jerry Bruckner she watched him at the deli counter and eventually concluded that she should proceed with caution. After that, when she spotted him at Jamail's, she usually veered off down the nearest aisle, hoping he hadn't seen her. Her theory that he was Aurora's lover was, at that point, just theory. Rosie Dunlup was of the opinion that they were close but that they hadn't actually "done it," as Rosie put it.

"What makes you so sure they haven't actually done it?" Patsy asked Rosie every time the subject came up, which was more or less every time she and Rosie went to exercise class together.

"It's just a feeling I get that they haven't," Rosie said. "I admit I could be wrong."

"Is it because he's so much younger than she is?" Patsy asked.

"It makes me uncomfortable thinking about how much younger he is, I admit that," Rosie said. "If it was me, and the guy was the age of my oldest boy, I don't think he'd be interested," she added, chewing a hangnail.

"Rosie, stop eating your fingers," Patsy said. Rosie stopped.

"In fact, though, it isn't you we're talking about," Patsy said. "It's Aurora. Anyway, you turned the question around. Forget about whether this man who's the age of your oldest son is interested in you, and tell me whether you would be interested in him."

"I don't want to talk about it anymore—old-age sex is too depressing," Rosie said. "If it don't work it's depressing, and if it does work you still wonder whether you wouldn't be better off playing racquetball."

Actually, to Aurora's astonishment and the General's delight, Rosie and Willie had joined a health club and had begun to play racquetball several times a week. Now the General was wanting to play too. He was finally off his crutches and was getting the athletic itch again. Willie was slow, but the General was slower—Rosie couldn't quite imagine a racquetball game slow enough that the General could contribute, but if it came to a choice between things to think about, she felt she would prefer to think about the General playing racquetball than to think about Aurora and Jerry doing things in bed.

"A surprising number of men choose women old enough to be their mothers," Patsy said. "They must enjoy *something* about it physically. It's puzzling, but it's a fact."

"It may be a fact, but you can take it and park it, for all I care," Rosie said.

Patsy might have elected to park her interest in Jerry Bruckner had it not been for a depression she fell into after coming back to Houston from L.A. Or perhaps the depression had begun in L.A. She had run into three of her old boyfriends in one day and had been appalled by all three of them. Bob, her sculptor boyfriend, had just seemed like an aging, sullen lout. Elias, her professor boyfriend, took her to lunch and talked pedantic gibberish to her until it was all she could do to stay awake and not drown in her vichyssoise. Henry, her rich patron-of-the-arts boyfriend, looked flabby and fucked out; he came across as a spoiled dope with a ponytail. It was discouraging to realize that she had once convinced herself she saw some magic in the three men, some talent or spirit or intelligence that was either no longer there or—more likely—had never been there.

Her thought on the plane, as it descended into muggy Houston, was that there had really been no period of her life when she had not seriously misled herself about men—nor, really, was there any reason to suppose that her judgment was getting any better. Her future might turn out to be just as full of jerks and failures as her past had been. Not only was she not likely to find Mr. Right, but it didn't even seem likely that she would manage to locate Mr. Halfway Right, or perhaps even Mr. Tolerable. Her marriages, so far, had been awful, and her love affairs insignificant. She hadn't written a good book, painted a good picture, composed a fugue, or even a lively song; she hadn't done any of the things she had once hoped she would do. She hadn't even nurtured a genius —Matt's translation of Rilke had petered out somewhere around the sixth Elegy, and Matt himself had gone to work in Sacramento as a staffer for the State Arts Council.

On the whole, if you excepted three more or less well-raised children, it wasn't much of a record. Patsy didn't think she was a bad person—in fact she was confident that she was a nice person—but it wasn't enough.

From snooping on him in the supermarket, plus the one time she had observed him at close range at Aurora's party, Patsy felt sure that Jerry Bruckner could be annexed more or less at will, should she decide to annex him. He looked like a passive man, of the sort who was perfectly content to accommodate whatever women wanted to crowd into his life, provided they themselves did all the work. He wouldn't be likely to take any initiative, but he would be even less likely to resist whatever initiatives others might take. If he was sleeping with Aurora, it was probably because she had insisted on sleeping with him.

Patsy had been depressed for three weeks before she concluded that her depression was serious enough that she might have to consider therapy. She had been in and out of therapy for most of her adult life; she thought no more about adopting a new therapy than she would about changing her shampoo. Of course, since she was beginning to feel that a spot of therapy wouldn't hurt, she had a perfectly valid reason for calling Jerry Bruckner and making a professional visit. There was no reason not to do it—after a session or two, if he still seemed seriously attractive, she could just let nature take its course, if nature had a mind to.

Perhaps if Aurora hadn't been in the picture she would have done it that way—but Aurora *was* in the picture. If she presented herself at Jerry's door as a patient he might casually report it to Aurora, which would create a complication. Aurora had always been suspicious of her, although on no clear grounds. Finding that Patsy had just become a patient of her boyfriend's would not be something Aurora would just lightly brush off.

Patsy decided it wasn't a complication she wanted—not yet, not until she sniffed the breeze with the man, at least. She didn't imagine that sniffing the breeze would take long, either. He looked to be the sort of man who would tell you his whole romantic history on the first date. If he was interested in adding a fresh chapter to his romantic history—well, that question could probably be answered rather rapidly, too.

She remembered that several of the times she had seen him in Jamail's had been around four in the afternoon—between the late-lunch rush and the early-evening shopping frenzy. She knew what his old station wagon looked like, so she started cruising the supermarket's parking lot about that time of day. She felt a little like a predator—after all, she was stalking her dead best friend's mother's boyfriend—but that didn't stop her. In fact, her depression began to lift the minute she began her stalk. By the third day, when she finally spotted the station wagon in the parking lot, her depression was mostly gone and she was impatient to conclude her ambush.

She walked in and headed right back to the deli counter, where Jerry was waiting, his hands in his pockets, for his corned beef to be wrapped up.

"Hello, remember me? I'm Patsy Carpenter," she said, putting her hand on his arm for a second, lightly.

"Hi," Jerry said. He had noticed Patsy in Jamail's several times, but she had seemed to want to avoid him—something he found mildly depressing. He remembered her vividly from Aurora's dinner party. She had been the most attractive woman there—hauntingly so, really, the haunting part being that he was pretty sure he had seen her several times before on the beach at Santa Monica. He thought so, but he couldn't quite be sure: after all, he had gone to the beach at Santa Monica hundreds of times, mainly to watch women. Indeed, in his L.A. years, it had been his main sport—lying on a towel, pretending he had come for a tan, while he watched women. He had watched hundreds and was pretty sure that he had seen Patsy more than once, picnicking with her two teenage daughters and an arrogantly handsome man who generally looked angry. Patsy, if that was who it had been, immediately lodged in his fantasy—there was no explaining it, but she was a woman who happened to look just right, to him. He liked the way she lifted her arms to pin up her hair. She seemed to be doing her best to ignore her husband's evident ill temper, but she didn't entirely succeed. Even when she was smiling and chatting with her girls, there was something slightly sad in her look. When left alone she simply gazed out to sea. Now and then she walked at the edge of the surf. Once he had started to walk parallel to her so he could watch her, but after a few yards he began to feel silly, and stopped. Why was he ogling a married woman? Even if she wasn't particularly happily married, that didn't mean she was going to get divorced just because he liked her face or the way she lifted her arms.

Now the same woman—he was almost certain it was the same woman—with the same liveliness in her eyes, and the same sadness in her face, had walked up to him in a supermarket in Houston and put her hand on his arm. The few times he had spotted her in the grocery store he had hoped they would bump into each other by the vegetables or something, so that he could at least find out if she *was* the woman he had seen and remembered—at least he could ask her if she had once lived in Santa Monica. But she seemed to want to avoid him, and he was too shy to chase her. A few times he had even wondered why she wanted to avoid him. Once, driving home from the grocery store, it occurred to him that she might have seen *him* on the same beach, and been put off by one of the women he was with. Few of them had been as good-looking as Patsy or her husband or, for that matter, her children. They were just the girlfriends of the moment. A few had been a little on the vulgar side. For a time, when he first moved to California, he had been attracted to loud, brash, energetic California girls, none of them exactly elegant or graceful, or possessed of good taste in the way that Patsy was.

But he didn't know—it was all speculation; he wasn't even positive that Patsy was the woman he had seen and fantasized about. Once he thought it over a bit, he realized he was probably stretching things to think that Patsy Carpenter was avoiding him because his girlfriends of several years ago had been a little coarse. If she *was* avoiding him, it might have been because of something he said at Aurora's dinner party, though he couldn't imagine what it would have been.

Now, there she was—not avoiding him. She had even touched him. Light as it was, it pleased him a lot. Though it might mean little, the mere fact that Patsy had approached him reaffirmed one of his most cherished beliefs, which was that whatever women he *really* wanted, the ones that most completely satisfied his idiosyncratic eye, that looked *just* right, would find their way to him eventually, or allow him to find his way to them. Here it was, happening again: an old image of someone not known, but seen and desired, had floated up from his beach days and materialized as a living woman at his side.

"You don't really want to eat that salty corned beef, do you?" Patsy asked—she had decided on an immediate strike. "Wouldn't you rather go to Galveston and eat some crab?"

The deli man heard the invitation. He had been just about to put the tape on the package of corned beef, but he stayed his hand and looked inquiringly at Jerry Bruckner.

"Sorry," Jerry said, to the deli man. "Looks like I just had a better offer."

"Looks like you just did," the deli man said, with a nod to Mrs. Carpenter. He had known her for many years and didn't really approve of her ways; in particular he didn't approve of some of the young guys she had turned up with over the years. But then, he had witnessed worse—far worse—in his years in Houston, and it was none of his business. He put the corned beef back in its proper tray.

"That meat man doesn't like me," Patsy said, as she and Jerry were walking out of the store. "I think he probably thinks I'm a slut because I've been known to go out with younger men."

"Well, I wouldn't worry about it," Jerry said.

Patsy found the remark slightly disappointing—actually she hadn't been worrying about the deli man in the least. She would rather Jerry had addressed himself, even jokingly, to the question of her presumed sluttishness—her younger men—or to *some* question. But Jerry just walked around the content of her remark. He did have a good head of hair, though. Once they got outside, the sunlight glinted in it nicely. She decided, what the hell, why be picky? We just met. Maybe he's scared.

If so, it wasn't of her driving. He got in her car as if it were a matter of course that they would go in her car, not his old heap, and he seemed to accept it also as a matter of course that she would drive. He easily let himself be picked up, as if that were the normal way, and seemed content to be delivered to wherever she wanted to deliver him.

"I'm pretty sure I used to see you on the beach at Santa Monica," he revealed, as soon as they got in the car. "You had two girls with you and a man who looked a little bit Mexican."

"Please, a little bit Spanish," Patsy said. "That was my husband, Tomas—he'd die at the thought that anyone might take him for a Mexican, though he *was* a Mexican.

"Then he died, anyway," she added, reflecting on what a weird thing she had just said.

"When I met you at Aurora's I thought I recognized you," Jerry said. At a stoplight just before they hit the freeway, Patsy hastily put her hair up; he found he still liked the way she lifted her arms. The movements of women, particularly the unself-conscious physical moments of women, who were, in the main, highly self-conscious, were a kind of sexual poetry—at least their little motions or gestures, such as pin-

356

ning up their hair, struck his eye as poetry. The smarter the women, the less likely it was that they would ever be able to forget themselves, and the more moving it was when they actually forgot themselves and did something simple and graceful.

"You should have spoken up," Patsy said, whirling onto the freeway. "I was pretty beaten down in those days. Tomas did everything he could to destroy my confidence in my looks, although he only married me for my looks. I would have been highly flattered to think that someone liked the way I looked on the beach."

Jerry had been feeling lonely and rather discouraged when Patsy walked up to him. He had been thinking that he might just move back to Las Vegas—maybe he'd run a bingo game for a while, something low key. He didn't feel quite up to the craps tables, much less blackjack or baccarat or anything very high stakes. He just might run a bingo game, and it wouldn't even have to be in Vegas, it could be Reno or Tahoe or even Elko. It would get him out of the sticky situation he was in with Aurora, and also out of his life as a therapist, which was beginning to seriously pull down his spirits. Maybe he'd run into a happy showgirl who liked to race-walk or something.

The move would require nothing more elaborate than putting his books in storage and maybe buying a couple of new tires for the station wagon. One morning he could just be gone. The people who showed up expecting to find him where they normally found him would be surprised, and he himself would be in El Paso or somewhere, heading west.

The power to leave—simply to leave, informing no one— was a power he cherished. He felt that within the next week or two, certainly within the next month, he would probably exercise it. His thinking had begun to focus more and more on Elko. He liked it that it was marginal—it was really just barely in Nevada, with Salt Lake a nice drive to the east. It was interesting to imagine what Elko women would be like, interesting enough that he spent quite a few happy hours imagining Elko girlfriends.

But now there was Patsy—she had apparently just decided to walk into his life. Now that he had the chance to see her up close, he wasn't totally sure she *was* the woman he had seen on the beach—there had been a lot of attractive brunettes with sexy, skinny arms on that beach, some of them with daughters and handsome husbands—but the fact that she might be and that he had already told her about it and convinced her already that he had once seen her and desired her meant that they had something going—something with a little bit of myth woven into it. He loved sitting back and watching her drive. Certain Texas women, like certain California women, seemed to be born to the wheel. Driving was like breathing to them—they did it with complete assurance, as Patsy was doing it now. He himself drove well enough, but he was nervous about being rammed, and he divided his attention about equally between the road ahead and the rearview mirror. Patsy was the fastest driver on the freeway—she seldom did more than flick her eyes at the rearview mirror. Now and then she also flicked her eyes at him. They were just quick glances, but Jerry felt nonetheless that he might have to put off finding out about the women of Elko, Nevada, until a little later in life.

"Let's have your life story," Patsy commanded as they were approaching the bridge to the island. By the time they reached the crab house and managed to get their order in over the din of Future Farmers and Future Farmerettes, she had heard a lot of the life story, enough to convince her that if anything he was even more aimless and easily led than she would have supposed. The affair he seemed to be mired in with Aurora—an affair he immediately confessed to—was a case in point. At times, listening to him describe himself, Patsy felt her spirits sag: the man was such a dishrag, did she even feel like buying his dinner, much less like taking him home? He seemed to be saying that he was fascinated by Aurora and had a kind of crush on her but didn't really want to sleep with her, although he *was* sleeping with her, of course.

"I guess I'm a little dense tonight," Patsy said. "I know

she's a bulldozer, but is she *that* much of a bulldozer that you have to make love to her when you'd rather not? Come on."

Jerry was uncomfortably aware that Patsy wasn't really liking what he was telling her about Aurora. She kept her eyes down, listening. The more he tried to explain that it both was and wasn't a big deal, the more he saw Patsy stiffening. The friendliness she had seemed to have in the grocery store and on the drive down to Galveston wasn't really there anymore. She was looking at him skeptically—even a little hostilely.

"Maybe I just have a class problem," he admitted. Class was something most of the women he went out with had never even thought about, and if he mentioned it as a possible explanation for some of his own dubious behavior it would sometimes distract them sufficiently to make them forget that they were on the verge of being angry with him.

"Come again?" Patsy said. "You're sleeping with a woman thirty years older than you because you have a *class* problem? Is your crush on her supposed to be a crush on her class, or what? I don't get it."

"I'm just not confident with upper-class women," Jerry said. "I doubt that I would ever have got up the nerve to speak to you in the grocery store—although I noticed you several times, and wanted to."

"Jesus Christ, I'm not an upper-class woman," Patsy said. "Neither is Aurora Greenway. I'm just a Dallas girl whose father made a little money in the oil business."

"Well, but Aurora *seems* upper class," Jerry said. "You do too. Maybe I'm just measuring from where I started out—I don't know."

"Come on, Mr. Shrink," Patsy said. "I doubt that it's class inferiority that prompts a man to sleep with someone his mother's age. There doesn't really have to be that weird an explanation, does there? The explanation is that Aurora's still attractive. I've never been crazy about her but even I can see that she's still an attractive woman. She's one of those greedy people who somehow manage to be appealing simply by being totally greedy."

She felt rather like throwing her plate at him—his conversation was so stupid that for a moment it made her miss her dead husband. Tomas had been perfectly capable of not saying a word to her for three or four weeks at a stretch, but when he did talk he was smart—mean, but smart. Tomas made her work for everything she got: sex, compliments, even domestic peace. She didn't like it, but at least it had a flavor. What would Jerry's flavor be if the best he could offer was a remark about his terror of high-born women, or women he supposed to be high-born?

"I mean educated," Jerry said. "Women like you and Aurora are much more knowing than I am. You've traveled, and you've been to school. It's not so much that you know which fork to use. You know which poems to quote, and you've been to all the museums and seen all the pictures. My mother was just a skater with a good figure—she left school in the seventh grade."

"What about you?" Patsy asked.

"I finished high school and went to casino school, but I dropped out," Jerry said.

"Casino school?"

"Sure—where they train croupiers," Jerry said. "I guess the best casino schools are in Europe, but I just went to one of the ones in Las Vegas. It's not everybody who can make it as a croupier. Most of the people I went to casino school with didn't make it."

"I thought you were a shrink," Patsy said. "Actually I didn't think you were a shrink at first, but spying on you in the supermarket almost convinced me you might actually be one. So are you a fake shrink, or what?"

"At least I have you confused," Jerry said. "Can we get out of here? I hate this noise."

They drove to the south end of the seawall and watched the ocean for a while. Patsy had ceased to feel hostile. Jerry had disarmed her with his remark about Aurora's knowingness, and her own. Their knowingness had nothing to do with class—or maybe it did, though not in the old Continental sense. She knew she wasn't upper class, but on the other hand she *had* traveled, *had* read some poetry, had seen all the pictures in all the museums. She had never thought of her traveling or her museuming or her reading as being definitive—in fact, all that had just made her feel dilettantish and shallow—another sign that she could never really rise above the decorative, because her mind itself was only decorative. Such little learning as she had enabled her to hold her own at upper-middlebrow parties the world over, but that was as far as it took her. She could read, but she couldn't write; she could look, but she couldn't paint. She was a first-rate dinner partner, though—the many rich or famous men who had been seated beside her at parties in L.A. or London or Madrid had not gone home disappointed. They *liked* sitting beside her and chatting with her, and yet that in itself was a damning fact. It just meant that her mind matched her looks—both were highly decorative, but neither had even the slightest hint of the exceptional.

But to Jerry Bruckner, son of a showgirl, she and Aurora Greenway, two fairly ordinary women, were empresses of the *haut monde*. The touching part of that was that the man, for once, was undoubtedly sincere. He really *was* awed by semi-educated women who were just smart enough and well-trained enough to go into Hermès or Fendi and buy a decent handbag.

Patsy was glad he had come out with that remark—maybe, after all, he wasn't totally uninteresting. Also, he had a nice way of being quiet—at least he did if the sea was there to look at and listen to. He wasn't bored, he wasn't sullen, he wasn't nervous, and he wasn't too attached to his own observations or anxieties. They sat for half an hour without speaking. Patsy felt that her irritation had been a little silly. She had violated one of her own beliefs, which was that speculating about men was foolish. She could have grabbed Jerry Bruckner at almost any time and whirled him off to Galveston to eat crabs. She could even have grabbed him the night after she met him at Aurora's dinner party. Instead, she had speculated and fantasized. She had sort of invented Jerry as she had wanted him to be, and had then been annoyed to discover that he didn't resemble the guy she had invented. Knowing nothing about him, she had let her imagination advance him a notch or two socially. She had invented him as the kind of man *she* liked to sit next to at dinner parties—someone who was lively and at the same time dazzled by her. Such men often turned out to be more fun at the dinner party than they were if she turned up in bed with them, but Jerry had looked so appealing, sitting by Aurora, that she had discounted her own rules, and also her considerable experience in such areas.

"Does the fact that you went to casino school mean that you aren't a real shrink?" Patsy asked.

"I'm not accredited," Jerry said. "I never went to college, much less to medical school. But the man who was sort of my stepfather was a psychiatrist. He talked to me a lot about psychiatry, and he also left me his books. When I was in New York trying to be a comic I did analysis routines. I went into analysis myself, but my analyst got killed before we got very far."

He stopped, feeling it must all sound really flimsy to Patsy. He could easily be a convincing shrink to people like the woman whose daughter had had all the strokes in the same side of her head, or to the old man who kept trying to convince him that Jesus had come back and was living in the neighborhood; but he hadn't been a convincing shrink to Aurora, and he didn't think he'd have any better luck with Patsy.

Down the beach, a mile or two away, he could see the lights of the big hotel where he'd worked as a concierge after hitchhiking to Galveston for the first time. That was the day he left Cherry, a girl he still sort of missed.

For a moment, he not only sort of missed Cherry, he missed her a lot. If it had been Cherry in the car, and not Patsy, he wouldn't feel so tight in his chest or be so worried about saying something stupid or uninformed. He knew that he had a weak grasp of historical chronology; he was always confusing artists or composers who lived in the eighteenth century with those who lived in the nineteenth. Errors of that sort marked you as a booby if you ran with a certain crowd. With Cherry it had been no problem. Cherry was a nice, boisterous American girl who liked to do things top speed. She didn't know much about anything, and probably would have placed the eighteenth century as way back before the birth of Jesus, in whom she believed fervently if vaguely.

"You don't need to be quite so wary of me, Jerry," Patsy informed him. "I'm just trying to get to know you. I'm not going to turn you in to the thought police for practicing shrinkery without a license. I was just kind of wondering how you got started in it."

"I made a sign and put it on my porch," Jerry said. "Most people believe signs, you know. if the sign says 'Therapy,' they don't question it. All they want to know is how much you charge.

"I used to be concierge at that hotel," he added, pointing down the beach. They had never had a concierge until I came along. I said I'd work for tips if they'd let me try it. The first day I made four hundred and twenty dollars. I probably should have stayed a concierge."

"Are you an altruist?" Patsy asked. "Did you give up being a concierge in order to help suffering humanity? Or was there just more money in shrinkery?"

"I guess I thought it was a little more intellectual," Jerry said. "Trying to sort out people's problems seemed more enterprising than just trying to sort out restaurant reservations for old ladies from West Texas."

"I see, you're the neighborhood priest," Patsy said. "So much for my quiz." Her hair felt sticky from the moisture of the sea—also, her ambush felt like a failure.

Going north, back to Houston, she drove at speeds above ninety. When they arrived at Jamail's, Jerry's station wagon was the only car in the parking lot, although beside the store a big produce truck was purring. A team of men with handcarts wheeled vegetables from the fertile valleys of Texas and California into the depths of the store.

When Patsy stopped, Jerry tried to kiss her, but she drew away.

"I'm not one of your parishioners yet, Father," she said.

She felt irritated with him, as she had for much of the evening.

Jerry just felt confused—not a new feeling. He felt that once again he had tried for a woman who was out of his class. Even so, he knew he would be sad if he just let her drive away.

"Can we do this again?" he asked, his hand on the door.

"You mean eat crabs?" Patsy asked.

"Well, eat something," Jerry said.

"Don't know," Patsy said. "I do know that I'm not dating someone who has to two-time Aurora Greenway to date me."

Jerry wished he had just kept his fantasies of the woman on the beach at Santa Monica. Feeling tired and feeling sad, he got out.

"It was a nice evening," he said politely.

"You're a hypocrite, Father," Patsy said, as she whipped away.

21

Bump had learned to talk. To the delight of both his mother and his father, he had beautiful enunciation, and his talk, from the first, was interesting. Usually, he even spoke in complete sentences. But there was a catch: he didn't want to talk to them. He only wanted to talk to his best friend, Kermit the Frog.

"I'm a Frog too," he told his Big Granny, one day. "I'm going to live in Frog Town, where Kermit lives."

His Big Granny had bought him Kermit and showed him how to slip his hand inside Kermit and wiggle his mouth, so he could speak. His Big Granny had only had to show him once. After that, Kermit went every place Bump went. One day at Big Granny's, Bump saw Kermit on a picture machine his big Granny had in her bedroom. There was another, smaller picture machine in the kitchen, which Rosie let him watch. At first it astonished him to see Kermit on the picture machine at the very moment that he had Kermit on his own hand and was making him talk to Rosie and Big Granny.

"Why is Kermit two?" he asked.

"A good question," Aurora said. She was very pleased with

her great-grandson, now that he could talk. "Kermit is two because the world is weird."

"Is that Frog Town in that picture?" Bump asked, pointing.

"I think so," Aurora said.

"I want Kermit to be one," Bump said. "I want him to be just *my* Kermit." He knew numbers, and how they looked, and he also knew the days of the week, although he didn't find the days of the week particularly interesting. Nothing in the world was as interesting as Kermit, his friend.

"Why are you in there?" he asked Kermit, pointing at the picture machine.

Big Granny borrowed Kermit long enough for him to answer Bump's question.

"I'm just a poor Frog, that's where I work," Kermit said.

Bump took Kermit home with him that night, a little troubled. He didn't like it that Kermit was so tricky that he could be in two places at once. He didn't tell his Bigs this, though. They weren't really friendly to Kermit. If he gave Kermit too many hugs and kisses, his Bigs didn't like it. They wanted him to give *them* the hugs and kisses. His mother was always grabbing him and making him sit in her lap and listen to stories. She didn't understand that he would rather spend his time with Kermit in one of their hideaways. Their best hideaway was in the yard, under a hedge, but they also had a hideaway in the closet. Sometimes when his mother grabbed him he would try to kick his way out of her lap so he could get back to his life with Kermit, but his mother was strong, and it didn't always work. She just hung on until his legs grew tired of kicking. If he tried to bite her and tried to make her let him go back to Frog Town she just held him up in the air and laughed. Usually Claudia laughed too, but she rarely tried to make Bump sit in her lap.

"My daddy's hands shake when he reads me stories," Bump informed Kermit one day. "I think he's sick."

When he talked with Kermit, he had to make Kermit's words too, unless he saw Kermit on the picture machine—then Kermit made his own words. At Bump's house there was no picture machine and Kermit never made his own words there.

Bump wished his parents would get a picture machine so maybe Kermit would make his own words more often, but his parents didn't like picture machines. Once when he and Kermit were playing with his Greek blocks, Big Granny came over and argued with his parents about picture machines, while Bump and Kermit listened.

"I never thought I'd have relatives so high-minded they won't even allow a child to watch television," Big Granny said. "No wonder he took so long learning to talk. They have to *hear* speech before they do it."

"He hears speech," Jane said, annoyed. She was in the mood to go over to Claudia's apartment and bag family life for an hour or two.

"Yes, but how often?" Aurora asked. "It's my impression that you two mostly pore over your classical texts. If you aren't going to talk to your child you might at least get a television set so he can hear his own language spoken."

"I would risk getting one but Jane doesn't want to," Teddy said.

"Why is it risky?" Aurora wanted to know. "*I* watch television—do you consider me intellectually stunted?"

"You're not intellectually stunted but you're not a two-year-old, either," Jane said with some vehemence. "I don't want Bump to grow up watching violent garbage, and that's all that's on television now. Even the cartoons are violent garbage."

"Well, I disagree," Aurora said. "As it happens I'm almost as fond of Kermit as Jonathan is. The day seldom passes without my watching Kermit. What he has to say can hardly be described as violent garbage."

"There are exceptions, but not enough," Jane said grudgingly.

Bump thought his mother might be about to be a beast, but then the telephone rang and he ran to get it. His father had explained to him that if everyone else was busy, then answering the telephone was his job. But he usually tried to answer all phone calls now himself, even if the Bigs weren't in the bedroom with the door shut. This time it was Claudia.

"Hi, Bump, is your mom there?" Claudia asked.

"I live in Frog Town now," Bump said, but he carried the phone over to his mother, who began to talk low. Big Granny got up to leave, and he and his father and Kermit went down the stairs with her to her car.

Big Granny picked him up and gave him some kisses—Bump didn't mind, because she smelled good. She gave Kermit a kiss too.

"I like Big Granny," Bump said to Kermit, after he and Kermit had gone out on the lawn to be by themselves. They sat down in the grass. Bump was wearing only his underpants, so the grass tickled.

"I wish she'd bring us some storybooks," Kermit said. "Go tell her."

Bump got up and ran over to Big Granny, who was still standing on the sidewalk talking to his father.

"Kermit wants you to bring us some new storybooks," Bump said, pulling on Big Granny's skirt. "We don't have any new stories."

"Of course, you must have new stories," Big Granny said. "I promise to attend to that promptly, Jonathan."

"She calls me Jonathan—it's her name for me," Bump told Kermit, going back out on the prickly lawn.

"I wish I had an airplane," Kermit said. When they rode in the car they kept their eyes on the skies, hoping to see an airplane.

"Whether she likes it or not, television is part of our culture now," Aurora said. "It's not going to hurt him to watch a few cartoons—nor would it hurt you and Jane. From the looks of things, you two could stand some laughs."

"I don't think Jane would ever laugh at something that was on television," Teddy said. "She used to like Carol Burnett but Carol Burnett's not on anymore."

To Aurora's eye, Teddy looked ground down. There was no light in his eyes—not even the manic light that appeared when he became unstable. Now he didn't look unstable, he just looked sad. He had always been sweet but not strong, and he still was sweet but not strong.

"What is it?" she asked, hoping she might surprise him into talking about his problems.

"It's not anything in particular," Teddy said. "I guess it's just life."

Jane came down the steps and waved at them as she turned along the sidewalk.

"She's going away," Bump said to Kermit. "I hope she never comes back. She shakes me when she's mad."

Sometimes he loved his mommy more than anyone, but he could not forget that she was apt to turn into a beast, which was scary. Once when she was scary she had grabbed Kermit and thrown him out the window. Bump had had to hurry down the stairs to get him. Kermit hadn't been hurt, but Bump hadn't forgotten or forgiven what his mommy had done. His daddy would never become so scary that he would throw Kermit out a window. His daddy only shook, and talked in a high voice, when he got angry.

"I think she's just going over to Claudia's," Teddy said. His grandmother had not asked, but he still felt that he ought to explain his wife's silent departure.

"Oh, yes, the girlfriend," Aurora said. "Is that why you're looking so miserable?"

"No," Teddy said quickly. "I don't mind her seeing Claudia."

"Ted, are you sure?" Aurora asked. "I myself am not at all possessive, in theory. It's my firm belief that human beings belong to themselves—what they do with others is strictly their business."

"I bet what *you* do with others is strictly your business," Teddy said, smiling for the first time since his grandmother had come.

Aurora smiled too, a little relieved. At least he was not so sad as to be unable to appreciate certain aspects of the human comedy.

"Yes, absolutely my business," she said. "Still, there's theory and there's practice. In practice one is always wrestling with one's demons. Mine happen to be quite possessive demons, despite my admirable theories. So are the General's. In theory he and I are in perfect agreement about the value of individual freedom, but in practice he's mad as hell at me because he suspects I have a lover.

"Which I do," she added, after a moment. "In his finer moments Hector would probably admit that the game is over, for him, and that I need a lover and have every right to have one. But in practice he's mad as hell and he won't admit anything except that he'd like to bash my head in with one of his golf clubs."

"We're younger, though," Teddy pointed out. "Jane's not neglecting me or anything. I really don't mind about Claudia —sometimes I even think I like her better than Jane."

"She does seem pleasant," Aurora said. She had met Claudia—a small woman with mild blue eyes—only once.

"Jane can be a little rigid—like she is about television and stuff," Teddy said. "She's also mad.

"I don't mean crazy, I mean angry," he added, seeing anxiety in his grandmother's eyes. "I'm not sure I could live with Jane right now if Claudia wasn't in the picture. It doesn't mean we have a bad relationship or anything, though."

"Of course it doesn't," Aurora said. "I've always considered it rather ridiculous, this penchant human beings have for taking vows which, if held to literally, mean they would only see one other adult naked for the entirety of their lives."

Again Teddy smiled, this time with a little light in his eyes.

"Jane and I didn't marry, though," he said. "I'm pretty sure she plans to see more than one person naked in the course of her life."

"Well, I approve—but I can approve and still be a little worried about you, can't I?" Aurora said. "I want you and Jonathan and Jane to flourish. Jonathan's fine and Jane's fine, but I'm not sure I think you're exactly flourishing, Ted."

"It may just be the job," Teddy said. "Selling coffee and toilet paper's okay, but it's not too stimulating. I've been thinking of going back to school."

"Bravo," Aurora said. "I hope you will."

She gave him a hug of encouragement and blew Jonathan a kiss before getting into her car. Both Jonathan and Kermit the Frog blew her a kiss back.

"What if I just bought the three of you a television set as a present and brought it over?" she asked, looking up at Teddy. "Do you think Jane would throw it out the window?"

"Wait a month or two," Teddy advised. "Right now I think she'd throw it out the window. But if you'll give me a month or two, I'll work on her."

Driving away from Teddy was never easy—Aurora almost always wanted to cry when she left him. There was just something sad in Teddy, even when he seemed fairly happy. Sometimes she found herself wishing Jane would just disappear with a lover of some sort, leaving her Teddy and Jonathan. It seemed to her it would be nicer at home if only some younger people were there.

She sniffed back a tear, braking for a cat that was idling in the street. She thought she might go see Jerry, though he would be annoyed if she showed up. He was almost always annoyed when she showed up, though he tried to suppress it. It took all her wiles to override his annoyance, make him pleasant again, and get him to touch her.

She felt quite low, as she often did when leaving Teddy— she felt she might not be able to muster a sufficiency of wiles to overcome Jerry's pique just at that time. Yet she didn't feel like driving home in resignation to quarrel with Rosie or Hector. She didn't want to go home and be an old person, with other old people.

Her last resort at such times, when she didn't feel like trying to get Jerry Bruckner to unfold the bounty of his sex one more time, was the Pig Stand. It was a resort she seemed to be having recourse to more and more often lately—but, at least, the mince pie was excellent.

"I won't have but one piece," she said to herself as she turned the car toward Washington Avenue.

"And you should move a little faster when you cross the street," she said out the window to the idling cat.

III

Aurora's Project

1

"You sure do own a lot of gowns," Jerry said, rolling over. "I don't think I've ever seen you in the same gown twice. You're sort of a Scheherazade of gowns."

Aurora pulled the gown of the moment back down over her hips. It was a pale peach gown she had bought in Paris some ten years back.

"I'd like to think that means I'm going to get a thousand and one nights out of you," she said, stroking his stomach. She had become too fond of him to conceal many of her feelings, although she knew her feelings disturbed him. He would have been more comfortable if she concealed nine-tenths of her feelings, and she knew it, yet she couldn't conceal them—or, at least, she refused to. She felt them, she wanted to feel them, she let them go on and brim over—it seemed unlikely that she would ever brim again in quite that way, and she had no intention of slapping a lid on what she felt, bleak though the ultimate consequences might be.

Jerry said nothing. It was at such moments, after lovemaking, when he felt most strongly that life would have been more comfortable if he had followed his instincts and headed out to Elko. There were probably some cute, skinny wait-resses in Elko.

"I do have some very nice gowns," Aurora said. "In my day nice gowns were thought to be a necessary accouterment to seduction—I'm sure that view has long since gone by the way. Somehow I doubt that I'm going to get anything like a thousand and one nights out of you despite my well-chosen gowns."

They were lying in his bed at dusk, with no lights on—the sun had set, but birds were still chirping in Jerry's backyard. Theirs was not an affair of brilliant mornings or sunny noons—theirs was an affair of dusk and gowns. Aurora managed it that way—relentlessly, but with a nice tact.

Just when Jerry was beginning to feel surly, resenting her, telling himself it was time to dig in his heels and not let her make it happen again, she arrived and somehow made it happen. She would bring over a good bottle of wine or a thermos of margaritas of her own making. He liked good wine and good margaritas—they helped him get his mind off a long day of patients whose miseries were endless and ineradicable. He was pleasantly fuzzy from the wine, or pleasantly tipsy from the margaritas; Aurora would materialize in her gown and bite his neck or something. Even when he was at his stiffest, determined not to allow her to surprise him, she would quickly worm her way around his resistance and surprise him.

At such moments she somehow wiped out the age gap and all other gaps, just with sheer appeal. Sometimes she was delicate and sometimes she was bold, sometimes she got him a little drunker than other times, but always, little by little, she dissolved his resistance. She made him forget that she was a lot more fleshy than the slim, trim exercise addicts he usually had for girlfriends. The slim, trim beauties went to no such trouble. They assumed he'd break his neck trying to seduce them, and if he didn't, they could always race-walk away and some other guy would. Their bodies were exactly the kind of bodies he liked, and Aurora's wasn't at all, and yet, again and again, she coaxed him into bed.

Once he had allowed it to happen yet again, Jerry felt half annoyed, but also a little flattered. Who else had ever put that much thought, or that much tact, or anything like that much skill, into seducing *him?* Aurora never let it become just the same old thing—at least, she hadn't so far. She took some pains with her preludes, bringing him tasty things to eat, or books and records she knew he wanted. She didn't call too often, she stayed clear of him during working hours, she spaced her visits, she was responsive to anything he wanted to do, and often had things *she* wanted to do—erotic things—that took him by surprise.

It was odd to think of a woman her age as his mistress, but the word "girlfriend" didn't work either for a woman her age. He didn't quite know what to call her, but he had to admit that if a mistress was what she was, she was pretty nearly an ideal mistress. Once his resistance dissolved on a given occasion, he sometimes suddenly felt that he loved Aurora— loved her very much. He felt touched emotionally in ways that he had not been touched before.

Still, the fact remained that he was sleeping with someone he indeed might love but didn't really want to sleep with. Sometimes he would spend half a day trying to rehearse a nice way to tell Aurora that he didn't want to sleep with her anymore, but he never came close to actually telling her such a thing. Half an hour after rehearsing things to say that would help him get rid of her, she would show up and make him forget all his plans. There would be moments when he even felt that he was in love with her—*really* in love. Several times he felt it so strongly that he told her he was in love with her. Aurora usually received these declarations lightly —so lightly that it annoyed him.

"I don't say that very often," he complained. "I don't tell just anybody that I'm in love with them. Doesn't it matter to you?"

They were standing by the bed—they had been kissing, but Aurora moved back a step. She looked inaccessible, and less fond of him than she had seemed only a moment earlier.

"That's flattering to hear, I suppose," she said.

"You suppose?" Jerry said, startled. "Don't you want me to love you?"

"Why, yes, I suppose," Aurora said again, with a cool little smile.

Jerry began to feel tight in his chest. He also felt a sense of déjà vu. it was to avoid just such scenes or just such moments that he mainly kept on the move. He had been afraid one might develop with Aurora, which was why he had been planning to get rid of her. Now the ground between them was splitting—a crevasse had just opened between them, and it was widening, all because he had suddenly felt himself in love with this devilish, aging woman, and had said so.

"What are we doing here, then?" he asked. "Why do you come to my house, if you don't want me to love you?"

"To get laid," Aurora said.

Jerry flinched, not so much at the statement as at her tone, which was still light. She wasn't angry or hard—moments ago they had been kissing—but she didn't seem to take his declaration of love seriously. Nothing very strange had happened—feeling had risen up in him and he had said, "You know what? I love you." Why had that made her step away?

"You're joking," he said. He decided that must be it. She was always teasing and joking, making remarks that were ironic, or sarcastic, or vulgar, or silly. Often her joking took him off guard—he was aware that she was quicker than he was, that he could never get quite in sync with her humor. Maybe instead of a widening crevasse, all that was going on was a leg pull. Maybe she was pulling back in order to suck him in a little deeper.

"Am I joking?" Aurora asked. She came back closer to him and put her arms around his neck.

"Tell me," she said. "Am I joking?"

"I think you're crazy," Jerry said. "All I did was tell you I love you. Most women like to hear that."

"Here we go, a generalization," Aurora said. "I expect it's a true one, of course, for once. Most women do like to be told they're loved, but only when it's true, my dear. Only when they can believe it—otherwise it can be rather off-putting, as you have just discovered."

"You don't believe me?" Jerry said. It had not occurred to him that his "I love you" would be disbelieved, although his own words, in this instance, took him by surprise—he had not really planned or expected to say it.

"Nope," Aurora said, moving even closer. Then she bit his neck so hard he tried to jerk away. But she didn't let him. For a moment he felt like shoving her through the window—who was she to disbelieve him so casually? But he didn't shove her through the window—there was a rather hostile wrestling match that led to a sweaty, sticky embrace. When it was over Jerry still felt aggrieved that Aurora was so skeptical of his feelings at the moment when he felt so strongly.

"I suppose I was rather hard on you," she said, rubbing the bite on his neck. She had broken the skin just slightly.

"You were horrible," Jerry said. "I do love you—I wouldn't even still be in this town, if I didn't love you."

Aurora didn't look inaccessible anymore, at least. But her look now was a little sad.

"Planning to leave soon?" she asked.

"No, not really planning," Jerry said. "But you *are* a big factor in my life, even though you don't believe it."

"What about your patients?" Aurora asked. "Were you planning on chartering a bus and taking them with you?"

Jerry didn't answer. Actually, when contemplating Elko, he did feel guilty about his patients. He wasn't really curing any of them—he was just sort of maintaining them, listening a lot, advising a little. Patsy had been right to call him the neighborhood priest. He wasn't making anybody well—he was just providing a kind of consistent reassurance. Still, his parishioners *did* depend on him. A little reassurance was better than none.

"Say something," Aurora demanded. "Were you just planning to run out on me and your patients too, and if so, why did you profess such shock when I made free to disbelieve your little declaration of love?"

"It wasn't so little," Jerry said—her immediate step back, when he'd said it, still hurt—and so did the bite on his neck.

"That's for me to judge, and I judge it to have been modest," Aurora said. "Your patients all sound rather crushed. I imagine they think of you as a doctor. I doubt many of them realize what a trifler you are."

"I haven't actually gone anywhere," Jerry said. "How am I trifling?"

"You're the psychiatrist," Aurora said. "I've done my best not to start explaining you to yourself. That would be quite presumptuous, since I'm not a psychiatrist. I'm just a picky woman."

"You are picky," Jerry said.

"Yes, I know," Aurora replied. "Men have been complaining about my pickiness since I was fifteen. I've heard my flaws described hundreds of times over the years."

She fell silent. Jerry wished she'd go home, but on the other hand he knew that if he let her go home looking so sad he'd be miserable and feel guilty all night, although he really hadn't done a thing to feel guilty for, that he could remember.

"Picky or not, I recognize that you're a very sweet man," Aurora said in a subdued voice. "It's because you're so sweet that I've developed this awkward crush on you. Because you're sweet you've even let me indulge my crush—a generous thing for you to do. It may well be my last crush, and it's meant a lot to me. But I've never been fool enough to assume it could mean much to you. I suppose that's why I have a tendency to withdraw when you suddenly decide you love me. I feel you're only saying it for your own benefit."

"You mean you think I only love myself?" Jerry asked.

"No, no," Aurora said, getting off the bed. She picked up her dress rather wearily and went into the bathroom to change. Jerry sat up, but he didn't get out of bed. He felt it was likely to be a night he would mainly spend being depressed. Maybe he'd walk to the video store and rent a kung fu movie, as good an antidote as any to certain kinds of depression.

Aurora soon emerged from the bathroom, buttoning her dress.

"Where were we in our debate?" Jerry asked pleasantly. There was still hope that he could work her out of her low mood before she left.

Aurora sat down in a chair across from the bed and picked up a stocking. She had been to see Pascal before coming to see Jerry, and she tried to keep up certain dress standards when seeing Pascal. He had been extremely surly with her since leaving the hospital—he never failed to point out that she had dropped him for a younger man after he had cracked his skull while coming to her rescue.

Still, there was no telling—Pascal might yet be her lot in life, so she tried to keep up her standards. She wore stockings when she went to see him, and despite his surliness they managed to have a certain amount of fun.

But at the moment, with the day waning and gloom in her heart, she didn't feel like getting back into stockings. Instead of putting them on, she wadded them up and stuffed them in her purse.

"Well, we were discussing your career as a trifler," Aurora said. She transferred herself to the edge of his bed and turned on the bed light so she could see him better. Trifler or not, he was appealing, and never more so than when he was feeling aggrieved, or misunderstood, or pouty at the thought that he was not being taken seriously. She touched his face fondly to show that she bore him no hard feelings.

"Thanks to your indulgence I've become profoundly fond of you, young man," she said. "You allowed me to take an interest in you, and now I have."

"I've taken an interest in you, too, although you don't seem to believe it," Jerry said.

"If you don't stop being so defensive I'm going to bite you again, and this time it will *really* hurt," Aurora said.

"I'm not defensive," Jerry said defensively. "I just don't have any idea what you want."

"I want you to be good," Aurora said. "I'm having my fun and that's fine, but I don't like to think that I'm having it with someone who won't bother to be good."

Her remark was so unexpected that Jerry didn't know quite what to say. At least she was not looking so sad. He took one of her hands and she let him hold it.

"Expense of spirit," she said. "Remember the line? Most of the men I've loved haven't been much, professionally.

Hector was a minor general. My husband, Rudyard, was a minor executive. Pascal is a minor diplomat. Trevor, my most dashing beau, was a minor yachtsman. Vernon Dalhart was a minor oilman. The only first-rater I've ever been involved with was Alberto, my tenor, and he was only first-rate for a few years in his youth. He ended his days running a music store."

She pursed her lips, looked away, then looked back at him. "I thought I'd do better, but when all's said and done I didn't do better," she said. "Now I've flung myself at you just because you're cute.

"I'm continuing my pattern of not doing better," she added with a wry grin.

"I see—I fit right in with the rest of your guys, don't I?" Jerry said—he liked her wry grins. "I'm as minor as the rest of them."

"Yes, but you can still be good," Aurora said. "You started out as a fake shrink, but now, like it or not, you're a real shrink. People become what they do, and you *are* treating your patients. I like that. In fact I like it a lot. But now you have to live up to it, don't you? I don't mean with me. You can cast me out any day and go back to your working girls. I've never exactly been a working girl, but I respect them. You can have as many of them as you want, once this is done."

"Please stop talking like that," Jerry said. Although he knew very well that he wanted the affair to be over, he didn't want to admit that fact to Aurora. Instead, he felt a need to deny it, even to make it sound ridiculous. He knew that Aurora's way of looking at their situation was a good deal more honest than his own. That was no novelty, either—women were always more honest about impending breakups than he was able to be. It left him feeling conflicted, which was how he felt when he looked at Aurora as she sat sadly beside him, rubbing the back of his hand.

"This isn't finished," he said.

"Perhaps not," Aurora admitted. "But you mustn't lure me away from my point."

"I guess I've forgotten the point," Jerry said.

"Your patients," Aurora said. "They're the point. Being a doctor is not like being a concierge."

"Well, there are similarities," Jerry said.

Aurora let go his hand and stood up.

"You only want to quibble," she said. "I frequently enjoy quibbling myself, but this is not one of the times when I'm likely to enjoy it. So I'm going."

She picked up her purse and walked out. Jerry jumped up and grabbed a pair of shorts. He caught up with Aurora just as she was getting into her car.

"I didn't mean to make you mad," he said.

"You didn't," Aurora said. "I'm not angry. I suppose I'm just disappointed—you're so afraid of serious talk, or serious anything.

"But perhaps you aren't, with your patients," she added. "If I had just had the good sense to stay a patient, I might have got seriousness out of you. I'm sure not getting it this way."

"I haven't done anything," Jerry protested. "You've got me leaving town and deserting my patients, and deserting you, too, but I haven't left. I may not be doing that much good, but I'm still here, doing my best."

"Perhaps it's just energy," Aurora said, deciding that she wasn't quite up to managing her seat belt.

"What's that mean?" Jerry asked.

"It takes immense energy to remain decent," Aurora said. She put her key in the ignition and wiggled it a few times to encourage it. "Some people just don't have it.

"I scarcely have the energy to be decent now myself," she added. "It's no job for the lazy. The truth is that Hector Scott would be completely justified in bashing my head in with a golf club, and you know why? Because dealing with him decently in his present state takes more energy than I have. To my shame I've diverted much of my energy to you. There's almost none left for poor Hector—but at least I'm decent enough to feel ashamed of my neglect."

"Aurora, I don't think I'm neglecting anybody," Jerry said.

Aurora just looked at him standing by the car in his shorts. For a moment, he reminded her of Teddy. There was something hollow there—something that might break. She wondered if, Hector Scott apart, she had ever been attracted to anything but weakness? Why couldn't she, for once, be attracted to strength? Why did so many men look so quivery when you looked at them hard? Why did the sight of a man she liked, or perhaps loved, make her feel so alone?

"When will I see you?" Jerry asked. He had a sense that she might be leaving not to return, and it made him feel panicky, suddenly. He forgot that he didn't really like to sleep with her, forgot his dreams of Elko. He didn't want to hear Aurora say that she was never coming back.

"I don't know," she said. "I'll have to think about it."

"I wish I knew what I'd done," Jerry said.

"Oh, you've been fine," Aurora said. "You've indulged me quite a lot. In your own way, you're exemplary."

She started the car and let it sit for a minute, idling. She looked steadily at Jerry while it was idling, thinking that a steady look might drive him back into the house. But he just stood there looking youthful and appealing, hangdog, worried, sad.

"Are you sure you aren't the kind of fellow who goes off to the store to get a loaf of bread and is never seen or heard from again?" she asked.

At home, later, when she told Rosie she had asked him that question, Rosie looked shocked.

"What did the poor man say?" she asked.

"The poor man said nothing," Aurora said.

"Good lord," Rosie said. "What got into you?"

"Fatigue, I suppose," Aurora said. "Sometimes I feel like I'm holding up both ends of this unfortunate passion."

"You say even worse things to men than I say," Rosie said. "I thought I was the worst, but maybe I ain't.

"So is that where you left it?" she asked, when Aurora didn't elaborate.

"I'm afraid that's where we left it," Aurora said.

2

The General had begun to wonder if the gloom would ever lift. Aurora had stopped singing opera in the bathroom, a bad sign. Rosie still did his eggs impeccably, but after that she surrendered herself to television for the rest of the day. No amount of coaxing could persuade her to play dominoes. He was so bored and so tired of the gloom that he even attempted to get Aurora to ask Pascal over for dinner, or a game of cards, or anything.

"You hate him and he hates you, why should I invite the little trifler over for dinner?" Aurora said. "I might get annoyed and stab both of you and have to spend the rest of my life in a rotten jail."

"Aurora, that's nonsense," the General said. "It's hard to stab a person seriously. It takes training. Mostly when a person gets stabbed the knife hits a bone and they bleed a little and that's it."

"Yes, I'm sure that's what would happen if I stabbed you, since there's nothing left of you but bone," Aurora said. "Every night your bones stab me in five or six places. Your elbows are particularly lethal—they're so sharp I could carve a turkey with them."

"Shut up, I wish you would both hang yourselves," Rosie said. They were all at the breakfast table, waiting for Willie, who was out in Rosie's room, packing his bag. Willie refused to fly, and so was being sent by bus to a drug rehab center in Huntington, Alabama. Gallantly, he was leaving Rosie his pickup for her own personal use. Insofar as Rosie could remember, Willie's leaving her his pickup was the most generous thing any man had done for her in her life. The fact that he was doing it rendered her even more heartbroken than she would have been anyway at the thought of his departure.

"What an original contribution to the conversation, and how like you," Aurora said. "I don't intend to hang myself, but if Hector feels that he'd enjoy hanging himself, it's fine with me.

"Just kidding, just kidding," she added hastily, feeling that a tear storm was gathering in her maid. She scooted her chair over closer to Rosie and hugged her, just as the tear storm broke.

Willie stumbled in just at that point. He himself had been crying more or less continuously for three days at the thought of his departure for a foreign land; he had never set foot beyond the Texas border in his life and could hardly believe he was going to get on a bus and leave Texas.

"It's the land of my birth and I hope it's the land of my death, too," he said several times, exasperating Aurora.

"Willie, you need to lighten up," she informed him. "You're not going to die, you're going to be cured."

"It's such a long way from home, though," Willie said. "I wisht I'd never taken heroin in the first place."

Now, at the sight of Rosie sobbing miserably, he began to sob miserably too. Aurora hung grimly to Rosie, whose small body was shaking violently. The General looked on in dismay—all around him, people were crying—and a tear or two even leaked down his own cheek. He knew he was going to miss Willie. The man might be incompetent, but at least he was male, and having another male on the property was a nice change from nothing but the same old cranky females.

"My God," he said. "Why are we all crying? He's just

going to Alabama. He'll be back in forty-five days. There weren't this many tears shed on Omaha Beach."

"Hector, don't you understand anything?" Aurora asked. "Willie's part of our family now—we're going to miss him cruelly for forty-five days. No wonder we're crying."

"You aren't crying," the General pointed out.

"That's because I have to drive," Aurora informed him. "I can't drive when my eyes are red."

"You can't drive when they're blue, green, or purple, either," the General told her. "You can't drive no matter what color your eyes are."

"Hector, if you provoke me at a tragic moment such as this, you'll regret it," Aurora said.

"What town is it I change buses in?" Willie asked, drying his face on a napkin. "What if I sleep through it? Where will I end up?"

"You change in New Orleans," Aurora said. "Perhaps I should write that down for you."

"Would you please?" Willie asked. "I don't want to ride off and just get lost out there. I been having bad dreams, and they're all about getting lost."

"He's got no more sense of direction than a bird," Rosie said, wiping her eyes on a napkin.

"Rosie, birds have an excellent sense of direction," the General said. "They fly thousands of miles and arrive year after year at the same pond."

"Well, then he's got no more sense of direction than a hippopotamus," Rosie amended. "I don't guess hippos fly no thousands of miles."

"Hector has a point, though," Aurora said. "Forty-five days isn't forever. Before we know it Willie will be coming home, cured. We should all keep that in mind and try to get a grip on ourselves."

"I never lost my grip on myself," the General pointed out.

"No, of course you wouldn't, Hector," Aurora said. "You're our rock. You've a veritable Gibraltar. Human emotion rarely sways you. In all my years with you it's only swayed you once or twice, and then only by a few millimeters."

"Don't pick on him, he's as human as the rest of us, he's

just older," Rosie said. Lately, for some reason, Aurora had been savage with the General—so savage that Rosie herself was beginning to feel protective. In her view the General had been behaving better in the last few weeks. He seemed even to have gotten beyond flashing and he rarely appeared naked anymore. There was no reason for Aurora to slam-dunk him every time he opened his mouth, but that was usually what she did.

"Come along, Willie, let's see how my car's feeling," Aurora said. "I don't know what I'll do for a mechanic while you're gone."

"Use Rosie," Willie suggested. "She's a better mechanic than me anyway."

"Yes, but she doesn't approve of me, and I happen to be in a period when I require a great deal of approval," Aurora said. "Your absence will deprive me of most of the approval I get, I'm afraid."

"Why should we approve of you? You don't approve of us," the General remarked.

The ride to the bus station was grim. The only sound was the General's snoring. The motion of a motorcar invariably put him to sleep now, usually within a mile or two.

"He used to cling to the edge of his seat in terror when I drove him somewhere," Aurora remarked. "Now he just snores. He used to merely snore at night. Now he snores most of the day as well."

"Honey, he's old," Rosie said. "You ought to treat him nicer. You and me will be old someday."

"You may not be no spring chickens, but you both still look good," Willie observed. He hoped the bus would be ready to leave when they got there. The women were not in a very good mood. Any moment one of them might be sawing at the other's throat. He wished he had some drugs with him. At least on the ride, even if he got lost in a foreign state, he wouldn't have to worry about a big fight breaking out between Rosie and Aurora.

At the bus station they were greeted by the news that Willie's bus would be an hour late—it had had a flat near Luling, Texas.

The General, having been awakened before he had his nap out, was feeling cranky.

"I abhor lengthy farewells," he said. "This pampering is ridiculous. Willie's a grown man. He's perfectly competent to get himself on a goddamn bus. Why can't we just go home and let him manage this for himself?"

In fact, the thought of all four of them having to endure one another's company for another hour while they waited in the chilly bus station was not a thought Rosie was happy with, either. Aurora was being too nice to Willie, for one thing. It always annoyed her when Aurora was too nice to one of her boyfriends. After all, it was *her* boyfriend, Willie, who was leaving to go be rehabbed off heroin. She didn't see why Aurora should get to horn in on the emotion at such a moment.

"You two go on home and watch your soaps," Rosie said. "I'll come home on a bus, if Willie ever leaves."

"If I ever leave?" Willie said, startled by her comment. "I thought you didn't want me to leave. You mean you want me to leave?"

"Shut up, Willie—my nerves are on edge and it just came out wrong," Rosie said. "I'm trying not to have no breakdown, if you don't mind."

Aurora saw that Rosie was indeed not far from the point of serious sorrow. She had been low for days, worrying about Willie's departure, worrying that they would lock him in his cell and do horrible things to him in Alabama, worrying that he would be raped by gay drug addicts and have AIDS by the time he came home—if he came home.

It was not hard to see that, in fact, Rosie's deepest fear was that Willie just might not come home. He might find someone younger and prettier in Alabama—a nurse in the rehab center, for example, someone who was only forty-five or fifty. He might never come back at all.

At the moment, Rosie was staring at Willie—all two hundred and thirty pounds of him—with a look of woe, as she stood in the bare bus station, holding one of his large hands. All around them, little clumps of families were not much less woeful; they cried and blew noses and looked forlornly at whichever family member was about to depart—usually a boy, usually to the army. One fat girl with hair exactly the color of Melanie's was clinging to a boy who looked no more than fifteen.

The thought of Melanie, so young and so far away, pushed Aurora's own spirits suddenly downward. All around them was evidence of what she knew in her own heart: that life was nothing but a matter of innumerable comings and goings, separations and separateness, of departures from which there might be no certain return. Rosie, a woman of erratic taste but profound common sense, was right to worry about Willie's return. The fact was, sometimes people didn't return. Rudyard, her husband, had gone to cash a check and died of a heart attack in the bank; Emma, her daughter, had not returned from her agony with the cancer. Trevor had not returned from his yacht, Vernon had not returned from Alaska, and Alberto had not returned from Genoa, where he had gone to visit his kin. She had seen her lovers off gaily—she felt that was how one should send lovers off—but one by one they had departed, with her blessings, and had not returned. She had not been able to protect them, either at home or on their rambles; the end of it was that journeys that had seemed temporary at the time had merged into that great journey of the spirit which all must make. People left, they died, they didn't come back.

Fearful suddenly that one of the dear ones left to her—Melanie, Teddy, Tommy—might journey on, might not come back, Aurora realized that she didn't want to stay in the bus station a moment longer. She had to get out, away from all the departures, all the going away.

"Hector, Rosie and Willie might want to be alone," she said. "Let's wait outside."

She grabbed Willie and hugged him, tears in her eyes.

"Willie, I'm counting on you to do exactly as you're told," she said. "We'll all miss you. You get well as promptly as possible, and come back cured."

"Do my best, Miz Greenway," Willie said. He felt sad to be leaving, but what he really wished was that people would go away and leave him alone—all the hugging and crying and sad looks made it difficult for him to concentrate on the one name he had to remember: New Orleans, the town where he had to change buses. Leave-taking was one thing, but as he saw it, his life depended on making the change correctly in New Orleans. If he didn't, he'd just be lost, and it wouldn't matter whether he was a heroin addict or not.

"Aurora, it's broiling out there," Rosie said. "That bus ain't due for a good forty-five minutes. You'll melt and so will the General. Why don't you just go on home? I can ride a city bus. I rode 'em most of my life. Riding one more ain't going to hurt me."

"We'll wait," Aurora said. "We'll be right outside."

In the car the General quickly discovered that Rosie's description of what would happen to him was as deadly accurate as most of Rosie's descriptions. It *was* broiling, and though there was little of him that was meltable, he thought he might melt.

"Why do we have to wait?" he asked. "The bus might have another flat. We might be here for hours, in which case we'll both die of heatstroke."

"I'll employ my air conditioner if it gets too bad," Aurora said.

"Then the goddamn car will have a heatstroke and we'll all have to ride a goddamn bus," the General said.

"If you're going to be rude, then I don't think I will employ my air conditioner," Aurora said.

But she said it mildly, and, to his surprise, she took his hand and put her cheek against it. It had been weeks since she had done anything but bark at him. This tender gesture took him by surprise to such an extent that he almost jerked his hand away. He looked into her eyes, something he rarely ventured to do in periods when she was in a bad humor. Her eyes seemed to have grown larger since the last time he looked into them. They were very large and very sad.

"They shouldn't call them bus terminals," Aurora said. "They should just call them bus stations, like they used to. Calling them terminals is a very bad idea."

"What are you talking about?" the General said. "What's wrong with calling a bus terminal a bus terminal? It just means it's a place where buses stop."

Aurora stared at him gravely.

"Think about it," she said. "What does the word terminal suggest to you, at your advanced age?"

The General saw the point, but it was hot, and he was still annoyed, despite the encouraging fact that Aurora was still pressing his palm against her cheek.

"I know, dying," he said. "But it could also just suggest a place where the buses stop."

"Think about it some more and I'm sure you'll see that stations is the better word," Aurora said. "Stations is so much more romantic. We all proceed from station to station, after all."

"If it's romantic, I'm surprised you like it, then," the General said. "You've been about as romantic as a goddamn fireplug lately—at least to me."

"That's because you're so difficult that you make me forget that I love you," Aurora said, looking straight at him.

The General, feeling shy suddenly, said nothing.

"But I do love you," Aurora said. "Despite your difficulty and despite my little lapses."

"*Little* lapses?" the General said. "Some of them aren't so little, at least not from where I sit. Some of them go on for years."

Despite the heat, Aurora scooted closer and put her arm around him. It seemed to the General that she must be feeling very insecure to be scooting closer to him on such a hot day.

"Even if they aren't little, I was hoping you'd overlook them," she said.

The General gave it some thought. He rubbed her hand a bit.

"Okay, just don't start crying," he said, at the very moment that she put her face against his neck and started crying. A white bum so drunk that he could scarcely walk staggered over to the curb and held out a Styrofoam cup, hoping the

General would put some money in it. The General ignored the cup. Aurora slipped one of her hands inside his shirt, a thing she liked to do. She continued to cry. The bum was reluctant to leave without any money, though finally he did. Aurora had more staying power than the bum; she sobbed for a good while, but finally she stopped.

"I don't suppose I'm perfect either," the General allowed.

"What a generous admission," Aurora said, resting comfortably against his shoulder, though thanks to his boniness she had to wiggle around for a bit before she could get comfortable. When she glanced up at Hector, she saw that he was wearing his wary look, the look he assumed when he couldn't figure out what she might do next.

"Are we going to take any more trips?" he asked, by way of changing the subject. He didn't know what the subject of the moment was, exactly, but with Aurora in such an emotional state he felt it might be a good idea to change it, just on general principles.

"Well, we're here at the station," she said. "Where would you like to go?"

"Nowhere you have to go on a goddamn bus," he said. "I meant a cruise or something.

"I'm at my best when I'm on the water," he added. "I feel sexier. All we ever did on our cruises was screw. If we hadn't stopped taking cruises I doubt we would have had any of these problems."

Aurora found herself wondering if Jerry Bruckner had left town yet. Every time she dialed his number or drove to his house, she expected him not to be there. His assurances that he wasn't about to leave either her or his patients were lies, she knew—though probably he was lying to himself and believing his own lies, as men so often did. Meanwhile, here was Hector, still hoping for one more sexy cruise. Maybe he was right. Maybe they ought to try it, though the prospect held a large potential for melancholy. Their last sexy cruise had been eight years before, when Hector was in some respects a different man.

"We could splurge and get one of those staterooms with a

big bed," the General said—he was getting excited about his own idea. Mainly he thought it might help if he could just get Aurora to himself again. In Houston he just didn't seem to be able to get her to himself.

"What do you think?" he asked.

"About the cruise, or the big bed?" Aurora asked.

"Well, both," the General said. A huge, puffy Gulf cloud floated over, making it briefly cooler.

"Yes, why not?" Aurora said. Hector needed encouragement, and if Jerry Bruckner was about to skip out, as she suspected, she would prefer to be far away. Asia would be a nice distance—Hong Kong, the South China Sea, the Seychelles, anywhere. Perhaps by the time they returned she would have ceased to ache so much for Jerry. Her ache was unseemly, of course, but still, she had it.

"By God, this is a miracle," the General said. "It's the first time in all our years together that you've wanted to do something that I want to do."

"Not true and you know it," Aurora said. "I can assure you that our sexy cruises wouldn't have been so sexy if I hadn't wanted to do them or it both."

"So what will it be, the Greek islands?" the General asked. He took out his handkerchief and wiped his sweaty face, feeling like a new man. Aurora borrowed the handkerchief, wiped hers, and then scooted back behind the wheel and started the car.

"No, someplace further," she said. "Since you're being nice for a change I think I'll employ my air conditioner for a few minutes."

Inside the bus station, Rosie and Willie had sunk steadily downward to a level of misery neither could remember ever having reached before. Rosie sat on a bench. Willie shuffled around, smoking. From time to time he sat down, too, only to pop up a moment later and resume his shuffling. Rosie was remembering the time long ago when she had finally given up on her marriage and gone home to Bossier City in despair. Royce, her husband, had been seduced by a slut, her children were driving her crazy, so crazy that she had even quit her job at Aurora's and started car-hopping at a drive-in on McCarty Street. One day it all simply became too much. She stuffed her few clothes in a suitcase and came to this same bus station, to depart Houston forever, she hoped.

It hadn't been forever—she had come back. But now the wheel had turned again, and she was back in the same bus station, feeling even more despairing. Why, of all the prison guards on the face of the earth, had she had to choose Willie, a drug addict, to fall in love with? Now he was going away for forty-five whole days. Life could change forever in a lot less time than forty-five days, and if it did, she had no doubt that it would change for the worse. Willie was no more slut-proof than Royce had been—possibly less slut-proof, since Royce had been lazy and Willie wasn't.

"I just hope I can remember to do it right in New Orleans," Willie said for perhaps the hundredth time. "That's the part that's worrying me, mainly."

It seemed it was the wrong thing to say, though Willie didn't know why. The next thing he knew Rosie jumped up, hugged him, and gave him a hasty kiss.

"Come back safe, hon," she said, and then she walked away, not in too straight a line either, holding her hand over her mouth as if she might be going to vomit. Willie didn't know what to make of it, but he didn't follow her. If Rosie needed to go, it was best just to let her go—in a way it was a relief. At last he could settle his mind and start concentrating on the bus change he had to make in New Orleans.

When Rosie reached the car she still had her hand over her mouth—at the last second, just as she was reaching for the door handle, she veered off behind the car and vomited in the gutter.

"Where'd she go?" the General asked. "She was almost here, and now she's run off."

"Open the glove compartment and see if we have any Kleenex," Aurora said.

"Why, who's sneezing?" the General asked, but he did as he was told.

"Nobody's sneezing—it's just that Rosie's nerves are more

delicate than ours," Aurora said. When Rosie finally got in the car, Aurora handed her the Kleenex.

"I left, I couldn't take it no more," Rosie admitted. "I just left the poor man standing there. I hope he gets on the right bus."

"He'll get on the right bus," Aurora said. "After all, they're professionals in the bus station. They don't want to be hauling people around in the wrong buses and then having to bring them back. They'll see that he gets on the right bus."

"Good God, he's a grown man, of course he'll get on the right bus," the General said. "I never heard such a fuss about getting on a bus."

"Hector, we're upset, we have to talk about *something*," Aurora said.

"Do you think it will be like it was with Frank Sinatra?" Rosie asked.

Aurora knew exactly what she meant—the two of them had rented a video of *The Man with the Golden Arm* and watched it in secret. The horrors of Frank Sinatra's cold-turkey withdrawal from heroin made a big impression on them. Although Aurora had hastened to assure Rosie that methods had improved and that modern drug rehab wouldn't involve Willie in any such tortures, neither of them believed what she said. Both continued to imagine Willie writhing around on a cot, going through exactly what Frank Sinatra had gone through.

The General, who had met Frank Sinatra once on a golf course in California, had no idea what Rosie was talking about.

"What are you talking about?" he asked. "Like *what* was with Frank Sinatra?"

"Hector, mind your own business, it's just a private joke," Aurora said.

"I see, another one," the General said. "Everything you two say nowadays is some kind of joke. I like jokes too. Why can't there be public jokes so I can enjoy them too?"

"I wouldn't call it no joke," Rosie said. "I'd call it hell, if I had to call it anything."

"If you mean the temperature in this car, it is a lot like

396

hell," the General commented. "That has nothing to do with Frank Sinatra, though. It has to do with the fact that Aurora didn't turn on the air conditioner until just a minute ago."

Rosie sniffed loudly a few times and began to cry. Then she began to beat her fist against the seat in front of her, which happened to be the seat the General was sitting in. Every time she hit the seat it caused his head to bounce.

"Stop hitting my seat!" the General said, annoyed.

"Hector, can't you be a little patient?" Aurora asked. "Rosie's very upset."

"I know she's very upset," the General said. "But why can't she beat on her own seat? The one *she's* sitting on, not the one I'm sitting on. If this keeps up I'll have whiplash."

Obediently, Rosie stopped beating on the General's seat, but instead of beating on her own, she began to beat on the door, which alarmed Aurora.

"Don't beat on the door!" she commanded. "It might come open and then you'll fall out and be killed."

"I doubt I could be so lucky," Rosie said between sobs.

"I didn't want to come on this trip," the General said. "I was forced to come, and now I regret it, just as I knew I would."

With all the beating on seats and doors, Aurora was having trouble steering a firm course. Several cars honked at her because they seemed to consider that she was in their lane. Also, while she had been seated close to Hector, she had twisted the rearview mirror around in order to take a reading on her looks and had forgotten to twist it back, which meant that she had only her instincts to inform her about what might be lurking to the rear. Her instincts told her there were probably large garbage trucks not far behind. A great many garbage trucks seemed to rove through Houston—it took constant vigilance to keep safely ahead of them, and with her rearview mirror in the wrong position she could not be sure that she *was* safely ahead of them. It was rather nerve-racking and became more so as she proceeded. She made an abrupt decision to switch lanes, hoping that whatever garbage trucks were behind her would use the opportunity to go on by, but instead, all that happened was that several more people honked at her and a few even seemed to be screaming at her.

The honks and screams of the people behind and on either side of her had the effect of making both Rosie and Hector forget their own troubles. They both looked out the window and saw signs of chaos on either side, which increased when Aurora, who decided she had given the garbage trucks enough time to go by, swung back into the fast lane.

"Don't do it!" Rosie and the General said at the same time.

"What are you, a Greek chorus?" Aurora said, annoyed. "I will so do it, and you can both shut up if you can't be helpful."

There were screechings of brakes, and a lot of honking, but the traffic parted.

"She's a maniac!" the General said over his shoulder to Rosie. "I don't ride with her much anymore, so I tend to forget. She's a goddamn maniac."

"You ain't telling me nothing I don't already know," Rosie said. "Is there any Kleenex up there?"

The General handed the whole box of Kleenex over to Rosie.

"Who said she could have the whole box?" Aurora asked. "Those are my Kleenex. I might need to cry soon myself if I'm not spoken to more kindly than I'm being spoken to at the moment."

"Yes, and we'll all need to cry if you don't watch your goddamn driving," the General said. "We'll be lucky if we're even alive so we *can* cry."

"Hector, you are rarely alive enough to cry, no matter what's happening," Aurora pointed out. "Many's the time I would have welcomed a few tears from you—tears that never fell."

"Maybe he don't have no oil in his tear ducts," Rosie volunteered. She had begun to feel a little better. "I had an aunt that had that problem. It's like a condition. We had to squirt stuff like window-washing liquid in her eyes before she could cry."

"At least it's a solution, no pun intended," Aurora said. "I think I'll get some and squirt it in your eyes, Hector—then we'll see if you can think of anything to cry about."

"Did you tell Rosie about our cruise?" the General asked in a bald attempt to change the subject. His tears, or the lack of them, was a subject they had been on long enough, it seemed to him.

"No, because it isn't settled," Aurora said.

"Of course it's settled," the General said. "You said yourself we ought to go to Asia."

"That was before you made free to criticize my driving," Aurora said. "You know how touchy I am about it. How dare you treat me with derision and then expect me to sail off to Asia with you!"

"You mean you're going to go away and leave me?" Rosie said, panic in her voice. "I thought you'd at least stay around until Willie gets back—if he gets back."

"Relax, we will not go away and leave you before Willie gets back," Aurora said. "An Asian cruise requires months of planning. Since Hector just said he thinks I'm a maniac, he obviously won't let me plan it, which means he'll have to do it himself. He's never planned anything, unless you count the invasion of Normandy, and I doubt he was allowed to plan much of that. So the planning stage for our Asian trip will probably take several years, by which time Willie will have been able to take a dozen cures, if he wants them."

"You mean you think he won't be able to kick it on the first try?" Rosie said. She herself had some doubt that Willie would be able to kick it on the first try, and was alert to any hint to what others might be thinking on that score.

"Rosie, it was a slip of the tongue," Aurora said. "Must you seek the darkest possible implications in every word I utter?"

The General was contemplating how much he hated travel agents, or buying plane tickets, or trying to figure out which hotels Aurora might hate the least. If he had to make all the arrangements and things went wrong on the trip, Aurora was sure to go into a towering rage; sometimes she went into towering rages even if *she* had done all the planning and chosen all the hotels. Her towering rages were often followed by days, if not weeks, of deep chill. The time they went to Cairo she had scarcely spoken to him all the time they were there, all because of a mishap or two that hadn't really been his fault.

It occurred to him that they were both getting on: the trip to Asia might turn out to be their last cruise. Having a large stateroom and a big bed wouldn't do him much good if Aurora was pissed off before they even started. He decided that, for the sake of harmony, he would apologize for calling her a maniac, and he immediately acted on his decision.

"For the sake of harmony I'm apologizing," he said. "Obviously you're not a maniac, you just happen to drive like one."

"Oops, you shouldn't have said that last part," Rosie told him. "It kind of cancels out the first part, even though the first part was real sweet."

"Oh, never mind, I suppose he meant well," Aurora said. "He knows he can't plan a trip, so the fact that he worked up to one of his rare apologies counts for something, even if he botched it."

The General felt a little relieved, but suddenly, peering out the window, he noticed that the street they were driving along wasn't bordered by large green lawns with huge houses behind them, as the streets in River Oaks were. This street was bordered only by a warehouse or two, lots of weeds, a railroad track, and a few saggy, paintless frame buildings.

"This isn't the way home," he announced. "Are you lost, on top of everything else?"

"Hush up before you get in worse trouble than you're already in," Rosie said. "She ain't lost, she's just headed for the Pig Stand."

"That's good advice, Hector," Aurora said. "This has all been an ordeal, and the healthiest thing to do after an ordeal is eat. I'm sure once you've had a piece or two of mince pie you'll realize that I'm right."

"I don't like mince pie, but you two can stuff yourselves all you want to," the General said. "Then maybe we'll finally get home."

In the cool green booth at the Pig Stand, after allowing Aurora to feed him a bite or two of her mince pie, the General began to feel very, very tired. Probably it was all that quarreling with Aurora, or waiting in the hot car or something. Thinking about Aurora and the large stateroom and the bed was nice, but just at that moment he was so tired he could hardly lift his iced-tea glass. His energy seemed to be leaving him, and he wondered for a moment or two if he was really up to a trip to Asia. He had served in Manila and, more briefly, in Burma. Thinking about Asia made him remember what a difficult time he had had working with MacArthur—and working with Vinegar Joe Stilwell hadn't been any cakewalk either. Both men had been impossible to satisfy—at some point he had developed a bleeding ulcer from the strain, though he couldn't quite pinpoint whether that had been when he was with Stilwell or with MacArthur. What he remembered more clearly was his immense relief when he was finally transferred back to the European theater. Still, going to Asia with Aurora in a large stateroom with a big bed would be a good deal easier than working for either Stilwell or MacArthur. His energy might pick up, though now, sitting in the booth, it did seem as if his energy was all sliding rapidly away. It had been an effort to chew the last bit of pie. Now it was an effort just to keep his eyes open and to sit up straight in his booth. He looked over at Rosie and to his shock and surprise saw General Stilwell's head where Rosie's should have been. He was afraid to look up at Aurora, for fear she might have come to resemble MacArthur. The General felt sad, suddenly—deeply sad: life was passing strangely. Just because he and Aurora were thinking about going to Asia was no reason for his old commanders to start popping up in the Pig Stand. He had not liked them when he was young, and he didn't want them showing up now that he was old. It was very confusing—he wished for a moment that Aurora could have been persuaded to pass up the Pig Stand and forgo her pie. If she could have been persuaded, they might be home by now and he could nap in his own chair. Of course, Aurora could never be persuaded—that was her charm, that was what he still found delightful about her. Even Rosie was not easy to persuade. So there they were at the Pig Stand, with his energies draining out of him like blood from a deep cut, and his old commanders were calling, and he felt very, very confused. The room turned a piercing blue for a moment—he thought perhaps he was imagining the harbor at Hong Kong as it might look when he and Aurora sailed into it aboard their ship. He saw himself wearing his white ducks—he would have to get some new ones. They could stand at the rail as the great harbor came into view. But then, slowly, the brilliant blue faded and a grayness long as the ocean, wide as the sky, spread before his eyes. A few shadows cut the grayness for a moment as waitresses moved around the room, clearing the tables, but then the shadows grew more faint, the grayness seemed restful, and he slipped gratefully into it as into a warm pool.

The General's head tipped and rested against Aurora's shoulder. She was, at the moment, occupied with finishing a crossword puzzle she had begun earlier in the day. She had often found that when stumped on a crossword, working on it at the Pig Stand often got her going again. Words that she would never have thought of at home just popped right out of her brain when she was at the Pig Stand with a piece of pie handy to help her think.

Rosie looked across the table and saw that the General had gone to sleep. She didn't mind. Let the poor old thing nap. She also didn't mind that Aurora was doing her crossword and ignoring everything else. As far as she was concerned, they could stay at the Pig Stand all day. The General could nap, Aurora could do her crosswords, and she herself could sip coffee and put off the moment when she would have to go back to her little house and face the fact that Willie wouldn't be there to sit in it with her for forty-five days and also forty-five nights.

"Are you really going to drag that poor old man to China,

or wherever you're thinking of going?" she asked, emptying another Sweet 'n Low into her coffee.

"Look how tired he looked," she added, bracing herself slightly for the moment when the General would start snoring. He seldom napped for more than thirty seconds without emitting his penetrating snore. His mouth just dropped open and out came the snore.

"A cruise was his idea, but I'd rather not think about it while I'm trying to do my crossword, if you don't mind," Aurora said.

"You ought not to have agreed to it unless you meant it," Rosie said. "You know how he is once he gets his heart set on something."

"Yes, I should know," Aurora said. "After all, he's had his heart set on me ever since I can remember."

Lorna, an elderly waitress who had served the two women often, came tripping over to the table with a steaming pot of coffee. She meant to freshen their cups, and was just about to tip the pot and pour a little coffee over Rosie's Sweet 'n Low, when for some reason she happened to glance at General Scott, who was dead.

Lorna had worked at the Pig Stand for many years, and had seen much, but even for a woman of her experience it was a shock to see a dead general sitting in one of her booths.

"Oh, good lord," she said, in a tone that caused Rosie to look up. The same tone had no effect on Aurora, who, when engaged with a crossword, seldom looked up.

Rosie thought for a second that Lorna must have spilled the coffee, which would have been unusual. Lorna was such a good waitress that she could pour coffee from ten feet away. But there was no spilled coffee on the table, and when Rosie looked up Lorna tactfully inclined her head, with its blue perm, in the direction of the General, who seemed to be napping comfortably against Aurora's shoulder. His mouth was open, it was true, but he wasn't snoring.

A second later, Rosie realized why the General wasn't snoring—why he would snore no more. Shock hit—she felt dizzy for a second, but only for a second. There was Aurora to think of—Aurora hadn't realized yet that a dead man, not a live man, leaned against her shoulder. She was tapping one finger impatiently against the table—she often tapped one finger when she was about to get a word.

Rosie looked to Lorna for help, but Lorna was finding herself a little more unnerved by this development than was good. The hand that held the coffeepot began to shake, forcing her to give up the idea of pouring Rosie some more coffee.

Rosie looked at Aurora, hoping she would look up—one look would do it.

"Hon," Rosie said, and stopped.

Aurora began to get a feeling she had had before—a sense of disquiet. Her feeling told her that something she wasn't going to want to know about had happened. Around her in the restaurant there had been a change of atmosphere. Things had become too quiet. No glasses were rattling. Silence was spreading through the Pig Stand, a place that was usually full of the noise of life.

"Hon," Rosie said again.

Aurora reluctantly looked at Rosie, who was very pale. She looked at Lorna, who had been forced to set the coffeepot on a nearby table. Lorna was also pale—she seemed to be trembling. Finally, Aurora looked at Hector, who was leaning rather too heavily against her shoulder. She knew at once that she wouldn't be finishing her crossword, not just then. The reason for the quiet in the restaurant was clear, and her feeling about the something she didn't want to know had been accurate.

Carefully, Aurora put the cap back on her fountain pen.

"Well, Hector, you would," she said in a small voice. "You . . . would, and just when I was beginning to like you again, too."

"He had a good life, I guess, your old boyfriend," Rosie said.

404

3

Melanie had only been back from the General's funeral two hours when Bruce told her he was sleeping with Katie. He had been pretty distant when he met her at LAX, and that was why. On the drive over to the Valley they had a hard time making conversation—even before they got to the apartment Melanie had begun to wonder why she had even come back. She had stayed in Houston ten days—her granny and Rosie were adjusting, there was no real reason for her to stay longer. When she talked to Bruce on the phone it made her nervous—it kind of made her wonder. He wouldn't tip one way or another on the question of her coming back. He wouldn't say he wanted her to, but he also wouldn't say he *didn't* want her to. His voice had an aggrieved tone, as if talking to her at all was this enormous burden. After just about every conversation, Melanie cried. She missed him and wanted him to say he missed her, but he didn't say it, and if his tone of voice was any indication, didn't miss her either.

"So why go back?" Rosie asked once, when Melanie was crying. "If he can't come up with a better conversation than that, then he's a jerk, and if he's a jerk, why go back? Stay here and help me with your grandmother."

"Stay here and help you with *you*, I believe you mean," Aurora said. "Sometimes I think you miss Hector more than I do."

"I do, I miss him terrible, I don't know why," Rosie said. "I wish I could just hear his cranky old voice one more time."

"People are odd," Aurora said. "But that's not Melly's problem. There's no reason she should sit around here being depressed by two moldering old women."

"But Bruce is a jerk," Rosie said. "He's a stupid little two-timing jerk, and I thought so the minute I saw him."

"That description more or less fits the male gender, you know," Aurora said.

"It didn't fit Willie, I just wish he was back," Rosie said, wiping her eyes. She had to wipe them every time Willie's name came up.

Aurora sighed, but she didn't cry. She looked at her grand-daughter, chubby and dispirited, and considered what to advise. Very probably Rosie was right about the young man, Bruce, but the fact that very probably she was right was no help to Melanie, who seemed to love him.

"Why don't you two run off to your gym and bob up and down for a while?" Aurora said to Rosie. "Melly could stand to lose two or three pounds, and you need to get your mind off Willie, if it is humanly possible for you to get your mind off Willie."

Only the day before they had received the bad news that Willie's therapy was not going well and that he might have to be in Alabama for as much as another month. The news convinced Rosie of what she had been more or less convinced of anyway, which was that Willie, cured or not, didn't want to be her boyfriend anymore and would never come back. Willie called collect every two or three days and said exactly the opposite—that he couldn't wait to come back, that he *did* still want to be Rosie's boyfriend—but Rosie in her heart of hearts didn't believe him.

The next day, Melanie began to get the feeling that it was

now or never. She made a plane reservation, called Bruce, and flew into LAX. Another bad sign was that Bruce hadn't really wanted to come meet her plane. He said he had been working a double shift at the gas station and was too bummed to drive that far. He actually tried to talk her in to taking a bus over to Hollywood-Burbank airport, which would be a lot easier for him.

"Bruce, I'm coming in at eleven-forty—nearly midnight," Melanie explained. "Am I really going to have to ride a bus all the way across L.A. at midnight?"

Then Bruce suggested that maybe her grandmother could give her enough money to take a taxi—he acknowledged that getting a bus at midnight was no fun. Melanie was getting close to losing her temper—he was just being *so* reluctant— and she was also getting close to crying when Bruce finally gave in and said, rather meekly, okay, he'd come and get her.

He was there, too, looking nervous, and he didn't kiss her on the mouth when she came bouncing up to hug him. She didn't know if it was deliberate; maybe he was just shy, with all the strangers milling around them, but it sort of left her with a sinking feeling—not a good feeling to have when you were just getting home at midnight. It was hard to come back and start trying again, with Bruce acting so reluctant. She asked about his acting class, and what movies he'd seen and stuff, but Bruce just drove. He didn't look at her, he wasn't cooperative when she tried to hold his hand, and when they got back to the apartment and she made a pass—after all, it was her first night back—he just deflected the pass by saying he was tired.

"Okay," Melanie said. After all, it was one in the morning by then and he did work in a gas station, maybe he *was* tired. But the fact that he hadn't kissed her on the mouth at the airport and then had deflected the pass, too, had begun to get her down. It wasn't too often that Bruce deflected a pass— sex was kind of the one sure thing they had, and now the vibe she was getting was that maybe they didn't have it any- more.

Then, since she felt he wouldn't talk and she felt too jittery just to get in bed and try to sleep, she started unpacking her suitcase and went to hang up her funeral dress and stuff, and that was when she got the big shock. They had only one closet, and it was always jammed, but now it wasn't, and the reason it wasn't was that none of Bruce's clothes were in it anymore.

"Bruce, where's your clothes, was it a robbery?" she asked, panicky for a moment.

"It wasn't a robbery," Bruce assured her, looking guilty and hangdog.

"Then where's your stupid clothes?" Melanie asked, almost yelling—she was getting in a bad panic. Maybe she shouldn't have called them stupid, Bruce had some pretty good clothes, but still—

He was just acting real reluctant—he didn't even say one word.

"Bruce, where's your clothes?" she demanded. She couldn't help it, she was getting wrought up.

"I'm living with Katie now," he said finally. "I took my clothes to her house."

Melanie was so stunned she couldn't speak—but she should have spoken, because at that point Bruce just stood up, stuck a couple of twenty-dollar bills on top of the TV, and walked out. By the time she was ready to speak he was gone and there was no one to speak to—really there wasn't even anyone to call. Her one semi-friend in L.A. was Katie, the little skinny yuppie who had just taken her boyfriend. Melanie would have liked to spend about a hundred hours talking to either one of them, or to both of them together, but of course that couldn't happen—she was obviously the last person either of them would want to talk to. Bruce had had his chance, and probably hadn't uttered thirty words all told, in the two hours she'd been with him.

But it was so weird—the two of them had just been getting to know Katie a little. She had come out to her mother's beach house a lot while Melanie was there recuperating from her miscarriage. Usually she had a guy, and usually they surfed. Sometimes all four of them went down the road and had Chinese. All Bruce could talk about afterward was what a complete yuppie Katie was. Melanie had even defended her, pointing out that she came by her yuppiness naturally. After all, nice as Patsy was, she was still pretty much a yuppie, and Katie was her daughter. Bruce even made fun of Katie's skinny legs; Melanie had even said, Come on, she's nice, she can't help it if she has skinny legs.

Three days after Melanie got back to town, Bruce called and asked if she'd send him his mail, and Melanie couldn't help bursting out. "I guess you managed to get over your phobia about skinny legs, didn't you, asshole!" she yelled.

Bruce, since he wasn't there facing her—he was safe at the other end of the phone—came on real calm and mature, which, considering the mood she was in, didn't help matters at all.

"You told me yourself I needed to get over that," he pointed out.

"If you were falling in love with her, why didn't you tell me when I was in Houston?" she asked. "Why'd you let me come all the way back out here if you were already in love with Katie?"

"It's not so much that I'm in love," Bruce said—he seemed to be real calm. It was as if he had just decided to meditate now about it all over the phone with her, real calm, as if he had done yoga all night or something. Just when she was so wrought up she could have smashed him with a club, he was suddenly Mr. Cool. It was extremely irritating. Melanie had all she could do to keep from screaming into the phone at the top of her lungs.

"If you're not in love, why'd you do this to me?" she asked.

"Melly, it wasn't like this was aimed at you," Bruce said. "It wasn't aimed at anybody. It just sort of happened."

"It may not have been aimed at me, but it hit me," Melanie said. "Now I lost my job—they said at the restaurant that I stayed away three days too long. So now I don't have a job and I don't have you—I don't have anything. I wish you'd told me before I came back here. All I do all day is sit and feel like a fucking fool."

"You need to get a little more positive about things," Bruce said blandly.

"Positive about what, you fuckhead!" Melanie yelled. "What do I have to be positive about? I've got about five dollars, the rent's due, and now I'm going to have to ask Granny for money, which I absolutely hate doing."

"I don't see why you hate it so much," Bruce said. "She's your grandmother. She's not going to mind."

"She may not mind about the money but she's gonna mind that I wasted my time with an asshole like you," Melanie said. "I talked myself hoarse defending you and then this happened."

"Are my *Varietys* still coming to the apartment?" Bruce asked, trying to change the subject. "I sent a forwarding address but they haven't started showing up over here yet."

"Yeah, they're here, you wanta come and get them?" Melanie asked. For a moment she had the faint hope that if she could just get him in her presence for a moment he might come back to her. He might have just got dazzled briefly—Katie *was* very good-looking in her yuppie way. Also, Katie totally couldn't exist without a guy—she went through every second of her life being vulnerable—maybe Bruce had fallen for the vulnerability. Maybe if he came back to get his mail he'd get some perspective and realize that Katie wasn't really his type. At least it went through her head. At least she'd get to see him face to face. But a second later she was sorry she'd asked, because Bruce immediately made five or six excuses and got off the phone. When he hung up she felt so bleak she didn't even move for at least an hour. There was nothing to move for. Who knew if she would even get to hear his voice on the phone again? He was a total wimp when it came to pressure—the mere thought that she wanted him to come over would probably be enough to keep him from coming over.

While she was feeling so bleak she couldn't move the phone rang and it was her granny—she had just called on a hunch. Her granny often had hunches where Melanie was concerned, and her hunches were usually right. They were so right that Aurora didn't even bother chatting for a while to see if it came out that her hunch was right. This time she just bore right in.

"What's wrong with my girl?" she asked, as soon as Melanie said hi.

"I don't want to talk about it," Melanie said. "It's my problem, you can't help me, Rosie can't help me, it's just hopeless."

"That must mean that he left you for another woman," Aurora said.

"Yep, Patsy's daughter," Melanie admitted. Though she had meant to try to conceal Bruce's departure for a while, she was actually just as glad she didn't have to. Concealing things from a snoop like her granny took a lot of energy, and she didn't really have that much energy, not just then.

"Do you mind very much?" Aurora asked.

"Yeah, I mind very much," Melanie said. "Why would you ask me that? I love Bruce. What even makes you think I might not mind?"

Sometimes her grandmother could just say two words and piss everybody around her off. It was as if she always had the two perfect worst words right on the tip of her tongue. She didn't mind saying them, either.

"Just fishing," Aurora said. "What would you rather do, get the boy back or get revenge on the other woman?"

"Neither's going to happen, what does it matter?" Melanie said. "I'll probably never see either one of them again."

In fact, she *had* found herself wanting to beat Katie up. She had a dream in which she pushed her off the Santa Monica pier.

"Whose fault do you think it was?" Aurora asked.

"Come on, it's both their faults," Melanie said.

"I imagine it was largely Katie's," Aurora said. "She comes by man-stealing naturally. Would you like to know what her mother's doing at the moment?"

"Who, Patsy?" Melanie said, puzzled. What difference did it make what Patsy was doing?

"That's the one—Patsy," Aurora said. "Your mother's best friend."

"Well, what?" Melanie asked. She felt a little impatient.

Now that her grandmother had found out, Melanie was eager to hash over the Bruce-Katie business a little bit more, not hear gossip about Katie's mother.

"She's trying to steal my lover," Aurora said. "I don't think she's managed it yet, but she's trying."

"Who, you mean the shrink?" Melanie asked, confused. Although months ago, long before the General died, Rosie had confided in her that she suspected Aurora might be "seeing" her shrink, Melanie hadn't taken it too seriously, at least not at first.

"What do you mean 'seeing?'" she had asked Rosie. "Of course she's seeing him. How can he be her shrink if she never sees him?"

"Not *that* way, that ain't what I meant," Rosie said. "I think it's more like a romance."

"Come on, he's younger," Melanie said. "He must be a lot younger. Why would he want to go with Granny?"

"I don't know if they go out or what they do," Rosie admitted. "I think it's a romance, though. Pascal thinks so too."

"Pascal's no one to talk. Granny said she caught him with a twenty-year-old," Melanie pointed out.

"Okay, okay," Rosie said—it was obvious that Melanie wasn't thrilled with the confidences she was offering, and why should she be? "I just wanted you to know, in case they run off or something," she added.

Later, though, when she thought about it, Melanie decided she wanted to hear more. The thought that her grandmother was actually having sex with a man so much younger was slightly disturbing. Of course, why shouldn't she? She and the General weren't married, and her granny herself had told her that she would have liked to have sex with Pascal on the couch; there was no reason she shouldn't stay active, and certainly she was the type to stay active, if there was any way to manage it. But still, the thought of Aurora and a guy that much younger took some getting used to.

"The shrink," Aurora confirmed. "*My* shrink. I should never have invited them both to my dinner party. Now she's trying to get her greasy little hands on him."

"Granny!" Melanie said. She was startled—she felt really confused. What Rosie had been hinting at was *true*.

"Melly, I hope I'm not shocking you," Aurora said. "I thought it might help to realize that what just happened to you could also happen to me. But I suppose you would prefer to think that your grandmother is past all that—that I'm safe —that age brings serenity or something."

"You mean it doesn't?" Melanie said. That *had* been what she was thinking, when she thought of her grandmother— even despite Pascal and the couch.

"I suppose it might, for some," Aurora said. She was sitting in her window nook, looking out her window, wondering what serenity actually felt like. She remembered asking her own mother that very question, after having just been jilted by a cool New Yorker; she felt that she could never be happy, much less serene. Her mother had just looked back at her, her large eyes gray and sad. If she had said anything, Aurora couldn't remember it. Now Melanie had been jilted by a not-so-cool Houstonian and felt sure she would never be happy —and the possibility *did* exist that she would never be very happy, not unless she got tougher with boys.

"So you mean you just think she's trying?" Melanie asked. "You don't think she's actually seduced him yet?"

"I think she probably hasn't, yet," Aurora said. "Unfortunately, since I'm in mourning, I'm not in a good position to fight fire with fire just now. He's not a man with much backbone, I'm afraid. He's the sort who tends to flow with whatever flow is flowing. I'm afraid I'm not optimistic."

"I guess you are in mourning, aren't you?" Melanie said.

"Yes, I have to try to behave for a while," Aurora said.

The way she said it—her voice got sad—made Melanie feel better somehow. Her granny must really miss the General, although she hadn't talked about him much while Melanie was home. It was good that her granny thought of herself as in mourning, even if it meant that Patsy got to make off with the stupid shrink. The General had been with Aurora for a long time, all Melanie's life—in fact, even longer than her life—and he deserved to be mourned. Certainly Rosie

413

mourned him—she sort of turned into a wet mop every time he was mentioned. With her granny it was harder to tell. She kept her cool better. But if she was willing to risk a boyfriend in order to mourn the General for a while, it must mean that she really had loved him despite all their bickering, some of which had gotten pretty intense.

"I hope she doesn't get him," Melanie said.

"You see what I mean, though, don't you?" Aurora said. "If the mother feels free to take another woman's man, then the daughter's very likely to do the same."

"I guess, but it still makes me mad," Melanie said.

"I wasn't suggesting you shouldn't be angry," Aurora said. "Of course you should be angry. I find I have a touch of sympathy for Katie, though, despite her treachery."

"Why?" Melanie asked.

"Because she lacked a proper upbringing," Aurora said.

"Baloney, she did not," Melanie declared. "She went to the best schools in L.A. What's so bad about her upbringing? At least she had a mother."

"Well, she had a weak mother," Aurora said. "I don't suppose I actually despise Patsy, but her character has certainly never impressed me."

"She was nice to me when I had my miscarriage," Melanie pointed out. It was a little annoying the way her granny took every opportunity to attack Patsy.

"I don't see what's so bad about her," she added. "She bought me some new clothes. I sort of feel like she's my aunt."

"Okay," Aurora said. "Those things I grant you. I won't run her down anymore. I would merely point out that it's rather unusual for a daughter to exhibit more character than her mother has, particularly where men are concerned."

"Katie may be bad, but so is Bruce," Melanie said. "He did the same thing with Beverly. We were getting along fine, and the minute Beverly got a Ferrari, he split.

"I guess he just likes yuppies," she added, remembering the whole Beverly episode more clearly. Dresswise, Beverly and Katie were sort of two peas in a pod. Probably Bruce did just like yuppies—he was always criticizing her for not being neat enough, or not picking up the house often enough—stuff like that.

"I think I'd better send you a little money, Melly," Aurora said. "I doubt you have any."

"Not much," Melanie admitted.

"Are you in the mood to come home?" Aurora asked.

"No!" Melanie said fiercely.

"Calm down, I just asked," Aurora said. "I do think Rosie's going to drive me crazy if Willie doesn't get back here soon."

"Is he nicer than C.C.?" Melanie asked—she had not had the pleasure of meeting Willie.

"Well, he's more modest," Aurora said. "C.C. had a tendency to get bigheaded every time he made a few hundred thousand dollars. Willie's never had a dollar to his name and has few reasons for getting bigheaded. He knows it, too."

They chattered on for a while. Melanie kept the conversation going—she didn't want to go home, but on the other hand she missed her granny, and Rosie. When her granny finally got off the phone, Rosie came on for a bit.

"Don't criticize Bruce!" Melanie insisted. Although Bruce had behaved horribly, she wasn't in the mood to hear him criticized.

"Okay, I won't until the next time I see him," Rosie promised.

"Why would you ever see him?" Melanie asked. "He'll probably marry Katie. Then he can wear polo shirts for the rest of his stupid life."

"You may think you're rid of him, but you ain't," Rosie assured her. "He'll come back one of these days, acting like a wet dog."

"How does a wet dog act?" Melanie wondered.

"Guilty," Rosie said. "He'll be trying to find a nice place to get warm."

When Rosie hung up, Melanie found that she felt a little better. Both her grandmother and Rosie seemed to be convinced that Bruce would be showing up again someday. They weren't wrong too often, so maybe he would. After all, he had showed up when he got tired of Beverly, Ferrari or no Ferrari. Katie didn't have anything resembling a Ferrari to offer, either—she just drove a Honda. Also, Bruce hated the ocean—he sort of hated water in general—and Katie couldn't live without surfing. That was a potential incompatibility, right there.

Since she was feeling a little bit forgiving, she decided she would just bundle up his mail and send it to him. It consisted almost entirely of copies of the daily *Variety*—since a copy came every day they were piling up. In a few more weeks, if she didn't do something, the apartment would be full of daily *Varietys*.

Bruce's plan in subscribing had been to find out what plays and TV series and stuff were being cast, but so far as she knew he had never actually shown up for a casting call. He kept putting it off until he got a little farther along in his acting class.

Having nothing better to do, Melanie decided to read a few of the casting notices herself. She had done some acting in high school—probably 90 percent of the people who showed up for casting calls were just kids who had done some acting in high school. Maybe she'd go to a few. Even if she didn't get a part and become famous, she might make a few friends.

Leafing through a few recent issues she saw that two TV pilots were being cast in the Valley, the first one at Warner Brothers the very next day. That was neat—she wouldn't even have to get herself over to Hollywood, she could just take a bus, or even walk. One of the pilots had a part for a maid—it caught her eye because the last thing she would ever be likely to be good at in real life was being a maid. What she might do, though, was a Rosie-imitation. She and her granny, when they were feeling lively and were just free-wheeling around, often competed with one another to see who could produce the most far-out Rosie imitation. Maybe she could reel off one for the casting director and become a famous TV star.

The thought definitely made her feel better—at least she had something to do for the next few days. The day was overcast and chilly; the thought of how miserable Bruce would be if Katie forced him to go surfing on such a day didn't hurt her spirits, either. Bruce really hated water, and yet had picked a little yuppie surf bunny to be his new girlfriend. The thought of Bruce shivering on the beach made her feel not quite so mad, actually. It was hard to feel totally mad at a guy who could make such a major mistake. Maybe it would teach him a lesson, if he didn't drown or something.

She was so excited by her idea of going to the casting call and doing a Rosie-imitation that she called her granny back, collect, and told her about it. It occurred to her that Rosie might have developed a few new mannerisms that she hadn't noticed when she was home.

"Why, yes, in fact she has," Aurora said. "Now she spends much of the day standing on her head. This is not a mannerism I feel I can imitate successfully but you're younger, you could probably make it work if you practiced a little."

"You mean she does housework standing on her head?" Melanie asked. Rosie had not stood on her head that she had noticed while she was at home, but then the General had just been buried and they were all being pretty decorous.

"No, she just stands there on her head," Aurora said. "I find it disconcerting. One minute I'm looking my maid in the eye and the next minute it's her toes I'm looking in the eye."

"What else?" Melanie asked.

"She polishes Hector's medals," Aurora said. "Now that he's not here to gripe at her, she's decided he was a saint in disguise. If that man was a saint, it certainly was in disguise, and a good disguise too, but I can't say that to Rosie. She jumps on me often enough as it is for my alleged mistreatment of him."

"She polishes his medals?" Melanie asked. "I never saw any medals."

"Well, he had a batch, but I don't want to talk about it—I'll decide he was more gallant than he was, and the next thing you know your grandmother will be crying into your ear."

"Granny, do you miss him?" Melanie asked.

Aurora sighed. She didn't answer for a moment.

Melanie became fearful—perhaps it was the wrong thing to ask when a person has just died.

"I'm sorry, maybe you don't want to talk about it so soon," she said.

"Oh, no, that's fine," Aurora said. "I do miss Hector. He was my old soldier, after all. We had rather a lively dialogue for a good many years. I suppose we were fairly well balanced, as couples go."

"I've never seen you with any other man unless you count that time Pascal tried to strangle you," Melanie said. "It's just always been the General. When I think of you seeing this shrink I don't know how to imagine it. You and the General sort of fit, at least as I imagined you. I can't imagine anyone else fitting with you that way."

"I know what you mean," Aurora admitted. "I'm bound to say that a great deal of trouble arises in life when people start imagining other people's relationships. I suppose people can't help doing it, but I still find it unfortunate."

"Why, it's just imagining—what does it hurt?" Melanie asked.

"People tend to get carried away with their own imaginings," Aurora said. "Then when real people go and do real things with other real people, and the things they do clash with someone's cherished view of how they are or how they're behaving, there can be problems.

"In fact, it may be that that's the root of most problems," Aurora continued. "Rosie's currently imagining that Hector Scott was better to me than he was, despite the fact that she lived in close proximity to us for twenty years. She ought to know better, but she doesn't; now she's angry at me half the time because I took a lover or two to help me get through Hector's declining years."

Again Aurora sighed.

"I didn't mean to upset you," Melanie said hastily. "I mainly just called to tell you I intended to try this audition."

"You don't have to change the subject just because I'm a little discouraged," Aurora said. "If you and everyone else keep avoiding my discouragement I don't see how I'm ever to work out of it.

"Don't imagine me as invulnerable, but don't imagine me beaten, either," she added. "I'm not beaten. I'm just a little discouraged."

Melanie didn't know what to say. In fact, it did frighten her a lot when her grandmother became sad or when she cried or sank into despair. It didn't happen all that often, but it was frightening when it did happen.

"I know you have a right to be sad, I just don't know how to handle it when you are sad," Melanie said.

"Well, that's human," Aurora said. "*I* didn't like it when *my* mother faltered, either. She was supposed to be the strong one. She faltered terribly when her main lover died, and it scared me out of my wits."

"Was that Sam?" Melanie asked.

"Sam," Aurora said. "Her handsome gardener. When she lost him she stopped being strong, and the fact that the only strong person in my life wasn't strong anymore undid me to such an extent that I panicked and married your grandfather.

"People don't like it when the strong one suddenly goes weak," Aurora added. "I suppose we all need the illusion that there's someone who's always strong, but it's just an illusion. Right now I'm feeling discouraged and would be happy if someone else would take over and be the strong one for a while, but I don't think anyone is likely to leap to this task. Rosie certainly won't. She'd rather spend her days standing on her head."

"I wish I'd known your mother," Melanie said, hoping Aurora would talk a little more about the past. She wanted to know more about her great-grandmother and her lover, Sam the gardener. Of course she'd seen lots of pictures of her great-grandmother in the family albums—there were even a few pictures of Sam the gardener. But stories were better than pictures—stories just gave her more sense of what her great-grandmother might have been like.

"Well, she was a gifted woman, but in the end she only achieved her life, which is what most of us do," Aurora said.

"I hope you'll look a little harder before you marry, Melly. Don't marry a non-starter like I did. Try to find someone who'll do something."

"I probably won't marry at all," Melanie said. "There might not be anybody who likes me that much."

"There certainly will be somebody who likes you that much," Aurora assured her. "You're just blooming, you know. In the course of your blooming I'm sure you'll encounter several young men who will want to marry you."

"I doubt it," Melanie said. "I'm not pretty enough."

"As I said, you're blooming," Aurora said. "When you've finished the process you'll be more than pretty enough.

"Anyway, it's rarely prettiness that people marry," she added. "I was plump as a plum when I was your age, and yet scads of young men flung themselves at me. I had so many options that I became confused and chose your grandfather. When he died I still found myself with a bunch of options, and I became addled again and chose Hector, mainly because he insisted on being chosen. There are only two kinds of men, insistent and uninsistent, and I can't seem to resist either kind."

"What about the shrink?" Melanie asked. "What kind is he?"

"Uninsistent," Aurora said. "I practically had to take his pants off myself in order to get him in bed."

"Granny!" Melanie said, a little shocked.

"Well, you did ask," Aurora said. "I do still have a sexual appetite and I don't see why I should have to apologize for it, although in point of fact quite a number of people seem to think I should apologize for it. They seem to think I should devote myself to knitting bootees for my great-grandchildren, but I only have one great-grandchild and he's already past the age for bootees."

"You don't have to apologize for it to me," Melanie said nervously.

"I heard you—you sounded shocked at the thought of your grandmother peeling the trousers off an uninsistent psychiatrist," Aurora said. She laughed, mainly because she liked her own imagery.

"Do you think I'm too much, Melanie?" she asked.

"Uh, no—you're just you," Melanie said.

"Well, most people have always thought I was too much," Aurora said. "If I am, it's not calculated. I've just always thought I'd better keep trying. So many people stop trying, and the minute they do, they dwindle. I personally would rather not dwindle until I have to."

"Maybe you'll never have to," Melanie said.

"Oh, well, we're all just following the shadow," Aurora said. "Poor Hector had no idea he was so close on its heels. He had just been talking about taking me on a cruise to the Orient. We were going to have a big bed, in a stateroom, and make love all the way across the ocean. He didn't understand women at all, but he kept trying. His last thought was probably about sex."

"That's good," Melanie said. "I mean, maybe it's weird, since he was so old, but it's kind of good."

"Rosie thinks I killed him," Aurora said.

"How, by making him think about sex?" Melanie asked.

"No, by driving so badly that it caused him to have a fit," Aurora said. "However, she had a fit, too, and she didn't die. Hector had thousands of fits about things that were my fault, and he didn't die. Nonetheless, Rosie's angry with me. That's why she's standing on her head so much, I expect. Doesn't want to look me in the eye."

Then, to Melanie's horror, she sank into sobs.

"I . . . can't help it . . . that Hector died," Aurora said, her voice breaking. "He just clicked off. He was . . . very quiet about it. Neither . . . Rosie nor I . . . heard the click. I was trying . . . to finish my crossword, and when . . . I looked up he was gone."

"It wasn't your fault. Of course it wasn't your fault," Melanie said.

"What?—to Melanie—" Aurora said, trying to get control of herself. Rosie had heard her crying and stepped into the room.

"Don't tell her about my audition," Melanie said quickly. "It might hurt her feelings that I'm sort of going to imitate her."

"Well, we certainly wouldn't want that," Aurora said. "She's as touchy as Proust as it is."

Aurora sighed, but Melanie could tell she was calming don. "Are you okay now?" she asked.

"I'm functional—I imagine we'd better leave it at that," Aurora said.

4

"I was doomed even before I was born," Wilbur said in one of his many attempts to explain to himself and Tommy how he had ended up in prison. Wilbur was Tommy's new cell-mate. Joey, his old cellmate, had lost it one day in the dining hall, or pretended to lose it, Tommy was not quite sure which. He had gone beserko and started screaming at the top of his lungs, after which he had tried to stab himself in the jugular vein with a plastic fork. The fork broke, but Joey was dragged off to the psychiatric unit, where he regressed to the state of a three-year-old, or so rumor had it.

Tommy didn't buy most of the rumors. For one thing, Joey had never been much more mature than a three-year-old, except in the sexual area. Tommy thought he might have faked the beserko bit in order to get moved to a hospital, where he might find a nurse to fuck. Joey had already whored his way through pretty much the whole unit where they were kept—he was probably just looking for greener pastures, Tommy thought.

Unfortunately, that meant that Tommy ended up with Wil-bur for a cellmate, which involved listening to endless analyses of why Wilbur had been doomed before he was born. Joey had been all dick; Wilbur, who was fat, was all brain. Tommy was not quite sure he liked the change, but there was not much he could do about it other than kill himself, something he wasn't contemplating in the immediate future. If he did someday fling himself into space, it would be for political reasons, not because he had a fat, overeducated cellmate who considered that he had been doomed before he was born.

"Was your mother a dope addict?" he asked. For a week or two he had kind of stonewalled Wilbur, but that got to be boring, so he decided that he might as well find out why Wilbur considered himself so doomed.

"No, my mother was president of her Amity Club," Wilbur said.

"What's an Amity Club?" Tommy asked.

"It's a club for bored small-town ladies who like to think they're improving themselves by reading best-sellers and chatting about them," Wilbur told him.

"Is that why you were doomed?" Tommy asked. "Because your mom liked to read best-sellers?" In only two weeks he had developed a knack for making any statement Wilbur made seem absurd.

"That may have produced prenatal boredom, but it wasn't why I was doomed before my birth," Wilbur admitted. "I'm doomed because of my name. How would you like to be named Wilbur?"

"It's not great," Tommy agreed.

"Well, I hate it," Wilbur said. "I hate it, and I hate my parents for giving it to me."

"You could change it," Tommy suggested.

"Yes, but before I knew I had that right it was too late," Wilbur said. His face was so fat that his eyes were barely visible. Most of the inmates called him Squint, and so did the guards, though he probably didn't mean to squint. His eyes were just fenced in by fat.

"I've always felt like a Wilbur and I always will," Wilbur said.

"I don't see that it's that major a catastrophe," Tommy said.

Despite himself, he sometimes got amused by Wilbur, and he definitely enjoyed needling him.

"It is, though," Wilbur assured him.

"One of the Wright brothers was Wilbur," Tommy pointed out.

Wilbur ignored that comment.

"I imagine there are plenty of other people named Wilbur who just lead ordinary lives running hardware stores or something."

"I'm not attracted to the hardware business," Wilbur said.

What he was attracted to was opera. He listened to opera through earphones, but sometimes the opera leaked out around the earphones, or else Wilbur fell asleep and the earphones fell out of his ears, in which case more opera leaked out. Tommy didn't particularly mind, unless he was tinkering with his code, in which case having opera leaking into the cell was pretty distracting.

The person that minded was a black convict named Dog, who was in the next cell. Dog's nickname derived from the fact that he had beaten his wife to death with a frozen dog. When he decided his wife was fooling around on him, he killed her own pooch, froze it in a neighbor's deep-freeze for two weeks, and then one day took it out and beat his wife to death with it while she was standing at the bus stop waiting for her bus.

"Turn off that shit," Dog instructed Wilbur, several times. "I ain't listening to no screeching shit like that."

"You can just barely hear it," Wilbur pointed out—it was true.

"Barely's too much," Dog said darkly. He had just been moved to their unit after a long period in solitary, where he had been sent for slamming a cell door as hard as he could on another prisoner's head. Dog was large, and his victim, also black, had been small. Dog had held the man exactly where he wanted him so that when he slammed the door on his head it would achieve the maximum effect. In this he had succeeded so well that the other prisoner had remained in a coma for four days.

Wilbur was not entirely without sense. He turned the

425

opera he had been listening to down so low that only a faint sound could be heard, even when the earphones were not in Wilbur's ears. But he didn't turn it off, and Dog was not entirely mollified. "Ain't you got no normal music?" he asked. "I don't mind about normal music."

"The whole Italian nation thinks this is normal music," Wilbur informed him.

Dog let it go for the moment, but he didn't look happy.

"Italians may think opera is normal music, but this isn't an Italian jail you're in," Tommy pointed out later, when Dog was asleep.

"I turned it down," Wilbur said in an annoyed tone. Despite being in jail he still had some of the attitudes of a white kid whose family was rich. Having to play his operas at less than full blast struck him as a big inconvenience, and he didn't pretend otherwise.

"Dog beat his own wife to death with a frozen dog," Tommy reminded him. "He slammed that guy's head in the door and put the guy out for four days."

"I turned it *down*," Wilbur said crossly. "I have a right to listen to Verdi if I want to."

"Maybe you *were* doomed before you were born," Tommy said. "If Dog slams your head in the door a few times you won't be able to listen to Verdi anyway, because your brains will be running out of your ears."

"The guards are dying to beat the shit out of him," Wilbur said. "If he bothers me, I'll just yell."

Tommy didn't bother to point out that the guards were dying to beat the shit out of anything that moved—or, at least, anything that moved in a way that didn't strike their fancy. If Wilbur wanted to think they would make an exception in his case because he had gone to Kenyon College and studied music for a year, or because his family was rich, let him think it. In fact, the guards thought Wilbur was a fat priss, and it probably wouldn't be too long before one of them expressed his dislike by spitting tobacco in Wilbur's coffee, or something.

Meanwhile Tommy sometimes amused himself by interrogating Wilbur about his crimes, which had been about as stupid and incompetently planned as the various criminal acts many of the other inmates had been sent to prison for. The only thing different about Wilbur's crimes was both of them had occurred on Christmas Eve. The first Christmas Eve Wilbur had written a hot check for his wife's Christmas present, a new BMW. For that one, with a little help from his family, he got off with probation. His wife left him the day she found out that she had to give the car back.

When, the very next Christmas Eve, finding that he had no money and couldn't afford to buy either his ex-wife or his three children the lavish presents they expected from him, Wilbur walked into a bank in Mansfield, Texas, and tried to rob it. A security guard intervened, and Wilbur shot him with a ·44-caliber revolver, one of his large collection of handguns. After that, he went and sat in his car in the bank's parking lot, listening to a Haydn concerto through his earphones until the police came for him. The guard died, and Wilbur was given twenty years to life.

"I hate Christmas," Wilbur told Tommy. "There's all this pressure to act happy when you're not. If it wasn't for Christmas I'd be a free man right now."

"Are you sorry you killed the guard?" Tommy asked. He had recently become interested in the question of remorse, something the prison shrinks were more or less obsessed with. In their world remorse was the quality that divided the good from the bad. A maniac could cut somebody into bloody slivers, but if he felt terrible about it later, he was an okay guy, in the shrinks' view.

Wilbur looked surprised when Tommy asked him if he was remorseful about killing the guard.

"I didn't know him," Wilbur said. "In fact, I didn't even really notice him. I guess I killed him but I can't remember that part."

The only thing Wilbur really seemed remorseful about was that his robbery attempt had failed, and consequently his kids and ex-wife hadn't received any lavish Christmas presents from him. Not being able to give lavish Christmas presents was the real failure in his view. Killing the guard was just an incident that he didn't remember too clearly.

Joey, Tommy's former cellmate, though mainly only interested in sex, did occasionally have wild fits of remorse about having killed his brother and his best friend. Tommy concluded from that that Joey would probably get paroled in another year or two, whereas if Wilbur got paroled it would only be because he was white, or because his family bribed someone on the parole board, or because everyone in the prison was bored shitless with him. Lots of convicts got shoved out the door because they bored the shrinks, or the staff, or both.

"He's too self-absorbed to make a good cellmate," Tommy told Teddy, on one of the latter's visits. Since his grandmother had stopped coming, Teddy had come faithfully, which was an improvement. Teddy didn't bother hassling him about improving his attitude. Teddy knew him better than anyone and had no desire to improve him.

"Well, most people think you're pretty self-absorbed yourself," Teddy said.

Tommy smiled. He liked his brother and had even begun to sort of look forward to his visits to the prison.

"Most people are stupid," Tommy said. "I'm not interested in myself at all. I'm not even sure I have a self, in the ordinary sense."

"What is the ordinary sense?" Teddy asked. "Maybe I don't have a self either, in the ordinary sense."

"Sure you do," Tommy said. "You want a lot of things I don't give a shit about."

"I'm sure we have different likes except for baseball," Teddy agreed. Before they had got into selves, ordinary and otherwise, they had been discussing the fading hopes of the Cubs. "But I don't see why that means that you have less of a self than I do," he added.

"I have almost no self," Tommy insisted, with one of his small, arrogant smiles.

"I don't get it, you'll have to give me an example," Teddy said. "Something that will explain why I have a self and you don't."

"You want to have sex with Jane, don't you?" Tommy said.

"I do when I can get her interested," Teddy admitted.

Tommy smiled. "You want Bump to grow up and be healthy and happy, don't you?" he asked.

"I sure, do," Teddy said. Two or three other prisoners were in the visitors' room, talking in low voices to members of their families. Prisoners and families alike looked sad. The thought occurred to Teddy that there was at least a mathematical chance that Bump would grow up and do something criminal, as Tommy had, in which case Bump might be put in such a place. It was such a terrible, unexpected thought that it made him want to go home at once and be with his mate and his son. Maybe Jane would be feeling sexy, and after they made love they could bring Bump into the bed with them and read him stories.

For a second Teddy couldn't think of anything nicer than just being in a bed with Jane and Bump. Jane usually got playful after they made love—she would sometimes make up stories for Bump while in her playful mood. Bump's favorite story, an ongoing picaresque tale, was about a walking, talking car named Reddy, who was traveling around the world. Reddy's main problem was with a posse of carrot-obsessed vegetarians who wanted to make him into a carrot cake. It was a thrilling saga to which Bump listened intently, clutching both his mother's and his father's fingers anxiously during Reddy's moments of peril.

But of course Bump was just a little boy—he wasn't in prison. Tommy was the one in prison, claiming not to have a self. He was still smiling his arrogant little smile. Much as he cared for Tommy, Teddy was still sometimes shaken by his brother's way of looking at things. There was no disguising the fact that it was a cold, cold way.

"So, that's all I meant," Tommy said. "You do have a self in the ordinary sense, because you have normal desires and normal hopes. I really don't want anything."

"What about your code?" Teddy inquired. "You seemed once to really want your code, at least for a while."

"I think I wanted to do something to set me apart," Tommy said. "That's when I was first adjusting to jail. I think I may have been competing with the shrinks a little."

"Did the shrinks know about your code?"

"No, but they would have thought it was pretty interesting if they had known about it," Tommy said. "They would have flipped out trying to break my code and find out what I was really like, or whether I was planning to blast someone else, or what."

Teddy didn't quite get it, but he didn't want to say so. Growing up with Tommy, he had often found himself not quite getting it. Sometimes he asked Tommy to explain what he was doing, or what some statement meant, but mostly he didn't ask. Mostly he just faked it, hoping Tommy wouldn't realize how in the dark he really was. One of his big fears was that Tommy would conclude that he was too dumb to be worth sharing secrets with. If that ever happened Tommy might stop sharing anything with him, in which case he wouldn't really have a brother.

Tommy saw that his brother was confused about the shrinks and the code and was a little bit sorry he had mentioned it, mainly because it annoyed him that he had even momentarily wanted to play to the prison shrinks, even to the weird extent of making up a code they would never see. Once he decided that the shrinks were too uninteresting even to bother impressing in the secrecy of his own mind, he began to lose interest in the code—lately he had only fiddled with it when he needed an intellectual toy to fiddle with for a few minutes.

"It's too existential for me, I guess," Teddy said. "Not wanting to have a self in the ordinary sense *is* sort of what you want, right? That still means you have a self in some sense, though. Granny certainly thinks you have a self, and so do Jane and Rosie and everyone who knows you."

"I guess," Tommy said. Actually it was a lot more interesting to talk about the Cubs. "I guess everybody wants something but I still think I'm about as wantless as anybody I know.

"On the other hand, there are millions of things I *don't* want," he added. "I don't want Wilbur in my life, for example. Right now that's the main thing I *don't* want."

"What can you do about it, though?" Teddy asked. One of

his main hopes was that someday Tommy would be out of prison, leading some sort of accessible life. It worried him that Tommy was only going to be a myth to Bump, for example. He wished Tommy would behave and get paroled as soon as possible, so he could meet Bump and read him stories or play with him or something.

Yet, deep within Teddy, lurking wherever nightmares came from, was the fear that Tommy *wouldn't* behave—that he *wanted* to stay in prison, inaccessible to everyone. Teddy more than once dreamed that Tommy might kill again. Once he even dreamed that Tommy killed another prisoner the day before his parole hearings began.

"I'm not planning to kill him, if that's what you're worried about," Tommy said. "I wouldn't waste my time on Wilbur. He's a dick, but I can put up with him."

Their time was almost up. They returned to baseball talk, which sort of made it easier when Teddy had to go. Baseball was a topic they could pick up or drop with ease—it was really the only topic they had which was easy. Almost everything else there was to talk about led back to the fact that Tommy was in prison, while Teddy was free.

"Any messages for anyone?" Teddy asked, when his time was up.

Immediately he wished he had kept himself from asking it, because Tommy just shook his head. He had asked no questions about anyone, either—not about the General's death, or his funeral, or how their grandmother was taking it; not about their father, not about how Melanie was doing in California—not about anything.

Driving home, Teddy felt a moment of anger at Tommy for being that way—for never admitting, even to the extent of one question, that he had a family out in the world, trying to live their lives. But between one freeway exit and the next, Teddy's anger gave way to sadness, as it always did. Anger was not an emotion he could sustain for very long. There were times when he *wanted* to be angry at Jane, and certainly times when he had good reason to be angry at Jane; yet he could never be sure it was *really* anger he was feeling

—maybe it was just the idea of anger that ran through his head.

When his anger at Tommy passed, Teddy felt a sadness so deep that he wondered if he was going to be able to avoid going crazy again. His sadness gave him a kind of quivery feeling with a lot of anxiety in it. Sometimes, driving home from the prison, he started worrying that he would never get home. Maybe an overpass would collapse; maybe two wheels would fly off his car; maybe there would be a flood and he'd be swept off the road into a swamp. He knew these were silly fears: the overpasses weren't going to collapse, the sky was clear, and even if a wheel or two did come off the car, he could probably get stopped before anything fatal happened. He always drove in the right-hand lane because he wanted to be able to get across the road quickly, in case anything *did* happen.

But just because his fears were silly didn't mean they were not powerful: he felt quivery all through his body. Part of it was hating to get home, where he would have to disappoint everyone's expectations. Once again, he would either have to lie, which he didn't do well, or admit that Tommy, once again, had not asked a single question about any of them or sent a single message. Either he didn't care at all or, if he did care, he didn't want them to know it.

"You're such a sucker for him," Jane said, when Teddy finally got home. She was annoyed with him, as she often was when he got home from a prison visit. He always came in with a migraine, so pale and quivery that he could hardly make it to the bed. Bump, who could tell instantly that his father was in a bad way, grabbed Kermit the Frog and retreated to his closet, where he could hold Kermit and whisper to him in his strange Kermit-babble, sometimes for hours. Jane would always put Teddy to bed, ice down his forehead, rub his stomach, and wait for him to stop shaking, for a little color to come back, a little life to return to his eyes. What started as therapy almost always ended as foreplay—Jane would start to get angrier even before Teddy had really recovered—she hated the feeling that Tommy, seventy miles away in a prison, was sucking her husband away from her with his coldness or his arrogance or something. The anger stirred her until pretty soon she would be sucking on Teddy herself, or squatting over him, trying to stuff him in her. Her desire to pull Teddy back, to counter Tommy's suction with her own, to get Teddy inside her, out of Tommy's reach, made for some powerful sex. Teddy came out of it recovered —Jane was always the one who was left shaken for a bit.

"You sure know how to clear up my headaches," Teddy said, thinking he might try to coax Bump and his friend Kermit out of the closet. Maybe they would want to come to bed and hear some stories about Reddy the car.

"Shut up—I don't want you going to that prison anymore," Jane said. Sex or no sex, she didn't like it—she didn't feel safe.

5

Despite telling herself that nothing was going to happen, Patsy couldn't stop ambushing Jerry Bruckner at the grocery store. After their trip to Galveston she stoically waited two weeks before swallowing her pride one afternoon. She finally decided that her pride was sort of anachronistic—it didn't fit the spirit of the age, which allowed women to hit on men if they wanted to.

Aurora Greenway had hit on Jerry, after all—and Aurora had looked down her nose at Patsy on some sort of vague moral grounds for most of Patsy's life. But once Aurora decided that she wanted Jerry, she didn't waste any time taking him, and she didn't make any bones about it, either.

What was fair for Aurora was certainly fair for her, Patsy felt, so once again she took to cruising Jamail's parking lot in the late afternoons. If his station wagon was there, she marched right in and found him, usually staring vaguely at an array of frozen dinners, or pondering how many tomatoes to buy, or looking solemnly at the mustards. Jerry ate a lot of sandwiches and liked to try unusual mustards.

"Let's pretend this is a game," Patsy said the second time she ambushed him. "The name of the game is Find-Jerry-at-the-Grocery-Store. I'm the hunter and you're the hunted. The rules are simple. If I find you you have to take me someplace."

Jerry looked slightly flattered in an unaggressive way. "This could be a fun game," he said. "How often will we play it?"

"The hunter controls the frequency," Patsy informed him. "We play it whenever I'm in the mood."

"It doesn't sound as if the hunted has much choice," Jerry said.

"Sure he does," Patsy said. "This isn't the only grocery store in Houston. If you don't want to be hunted just buy your stupid Algerian mustard somewhere else."

The evening of the second ambush they drove to Austin and ate barbecue at a fashionable barbecue joint in Dripping Springs. They returned to Jamail's parking lot at three in the morning. Again, the great produce trucks were parking at the loading docks. They had been together nearly ten hours and had talked constantly the whole time. On the way to Austin they had talked quite a bit about art. Jerry enjoyed museums, and had been to many, though he didn't have strong opinions about art. He liked to drift past pictures until he found one that he liked. Then he would pause a minute and drift on.

"That's you, Mr. Drift Along," Patsy said. "Always looking, never touching. Why do you even go to the museums if you're that casual about art?"

"I think I just like being in nice buildings," Jerry said.

"Name a nice building," Patsy demanded.

"Well, the Menil museum," Jerry said, mentioning Houston's newest.

"I have to admit it's a nice building," Patsy said.

"Why would you mind admitting it?" Jerry asked.

"Because I'm ticked at you and I don't like agreeing with anything you say," Patsy said.

Jerry didn't answer, though he did smile sadly.

"Have you always gotten by on wistfulness?" she asked. They were blazing down the dark road at close to ninety.

"Mostly," he said.

"Psychiatrists are supposed to be able to deal with anger, their own and other people's," Patsy said. "Why are you so reluctant to deal with mine?"

"I just am," Jerry said.

"Do you have any notion of why I'm angry?" she asked.

"Well, yes," Jerry said. "You're offering and I'm declining, sort of."

"Sort of?" Patsy said. "How can you 'sort of' decline a woman who offers herself? You either decline or you don't, no sort of about it."

"Well, I'm in the car with you," Jerry said. "I ate barbecue with you. It may not be much, but it's not nothing, either."

"From where I sit there's a pretty thin line separating this from nothing," Patsy said.

Fifty miles passed in silence, and Patsy began to ask about Aurora.

"Did the General's death change anything?" she asked.

"It ended the affair," Jerry said.

"Well, that's news," Patsy said.

"Why did it end the affair?" she asked a minute later, after waiting in vain for Jerry to amplify the information.

"Aurora's in mourning," he said.

"As well she should be," Patsy said. "The General stood by her through some pretty thin times."

"Yes, that's what she said," Jerry agreed. "I only saw the man three or four times myself."

"They were an odd fit, but I guess they were a fit," Patsy said. "Did Aurora ever think you were really going to be her therapist, or was that just a ruse?"

"Aurora's not much for ruses," Jerry said.

"Well, neither am I, unless you consider hitting on you in a grocery store to be a ruse," Patsy said.

Jerry didn't respond to that remark—he let a minute go by in silence.

"Is it that you'd just rather not be wanted, or that you're at a loss for words when you discover that you *are* wanted?" Patsy asked.

"I think of myself as the prime wanter, actually," Jerry said.

Patsy thought he must be joking, but when she looked at him he looked back at her gravely.

"The prime wanter?" she said. "If that's how you think of yourself you certainly disguise your wantings pretty well. Other than Algerian mustard, I'd be hard put to name a single thing you seem to want particularly. You certainly don't appear to want me."

"I want you but I'm blocked," Jerry said, still solemn. "You're too educated. I know it's silly to be so scared of educated women, but I can't help it."

"Uh—hum, and how long have you had this problem, Doctor?" Patsy asked.

"Since I left Las Vegas," Jerry said. "When I went to New York to try and be a comic I had it really badly."

Patsy waited. Jerry seemed to have forgotten that they were talking, but then he sensed her impatience, looked over at her, and grinned.

"In New York I went out with a beautiful widow," he said. "Her husband had been a socially prominent stockbroker—he lost a lot of money and jumped out of a window. She had been to medical school and was a top cancer researcher. She was one of the most beautiful women I've ever gone out with, and she was nice, too. She had been to school in France, and also to the Harvard Medical School."

Again he stopped, shrugged, and said no more.

"Well, those things aren't sins," Patsy said. "So what's the deal? What happened?"

"I was paralyzed—I just couldn't deal with that much education," Jerry said. "I think we went out eighteen times and I never so much as kissed her."

"If it's any help, I didn't go to school in France, or to the Harvard Medical School either," Patsy said.

"The General told me something interesting the one time I saw him alone," Jerry said.

"You're the worst sidestepper I've ever known," Patsy said. "I'll bite, though—there being nothing else to do. What interesting thing did the General tell you?"

"That if Aurora died suddenly he intended to try and marry Rosie," Jerry said.

"Men are lazy," Patsy told him. "Why go to all the trouble of looking for a new woman when there's one you've known for twenty years right in the house? I think that's how men reason, if you can call that reason.

"So what about Aurora?" Patsy asked. She had killed her motor—they were just sitting in the empty parking lot, watching clouds roll over. "Do you think the affair's *really* ended?"

Jerry considered. The truth was, sorrow lent Aurora something. She was more silent, for one thing. She wasn't always talking, chattering, singing. From being sexually bold or even coarse, she had become dignified, reserved, and withdrawn. She took her mourning seriously enough to dress more soberly, too. She wasn't always in black, but she avoided wild colors and often wore a scarf over her hair.

She wouldn't let Jerry get near her, either—not even to hold her hand or offer a comforting hug.

"I suppose I feel a certain guilt," Aurora admitted to him. "Death often makes much of life seem unseemly, you know."

Jerry, who had never particularly wanted to sleep with Aurora when she was pursuing him, now found that he missed being in bed with her; but instead of waiting for a moment when Aurora might feel yielding again, he had started going to the movies and then to bed with another tall country girl with slightly crooked teeth. Her name was Lalani, she was twenty-two, she hoped to be a beautician, and she worked at the Winchell's Doughnut House six blocks from his home, where he often went for coffee. Lalani had grown up in Odessa.

"Oil-field trash and proud of it," she said brightly. "I guess that's why I like this dirty ol' fucking so much." She had greenish eyes and a large collection of Harlequin romances, which she added to, on her afternoons off, at a paperback exchange on Airline Road.

"It's a long way to drive but they got the most Harlequins," Lalani said. She lived on onion rings, cheeseburgers, and Winchell's doughnuts; she had no interest in exercise, unless activities of a sexual nature counted as exercise.

"Why'd I want to run around pounding my legs on the

pavement when I can sweat off just as much weight bouncing on this nice old bed with you?" she asked, when Jerry invited her to jog with him.

Jerry decided not to mention Lalani to Patsy—Patsy was irritated enough as it was. He eased out of the evening by offering to lend her a book she had happened to mention, which he happened to own. It was a book on subconscious language, by a Hungarian analyst named Thaas-Thienemann.

Patsy drove home thinking Jerry was a jerk—it was too humiliating, she would never attempt to ambush him at Jamail's again; but—again—she changed her mind and they sparred through six more lengthy evenings before she finally decided that the only way it was going to happen was if she took matters into her own hands, which she did one afternoon not five minutes after Aurora Greenway had walked out of Jerry's door. Patsy had been on her way over, meaning to return Jerry's book, saw Aurora's Cadillac at the curb, and was about to drive on, more annoyed than ever, when she saw Aurora step out of his house. She quickly turned right, hoping Aurora hadn't seen her, and then drove around the block, and around another block, wondering why she was bothering with this man. Anyone who liked Aurora Greenway as much as Jerry seemed to couldn't be that interesting, anyway.

But, after whistling along several nondescript sururban blocks, she turned back to Jerry's street. The Cadillac was gone. Patsy was too annoyed to reflect, and one of the things she was annoyed with was her own tendency to last-minute timidities. She was always backing out at the last minute; both her girls were always telling her she was too chicken, too conservative, when it came to men. Both girls were appalled, or, at least, professed to be appalled, by their mother's long celibate stretches, the most recent of which was getting on toward a year and a half.

"You just need to get laid, Mom—maybe you wouldn't be so critical," Katie told her in their most recent telephone conversation.

Patsy started to ring Jerry's doorbell, but then decided to

try the door instead. It opened, and she stepped into his house. Jerry sat in the living room, in shorts and an old blue T-shirt. He had been reading the sports page. He looked up at Patsy, a little surprised but not alarmed.

"I brought your book back," Patsy said, her timidity rising. What was she doing, marching into this man's living room?

"What'd you think of it?" Jerry asked.

"I'm not thinking just now, I want to kiss you," Patsy said, taking his paper and folding it carefully before she trapped him on his couch, her body across his legs.

"I don't want you to give me any trouble—I don't want you to deny me anymore," she said, sliding her fingers up his neck, into his hair.

6

When Aurora walked into Jerry's house early the next morning, the first thing she noticed was Patsy Carpenter's yellow belt lying on Jerry's old couch.

Since Hector's death, she had formed the habit of driving over to Jerry's early to have a cup of coffee with him before his first patient appeared. She seldom stayed more than fifteen or twenty minutes. Willie was back, apparently cured, and he and Rosie had taken to staying in bed rather late, which left Aurora with no one in the early mornings, a time when she particularly liked to have someone to have a cup of coffee or a bite of breakfast with. On a few occasions she had summoned Pascal, but Pascal was not what one would call a morning person. He was either silent and half-asleep or he was wide-awake and petulant, at a time when a petulant man was the last thing Aurora was interested in seeing across her breakfast table.

Jerry Bruckner was not much of a morning person either, but he wasn't French, and thus was far less likely to ruin her morning with complaints, as Pascal so often did. At their most recent breakfast Pascal had upbraided her bitterly because she had allowed herself to run out of raspberry jam although she was well aware that raspberry was his favorite jam.

"Pascal, I'm in mourning, don't talk to me like that just because I forgot your raspberry jam," Aurora said before crying briefly.

Patsy Carpenter's yellow belt had a certain dash—sufficient dash, in fact, that Aurora had once been moved to compliment her on it. She had even asked Patsy where she got the belt, thinking she might want to locate something comparable for herself.

"I got it at the Broadway in Sherman Oaks," Patsy said. "I went to shop for towels and ended up buying this belt. Want me to get you a swell belt, Aurora, next time I go?"

"Well, if you see one that says 'Aurora' to you, you might," Aurora said.

Now the same yellow belt was lying on Jerry Bruckner's living-room couch, and the somewhat squashed cushions of the old couch caused Aurora to picture the two bodies, Jerry's and Patsy's, fervent and sweaty, in the act of love. The image had such impact that she felt weak—she didn't take another step forward. Jerry had left the front door open for her, but he was not in the room. Often she slipped in while he was showering; she would be sitting at the kitchen table, sipping tea, when he appeared, looking clean-shaven, boyish, a little sleepy, his hair still wet.

The morning there would be no coffee. Aurora could hear the shower running down the hall. She felt as if she had been kicked in the gut. Quietly, hoping Jerry wouldn't hear her, she backed out the door and closed it behind her. Her main hope was that her car would start smoothly so she could make her way off and not have to see or speak to Jerry Bruckner just then. The Cadillac had been rather prone to stalls lately —it often didn't seem quite ready to start when she turned the key. Her one hope, this time, was that it would at least run long enough to get her around the corner, out of sight, so that her humiliation would not be witnessed by the young man she had so foolishly insisted on flinging herself at. Again, the image of his body and Patsy's on the couch came to mind, so clearly that she could scarcely see the sidewalk ahead of her.

Fortunately, the Cadillac started immediately and she was able to ease away. At the corner she looked back, fearing she might see Jerry running down the sidewalk after her, or else just standing on his front step, wondering why she was leaving without so much as a sip of coffee. But there was no one on the sidewalk or on the step. She was safe.

She thought of going to Pascal's—there was a chance he would rise to the occasion and provide her with an emotional refuge for a bit. For all his petulance about raspberry jam, he was rather a knowing man—that was the good part about his being French.

On the other hand, he was a very selfish man—he might try to take advantage of her in her distress. In fact, that would be just like him. He had already offended her several times by being callous about Hector's death. Only last week he had offended her at lunch by suggesting pointedly that she had mourned long enough.

"Life is for the living," he said.

"Yes, I know, I'm living right now," Aurora said.

"You are not living—you are not active," Pascal said. "My wife died, I was sad, but I put it behind. I became active again."

"I've had a sample of your activity," Aurora reminded him. "It's fine, but for the moment I prefer my grief, if you don't mind. For all his persnickitiness Hector Scott meant a lot to me. I hope I don't have to remind you of that too many more times, Pascal."

His views on activity and inactivity being what they were, she decided it was not the moment to present herself to Pascal. She thought of the Pig Stand and of a waffle house she was fond of, but with no enthusiasm: the punch she had just received seemed to have taken away her appetite. She felt too punched to eat, or cry. She thought of going to Galveston and watching the ocean all day, but there would be traffic, her car might stop, it was a long way to drive. She had come out barefoot, in her gown and housecoat, which would leave her feeling at a disadvantage if she had to talk to policemen or tow-truck people, which could well be the case if her car did stop.

Carefully, using an old route remembered from the days when Houston had no freeway, Aurora inched north across the bayou and east through the railroad yards until she was in the region of the Ship Channel. Somewhere on McCarty Street she remembered seeing an open-air Greek bar where the sailors came to drink and play cards. It was in sight of the great refineries to the south—the air smelled of oil and salt. But she remembered it as friendly, and friendly at the moment was all she hoped for from life.

Sure enough, the bar—actually, little more than a shed—was there, open to the breezes from the Gulf, and to the traffic from McCarty Street as well. Two old Greek men in undershirts were sitting at a little rickety table, shuffling little ivory dominoes. Both were stocky, both had white hair, both were smoking, and neither seemed at all surprised when a large barefooted woman in a gown and housecoat got out of an old Cadillac and picked her way across the strip of shaley gravel that functioned as their parking lot.

"Got any retsina this morning?" Aurora asked, with the best smile she was capable of.

The Greek on her right raised his eyebrows and smiled. "You lose your shoes?" he asked.

"Shut up! She left them at the dance," the Greek on her left said. He rose and went to retrieve a wobbly-looking green chair that someone had kicked into the parking lot in the course of the night. Aurora had almost hit it while attempting to park correctly. The man set it carefully on the somewhat uneven concrete floor of the bar.

"Sit, be comfortable," he said. "It's a beautiful day."

The other man got up, disappeared briefly, and returned with a bottle of retsina and a glass.

"Don't drop it, it's the last glass," he said, setting bottle and glass in front of Aurora. "I may go buy some more today if it don't get too hazy.

"It's a beautiful day, it ain't gonna get hazy," he added, for Aurora's benefit.

It *was* rather a beautiful day, Aurora decided. Sunlight was slanting through a number of holes in the roof, which seemed to be affixed to the walls at a rather tipsy angle.

"The hurricane blew the roof off, but we stuck it back," the other man informed her. "We didn't stick it back too straight."

"It don't look heavy, but it's heavy," the other man informed her.

"It's also rather punctured," Aurora observed, pouring herself a retsina. "Don't you get wet when it rains?"

"We don't come here when it rains," one of the Greeks admitted.

Aurora quickly drank about half of the glass of retsina, watched impassively by the two men. Both had huge bags under their eyes—identical bags. The longer she inspected them, the more identicalities she noticed. They had identical bellies, identical undershirts, identically muscular shoulders, and identical white hair. Besides, the looks they fixed on her were also identical: profoundly world-weary, and yet alert. They were men, she was a woman, she had walked into their lives, and they were sizing matters up.

"My goodness, I've figured it out, you're twins," Aurora announced.

The two men shook their heads. "Brothers, not twins," one said.

"Do I get to know your names?" Aurora asked.

"Petrakis," one said. "I'm Theo and he's Vassily."

"Well, I'm Aurora. I like this retsina, but I hate to be the only one drinking, particularly at such an early hour," she said.

"It don't matter when you drink," Theo said. "Your stomach don't know what time it is."

"Are you sure this is the only glass?" Aurora asked. "What kind of bar just owns one glass?"

"A Greek kind of bar," Vassily remarked. "Everybody that comes here thinks he has to be a Greek and break glasses. I wanted to get plastic but Theo won't have no plastic."

"We argue," Theo said. "I think plastic is tacky."

"I absolutely agree," Aurora said, just as a large oil truck, running a bit too close to the edge of the road, whooshed a gust of hot exhaust into the bar, causing her to cough.

When she stopped coughing, the two Greeks were still looking at her.

"You two look as if you've seen it all, and I guess if it's Western civilization we're talking about, you have," Aurora said.

The men had no comment on that observation.

"If you two are not twins, who's the elder?" Aurora asked, hoping to milk a little volubility out of them.

"I was born first," Theo said. "I beat him by a year."

"It's my bar, though," Vassily said. "He just works here."

Aurora drained the glass and turned it upside down.

"I think I'll refrain from breaking it, since it's your last," she said. "I've had rather a bad shock today and I would rather not drink alone. Let's spare the glass and drink out of the bottle."

She took a swig from the bottle and handed it to Vassily, who drank a good swallow and handed the bottle to Theo.

Two grimy young sailors came walking up the road from the direction of the Ship Channel. They ignored the retsina drinkers and fed a few quarters into a dusty soda-pop machine. Nothing happened for a bit until they began to punch the pop machine. One kicked it and the other shook it. Finally a single 7-Up clattered out. The two sailors stationed themselves at the bar's other table, popped open the 7-Up, and shared it.

"If you hurry before I get drunk you could probably teach me to play that interesting-looking domino game you were playing when I drove up," Aurora said. She took the last swallow from the bottle of retsina.

Theo got up and returned in a moment with another bottle.

"I can tell you a curious thing about ivory," Aurora said, playing with one of the little dominoes. "It turns black if it doesn't get sunlight. Of course, there's not much danger that your dominoes won't get sunlight here."

"You don't want to play with Theo, he cheats," Vassily said.

"Shut up—*you* cheat," Theo said, with no heat.

"That's how I lost the bar," he added, to Aurora. "He cheated."

"Oh, well, if I get him drunk, Theo, perhaps you'll win it back," Aurora said. She found herself rather warming to Theo as the retsina began to take effect. Though Vassily and he looked identical, Vassily did not quite seem to have Theo's sparkle—even if, at first glance, sparkle might seem an odd word to apply to a fat old Greek with bags under his eyes.

Still, Aurora thought she detected sparkle in the way Theo looked at her.

"What happened, your boyfriend leave you?" he asked, handing her the new bottle.

"In a manner of speaking, yes," Aurora said. "The son of a bitch left me for my daughter's best friend."

7

"I'm looped, I'm plastered, I'm God's own drunk!" Aurora said, wobbling into her kitchen. Though everything was rising and falling, swirling and heaving as if an earthquake was in progress, she felt sure she could make it across the kitchen floor under her own power.

A second later, her conviction proved to be hubris: the floor seemed to bubble, flinging her feet out from under her. She fell flat on her face and cracked her head solidly on a doorjamb. Then she rolled over, sprawled out more or less in the starfish position on her own kitchen floor, and tried unsuccessfully to focus on Rosie and Willie, who had been sitting at the table playing rummy when she wobbled in.

"Oh shit, I hate him," she said, before passing out.

"Her boyfriend left her, she don't hate me," a voice explained from the doorway that connected the kitchen to the garage.

Rosie hadn't even had time to put her cards on the table. She looked down briefly at Aurora and then over at the person who had spoken—a small, stocky, white-haired man in an undershirt and old pants. He wore sandals, but no socks,

and had bags under his eyes. Rosie had never seen him before and didn't know how to evaluate his statement, or Aurora's. For a second her instinct was just to try and go on with
the rummy game, hoping that what had just occurred was a
hallucination of some kind.

"Willie, are you ever gonna play?" she asked in a neutral
voice.

Willie, meanwhile, suddenly felt in terrible peril. Aurora
was sprawled on the floor, right beside his chair, lying on her
back with her legs spread wide. He had glanced down once,
just as she had rolled over and passed out, and, through no
fault of his own, had seen practically up to her crotch.
Though the glance had only lasted about a tenth of a second,
it wouldn't go out of his mind, which is why he felt in terrible
peril. If he glanced down again and actually saw Aurora's
crotch, that would be the end, so far as Rosie was concerned.
Rosie would notice, and as soon as she informed him that
she'd noticed, she would probably never speak to him again.
If she did speak to him again, it would only be to tell him
what a terrible person he was. It was even conceivable that
she would make him move out.

The one certainty Willie clung to in his dilemma was that
he must not—absolutely must not—glance down at the large
female body lying just beside his chair. The briefest glance
would invite calamity—yet, even so, he had a terrible urge
to glance down briefly just once more.

Theo Petrakis, from the doorway, saw that the two people
in the kitchen were in a stunned state, to put it mildly. In his
view they could be excused: it was probably not every day
that their boss came home drunk and fell down and knocked
herself out. He had seen people sitting at his own bar become stunned for long stretches just because they happened
to witness a car wreck on McCarty Street in which only one
or two people were killed or mangled. In the early months of
the war he had often been stunned himself by seeing people
killed; but, after he had seen a few hundred killed, as he had,
he ceased to be easily stunned, and remained not easily
stunned throughout his years in Houston, during which he

had witnessed almost as much violence as he had seen in the war. In the war it was clear why the violence was occurring, and in Houston it often was not clear, but in either case the effect on Theo was slight.

In the present situation, Theo realized that he would have to be the one to act, so he left his position in the doorway, walked around the table, squatted by Aurora, decided she was really out cold, and carefully pulled her gown and housecoat a little farther down over her legs.

In the four hours Theo had spent watching Aurora get drunk he had fallen deeply in love with her, much to the disgust of his cynical brother, Vassily, who, when she passed out briefly without paying for the first three bottles of retsina —she had a short nap, with her head on the green table— actually suggested that they call the police and have her taken to jail.

"Yeah, jail, where drunks belong," Vassily repeated, when Theo asked if he had heard him correctly.

"You were a drunk for thirty years, did you belong in jail?" Theo inquired.

"No, I'm your brother, this lady ain't your brother," Vassily pointed out. He hated it when Theo fell in love. It had happened many times in their long life together, and its consequences were always painful and expensive. Now it was happening again, right before his eyes, and it irritated him. His one hope was that the police would come and drag the drunken woman away before Theo went completely over the edge. Once Theo went over the edge, wild disorder followed, and business always suffered. Besides, Vassily had been with Theo all his life, except when Theo ran off in order to be in love. Though he acknowledged that Theo had a right to be in love, Vassily still resented the separations.

When Theo walked around the table, Rosie came out of her shock, only to discover that, on the whole, she was more shocked than she had been when she was actually in shock. The small man squatting by Aurora, attempting to see that her unconscious body was modestly covered, was clearly no hallucination. Something dreadful had happened, and whatever it was, it was real. Aurora had actually come in drunk and knocked herself out cold. Besides that, she had come in with a stranger, a little fat man in an undershirt. At first glance Rosie had feared that he was just some aging sex fiend that Aurora had somehow fallen prey to, but since he seemed to be trying to cover Aurora up, rather than uncover her more, perhaps that judgment was too harsh. Perhaps he wasn't a sex fiend.

"You gotta washrag?" he asked, looking at her from his squatting position near Aurora.

"Sure, what am I doing, I guess I've gone crazy, it ain't like this is the first drunk I've ever seen," Rosie said, jumping up.

Willie got up too and stumbled over to the corner of the kitchen so as not to be in the way. One of his lifelong rules had been to try and stay out of the way while serious matters were being attended to, and it certainly seemed to him that Mrs. Greenway lying unconscious and only partially dressed on the kitchen floor constituted a serious matter.

Rosie didn't take that view—Willie's habit of doing as little as possible just when things really needed doing had more than once caused her to want to punch him in the nose.

"Willie, you could be helpful, go upstairs and get a couple of pillows," she commanded.

She herself immediately got a bowl of ice cubes, a dish towel, and a couple of washrags, all of which she passed to Theo.

"Thank you, are you Rosie?" he asked gravely.

"Sure am, what's your name?" she asked.

"I am Theo Petrakis," he said, reaching across Aurora's prone body to offer his hand.

"Rosie Dunlup," Rosie said, shaking hands with him. "Can I just call you Theo? I think I can remember that."

"Of course," Theo said gravely. "Now that we are introduced I guess we better get to work. You got a dishpan?"

"Did you mean a bed pillow or a couch pillow?" Willie asked. He had moved to the foot of the stairs. At such a moment of crisis he didn't want to make any mistakes, and the only way not to was to ask.

"A bed pillow, Willie—I mean two bed pillows," Rosie

451

said, trying not to sound as put out as she felt. "Why would I send you upstairs to get a couch pillow when there's couches all over the place?"

Willie, abashed that he had managed to annoy Rosie at a time of crisis, hurried upstairs.

Working from opposite sides of her body, Rosie and Theo began to bathe Aurora's temples.

"He was a prison guard until he got on dope," Rosie said, once Willie left. "He's cured now, but I still have to tell him everything."

"I am on dope too, Excedrin," Theo said. "I think you better get the dishpan. This lady drank four bottles of retsina. My brother and I, we drank too, but we didn't drink no four bottles."

"I don't even know what it is you're talking about, but if she drank four bottles of it we may need more than a dishpan," Rosie said. "We may need a bathtub."

"Wouldn't hurt," Theo admitted.

At that moment Aurora made a whimpering sound and gritted her teeth.

"Oh boy," she said, without opening her eyes.

"Willie, get down here with them pillows, she's coming to," Rosie yelled.

"Rosie, don't yell," Aurora said. "My head is splitting. I must have got a bump."

Her eyes were still closed.

"Hon, you fell and hit your head on the door," Rosie said, bathing Aurora's temple lightly with an ice cube held in a washrag.

Willie had made the mistake of attempting to decide which pillows were the most suitable, a hopeless task. In desperation he grabbed five and hurried downstairs.

Aurora yawned.

"That feels good," she said, as more ice was applied to her temples. "Did Theo leave?"

"Theo is at your service," Theo said.

"You sound as if you're also at my elbow," Aurora said, her eyes still closed.

"My God, I didn't say bring a hundred pillows," Rosie said irritably. It annoyed her that Aurora's boyfriends were always able to muster more presence of mind than her own. Theo seemed to be a source of great strength compared to Willie, who was mainly a source of great irritation.

"Couldn't decide," Willie said.

"Rosie, must you pick on Willie when my head hurts so?" Aurora asked.

"I wasn't picking on him much," Rosie said, trying to get a grip. "He just brought a few too many pillows, but we might need them before we're done."

"Theo, are you near?" Aurora inquired, tentatively opening one eye. The room immediately began to swirl like a merry-go-round. She tried to swivel a bit so as to counteract the swirl, but it didn't work; the swirl got faster, and she was forced to close her eye again.

"Oh boy, troops," she said. Though her eye was now firmly closed, parts of her body were still participating in the swirling of the room. She realized too late that opening the one eye had been a serious mistake—now the room wouldn't stop swirling and *she* couldn't stop swirling, even though she was lying flat on the floor. Very soon, and very ominously, her stomach showed signs of wanting to join the universal swirl.

"Could someone please assist me to the bathroom?" she said, or rather, whispered. She was afraid that any attempt to use her voice normally might precipitate the crisis.

Rosie looked at Theo, who surveyed the surroundings with the practiced eye of the barkeeper.

"The sink's close,"he remarked.

"Theo, I know you're just trying to be practical, but I would prefer not to be sick in a sink," Aurora whispered. She was still hoping against hope that somehow the swirling would cease, or at least slow down, but every syllable she uttered seemed to make the swirling speed up. It seemed to her that the room was already swirling through space at the speed of a galaxy or something—astronomy had not been one of her best subjects.

"Oh dear, I'm afraid the matter's become urgent," she said. "I'm afraid the wisest if not the only course is to get me somewhere quickly."

Even as she said it she marveled at her own capacity to speak in complete and even lucid sentences at such a moment of crisis—it had always been thus, and it often had a tendency to make the crisis worse, since her lucidity often infuriated her helpmates, most of whom could scarcely speak in a complete sentence at the calmest moments of their lives.

Theo decided he had better pick Aurora up to facilitate rapid transport, so he slid his arms under her and did just that, to the surprise of everyone, particularly Aurora.

"What's happening, is gravity annulled?" she inquired as she felt herself being lifted into the air.

"Shut up or you'll puke sooner," Theo advised.

"Theo, you're in great shape, I'll say that for you," Rosie commented, although Aurora's large body almost entirely blocked her view of the man she was complimenting.

"If Willie tried to pick Aurora up he'd be down in his back for a week," she added, with a baleful glance at the useless Willie.

"He gets down in the back just from bringing in a bag of ice," she continued mercilessly.

"Ice—that's it—I need ice," Aurora whimpered.

"Where are we going with her?" Theo asked—Aurora was carryable, but that didn't mean she was light.

"Think you could carry her upstairs? It's just one flight," Rosie asked.

"I could carry her for three days," Theo boasted, hoping Aurora was listening.

"Oh, Theo," Aurora said, peeking briefly, to observe herself in the bare muscular arms of her rescuer, who smelled of strong tobacco.

"Let's hit it," Rosie commanded, heading up the stairs.

Midway up the stairs Theo began to get a painful cramp in his left leg, but he limped stoically on upward, stair by stair, until he was able to deposit Aurora safely on a blue rug in her own bathroom—an easy crawl, in his judgment, to either the bathtub or the toilet. He limped out, but Rosie lingered with Aurora, trying to help with cold rags. Before he was well out the door Theo heard Aurora begin to throw up. Still Rosie lingered in order to flush the toilet as often as possible.

"Rosie, do go out, I don't require attendance while I'm losing my retsina," Aurora said in a very weak voice.

Theo looked only briefly at Aurora's bedroom before limping on downstairs. He didn't feel it was mannerly to inspect a lady's bedroom while she was ill. Bedrooms were for times of health, or for laying out bodies. He looked forward to seeing Aurora in her bedroom in a time of health.

Downstairs, he dropped into a chair and began to massage his cramping leg.

Willie, very anxious, immediately set a cup of coffee in front of Theo.

"We got plenty," he said. "What's the verdict on Mrs. Greenway?"

"Drunk, that's the verdict," Theo said, just as Rosie came tripping downstairs.

"She swears she can crawl to the bed when she gets through puking, but I don't know—maybe, maybe not," Rosie said. "I left her a pillow and a dishpan."

"A dishpan?" Theo inquired.

"Yeah, in case she can't raise up high enough to puke in the toilet," Rosie said. "She says she thinks she might vomit all day, so she don't want to be bothered, but tomorrow night you and your brother are invited to dinner, for being so nice to her."

"I ain't bringing Vassily, I don't like him," Theo said. "When she passed out the first time, he wanted to put her in jail. Why should she feed him?"

"Oh, well, be that as it may," Rosie said, stealing one of Aurora's favorite phrases. "What do you take in your coffee? I'm glad Willie at least offered you some."

She felt increasingly ticked at Willie. He was a much larger man than Theo—why hadn't he carried Aurora upstairs?

"Blacker coffee, I'm Greek," Theo said.

"You're strong—do you exercise or are you a weight lifter or what?" Rosie asked.

"I don't do no exercise—I used to carry sacks off ships," Theo explained.

Willie began to feel sad—he wished very much that he could shoot up. Everyone in the world was more competent than he was, he knew. Rosie was more competent, and the Greek man, Theo, was also. He himself had not even been able to make the coffee black enough to suit their guest, which put him, in his own view, pretty much at the bottom of the ladder, competence-wise. It was depressing to be so useless, but dope made it better.

"Got any toothpicks?" Theo asked.

"Why, got coffee in your teeth?" Rosie asked, grinning. She liked Theo. A house containing no one but herself, Aurora, and Willie was, in her view, a pretty boresome house. Theo had a novel way of putting things, and, besides, he was cute. She had once considered Willie cute in a chunky sort of way, but she no longer thought Willie was particularly cute. He might be her problem, or her mainstay, but he wasn't cute. Theo had a brother—maybe he was cute too. Maybe she and Aurora and Theo and his brother could even double-date. What she would do with Willie if such a thing happened was a question she decided she would think about later.

"I can play cards too," Theo remarked. "If we ain't gonna play for money, at least we could play for toothpicks."

Two hours later, when they stopped playing cards, Theo had won the whole box of toothpicks. He attempted to teach Rosie and Willie several new card games, but their grasp of the games was imperfect, and Theo always won. The only sound from upstairs was the occasional faint flush of a toilet. When he had won all the toothpicks, Theo decided to go.

"I guess she ain't gonna come back downstairs today," he concluded, a little sadly. He had hung around hoping for one more glimpse of Aurora—he also wanted her to have one more glimpse of him. People who got very drunk sometimes didn't remember a thing about the experience. Certain levels of drunkenness often canceled all memory, both of the place and of the people who had been around during the drunkenness. Aurora had been at a pretty deep level of drunkenness —four bottles of retsina was not nothing. She might not remember him, his brother, or McCarty Street. If he turned up at her dinner the next night, with or without Vassily, Aurora might not have the faintest idea who he was. He himself had once forgotten a whole marriage due to drunkenness—one that had taken place in Egypt. He had married an Egyptian woman, lived with her for the better part of a week in a state of deep drunkenness caused by drinking too many Egyptian liquors that his system was not familiar with, and, once back to sea and sober, forgot all about it. He might never have remembered the marriage at all if it had not been for the fact that on his next trip to Alexandria he had happened to bump into his wife in a tobacco shop. She was with her new husband, an Englishman, and thus did not comment much on the fact that he had forgotten not only their nuptials but the whole week of their marriage.

All this led him to conclude that Aurora might be too drunk to remember him, which might mean that he would never see her again. Since he was now in love with her, this was a discouraging prospect, and he said as much to Rosie, who seemed trustworthy.

"What if she don't remember nothing?" he asked. "Lots of drunks don't remember nothing. She ain't gonna want somebody she don't remember showing up for dinner."

"Aurora won't forget you," Rosie assured him. "She's got a project, and it's to remember every single day of her life, even back to when she was a baby."

"Lots of luck," Willie remarked. "I can't remember nothing before third grade."

"And not much after," Rosie commented. "But then you ain't Aurora. Once she gets after something she's determined. It wouldn't surprise me a bit if she remembered every day of her life. She's got all her old calendars and she goes out in the garage and works at it."

"Sounds dopey to me," Theo said. "Why would anyone

want to remember every day of their life?" It would take up all the space in their head."

"I don't know, maybe you can ask her tomorrow," Rosie said.

"I can't remember but about three days of my life," Theo said. "The day the war ended was one."

The more he thought about Aurora's project, the weirder it seemed. Still, he wanted to see more of her if he possibly could.

"She said to be sure and get your phone number, in case she can't remember the name of your bar," Rosie said. "She said she might want to talk when she feels better."

She offered to call Theo a cab, but he looked at her as if she were crazy, before trudging off to catch the bus.

"He said he learned most of them card games in Yugoslavia," Rosie reported later to a very weak Aurora, pale as a ghost in her bed.

"That's fine, I like a well-traveled man," Aurora said.

8

For most of that day, Aurora was too sick to care whether she lived or died, recovered or perished, had a lover or didn't have a lover. Rosie peeked in about noon to see if she was well enough to consider a snack, only to discover Aurora lying on the floor midway between bathroom and bed.

"I'm not dead, I'm resting, go away," Aurora said.

"Hon, if you're too weak even to crawl, then you need help," Rosie informed her. She noticed that Aurora had pulled most of the bedcovers off the bed and had constructed a kind of nest for herself on the floor, near the window nook.

"I'll proceed to my nest in a moment," Aurora said. "Did my Greek leave?"

"Yeah, but what makes you think he's yours?" Rosie asked, annoyed by Aurora's habit of assuming that she could have whatever she wanted, at least where men were concerned. Having what she wanted in the way of men was exactly what had led her to be lying collapsed in the middle of her own bedroom floor.

"Of course he's mine," Aurora said. "How dare you challenge my right to him?"

"Good lord, I just asked a question," Rosie said.

Later, though, after a couple more painful crawls to the bathroom to attempt to empty a stomach that was already empty, Aurora began to remember the chain of events that had brought her to such a state. It was a short chain, actually, the beginning and end of which was the discovery of Patsy Carpenter's belt on Jerry Bruckner's couch. When she was strong enough to feel anything again, what she felt was a sense of betrayal, as bitter as the few drops of bile that seemed, after so much vomiting, to be all that was left of her bodily fluids.

The next time Rosie ventured to peek in the door, it was almost dinnertime. Aurora was in the bed crying, with just her bed light on.

Aurora, feeling lonely, hopeless, and old, told her about the belt on the couch.

"So it was really happening . . . I mean, you and Jerry?" Rosie said, relieved to have correct information at last.

"Oh, I don't know," Aurora admitted. "I guess it was only happening in the sense that it occurred."

"I don't get it," Rosie said. "What does that mean?"

"It means I wanted it and he didn't," Aurora said. "I was there, but he wasn't. So in a sense it wasn't happening at all. And what that means is that I made a very bad fool of myself, and now I've had my comeuppance," she added in a flat voice. "I knew I'd get my comeuppance eventually— I just didn't think Patsy Carpenter would be the one to deliver it."

"Maybe she didn't," Rosie said. "All you got to go on is a belt on a couch. Maybe she just got an itch and took off her belt to scratch it, and then she forgot the belt."

Aurora looked at her so grimly that Rosie was taken aback. What had she done now? Then it occurred to her that perhaps she shouldn't have mentioned itch and scratching.

"Or she could have just lost a button, or something, or eaten too much—you don't know," she added lamely.

Later in the night, sitting wakeful but blank in her window nook, Aurora realized that Rosie could be right. There could be an innocent explanation for the belt on the couch. She didn't for a moment believe there was, but it was possible. But did it matter? If Jerry wasn't sleeping with Patsy already, he would be sleeping with her soon, or with some other young woman soon. What seeing the belt had brought home to her had little to do with Jerry: what it had brought home to her was her own folly. She had cast aside her dignity for a few months of sex with a younger man who didn't really want her. Besides that, she had grasped the whole equation from the beginning and had done it anyway. Her lifelong tendency had been to overreach, but she could not recall an occasion when she had overreached so crudely, or been slapped down so hard.

"You're probably right, but you could be wrong, remember?" Rosie said at breakfast, while making pancakes for Aurora. Just then the phone rang.

Aurora, who was closest, ignored it. It rang several times.

"Want me to get it?" Rosie asked.

"You may, if you choose," Aurora said.

Rosie got it and immediately gave Aurora a scared look.

"It's Jerry!" she whispered, covering the receiver not only with her hand but with a pot holder too, for good measure.

Aurora didn't change expression or respond in any way.

"Hi, Jerry," Rosie said, thinking she might want to quit her job if she was going to be placed in the middle every time the phone rang from now on.

"Yeah, she's fine, but she just ain't come down yet. I guess she's probably in the shower, want her to call you?" Rosie said. Aurora frowned when she heard the want-her-to-call-you part.

"Please have her call me, she didn't show up yesterday and I've been a little worried," Jerry said.

"He says he's been a little worried," Rosie said, putting down the phone.

Aurora got up without a word, walked through the garage, and got into her car.

Once the car warmed up, she began to back it out of the garage. She had a grim look on her face, and it wasn't, Rosie felt, because of the familiar threat of scraping her fenders.

Rosie followed her out of the garage and down the driveway, determined to make one last effort to get her to be reasonable —or, if that took too much effort, at least to get her to reveal where she was going.

"Jerry sounded real concerned on the phone," she said, easily keeping pace with the car as Aurora crept backward down the driveway. "He sounded like he misses you."

This got no response at all, but Rosie, ever hopeful, kept following, all the way to the street.

"I hope you ain't gonna go get drunk again," she said, as Aurora curved into the street and shifted from reverse to drive.

"Your system is just going to get damaged if you keep getting drunk," Rosie continued by way of parting advice. Aurora ignored her, looked down the street to see if there were any obvious obstacles ahead, and drove off.

"It could have been somebody's else's stupid belt—it could have been a patient's," Rosie yelled after her, before going through the backyard to her own little house, to rout out Willie. She felt that bad things might happen before the day was over; she wanted Willie to be up and about—she didn't expect him to deliver any particularly wise counsel, but she did expect him to sit and drink coffee with her while she worried.

To her annoyance, Willie wasn't in their little house. At first she thought he had just misplaced himself. Lately he had been moping around the backyard a lot, trimming hedges —but when she looked, she discovered that the backyard wasn't where he was moping, if he was moping. She hurried back into the house, hoping to find him in the kitchen, but he wasn't in the kitchen and he didn't appear to be in any of the bathrooms either.

It came to her in a flash that Willie was gone—he had skipped, departed, run off. Once this simple thought occurred to her she realized she was not very surprised, though she was intensely annoyed. Now he would be even less useful than he had been when he was there!

Of course, Willie was slow; he had still been in bed when

she had gone in to try and coax Aurora into eating a few pancakes. He wasn't in the backyard, but maybe he was in the alley behind the backyard, wandering around indecisively, trying to decide which way to run like a rat when he ran.

Rosie darted into the alley, saw no Willie, and quickly jogged around the block, hoping to spot him at the bus stop. He had registered two DWIs lately and was no longer allowed the keys to his midget pickup. But Willie wasn't at the bus stop either. Slow people evidently moved faster when they were conducting an escape. She herself had never been slow, but when, years before, she had decided the jig was really up with her marriage, she had acted like greased lightning—and then had had to come back home anyway, due to the fact that her husband, Royce, had been disemboweled by one of his best friends.

She went back inside and made another inspection of the house, but she didn't really expect to find anyone there, and she didn't find anyone there.

"Gone where?" Aurora asked, twenty minutes later, when she returned, having merely driven aimlessly around the neighborhood for a while. She had meant to go to Jerry's and have it out with him as a prelude to forgetting him and getting over him, if she could. But she hadn't gone more than two blocks before she began to feel shaky; she parked for a while in a nice spot of River Oaks shade, but didn't become less shaky and soon was forced to admit that she wasn't up to having anything out with anybody, not just then. Her stomach still felt knotted, and she could detect only faint traces of appetite, a sure sign that she was in no condition to have very much out with a man.

Now, just when she needed sympathy on the home front, Rosie, who often gave it, had had the bad timing to become deserted herself, leaving her in no state to provide much sympathy.

"Oh, buck up," Aurora said. "He probably just went to buy shaving cream. If the world were made of shaving cream, men would still manage to run out of it just when one would prefer to see them shaved. At least that's been my experience with men, and I've had a lot, as you know."

"No, he left me," Rosie assured her. "I knew he was about to unless I stopped being mean to him."

"If you knew that precise fact, then why didn't you stop being mean to him?" Aurora inquired. "Did you want him to leave?"

"I did and I didn't," Rosie admitted, glancing at the stove, where a nice pile of pancakes was waiting, unconsumed.

"Them pancakes just went to waste," she added.

Aurora turned her attention to the substantial stack of pancakes on the stove—it seemed to her that her stomach might be becoming a little less knotted.

"Nonsense, those pancakes still look quite edible to me," she said. "Let's you and I split them. You know my principles."

"Yeah, eat as much as you can stuff down," Rosie intoned. "If I was to eat two bites, with my stomach like this, I'd vomit all day, just like you did yesterday. I'm just a bundle of nerves," she said, as Aurora divided the pancakes evenly and placed them on two plates. Aurora then proceeded to eat both her plate of pancakes and Rosie's, while Rosie sat, sipped coffee, and looked bleak.

"I wish I still smoked," Rosie said. "I'd be smoking right now, if I did."

"Well, we just have to face matters squarely, Rosie," Aurora said. "We've both been abandoned, and that's that. Do you think there could be another woman in Willie's life? Or did he just leave you because you were mean?

"You *were* quite mean, at times," she added. "I suppose it's because you have the advantage of having me as a teacher and model for some forty years."

"Naw, it ain't your fault, I just get mean sometimes anyway," Rosie admitted.

"What about my other woman theory?" Aurora asked again.

"It's possible, but it ain't likely," Rosie said. "Willie is too lazy. My guess is he'll just go back on dope. I don't know about that cure he took—I don't think it really worked."

"Probably not," Aurora agreed. "I disapprove of these cures anyway. People should be given all the dope they want, in my view—whatever it takes to keep them stable."

"Oh, poor Willie ain't up to being stable," Rosie said, looking suddenly very much sadder. "That man's like Jello inside —you know, quivers constantly. If I had it all to do over again I wouldn't have been so mean."

"Look at it this way—at least he didn't sleep with Patsy Carpenter," Aurora commented.

"That could have been an accidental slip on Jerry's part," Rosie said. After all, she had known Patsy as long as Aurora had and was not disposed to be as hard on her as Aurora was. Whatever else she might be, Patsy was unarguably attractive, and what else did it take where men were concerned?

"Baloney—Patsy's a determined predator, like me," Aurora said, wishing there were more pancakes and wondering if she would still feel hungry if she got up and made some.

"She passed along the gene, too," she added. "Don't forget that Katie just stole Melanie's heartthrob."

"Some heartthrob, the little jerk," Rosie said. "I'm never gettin' involved again, it's too much torment when it ends."

"Wrong, totally wrong," Aurora said, jumping up. She had decided to go for the pancakes while her appetite was on the upswing.

"What we both must do is seduce someone else as soon as possible," she said. "It's the principle that my mother always applied when her horse threw her. No matter how painful the fall, she always got up and got right back on the horse so as not to lose her nerve."

"Yeah, but what if you lose your nerve anyway?" Rosie asked. "This ain't my first rodeo, you know? If you get thrown a hundred times, maybe the smart thing to do is stay off horses."

"Well, if you want to be an old woman, okay," Aurora said. "You *are* an old woman, but if you give up and start acting like one, I can assure you you'll be a lot older in a matter of weeks."

Rosie pondered that observation for a moment—she didn't disagree with it. It was just that at the moment the weight of life seemed so heavy that the most restful course seemed to be to go on and sink beneath it.

"I ain't no woman of steel," she pointed out. "I don't know if I can get my nerve up again, and anyway, who would I get it up for?"

Aurora suddenly remembered that she had invited two Greeks to dinner. Actually, all she could remember about them was that they had bags under their eyes, wore undershirts, and had muscular shoulders—and also that oil trucks drove almost through their little shed of a bar on their way to the Ship Channel.

"Didn't Theo lift me or something when I was extremely drunk?" Aurora asked. She had a vague sense that one set of muscular shoulders had been put into play on her behalf.

"He not only lifted you, he carried you all the way upstairs," Rosie said. "Got a cramp in his leg, though."

"I have not been lifted in many years," Aurora said. "What a pity I was not sober enough to enjoy the sensation."

"He used to carry sacks off ships, but he don't do no exercise now," Rosie said.

"You seem to have got to know him rather well while I was drunk," Aurora said, casting a glance over her shoulder as she turned a pancake.

"No, and I ain't after him or nothing, leave me alone when I'm brokenhearted," Rosie protested, deciding not to mention that she and Theo had played cards for several hours. Then she remembered that she already *had* mentioned it when she told Aurora that Theo had learned his card games in Yugoslavia.

"I'll finish them pancakes, you sit down and eat," she said, hoping to deflect any jealous thoughts Aurora might be having before they picked up momentum.

"Yes, I'm starving," Aurora said. "We have the Petrakis brothers coming to dinner, we have to start thinking about our menu."

"No, just Theo's coming," Rosie said. "He said he wasn't bringing his brother because he doesn't like him."

"Well, that's another confidence he delivered to you instead of to me," Aurora said. "It's my dinner party and I want them both here so I can look at them when I'm sober. For all I know, Vassily might be the cuter."

"Vassily wanted to call the cops and have you arrested when you passed out—that's what Theo said," Rosie revealed. "He said Vassily wasn't even nice to you—why should you feed him?"

"Rosie, most men aren't nice to me, but I've fed millions," Aurora pointed out.

"Yeah, but most men don't try to have you put in jail just because you're passed out," Rosie countered. Vassily sounded like a bad egg to her.

"Well, I don't know, Vassily may have had his reasons," Aurora said.

"Reasons for having some stupid cop drag you off to jail?" Rosie said, her anti-cop bias surging to the surface. "What kinds of reasons would make him want to do that?"

"I was not too punctilious yesterday morning," Aurora said. "I may have neglected to pay for my retsina before passing out. Perhaps he concluded that he was going to be stiffed, a not unreasonable fear, since I was barefooted and in my gown."

"You showed up in a Cadillac, I doubt he thought you was broke," Rosie said. "Anyway, you better call Theo and work all this out, because he don't intend to bring nobody but himself."

"I believe Theo became rather sweet on me before I got so drunk," Aurora said. "I'm sure the real reason he doesn't want to bring his brother is because he doesn't want me to conclude that his brother is cuter."

"Okay, you can do what you want with the Greeks, I wish Willie would come back," Rosie said, getting up. It seemed to her that she had better launch into some housekeeping or else she was just going to spend the morning crying and being depressed.

"I wish you'd call Jerry and relieve his mind," she said. "He sounded pretty worried."

"What mind? I certainly won't call him," Aurora said. "He

knows where I live. If he has any interest in working this out, let him try. And if he's too big a coward to come and try, then the more he suffers the better."

"Woman of steel, that's you," Rosie said. "I feel sorry for Jerry. He probably just got broadsided by Patsy and now he's miserable and wishes he had you back."

"I seriously doubt that, Rosie—they're probably tupping right now," Aurora said. Again for a moment she was afflicted with a tormenting vision, two bodies younger than her own joined in urgent union.

"Doing what right now?" Rosie asked.

"Tupping, you know what it means, even if you don't read Shakespeare," Aurora said. "I'm disgusted with you anyway, even if you are heartbroken."

"Why?" Rosie asked.

"For feeling sorry for that son of a bitch who jilted me," Aurora said, slapping several fresh pancakes on her plate. "You're always feeling sorry for men who don't deserve even a dollop of sympathy. We're the ones who deserve the sympathy. When are you going to grasp that obvious fact?"

Rosie squatted by the sink, surveying the array of detergents she had stashed underneath it. What she really felt like was crawling under the sink herself. If she could just hide there for a few more hours, maybe Willie would decide to come home and one problem would be solved. What Aurora said was true: men did cause endless trouble and pain, women were the ones who deserved sympathy, and yet, mad as she got at men, and mean as she could be to them individually and briefly, she could never withold her sympathies from them for very long. There was just something about them that sooner or later prompted her to ease up.

"It's like they're just boys," she said. "Emma was a girl, you never had no boys, you don't know. But I had four boys."

"Yes, and from what I can tell, every one of your sons is more grown-up and more responsible and better to their women than any of your boyfriends have ever been to you," Aurora pointed out. "Why does the fact that you raised responsible sons mean you have to excuse every weak male that comes your way?"

"You ask too many questions, hon," Rosie said wearily. She went to the little closet where she kept the vacuum cleaner and began to put it together. Vacuuming might be the most soothing thing she could do just at the moment. At least it would drown out Aurora's questions, which had a tendency to become more difficult to answer the worse they both were feeling.

"Undoubtedly I do, that's because I need to find out what's wrong with the world, and why," Aurora said. "Go away, run your machine, close me out if you want to."

She smeared her fresh pancakes liberally with butter and then doused them in an even more liberal gush of maple syrup. Her mood had been rising at the thought of her Greeks, but it suddenly turned around and began to sink at the thought of what Patsy and Jerry might be doing just then, or, if not just then, then later in the day, or, if not this day, then sometime.

The factor that was causing her spirits to take their dive was the sense that Patsy and Jerry had just knocked her out of the mainstream. Why making love occasionally meant that one was still in the mainstream, she didn't know—it just seemed to her that it did. And in the last few years she had struggled mightily—or so it seemed to her—for just that: just to stay in the mainstream a little longer. Often she got no great pleasure out of her activities; often her partners were at best inadequate and at worst pathetic; often her self-esteem took a battering of one kind or another, as it had when she had cast aside good sense and seduced Jerry—but she could at least have the momentary sense of swimming where she ought to swim, rather than feel that she was merely creeping along like an old turtle, in the shallows, the mud, the ditch.

Now Jerry and Patsy were the swimmers: whatever they were doing, and however or whenever they did it, would likely be better than anything she was apt to be doing for some time to come, perhaps forever.

"I'll leave you alone and let you eat," Rosie said, carrying the vacuum cleaner to the foot of the stairs. It was hard to worry too much about Aurora when she was eating—and, with a second stack of pancakes in front of her, she definitely *was* eating.

"Yes, go," Aurora said. "I'll sit here with my pancakes and do your work for you."

The remark puzzled Rosie. She was halfway up the stairs, vacuum cleaner at the ready, about to do her work for herself. What did Aurora mean? That she wanted to take over the vacuuming? Nobody could eat pancakes while vacuuming—but then maybe Aurora meant that she wanted to do the vacuuming after she ate the pancakes. On rare occasions she did get in the mood to do housework. Maybe this was one such rare occasion.

"No, go clean," Aurora said, seeking her maid's look of puzzlement. She waved her hand at Rosie vigorously.

"Okay, but what did you mean, do my work for me?" Rosie inquired.

"I meant your philosophical work," Aurora said. "Someone has to figure out what's wrong with men, and why. Obviously you'd rather take refuge in mindless labor than trouble yourself with these eternal questions."

"If they're eternal questions I guess a lot of people who are a lot smarter than me have worked on them," Rosie said. "If Shakespeare and Eric Hoffer can't figure them out, I couldn't have a chance in hell."

She had seen Eric Hoffer on television several times and had been much impressed by his ability to explain why things were as they were.

"What about Sir Kenneth Clark?" Rosie asked, remembering another television star whose ability to explain things had impressed her. "He explained nearly every single thing about civilization," Rosie reminded her boss. "Maybe you could just write him a letter and ask him why men are jerks."

"No, thanks," Aurora said. "Since he's male, there's every likelihood that he's a jerk himself. Anyway, I've spent most of my life questioning men about their own failings, and what have I got to show for it?"

"You got two Greeks coming to dinner—or one Greek at least," Rosie reminded her. "Maybe one of them won't be a jerk."

"It's a faint hope, but I have to start somewhere, if I intend to start," Aurora said. "Do you think we should invite Pascal, since we're cooking?"

"Good lord, no, you know how jealous he is," Rosie said. "He'd probably be twice as jealous of somebody who was a Greek, much less two somebodies, if the mean one comes."

"Nonetheless, I think I may invite Pascal anyway, over your protests," Aurora said, as Rosie, seeing that her boss seemed to be in an improving humor, lugged the vacuum cleaner on up the stairs.

9

"Greeks?" Pascal said, horrified. "You want me to share you with Greeks? Where did you pick up these Greeks?"

"At a bar on the Ship Channel," Aurora said calmly. "Where would you expect me to pick up Greeks in this town?"

In the mood to torment someone, she had telephoned Pascal to inform him that he was being invited to dinner to meet her new friends. She was seated in her window nook, looking in the mirror. It seemed to her that, despite all her efforts to be gallant and press ahead with life, her eyes lacked luster. Indeed, everything about her appearance lacked luster, and trying to provoke Pascal was not really much fun. He was so predictable and she was so obviously depressed that the effort seemed hollow.

Several times she had been on the point of calling Jerry Bruckner. Once or twice she had even picked up the phone, only to put it down gain. Once she had even started for her car meaning to drive over and catch him in the ten minutes he allowed himself between patients, but before she even got into her car, she did an about-face and retreated to her bedroom. Sooner or later she supposed she would have to talk to Jerry, or even see him, but she wasn't ready for it and had no way of predicting when she would be ready.

"All over the place you pick up everyone you see that's wearing pants," Pascal said.

"The pants these two had on were nothing much, I can assure you," Aurora said. "Still, having nothing better to do, I picked them up."

"You're a horrible woman!" Pascal burst out, his temper getting the better of him. "Anybody you pick up, you treat him better than me."

"That's not true, and it was ungrammatically put, besides," Aurora countered. "How do you hold down a job in a respectable consulate if you can only manage to speak broken English of that sort?"

"I can speak English better than you can speak French, any day of your life," Pascal said.

"I do not attempt French now, although I did once," Aurora said. "You attempt English and the results speak for themselves. This is a stupid squabble. I asked you to dinner. Are you accepting or are you declining?"

Pascal was silent for a moment, trying to master his anger.

"Take your time, there's no pressure," Aurora said. "It's just an invitation. You're quite free to accept or refuse. But if you happen to be refusing, I must say you're doing it with singular lack of grace."

Rosie wandered in. She had taken up smoking again and was smoking. Aurora waved her out, but she only stepped back a foot or two so as to be technically in the hall.

"Willie has left Rosie and it's had a bad effect on her," Aurora said. "She's smoking again."

Pascal received this news in silence. He was filled with bitterness at the thought of how badly Aurora was treating him. The only thing that kept him from telling her off in no uncertain terms was the knowledge that it would only lead her to redouble her efforts and treat him even worse.

"Greeks have filthy habits," he pointed out finally. "They make love to goats."

"Many do, I'm sure, but these two Greeks of mine are not goatherds," Aurora informed him. "They are retired from the shipping business and have established a delightful bar."

"Delightful to you, maybe," Pascal said. "Anywhere there's men in pants, you are delighted."

"Accept or refuse, eight o'clock, informal?" Aurora said.

"Accept," Pascal said, feeling miserable.

"The fat's in the fire now," Rosie said, when she saw Aurora hang up.

"What else do I have to do other than fling the fat in the fire?" Aurora inquired. "Anyway, what do you care? It's not your fire."

"It sort of is, I live here," Rosie reminded her.

The phone rang, and it was Melanie, wildly excited.

"I got it—I got the part! I'm going to be in a TV series," Melanie said. "I was too scared it wouldn't happen to call you sooner.

"I mean, I'm in a pilot," she added hastily. "But it will be a series if it's good, and people like it."

"Melly, this is little short of miraculous," Aurora said. "I'm very proud of you and so will Rosie be, once she's heard this news."

Rosie raced to the phone and heard it. They both heard it for almost an hour—all about Melanie getting called back for a second tryout, and then a third; about her eventual triumph and Bruce's intense jealousy; about his breakup with Katie and his attempts to return to Melanie, her rejection, his despair, and her new boyfriend Lee, a young assistant director who knew many wonderful cheap places to take Melanie to dine. The last item in the report was that Melanie had lost sixteen pounds, mainly from being too nervous to eat.

"I mean, once I knew there was some kind of chance I *might* get the part, the thought of not getting it was the worst," Melanie said. "It was so nerve-racking it just sort of melted me."

During the call both Aurora and Rosie grew cheerful almost to the point of bubbliness, but neither the bubbliness nor the cheer lasted much more than half an hour once Melanie hung up. They chattered on for fifteen minutes about how wonderful it was that Melanie had finally had a triumph —and then both sank swiftly back into depression.

"The downside is she won't never be coming home to cheer us up," Rosie pointed out. "Lord knows we need it, too."

"Oh, well," Aurora said. "You're only young once."

Rosie gave her an odd look. "That ain't what you used to say," she reminded Aurora. "You used to say you were young as long as you could manage it."

"Yes, that was a correct statement, too," Aurora said. "I was managing it fine right up until Jerry slept with Patsy. That took the wind out of my sails. In fact, it took the sails right off the ship."

"You still don't really know he done it," Rosie said. "All this suffering could be for nothing."

"If he hasn't done it, then where is he?" Aurora wanted to know. "What's to stop him from driving over here to affirm his innocence?"

"Aurora, he don't even know he's being accused," Rosie said, wondering why she was bothering to argue so hard for Jerry Bruckner, a man she scarcely knew. For all she knew, he was guilty as hell—one indicator pointing in that direction was that Patsy no longer came into the house for a chat when she came to pick Rosie up for exercise class. She now showed up at the last possible moment, got Rosie at the curb, drove like a bat to Bellaire, and said little—all signs of guilt, in Rosie's view. Once or twice she had been tempted to ask Patsy about it point-blank, but so far she hadn't.

"He knows he's accused of *something*," Aurora pointed out. "I was seeing him every morning and now I'm not. A moron would know that suggests that all is not well."

"I don't know why I'm carrying on about this," Rosie said. "Whether he did or whether he didn't ain't gonna bring Willie back."

"Rosie, Willie's only been gone a few hours," Aurora said. "He may have just gone on a bender."

"Naw, he don't drink, except wine coolers," Rosie said. "If it's a bender it's a dope bender."

"Do you really want him back, or are you just annoyed that

he managed to wrench himself from your embraces?" Aurora asked.

"What embraces?" Rosie said.

"Well, I suppose I just assumed there were embraces," Aurora said.

Rosie looked very downcast. "Once, since he got back from Alabama," she said. "I don't call that a sex life. I don't call it nothing."

"No wonder you don't want him back," Aurora said.

"I don't, particularly," Rosie admitted. "But I'd still like to know if he's alive or dead."

"This news about Melly is very good news," Aurora said. "If we weren't such selfish old hags we'd be happy as larks just knowing she's had this success."

"I'm happy as a lark for her," Rosie said. "I just ain't happy as a lark for me."

"It's an upswing, though," Aurora said. "I can remember whole years when there was not the slightest hint of an upswing. Now if Teddy could stop shaking, and if Tommy could get paroled, we'd be almost out of the woods.

"Also, it would help if we could both find beautiful, distinguished, desirable men to fall in love with," she added. "It would sure be a big improvement on what we've had."

"I like Theo but I wouldn't call him beautiful," Rosie allowed. "What's the mean brother look like?"

"Identical," Aurora said. "Identical to Theo, that is. While I was in the process of getting drunk I thought they might be twins."

The phone began to ring, and it rang several times. Aurora's hand was a foot from the receiver, but she made no move to pick it up.

"Pick it up, maybe you won a cruise to Turkey," Rosie begged. It maddened her when Aurora became reluctant to answer the phone. She herself had never ignored a ringing telephone in her life. How could anyone just sit there and pass up a chance on a cruise to Turkey?

"Pick it up!" she pleaded. "It could be Willie!"

"If it's Willie, then it's for you, and you should pick it up," Aurora said. "My own strong suspicion is that it's Pascal."

Rosie dashed over and got the phone on the seventh ring. "Hello, Greenway residence," she said.

"I'm not coming," Pascal said. "I don't want to see Greeks. I lived in Greece, I know what they're like. Tell her not to use the silver, they'll put the spoons in their pockets."

"You tell her," Rosie said, trying to hand the phone to Aurora, who resolutely refused to take it. When Rosie thrust it at her she batted it away.

"I can hear him, I'm not speaking to him," Aurora said. "He's just maligned my guests."

"She won't take the phone. If you're not coming you're not coming," Rosie said. "Is your decision final?"

"Final today, final tomorrow, final forever!" Pascal said, so annoyed by Aurora's refusal to take the phone herself that he immediately hung up. Just as he did, Aurora changed her mind and reached out her hand for the receiver.

"He hung up and I give up," Rosie said. The tensions of the morning made her feel like crying. Lately, it seemed, tension had become virtually the sole ingredient of her life: tension with Willie, tension with Aurora, tension within herself over her wishy-washy policies in regard to Willie. On the rare occasions when one of her children called, it was always to announce a calamity: a smashed car, a wounded grandchild, a huge hospital bill, a dead pet. None of her daughters ever called unless they were in tears; none of her sons unless they were at a point of despair—any way you colored it, what it added up to was more tension.

Though she knew she was bored with Willie, it hurt a lot that he had just crawled out of bed, put his clothes on, and run off. And now Aurora wouldn't even talk to Pascal, a nice enough man who was just a little too prone to flying off the handle.

Overwhelmed, engulfed, beleaguered, broken, Rosie thrust the dead receiver in Aurora's general direction and burst into tears. She ran out of the room, sobbing heavily, and crashed into the vacuum cleaner, which she had foolishly left at the head of the stairs. The vacuum cleaner began to topple down the stairs. Rosie made a grab for the hose but stepped on a little attachment she only used to dust the insides of lampshades, and fell after the vacuum cleaner head first. She somehow overtook the vacuum and passed it on her fall, so that when she came to rest at the bottom of the stairs, the cleaner caught up with her a second later and walloped her on the back of her head. Then, as she attempted to turn over and get the vacuum off her, the hose caught up with the parent machine and the long, heavy attachment that was on it at the moment whipped around and whacked Rosie hard in the eye, shocking her so that she sat helplessly while the world around her went blank, and she sank into a faint.

Aurora, in the process of calling Pascal back to give him a sound chewing out, heard a horrible crash on the stairs. The sound of crashing went on for some time. She hastily got up and ran to the stairs, only to see Rosie, apparently lifeless, lying at their foot, the vacuum cleaner on top of her.

"Rosie, wake up, are you alive?" Aurora asked tentatively. "However rude I may have been, I still hope you're alive."

Rosie neither moved nor spoke. She was out. Aurora managed to recall that only the day before she had knocked *her*self out, and had turned out not to be dead. Perhaps they had both simply slipped into the habit of knocking themselves out. On the other hand, Hector, whom she missed deeply and never more so than at this moment, had passed out quietly in the Pig Stand and had, in fact, been dead. Since that moment when she had looked over to discover Hector dead against her shoulder, not a single thing had been right: Jerry had betrayed her, and she had invited two Greeks to dinner although she didn't know them and there was a good chance that they would look ridiculous and out of place and not at all appealing to her—*if* Rosie wasn't dead and the dinner party happened and the Greeks actually showed up.

"Rosie, Rosie!" she said sharply, in her most military voice, before inching carefully downstairs, taking care not to trip on what seemed like miles of vacuum-cleaner cord curled threateningly down the whole length of the stairs.

Rosie didn't respond—she failed to so much as twitch. Aurora removed the vacuum cleaner, knelt by her maid, and tried to detect vital signs. She felt Rosie's forehead—it felt alarmingly cold—then tried to feel her pulse, but couldn't remember which arm the pulse was supposed to be in. At any rate she located nothing to indicate that Rosie was alive.

Panicked, she ran to the kitchen, thinking first Hector, now Rosie, what if I've lost them both? She grabbed the kitchen phone and immediately dialed Jerry: there was a time for pride and a time to put aside pride, and this was the latter. But the phone rang again and again and no one answered. Finally his message machine clicked on—she remembered that he had set it at ten rings so as to discourage all but the most desperate patients. She hung up—what good would it do to leave a message? Fortunately she had taped the name and number of the Petrakis brothers' bar on her refrigerator door for easy reference. Aurora dialed it rapidly while in her panic, missed a few digits or transposed them, got a wrong number, and woke up a woman who said, "I'll kill you if this is you!" Aurora hung up, redialed more carefully, and could almost have fainted with relief at hearing Theo's voice.

"Theo, it's urgent, Rosie may have killed herself, would you and Vassily mind coming to dinner a few hours early?" she asked.

"Why, you having the funeral tonight?" Theo asked. He had been thinking about the dinner party so much that he had become nervous, and when he was nervous he was apt to become a little sarcastic.

"Of course not—I need you to help me determine if she's alive," Aurora said.

"Her maid may be dead," Theo said to his brother. "You want to go over with me now?"

"Why?" Vassily asked.

"To see the body, I guess," Theo said, covering the receiver with his palm.

"I don't work for no ambulance company," Vassily reminded him. "Tell her to call an ambulance company if she want someone to examine the body. Does this mean the dinner's off?" he asked, annoyed. Though Vassily didn't much like Aurora, he did like free meals. He had had it in mind that Aurora might make veal française, one of his favorite dishes. Now it sounded to him like the dinner was off just as he had been looking forward to some mouth-watering veal française.

"Not necessarily," Theo said. "I don't know what happened yet."

"So why are you asking me? I don't know what happened neither," Vassily told him.

"What was the cause of her demise, if she demised?" Theo asked Aurora.

"Falling downstairs—I would appreciate it if you'd hurry on over," Aurora said.

"Uh–oh," Theo said. "That's what killed old Grandpa Paki. He fell down almost a hundred steps and died that night."

"Goodness, you must have had a large house if it had a hundred steps available for someone to fall down," Aurora said, just as Rosie came walking into the kitchen. Though upright, and clearly alive, she was rather unsteady on her pins.

"It wasn't a house, it was an island," Theo said. "There was a hundred steps going down to the water and Grandpa Paki fell all the way down them."

"Oh, false alarm, here's Rosie, she's apparently not dead," Aurora said, losing all interest in the fate of Grandpa Paki.

"She ain't dead, the dinner's on," Theo said to Vassily.

"Boy, am I gonna have a shiner," Rosie said, trying to tug an ice tray out of the refrigerator. "I ain't been hit in the eye that hard since Royce clobbered me that time I tried to stab him."

Despite her efforts, the ice tray wouldn't come out—it was frozen to its place.

"Sit down, sit down, I'll get you some ice," Aurora said. "I don't think you should move around too much—you may be injured internally."

"I am injured internally—Willie injured me internally by running off," Rosie said. Instead of obeying her boss's order not to move around, she demonstrated why she was the star of her exercise class by doing a back bend over the sink and letting a stream of cold water pour straight down on her injured eye.

"She's amazing—moments ago she was so injured I took her for dead, and now she's doing gymnastics of the sort no sane person would attempt," Aurora told Theo.

"I guess the crisis is over, but if you need help with the veal française, Vassily and I could come a little early," Theo said. He felt rather proud of the tactful way he had let Aurora know what his brother expected to be fed.

"We're not having veal française, we've having agneau à la grecque," Aurora corrected. "What makes you think I would serve two lively men a boring dish such as veal française?"

"Nothing makes me think it, it's just something Vassily had his heart set on," Theo said, winking at his brother.

"Well, let him reset his heart, and you can reset your clock, if it isn't set correctly," Aurora said. "Rosie and I are having a taxing day and we expect you promptly at eight.

"Almost nothing annoys me more than a man who presumes to tell me what to cook," Aurora said to Rosie, after hanging up. "If you start letting them tell you what to cook, the next thing you know they'll be telling you *how* to cook," she went on. "They'll be telling you to leave out the onions just when you should be putting in the onions. I find it very vexing."

"I don't think it's no worse than falling downstairs and knocking yourself out with your own vacuum cleaner," Rosie said. The faucet was still pouring water on her eye. Some of it splashed in her mouth as she was speaking, causing her to splutter. She kept her eye directly under the faucet, though —if she didn't cool down her eye, she knew she could expect to look horrible for a week.

"I said I'd get you some ice," Aurora said.

"Yeah, but where is it?" Rosie asked.

Aurora got up, and with a mighty yank managed to break the frozen tray loose from its moorings.

"It's here, and I wouldn't mind hitting a Greek with it," she said.

Across town in the salty breeze wafting off the Ship Channel, Theo looked at Vassily and shook his head.

"No veal française," he said. "We're having Greek food."

"Greek food?" Vassily said. "What does she know about Greek food?"

"I guess we'll find out," Theo said.

"I don't see why you like her, she's fat and bossy," Vassily said.

"What do you think your wife is—Angela?" Theo asked.

Vassily ignored the comment about his wife, who was undeniably fat and bossy, as well as being in the process of divorcing him. His mind was on the food issue. It was annoying that Theo's new River Oaks girlfriend had decided to feed them exactly the kind of food they could eat at home.

"It's an insult," he commented. "She must think we're too dumb to eat anything but feta cheese and little lambs."

"She only asked you to be polite—besides, she might be a good cook," Theo pointed out.

"If she asked me to be polite, how come she ain't polite enough to cook what I want to eat?" Vassily asked.

"Shut up about the veal française, maybe she'll cook it next time," Theo said, wondering if it would be correct to bring flowers.

"If there is a next time," Vassily said. "The woman's had time to sober up. Once she gets a good look at you sober she might decide you ain't so cute."

Theo ignored his brother. He was still thinking about the flowers. He thought he might bring a few, correct or not.

"I hope she has French wine," Vassily said.

10

The Greeks arrived promptly at eight, wearing black coats and smelling not so faintly of attar of roses, thanks to a Balkan cologne they both saved for fancy occasions.

Rosie met them at the door wearing a dramatic black eye patch over her developing shiner. Aurora remembered just in time that she had an eye patch among her memorabilia. Except for a few faint memories it was all that remained of a fling with a skinny professor who taught briefly at Bryn Mawr before dying young. His name was Justin, and he had been more refined than ardent, she remembered.

Still, she had kept the eye patch for a very long time, and now it had finally come in handy.

The only unhandy part was that Rosie seemed to depend unduly on the eye that the eye patch covered. She had difficulty seeing chairs, or even walls, and bumped into several on her way to greet their guests. Her bumpings were partly due to the eye patch and partly due to nerves. At the last minute Aurora had decided to press her into service as Vassily's date, a role that made Rosie more than a little uncomfortable.

"What if Willie shows up while we're eating and sees me with another man?" Rosie asked. "What kind of slut is he going to think I am if I wouldn't even wait one day before dating somebody?"

"He'll probably think you were a victim of my whim, which is in fact the case," Aurora said. "Besides, it would not be wise for you to live your life—or, rather, *not* live it— because of Willie or what he might think, if he can think," she added, heading upstairs to dress.

"It might not be wise to get involved with no Greek either —and I mean either one of us," Rosie said. She had never been to Greece, but she had followed a number of stories about Greek politics on CNN and she was not entirely sure that she liked what she saw.

"Who said involved, it's just one dinner," Aurora pointed out from the stairs.

She had been in the process of putting the finishing touches on herself when the Greeks drove up. They arrived in a rattly white pickup that looked as if it might be held together with chewing gum. From the safety of her window nook, she watched them disembark. Theo held a small bouquet of flowers. If they were impressed with her house, or with the neighborhood, or with anything at all, they didn't show it. While she watched, they trudged slowly up her sidewalk. From what she could tell of their demeanor, they might have been delivering themselves up to be pall-bearers.

"Rosie, they're here, give them drinks and make conversation," she commanded from the head of the stairs, before returning to her dressing table, where she sank unexpectedly, just at the least opportune of moments, into an almost paralyzing depression. Her body, heavy enough in its own right, seemed to grow heavier, and she felt an ache—a hopeless ache—for Jerry. Theo and Vassily, the new men who were supposed to make her stop wanting Jerry—to make him vanish from her consciousness—had had, merely by arriving, the opposite effect. Instead of missing him less, she seemed only to exist to miss him; instead of vanishing from her consciousness, he suddenly filled it. Instead of ceasing to want him, all she could think of was that she wanted to see him, be with him, touch him.

The feeling came over her so strongly that for a time all she could do was sit with her newly made up face in her hands, waiting for the feeling to pass. Along with the old need, and the knowledge of need, came a certain anger with herself. His house had been open to her, still. All the possibilities—loving him, having him—had been open to her, still. Yet, instead of fighting when she had caught the first whiff of Patsy, if it had been Patsy, she had run. It had not been her way to give up easily, and yet this time she had fled —if only she had stayed instead. Jerry would have stepped out of the shower soon. She could have confronted him, asked him questions, fought with him, grabbed him. She might have wrested him back then and there. But she hadn't, and why? The worm in the rose, the parasite that weakened her, sapping her impulse to fight, what was it but age? The affliction that had caused her to hesitate at the beginning also caused her to flee at the end—when, in all likelihood, there had not needed to be an end.

She had more force than Patsy—she knew she had. And yet she had immediately ceded Patsy the victory, for no better reason than that Patsy was younger. She had meekly accepted her own impotence at the very moment when she ought to have asserted her potency.

"Hon, they're here, ain't you coming down?" the eye-patched Rosie suddenly asked from her doorway.

"Yes, certainly, this is a farce," Aurora said, jumping up. She had guests—social duties. She couldn't simply sit and feel hopeless.

Five minutes later she got herself downstairs to find that Rosie, scared of the living room, had taken the Greeks into the kitchen to give them drinks. The smell of lamb from the oven mingled with the smell of attar of roses from the Greeks.

"Why this black, is this a funeral?" Aurora asked, feeling the material of Theo's coat.

"He thought it might be formal," Theo said, nodding at Vassily.

"Yeah, but now that I'm here I'm feeling no pain," Vassily reported.

"He oughtn't to be, he drinks vodka like some people drink orange juice," Rosie volunteered. Indeed, she was somewhat stunned by Vassily's thirst for vodka. She had offered it casually, and before she could turn around he had drunk half a bottle, which made her nervous about her hostessing abilities. What if Aurora came down from dressing to find both of her guest stone drunk? Theo, noticing the wine Aurora had chosen for their meal, had asked suavely if he could have a little of it for starters.

"I'm a man of the grape," he said. "Vas, he likes the grain."

"Gets you there quicker," Vassily commented.

"Gets you there quicker if drunk is where you're headed," Theo remarked.

Rosie was so nervous that she felt drunk might be where she was headed, too, so she drank a little vodka with Vassily. Theo opened a bottle of wine and smoothly consumed half of it while they were sitting around the kitchen, adjusting to one another and waiting for Aurora. In her nervousness Rosie had even considered bolting back upstairs and suggesting that Aurora hurry—she didn't feel she was up to handling foreign guests, solo, too much longer. On the other hand, hurrying Aurora almost always backfired. Fortunately Aurora floated downstairs just as Rosie was approaching panic.

"I see Theo's been clearing his throat with a little wine," Aurora said. "Perhaps I should clear my throat the same way."

Theo immediately rose and poured her a glass.

"Vassily's never been in this neighborhood," he remarked. "Me neither, till I met you."

"Well, you're men of the sea, the wine-dark sea," Aurora said. "I wouldn't expect to find you this far inland except in a good cause, such as cheering me up."

"Vas needs to cheer himself up," Theo said. "He's been in the dumps lately."

"Yeah, I'm getting divorced," Vassily said. "I hate my wife."

It seemed to Rosie that Vassily looked at her significantly as he said it. She had been hoping no one would look at her significantly until she straightened out her situation with Willie—if she had a situation with Willie. Unsettled by what seemed to be a significant look, she gulped a little more vodka.

"Rosie, I see you're being a brilliant hostess—our guests look as happy as Greeks can look," Aurora said. "This seems a perfect occasion for a little role reversal—you continue being the hostess and I'll attempt to function as the scullery maid. If I get in over my head, Theo can help me. He has the look of a man who's had experience with scullery maids."

"Okay, fine," Rosie said. She had no idea what that meant she was supposed to do.

"It's cooling off—why don't you take our guests out on the patio?" Aurora suggested. "The scullery maid will be along in a bit with some *fruits de mer*."

"Shrimp, I bet," Vassily said, as he got up and followed Rosie and Theo out.

"Shrimp, among other delicacies," Aurora said, noting that Vassily was now looking significantly at her. "And then we'll have some excellent lamb."

It proved, indeed, to be excellent lamb. The brothers Petrakis consumed it in satisfying quantities—satisfying both to them and to the cook—while Rosie, animated by uncertainty and drink, chattered with the two of them about the one subject they found they had in common: Shreveport, Louisiana, where, it turned out, the brothers had once had what Vassily described as "business interests." Rosie's hometown, Bossier City, was just across the river. The fact that she and the two Greeks had spent time in the same place made Rosie feel much closer to them than she had expected to. She drank a good deal of vodka and then a glass or two of wine and ceased to worry too much about Vassily's significant looks.

Indeed, even by the time the lamb was served, Rosie had

begun to feel that it was the best dinner party Aurora had ever had. Amazingly, Aurora had meant what she said about the role reversal. Rosie actually found herself leading the conversation, for once. It might have been only geographical reminiscences on the order of which store was on what corner in the Shreveport-Bossier City area, but she was the woman doing most of the talking. Aurora was up and down, serving; when she was down she was pleasant, but not especially talkative.

"Usually she does all the talking at these dinner parties," Rosie confided to Theo at a moment when Aurora was out of the room. "I don't know what hit her tonight."

"Nothing's hit me—when one is lucky enough to have a Greek chorus, one should shut up and let it chorus," Aurora said, popping back in just in time to overhear the remark.

In fact, something *had* hit her: a fatigue of the spirit; a sense that she was on a treadmill and that the treadmill was slowing down. She could not quite get her brights to click on, or her partying spirit to kick in. She did her best, but her best on this occasion was far beneath her normal best. Of course her guests had never seen her at her normal best, and they munched their lamb and drank their wine contentedly, unaware of what they were missing.

"I must say you're a laconic chorus, as choruses go," Aurora commented, as she and Rosie were seeing the Greeks to their pickup.

"It's your fault," Theo said. "There was so much to eat we didn't get time to talk."

"I like this neighborhood," Vassily said, looking around at the well-kept lawns. "It's nice, you know. It ain't dusty."

"Anyway, you was quiet yourself," Theo said, eying Aurora closely. "I guess you're still upset about that jerk that jilted you."

"I am, a bit," Aurora admitted. "How shrewd of you to notice."

"It's plain as day," Theo said. "You're here, only you ain't. Vas gets that way when he's depressed about his girlfriend."

"Girlfriend?" Aurora said. "I thought it was his wife he's depressed about."

"Naw, he ain't depressed about Angela, he just wants to kill her," Theo said.

"I see," Aurora said.

"You'd see for sure if you met Angela, she's a terrorist," Theo said.

Rosie and Vassily had wandered off down the sidewalk, indulging in yet more reminiscences of Shreveport while Vassily admired the neighborhood's houses.

"I'm sure Vassily can hold his own, even with a terrorist," Aurora said. "I'm not so sure about you, though." She put her arm lightly over his shoulder as she said it.

"No, I'm fine," Theo said. "I'm just fine."

"Well, you look like a soft touch to me," Aurora said. "Tell me about your heartbreaks."

Theo considered. Aurora took her arm off his shoulder and walked over to the pickup. She thought she might examine it while Theo gave some thought to his heartbreaks. She kicked a rear tire once or twice to see if it was solid, and found that it was.

"The worst was my second wife, she was German," Theo said. "Then there was Becky, but I shouldn't have never got involved with her, she was too young for me—she liked to kick up her heels and dance all night, which is okay if you're young, but I wasn't."

Aurora was silent, watching him across the sidewalk. Their pickup smelled like a sea creature.

"I'm afraid that was the problem with my jerk," she said. "He was young and I'm not—although in this case I was the one who wanted to kick up my heels. He didn't seem to want to do much of anything."

"A deadhead," Theo said. "These kids you see nowadays, they don't have no energy. It's like they don't know how to live."

"Well, at least I know that much," Aurora said. "I think I know how to live.

"I guess the real problem is that I don't know how to *stop* living," she added. "Most people would be relieved if I'd just stop, but I don't want to stop." She felt, for a moment, undone by the accuracy of her own insight.

"Even when I was younger, they wanted me to stop—twenty years ago they were wanting me to stop," she said, almost tearful.

"Why should you stop? You're beautiful!" Theo said. He could hear sadness in Aurora's voice and felt like rushing to her. But then, just as love was about to overwhelm him, his brother and Rosie wandered back up the sidewalk.

"I like the area," Vassily said. "Soon as I get rich, this is where I'm moving."

"Your pickup smells like a rolling fish," Aurora said, hastily struggling up from her sinking spell. "Why's that?"

"Because we haul fish in it when we ain't got nothing else to do," Vassily said.

Theo had a hard time choking down his sense of overwhelming love for Aurora. For the millionth time in his life he was reminded that his brother had no sense of timing, and no sensitivity to what was going on around him. He could have taken Rosie on a little longer walk—five minutes more—but here he was, back, and before Theo could find a way to say anything nice to Aurora, courtesies had been exchanged, the evening ended, and he was driving back across Houston with Vassily, who was fairly drunk and happy as a lark.

"Don't you ever notice nothing?" Theo said, exasperated.

"I noticed—I said it was a nice neighborhood, didn't you hear me?" Vassily said contentedly.

"It's interesting they lived in Shreveport," Rosie said, as she and Aurora were washing up together. "I ain't talked that much about Shreveport since F.V. D'Arch was alive.

F.V. D'Arch, a Shreveport native, had been General Scott's driver for many years, until one day in the garage a heart attack struck and carried him off.

"They're nice, our Greeks, aren't they?" Aurora said, her hands in the dishwater. Rosie was drying wineglasses. Just the way Aurora said it—our Greeks—gave Rosie a good feeling, a really good feeling. It was as if after all these years, she and Aurora had finally had a double date.

11

The next morning when Jerry Bruckner stepped out of his front door to get the paper, Aurora was sitting on the steps. He was startled and a little scared, though she looked at him calmly. There was something girlish and a bit demure in her look.

"I thought you'd never return," he said, feeling silly.

"I haven't returned," Aurora said. "Was it Patsy who left the brilliant yellow belt on your couch?"

"Yes, she forgot it," Jerry said.

"Did you fuck her before she forgot it?" Aurora asked.

"Uh—huh," Jerry said.

"That means yes, I take it," Aurora said.

"It means yes, I'm sorry," Jerry said. "I've missed you."

"Now you can really start missing me," Aurora said, standing up. "Goodbye."

She walked quickly down the sidewalk, not looking back —nor did she look back once she was in her car. She just started the car and drove off. Jerry had started to follow her as she was walking toward the car—had started to argue. But it didn't seem that Aurora had come for discussion, so he didn't. He watched and then went back inside, forgetting the paper.

"Of course she didn't come for discussion, she came for confirmation, nothing else," Patsy said as they were discussing it, later that day. They were on Patsy's bed, in her spacious second-floor bedroom. When Jerry got up to adjust the air conditioning he looked out the window and saw Katie, Patsy's younger daughter, who was visiting from L.A. Katie, topless, was floating on a pool mattress in the middle of her mother's large pool. Like her mother, Katie had small breasts. Unlike her mother, she was too young to have cares.

Jerry returned to the bed, thinking—as he had been almost constantly lately—that it was really time for him to leave town. He had been honest when he said he missed Aurora. He missed her quite a lot. Patsy was younger and more beautiful, but she was also less free and less fun. Patsy had many cares, and despite all her efforts to relax or let go, her cares seemed to restrain her. Even in lovemaking, for which she was almost desperately eager, there was some restraint, not in regard to his needs and pleasures, or her own either, really —she was not inhibited—but, still, there was something a little sad in Patsy's sex: she was greedy but seemed displeased by her own greed. It was in that that she differed most from Aurora.

"I knew she knew—she's not dumb," Patsy said. "It's been a month. Aurora doesn't just stop speaking to someone for a month unless she thinks she's got a powerful reason. I'm the reason. I wonder if she'll ever speak to me again."

Jerry was thinking of Lalani, his doughnut-shop girlfriend. Lalani had much larger breasts than Katie, and, like Katie, she was too young to have cares. Deplorable though he knew it was as an element in his character, Jerry had long known that when it came right down to it he really preferred women who were either too young or too dumb to have cares.

"So what if she found out?" Patsy asked, raising up on an elbow to study Jerry's face—his face fascinated her. It was attractive and intelligent, and yet also passive and empty. The parts were there, but she couldn't get a grip on the

492

whole. She had once hoped that kissing him would make him reveal the whole, but it hadn't. Kissing, fucking, the entree, the main act, usually told her something, but kissing Jerry only told her that she was kissing a pretty odd, though seriously attractive man.

"Suppose I hadn't forgotten my stupid belt and she hadn't found out?" she asked. "What would you have done? Would you have just gone right on sleeping with us both?"

"I wasn't sleeping with her," Jerry said, reminding her what he felt was an important, or at least a significant, point. "I hadn't slept with her since General Scott died."

Patsy regarded this distinction, of which Jerry was so proud, as a wimpy, bullshitty point, and she had said as much before.

"A lapse isn't the same as breaking up, so don't try to tell me you had broken up with her," she said emphatically. "I'd stop screwing my new guy too if my old guy lay down and died. I'd go into mourning too. But I wouldn't stay in mourning forever. By and by I'd want my new guy to take me to bed again, if he was still around."

Jerry said nothing. Often, when Patsy made a point that she considered important, he just said nothing. The most important-seeming points in a given conversation might not seem to matter at all if they were let lie for a day or two.

"So what would you have done when she wanted you again?" Patsy asked. "Tell me. This is not a question I intend to let you duck."

"Maybe I would just have left town," Jerry said.

"That's the coward's way," Patsy said.

"But it could still be the best way," Jerry said. "Cowards are sometimes survivors, you know."

Despite her nice breasts and lack of cares, he wasn't seeing much of Lalani anymore, though on the whole Lalani made a nice balance to Patsy: she was coarse where Patsy was over-refined; she had solid instincts in areas where Patsy's were shaky; she had no interest in things Patsy knew too much about; and she had no emotional restraints, whereas Patsy had too many.

He might have continued to see a lot of Lalani had it not been for a new discovery in the perennial pretty-women-without-cares sweepstakes. His new discovery was a nineteen-year-old Hispanic girl named Juanita, a countergirl at a little all-night tamale stand in the Heights. By a geographical irony too serious for Jerry to ignore, the tamale stand was just across the I-10 from the freeway ramp he had walked down the morning he hitchhiked away from Julie, his first Houston girlfriend. In fact, when he stood at the tamale stand, eating a tamale or a burrito and attempting to flirt with Juanita, he could look across I-10 and see the very spot where the black nurse had stopped to give him his ride to Galveston on the wedding day of Julie's sister.

He tried to convey the richness of this irony to Juanita, mainly because it gave him a chance to prolong their conversations, but Juanita couldn't get interested and didn't pretend to. Why should she care if this nice-looking Americano used to hitchhike from the other side of the freeway? She knew all the talk was probably just his way of showing interest in her—she was petite, beautiful, and full of talk herself; lots of guys came to the tamale stand and showed interest—but she would have liked it better if he had asked to take her dancing or something.

Juanita was an illegal, but she wasn't too worried about it—Immigration wasn't likely to come around hassling any girl as pretty as she was.

Jerry kept dropping by, though, and she began to like him, even if he did talk sort of boring. One day she confessed her dream to him: her dream of living in L.A. She had learned her English reading movie magazines, and she wanted to go to L.A. real bad. Jerry was a good-looking guy: Juanita picked up right away that he was mainly showing up to see *her*, not to eat tamales—which was fine. He looked like a guy who might be moving along soon. Maybe if he liked her so much he'd take her with him. If he didn't take her all the way to L.A., he might at least take her closer. Juanita was hoping for Phoenix or Tucson, at least. If some guy would just take her that far she was pretty sure she could make it the rest of the way on her own.

Of course, her boyfriend Luis had offered to take her to L.A., but Juanita didn't think that had much of a chance. Luis was a busboy at a fried-chicken place—he was an illegal too. Juanita had already pretty much decided not to go running off to California with him. Even if he could save the money for bus tickets, they'd never make it. Luis had the smell, or something—Immigration had already sent him back to Mexico twice.

Fortunately, working double shifts at the fried-chicken place kept Luis pretty busy—otherwise he could be trouble. He was so in love with her that he liked to lurk around the tamale stand on his day off, spying on her to see if she was too nice to customers. If she was even a little bit nice to some customer who was a male, it meant a big fight the next time they were alone together. He was so obsessed with keeping Juanita to himself that if he saw her being nice he would usually threaten to kill her, and the customer too. Once or twice at the tamale stand he got so enraged watching her be nice to customers that he blew up, threatened guys he had never seen before, threatened Juanita, threatened the manager of the tamale stand. Once he even pulled a knife and threatened a black guy. The manager called the cops, but Luis got away before they came. If they had caught him he would have been sent back to Mexico for sure.

Juanita didn't really mind that much that Luis was obsessed with her—sometimes she even sort of liked it. But that didn't mean she intended to set off for L.A. with him. She liked to think she had a little more common sense than that. The nice quiet Americano, who was showing up at the stand every day or two now, seemed like a much better bet. One night she got up her nerve and asked *him* if he'd like to go dancing—maybe the guy was too shy to ask her, or maybe he thought she was too young. He looked kind of startled when she asked him, but he didn't say no. He said he'd do it if he wasn't too busy on the weekend. The weekend was coming along in a day or two, and Juanita was getting excited, wondering if she'd have a new boyfriend to take her dancing. Fortunately Luis had to work on Saturday night—he wouldn't be around.

"Sometimes I wish I could be a virus in your brain," Patsy said to Jerry—she didn't bother to conceal her annoyance. "You're always drifting away from me, and I have no idea where you're drifting to. If I were a virus, at least I'd be there. I'd wiggle in so deep you'd have to think about me once in a while."

"When I think of you too much, I feel guilty," Jerry said.

"Guilty," Patsy said. "Baloney. You don't look as if you feel very guilty—of course you probably aren't thinking of me, either.

"Who were you thinking of, if not me?" she asked after a moment.

"Bruno Bettelheim," Jerry said—a stock answer. In fact, he had been thinking about Juanita's invitation. Maybe he *would* go to the dance with her on Saturday night. Then maybe they would just head down the road—instead of taking the east ramp onto I-10, perhaps they'd take the west ramp. They could drive most of the night and then sleep most of the day in some small-town motel in West Texas. It seemed like time to get back to Nevada, but getting back to Nevada wasn't so urgent that he would need to go straight there—he could take the talkative and curvaceous Juanita to L.A., city of her dreams, and help her get settled before wandering on north to Tahoe or Elko or wherever he decided to wander.

"I don't believe you feel guilty. Why should you? You haven't hurt me," Patsy said.

"I feel guilty generally when I think about women," Jerry said. It was mostly true, he mostly did. "And I usually feel specifically guilty when I think of a specific woman."

Patsy got up and put on a robe. She had the oppressed feeling she always got when the hour of breakup was close at hand. Part of the oppression consisted of all the unanswered questions that seemed to circulate through her system—first among them, why she had wanted Jerry so much in the first place. Why had she invested so much time and so much hope? She had had to drag him virtually every step of the way she had gotten him to go, and even so the affair had lasted only a month. She had once had men in her life who made her feel interesting; now she seemed only to be able to get men who made her feel the opposite, and at the moment she felt the opposite. She felt dull and a little stupid, but why? Maybe she had only wanted Jerry because Aurora Greenway had him. So she went after him and got him, they had a little nice sex, one or two lively conversations, one or two excellent dinners which she either cooked or paid for, and that seemed to be that. A breakup loomed, but there was nothing urgent about it, much less tragic—they had barely got to know one another anyway. In a sense, the most interesting thing about the affair was Aurora's absolute silence with regard to both of them: the thought only made Patsy feel more oppressed. If the defining thing about a love affair was that Aurora Greenway, aggressive as she was, hadn't even bothered to issue a challenge to it, what did that say?

"Would you like to just forget that we know one another?" Patsy asked, coming back to sit on the bed. She sat far enough from Jerry so that he couldn't touch her—not that he would be especially likely to try. What was more likely was that she would forget her annoyance and touch *him*. It wouldn't be the end of the world if she forgot and touched him, but right at the moment she would rather not.

"I don't think I could forget that I know you," Jerry said. "I *do* know you, and I have a good memory. I'm not going to forget that I know you."

"That's a dishonest statement," Patsy said. "Your good memory isn't the point. I have a good memory too, but I've had lovers that I've forgotten utterly—I mean utterly. If I met them on the street I wouldn't recognize them, and if one of these guys I've forgotten came up to me at a party and said, hi, we used to fuck, how are you? I'd probably slug him."

"I still don't get the point," Jerry said. "I'm certainly not going to forget you—not ever."

"Why not?" she asked, though his remark made her a little hopeful. It was possible that she was mistaking low key for no key.

"For one thing, you know more about Rilke than anyone I've ever met," Jerry said.

"Oh, fuck you!" Patsy said, stung. "All that means is that I had a boyfriend who was translating him. Read that new biography and you'll know as much about Rilke as I do."

"Yes, but you forget, I mostly don't know women who read biographies," Jerry said. "I mostly know women who wait tables. If they read anything it's usually just their horoscopes."

"So what you're going to remember about me is that I was overeducated—thanks a lot!" Patsy said. "I'd almost rather be remembered for giving good blow jobs."

"I didn't mean to make you mad," Jerry said. "What's wrong with being remembered for knowing a lot about something? Most people don't know much about anything."

"You're so goddamn passive I have to force you to explain yourself," Patsy said. "Then when I do force you, I hate your explanations. I think you better just get out of here, and don't be looking out the window at my daughter's tits while you're going."

Angry, she hurried downstairs and opened a bottle of red wine. While she was drinking a glass of it, trying to calm down, Jerry came into the kitchen. He looked mopey and depressed, but not depressed enough to suit Patsy.

"I really didn't mean to upset you," he said. "It was just kind of a philosophical conversation."

"All your conversations are philosophical conversations," Patsy observed. "Even beaten down as I am, I'm still an emotional person. Maybe I'd like an *emotional* conversation once in a while."

"Can't they be a little mixed?" Jerry asked.

"Sure, but yours aren't mixed, they're just philosophical," Patsy said. "They make people depressed—or at least they make me depressed. I come out of every single one of them feeling that my life is a complete failure. That's a terrible effect to have on a woman."

"But your life isn't a complete failure," Jerry said.

"How would you know?" Patsy asked. She felt like throwing the wine bottle at him.

"Didn't I tell you to leave?" she yelled. She felt that if he stayed she would just get angrier, and there would be a really ugly fight—ugly enough that Katie would hear it, which she didn't want. Her children had heard too many ugly fights when she was married to their father.

On his way home Jerry decided to cut by the tamale stand and accept Juanita's invitation to take her dancing. He was in the mood for someone younger—someone with fewer cares.

12

The subject that interested Bump most was his own future.

"Do you think I should live in Iran?" he asked his parents one morning as they were getting ready to go to the park. His father, at least, was getting ready. His mother was still in bed. She was awake but she still did not seem to be in a hurry to get up and go with them to the park.

"Well, if you want to live in Iran, we'll have to start you on Farsi," Teddy said.

"Is that the language they speak in Iran?" Bump asked. He was annoyed with his mother for being lazy. One of her bare feet stuck out of the covers. He grabbed it and tried to tug her out of the bed. But it was no use—she was much too heavy.

"You're supposed to come," he said firmly. "Get up and come."

"You're not the boss of me, Bump," Jane informed him.

"No, but you did say you'd come to the park," Teddy reminded her.

"I said I'd come but I didn't say when," Jane said with a smile. "It's Sunday morning and I don't have to work—I feel like staying in bed a little longer."

"No, you have to come *now!*" Bump said. "You're supposed to obey."

"Obey who, kid?" Jane said, amused. "I certainly don't have to obey you."

"Yes you do—I'll bite you," Bump said, in a fury because she just kept lying in bed. He tried to bite her foot, but she was too quick, jerking her foot back under the covers. Then, before he could move, she yanked him up on the bed and shook him—she was a quick, bad beast when she was angry.

"You are *not* to bite me, understand!" Jane said.

"Don't shake him so hard, he didn't actually bite you," Teddy said. He had already begun to hate the frequent, violent confrontations between his mate and his son.

"He bit me the other day and broke the skin," Jane said. "He wasn't sorry, either. I think he's a little sociopath."

"Come on, he isn't even four yet," Teddy said.

"I want to go live in Iran," Bump said, once his mother released him.

"Go, and I hope the ayatollah gets you," Jane said.

"If you don't come to the park I'll bite you next time you go to sleep," Bump threatened, angrily sliding off the bed. He wished he had some means of injuring his mother, but he didn't, and by the time he and his father had reached the park he had become less angry.

"She said something would get me if I go live in Iran," Bump said to his dad. "What is it that might get me?"

"An ayatollah," Teddy said. The park was peaceful, almost empty—just one or two other parents were out early with their kids. Bump could have had the slide completely to himself, something he rarely got, but he seemed to be more in a questioning mood than a sliding mood.

"What does the ayatollah do?" he asked from the top of the slide.

"An ayatollah is a holy man," Teddy said, just before Bump went down the slide.

Once in the park, away from Jane, Teddy felt much calmer. Seeing Bump glide happily down the slide, just as any little boy might, renewed his sense of normalcy, or order—it was something he was apt to lose whenever Jane and Bump had one of their confrontations. Some of their confrontations frightened him badly, because neither of them held back. What if Jane broke Bump's neck or something while shaking him? What if Bump snuck up on Jane while she was asleep and stabbed her in the eye with a pencil? He told himself he was letting his imagination run away with him, but he couldn't help it. His deepest fear was that Jane or Bump would really injure one another in one of their confrontations. If that happened, life would never be the same—not his life, anyway. Then it would become a life sort of like Tommy's, only outside a prison rather than inside one.

Bump reached the bottom, but he didn't get off the slide.

"What does a holy man do?" he asked, preoccupied with the question of Iran, a place he had often heard mentioned on the radio.

"They worship—they're like ministers or priests," Teddy said, realizing that that was probably not a terribly helpful description, since Bump had never been inside a church.

"Do they cook little boys in big ovens?" Bump asked.

"No, they don't bother little boys at all—you'd be perfectly safe even if there were a hundred ayatollahs in this park right now," Teddy said, "Where did you get that idea?"

"My mother said she cooked me in her stomach," Bump said. "She cooked me but I came out before I burned."

"Your mother said that?" Teddy asked. He didn't believe it. As soon as he had learned to talk Bump had started saying things like that and attributing them to Jane, who denied having said any of them.

Bump nodded as he eased off the slide. "I'm going to make poison and give it to her and she'll turn black," he said. "Then she can't get me back in her stomach and cook me till I burn."

"But she can't get you back in her stomach anyway," Teddy said. "You're much too big to fit in anyone's stomach."

"I could fit in a giant's stomach," Bump said, starting back up the ladder to the top of the slide. "I could fit in a whale's stomach or a grizzly bear's stomach or an elephant's stomach."

"Yes, but your mother is just a human woman," Teddy

said. "She isn't a giant or a whale or a grizzly bear or an elephant."

"She could blow herself up and become a giant," Bump said, looking down at his father again from the top of the slide. "She told me she could."

"Oh, Bump, I think you're fantasizing," Teddy said. "I don't think your mother told you she could blow herself up and become a giant."

"She told me it in a dream," Bump said. "She said she could swallow me and cook me in her stomach until I burned completely up."

Then he went down the slide again.

"I think you just had a bad dream," Teddy said. "Your mother is not going to swallow you and cook you in her stomach. It's impossible, and anyway she doesn't want to."

"I don't trust my mother," Bump said. He had stopped himself just at the bottom of the slide, and was swinging his legs.

"Well, you should trust her," Teddy said. "She's a very good mother."

"I may drop a bomb on her head and blow her head off," Bump said. "Are the ayatollahs black all over their skin?"

"No, they just wear black clothes," Teddy said.

"I might go live in Iceland where the seals live," Bump said. "Seals don't eat little boys."

"Hey, when did you get so worried about being eaten?" Teddy asked, as Bump jumped down and walked toward the swings.

"I felt my mother's stomach and it was hot like an oven," he said, taking Teddy's hand as he walked.

"Everybody's stomach is hot, more or less," Teddy said. "Your own stomach is hot as an oven, sometimes."

Bump put his hand under his T-shirt and felt his stomach. "If I could find a tiny little boy who was only as big as a bug I'd put him in my stomach and cook him," he said with a grin.

They played in the park for over an hour, but Jane did not appear. When they finally walked home they saw Claudia's car parked outside the apartment. The door to the bedroom was shut when they went up. On the way home Teddy had bought a paper from their own 7-Eleven so he could devote some study to the want ads. Three convenience-store clerks had been blasted in Houston within the week, one of them only six blocks from where he and Jane worked. They had talked it over and decided it might be time for one or both of them to change jobs.

While Teddy read the want ads Bump went into his closet and had a long conversation with himself. Later, when Jane and Claudia emerged from the bedroom, Bump emerged, too, and said he wanted to be an ayatollah.

"Give me some black clothes," he demanded. Jane draped him in a black shirt and made him a hood out of an old black scarf. There was a full-length mirror in the bathroom—Bump went in and studied himself for a bit. When he came out he was all smiles.

"I like being an ayatollah," he announced.

Jane and Claudia were in a rollicking mood. After some debate about what would constitute the ideal breakfast, Jane made French toast.

"I shouldn't eat it, I'm getting fatter by the day," Claudia said. It was true—Claudia was heavy—but she more than made up for it by being cheerful and upbeat. Although Teddy experienced a bad moment or two of jealousy when he came home and saw the bedroom door shut, he was, on the whole, glad that Claudia was in Jane's life, and thus in their life as a family. Claudia was really the only person who could coax Jane out of her mad, bad moods. If Claudia had not come over, Jane could easily have remained in her confrontational mode all day, which would have meant more fights with Bump, more shakings, and probably fights with Teddy as well. His stomach was in a knot as it was, and if Claudia hadn't come it would only have been in a worse knot before the day was over.

"He looks like a midget rock star," Claudia said, meaning Bump—he had gotten tired of his black ayatollah hood and had taken it off temporarily. He was messing around in the syrup, trying to draw letters in it with one finger.

"I'm trying to make the alphabet but my syrup keeps drowning it," Bump said, giggling. His hair had never been cut in his life; long brunette curls hung almost to his shoulders. Sometimes he liked to shake his head rapidly in order to make the curls swirl.

"Maybe we should cut his hair this morning," Jane suggested. She looked rosy and very cheerful. Once in a while she reached under the table and tickled Teddy's thigh a little in hopes of convincing him that, despite Claudia, she still wanted him around.

"Maybe," Teddy said. "Or we could just take him to a barbershop sometime and let a professional do it."

"Nope, no barber's touching my little boy's hair," Jane said.

Bump was still making letters in the syrup. "Do you think I will ever have wings?" he asked.

"Why do you want wings, sweets?" Jane asked, nuzzling his neck.

"If I had wings I could fly up in the sky with bombs and drop them on people," Bump said. "Then when all the people were killed I could live with the vultures."

"Yes, but birds can peck," Jane pointed out.

"What would you do if a big bird pecked you?" Claudia asked him.

Bump reflected for a moment. When he was in a good mood he had an angelic grin. "I'd get some French toast, and if the bird pecked me I'd drown it in syrup," he said, grinning his angelic grin.

"He's got an imagination, I'll say that for him," Teddy said that night. He had just finished reading Bump about a dozen stories, the last one a Tomi Ungerer story whose hero was a vulture. The vulture, Hugo, was now Bump's favorite literary character.

"If everyone in the whole world died, would there be enough vultures to eat all the bodies?" Bump asked with a big, long yawn. Before Teddy could answer, or at least speculate, Bump had gone to sleep.

"It's good that he's imaginative," Jane said.

"I know it's good," Teddy said. "I wish I could remember

my fantasies from when I was his age. His are so violent. I just wonder if mine were that violent."

"Does it worry you or something that Bump has violent fantasies?" Jane asked. She was in bed, but she hadn't put on her gown, often a sign that she might welcome a little sexual attention.

Teddy was more than willing to give her some sexual attention, but he felt hesitant, too. Sometimes he felt that Jane only wanted Claudia now. It was after Claudia's visits that she was in her best moods.

"I guess it does, a little," Teddy admitted, taking his shoes off. "He only seems to fantasize about poisoning us or bombing us."

"You want to hear about a fantasy I had when I was about seven or eight?" Jane asked. He was sitting on the edge of the bed with his back to her. She slid over a little and reached around him to unbuckle his belt. Once that was accomplished, she began to unzip his pants.

"Sure," Teddy said. "You think I'm not going to want to hear my own wife's fantasies?"

"I dreamed that Santa Claus drove his sleigh right into my bedroom," Jane said. She lolled on her back while Teddy stood up to finish undressing.

"So he could bring you your presents in bed?" Teddy asked.

"Nope, he got out of his sleigh and jumped in bed with me and ate my box," Jane said, smiling. "Boy, I can't tell you what a powerful fantasy that was. I got about five years' mileage out of that one."

"Lucky you," Teddy said. "So do you want to play like I'm Santa, or what?"

"You're kind of shy with me now, Theodore," Jane said later, after their play. "I mean, you're a beautiful lover—if you weren't, I wouldn't be living with you and I wouldn't have had a child by you, either. What's causing this shyness?"

"Maybe I'm just an inherently shy person," Teddy suggested.

"No, you aren't—it's something more," Jane said. "Once you're going, you're the best—I just wonder sometimes if I'm gonna be able to get you going."

"You got me going immediately," Teddy said, though he did feel a little melancholy. Sometimes after sex, he felt himself receding. It was as if a normal thing—his penis, receding out of Jane—took on an abnormal twist, or an abnormal momentum, or something. He felt as if he might be receding from happiness, from his mate, from his child, from normal life. He felt himself slipping away toward the edge of the world—he had felt that same sense of slippage just before he had to go to the mental hospital for the first time.

"I get you going on the outside, sure," Jane allowed, her large eyes searching his face. "But it's on the inside that you're shy."

Teddy didn't answer. He thought maybe Jane would start reading or go to sleep, but she didn't.

"There's nothing wrong with wanting a little girl nooky in the morning and then a little boy nooky at night," she pointed out. "Or do you disagree?"

"I don't disagree—I don't anything," Teddy said. "I like Claudia.

"I don't even know if I could handle you now, if Claudia weren't in our life," he added.

"I don't know if you could either," Jane said. "But if that's the case, why do you look so worried? Claudia's here to stay."

"I wasn't worried about Claudia," Teddy said. It didn't seem as if Jane wanted to read, so he turned off the bed light. She got up, went to the bathroom, came back, and stood by the bed a moment, pulling on her gown.

"So what *are* you worried about?" she asked.

"Going crazy, I guess," Teddy said.

"Teddy, don't you dare go crazy," Jane said, straightening her gown. "Don't you dare. I'll never forgive you if you do."

13

Shirley, a nice redhead who worked in wardrobe, more or less saved Melanie's life, or at least her sanity, by arranging to get Bruce a job as a gofer on a little cheap horror move that was being shot in Azuza. Up until then Melanie had been trying to save all her strength for her job as an actress in the sitcom pilot, and Bruce had been slowly but surely dragging her down. Half the time she didn't get back to her apartment until nearly midnight, with a six o'clock call staring her in the face, and there Bruce would be, waiting to argue with her about the fact that she had deserted him and had a new relationship already. He hated it that she had a new relationship—she didn't even dare bring Lee, her new boyfriend, home with her, for fear Bruce would attack him or something —but what was really driving Bruce crazy—the *real* bottom line—was that she had a job on TV and he didn't.

"I know they'd take me on if you'd just ask," he said maybe a thousand times. "Can't you just ask?"

"No, asshole, I can't just ask!" Melanie said, over and over again. "It's a miracle I have a job myself. I've never acted before, I don't know anybody, I have no pull, and I could get replaced in a minute if I do anything they don't like. It's not like I'm Greta Garbo or Madonna or somebody. I'm not even a trained actress."

None of that mattered to Bruce, who sat on the couch, smoked grass, and sulked.

"Look, nobody in Hollywood has less leverage than I do, can't you understand that?" Melanie pleaded.

"You could get me a job, you just don't want to," Bruce said, before stomping out. "You don't want to because of *him*."

Usually Melanie cried when he left—partly from fatigue. Bruce was wrong to think she could just walk up to the producer or the production manager and get her old boyfriend a job, but the part about Lee wasn't so wrong. The last thing she wanted as to have to deal with Lee and Bruce at the same time, on the same set, when really it took all the stability she could muster just to concentrate on her scenes so she could try to perform when the time came. The set was like a movable slum, the hours were endless, she was too low on the totem pole to have a trailer, a dressing room, or even a folding chair to call her own—it was all she could do to keep sane anyway without having two jealous men to worry about: not that there weren't ample possibilities for jealousy arising with the crew itself. A couple of the carpenters and the head grip had been giving her looks of a sort that indicated interest. Lee was the youngest A.D. on the set, he was fresh out of NYU film school, and was a little too brash and Eastern and apt to get a little too imperious with the crew sometimes, so naturally they hated him; several of them would have been glad to pick off his girlfriend, just to bring him down a little.

The time the crew—or most of the crew—laughed at one of her scenes, Melanie was so totally into the scene that she didn't even notice. When Shirley told her about it later, Melanie almost didn't believe it.

"They like you, honey—they realize you're gifted," Shirley said. Shirley was about fifty and had had her ups and downs. She had four daughters herself, by four different men, and she immediately took a motherly interest in Melanie. It made a big difference. Melanie had felt totally lost the first day or two—she didn't know the terminology, didn't even know what a master was, didn't know anything. At first she was just doing her best to be a quick learner, and she tried to be very careful, like you try to be in a frightening dream. Underneath, she still had a little bit of fear that getting the part had been some combination of dream and mistake; she was worried that the mistake would be discovered or the dream would end, and then she would have to go back to being clunky old fat Melanie, an unemployed person with no boyfriend.

Sometimes, too, she felt that the only reason Lee liked her was because she was so un-Hollywood. Lee had a smart New York lip; he didn't bother to conceal the fact that he thought southern California really *was* La-La land. He bought magazines such as *Cahiers du Cinéma* to the set with him and left them lying around so nobody could miss what a highbrow he was. He also made it clear that he wasn't planning to be a second A.D. forever—all of which added up to several reasons why Lee wasn't exactly popular with the crew, especially not with the older members of the crew, most of whom had had to put up with dozens of New York kids with smart lips in the course of doing their jobs for thirty or forty years.

When Shirley made the remark about the crew's recognizing that Melanie was gifted, Melanie's heart bounced up— until that moment the only time in her life when she had felt herself to be the least bit gifted was in the eighth grade, when she won a national math competition. After Shirley said it, Melanie started noticing when someone on the crew laughed at one of her scenes. Once, when she had just finished a take in which she outdid herself with her Rosie routine, nearly the whole crew broke up. It made her feel really wonderful, particularly since several people came up afterward and gave her a hug or a smile, or made a comment. After that, she could sort of allow herself to believe that what was happening wasn't a dream or a mistake; it might be something that would last. Maybe she was actually an actress. Maybe she had a talent, after all, and to feel that was so wonderful that it more than canceled out the negatives—the slummy set, the hours, no place to sit, Lee's unpopularity, all of it. Instead of hating it, as she had the first two weeks, she began to love it and to hope it would last forever.

Almost the luckiest thing of all, though, was that one of Shirley's former husbands was a production manager, and a good one.

"Eddie's always got a picture," Shirley said. "He don't always have a *good* picture, but Eddie's always got a picture."

Fortunately Eddie was also still sweet on Shirley—apparently he was the only one of the four husbands who was. He was happy to do her little favors, such as providing a gofering job for some kid he had never met.

From Melanie's point of view, that one little favor changed everything, vis-à-vis Bruce. From being sulky, belligerent, and disparaging, Bruce underwent a total transformation and became almost too grateful. Despite his resentment of her relationship with Lee, it turned out, after some investigation, that he had not *really* bothered to *really* break up with Katie.

"She sort of came back into the picture," he admitted finally. Just hearing it made Melanie feel better. Though she had no reason to feel guilty about the fact that Bruce was lonely and girl-less, at some level she felt guilty about it anyway. Right away she felt a little more free to enjoy life with Lee.

What made it all seem even luckier was that Eddie actually took a liking to Bruce, and when the horror flick wrapped he took Bruce along to his next job, a spy movie being made at one of the majors.

Getting the second movie job produced such a sense of good feeling in Bruce that he himself actually suggested that he and Katie and Melanie and Lee have lunch sometime. Melanie wasn't so crazy about the idea, but she put it to Lee and Lee agreed. They decided to go to Venice some Sunday and eat sushi.

When the Sunday came, one effect of the lunch—Melanie knew she should have predicted it—was to get Lee interested in Katie, who was still sporadically attending UCLA and taking the same kind of film classes Lee had taken at NYU. They started debating the UCLA film school versus the NYU film school, and then went on to talk about Czech directors and new Russian directors and even Dutch directors. Melanie did not exactly take a prominent part in the conversation, since she had not seen a single film by any of the people they were talking about.

The surprising aspect of *that* conversation was that Bruce contributed a lot more than Melanie would have expected him to. Evidently he spent his spare time at Katie's house by watching videos of all the right foreign movies, or else reading all the hip film magazines that Katie's mother subscribed to and that Katie filched from her mother's L.A. town house.

Watching Bruce transform himself into a highbrow who looked as if he'd been reading film history for a hundred years was pretty amazing; no less amazing, at least to Melanie, was how quickly the big sexual rivalry between Bruce and Lee died down. By the time they finished their raw octopus, they had more or less become buddies. All three of them, Bruce, Lee, and Katie, did their best to talk over Melanie's head, behavior which ordinarily would have really pissed her off. It didn't piss her off this time, though—she stuffed down a lot of sushi and felt really sort of serene. What made her serene was her sense that the real point of all the knowing chatter was to impress *her*—after all, however much the three of them might know about the new Dutch cinema, she was still the one who had a part in a TV pilot. *She* was the one working as an actress—never mind that it was just a pilot for a series that might never happen. Meanwhile, Lee was only one of about a million A.D.s, Bruce was only one of several million gofers, and Katie was still just in school, and in a half-assed way at that. But Melanie was the one with the real part in the real show, and they were all jealous and envious and showing it the only way they knew how, which was to try to snow her with their vast knowledge of everything having to do with cinema. Melanie ate and let the vast knowledge fly on by. She knew she herself didn't have very much knowledge, but on the other hand she also knew that she seemed to have something none of them had—the ability to be funny on camera. It might not be something she would have forever—how could she know about that?—but at the moment she had it and it gave her the upper hand in her little peer group of sushi eaters.

Later, though, when she and Lee were back home and Melanie was about to drift off into a pleasant nap, Lee suddenly strutted out of the bathroom with his dick sticking out in front of him. Before Melanie could even reverse directions and get herself back into a wakeful and receptive state Lee revealed that what he had in mind as a little Sunday afternoon treat for both of them was anal sex.

"Nope, get that idea out of your head," Melanie said. She had made a few experiments along that line and they had not been very successful. Of course, someday she might get in the mood to make more such experiments and maybe they would be more successful, but right at the moment, she definitely wasn't in that mood.

"Why not, what's wrong with it?" Lee wanted to know. He instantly got a pissed-off, petulant look, as he was apt to do if denied whatever he happened to want at the moment.

"I didn't say anything was wrong with it, if you mean wrong in capital letters or something," Melanie said. "I just said I didn't want to."

"But *I* want to," Lee said. "Can't we ever do anything I want to do?"

"Will you just not get mad, please?" Melanie requested. "We can do a lot of things you want to. We *do* do a lot of things you want to. I just don't happen to be in the mood for butt-fucking this afternoon."

"How do you know? We haven't even started," Lee said, looking even more petulant and even more pissed off.

"I know what I don't feel like," Melanie said, getting annoyed herself. Despite her plain statement, Lee had hopped behind her and was definitely trying to mess around. Melanie thwarted that simply by flopping onto her back and raising her feet as if she meant to kick him. Her move enraged him, he kept trying to mess around, and finally Melanie did kick him with both feet. Despite the fact that she had raised her feet in warning, it seemed not to occur to Lee that she might actually kick him. He was too preoccupied with pointing his dick at her. Both her heels caught him in the chest and knocked him right off the bed—Lee was not a large guy.

"Oops, I didn't really mean to do that, I'm sorry," Melanie said, but quick as her apology was, it wasn't quick enough. Before she could move Lee yanked her off the bed and began to hit her with both fists.

"Lee, stop! It was just an accident," Melanie yelled, covering her face with both arms. Immediately what went through her mind was that if she showed up on the set at seven the next morning with a black eye and a fat lip or something, that might be that: she might be replaced on the spot. At all cost she wanted to protect her face, and she did protect it—she got a hard bump to the back of her head when he jerked her off the bed, and also some bruises on her arms, but Lee was mostly just flailing; he was too mad to aim his blows. He smoked too much and wasn't in good shape anyway—it probably wasn't thirty seconds before he wore out and stopped trying to hit her. He was still plenty mad, though. Before Melanie could really recover from the storm of blows, he called her a cunt and a bitch and three or four other choice names—then got up and stormed out the door.

Melanie didn't try to stop him—she felt too stunned, and once she got over being stunned, too disappointed. Because of the Bruce factor, it had been almost the first time she had brought Lee home with her for the day. When they got to her apartment after the meal she had felt at peace—she was just looking forward to being comfortable with Lee for a while in her own setting. It seemed like a big luxury she was getting to have, just being at home with Lee. She had been thinking she might make him pasta for dinner—they had never just had a simple meal at her apartment before. Sex would have been fine, too; she would have probably been in the mood after her nap, although so far sex with Lee had not really been world-shaking—being tired from the long hours, or worrying about Bruce or something, had sort of put a hitch in her response. Lee was a little to rabbity, he was not one for much foreplay, but Melanie was confident that if she was just a little patient they'd hit a groove—she was actually real attracted to Lee; she took the optimistic view that their love-making was going to get better once they could relax and she could get him to take a little more time with her.

But now it was ruined—he had hit her with the wrong suggestion at the wrong moment, he would probably never forgive her for kicking him off the stupid bed. Before she knew it she was crying, which is what she mostly did for the rest of the afternoon. She looked in the mirror many times to be sure she wasn't getting a black eye, and when she wasn't looking in the mirror or crying she was mostly looking out the window, hoping Lee would get over it and come back. She didn't really think it would happen—he was too arrogant —but for an hour or two she did keep hoping.

Later, feeling really lonely and shocked because a relation-ship she mainly enjoyed and was sort of banking on had been ruined in less than five minutes and for a stupid reason at that, she called Rosie and told her what had happened.

"Anal sex, yuk!" Rosie said.

Aurora happened to be in the kitchen at the time, sniffing some sweetbreads she had decided to cook for Pascal. He had apologized for his rudeness so many times that Aurora finally decided enough was enough and invited him to din-ner.

When she heard Rosie say the words "anal sex" she looked around, surprised.

"He sounds like a little macho jerk to me," Rosie added. "You'd be better off without him."

"Rosie, you and Granny are always telling me that," Mel-anie complained. "Every time I get ditched you try to tell me I'd be better off without the guy."

"Yes, and it's true, specially if anal sex is all they can think about," Rosie insisted. Then she remembered her own prob-lems with C.C. and oral sex, preferably in cars; she felt sad for a moment. Other than that, C.C. hadn't been so bad.

"Men are weird, nine tenths of them," she said.

"Maybe they are, but I still need one," Melanie pointed out. "I don't make a good loner. I do a lot better when I have a guy around, even if he's not perfect."

"What's that about anal sex?" Aurora inquired, looking up from her inspection of the sweetbreads.

Melanie hadn't known her grandmother was in the room with Rosie until she heard her voice, distantly but distinctly.

"Uh—oh, is Granny hearing this?" she asked.

"Uh, she's cooking," Rosie said, feeling awkward. "I guess Pascal's come back into the picture."

"Rosie, that's really premature," Aurora said. "The mere fact that I'm letting him come to dinner doesn't mean that he's in the picture.

"At the moment there isn't a picture," she added, with a bit of a droop in her voice. "At the moment there's just a blur."

"Pascal might snap things back in focus, though, if he plays his cards right," Rosie said, determined to be the optimistic one for a change.

"His cards are mainly deuces," Aurora said. "Why is Melanie questioning you about anal sex?"

"Don't tell her! It'll just make her hate Lee if she ever happens to meet him," Melanie said. She heard her grandmother's voice growing louder.

"I think she wants to talk to you herself," Rosie said, since it was obvious that Aurora expected to do exactly that.

"Shit!" Melanie said. "I didn't want to talk to Granny right now. I just wanted to talk to you."

"Hon, she's just upset, her new boyfriend's just left her," Rosie said to Aurora, covering the receiver with one hand and trying to indicate with a look that it might be better if, for the moment, Aurora left well enough alone.

"Well, if I'm not wanted, I'm not wanted," Aurora said, getting the message plainly enough; indeed, too plainly. She went back to her sweetbreads, but not with the light heart she usually brought to the early stages of cooking.

"You might be wanted in a minute," Rosie said, not liking

the look on Aurora's face. "Right now she just wants someone to confide in."

"Is she mad?" Melanie asked, biting a hangnail. She hated trying to talk to Rosie about personal stuff when she knew her grandmother was in the room.

"No, now she's crying," Rosie said with a sigh—she was not unsympathetic either to Aurora or to Melanie. She was just in the middle, as she had so often been.

"It could be the onions, we're just starting to cook," she said. She began to feel sad herself—it was awful to be in the middle when grandmother and grandchild were both unhappy.

"It's not onions," Aurora said, but not loudly enough for Melanie to hear. The fact that no member of her family wanted to confide in her in times of crisis, or had ever wanted to confide in her at such times, made a pain in her breastbone. Year after year, decade after decade, it seemed that Rosie received the confidences—first it had been from Emma, now it was from Melanie. She felt shut out, always had. What *was* she, if not a mother and grandmother? It seemed too much to bear, but she went on cooking anyway, unhappy, but for the moment stoic.

Later, after the dinner with Pascal had been negotiated adequately, if, on Aurora's part, a little numbly, Melanie did call her to apologize for not talking to her that afternoon.

Melanie was feeling better. She had spent several hours thinking over her relationship with Lee and had found that she could only remember one occasion when he had been really nice to her. All the other times he had been borderline, at best.

Also, she felt guilty about her granny—it was no trick to tell from Aurora's voice if she was happy—and she was not happy.

"Are you just upset because I didn't talk to you this afternoon?" Melanie asked. With her grandmother there was no point in beating around the bush; better just to come right out and say it.

"Well, I'm upset about a number of things, Melly," Aurora

admitted. "That's one of them, but it's not really the most major."

"Granny, you're my parent," Melanie explained. "Daddy doesn't want to be my parent, and my mother's dead. You're the only person I have to hide things from—and everybody needs to hide some things from their parent, don't they?"

"I'm sure it's unusual, but that was not the case with me," Aurora said, reflecting. "At least it wasn't the case in regard to my mother—I never told my father a significant secret in my life."

"But you could tell your mother? Even things about sex?" Melanie asked, curious.

"My mother was the one person I could tell anything to," Aurora said. She instantly forgave Melanie, whose voice was that of a sad, hurt little girl.

"Now that I look back on it, I'm sure it was odd that I could tell my mother anything," Aurora reflected. "I can't remember holding back at all."

"You were lucky," Melanie said. "It must have been wonderful to be able to tell your mother anything."

"It *was* wonderful," Aurora agreed. "She was a very frank woman, with a remarkably open mind—very remarkably open, considering her time and her place."

She was silent for a moment, remembering her mother, and the long talks they had once had.

"The pity is that I was very young then," she said. "I didn't have anything very complicated to tell her. But I did once have a very minor venereal disease, and I told her that."

"You *did?*" Melanie said.

"Yes, I did. She was quite unfazed, and very practical. She took me to the doctor herself."

"I guess you'd have more complicated things to tell her now," Melanie said.

"I certainly would," Aurora agreed. "Later life itself is a complicated thing. But Mother died before she could have learned much about it, and the upshot of that is that I've had inadequate counsel and have not coped particularly well."

"I think you've coped fine," Melanie said.

"Nope, I haven't—lack of counsel has resulted in many setbacks," Aurora assured her.

"Isn't that what shrinks are for? Counsel?" Melanie asked.

"Yes, presumably that's what they're for," Aurora said. "But since mine allowed me to seduce him and then allowed Patsy Carpenter to seduce him, too, only a short while later, I don't think I can expect adequate counsel from him."

"You could change shrinks," Melanie pointed out.

"I could, but I think I prefer just to change the subject," Aurora said. "Am I ever going to be allowed to know why Rosie was talking about anal sex this afternoon?"

"I guess you can know," Melanie said. "My boyfriend wanted to have it and I didn't, which is why we broke up.

"I mean I didn't want to have it *today*," Melanie added. "I didn't mean I was against it per se."

"It does require rather a special mood," Aurora said casually. She was still thinking about her mother, remembering the way she played with her rings, twisting them round and round on her fingers when she was thinking about some problem Aurora had presented her with.

Melanie tried to imagine her grandmother having anal sex, but her imagination wouldn't go near it—her imagination wouldn't even provide much in the way of a sensual aid when she tried to imagine herself having it with Lee.

"Anyway, I'm back to no boyfriend," she said. "I guess I shouldn't complain. I'm sure there are worse fates."

"There are, but not many," Aurora said, remembering how flat and bored she had felt that very evening, trying to get through a dinner with Pascal.

"What does that mean?" Melanie asked. "Are you really that unhappy?"

"I'm not frolicking much these days," Aurora admitted. "I'm afraid I'm a very needy person, and this has led me to accept the wrong people in my life. Even when I know quite well that they're the wrong people I often accept them anyway, rather than be without.

"I really don't seem to be able to flourish when I'm without," she added.

"Are you going to get your shrink back from Patsy?" Melanie asked. "I bet you could if you tried."

Aurora let that one sit for a moment. She had the sense that it might be the wrong sort of thing to be talking about with her granddaughter. But, on the other hand, she had just praised her own mother for being open to discussion of just such complexities. Also, the question was a hard one: Was she or wasn't she going to actively compete for Jerry? For the past few weeks she had not supposed she would, but, now that Melanie had asked, she realized she was not exactly settled in her mind where he was concerned.

"I might be just that foolish," she said. "At this point my options seem to be folly or resignation, and I actually think folly might be the more honorable option. I've been a fool before, and in a way it's kept me going. I may just have to be a fool again."

Melanie tried to chatter about her job, or anything that might cheer her grandmother up, but Aurora was still rather gloomy when the conversation ended.

Melanie stayed awake until nearly two o'clock, hoping Lee would call and make up, but he didn't. The next day she saw him at a distance as she was walking to the makeup trailer. She started to wave, but he wasn't looking her way, so she didn't. Then, while she was being made up, he smart-lipped one of the stars and was fired on the spot. By the time Melanie walked to the set for her first scene he was already gone. It was sort of stunning how quickly you could vanish if you were just an A.D.

"Sweetie, you're better off without him," Shirley said when she heard about the breakup.

"You sound just like my grandmother!" Melanie said, a little bitterly. She was still upset, it was a raw wound, you'd think people would notice!

Still, she wasn't really mad at Shirley. After all, Shirley had gone out of her way to get Bruce a job, and that was still the nicest thing anyone had done for either one of them since they moved to Hollywood.

14

After having struggled to remain on his best behavior during Aurora's dinner, Pascal reflected for the better part of a day and decided that he was bitterly dissatisfied with the tenor of the evening. He felt sure he had been slighted in a number of subtle but nonetheless significant ways: his hug upon arrival had been perfunctory, and his kiss upon departure even more so. Conversation, usually so challenging as Aurora let her mind dart here and there, had been indifferent, as perfunctory as her embraces. She had even asked him again for gossip about Madame Mitterrand, probably the most boring question it was possible to ask a member of the French diplomatic corps.

He was in a bad mood the day after the dinner; that evening he started drinking cognac and kept drinking it until he fell out of his chair while reaching for the little instrument that flicked the TV channels. Somehow he had dropped it and had kicked it just out of reach. He leaned over to reach for it, fell out of his chair, went to sleep, and woke up with a splitting headache just in time to shave and go to work. He cursed his secretary because of a typo, and almost spat at

Solange, who was unable to get the fax machine to work immediately.

"It must work now!" Pascal demanded, his head still splitting.

Solange stared back at him icily—she was, on the whole, an extremely composed young woman—too composed, in his view.

"As you can see, it doesn't work *now*," she said. "I guess it has not heard this news."

"What news?" Pascal asked. He wondered apprehensively if some dreadful thing had happened somewhere in the world of which he had not informed himself. Perhaps it was even something that bore on the destiny of France.

"The news that Monsieur Pascal wants it to work *now!*" Solange said, looking him over with evident distaste.

At the moment the man looked grotesquely ugly to her: red-eyed, red-faced, jowly. She found it a little hard to believe that she had once found the same ugliness attractive; but—no getting around it—she had. Of course, having an affair with a man with a crooked penis made a good story to tell to her girlfriends; even some of her boyfriends laughed at her descriptions of the crooked penis, though normally the last thing she would have mentioned to a lover was another lover's penis.

"Oh," Pascal said, relieved that France had not been disgraced without his knowing about it immediately.

"I drank cognac," he added, by way of apology for his surly behavior.

Solange continued to stare at him icily. She popped open the fax machine, discovered there was no paper in it, tapped off down the hall, came back with a roll, stuck it in the machine, and snapped it shut with a loud pop.

"Now it will respond to monsieur's every command," she said.

"Why can't you be kind?" Pascal asked. "I ache all over this morning. I had a bad night. I am old and lonely. Once you were kind to me but now you aren't."

"Because you behaved like a pig," Solange informed him. "Go get a lady pig to be nice to you."

She started his fax and left. While the fax was running, the machine began to make a little *grrr* sound, like the growl of a small animal. Pascal began to feel desperate. He was afraid to summon Solange again, and yet the fax was not moving smoothly through the machine as it ought. It was merely sitting in its slot while the machine growled.

Finally, feeling that the growling sound, Solange, his job, Houston, and in fact his whole life were collectively intolerable, Pascal simply walked away. The fax was too stupid to send, anyway. The mayor of Houston wanted President Mitterrand to attend the Fat Stock Show next year. There would be a special barbecue in his honor, if only he would agree to come. Better yet, the Concorde would be allowed to bring him, though normally the Concorde was not permitted to land in Houston because of its noise. None of this would ever happen—what did it matter if the fax reached the Quay? Let the next person who wanted to send a fax fix the growling machine. Solange's icy looks were like stabs to the heart. He felt he might sob—if he sobbed, perhaps his head would feel better. He shut himself in his tiny office and remembered that Aurora had insulted him with her indifference, and suddenly his anger rose so fast he couldn't control it. He grabbed the phone and called her, meaning to bury her in curses.

"Hello," Aurora said. She was in her bed, attempting to make her way through a few sentences of Proust, something she rarely attempted unless she happened to be so low in spirit that she couldn't think of anything else to do.

"You were like a slug!" Pascal burst out. "A big white slug. I'm calling to say I am never coming again—I will not be insulted in this way."

"Wait a minute now, start over," Aurora said. "Did I go to the trouble of picking up my phone just to hear you call me a slug? Of course I'm slightly large, and I'm certainly white, but in just what manner do you think I resemble a slug? Isn't a slug some form of worm? Am I really such a fool as to have fixed sweetbreads for a man who equates me with a worm?"

"You didn't think about me," Pascal said. "Is it because of the Greeks?"

"No, it's because you're a dull old fart," Aurora said. "I tried to think about you several times during what I admit was an indifferent dinner, but the truth is it was like turning to an empty channel. There's not much there to see, and even less to think about."

"My head aches, I'm old and lonely," Pascal said, his anger draining out of him. He was horrified that he had lost control of himself so completely; he had even called Aurora a slug. A slug? Why had those words come from his mouth? She would never forgive him, probably. He felt that his only hope was to appear as pitiful as possible, which was not hard, because he felt pitiful.

"You deserve to be lonely, if the best you can do is call me a slug," Aurora said. "I'm going to tell Rosie you said that, and we're going to fix you."

"Don't fix me, I'm a broken person," Pascal said. His life was a wreck, he had nothing, he began to weep.

"Oh, shit, now you're crying, just because I was mean," Aurora said. Rosie came into the room, her arms filled with crisp clean sheets, a sure sign that Aurora would soon be asked to move so the bed could be changed.

"Pascal called me a slug but now he's sobbing," Aurora said, holding the receiver in Rosie's direction in case she wanted to hear the sobs.

"I don't want to hear it, who wants to listen to a Frenchman cry?" Rosie said. "You have to move so I can change this bed."

"Now, when I'm only on my second sentence of Proust?" Aurora asked, grinning. "Usually I read at least five or six sentences before I give up."

"I don't care, move it, I'm already half a lap behind where I like to be this time of day," Rosie said.

"It would be better to be dead than to live like this," Pascal said, his sobs subsiding.

"Well, that's pure speculation, Pascal," Aurora said. Somehow his sobs were having a tonic effect on her spirits.

"It might be a good deal worse to be dead," she continued. "Do you think the French government could spare you for a few hours?"

"Why?" Pascal asked. Her threat to "fix" him was not one that he felt he should take lightly.

"Pascal, if you're going to question me, let's forget it," Aurora said. "Just answer my question: Are you free for lunch, or aren't you?"

"Yes, I am free for lunch," Pascal said. "I am free for all lunches. Solange was cruel to me because of the fax."

"Well, that's between you and your young mistress," Aurora said. "Pull yourself together and get yourself over here about twelve."

"Okay, but I don't want you to fix me," Pascal said. "I'm already fixed enough."

"If you behave correctly I might not fix you, but I'll certainly fix you if you're not here on time," Aurora said, before hanging up.

"I knew he was back in the picture," Rosie said.

Aurora reluctantly yielded the bed and deposited herself in her window nook, sticking Proust back on her bookshelf first. It was not to be a six-sentence day, it didn't appear.

"He's rather crushed today—I suppose I was moved to pity," Aurora said. "I thought we might take him over to meet our Greeks."

"We? Why do I have to go?" Rosie asked.

"Well, they're brothers, and we're almost sisters," Aurora said. "I thought we might continue our tradition of double-dating where our Greeks are concerned."

"I don't know, I'm scared it will get messy," Rosie said. "Suppose I fall in love with the same one you fall in love with? Then if I win you'll fire me. But if I think I'm going to be fired I won't be able to let go and enjoy nothing anyway."

"Whoa! That's racing ahead if I ever saw racing ahead," Aurora said. "Nobody's in love yet—I doubt we'll be so lucky."

"I still think it'll get messy," Rosie said. "Everything you start gets messy in five minutes and everything I start is messy before I even start it. It just seems like we're asking for trouble."

"Even so, I prefer trouble to endless nothingness," Aurora said.

"What's so bad about nothingness?" Rosie asked.

"Do you really want to live out your life just changing my sheets?" Aurora asked. "Wouldn't a little mess be preferable to day after day of the void?"

"If Willie would just work himself up to one phone call, then I'd feel better," Rosie said. "I know he ain't calling, because he feels guilty about running out on me. It ain't that I want him back, either. I'd just like one phone call so I'd know the poor sucker's still alive."

"I agree that Willie has not been thoughtful," Aurora said. "On the other hand he hasn't phoned out of a clear blue sky and called you a slug, either, as Pascal just did to me."

"So what are we supposed to do when we get over there where the Greeks live?" Rosie asked. The idea of going to see them had startled her at first, but now that the prospect had been rattling around in her mind for a few minutes she had ceased to find it frightening. After all, it was broad daylight, and she did like feta cheese. Maybe a little visit could be managed without too much mess.

Aurora had kept the Greeks' phone number taped to her telephone for the last few days in case of emergencies; she dialed it and got Vassily.

"Boys, it's us," Aurora said. "We're coming over to visit."

"Bring some more of that lamb à la grecque, if you got any," Vassily said. "That was first-rate lamb à la greque."

"That's what I like about Greeks, they're men of appetite," Aurora said. "Also, they snap right into a conversation, which is more than I can say for the males of most nationalities. What's become of my friend Theo?"

"We got new glasses for the bar," Vassily said. "Theo's polishing one."

"Well, tell him hello," Aurora said. "Rosie and I will be along about noon, and we may bring an old Frenchman I want you to meet."

"I hope he ain't from Paris, I hate people from Paris," Vassily said.

"No, he's from Brittany," Aurora said. "If he says anything rude to me I hope one of you will beat him up."

"Theo can, I don't fight no more," Vassily said.

"Why not?"

"Because I lose," Vassily said. "Theo loses, too, but he's a scrapper. He might be able to whip this old guy from Brittany."

When Pascal stumbled up to Aurora's door precisely at noon, trying to look as pitiful as possible, she opened it and immediately slammed him on the chin with her fist. Though she didn't really hit him very hard, it gave him a shock—also, her ring cut his chin slightly.

"There!" Aurora said. "I've spent my morning remembering all the bad things you've called me over the years. You deserve to be socked, and now you have been."

Pascal was so shocked to have been hit that he didn't say a word in his own defense. He couldn't think of one.

"May I borrow a Kleenex?" he asked finally.

On the drive over to McCarty Street he had to borrow two more. The cut was tiny but deep. Aurora and Rosie seemed to be in fine moods, but Pascal wasn't in a fine mood. He had been relegated to the backseat—Aurora claimed she needed Rosie in the front to help her with directions. Pascal thought there was more to it than that; first he had been hit, now he was being exiled. In his depression he could hardly follow a word the two women were saying. Also, the neighborhoods they were driving through looked alarmingly violent. They were the types of neighborhoods he never went into no matter where he was in the world. Aurora stopped at a great many stoplights, which seemed to him a risky policy. Murderous-looking men, young and old, black and brown and white, stared at them from the sidewalks. The two women paid no attention—they had dressed up, and were chattering as happily as girls.

Finally, still unmurdered, they arrived at a little green shed sitting just off a dusty street, from which he could see the tops of ships at dock in the Ship Channel. Two men in undershirts sat under the shed, staring at them.

"They're in their undershirts," Rosie said, considerably shocked. She had once lived not very far from where they

527

were—indeed, had spent her whole twenty-two-year marriage not very far from where they were—and she knew that dress standards in the McCarty Street area were apt to vary; still, seeing the Greeks in their undershirts gave her a start. To her it seemed provocative, and she remembered her own prediction, which was that things might get messy. Men who showed up for dates in their undershirts were looking for something, in her view, and there was little mystery as to what it was.

"Nonsense, it's just their national dress," Aurora said, when Rosie revealed why she was taken aback.

"Pascal, are you bleeding to death? If not, why are you so quiet?" Aurora asked, whipping around to give him a good looking over.

"I will live for a while," Pascal said.

"Well, we're going to have a nice time with these Greeks, don't you be gloomy," she said, opening her door.

Pascal had every intention of remaining completely gloomy, but within ten minutes, to his great surprise, he had stopped being gloomy and was having a good time—even a wonderful time. Business was slow at the Acropolis Bar that day. The Petrakis brothers had taken advantage of the long morning lull to procure a few refreshments. Theo and Vassily proved, to Pascal's surprise, to be charming men. Retsina was provided, Theo had polished the bar's new glasses to perfection, there was excellent feta, olives, some tasty little sardines. The two men treated Pascal like a friend; they refused to let him pay for the retsina, or for anything. Theo thumped a dusty jukebox a few times and it began to emit tinkly Greek music. Soon everyone was dancing, Aurora with Vassily, Rosie with Theo; then Aurora made Pascal dance—the Greeks even gave him a Band-Aid for his chin, which still dribbled blood occasionally. Pascal decided that the Greeks were fine men: Europeans, after all, like himself. Though previously he had not particularly cared to regard Greeks as Europeans, Theo and Vassily treated him with such consideration that he changed his mind and accorded them European citizenship. They were civilized men—they might even have been French.

"What do you think about her French boyfriend?" Vassily asked Theo after the party had piled back into the Cadillac and lumbered away.

"Who says he's her boyfriend?" Theo asked.

"Well, he was with her—unless you think he was with Rosie," Vassily said. He found that he had developed an interest in Aurora, but he didn't say so—better to wait and see which way the wind blew, the next time it blew.

"He looked half dead to me," Theo said, feeling a little melancholy. He sensed that complications might lie ahead. Usually when he spotted complications on the horizon, he moved to another country—but he had about used up the countries, and just at that moment didn't feel like moving. Still, it seemed to him that a hurricane of complications was building up, just offshore.

"I hope the dead half is from the waist down, then," Vassily said.

"Uh–oh, I knew it, you're falling in love," Theo said.

"I ain't falling in nothing, I just don't trust no Frenchman," Vassily said.

15

When Jerry took Juanita to the Saturday night dance, as agreed, he expected to feel like a grandfather dancing with a teeny-bopper, and he did sort of feel that way, but he was the only one who noticed. The dance hall was a barn of a place on North Main; it was packed with people, many of them Mexican-American couples as old as he was or older, all dancing vigorously and many dancing well. At first Juanita, dressed to the nines and chewing gum like crazy, was a little dismayed by the stodginess of Jerry's performance on the dance floor, but then she discovered that, unlike Luis, he didn't become jealous or enraged when she danced with other men, so she danced with a steady stream of young guys while Jerry stood on the sidelines, happy just to drink beer and watch. Juanita got a little drunk and very sweaty, but she was having a good time—Jerry's limitations as a dancer didn't really bother her much. When she'd had her fill of dancing she grabbed his hand and took him home—or rather, she took him to a home she had borrowed for the occasion, mainly because she was still a little nervous about Luis. He hadn't showed up at the dance, but that didn't mean he wouldn't be trouble if he showed up at her apartment and caught the two of them in bed.

"You're gonna be my boyfriend now, I want someplace where we can be peaceful," Juanita said.

The place was a girlfriend's hot one-room apartment on 7½ Street. Becoming boyfriend and girlfriend turned the bed into a puddle of sweat, but their sleep was peaceful, as Juanita had wanted. The next morning Juanita awoke in the mood to see Jerry's house.

"Luis won't find us there, we can fuck all day," Juanita said, though in fact her sexual interest was perfunctory—it was just part of being a boyfriend and a girlfriend. It left her not deeply stirred.

On the way to Jerry's house they stopped for pancakes. While they were eating, Jerry told her he had decided to leave town—then, between bites, as her young face fell, he asked her if she'd like to go with him to Los Angeles.

"Oh, man, you bet—my dream is coming true," Juanita said, her black eyes shining.

Jerry wanted to pack a thing or two and leave that afternoon, but Juanita, despite her eagerness to be in L.A., the city of her dreams, got a little scared by the suddenness of it all and asked if they could wait a week.

"My sister, she works in Galveston, she was coming up for the dance next Saturday—I guess I oughta see my baby sister one more time before we split," she said.

She was a very pretty girl, and the knowledge that the main dream of her life was about to come true made her prettier. They spent the whole day at Jerry's house, watching television or sitting around his backyard draped in towels, drinking sun tea. The feeling of being a grandfather with a teeny-bopper arose in Jerry again—without makeup, Juanita looked like a bright-eyed girl of fifteen. She was all animation, chatter, excitement, happiness. He watched her, entranced, and yet with a little edge of sadness beneath his affection. As he listened to Juanita chatter and chirp, he also thought of his patients—the patients he would be leaving in a week; the patients he would have preferred to leave that very day.

His patients, it seemed to him, were at the opposite pole of being from Juanita. She was a pretty girl on the rise, all energy, frivolity, bounce. His patients, on the other hand, were all people on the slide, people whom the downward curve of life had caught and would never release. The force of the curve would only take them down and farther down, until the bottom stopped them.

His new fondness for Juanita made him wish that he could really help her escape the downward curve. He wished it could be that her friendliness and spirit would buoy her up, let her keep rising. It was their first day as lovers. Jerry wished he could make a wish for her and have it come true; yet he felt sad, because he didn't think his wish for this lovely girl *would* come true. The downward curve of life caught everybody—the wasting of the generations would soon bruise Juanita too.

That night they went to a movie with one of Juanita's girlfriends, the one who had lent them the tiny hot apartment on 7½ Street. The friend was a tall, skinny girl named Maria, who talked nonstop, including during the movie.

Driving home later, Jerry thought of Aurora. He missed her, as she had predicted he would—for a moment he had the impulse just to drive by her house and knock on her door. He realized that he wanted to tell Aurora goodbye—though rarely, in his many leavings, had he told anyone goodbye. He had been moody most of the afternoon, and he knew it had to do with delay: he had wanted to be out of Houston that morning. Waiting a week so Juanita could go to one more dance with her sister didn't feel quite right to him.

Leaving meant going: pure freedom. Any hitch made him feel a lot less free. So, by the same token, did saying goodbye. Telling people you were leaving moved leaving into a whole different category. It civilized it, which sort of contradicted the point.

Jerry had no intention of saying goodbye to Patsy, or Lalani, or Sondra, or any of his patients. But he would have liked to see Aurora again and hear her voice for a few minutes, even if her voice was saying cutting things about his character and behavior. If anyone held her own against the downward curve, it was Aurora.

He let himself drift to the edge of River Oaks, but then he caught himself and went on home. Aurora didn't want to see him, and no reason she should. He sat on the couch and watched television until three in the morning—*The Late Show* and then *The Late Late Show*. There was a Doris Day festival in progress—both movies featured Doris Day.

During commercials or when his interest in Doris and her antics flagged a little, Jerry went through the files of his patients. Since he was going to be here another week, he felt he might try to connect one or two of the more severely troubled patients with another psychiatrist. But sorting out the more severely troubled was not easy, since mainly what they all suffered from was neglect. Mrs. Fry was a typical case: her husband hadn't shown any interest in her sexually in eighteen years. Mr. Milbank, same story: his wife got sick at her stomach every time he tried to make love to her. Mrs. Henwood's three children never called her, even on Christmas, even on Mother's Day. She lived alone. Mrs. Dawson also lived alone—the daughter who had had thirty-seven strokes had to be sent to a "place," as Mrs. Dawson called it.

It occurred to Jerry that he ought simply to mail his whole file to some young doctor who was just getting started. If he or she took on all of Jerry's patients there would be an immediate income, and also a solid introduction to the psychiatrist's life work.

His patients mainly were people in whom everyone had simply lost interest—all interest. They were just people who were getting older. Most of them had never been particularly interesting to begin with, even in their prime, but as they slipped past their prime they became even less interesting—to neighbors and friends, mates and children—than they had once been. In time, once everyone around them lost interest in them, they began in consequence to lose interest in themselves: to slip, to not take good care of themselves, to skip little duties, to abandon their modest schedules, to ignore their bills. But the slippage wasn't total, else they wouldn't have bothered coming to him. The thought that they must be at least a little interesting, that someone ought to pay their troubles at least a little attention, seemed to be what brought them to him.

Now he, too, was going to fail them: to demonstrate by vanishing that he hadn't been able to become very interested in them either.

That was the story—sad, but common—of most of his patients—but it wasn't the story of Mr. Mobley, who, in 1946, had run over and killed his own baby son while backing the family car out of the driveway in order to pack it and leave on a big family vacation to Colorado Springs, Colorado. Mr. Mobley had only been married five years at the time, his young family had never been able to afford a vacation before, and, in the excitement of packing for it, everybody somehow lost track of the baby, who was crawling in the driveway, trying to catch a grasshopper, when he was run over and killed.

Five years passed. The Mobley family had not quite recovered, but they were functioning and were even planning a big Christmas for their two daughters, May and Billie, eight and nine respectively. But something went wrong with the Christmas-tree lights. May and Billie had two little girl-friends over for a slumber party and all the girls had just gone to sleep. Mr. Mobley was gone, hauling lumber to Alexandria, Louisiana, for the lumberyard where he worked. Mrs. Mobley slept upstairs. When she realized there was a fire, the smoke boiling up the stairs was so thick she couldn't face it: all she could do was jump out the window. Later the coroner told her the little girls were likely all dead by then anyway because of the smoke. All four died, the worst tragedy the little town of Cypress, Texas, had ever experienced during the Christmas season. Mr. Mobley heard about it on the truck radio as he was hurrying back from Alexandria to be with his family for Christmas.

Mrs. Mobley died of a stroke a few years later. Mr. Mobley, who described himself as "off and on a Christian," considered that it was merciful of the Lord to take her. He himself had not partaken of this mercy. He was in his eighties, still dressed neatly, lived on Social Security, watched a little television, gardened a little, smoked a lot, drank occasionally, and was tormented, night after night, year after year, with intolerable visions of his children's deaths.

"If I had known something could have happened this bad, I would never, no way, have had no children, bless their little hearts," he said to Jerry on every visit, when he had gone, once again, through the preludes to the deaths, in a hopeless, repetitive attempt to try to find the clues to whatever slippage of attention had destroyed his children and ruined his life.

Those words were Mr. Mobley's chorus, his lament, his cry. He came to Jerry once a week to say them—always, as he started to talk, he lost control of his voice, cried a little, recovered himself, and jerked on through the terrible story.

"I'd like to die tonight," he always said at some point during his hour. "Hell, I'm ready to die this afternoon. It's all I'm waiting for."

Once, tentatively, wondering if the old man felt anything at all that could be called hope, Jerry asked him his views on the afterlife. Did he expect to be reunited with his wife and his little ones, once the knell had finally rung?

Mr. Mobley shook his head. "Heaven? I 'spect that's just stories," he said. "If I can just die and it'll make my mind go blank, that's enough. You know, switch it off like it was the TV, so I won't be seeing them terrible pictures no more."

Jerry wrote a short letter to a young psychiatrist he had met in the Astrodome one night at a baseball game. He gave him Mr. Mobley's address and phone number and asked that he give him a call. Then he wrote a note to Mr. Mobley, giving him the young psychiatrist's name and phone number; he mentioned that he had asked the young doctor to call him. He added that he was sorry not to be able to treat him anymore, but he felt that the time had come for him to move back to Nevada, his home.

He sealed the letter and then, on impulse, took another sheet of paper and wrote "Dear Aurora," at the top of it. He put in the date as well. Then his mind seemed to stick. He could not think of what he wanted to say—could not decide whether he really wanted to say anything, could not even come up with a first sentence.

The piece of paper with Aurora's name on it lay on his desk all week, untouched. One by one his patients came, one by one they left. Mr. Mobley shuffled in and uttered his cry against the fates one more time; after he left, Jerry mailed the letter referring him to the young doctor, and mailed the note to the young doctor, too.

On Friday, after the last patient was gone, the three neighborhood teenagers he had hired to pack and store his psychiatric library began their work. They worked all night and took the last load to the storage bin on Airline Road about the middle of the morning. One of the teenagers had been given the key to the house the week before, when Jerry had first thought he was leaving. They had been put on hold for a week. They were restless—Jerry had told them they could have a party in the house whenever he did leave. They were to clean up, take the furniture to the Goodwill, and give the key to the landlord. They had been well paid and they tolerated the delay, but it was clear that they were anxious for him to go. They wanted to have their party.

Finally, just before he was to go get Juanita and her sister to take them to the dance, Jerry picked up the sheet of paper with Aurora's name on it. He had been carefully moving it around all week, but now that he was going, he couldn't leave it around any longer. Using an empty bookshelf as a desk he quickly wrote:

DEAR AURORA:

You were right. I've missed you very much. I'm leaving Houston today—moving back to Nevada, I think. I don't plan to go straight home, but I imagine I'll end up there eventually.

You were a great help to me, I just want to thank you.

Love,
JERRY

On his way to the Heights he jumped out of his car at a red light and popped the note into a mailbox. He knew it wasn't really a letter or an assessment he could be proud of, but at least he had made an acknowledgment. He drove on to Juanita's apartment with a lighter heart.

Marietta, Juanita's little sister, was a tiny version of Juanita. She claimed to be sixteen but Jerry suspected she was more like fourteen. As a special treat before the dance, he took the girls to a very expensive yuppie eatery, very nouvelle. The girls were excited but nervous; confronted with such a posh Anglo setting, they fell uncharacteristically silent. Jerry had to strain to keep a trickle of conversation going, but once they hit the dance floor, all constraint vanished. Both girls were soon doing what Juanita had done the week before: dancing with any young man who could get up the nerve to ask.

Jerry danced with Juanita a few times—she would have felt disgraced if he hadn't—but mostly he stayed on the sidelines, drinking beer. His thoughts were of the freeway. The dance hall was only two blocks north of it; from the plywood bathroom, when he went to piss, he could hear the freeway's roar. It stretched west, all the way to Santa Monica. In two days, three, if they dawdled, he and Juanita could be eating burritos on the Santa Monica pier. In between there would just be the desert, the long road, and the sky.

Finally the two girls danced themselves out. On the walk to the car Marietta began to cry a little at the thought that her big sister was leaving for far-off California.

"It's okay," Juanita assured her. "You can come too, soon as I get a good job. We can get an apartment together."

They were going to drop Marietta off at Maria's, on 7½ Street—in the morning Maria would take her back to Galveston, where she lived with an aunt and many cousins.

Because of the crowd at the dance hall, they had had to park nearly three blocks away. Jerry walked a little ahead, so the girls could have some privacy in which to say their goodbyes. Juanita was as excited about leaving as he was—she was ready to go, but she didn't want to appear indifferent to Marietta's sadness. She tried to chatter happily about their mutual future in L.A. as she walked along with her sister, a few steps behind him.

As Jerry bent to unlock his car, he dropped his keys. They hit the curb and bounced under the car. He had to squat in order to reach under the car and retrieve them, but squatting proved not good enough. He finally knelt on the curb and leaned far over, groping under the car as far as he could reach, hoping to touch the keys. Finally he reached them, way back by the rear wheel. He started to get to his feet, but as he did someone jumped in front of him, waving a hand in his face. Startled, Jerry looked up and saw a skinny Mexican teenager. He had seen him sitting on the curb across the street, a block or so back; or perhaps that had been another skinny teenager, he couldn't tell. The boy waved again, just a quick motion, in front of Jerry's face. As he did, Juanita, a few steps away, saw the boy and shrieked.

"Luis, don't—you go away!" she yelled.

The boy screamed something at her—Jerry didn't get the words. He was still on one knee. As he stood up, Juanita shrieked again.

"Oh lord, oh my God!" she said. She turned and tried to run, but the boy caught her before she had gone more than a few steps. Marietta began to yell too—she started trying to pull her sister away from the boy, who turned quickly and made the same waving motion at Marietta.

"Hey, wait!" Jerry said, or tried to say—in the confusion he didn't think he had made himself heard. He had been scared for a moment when the boy leaped in front of him—he thought he might be a mugger—but now he realized he was Luis, the jealous boyfriend, showing up a week later than expected. He was just a skinny kid, no taller than Marietta and probably not much older. The girls needed to stop yelling and just get in the car so they could leave. The boy would calm down once they were gone.

Luis grabbed Juanita by the hair and waved at her as he had at Marietta. Both girls had stopped shrieking. Jerry could once again hear the music from the dance hall three blocks away.

Jerry started toward the three teenagers, meaning to intervene, but he realized that he wasn't walking straight. It had been very hot in the dance hall, he had drunk several beers —probably he was a little drunk. Before he could reach the group he saw Juanita fall to the sidewalk. Marietta ran off the curb into the street—then she fell too.

Jerry wanted to walk the few steps to where Juanita lay and help her up, but instead he veered off the curb. For a moment he felt as if he were in one of those dreams where you never quite get to where you want to go—never quite, never precisely. The destination is in sight but unreachable. As he veered he almost stepped on Marietta; then he stumbled on around in a complete circle and arrived at the passenger side of his own car. He felt that he was about to lose consciousness—that he was about to fall. He couldn't imagine how he had got so drunk—passing-out drunk—on just a few beers. Then he went black for a moment and fell across the hood of his car. He opened his eyes and tried to grasp the radio antenna to steady himself, but he couldn't hold it, and he dropped his keys again. He began to slide along the side of the car as he would down a long slope. The street tilted and the slope stretched out far ahead, like a freeway ramp, like the ramp leading to the long road he wanted so much to travel—the road to El Paso, to California, to his home in Nevada.

As he began to choke he felt a sadness—the sadness of knowing that he had not gone down the road when he should have, that he had not left when he really wanted to leave.

His car keys lay near his face, not lost this time, not under the car. They were only a foot from his eyes. The gleam of the streetlight touched them, as it touched the skim of blood spreading underneath them. The girls were not shrieking, Houston was peaceful, Luis was gone, and the great highway, I-10, two blocks away, roared in his ears like surf. He was looking at his car keys when he closed his eyes.

16

Aurora and Rosie were in the Beverly Wilshire Hotel when Patsy called. They had flown to California on the spur of the moment at Melanie's invitation to visit her on the set. The sitcom pilot was about to wrap. Melanie felt she was doing good work, at least everyone told her she was; she finally felt confident enough to invite her granny and Rosie to visit the set for a day.

It worked well, too, at first. Aurora and Rosie were soon made welcome on the set. Before the morning was over they were yakking it up with the cast and the crew. The trouble only arrived when Melanie did a scene and Rosie realized, to her horror and shame, that Melanie's character was a parody of herself at her most manic. Melanie in turn was horrified to learn, when she finished the scene, that Rosie had gone outside and burst into tears. "That's all I am, that's all I've ever been, a clown!" she said to one of the security guards, who had no idea who or what she was talking about. She finally hid in the wardrobe trailer, where she was comforted by Shirley and others.

Hours later, after Melanie and virtually everyone on the picture had told Rosie that what Melanie was doing was an act of homage, and that the character based on her was the only admirable person in the story, and also that America was going to love her and recognize her true worth, Rosie finally shook it off and began to enjoy life again. Many hugs from Melanie and a few from other people preceded her recovery. Aurora was slightly disgusted that Rosie had managed to commandeer so much attention, but she contained herself, and later even took Rosie shopping on glamorous Rodeo Drive.

Rosie agreed that Rodeo Drive was pretty glamorous, all right, but what she really liked were the free toiletries at the Beverly Wilshire Hotel. They even provided free Q-Tips, a luxury Rosie had never expected to live to enjoy. Aurora liked the free toiletries too. They were sitting in her room, looking out at the Hollywood hills and waiting for Melanie to show up so they could all go to dinner, when the phone rang.

"That must be Melly, she's probably downstairs," Aurora said. They were planning to go to Venice for dinner—Melanie had assured them they would like it.

Rosie was closest to the phone and picked it up. Aurora looked around expectantly, only to see Rosie's face change instantly, and in a way that did not presage a happy evening.

"He was?" she said.

"It's Patsy," she continued, looking sadly at Aurora.

Aurora's first thought was that perhaps Willie had died or been killed. She had been slightly fearful ever since Willie's departure that one day they would pick up the phone and be told that he had died or been killed.

"Is it Willie, dear?" she asked, coming across the room to take the phone.

"No, it ain't Willie, you better sit down," Rosie said. She looked rather numb, although a moment earlier she had been happily painting her fingernails. She held out the phone, and Aurora took it.

"Yes?" she said quietly—the look on Rosie's face made her feel unsteady.

"Aurora, I have to deliver some bad news," Patsy said. "I

didn't realize you were out of town or I would have found you sooner."

"I guess now is soon enough," Aurora said. "Who's dead?"

"Jerry Bruckner was killed Saturday night," Patsy said. "He had his throat cut on Washington Avenue. Apparently he had been to a dance with two young Mexican women. The girls were sisters, and they're dead too—same cause of death."

"Do they know who did it?" Aurora asked, imagining a serial killer, Jack the Ripper, she didn't know what.

"Yes, he's in custody—he's nineteen," Patsy said. "He was dating one of the girls—it appears that she was about to leave town with Jerry. I've seen the boy's picture in the paper. He's just a kid. The girl Jerry was involved with was nineteen, and her sister was fifteen."

Rosie watched Aurora to see if she was likely to faint. She didn't faint, and she still held the phone, but she said nothing. She had dropped her head.

"Jerry's car was packed," Patsy added. "He had made arrangements to have his furniture given away and his books stored. I guess they meant to leave town that night. The boy-friend just ambushed them. If they hadn't gone to the dance they'd probably be alive."

There was a long pause.

"I'm sorry to be the bearer of sad tidings," Patsy said. Then her voice broke—it had taken a lot to work up to calling Aurora, and now that she had done it, all the sadness and confusion she felt began to break through.

"I'm sorry about more than that," she said in a trembling voice. "I'm sorry I ever slept with him—I wish I'd let him alone. You're better at holding people than I am. If I'd let him alone maybe he'd still be with you and this wouldn't have happened."

"If you mean the girls, I suspect that part was probably happening while he was with me," Aurora said. "I doubt that I ever had his exclusive attention. In fact, I doubt that either of us had it, or that anyone ever had it for long. He was not that kind of man."

"No, but I still feel that it's all my fault," Patsy said, desperate to apologize. "I've never known when to stay out of things . . . or I can't manage to. I don't know."

Aurora felt she must try to keep a grip—her mind seemed to her to be gyrating wildly. At one moment all was confusion, but the next she seemed to see things too clearly—far too clearly. Still, she wanted to stop the gyration at a point of clarity. The confusion frightened her too much.

"You may as well stop iffing, Patsy," she said. "Our iffing won't change anything now. You've always had a tendency to assume blame, but you should try to control it in this instance."

"I can't control it—it's all I can think about," Patsy said.

"If he was at a dance with two young girls, then I hardly think it's all your fault," Aurora told her. "Most of it was *his* fault—although of course that doesn't mean I'm not sorry it happened."

She felt she should take the opportunity to lecture Patsy more sternly about her odd tendency to assume blame for all the mishaps of life, all the thorns it scattered in one's path, all the tragedies. She had been lecturing Patsy on her failings since Patsy herself had been a teenager no older than the girls who had been killed. It was a familiar thing to do—she felt she must stick with the familiar as long as she could—keep on lecturing Patsy, do anything that was familiar.

That was the safest course at such a time, but it was a course that she proved, moments later, to be unable to hold to. The spinning of her mind got faster—she no longer had a clear view of anything—all she could do was thrust the phone at Rosie and grab a pillow to bury her face in.

Rosie took the phone. "I guess the dam just broke," she said. She tried to put an arm around Aurora, but Aurora rolled off the bed and stumbled to the bathroom.

"Well, it was bound to break," Patsy said. "Is Melanie there?"

"No, but she's coming," Rosie said. "I'll be glad when she gets here. We're looking at a long night."

"Do you think Aurora hates me?" Patsy asked. She knew it was an unworthy question to ask at such a time, but she felt bereft—she had to ask it.

"Aw, no, she'll get over it," Rosie said. "I don't imagine she'll trust you around her boyfriends no more, but then she never did. She don't even trust me around her boyfriends, and look how harmless I am."

From the bathroom she heard the sound of water running, at full force, it sounded like. Aurora often did that if there was a bathroom handy when tragedy struck. She didn't like anyone to hear her cry. Rosie remembered the water running and running in their miserable motel in Nebraska the night Emma died. More recently, a lot of water had flowed down the pipes the day General Scott passed away.

"All these tears she cries for me, they're wasted," Patsy said. "I didn't really know Jerry very well, but I don't think he was bad."

"He got two girls killed," Rosie pointed out. "A grown man that's supposed to have sense enough to be a doctor ought to do a better job of looking after his girlfriends, specially if he's gonna have girlfriends that young."

Patsy decided to get off the phone—she didn't want to hear Rosie's judgments of Jerry, not just then. She had a need to think well of him still.

"Do you think you'll come home?" she asked. "There's going to be a little funeral tomorrow."

"Oh, we'll come home," Rosie said. "We were coming anyway. What else can we do? It's where we live. Who arranged the funeral?"

"I did," Patsy said. "I just told them I was a friend."

Later, after Melanie had come, been awed by the news of the tragedy and by the change in her grandmother, been fed room service and sent home, Rosie and Aurora sat by the windows in Aurora's room, looking out at Beverly Hills. Rosie could not get it out of her mind that the girls had been so young. To her that seemed the worst part—that the man would go to a dance in a dangerous part of town with girls so much younger than himself and not take better care of them.

She raised the issue several times, but Aurora didn't respond. She just sat looking out the window.

Rosie couldn't seem to stop, though—she couldn't help it. All she could think about was the youth of the two dead girls, and how pretty they had probably looked in their party clothes.

Finally, after she had mentioned the girls four or five times, Aurora looked up at her with a glint of anger.

"Stop talking about them!" she said. "Don't say another word. Young as they were, they were still closer to his age than I am. Don't you realize that?"

Rosie hadn't realized it—it just hadn't occurred to her.

"Oh lord, I'm sorry," she said, wishing she had never said a word about the girls or anything else. In a way she saw what Aurora was getting at, but in a way she didn't see what difference it made. Aurora was old enough to take care of herself, and the dead girls hadn't been.

It was no time to argue, though, Rosie knew. Neither of the women said anything else for a very long time. They sat looking out the window, down Rodeo Drive and down the years, until the sky began to turn again, and cars to honk in the busy street below.

17

When they got home, tired and sad, the next afternoon, Jerry's letter was among the mail. Aurora thought the handwriting on the envelope looked familiar, but there was no return address and it took her a moment to realize that the handwriting was Jerry's. When it finally struck her she immediately tried to hand the letter to Rosie.

"Please read it for me," she said. "It's from Jerry."

But Rosie wouldn't take it. She drew away.

"It's from beyond the grave," Rosie said. "I'm too superstitious to read something like that."

Aurora took the letter upstairs and read it in her bathroom with the door shut. What saddened her most was that it was just written on plain paper—Jerry had never felt legitimate enough as a doctor to have letterheads printed. He wouldn't award himself even that much of a title—it led her to reflect, with increasing grief, how empty the man must have felt. He had been smart enough and kind enough, in her view, to have earned a few little victories, or to have acquired enough sense of his own value as a counselor to grant himself official stationery at least. Yet he hadn't. He even told her once that he felt more like a psychiatrist when he had been doing stand-up comedy than he had since he began his unsanctioned practice. The fact that his patients sanctioned the practice by coming back again and again had not been enough to make him feel legitimate.

It seemed very sad—too sad to keep to herself. Also, the note was cryptic. Though he had clearly meant to compliment and thank her, she didn't understand the compliment. How had she been a great help to him? Puzzled, but under control, she took the note down to Rosie, who consented this time to read it.

"It's nice, it's just real short," she said.

"Yes, that's what I'm feeling," Aurora said. "I never felt that I knew the man very well, and now I feel that I must not have known him at all. He said that I was a great help, and I would like to have been, but right now I can't feel that I was any help at all."

"He probably just meant that if you hadn't fallen in love with him he wouldn't have had no happiness at all in the last part of his life," Rosie said.

"Of course he had no idea that it *was* the last part of his life," Aurora said. "I wonder if Patsy got a note—after all, she was in love with Jerry, too."

"I guess we can ask her at the funeral," Rosie said.

"No, we mustn't," Aurora said. "If she didn't get one, and we reveal that I did, it will just make her inferiority complex worse. Treacherous as she was, we still don't want that."

"Does that mean you're ready to forgive and forget?" Rosie asked. She was hoping that someday Patsy would be allowed back in the house, so that they could have a little tea and a chat before running off to the exercise class in the morning.

"I seem to be the type of person who can forgive more than I'm able to forget," Aurora said. "The man's dead—why hate Patsy? On the other hand, I won't be forgetting what she did anytime soon."

"Maybe she'll tell me if she got a letter," Rosie said. "I doubt he wrote her one, though. You're more the type that a man like that would write letters to."

"Someday I may ask you to clarify that statement," Aurora

said. "He didn't write letters to me. He only wrote me one short note. I don't know what you mean at all."

Once she thought it over, Rosie didn't either, though she still felt it was probably true in a general way.

A copy of Jerry's will had been found in the glove compartment of his station wagon. He had requested cremation and that had been done; since he had no living relatives, or none anyone knew about, Patsy signed the order. Then, unable to resist the best taste she could get, she had arranged a little service, to be held in the Rothko chapel. Several of Jerry's patients came. Except for one, a tall, nervous boy who reminded Aurora uncomfortably of Teddy, all the patients who showed up were elderly. None of them looked well off. They were also very ill at ease in the setting—most of them had clearly never been in the Rothko chapel before; indeed, it seemed unlikely that many of them had ever heard of Mark Rothko or would know what to make of his huge, somber paintings.

"Patsy always overshoots," Aurora whispered to Rosie. "She can't stop being arty, even when somebody dies. Why couldn't she have found some simple little nondenominational church? Most of these people don't know where to put their feet."

She had insisted that Pascal accompany them, and he didn't seem to know where to put *his* feet, either. He kept shuffling around nervously, although they were only in the chapel ten minutes.

Among the mourners were three tall, toothy young women —they were cheaply dressed and red-eyed from crying, unlike the more elderly mourners, who accepted Jerry's passing with a tired stoicism.

"How old do you think those girls were?" Aurora asked, as she watched them walk away across the green lawn once they were all outside again.

"Mid-twenties," Rosie ventured. "They all look like waitresses."

"Well, but nice waitresses," Aurora said. "They look healthy—not sicklied over, like we are."

"Speak for yourself, I ain't sicklied over, I just get head-aches once in a while," Rosie declared.

"Who was this man that was killed?" Pascal asked. In life he tried to avoid the kind of people who would go to places where they would get their throats cut, and he would have preferred to avoid such people even after they were dead.

"One of my doctors—you shut up," Aurora said. She didn't want him probing.

Feeling weary, and wondering what the point was of knowing such a woman, Pascal trudged back to his consulate, which was only a few blocks away.

"I guess that's that," Patsy said, walking over, a little nervous—Aurora seemed friendly, but she wasn't sure she could trust it. "Do the two of you want to come with me to scatter his ashes?"

"I don't, not me," Rosie said. "I ain't touching no ashes, if it's ashes of a person."

In fact, she had a horror of cremation. What if a person was just in a deep coma and came out of it to find themselves in some kind of oven being burned up? She couldn't think of anything she'd rather not risk.

"I didn't know that was part of the plan," Aurora said. "Where would we scatter them?"

"In Galveston, in the sea," Patsy said.

"Let's stop at the Pig Stand first," Aurora said. "I'd like to fortify myself with a piece of pie."

Rosie agreed to accompany them, but only on condition that she didn't have to touch Jerry's ashes, or even see them. They were put in the trunk of Patsy's car, and Rosie was allowed to sit in the front seat as far from the remains as possible. Even so, she spent the short ride to the Pig Stand hunched against the dashboard. "I just get nervous when I think about being dead," she said.

At the Pig Stand, Patsy choked up and became so upset that she couldn't finish her pie. Embarrassed, she got up and walked around outside until she stopped crying.

Rosie smoked and drank coffee. Aurora, unusually silent, ate three pieces of pie. Dolly, the waitress, attempted to be friendly, but was a little unnerved. Rosie revealed that they had a human's ashes in their car. Dolly remembered that Aurora's old boyfriend had died right there in a booth—and now she was carrying ashes in her car! Mostly, Dolly liked Aurora—she was friendly and she left good tips—but she seemed to always have people dying around her, and that was not a good sign.

After the meal, Aurora insisted on driving by the Acropolis Bar. She thought they ought to have a wake, and the Acropolis Bar was, in her view, a good place to have it.

"I'll just get out and give the Petrakis brothers a little warning," she said.

Theo and Vassily were there, sitting on their stools.

Aurora got out of the car, Rosie waved, and Patsy, feeling miserable, merely sat.

"We're taking a comrade home to the sea," Aurora said to the brothers. "His ashes are in my trunk. I thought on our way back we might stop by and have a little wake. Life for the living, after all."

"Life for the living," Theo agreed. "Do you want a band?"

"Well, is one handy?" she asked.

"Across the street and back a block there's a band," Theo said. "That's handy enough."

"Most of a band," Vassily corrected. "Bobby's in jail."

"Well, he can't play anyway," Theo said.

"We'll be happy with whatever you care to arrange," Aurora said.

Once in Galveston, she took off her stockings and waded with Patsy into the warm, dirty gray surf. Patsy did most of the scattering. Aurora walked behind, wishing Jerry could have brought himself to write a longer letter; but he hadn't —the mystery of his character would never be revealed.

"We should have just scattered him along the highway," she remarked, driving back. "He was more of a man of the highways than he was a man of the sea."

"I know, but the sea's nicer," Patsy said. "The sea's supposed to be our home."

"Speak for yourself, it ain't mine," Rosie said. She had a

headache and wished she could be home. Taking a whole afternoon to get a funeral over with was not her way of doing things.

As soon as Theo saw them coming back, the band started playing under the shed that was the Acropolis Bar. By a miracle, Bobby's girlfriend had made bail for him that morning, so the band's force was undiminished.

Still, in Aurora's view, the band didn't generate enough force for a proper wake.

"They're so music-boxy," she said to Vassily. "I was hoping for something a little more elemental."

"More Dionysian," Patsy said.

"Oh, these boys are good boys," Theo said, not sure how to take Patsy's remark. "It ain't often they get in trouble. Bobby just let jealousy get the best of him—that's what got him sent to jail."

Aurora had sand on her legs; so did Patsy. Vassily noticed —the sight produced a little erotic thrill. The sad woman, Patsy, had skinny legs, but that was all right. In fact, it even sharpened the erotic thrill. Theo kidded him about it, but he liked women with skinny legs.

Aurora belted down seven or eight glasses of retsina, but she didn't dance, and she seemed remote. Theo felt a little hurt. The promise of their first meeting had not been fulfilled, and he was beginning to fear that it never would be. Probably she had been in love with the man whose ashes they had scattered. If that was the case, his death might take a while to wear off. It was easier to stay in love with dead people than with living people for the simple reason that they weren't around to irritate you. He himself was still in love with his third wife, Eta, a Yugoslav. Eta had been killed in a car wreck in Brighton, England. She had refused to accept the English penchant for driving on the left side of the road. She was stubborn, like many Yugoslavs. Eta had frequently cursed him, but their love had been passionate and he could not stop being in love with her—though he felt he might succeed in stopping if only Aurora would be a little less remote.

"You're chilly today, crispy," he said, looking at her mournfully.

"Well, I lost a friend, leave me alone," Aurora said.

"You were mean to Theo, after he went and got cheese and the band and everything," Rosie told her on the way home. The retsina had gone down too smoothly—she had a feeling she might be drunk.

"I don't know if I want a lot of people getting drunk when I die," she said. "It don't feel respectful, not to me."

"Then you better stay alive until I'm gone," Aurora said. "I certainly plan to get drunk when you die, if I'm around."

"I can't imagine how you found those Greeks," Patsy said. "They're cute, you know. I liked them."

"Greeks are always simple to find," Aurora said. "Just go to the nearest port, and there will be a Greek, if not several."

That night, wakeful, she called Theo and apologized for being sharp with him. In the background she could hear the band—probably the same band—tinkling away like a music box.

Theo was glad she called—he had been ill at ease and low ever since she'd left.

"I wish I could come see you," he said. Though he knew it was far too soon to declare himself—after all, a man she had probably loved had just died—he was still having trouble not declaring himself.

"Well, I'm up, come and see me," Aurora said.

"Get the number of the one with the skinny legs," Vassily requested as Theo, dumbstruck by his good fortune, was making a hasty departure.

He raced to Aurora's, but to his dismay, nothing had changed. She was wrapped in a robe, she gave him brandy, but she was remote.

"You left, where'd you go?" he asked, trying to joke. She had brought him into her brightly lit kitchen, to give him the brandy.

"Perhaps I've gone into reverse," Aurora said. The look on her face was friendly, yet not encouraging.

"Life for the living," Theo reminded her.

552

"Reverse isn't death," Aurora reminded him. "I *am* living, I've just changed gears."

"I wish you'd change back so we could get together," Theo said. "I mean, I know it's the wrong day to say it, but if you've got a feeling it's better to say it, right?"

"It certainly is better to say it," Aurora agreed.

"Well, I've got a feeling, now I've said it, you gonna throw me out?" Theo asked.

"No, I'm going to make you into my hand-holding friend," Aurora said, reaching over to take his hand. His hand felt comfortable to her—it bore two or three scars, one of which she traced with her finger.

"That's from when I ran a lathe," Theo said.

Aurora didn't comment.

"You mean, that's it—hand-holding?" Theo asked. He had popped off, and now he felt on shaky ground.

"That's it—take it or leave it," Aurora said. "Youthful as you are, you probably should leave it."

"I ain't leaving it," Theo assured her—he was too much in love. Besides, women changed their minds.

"Don't waste too much of your youthfulness waiting for me to change my mind, either," Aurora said immediately. To Theo she looked sad—too sad; he didn't care if she didn't change her mind.

"Vassily wants the phone number of that girl you had with you," he said, feeling in a hurry to change the subject.

"That girl has three grown children," Aurora informed him. "Your brother's what I mean by elemental. I don't know if he'd be interested at the level of hand-holding."

Theo shrugged. "I've seen him when he'd be glad to get it," he said. "His next to last wife didn't let him touch her for four years."

"Such times come to us all, I guess," Aurora said.

"Yeah, they came to me after Eta was smashed in the wreck," Theo said. "I went six years."

"Goodness," Aurora said.

"I lived, it don't kill you," Theo said. "Vassily has bad judgment, he's better off when he don't have no woman."

The next morning Patsy called Aurora. She sounded rather flustered.

"One of your Greeks just called and asked me for a date," Patsy said.

"Yes, Vassily," Aurora said. "Since they provided us with a free wake I felt I couldn't refuse him your phone number."

"I don't know what to do," Patsy said. "I mean, I liked them, but we just met once, and the circumstances were a little unusual. I don't know what we'd talk about on a date."

"Though it's none of my business, I hope you accepted," Aurora said. "It might be interesting for you, just once, to go out with someone who wasn't an artist or an artist manqué.

"A man of the people, so to speak," she added.

"Actually, I've had a few of those," Patsy said. "Remember my rodeo clown? There was also my carpenter—actually, several carpenters—and my Vietnam helicopter pilot and my semipro baseball player," she said, remembering her several efforts with men of the people.

"Well, this ball is in your court," Aurora said. "Return it if you choose."

Later, when she told Rosie that Vassily had asked Patsy for a date, Rosie evinced no surprise.

"I seen him looking at her legs," she said. Secretly, she was glad it was Vassily, and not Theo. She was harboring a soft spot for Theo herself. Despite his obvious crush on Aurora, he sometimes smiled at her in a way that seemed to mean he might be interested. And if he was, she was, Aurora or no Aurora—that Theo just had a really nice way about him.

18

"Hon, this don't make no sense," Rosie said. "You'd already stopped dating him, and he was on his way out of town anyway. You might not have ever heard from him again, other than that little note."

Aurora had only eaten an orange for breakfast. In fact, she hadn't even eaten all the orange—she just sort of picked it to pieces. In the months since Jerry's death she had lost over twenty pounds. She had stopped doing all the things she had done all her life, and it worried everyone. She had stopped watching television, stopped buying clothes, stopped wearing makeup, stopped going out, stopped having romances, or even flirting, and she had even virtually stopped eating. The change alarmed neighbors and friends, suitors and grandchildren, but it alarmed Rosie most, she being the one person who had to watch it every single day of her life, and at close range to boot.

"Are you speaking for yourself, or have you been appointed a one-woman committee to harass me at my own breakfast table?" Aurora asked, looking up.

"Well, everybody's worried, this ain't like you," Rosie said.

"On the contrary, it's precisely like me as I am at this time in my life," Aurora said. "I'm aware that you all liked me better the way I was before, but there's nothing I can do about that because I'm no longer the way I was before."

"You could be, though, if you could just get over Jerry," Rosie said. "You hounded me till I finally got over Royce, why can't I hound you till you get over Jerry?"

"Bad comparison," Aurora said. "You were young and active when Royce died. You had many productive years ahead and I was determined that you not waste them. I admit I expected you to do better than C.C. and Willie, but that sort of bad luck couldn't have been predicted."

"That's another thing we need to talk about," Rosie said, uneasily. "Arthur's proposed three times now—I gotta decide what I'm gonna do. But I can't decide, not with you like this."

"What do you mean, 'like this?'" Aurora asked calmly. "I'm clean, you know! I bathe every day. I brush my teeth. I go to my doctor for my checkups and no one has informed me of any structural flaws. My vital signs are as vital as ever. I don't know why the mere fact that I'm living the life of my choice gives people the notion that they can refer to me as 'like this.'

"Besides that, I'm still concerned about the people I'm concerned about," she added, after a pause.

"I'm sorry I ever brought it up, I'm just confused myself," Rosie said, sitting down at the table.

"I think it's horrible of all of you to pester me to lose weight for decades if you're only going to accuse me of being 'like this' when I finally do lose a few pounds," Aurora remarked. She got up and was about to make her way out to her little garage office where she spent her days, working on her memory project on the new word processor Teddy had taught her how to use. Rosie looked more than confused— she looked as if her heart were breaking.

"I've been here working for you over forty years," Rosie said. "I thought I'd just go on living here and working for you and we'd never change from being how we've been. I guess it scares me to think of marrying Arthur and moving away."

"Rosie, Arthur Cotton lives across the street," Aurora said, touched by her maid's sad eyes and quavery voice.

"Across the street and down two houses," Rosie corrected, though she knew the correction sounded ridiculous. From her suitor Arthur Cotton's bedroom windows she could look across a long-familiar street and see Aurora's bedroom windows. The move—if she undertook it—might seem like no move at all to some people; but the thought of it frightened Rosie more than any move she had ever contemplated in her life.

"It's just that I wouldn't be working for you no more," Rosie said. "If I wasn't still your maid it might be different. You really don't like Arthur much—you know you don't."

"No, but it's not as if I *dislike* him," Aurora said. "Somehow I've managed to remain largely indifferent to Arthur Cotton all these years. What I did dislike was his late wife's name."

"Eureka, what's wrong with that?" Rosie asked.

"Nothing, in the abstract," Aurora said. "It's just that having a Eureka and an Aurora on the same street seems a bit much."

"Anyway, if I marry him and move over there, who knows what will happen?" Rosie said. "It might change things too much."

"Why should it?" Aurora asked—through she had had the same thought a few times.

"Well, I wouldn't be right here in the kitchen to nag you," Rosie said. "We might drift apart. Someday we might not even be friends no more."

Aurora sighed, came back, and sat down at the table again. Arthur Cotton was an insurance man, and a very wealthy one. He loved his lawn, and in the course of mowing it for the past thirty years had often stopped to chat briefly with Rosie, if she happened to walk past on her way to the bus stop. Five months before, his wife, Eureka, had dropped dead. Three weeks after her funeral he asked Rosie for a date. On the third date he proposed. He told Rosie he had secretly yearned for her for many years. Rosie couldn't—and didn't—pretend to Arthur that she had yearned for *him* for thirty years—all her passion amounted to was having once or twice mentioned to Aurora that she thought Arthur was cute in his roly-poly way.

She wasn't entirely unmoved by his proposals, though. Willie had never called—not once; she felt in limbo and wanted to get out. What scared her was the thought of leaving Aurora's employ after forty years. What would she be if she was no longer a maid? The question stuck in her mind and she couldn't stop asking it.

Privately Aurora wished that Eureka Cotton could have managed not to drop dead for a few more years. A little more longevity on her part would have spared them all a painful dilemma. But Eureka hadn't managed it, and there they were.

"Rosie, listen to me," Aurora said finally. "You and I have survived together in this kitchen for forty-two years. You were with me the night my husband died. You were with me the night my daughter died. You were with me when we found out that Tommy had killed his girlfriend. I like to hope that I've been some support in various of your family trage-dies, too. You're not only my friend, you're my dearest friend, and that isn't going to change. What you should be asking yourself is whether you think you can be happy living with Arthur Cotton. That's the real question."

Rosie began to cry. It was sweet of Aurora to tell her that she was her dearest friend—and, of course, Aurora had long been *her* dearest friend. And yet she felt uncertain. A mar-riage could change things around and end up making every-thing different. Little things that she enjoyed doing with Aurora, such as watching certain soaps, she might not get to do anymore. Just sitting and talking at the table might not be quite the same if she was living way off down the street.

"I know Arthur's important, but it's the thought of leaving you that makes me nervous," Rosie said. "You're still upset about Jerry, you ain't eating right, and you don't pay atten-tion to yourself like you used to. I'd just feel like I was de-serting you in your time of need."

"Rosie, I'm not starving," Aurora pointed out. "I'm just

more interested in my memory project than I am in eating right now. I've spent a great many years stuffing myself, as you should know better than anyone. Why can't I just let it go for a while?"

Rosie abandoned that point and moved to another.

"Another thing is, Arthur's rich, and I've always been just a working woman," she said. "He wants to fly me off to Paris and buy me fur coats and emeralds—the only place he'll even take me to eat is Maxim's and my stomach can't handle all that rich food. I keep telling the poor man he's trying to make a silk purse out of a sow's ear, but he won't listen."

"It certainly won't work if you go into it with that attitude," Aurora said. "What's wrong with a few fur coats and emeralds?"

"Maybe I'm just too old to change sides of the street," Rosie said. "Now, if he'd just let me go on working for you, I might do it, but he won't, will he?"

"No, Arthur's much too custom-bound to allow his wife to be a domestic," Aurora said. "In fact, instead of being a maid, you'd undoubtedly be required to *hire* a maid."

"Well, that'll never work, I'd die before I'd give another human being an order," Rosie said.

"I find that hard to believe, since you've given me millions," Aurora said. "For forty years you've been driving me from my own bed, where I was perfectly comfortable, just so you could make it up in keeping with some arcane schedule you seem to feel you have to keep to."

"Oh, well," Rosie said. It was true that she sometimes bossed Aurora, a bit.

"Oh, well yourself," Aurora said. "You crack the whip perfectly well, when you feel like it. I'm sure I would have finished Proust years ago if you hadn't always driven me from my bed just as I was getting settled in with his book."

In the three weeks after Jerry's death, Aurora had shut herself into her little garage office and read Proust straight through. At times she put the book down and brooded; at other times she put the book down and wept, not so much for a lost Paris, or her own lost love, as from a profound sense of wasted time. Somehow she had let her life slip by, achieving nothing. She did not suppose, in her hours of regret, that she had ever had mind enough to achieve a great work, like Monsieur Proust. Perhaps she hadn't mind enough to achieve a work of even modest scope—yet it did seem to her that she had mind enough and sufficient individuality that she ought to have achieved more. Her mother had always hoped she would write, or, failing that, sing, but she had done neither. She had, in the end, merely lived, partaking rather fully of the human experience, absorbing it, and yet doing nothing with it. That was the common way, of course, and yet the knowledge that she had not transcended the common way left her discontented, restless. It seemed to her that her problem may have been that she absorbed experience too avidly —so avidly that she had never taken time really to think about it.

As she saw it, the memory project was her last chance. Whatever she achieved with her new computer and her huge archive of social calendars, desk diaries, baby books, cruise journals, concert programs, playbills and the like—counting Emma's few jottings, the collection spanned four generations —would not be a great work of creation and re-creation, such as Proust had done, but it would be something that would reflect the deeper side of her nature, or at least show that there had been a deeper side.

"I can't keep the poor man hanging, I've got to say yes or no," Rosie said, still tortured by the thought of Arthur Cotton.

"Pardon my bluntness, but have you slept with him yet?" Aurora asked.

"Well, nearly," Rosie said. "He's been nervous. He says he's nervous because he's afraid of getting his heart broke at the last minute.

"I don't really care, I ain't very attracted to him anyway," she added. "I think he's cute, but cute's kind of got its limits."

"Then why won't you give Theo a chance before you handcuff yourself to this rich man?" Aurora asked. "Theo's dying to take you out."

"It's just because he's given up on you, though," Rosie said. It was true that she still had her soft spot for Theo, and it was also true that he had been asking her for dates and even bringing her little presents lately—usually just some particularly good olives, or some feta or something—and yet it didn't feel right, she knew it was just because of his despair about Aurora. Like everything else that happened to her, Theo's little suit seemed to involve impossible complications.

"It all just comes back to what I wanted to talk to you about in the first place," Rosie said.

"Oh, yes, my state of mind," Aurora said. "I'm aware that practically everyone in the universe is dissatisfied with it, but I don't know why. I'm healthy, stable, and busy—isn't that enough?"

"No, because it's like you ain't trying anymore," Rosie said. "All these years, when one of us got ground down and just wanted to give up, it was mainly just that you always kept on trying that got us though."

"What that boils down to is that I'm a very selfish woman and I've brought a certain amount of energy to what was mainly just selfishness," Aurora said. "I was grabby and you all liked it, although you complained about it constantly. Now I've stopped being grabby, and none of you know what to do with yourselves."

"That's it," Rosie said. "When are you going to start being grabby again?"

"What if I never do?" Aurora asked. "The years have slipped by in a twinkling, and now you and I are old women —at least we are women who are not young. I don't feel like being grabby any more. Since we're talking about my state of mind, I want to point out that what seems to shock all of you is that a state of *mind* is what I've acquired. If I feel that I've lived my life fully enough, what I want to do now is *think* about it. Just *think* about it, got it?"

"I got it, I just don't understand," Rosie said. "What if you do sit out there and go through them old calendars until you remember every single day of your life? What if you remember everything? It's still all just stuff that's passed. What'll you have, when you do remember it?"

"Why, I don't know," Aurora admitted cheerfully. "I haven't gotten very far with my memory project yet. I've just assembled a few scraps. But I do know that working on my memory project is what I want to do. I don't care about society, I don't want to travel, I'm not interested in males and their penises anymore. I just want to work on my project. I may be at it for months, or I may be at it for the rest of my life. I don't know, and I also don't know why it should throw the universe off just because I've chosen to use my mind for a change, instead of just indulging my body."

"You used to want to be happy," Rosie said. "It's what made you such fun to be around, even if you were a little bossy sometimes. You were just *determined* to be happy. I guess that's what I miss."

"Yes, I know what you mean," Aurora said—often she missed her old high spirits too. In her memory it was not so much that she had been determined to be happy as that she had been determined to fight clear of the constant drag of unhappiness that she supposed to be merely the common affliction of adult life.

"I didn't want to be defeated," she said to Rosie. "I didn't want to be, and I wasn't—at least I never was for very long."

"But now you don't care, right?" Rosie asked.

"I wouldn't say I don't care," Aurora said. "I suppose I'm like an old dog. I've mostly got my eye on the other place now."

"Well, I hate it," Rosie said. "I'm about as old as you and I'm thinking of getting married. I might even go to Paris, over in France. I ain't happy but I ain't quitting, either. We *are* sort of in this together—it ain't fair for you to quit, and leave me to struggle alone."

"Being in neutral isn't quite the same as quitting," Aurora quibbled. "The motor's still running. The car could jump in gear and run over somebody anytime."

Rosie shook her head. "The bottom line is, you quit," Rosie said. "I still think it's all because of Jerry, even though you wasn't dating him and he was about to leave town."

"Well, this is where I came in, goodbye for now," Aurora said. "I've got to go organize my concert programs. I seem to have over a thousand, which is odd."

"I don't think it's odd," Rosie said. "You was always going off to the symphony."

"But I don't remember it that way—it's what makes my memory project so interesting," Aurora said. "I have the programs, so I must have gone to concerts constantly, but I don't remember getting to go to concerts that often. Rudyard hated having to go out—I always had to coax him or trick him when there was a program I really wanted to hear."

"If that's the way you remember it, your memory project's got a long way to go," Rosie informed her matter-of-factly.

"Meaning what, may I ask?" Aurora inquired.

"You never coaxed Rud or tricked him when I was here," Rosie said, a little too vengefully, Aurora thought. "You mainly just told him to get up and get dressed—he was going to a concert with you."

"Oh, well, I may occasionally have been a little peremptory, if there was a good soloist or if a conductor I happened to be mad about happened to be conducting," Aurora said. "How tactless of you to remember the few times when I was peremptory with Rud and forget the many times I was forced to coax."

"I notice you didn't pester Rud to go along when that old fat Englishman you were so crazy about happened to be conducting," Rosie reminded her.

"Sir Thomas Beecham, of course I was crazy about him," Aurora admitted. "Of course I didn't drag Rud along on those occasions. In fact I was saddened that Sir Thomas had been forced by circumstance to spend his declining years conducting in front of barbarians, and I was quite prepared to make it up to him any way I could."

"So did you?" Rosie asked. Sir Thomas Beecham had come to dinner a number of times in those years. Rosie remembered that he was very forcefully spoken, and also very hard to please when it came to food.

"There's no food outside New York," he had said, not once but several times, even as he was eating Aurora's delicious

563

food, and eating it heartily, too. Rosie found that sort of behavior disgusting. If she had been the boss, and not the maid, she would have told him he ought to stop taking third helpings if he didn't like the food. He could have run on back to New York any time, it would have been fine with her. But she had not been the boss, most of her kids were still at home in those days, and she needed the job. The Beecham dinners usually took place when Rud, Aurora's husband, was away on one of his mysterious fishing trips—the mystery being why he never came back with even a single fish. It was plain that Aurora would have jumped in bed with old Sir Thomas in a minute, but he had soon moved away and Rosie had never been quite sure whether Aurora had or hadn't been able to make matters up to him in that particular way.

"Pardon me, did I what?" Aurora asked.

"Sleep with that old white-haired fart?" Rosie said. Since Aurora had just asked her if she'd slept with Arthur, she thought she might get away with asking if Aurora had slept with Sir Thomas Beecham.

"Nope," Aurora admitted. "Apart from some fumblings once, nothing came to pass."

"Is that what you're doing, sitting out there with all those old date books?" Rosie asked. "Trying to remember who you fumbled with and who you didn't?"

"No, because I never fumbled—as you put it—with anyone very noteworthy in my whole life," Aurora said. "As a seducer of the illustrious I have a very poor record—in fact, no record."

"I wouldn't lose no sleep over it, they're probably just duds, like most men," Rosie said.

"You're probably right, oh sage," Aurora said. "I would have liked to try just one celebrity, though, just to be sure, and Sir Thomas Beecham would have been high on my list. It's unlikely that anyone of that caliber will come my way again."

"Yeah, but you never know," Rosie said. "I sure never expected Arthur Cotton to come my way, but he showed up, and now look what a jam I'm in."

Later, in her little office, her hands dusty from stacking and arranging the many hundreds of concert programs—hers, her mother's, and her grandmother's—Aurora reflected that if nothing else her memory project would show how profoundly important music and the theater had been in the lives of the women in her family. The concert programs went back almost a century, and she still had, boxed, almost an equal number of playbills.

It occurred to her that if she cared to type every concert program into her computer, she would know, at the end, exactly how many times she and her mother and her grandmother had listened to a given piece of music, or been charmed by a given conductor or soloist. How much Debussy, how much Mozart, how much Haydn. Then, if she did the same with the playbills, she could also chart their dramatic loyalties: Shakespeare, O'Neill, Ibsen, Shaw.

It was a daunting mass of concert programs, though—they covered the floor, and so would the playbills, when she got around to unpacking them. It seemed to her that she might need an assistant—even two assistants. She thought of Teddy and Jane—they both had computers and also, both had time on their hands. They had quit their jobs at the 7-Eleven, where danger had increased to the point that they had to make change for the customers from behind a plexiglass shield.

"Sort of takes the fun out of it," Jane said. At the moment they were both drawing unemployment; they seemed to do nothing except study dead languages and indulge their brilliant child. Aurora decided she might visit and offer them temporary employment on her memory project. Jane liked music—she could do the concert programs, and Teddy, who, despite his antidepressants, still showed signs of shakiness, could do the playbills.

What that left was eight shelves of social calendars, desk diaries, and other memorabilia, source of the raw chronological data from which Aurora hoped to extract a more or less day-to-day record of her existence. She realized that it was an eccentric hope: after all, she had lived twenty-five thousand days or more, and might not have time enough left in which to work back through the years and months, the weeks and days, to her unremembered beginnings.

The truth was that most—indeed, almost all—of those days were unremembered, and she knew already that the calendars and desk diaries stacked on her shelves were not going to bring many of them back in much detail. Like herself, her mother and grandmother had taken a severely minimalist attitude toward diary keeping. So brief were their entries— and hers, too—that the really odd thing was that they had felt the need to make even a faint scratch on the rock of time as it rolled past. Yet all three of them had scratched—they seldom missed a day, even though they seldom scratched even as much as a complete sentence.

A typical entry for her grandmother, Catherine Dodd, might simply read "Left Boston," or "Got home, beds dusty." A New England picnic, of the sort Renoir ought to have painted, might receive from Catherine Dodd only one brusque stroke: "Bad clam, Charley sick."

Her mother, Amelia, was equally terse. One entry, made when Aurora was five, merely said, "Aurora spat on Bob." Aurora could not even recall who Bob might have been—she had no cousin named Bob. Though she searched carefully through the diaries of that period hoping for other references to a Bob, she found none. Try as she might, she could not remember spitting on a little boy—though, she had to admit, it was well within her potential: she did recall being often angry with little boys when she was around six; she was violently jealous because they had so much more freedom and more fun than little girls. Probably she had spat on one —but why, precisely?

Her own diaries, she had to admit, were no improvement. She had rarely been moved to jot down more than three or four words about any day, often saying no more than "Trevor, lobster," "Edward, wretched dancer," or "Beulah overcooked the fish." The majority of her jottings reflected her critical nature. She had always maintained that her critical nature was merely a by-product of high standards; but after leafing through a decade or so of her desk diaries she was forced to conclude that an impartial judge—a biographer, say —would probably conclude that she had been a woman with a very critical nature. Year after year, the three or four words she had allotted to a given day were words of complaint: overcooked fish, suitors who couldn't dance, policemen who gave her tickets, concerts where the woodwinds were weak or the soloists unprepared.

Such records as she had left, viewed in the main, were sobering to such a degree that she wondered at times why she had ever supposed that she wanted to remember her life. She thought she had had mostly a happy, even an exuberant, life, and yet none of her esprit or her appreciation of human vicissitudes seemed to be reflected in her jottings.

It made what she was determined to undertake seem even more eccentric: Why spend months or years remembering a life if all it had consisted of were people who couldn't dance or didn't know how to cook fish or woodwind sections that weren't up to snuff?

Tired of thinking about it, or of preparing to think about it, Aurora opened the drawer where she kept her little note from Jerry and her one photograph of him, a snapshot she had taken herself, of him sitting on his back step in a bathrobe, looking like a large, sleepy, slightly sulky child.

The little picture and the short note said more to her of her life—or, at least, touched her more—than all the memorabilia she had unpacked and arranged.

What the picture and the note made her feel was that it hadn't after all been so wrong, her pursuit of Jerry. He had been, though a strange man, also a nice man. Better still, it had not been desultory—not from her side at least—and so many last loves *were* desultory, as she felt hers might have been had she had it with Pascal, or one of the Petrakis brothers.

At least her last real love had not been desultory. She had the feeling that one of the sadnesses of Jerry Bruckner's was that *all* his loves were, in a manner, desultory. Probably he had simply been one of those passive men who accept all women, each in her turn, much as he might accept the weather.

Then, out of nowhere, while she was thinking about Jerry —how comforting it had been that he had thought enough of her to write her the note—she remembered Hector Scott and the pointless quarrel they had had just before he keeled over in the booth at the Pig Stand. With the memory came a wave of weeping—there seemed to be no staying steady, in life, not really. Feeling better about Jerry led to feeling worse about her old soldier, who, after all, had struggled loyally with her for many years.

"I'm feeling better about Jerry but I just cried my eyes out thinking about Hector," she said to Rosie when she was back in her kitchen, sipping tea.

"The General's dead, it don't do no good to feel bad about him and besides he didn't have a lot of mercy himself," Rosie said. "Why can't you help me with some of my problems instead of just worrying about old dead and gone boyfriends?"

"I don't know that I'm feeling *that* much better," Aurora said.

"Do you wish you hadn't done it?" Rosie asked—she had always been curious as to how Aurora justified sleeping with Jerry.

"No, I'm proud that I did it," Aurora said. "It took true courage, and I don't think I've done too many things that took true courage."

She swirled her finger in the tea and licked it, a new, strange unladylike habit she had acquired.

"For a while I was wishing I hadn't done it because it hurt so much," she admitted. "But now I'm glad I did it, even if it does hurt."

"Yeah, but the big question is, will I be happy if I marry Arthur Cotton?" Rosie said. "Or, if I do marry him, will I wish I hadn't done it for the rest of my life?"

"If only Willie would have called, just once, it would never have come to this—at least I don't think it would have," she added.

"Do you really still think of Willie as much as you did?" Aurora asked.

"Every night—every single one, whether I'm with Arthur or not," Rosie admitted. "I was in love with Willie, only I didn't realize it until it was too late."

"I doubt he realized how deep it cut, either," Aurora said. "Willie was not greatly perceptive."

"He was worse than that, he was just plain dumb," Rosie said. "But it didn't matter. Something about Willie touched me . . . do you know what I mean?"

Aurora thought of the boyish Jerry Bruckner, sitting on his back step in his bathrobe.

"Yes, dear, I know what you mean," she said.

19

Tommy's personal rule for surviving prison life was never to voice an opinion—any opinion, on any topic. Prison society was like a lake of kerosene, from whose surface fumes of rage and hatred rose continuously. An opinion that happened to strike someone wrong, happened to nudge some grudge or prick some prejudice, could ignite the fumes and leave one wrapped in flames.

Tommy's problem, as he well knew, was that he was not quite the perfect master of his own disdain. Certain levels of repulsiveness or stupidity were apt now and again to tip him into sarcasm, or at least, cool rebuttal. Besides, though he didn't much want to be human, he was, and he could not always resist voicing an opinion, nor could he easily conceal his total disdain for Mickey Cleburne, his cellmate Wilbur's new disciple.

Mickey was, in Tommy's view, the prototype of the Southern chain-saw massacre hulk—the word "hulk" could have been coined just for Mickey, a fact Tommy and Wilbur agreed on. Mickey was so far beyond mere redneck behavior, or even redneck beliefs, that the term could not accurately be applied to him. He was more the white trash swamp rat, size extra large. Besides being large, he was never clean, had bad breath and bad acne, and was an obsessive cracker of his own knuckles, across all ten of which he had Confederate flags tattooed.

Mickey Cleburne hated almost everything and almost everybody. He hated Tommy immediately because Tommy was educated, but even if he hadn't been educated, he would have hated him because he was from the city. Mickey hated all people from the city, and was not much more tolerant of people from the small towns. The only good thing about small towns in his view was that they contained all-night convenience stores. Mickey liked to rob such stores; he also liked to hold his shotgun under the chins of the terrified clerks for a minute or two just to see them quiver, before heading back into the great piney woods and the safety of the swamps, where he could hunt alligators and coons. Before he discovered the pleasures of robbing small-town convenience stores he had made a living catching poisonous snakes—he would snare fifty or sixty cottonmouths or swamp rattlers, drop them in a barrel he kept in his pickup, and sell them to a laboratory in Lufkin, Texas.

The tattoos of the Confederate flags had been acquired on a trip to Texarkana—they had all still been bleeding a little when Mickey lost it, went on a hate rampage, and shot five people in one 7-Eleven, all because the young woman who was clerking that night asked to see his driver's license when he walked up with a six-pack. None of the five people died, but Mickey Cleburne soon found himself in a place filled with all the kinds of people he hated most, black people and brown people being at the top of the list. In such a place it was not necessarily an advantage to have ten Confederate flags tattooed across one's hands, but Mickey made no attempt to conceal his tattoos. The thing he would have been most proud of was to die for the South. Mickey could read only a few words, but he could listen, and the song he took as his battle hymn was Hank Williams Jr.'s "The South Shall Rise Again."

Mickey Cleburne believed every word of that song and was ready to fight for its sentiments. The reason he had become a disciple of Wilbur's, overlooking the fact that Wilbur was a town person and also an educated person, was that Wilbur, too, loved the South, and knew its glorious history. Wilbur was a Civil War buff, and had been, a little earlier in his life, a collector of medals. He liked to think of himself as the prison's leading authority on Civil War battles, and he could spend hours describing to Mickey the glorious feats of all the dashing Civil War heroes, Forrest and Beauregard, Mosby and Jackson. Tommy, who listened with a more critical ear than Mickey Cleburne, suspected that Wilbur was making most of it up, but he kept his suspicions to himself and tried not to look at Mickey at all when Wilbur was doing one of his Civil War spiels. He knew Mickey hated him. In Mickey's bloodshot eyes was the hatred of the despised—the not-good-enough southern swamper, more scorned even than Negroes in the small towns strung around the wetlands of the South.

Tommy didn't feel that he needed to analyze Mickey's hatred too closely. He had heard that a mad dog wouldn't attack if you didn't make eye contact with it, and he adopted the same principle toward Mickey. He didn't look him in the eye. If Mickey wanted to worship Wilbur because Wilbur could bullshit about Civil War battles, that was fine. Tommy just avoided wanting to strike the match that might ignite the kerosene fumes of Mickey's hatred.

But Tommy slipped. One day in the exercise yard Mickey was talking about his dream—he only had one, and Tommy and Wilbur had heard about it often. It was to escape from the prison, make his way through the woods to Idaho, and become a humble private in the army of the Aryan Nation.

"That's noble," Wilbur said. "You've got the right stuff, Mick. There's one problem with your plan, though."

"What?" Mickey asked.

"You're gonna run out of woods long before you reach Idaho," Wilbur said. "Isn't that true, Tommy?"

"That's true," Tommy said.

"Lots of wide-open spaces out west," Wilbur said. "Still, maybe you can hitchhike. If you could hook up with the right trucker, he might take you all the way. Some truckers are pretty sympathetic to the Aryan Nation."

Mickey thought that over. He had never been out of East Texas—a world without trees was beyond his ken. But if he had to travel through a treeless world in order to enlist in the army of the Aryan Nation and help the South to rise again, he was willing.

"I could steal a pickup," he said. He knew he didn't want to hitchhike. He had tried hitchhiking several times when one of his old cars broke down, but it hadn't worked. People just ignored him. In one case, two of his own brothers passed him without even looking at him. If he tried to hitchhike to the Aryan Nation, it was possible he would never get there. His new plan, then, was to steal a pickup from somebody's driveway and to drive all night until he reached Idaho.

"They might want you for a suicide soldier," Wilbur said, looking at Mickey. He liked to test big Mick's devotion to the Southland—the only thing he had any devotion to.

"I've never heard of the Aryan Nation having suicide soldiers," Tommy commented. He didn't really want to be in the conversation, but Mickey Cleburne was staring at him sullenly anyway, and he didn't feel it was safe to be too conspicuously out of it, either.

"No, but they need a few," Wilbur said. "They could wire Mick up with a little plastique and he could probably take out the whole Supreme Court, if he was willing. It was the Supreme Court that destroyed the South, when they started letting niggers into white folks' schools," Wilbur reminded them. He often treated Mickey to short civics lessons, letting him know what institutions had contributed most to the South's decline.

Mickey hadn't been thinking about blowing himself up in order to destroy the Supreme Court—what he had in mind was doing some shooting first. He hoped to kill some blacks or, failing that, some gooks or Mexicans. Just a few days before, a white man had lost it in some town in California and fired his machine gun into a schoolyard filled with children, killing several. Most of the dead children were Asian, which made Mickey think maybe the Aryan Nation had been behind the massacre. He had been told by several inmates that in California gooks were as thick as niggers were in the South —maybe the Aryan Nation had had a few gook children massacred in order to give the gooks warning that soon they would all have to leave America or die.

"I'd plan on killin' niggers, mostly," Mickey said, thinking ahead to his life after prison. "Hangin' them's right—it's what they deserve. I'd like to see every nigger in the world hung up on a tree with their tongues hanging out."

"Wow, that's a vision," Wilbur said. "After niggers, who would you kill? Mexicans or gooks?"

"Goddamn yellow gooks," Mickey said. He had seen very few gooks in real life, but on TV they looked as bad to him as niggers.

"You better be careful if you go after Asians," Tommy said. Mickey just looked at him.

"Why's that?" Wilbur asked.

"Because they're smarter than us, that's why," Tommy said.

He knew instantly that he shouldn't have said it, but he was too disgusted with Wilbur to hold back. Wilbur liked having Mickey for a disciple; he liked dazzling him with his Civil War stories and he enjoyed helping him build fantasies about all the killing he would get to do once he had become a foot soldier in the Aryan Nation. It was all a tease on Wilbur's part—Tommy couldn't resist taking a little cool cut at it.

"Who invented kung fu? Not us," he added as a clincher. "One good Ninja could take out half the tough guys in this prison, and all the guards, too."

"Oh, the guards, sure," Wilbur agreed. "Mickey could probably take out the guards—he wouldn't need a Ninja."

"Why do you want to get him worked up?" Tommy asked Wilbur in their cell that night. "He'll never get near Idaho. He's too dumb. I don't even think the Aryan Nation would have him."

"He's big, dumb, and ugly, all right," Wilbur agreed. "You shouldn't have said that about Asians being smarter than us, though. Mickey doesn't like to think that a yellow gook could be smarter than a white Southern American."

"Too bad," Tommy said. "Asians are smarter than us. Look at the math stats."

Wilbur just looked at him and smiled. "Math stats don't cut much ice with big Mickey," he said.

Tommy decided he had indeed been incautious. Mickey Cleburne started watching him, saying nothing, just watching him, if they happened to be in the exercise yard or taking their meals. His worship of Wilbur didn't diminish, either. He still hung out with Wilbur in the exercise yard, he still took his meals with Wilbur, he still listened silently as Wilbur spun stories about the great Southern cavalrymen or the great Southern victories.

There was one moment when Tommy thought maybe big Mickey was going to be distracted by a more worthy target than himself. Wilbur was giving one of his raps about the South ascending when Dog, the black man in the next cell, who didn't like Wilbur at all, and had such contempt for Mickey that he wouldn't even look at him, stopped as he was passing and gave Wilbur a little thump on his skull, just with a knuckle—the kind of little thump an experienced farmer gives a watermelon, to see if it is ripe.

"You talk all that shit you want to, motherfucker," Dog said. "The South's gonna rise again all right, but you ain't gonna get to see it, because all you white motherfuckers are gonna be dead. Gonna be a *black* South that rises this time."

With that he walked on. Wilbur was so scared he was shaking. Wilbur might be arrogant when he was with whites, but he wasn't too arrogant to be scared—he knew he had an enemy, and the enemy lived next door.

"That son of a bitch needs to be hung up from a tree till his goddamn black tongue falls out of his head," Mickey said.

Neither Wilbur nor Tommy said anything.

For a few days Tommy watched Mickey to see if he was going to make some effort to kill Dog. It seemed to him that Mickey might try it. After all, Dog had belittled his chief, the priest of his religion. Another Hank Williams Jr. song Mickey liked was called "A Country Boy Can Survive." It praised the general competence and resourcefulness of country boys —they could skin deer, run trotlines, defend themselves against city dudes with switchblades. Tommy thought Mickey might try to demonstrate his country-boy competence and resourcefulness by trying to kill Dog, but this didn't happen. He let Dog strictly alone and continued to stare at Tommy out of his pale, swamp-water eyes.

"I wish you'd call off your pit bull," Tommy told Wilbur one night. "All that staring's beginning to bug me."

"Well, why don't you just have a word with him about it, then?" Wilbur said.

"Because it would just make it worse," Tommy said. "He only minds you—the Grand Dragon of the South."

Wilbur smiled his self-satisfied smile. "I like that," he said. "The Grand Dragon of the South. It rolls off the tongue nicely. Maybe I'll join the Klan when I get out of here. I bet I could rise rapidly through the ranks of the Klan."

"I'm sure you could," Tommy said. "Just start practicing by telling your disciple to keep his dumb eyes to himself."

"Why don't you just tell him that you didn't really mean that gooks are smarter than us?" Wilbur asked. "Tell him you were just teasing. He might believe you."

"They are smarter than us," Tommy said.

"I'm glad you're ready to die for your beliefs," Wilbur said, yawning.

For the next few days Tommy decided to counterattack, at least in the form of eye contact. Instead of avoiding Mickey's eyes, he started staring at Mickey before Mickey could stare at him. When their eyes locked Tommy stared right into Mickey's eyes until Mickey finally turned his head and shuffled off.

After that, Tommy felt a little better. He knew Mickey still hated him, but he thought he might have backed off a little. Mickey stopped spending quite so much time with Wilbur. He stopped talking about his plan for joining the Aryan Nation. He was still a menace, Tommy knew, but at least he was a slow menace. In group situations Tommy knew he had to remember to keep Mickey in sight—keep him in front of him. As long as Mickey was in front of him Tommy felt sure he could out-maneuver him if he attacked. He even began to exercise a little in preparation. In high school he had had a martial arts phase; he lost interest before he could become a black belt, but he had worked up to yellow belt. He began to do judo exercises in his cell.

Wilbur did no exercises. If he even shot a basketball twice he was out of breath. When Tommy did his exercises, Wilbur watched from his bunk, looking bored.

"Gook exercises won't save you when big Mickey comes," he said.

"That's your opinion," Tommy said. "They might save me. Just because your fat disciple knows how to run a trotline doesn't mean he can just walk up and strangle me."

"You put too much faith in math scores, asshole," Wilbur said.

Tommy kept on exercising. For a while he had accepted prison, and had even liked it. It was a place where he could withdraw, be invisible, and think his thoughts. Dealing with the discomfort and the regimentation took discipline, but then he rather liked that.

What was beginning to weigh on him was the company. He was tired of having to deal with spoiled brats like Wilbur or dangerous troglodytes such as Mickey Cleburne—and Mickey was not exactly the only troglodyte in the prison, either.

Now and then Tommy began to have thoughts of getting out. It wouldn't be real soon—he wasn't eligible for parole for nearly two more years—but it wasn't hopelessly distant, either. Time did pass. One day by accident he had helped one of the prison technicians fix a computer. Tommy had been a precocious hacker—he hadn't really kept up too energetically, but it turned out that he had more of a touch with computers than anyone else in the prison. Lately he had been getting asked to unsnarl some program or restart some computer on an average of once a week. Getting Tommy to do it was better than paying a computer man to come all the way from Houston—and Tommy was quicker than most of computer repairmen anyway. He found he liked it when the prison people came and got him to help with some problem. It was good being back with computers. He didn't tell Teddy what he was doing, but he began to think that maybe he and Teddy ought to do something with computers when he got out. They could invent computer games or something, maybe start some little business.

As Tommy began to let himself fantasize a future out of prison, he also began to let his attention slip a little. More than once he felt a moment of panic when he was outside in the exercise yard and realized that he had lost sight of Mickey. It happened in the dining hall, too. Tommy knew he had to stop drifting off that way, in his mind; the whole point of all his discipline and his exercising was to equip himself to be constantly alert. Even if he only slipped once a week for five minutes or so, it was still not good. He was in prison, and he had an enemy, and he had to make remembering that one fact his first priority. At night, when he was safely locked away from Mickey, he could let his new interest in the future blossom a little.

A moment or two, maybe only a second or two, before the pain came and tore a scream out of him, Tommy sensed that he had slipped again. He was in the exercise yard, bouncing a basketball—they had just had a little game. Though short, Tommy was not a bad basketball player—he had a turnaway jumper that was pretty effective. He was just about to whirl and shoot it, just practicing, when he happened to notice that the guys near him were all looking away. There had been a shift in density that he hadn't picked up on quickly enough. He had been in the midst of a crowd, but now he wasn't. The other guys were there, but they weren't as close to him as they had been—they were now at a little remove, and they were all looking away. Too much space had spread around him.

Quickly Tommy tried to locate Mickey Cleburne, but before he could even turn his head to scan the prison yard the pain struck and he began to scream. It was searing pain, as if a large hot needle were being jabbed, jabbed, jabbed into his spine. He fell, trying to get away from it. As he fell he tried to hold onto the basketball, but it rolled away. Then he flopped over, trying to get away from the pain, and saw Mickey Cleburne looking down at him.

"Ol' gator got a sharp tooth," Mickey said, as he turned away.

Even as he lay hurting, and as the first guard tentatively moved toward him, Tommy's main feeling was one of surprise.

What surprised him was that the swamp boy Mickey Cleburne could put something that well.

20

Aurora and Rosie were in the prison hospital for almost nine hours, pacing and sitting, but the news, when it finally came, was that Tommy would live. They had failed to locate Teddy and Jane: it turned out that they had taken Bump to the beach that day. Rosie's wedding—she had finally bitten the bullet, she was marrying Arthur Cotton—was taking place the very next day. There were a million things to do, but Rosie absolutely would not hear of Aurora going to the prison alone.

"That's Emma's boy that's hurt," Rosie said. "I feel like he's my kid, too."

Mickey Cleburne had stabbed Tommy with a five-inch piece of wire that he had found somewhere, probably only that day. He had twisted a loop for his finger to fit into, and still had more than enough wire left for an effective skewer. He stabbed Tommy six times. One lung and one kidney were punctured, and the spleen had been nicked.

Still, when they walked out of the prison into the muggy night, both women felt some relief—a lightness, really. They had been allowed, for a moment, to stand by Tommy's bed in the prison hospital and he had smiled at them. It was a

580

brief, wan smile, but it brightened them both like a sunrise. They had both been afraid that Tommy, if he looked at them at all, would look at them hostilely or indifferently, as he had so many times.

But Tommy hadn't been hostile—he had tried to smile. Rosie was so moved that she became weak. Aurora had driven them to the prison, and Rosie had had every intention of driving them home, but the weakness undid her.

"You'll have to drive back, hon," she told Aurora. "I might get out there on the highway and faint."

"I can't remember when I've seen Tommy look that welcoming," Aurora said. "I suppose we'd better not get our hopes up too high, though. He was pretty sedated. Next time we come he might be the other way again."

"It don't hurt to hope a little, though," Rosie said. The freeway south through the pines was almost empty, though now and then a truck or two purred smoothly past them.

"I've always tried to be hopeful," Aurora said, feeling quite drained. "I've certainly been far more hopeful than you over the years. I've got slapped down a lot, though, particularly by the children."

"Kid's don't live for nobody's hopes but their own," Rosie reminded her. "None of mine ever cared about what I hoped. You think this marriage I'm about to do is a big mistake, don't you?"

Aurora was trying to go around a small pickup. The pickup had appeared to be going rather slow, but now that she had committed herself to passing it, it seemed to have increased its speed. The Cadillac managed to pull even with it, but that seemed to be the best it could do. Efforts to edge ahead were unavailing, yet she didn't feel like giving up and slipping behind again. It was a very annoying pickup; also, somewhere behind, she felt sure that large trucks were massing, getting ready to honk at her if she didn't get out of the fast lane. On the whole, it was not a moment in which she wished to be bullied yet again into a discussion of Rosie's chances of finding happiness across the street as the wife of Arthur Cotton.

"Rosie, I'm passing a car, or rather, a pickup," Aurora said. "I've told you repeatedly that I take no position on this marriage. I scarcely know Arthur Cotton. I've heard he's a man of probity—for all I know he may make you very happy. What else can I be expected to say?"

Rosie sighed. "I ain't seen much of this probity, if it means what I think it means," she said. "I wish I knew if I was doing the right thing. It ain't like you not to tell me what you really think, either—but you ain't telling me what you really think. Not what you *really* think."

"You know something? I stopped *really* thinking several months ago," Aurora said. "I got old or something—I don't know. But you might as well not ask for real thinking from me, because I can't do it anymore. When I try, I get a headache, or else I drift. Half the time we were in the waiting room I wasn't even thinking about Tommy. I've always liked to try and count for something, but I don't know if I do count for anything now. Do you know what I mean?"

"No, but let's go to the Pig Stand, if we ever get around this pickup," Rosie said. "If I don't get something in my stomach pretty soon I think I might faint from all this worrying."

The lights of the Pig Stand parking lot were orange in the Houston mist. Dawn was not far away. Despite the late hour, two men in baseball uniforms were lazily tossing a softball back and forth to one another under the orange lights.

"Do you think there's something wrong with those men?" Aurora asked, watching them toss the softball. "Surely this is not a normal hour for baseball."

"Let 'em alone, they're just playing catch and it's a free country," Rosie said.

Inside, they were served immediately but watched nervously by the waitresses at the Pig Stand. Since Hector Scott had died in the number six booth, the easy camaraderie Aurora and Rosie had once had with the waitresses hadn't been quite so easy. The same words were said, the same questions asked, the same orders given, and the same food served, but something had changed.

"I think they expect somebody to die every time we come

in now," Aurora observed, watching the waitresses huddle as far away from them as possible. "I think it's a little unfair. After all, Hector is the only person who's died in all the years we've been coming here. I wouldn't have thought they'd hold it against us this long."

As they were paying, two of the waitresses and the elderly cashier congratulated Rosie on her upcoming wedding.

"You should of let us cater your reception," Marge, the elderly cashier, said reproachfully. "We cater receptions left and right and we do a bang-up good job, too. I usually serve the punch."

"It's just a small service," Rosie said, embarrassed by the attention.

"That was something of a lie," Aurora told her in the parking lot. The two men were no longer pitching the softball—the parking lot was empty, except for themselves and the gentle mist.

"Your whole family's coming, which alone means that it won't be a small wedding," Aurora added. "I admit that the groom would probably have been rather taken aback at the thought of the Pig Stand catering the reception, but I personally don't think it would have been such a bad idea. A few pig sandwiches and a lot of liquor might loosen Arthur and his set up a little—nothing I've tried seems to."

She had given two dinners for Rosie and Arthur, and neither had been a success. After each of them, Rosie had cried for a long time and kept Aurora up half the night worrying the question of whether the right thing or the wrong thing was being done. Aurora had tried inviting the Petrakis brothers, she'd tried inviting Pascal, and she had made Teddy and Jane come to both dinners, but for once—or, rather, for twice—her touch failed her and nothing clicked.

"Them waitresses all think I'm a silly old fool, I can see it in their eyes," Rosie said.

"Nonsense, I saw no sign of that, and I saw their eyes," Aurora said. "They've never met the groom—how would they know whether you're making a mistake or not? You don't even know yourself."

"I've been a waitress, you know," Rosie reminded her. "I

know how waitresses think. If they saw Arthur they'd think I drug his little fat body into bed because he's rich. Waitresses hate to see an old country girl like me get money all of a sudden. They all get to wondering why it never happened to them."

"Rosie, please try a little positive thinking," Aurora urged, starting her car. "You don't have to think positively forever —just try it as an exercise for twenty-four hours or so. If necessary, pretend you're me, as I once was. Sing an aria in the shower. You'll feel better, we'll get through the day, and for all you know you may be happy as a lark in your new status as my neighbor, rather than my maid."

"That's another thing that's gnawing at me," Rosie informed her, looking anything but positive. "Who are you gonna get to clean? You said you'd start looking for somebody, but here it is my wedding day and you haven't got nobody yet."

"Actually, I have a lead on a suitable Guatemalan," Aurora informed her blithely. It was a lie. What she had been concealing from Rosie was her recently taken decision to do her own housework, once Rosie married. Lately she had begun to feel that her memory project was making her too sedentary —all she did was sit in her garage, drink tea, and think about her life. Sometimes it was interesting to think about her life, but other times it wasn't. Lately she had begun to think more often about the lives of others, Jerry for one, Rosie for another, than about her own life. Rosie's continuing and profound anxiety about her upcoming marriage touched her, even though from moment to moment it might irritate her. She was beginning to wonder a little what it might feel like to be Rosie, and had concluded secretly that one way to find out might be to do her own housework. If she found she didn't like being Rosie she *could* always seek the suitable Guatemalan.

Also she had become curious about being alone—in her own house, alone. One of the few things that struck her forcibly, just reading through her own desk diaries, was how little of her life had been spent alone. Rosie herself had been in her presence virtually every day for forty-two years; that in itself said something. Hector Scott, as she remembered him, had scarcely seemed to leave the house during the years they lived together, and Rudyard had not been much better. It occurred to her that she had reached her eighth decade without having experienced solitude to any depth. She had always supposed it wouldn't suit her at all, yet she had never tried it, not really, not long enough to find out. Now, at last, through the advent of Arthur Cotton, she *could* try it. Far from fearing it, she had begun to suspect that she might rather like it.

"Nobody knows how to clean a house right no more—I don't care if they're from Guatemala or where," Rosie said firmly, as they pulled into their street. She looked out the window at Arthur Cotton's house, the house she would be moving into as a wife that very day, and felt sad, what her mother called "way down deep sad." Why had she done it? Why had she said yes when she didn't feel yes—not a real yes—not really?

"I'm going to be coming over every day, inspecting," she said, clinging in her sadness to the one thing she felt sure she knew, which was how to tell a house that had been cleaned properly from one that hadn't.

"You can inspect till you're blue in the face," Aurora assured her. "Anything you want to do in my house, do it. Just don't tell Arthur you're moonlighting, and I expect things will be fine.

"By the way," she added, picking up an old question left hanging some while back in the conversation, "what *do* you think probity means?"

Rosie looked embarrassed. "I shouldn't have said it," she said. "I don't have no idea what it means, really. I guess I could look it up in a dictionary, if I had a dictionary."

Aurora swung into the driveway, but stopped the car well short of the garage. Three squirrels sat looking at them from the center of her yard.

Aurora looked at Rosie, waiting.

"I thought it had to do with sex—that's what it sounds

like," Rosie admitted. "But I can't tell if Arthur's got much of it, because we still ain't done it yet."

"I see," Aurora said. "He's still nervous?"

"He's still nervous," Rosie confirmed.

"Good lord," Aurora said. "That man's had plenty of time to get it up. What do you think's the matter?"

"Well, he's out of practice, for one thing," Rosie said. "He didn't sleep with Eureka the last fourteen years before she died. That makes nearly fifteen years with no practice, counting all this time we've been courtin'."

"Good lord," Aurora said again. "No wonder you're having difficulty thinking positively about this union. You have to try, though. Maybe once you get him off in Cozumel he'll perk up."

Rosie and Arthur had decided to honeymoon in Cozumel rather than Paris, because Rosie had become enraptured by a poster she saw at the travel agency.

"Maybe, but what if it don't happen there either?" Rosie asked.

"Cozumel's pretty romantic," Aurora said, watching the three squirrels. "Surely Cozumel won't fail you."

"Yeah, but what if it fails me?" Rosie asked. "What do I do then? What if all he knows how to do is spend money? How many fur coats can you wear in a climate like this?"

"Not many," Aurora admitted. "Probably we should have talked of this sooner. I suppose I assumed there had been progress recently. I thought perhaps the progress was what prompted you to say yes."

"No, I just broke down," Rosie said. "He's sweet to me, you know. I finally just broke down."

Then, overcome by her sorrows, the deep-down ones and the smaller ones too, Rosie began to cry. At first she was merely crying gently—then she began to sob, deeply and more deeply. For a time Aurora thought it might be a minor cry, a wedding-day cry, but she soon realized it was going to be a major release. She scooted across the seat and put her arms around Rosie, her maid, her oldest friend, and let her cry out her worries and her fears. The squirrels on her lawn had stopped watching—they were going about their business. Rosie's thin chest heaved—she was very upset. Aurora held her and waited as the sun lifted its bright edge above the houses and touched the green lawns with light.

IV

Rosie's Problem

1

Four months and a day after Rosie Dunlup married Arthur Cotton she was diagnosed as having cancer of the pancreas. She developed a pain in exercise class, and the pain got worse—within two weeks she was having trouble with exercises that she had excelled at for years.

Patsy Carpenter insisted that she go to the Medical Center and have herself looked at.

"I don't want to, I've never been in a hospital other than to have my kids," Rosie said. "I'm superstitious about hospitals. Last time I was inside one was when Royce got disemboweled."

"Rosie, come on," Patsy said. "It's probably just something minor. Let's just go check."

"If I do, don't tell Aurora," Rosie said—the pain was actually pretty bad. "She ain't even got a housekeeper yet, that place is a mess."

"Oh, it is not," Patsy said. "For a woman who's scarcely lifted a finger her whole life other than to crook one at a man, I think she's doing pretty well being her own maid."

"I don't, there's.dust behind every one of them curtains," Rosie insisted.

But she went to the hospital, to be told that the cancer in her pancreas was well advanced and that there was really little to be done.

"Unfortunately, we can't transplant the pancreas," the young doctor said. "They're doing some experimental work in Canada on pancreatic cancers—it involves icing you down. If you want to try that, we'll help set it up."

"I told you I was superstitious," Rosie reminded Patsy, as Patsy drove her home. "If I'd never gone and found out, then I wouldn't know, and maybe it would just go away."

"A malignancy usually doesn't go away," Patsy said. "You go away."

"They say attitude makes a lot of difference," Rosie said. "Maybe I could try eating the right foods and stuff."

"I think you should go to Canada and give this new treatment a try," Patsy said. "It might just click with your metabolism or something. You might get the cancer stopped for a while. I'd try it, if it was me," she added. In deference to Rosie's condition she was driving more carefully than was her custom.

Rosie looked down at her expensive wedding ring and the even more expensive bracelet Arthur had given her right after their honeymoon. Neither looked right on her—neither ever would. She had the impulse to take them both off and throw them out the window, but she didn't. It would break Arthur's heart, and Arthur, after all, was sweet. Now, if what the doctor said was true, Arthur was going to lose her anyway, probably without ever having quite had her. Cozumel hadn't worked either—her marriage had only been sort of slightly consummated, once, and that once was, from her point of view, so brief and indefinite that she wasn't quite sure that it counted as a consummation. Arthur was constantly apologizing for his impotence, and now she had to go home and tell him she had cancer. "I wish I'd died already, then at least I wouldn't have to tell Arthur about this."

"Rosie, don't talk that way," Patsy said.

"Why not?" Rosie asked. "It's how I feel."

2

"Well, I knew something was wrong," Aurora said, later that day, when she had been given the news.

"Why, do I look like I'm dying, or what?" Rosie asked. It was on the tip of her tongue to ask Aurora if she could move back in. Even if it did break Arthur's heart, it was what she really wanted to do.

"You don't look like you're dying, but you haven't been bullying me lately," Aurora said. "For forty-two years you've bullied me virtually every day, but recently you stopped. I knew it meant trouble—I just didn't know it meant this."

"You don't take time to clean behind the curtains, but it's your life. I figured I'd try to let up," Rosie said. "You said you'd get a Guatemalan lady, but you didn't."

"No, but I still can if I find that I'm faltering seriously," Aurora said. "I just wanted to try it myself for a bit. Cleaning house gives me something to do."

"You got the out-of-sight, out-of-mind attitude, though," Rosie said. "You was born with it and you've still got it. If you don't want to see no dust, you just pretend that it isn't there. That'll always catch up with you, sooner or later."

"Let it catch up with me," Aurora said. "Now we have to deal with you and your problem, which is far more serious than a little dust behind my curtains."

Rosie shrugged. "It's got me—there ain't much I can do," she said.

"What does your new husband think?" Aurora asked.

"He wants me to have chemo and radiation," Rosie said. "He says they got real good hospitals here, which I guess they do."

"What about Canada and the new treatment the doctor

593

mentioned?" Aurora asked. "I'll go with you, if you want to try it. Arthur can come too, if he likes. We could leave tomorrow if you want to. It sounds as if speed might be of the essence."

"I ain't going to Canada, no way," Rosie said. "I don't know nobody up there and it's too far away, anyway. My kids would just get lost trying to visit.

"Thanks, hon," she said, looking at Aurora. "It's nice of you to offer to go with me."

"Of course I'll go with you," Aurora said. "What do you think I am?"

"Better in a crunch than Arthur, that's for sure," Rosie said. "That man's been crying constantly, ever since I told him."

"He just married you—I think he should be permitted some emotional display," Aurora said. "I've come to like him better than I thought I would, if it's any consolation."

Rosie shook her head. Unfortunately she herself had not come to like her new husband better than she thought she would. She didn't *dislike* him, either—it was just that, disappointingly, her affection had not really increased.

"He thinks it's because I ain't gettin' no sex that I got cancer," she told Aurora.

"How male," Aurora said.

"Yeah, ain't it?" Rosie said. "I told him if not getting any could cause it, half the world would be dead of cancer already, but he didn't listen."

"So, are you inclined to try the chemo and the radiation?" Aurora asked.

"I don't think so," Rosie said. In fact, she had not quite made up her mind on that score. "I think I'll just try eating the right foods and stuff."

"I'll cook you the right foods," Aurora assured her. "But it might be that you ought to try the right foods and a little chemo too."

"I'm thinking about it," Rosie said. "I guess right now it's pretty much all I'm thinking about."

"Sometimes I wish you'd married Theo," Aurora said. "Then we'd have a Greek around the house. A Greek might be rather convenient at a time like this."

"Theo was in love with you, not me," Rosie reminded her. "He just started looking at me that way because you broke his heart."

"It still might have worked, though," Aurora said. "You never know what will work until you try."

"You don't have to remind me of that, I just tried Arthur and he don't work," Rosie said. "Now I'm stuck and I got cancer to boot."

Later they drove over to the Acropolis Bar to see the Petrakis brothers. On the way they speculated on Vassily's frustrated courtship of Patsy Carpenter. There had been a flurry of dates. Then Patsy had gone to L.A. for several months. Vassily, as far as anyone knew, had not been invited to visit. But now Patsy was back in Houston and there had been more dates.

"Vas likes women with skinny legs," Theo explained, but the explanation did not entirely settle the question of whether Vassily and Patsy were, in all the usual respects, a couple.

At the bar Rosie immediately told the Petrakis brothers that she was dying.

"I thought I'd just get the bad news out of the way so we can have some fun," she said. "I wouldn't mind coming here and getting drunk every day for the rest of my life."

"That's the spirit," Aurora said. "I'll come with you. I'll also get drunk with you. Once we're drunk, Theo can drive us home."

"Why him? You don't like my driving?" Vassily asked. Aurora annoyed him. Theo also annoyed him. In fact, he and Theo had quarreled so much lately that they were thinking of selling the bar and going their separate ways. He himself was thinking of going to Nice—lots of French girls had skinny legs. He did not think, however, that it was the proper moment to inform the ladies that there might not always be an Acropolis Bar for them to get drunk in while Rosie died.

"Theo has a gentle spirit," Aurora said, looking Vassily in the eye. "I'm not sure I can say the same about you."

Theo had a hard time controlling his emotions. He had come to care for Rosie a lot. In the depths of his heart it might be Aurora that he coveted still, but Aurora was too much for him, and Rosie was such a nice woman. He would have married her anytime, but he didn't hold it against her that she had chosen to marry someone rich. He choked back his tears and persuaded her to dance with him a little.

"I guess we're all just passing through," he said.

"That's right," Rosie said. "I just didn't expect to get to the back door quite to soon."

3

Since Arthur pleaded so, Rosie tried chemotherapy and radiation. They slowed the cancer down some, but not much—they slowed Rosie down a great deal more. Aurora crossed the street every day—indeed, several times every day—bringing her the right foods. Often she stayed most of the day and much of the night. Patsy visited, the Petrakis brothers visited, Pascal visited, Rosie's children and grandchildren visited, but Rosie was only at peace when Aurora was there. Arthur and Aurora between them consumed most of the right foods.

After two weeks, Arthur Cotton crossed the street one morning while Aurora was out watering her flowers. He looked very tired, and had such difficulty lifting his feet that he stumbled over the curb. Even sitting in her kitchen, drinking the tea Aurora made for him, Arthur looked like a man who was tottering; his eyes were red and sad.

"She doesn't want to die in my house," Arthur said, looking at Aurora sadly. "She wants to come home."

"I've been wondering if that mightn't be best," Aurora said.

"I'm crazy about her but I shouldn't have married her," Arthur said. "We should have just gone on being neighbors —having our little talks on the lawn. Those were our best times, really."

"Yes, the salad's frequently better than the meal," Aurora told him. "You didn't give her cancer, though, and you mustn't bog yourself down with useless regrets. Let's just go get Rosie and bring her home."

"Can I visit a lot?" Arthur asked. He looked, if possible, more bleak than he had looked when he arrived.

"You're her husband, Arthur—you can visit as much as you like," Aurora said.

4

Aurora's bedroom was the nicest, airiest, brightest, most cheerful room in her house. That afternoon she installed Rosie in it, moving herself, for sleeping purposes, to the little room down the hall that had once been Emma's.

If Rosie moved at all, in the course of the day, it was usually just from Aurora's bed to Aurora's window nook, where she sat propped amid the huge, fluffy pillows that Aurora loved, and that she herself had kept cleanly pillowcased for so many years. She could look out the window at the sunny lawn and the flowers; she could look across the street to Arthur's house, or watch him as he trudged across the street and along the sidewalk, five or six times a day, to pay her the brief visits that he seemed to feel were all that he should be permitted.

"Arthur's aged," Rosie commented, watching him trudge back along the sidewalk and across the street after one such visit.

"Well, his beloved wife is sick," Aurora said. "That'll do it."

"I feel guilty thinking about him being lonely over there in that empty house," Rosie said. "It ain't cozy, like our house. Eureka had it decorated sort of too formal, you know."

"Eureka herself never struck me as being particularly cozy," Aurora said. "She was always rather stiff."

"Poor Arthur, his whole life has been like that—sort of formal," Rosie said. "I think that's why he can't do it."

"Could be," Aurora said.

5

In the next months Aurora worked tirelessly—keeping the house clean, keeping the meals cooked, keeping the bed changed and the linen absolutely fresh. Rosie sat propped up in the clean bed or in the airy window nook and watched. When she was feeling well enough to be awed, she was awed. Once in a while she tottered around, inspecting, and was stunned to find that there was no longer a speck of dust to be found behind the curtains, or anywhere else.

"It's clean," she said, in surprise. "It's really clean."

"I've had more than forty years in which to study the work

of a master," Aurora said. "I should hope I've learned a little something."

Back in bed, Rosie thought about all the things she herself hadn't learned, and became sad. Aurora saw that she was sad and tried to sing to her, but Rosie remained sad through several songs.

"I never learned nothing," she said. "I never learned how to live and now I don't know how to die. It's awful to live your whole life and stay as ignorant as I am."

Aurora sat down on the bed with her and took her hand.

"It may be that you were deeper than you were smart," she said. "I've had the opposite misfortune, myself. I've always been smarter than I am deep."

"I don't see what's deep about marrying two people like Royce and Arthur," Rosie said. "Now that I'm sitting here looking back on it, it just seems plain stupid to me."

"I'm not sure that the smart-deep equation applies to mating," Aurora said. "Mating is something else. In my experience it almost never adds up, but probably one shouldn't try to add it up. It's something else."

"Whatever it is, I wasn't no good at it," Rosie said.

6

In the early fall, Melanie's pilot was on TV. Rosie watched ten minutes of it and burst into tears. There it was, for all to see: she had been a clown, just one more crazy maid who acted weird and got in everybody's way.

Aurora, for once, didn't know what to say, and didn't say

anything. There was no point in telling a dying woman that the show was fiction. It was there, Rosie saw it, as far as she was concerned it was totally about her, and she believed that it was absolutely true: she had been a clown.

Though the pilot itself was a success, the sitcom failed to live up to it. After five episodes, it folded. Melanie came home to Houston to help her granny with Rosie, but it didn't work. Rosie loved Melanie, but her hurt feelings about the sitcom wouldn't go away. She couldn't help it—she made it clear that she only wanted Aurora to wait on her. After a week, Melanie, perplexed and in tears, went back to L.A. to look for another acting job. Aurora held her tongue—indeed, held it until Rosie couldn't stand it.

"I know I hurt her feelings," she said. "I don't know what's the matter with me. I know it was just a dumb TV show. I ought to get over it but I can't."

"If you can't, you can't," Aurora said.

7

Rosie became wakeful—she began to be afraid to go to sleep, for fear she'd die in the night. Aurora lay on the bed with her, holding her hand. They watched cable much of the night. When it began to grow light, Rosie would relax and go to sleep. Aurora would retreat to Hector's old chaise on her patio and nap a little.

Often, sitting in Aurora's window nook, amid a great pile of clean pillows, watching Aurora run the vacuum, or wash the windows, or mop the tiles in the bathroom, Rosie had a deep, sad urge to turn everything back and make it as it had been. She wanted to get up and take the mop or the vacuum cleaner or the Windex away from Aurora and do the work herself. It had all gotten backwards—Aurora ought to be sitting in the window nook, reading magazines or tormenting her boyfriends on the telephone, while she, Rosie Dunlup, one of Houston's premier maids, did the housework.

"Sometimes I just wish so that I could get up from here and have my old job back," Rosie said weakly, one morning.

"Well, honey, you can't," Aurora said, inspecting, with some pride, a clean windowpane.

"It don't seem right that you're doing everything and I'm doing nothing," Rosie said.

"It was the other way around for forty years, what's wrong with you having a rest?" Aurora asked incautiously.

"It's only because I'm dying, that's what's wrong with it," Rosie said.

"Okay, sorry, I concede the point," Aurora said sadly.

8

One by one, Rosie's children came, bringing their families. Bud, the oldest boy, a middle-aged man, ran a body shop in Abilene. Estelle, her oldest girl, had a beauty parlor in Navasota. The next girl, Jolene, was a nurse in Texarkana, and was married to a man who sold lawn statuary. Doak, the one who, to Aurora's eye, looked the most like Rosie, was in the well-service business in Wink, Texas. Annabelle, the most educated, worked in a pharmacy in Wichita Falls. Dotsie, the flighty one (as her mother described her) was with her fourth husband and was currently employed as a secretary at a high school in Beaumont. Little Buster, the last and most reckless, but also clearly the most prosperous, ran a small stock-car track outside Waxahachie.

The wives of the boys and the husbands of the girls were alike only in that they smoked a lot, were terrified of Aurora, and couldn't think of much to say to Rosie. The children of all the couples ran around Aurora's backyard, screaming. Whatever their ages, they seemed to converse in screams.

Aurora drew the blinds, but even so, most of the screams were audible. It was a relief to everyone when the visits ended, but particularly a relief to Rosie. Aurora had done a great deal of cooking, and Rosie's children, all of whom possessed serious appetites, had done a great deal of eating.

"Thanks for cooking for the kids," Rosie said, when the painful sequence of visits finally ended.

"Well, that's quite a brood you raised," Aurora said.

"My boys done better than my girls, don't you think?" Rosie asked.

"Yes, but then it's easier for boys to do better," Aurora said. "The world's set up for boys, after all."

"Now that they've come and gone I feel worse than ever," Rosie commented. "I raised them, but they come here and sit, and they're like strangers. They don't seem like my kids, you know what I mean?"

"Not exactly," Aurora admitted.

"They're like people I knew a long time ago, when I was young and healthy," Rosie said. "Now I'm old and sick, and they're grown up, and it's like we don't know one another, we're just pretending."

"You take a bleak view," Aurora said. "Your children are decent people. They seem to me to love you, even if they're not polished at expressing it. All seven of them drove away in tears, which indicated to me that they certainly think they know you and care about you. What more do you want?"

"I guess just something I used to have, or thought I had," Rosie said. What Aurora said chastened her a little. After all, her children had made long trips across great stretches of Texas, just to see her for a few hours. Perhaps Aurora was right. Perhaps she expected too much.

"They should have just waited and come for the funeral," she said. "It's a burden on them to have to come all this way twice."

"Rosie, you're being ridiculous," Aurora said. "Let your family be grieved in the way they need to be."

The visits had been very tiring. Rosie mainly dozed for the next few days. She hated to see the night come on, though. To cheer her up as much as possible, Aurora put one hundred and fifty-watt bulbs in all the lamps in the bedroom, doing her best to make the nights as bright as the days.

9

The one visitor Rosie really liked to see was Bump, although he was as wild as her own Little Buster had been when Little Buster was Bump's age. Despite the vigilance of Aurora, or Jane, or Teddy, or all of them at once, Bump always managed to elude his keepers at some point. He jumped on the bed or he ran into the bedside table and knocked over all of Rosie's medicine bottles. Once he crawled under the bed and refused to come out.

"I'm an ogre, I live under this bed," he told his Big Granny, when she demanded that he come out.

It made Rosie giggle that a tiny little boy could say a word like ogre.

"He reminds me a lot of Emma," she told Aurora. "Emma was full of mischief when she was that age."

"Yes, I could never quite manage Emma," Aurora said. "If I hadn't had your help I'm sure I would have done worse than I did."

"I guess kids are what it's all about," Rosie said one day, watching Bump, who had captured a spoon and was using it to try to pry open one of the window screens.

"I want to let the birds in," he said, when told to stop. "The birds want to come in and see Rosie."

"Well, they're among the many things it's all about," Aurora said, in response to Rosie's remark.

Then, as Rosie grew more fragile—she could not get up now without assistance—Jane and Teddy grew worried that Bump would get out of control and injure her in some way. They stopped bringing him for a week, but Rosie missed him and protested.

"I'm dying, what can he do?" she said. "I need to get this over with—Aurora's losing too much weight. About the only thing I got left that's any fun is seeing Bump. It's good for an old dying person to see a young person that don't have nothing on his mind but enjoying life."

"Bump has things on his mind," Teddy said. "He has breaking everything in sight on his mind, for example."

"Yeah, but they're different things from what I got on my mind," Rosie said.

Aurora weighed in on Rosie's side, and Bump continued to be brought upstairs for visits.

10

Soon, though, all visits stopped. One day Rosie told Arthur that she didn't want him coming across the street anymore.

"I'm sorry about how it all worked out, hon," she whispered. "I mean our marriage and all."

Arthur was too numb to answer. He shook his head; he cried. Then he walked slowly back home.

"I just don't want no emotion, you know what I mean?" Rosie told Aurora. "I just can't deal with no emotion no more. It wears me out."

"That's all right, dear," Aurora said. "If you can't, you won't have to."

That night, Rosie was afraid to sleep. She began to talk about her early days in Bossier City. She told Aurora about being bitten by a rattlesnake; about the time her little sister had been run over by a car and killed; about looking at her father across the dinner table and thinking he looked a little peculiar, just before he keeled over and died of his heart attack. She talked of Jody White, her first beau—he had died at Iwo Jima—and of the fact that her big sister Louise's first husband had made a pass at her, Rosie, on the very day her big sister married him.

"Not only then, but every other time he could catch me alone, the skunk," Rosie said.

"Goodness," Aurora said. "I suspect I should be focusing my memory project on your life rather than my own. Yours has been a lot more colorful."

"Yeah, colorful, and hard, too," Rosie said. "But all I can think about now is that I wish I could have more of it.

"I guess I should have been going to church and praying all these years," she whispered to Aurora, a little later. "What do you think?"

"Rosie, if it's eternity you're talking about, I have to confess I probably haven't given it the kind of thought I should have given it," Aurora said. "I've had too much to deal with, right here. I'm afraid I've just left eternity to sort itself out as best it can."

"Me too," Rosie said. "The thing is, Sunday morning's such a good time to do laundry. All that time I should have been going to church I was washing sheets and pillowcases."

She smiled a little—her eyes seemed to brighten, for a moment.

"I just hope if I meet up with the General somewhere up in the sky, he's at least got his britches on," she whispered.

"Amen to that," Aurora said.

11

Near the end, a nurse was required, as well as a certain amount of medical apparatus. Rosie submitted to the IV, but she froze out the nurse and looked balefully at the apparatus.

"Your bedroom don't look like your bedroom, no more," she said. "You ought to just pack me off to the hospital. I'm just bones anyway."

"Yes, but you're beloved bones, and you belong where you are," Aurora said.

Theo was there at the time. He was allowed to peek in the door. He had brought a few flowers which he held up for Rosie to see.

Late that night, around one, as Theo and Vassily were

counting receipts and getting ready to close down the Acropolis Bar, the phone rang.

"She's gone, my poor girl," Aurora said.

Though she sounded calm, Theo and Vassily hurried across town anyway. Aurora gave them whiskey, and lots of tea, and the three of them sat around in her kitchen talking about Rosie, or just about this and that, until the sun came up.

12

Rosie's children didn't particularly want her to be buried in Bossier City. After all, none of them lived there—none even lived close. When Aurora asked if she might bury Rosie in the Greenway plot, they quickly agreed.

"Perhaps it's selfish, but her children don't seem to care, and I do," Aurora said to Patsy. "If anyone stood by me, it was Rosie Dunlup."

"You did a certain amount of standing by, yourself," Patsy told her.

As they stood at the graveside—it was breezy and the great trees were rustling and waving—Aurora noticed a large man short of shuffling around at the rear of the small crowd. It was Willie Cotts, in a very ill-fitting suit.

"Willie, where have you been all these months? We were both worried silly," Aurora asked, going over to him the moment the service ended.

Where he had been was clerking at a convenience store on

Little York Road, scarcely five miles from Aurora's door, although admittedly in a very different part of town.

"I know I really ort to have called, Miz Greenway," Willie said. In his bad suit he looked not merely miserable; he looked bereft and pitiable.

"I thought about it a million times, but I couldn't work up my nerve," he added. "I felt too guilty about running off and all. What I mean is, I never dreamed she'd die on us," Willie went on, in tones so hopeless Aurora was glad Rosie wasn't there to hear them. "I just figured she'd be there in River Oaks, working for you, and I'd get to feeling better and make the call someday."

"Never mind, Willie," Aurora said quickly, putting her arms around him. "I'm afraid I was just like you. I never dreamed she'd die."

V

Last Love,
First Loss

1

The night Aurora had her stroke she dreamed that a mad dog bit her. It was a small, savage black dog, and it came at her snapping while she was on her knees in the backyard, weeding a flower bed. In her fear, she couldn't move—the fierce little black dog flung itself at her, biting her arms and breasts. Even when the dog faded and she realized she was having a nightmare, she was reluctant to wake up. For a time the dream was more convincing than her conviction that it was a dream. When she woke up she would have to go at once to the hospital and start getting painful rabies shots.

Then she became aware of a crashing headache, the worst of her life. She wondered if she were dying. Slowly, the nightmare released her, but the headache wouldn't. She tried to sit up and found that she couldn't move—at least, she mostly couldn't move. One hand still moved—she tried to grasp the receiver of her telephone but dropped it. The headache pounded like surf. Soon the phone began to make the sound it makes when the receiver is left off the book. Aurora couldn't stop it. She couldn't speak. She couldn't move.

2

Tommy and Ellen's baby was born the week Aurora had her stroke. They named him Henry—it was kind of a wry name, and Ellen thought the baby had a wry little face. No one in Ellen's family had been named Henry, and no one in Tommy's family, either.

3

By the time Henry was five months old it had become clear that Aurora would never make a full recovery from the stroke. She was, after all, pushing ninety. But she got well enough to be allowed to go home, where she had many visitors. She could read, play cards a little, work a CD player, and even now and then—with the assistance of Maria, the kind, stout Guatemalan woman who had worked for her since Rosie's death—move to her patio for the afternoon and see a different view.

But, to Ellen's sorrow particularly, she had not recovered her speech. Aurora was the one person in Tommy's family that Ellen really longed to talk to. Ellen kept hoping that someday a miracle would happen so that Aurora would be able to talk again.

4

Mainly Ellen wanted to know things about Tommy that no one but Aurora could tell her. Jane, who had been Ellen's roommate at Bryn Mawr, kept saying that she didn't really know Tommy well. Teddy obviously knew him pretty well —the two of them worked together in a very successful business, fixing defective computer programs for some of the largest banks and oil companies in the southwest—but Teddy was closemouthed with Ellen. He didn't seem to trust her entirely, even though Jane, his own mate, assured him over and over again that Ellen was one of the most trustworthy people on earth. Still, Teddy clammed up around her, particularly if Tommy was the subject of the conversation.

5

In a way Ellen figured it didn't matter too much if Teddy clammed up. Her sense was that if anyone in the family, other than herself, knew much about Tommy, it was probably Aurora. After all, Aurora had raised him. And Ellen could tell just by looking into Aurora's eyes that she still had her intelligence. In particular Ellen wanted to know if Aurora thought Tommy had killed her former girlfriend on purpose. No one in the family would come near that question, but Ellen had a feeling that Aurora might come near it, if only she could talk.

6

Of course, Aurora *could* write—or at least she could scrawl. Every day she scrawled requests on big legal pads and gave the requests to anyone who came to visit. Usually the requests were for books or music or a specific food Aurora wanted—and it was usually Theo, a sad-looking old Greek—who took the requests and filled them; though sometimes, if Ellen and Jane felt like spending an afternoon together, they might fill seven or eight of Aurora's little requests on a single shopping spree.

Ellen *really* wanted to know what Aurora thought about Tommy's having killed his girlfriend. She would have liked to ask Aurora flat out if she thought Tommy might do it again someday, in which case the most likely victim, assuming they stayed married, would be herself. But you couldn't expect an old woman who was nearly ninety to scrawl an answer to a question like that on a legal pad.

Much as Ellen wanted to ask the question, she knew she'd better wait for the miracle to happen—she'd better wait until Aurora could speak again.

7

Ellen had supposed she would spend her whole life in Minneapolis, where she was an art critic on a newspaper. She flew to Houston for a weekend with Jane, her old roommate, and met Tommy, who was just finishing his parole. Tommy and Teddy had already started their business, which was tiny at the time. Jane was teaching a class in Greek and a class in Latin at the University of Houston. Ellen had never had a really exciting romance before—not a *really* exciting romance. The next thing she knew, she had moved from the top of the country to the bottom. Work was no problem. Ellen knew her stuff—she was soon writing free-lance art criticism for a number of Texas magazines. The fact that Tommy had killed his former girlfriend was a huge problem, though, for Ellen's sober Midwestern parents.

But Ellen—as Jane put it—was really in a lather about Tommy. She married him anyway.

8

Aurora concluded that her luck had finally run out. It seemed that her future, what little there was likely to be of it, would mainly consist of frustration. She couldn't talk, and her capacity for movement was severely limited. At least she was home—she could watch TV in her own bedroom, and look out her own large windows at the beautiful sky. She was lucky in Maria, who cared for her very well. Hoping to get her more interested in life than she usually was, Maria even brought in some of the old date books from the little office in the garage. On dull days, when Theo was too down in his back even to drag himself across town, Aurora piddled a little with her memory project; she would flip through a few scrapbooks or diaries and would occasionally conjure up what she supposed was really a memory of some picnic on the Cape, seventy-five or eighty years before—her mother, Amelia Starrett, would be there, and a number of vague men with mustaches, wearing white trousers.

9

Aurora, though, was not much persuaded by her own dabblings in the past—she knew she was just wading in the

shallows of a memory that had never been particularly deep.
Despite the playbills and the concert programs, despite the
diaries and the scrapbooks, she had to admit that she could
remember practically nothing of her long experience of life.
The analysis of high moments, whether ecstatic or terrible,
that Monsieur Proust was so good at was far beyond her. She
could not get back in memory the life of her emotions, or of
her senses, or even of her society, to any important degree.
She really knew nothing of her mother, except that she had
loved a gardener, her Sammy. She had never understood her
daughter—she still found herself wondering why Emma had
chosen to marry an almost worthless man.

10

She did remember, with pain, how cold and colorless the
Nebraska sky had looked the day Emma died. It was a day in
which all the color—as well as all the hope—had seemed to
go out of life.

11

Of her time with men, Aurora could call back little, though she did recall the ambivalence that had always seemed to precede and impede seductions, or anything else she might want to do with a man. She had always wanted love to go both faster and slower—but men had never got it right. They made her impatient when they hurried; they made her impatient when they lagged.

Theo had fallen out of his pickup and hurt his back badly. He was more than half-crippled himself, but when he came to see Aurora he gave her such sad looks that she wanted to smack him. She didn't want to think of herself as sick—if she must, then at least she didn't want to forget what it had felt like to be well.

For that, a forthright man might have helped, but Theo Petrakis had forgotten how to be forthright. "Go away if you're going to look at me that way!" Aurora scrawled on her pad one day.

"What way?" Theo asked.

12

Vassily had died some years earlier. Theo had sold the bar, he had nothing to do, he loved Aurora, he kept coming. After all, her condition had improved a lot—she might keep on improving. They might even marry someday. When she looked at him angrily and scolded him bitterly, in notes, Theo consoled himself with the thought that at least—and at last!—he had no rivals.

Pascal, the last rival, had stumbled onto a rich widow, a Jungian or something. They married and moved to Switzerland, only to capsize in a boat and drown.

13

Though she was habituated to Theo and grateful for his loyalty, Aurora was often very angry with him. She was old and rather sick, yet she still found that when initiative was required—or, at least, when it would have been welcomed—she still had to supply it. If they wanted a special meal, she ordered it. If they felt like a change of scene—a little card game on her patio, perhaps—she made the decision and went to the considerable trouble of having herself moved. If they decided to listen to opera, she chose the opera.

Theo always agreed; he just never initiated—and there, it seemed to her, was the story of her life with men. She didn't need to remember it because it was still happening.

14

Once she wrote, "You don't provide, I never want to see you again," on her pad. But Theo was late that day, and she tore the page off and wadded it up before he came.

15

Aurora decided it would be wisest to stop hoping for anything beyond the simplest pleasure: an especially sunny day; a particularly good tomato. Cast about as she might, she could not find a focus for any larger expectation.

16

It was then, when she was very low, scarcely looking at Theo, scarcely responding to visitors, that new life came, in the person of Henry.

She had supposed herself to be beyond babies—and indeed, *had* been beyond Midge, Jane and Teddy's second child—well before she had her stroke. Midge had a blandness that stood in sharp contrast to the rather disturbing behavior of her brother, Bump. Before Midge was three months old, Bump—almost a teenager, and old enough to know better—had stuffed her in the toilet twice, flushing it both times. Jane and Teddy had hastily bought a one-level ranch-style house, a precaution against the moment when it might occur to Bump to throw Midge out the window.

Aurora hoped for Midge's survival, and hoped, too, that Bump would not follow in his Uncle Tommy's footsteps and kill somebody. But she could not really sustain much interest in either child.

When Ellen began to bring Henry to see her, Aurora was not, at first, very interested. Henry was over six months old before he began to hold her attention, and the first thing that attracted her to him was that *she* was holding Henry's attention.

Babies, of course, would stare at anything—babies could stare down panthers. But Henry didn't just stare. He seemed unusually curious for a person so young. Aurora had been forced to buy a hospital bed, one that raised and lowered itself. Henry was fascinated by the bed, not so much by the raising and lowering itself as by the sound the bed made when Aurora pushed its buttons. Henry soon figured out that the little buttons made the sound happen—be could feel the buttons but he couldn't push them—his fingers were too small. He would look at Aurora expectantly out of hopeful young gray eyes—they reminded her of Emma's eyes—and when she pushed the buttons and made the bed produce its sound, Henry would grin a big grin.

When Aurora gave Henry a spoon to play with, Henry banged it on the tray, but that produced no sound of interest. When, by accident, he happened to bang it on the metal railings of the bed, the sound that resulted was much more to his interest. Henry then banged the spoon on the railings many times. Aurora wrote "pan" on her pad and Ellen grabbed Henry for a moment and went to get one. Henry immediately banged the pan with his spoon. Then he slapped the pan with his hand, making a different sound. When he managed to make a particularly loud sound he looked at Aurora questioningly, wondering if she enjoyed the sound, too.

Sometimes Aurora pushed Henry on his back with her good hand and tickled him. Henry laughed and squealed. Sometimes he would try to tug the rings off her fingers. Other times he would crawl up on her chest and try to get her earrings. On the whole, he proceeded rather delicately with his investigations. He didn't try to yank her earrings off—she still tended toward elaborate earrings. Henry mainly liked to make her earrings sway.

Aurora quickly grew to like the little boy and to look forward to his visits. It seemed to her that Henry had an unusually long attention span for a child his age. Often Henry would sit on her bed for ten minutes or more, playing with a piece of wrapping paper or a ribbon from one of the packages she received. Sometimes he would flip the pages of whatever book she was reading. Frequently Henry attempted to speak to her, making confident remarks in his own language. Often he sat thinking, but when he decided to crawl somewhere he crawled with confidence. He crawled to get there, and he hated his mother or Maria to pick him up before he reached his destination. When they did anyway, he uttered a kind of war cry. If they relented and sat him down again, he immediately resumed his journey.

Ellen liked bringing the baby to Aurora's. It was some-place to take him. She also loved it that Aurora was interested in *her* baby. Jane was always complaining about Aurora's indifference to Midge—a perfectly nice little girl but, in El-len's view, nowhere near as interesting a child as Henry.

Though Aurora couldn't talk, she could produce a kind of murmur, faintly musical. Once she and Henry became chums, she would do her little singsong murmurings for him. Henry didn't find her murmurings as interesting as the bang-ings he could do with his spoon. But Aurora kept murmuring her little wordless song, and Henry grew more interested. He crawled up on her chest and put his fingers to her lips, trying to figure out how she made the sound. He could sput-ter, himself; when Aurora murmured, he sputtered, thinking that might be what the old woman was hoping he would do.

Aurora liked it that Henry seemed to enjoy her company. She liked the way he sat on her bed, perfectly at ease, play-ing with her scraps of paper. She also liked the way he dived off the edge when he decided to leave the bed. Henry was confident that some adult would always be there to catch him, and so far his confidence had not been misplaced, though once it was Aurora who performed this duty. She just managed to catch his heel with her good hand.

It amused her to watch Henry crawl away when he was tired of whatever adults happened to be in the bedroom—or if he merely wanted to see what he could find on the patio. The thought occurred to her that finally life had provided her with a forthright male. He just happened, at the time, to be slightly less than ten months old.

But Henry was happy, male, and forthright, that was for sure. He loved to bang on her wastebasket, or on the toilet seat in her bathroom, or on a hatbox he discovered in her closet. Unusual sounds fascinated him. Once by accident he dropped his spoon on a little brass doorstop at the entrance to her bedroom. The spoon struck the brass and produced what to Henry was a new tone. He had been outward bound, ready to explore the patio, but he stopped immediately and began again to drop his spoon on the doorstop. He succeeded in making the new sound fifteen or twenty times before he had heard it enough. Then he left the spoon and crawled away.

17

Aurora grew to love Henry—he became the only person she really looked forward to seeing, the only one to whom she would commit her interest or what energy she had left.

But Henry, so far, only came in the company of his mother. Aurora didn't really object to Ellen; she did feel rather sorry for her, though without quite knowing what Ellen's problems might be. Rumor had it that there had been a falling-out between Ellen and Jane—and Jane, besides being her sister-in-law, had been Ellen's main Houston friend. Aurora didn't imagine that Ellen's home life could be all that rich, either—Tommy had gone from being a murderer and an inmate to being a workaholic computer gypsy, much in demand, rarely at home.

Despite having produced such a bright, lively little boy, a charmer not even Tommy—a good resister—could resist, Ellen had a lonely, needy, undecided look. Perhaps to compensate for her sense of uncertainty, she was overdutiful, to a degree that made Aurora slightly restive. Ellen was very careful to give no cause for complaint, in itself a quality that Aurora, had she felt healthier, might have found to be a basis for complaint.

Mainly, though, what Aurora wanted was to have Henry entirely to herself. She wanted it to be just the two of them, if it was for only fifteen minutes a day. She didn't want Maria interfering, laughing at every cute thing Henry did. She didn't want Ellen around, either. She wanted more time with her new little male, alone.

18

One day Aurora scrawled on her pad: "Please leave me alone with Henry—thirty minutes. I want to teach him music."

She arranged with Maria to make her a kind of pallet on the floor, in a corner of her patio where it was lovely and sunny. It was the spot where Hector Scott had once had his chaise. Maria, who could lift Aurora as if she were no heavier than a feather pillow, carried her to the pallet and propped her up. If she was on the floor, Henry could not injure himself falling off the bed.

Ellen thought it was lovely that Aurora wanted to teach Henry music—she sure hadn't offered to teach Midge music. She brought Henry upstairs, plopped him on the pallet, and went back down to watch a Spanish soap opera with Maria.

19

Aurora had chosen *Petrouchka* for the first offering. She turned the volume up fairly loud. Henry perked up when the sounds began; he listened for a few seconds, but then he decided that he was more interested in the CD player on the floor by Aurora than he was in the sounds. He tried to get the CD player, but Aurora fended him off with her good hand.

Henry crawled around the room and pulled himself up by a large flowerpot with a green plant in it. He pulled a leaf off the plant and put it in his mouth. He looked at the old woman, to see if she was going to make him stop eating the green leaf. She did something that made the music louder, but she didn't try to stop him.

The leaf, however, was bitter, not tasty at all. Henry spat it out and crawled back over to the pallet. He managed to knock over one of the little black boxes that the sound came out of. Then the old woman rolled him on his back and put the black box close to his ear. Henry lay still for a minute, taking in the sound. It was some kind of game involving the sound. He grinned—he liked games, even if they meant tickling, which is what often happened when a Big rolled him on his back.

20

Aurora and Henry's half hour of music became a daily ritual, timed to coincide with Maria's favorite Spanish soap. One of the two women would bring the little boy upstairs, plop him down, fasten the little gate that kept him from tumbling downstairs, and leave.

Aurora would turn on the music—different every day. It might be Mozart, it might be blues, or jazz, or Debussy—and Henry would crawl around the patio, seeing what he could find. Aurora made sure she was provided with a bottle—at some point, when Henry crawled within reach, she would roll him on his back, stick the bottle in his mouth, turn up the music, and bring one of the speakers a little closer to his ear.

Sucking at his bottle greedily, Henry listened. Sometimes the old woman put a hand on his stomach. When she did he idly twisted the big green ring on her finger. But the sounds were interesting, too. They were different every day, and they were interesting to listen to while he sucked his bottle. Sometimes the old woman couldn't resist tickling him. When she did, he rolled over and crawled on her. He liked to touch the big yellow things that hung from her ears.

21

Sometimes, when Henry was crawling on the old woman, trying to play with the toys she hung from her ears, he would put his face very close to hers. He knew that most Bigs liked for him to do that. They liked for him to mash his nose against their faces—it always made them smile. He did it a few times with the old woman—she had interesting toys stuck in her hair, too, and he could sometimes get close enough to pull the interesting toys out of her hair so he could examine them.

While he crawled on her, the old woman sometimes made the sounds they were hearing a bit louder. Often she made them so loud that Henry would forget about the toys in her hair, or those dangling from her ears. The sounds became so loud that he had to stop and listen. They were interesting sounds—different, but always interesting. The old woman was a really interesting Big—none of the others he owned ever caused sounds that loud or that complicated to occur. The old woman didn't make the sounds with her mouth, either. She caused them to come out of the two little black boxes, and when the sounds got out they filled his ears and they filled the room. Henry had to listen to them closely, they were so complicated, but they were very pleasing, too. It was worth it, listening to them.

Sometimes, when Henry put his face close to the old woman's face in order to grab one of the toys she had stuck in her hair, she would murmur at him in her strange language. Her language was not like the goos and coos and oos of his other Bigs. Sometimes when she murmured it, Henry would stop his scrambling for a bit and look at her closely. Sometimes he put his hands on her face and peered right into her eyes, wondering if he could see where her murmur language came from.

The deep eyes of the old woman always startled Henry when he tried to peer into them. They were not like the eyes of his other Bigs. His Bigs' eyes only saw *him*—they smiled at him, or they laughed. They gooed and cooed and made silly faces, all for his amusement. They admired whatever he did, even if all he did was knock his toys off the high chair, or something.

The old woman, of course, saw him too. Everybody saw *him*. But the old woman saw more than other Bigs. When he looked into her eyes, with his nose almost touching her face, he suddenly thought he saw the Other Place—the place where there were no Bigs. The sight startled Henry—it confused and upset him a little. He was a busy boy. He had many places to crawl, many things to bite, much to investigate. The place he had come to, where his Bigs lived, kept him fully occupied, and yet when he looked right into the old woman's eyes and saw that she could see the Other Place, he felt confused, and not happy. Perplexed, he batted at his ear or rubbed his face unhappily, as he did when he wanted to go to sleep. Sometimes he made an indecisive sound—a sound part laugh and part cry. He wanted something, but he didn't know what. He tried to remember the Other Place, but he couldn't. He didn't understand the old woman but he wanted to stay with her anyway. In his confusion he lay back in her lap and held the sleeve of her gown tightly. He let her give him his bottle, while the great sounds she controlled surged around them. Often, lying there with the old woman, sucking, he slid into sleep. When he woke he would have forgotten about what he saw in the old woman's eyes. Usually he would crawl rapidly across the room and go after the big green plant again, the one with the bitter leaves.

22

Aurora grew very tired—in the time of her tiredness she roused herself only for Henry. When Theo came she could not even try to respond—it was all she could do to look at him. Melanie came from Los Angeles and hugged her and wept on her gown but Aurora could not respond to Melanie either. A woman came who seemed to be Patsy Carpenter, but, once she left, Aurora could not be sure that it had been Patsy Carpenter, nor was she really sure that she even remembered who Patsy Carpenter was.

Henry became the only person Aurora knew except Maria. Ellen wondered if she should stop bringing him. After all, Henry was a rowdy little boy, soon to be a year old. He was no respecter of persons, and Aurora was very frail. What if accidentally he injured her in some way?

When Aurora understood that they were thinking of keeping Henry from her, she wrote on her pad, with the last emphasis she could muster, "Bring Henry!"

Ellen was still uncertain: Aurora was so frail. But Tommy overruled her.

"If she wants him, take him over there," he said. "Maybe they're doing something pleasant."

Then he flew off to Boston, to correct the computer system of a giant bank. Ellen wondered why she had chosen a life that was so lonely. She tried to make up with Jane, but Jane was nasty to her. Jane didn't like it that Tommy was the boss of the business—she thought Teddy ought to be the boss, although he didn't want to be. Teddy was happy just being the administrator—it was okay with him that Tommy was the recognized computer genius. It annoyed Jane, but Teddy had long since come to terms with the fact that the way he was

annoyed Jane. Fortunately it didn't annoy her quite enough
to cause her to leave him.

23

One night Aurora dreamed all night of Henry. She wanted
very much to see him. In the morning she took her pad and
slowly scrawled on it, "Brahms Requiem." It caused a problem for Ellen because nobody in the family had a CD of the
Brahms *Requiem*. Besides that, most of the record stores in
Houston were out of it. She had to go to four record stores
before she found it. By the time she got to Aurora's, Maria's
soap was half over. It was a blustery day. Ellen had tried to
make Henry wear the smart French cap she had bought him.
It was a red cap, and Henry looked smashing in it, but he
didn't know that, or didn't care. He kept removing the cap in
order to bite its bill. Soon he had baby slobbers over most of
the surface of the cap, and it didn't look quite so smart anymore.

24

Henry was in a good mood. Sometimes the old woman let him crawl around for a while before she started the sounds. He was nearly eleven months old, he could walk fairly well, but for speed he sometimes still preferred to crawl. He crawled all the way into the old woman's bathroom, where there was a tortoiseshell wastebasket he liked to turn over. He could lift the wastebasket for a moment or two—then, when he dropped it on the tile floor, it made a loud, satisfying sound.

While he was dropping the wastebasket, making it ring against the tile floor, the sounds began from the other room. They were unusually loud and deep—the loudest and deepest they had ever been.

Henry walked back to the patio to see what was on the old woman's mind.

"Wow, she's really playing it loud today," Ellen said to Maria, when the *Requiem* began to resonate through the house.

Maria felt sad. She knew her job was ending. Soon she might not have such a bright, nice kitchen in which to watch her soaps.

The old woman let Henry take the big combs out of her hair. Then she took a comb from him and combed his hair a little. His hair was curly—the comb made a scratchy feeling. Henry grinned. He took the comb from the old woman and tried to comb his hair himself. But the sounds were so loud it became hard to do anything but listen. He lolled back in the old woman's lap. He thought that was probably what the old woman wanted, for him to lie there and listen to the sounds with her. She handed him his bottle but the sounds were so loud and interesting that after a swallow or two he dropped it. He had never heard such loud sounds. They seemed to be coming inside him—at least, they were as much inside him as outside him. He looked at the old woman to see if the sounds were inside her too. He started to wiggle off her lap, but she began to stroke his hair, and he stopped wiggling. She put one hand on his stomach—the great sounds seemed to be in her hand as she touched him. Henry carefully turned the big ring on her finger. Then the old woman took the big ring off her finger, and gave it to him. It was gold and green. Henry started to put it in his mouth, but the old woman stopped him. She made him hold up two fingers. Then she put the ring over his two fingers and folded his hand around it. From the way that she looked down at him Henry understood that the ring was a special gift and that the two of them were having a special time. He lay very still. He didn't want to do anything wrong. Being very still was best at such a time. As he lay on her lap the old woman made the sounds even louder. The sounds became the world, became his life, for the course of the special time, and he and the old woman were in them together. The old woman offered him a finger and Henry took it and held it very tight. He wanted to stay with the old woman, and to have her stay with him. He did not want to be lost. The old woman stroked his hair with her old hand; Henry stopped feeling scared and became comfortable and happy. He and the old woman floated together, in the world of the sounds. Still, he held her tightly. Something unusual was happening—Henry wanted to be sure that he and the old woman stayed together. He did not want to get lost.

25

Eight more times, Aurora played the Brahms *Requiem* with Henry. She played it almost at top volume.

In the kitchen below, Maria felt ever more sad.

26

One day, to his annoyance, his Bigs forgot to take Henry to the old woman. He was irritated; he fretted, but his Bigs, who were very inconsistent, just didn't get it. Henry was expecting to bang the tortoiseshell wastebasket and then to go sit with the old woman for a bit, playing with her combs and hearing the sounds. It was irritating of his Bigs to forget, but there was nothing he could do about it except fret. Sometimes his Bigs were really stupid. Also, they were very possessive, especially his mother. She wanted Henry for herself and she didn't take him to the old woman's at all that day.

The next day his Bigs forgot again, only this time they took him to a kind of park. After he wiggled and squirmed for a while they finally let him down to walk in the grass. There were quite a few bugs in the grass, but they were fast bugs. It took him some time to catch one, though he did catch a

little round one finally, only to have Jane, who often inter-
fered with him, come and take it away from him before he
could eat it.

27

In the next few weeks Henry often fretted—once or twice he
even screamed his war cry—because of his Bigs' stubborn
refusal to take him to the old woman's. It was a simple thing,
and it annoyed him terribly that they kept forgetting. He
missed the old woman and he missed the sounds.

In desperation, when fretting and screaming got no results,
Henry began to bump his face against the floor. It was a tactic
that filled his young mother with despair—if that didn't make
her get him back on schedule, nothing would.

"Oh, Henry, please don't bump your face against the
floor," Ellen said.

"He's probably just teething," Jane said. "Maybe it feels
good to him to bump his gums like that."

Jane had grown tired of being cruel to Ellen and was being
seductive again.

28

When Henry was twenty-four he moved to New York to try to make it as an actor. His Aunt Melanie, who had had a measly little career as an actress, but a pretty good career as a stage director, was working consistently off Broadway at the time. She gave Henry a little job as a gofer and made him start auditioning for every possible part: commercials, soaps, anything. He finally did get a part in a commercial, though it turned out to be a commercial shown only in Japan. Somebody must have seen it, though, because he got a call from an agent. The agent didn't immediately get him any good parts—but at least he had an agent.

His girlfriend at the time was a girl named Sid, a dancer. Henry had the maddest love and the biggest lust for Sid that he had ever had for any girl, but Sid resisted—not totally, but she resisted a lot. She didn't like it that Henry was so controlled. Sid was serious about music—her father played the French horn in the Philharmonic. Henry wasn't serious about music—he didn't judge it very well—but he did love it, always had, all kinds of music. He and Sid went to the symphony a lot. They had terrible seats, but they went.

One night when Henry had not been paying enough attention even to read the program all the way through, the Philharmonic played the Brahms *Requiem*. Suddenly, in the midst of the *Requiem*, to Henry's surprise and Sid's total amazement, Henry put his face in his hands and began to cry. His chest was heaving—he was overcome. Before he knew it, the music had taken him to another place—to an old place in his memory, to a place so old that he could not really even find the memory, or put a picture to it, or a face. He just had the emptying sense that he had once had someone or something very important: something or someone that he could not even remember, except as a loss—something or someone that he would never have again.

Walking home in the summer evening, Sid had not totally recovered from her amazement, nor Henry from the memory that had not quite been a memory. He was there—or mostly there—walking with Sid on Columbus Avenue. But some of him was in another place—some of him was absent. Sid knew it too—she held his arm and looked at him differently.

"Boy," she said. "You were really upset."